# THE
# BRIDE
# OF THE
# WILDERNESS

## By Charles McCarry

The Bride of the Wilderness
The Last Supper
The Better Angels
The Secret Lovers
The Tears of Autumn
The Miernik Dossier
The Great Southwest (with George F. Mobley)
Double Eagle
Citizen Nader

# THE
# BRIDE
# OF THE
# WILDERNESS

a novel

# Charles McCarry

NAL BOOKS

**NEW AMERICAN LIBRARY**

NEW YORK AND SCARBOROUGH, ONTARIO

 NAL BOOKS TRADEMARK REG. U.S. PAT. OFF. AND FOREIGN COUNTRIES
REGISTERED TRADEMARK—MARCA REGISTRADA
HECHO EN CHICAGO, U.S.A.

SIGNET, SIGNET CLASSIC, MENTOR, ONYX, PLUME, MERIDIAN and NAL BOOKS are published *in the United States* by NAL PENGUIN INC., 1633 Broadway, New York, New York 10019, *in Canada* by The New American Library of Canada Limited, 81 Mack Avenue, Scarborough, Ontario M1L 1M8

Library of Congress Cataloging-in-Publication Data
McCarry, Charles.
  The bride of the wilderness.
  I. Title.
PS3563.C336B75  1988      813'.54      87-31535
ISBN 0-453-00592-6

Designed by Sherry Brown

First Printing, July, 1988

1  2  3  4  5  6  7  8  9

PRINTED IN THE UNITED STATES OF AMERICA

*To Owen Laster*

*Mutate nomine de te*
*Fabula narratur.*

HORACE, *Satires* I.i.69

# I

# ENGLAND

# 1

**A**s soon as the candles were lit at the wedding feast, Henry Harding asked his daughter Fanny to sing. She had just learned to play a new Italian instrument, the viola d'amore, that had seldom before been heard in England. With seven strings to play upon, and seven sympathetic strings quivering beneath them, the viola made a thrilling foreign sound. Fanny closed her eyes as she sang "Tell me no more you love," her father's favorite song. She was seventeen years old and she looked like the portrait of her dead mother that hung above the mantelpiece: black hair, trustful eyes, slender neck, and a wheaten complexion that her father called the golden skin of Araby.

When Fanny opened her eyes at the end of the song she saw her father smiling at her in his boyish delighted way. The wedding guests were clapping their hands and calling out the names of songs. Fanny waited for them to be quiet. A man had entered the room while she was singing and now Henry got to his feet and held out his hand to welcome him. Fanny did not know the newcomer but she was not surprised to see him; her father was famous for his hospitality, and often invited strangers to supper. The man touched Henry's outstretched hand with a limp gesture and looked with boredom around the circle of flushed faces at the table. He was bony and tall and stood with one foot well before the other, like an actor playing a gentleman on the stage. The servant offered him a goblet of Canary wine, Henry's best; he sniffed it disdainfully and gave it back without tasting it.

Fanny began to sing again in her sweet soprano voice that was almost like a boy's voice. The stranger, standing well back in the shadows with his chin resting on a hand covered with jeweled rings, watched her intently. She continued for an hour until her throat grew sore, and then sang a tavern song, "I gave her cakes." The wedding guests joined in the chorus, shouting out the bawdy words and pounding on their goblets with their knives. The stranger's face changed and a wise little smile came to his lips, as if he had learned a secret about Fanny. If she knew this song, he

3

seemed to be thinking, what else did she know? He was looking straight into Fanny's eyes as she sang. She looked straight back until his gaze wavered. Henry had taught his daughter never to look downward when a bold man stared at her. "It makes them think they've made you yield," Henry said. "Don't give them even that much, Fanny; they have no right to it."

His stare broken, the stranger turned his back on Fanny and gazed studiously at the portrait of Fanny's mother. A chair scraped over the floor, and Fanny, knowing what was coming, swept her viola d'amore out of harm's way. The bridegroom, an immense rawboned man named Oliver Barebones, lurched out of his chair, pulled Fanny to her feet, and gave her a loud kiss on the cheek. His powdered wig was askew and he had spilled wine on his silk wedding coat. Fanny straightened the wig, which was brand-new and overpowdered, so that it had left a line of caked powder on Oliver's sweaty forehead.

"Fanny-my-love," Oliver cried. He kissed her again, bending down from his great height and pushing out his lips like a child who was just learning to kiss. His wig slipped again; it must be too big for him. That such a thing was possible made Fanny smile: how could any wig be too big for that enormous skull? She laid her palm against his stubbled cheek and kissed him on the lips. Fanny had known Oliver, who was her godfather, literally from the hour of her birth, and she loved him dearly. Her father kissed her too, and for a moment the three of them stood smiling at one another and holding hands. Across the table, the stranger watched, and the mockery had come back into his face. He opened his lips to speak. Fanny turned away before he could do so.

Beside her, Oliver Barebones' bride sat alone. A mirror hung on the opposite wall. Fanny saw that she was looking at herself in the glass. Henry stood up and raised his wine.

"The bride," he said.

The guests rose to their feet and drank. The bride herself, eyes fixed on her image in the mirror, did not acknowledge the toast. When it was over, she tugged Fanny's sleeve and whispered in her ear. Her eyes were on the stranger.

"What a wicked man," she said. "Did you hear what he said to you?"

"Who?"

"That man who's been staring at you."

"No," Fanny said. "I didn't hear."

Rose opened her lips to tell her, but before she could speak, Oliver picked her up like a doll and stood her on her chair.

"Another toast," he said. "To Missis Rose Barebones, the most beautiful woman in England, my bride."

While the toast was drunk, the stranger stepped backward through a doorway into the dark room that adjoined the dining hall. Rose pulled Fanny close and placed her lips against her ear.

"He said, 'You'll change your tune,' " she said. "He said . . ."

Rose did not finish the sentence. Something was happening. She shrieked and squeezed Fanny against her. A fuzzy white cat, all four feet extended as it sailed through the air, came flying out of the darkened room into which the stranger had disappeared and landed in the middle of the table, skidding and knocking over Venetian glass as it went. People grabbed for the animal. Its fur went up and it hissed and showed its claws as it looked frantically for a means of escape. Yowling, it leaped toward a window. The sash was closed and the cat went straight through it, punching a clean round hole in the glass about twice the diameter of its furry body.

"By God, Oliver!" Henry cried. "It's a day for cats!"

A white cat had appeared in the church that afternoon during the wedding ceremony and walked among the candlesticks. The guests were delighted. No one present had ever before seen a cat at a wedding, much less a cat that could leap through a pane of glass without shattering the whole pane. Were this cat and the cat in the church the same cat? Was it the ghost of Rose's first husband? Who had smuggled it into the house? Who had tossed it onto the table?

"Oh, Fanny," Rose said, clinging to her friend, "you know how I hate cats. He promised me there'd be no cats if I married him."

Although Rose was a widow who had borne two stillborn children, she was only two or three years older than Fanny, and she looked and behaved like a maiden instead of a woman who knew what marriage was. She did hate cats. All her life they had brought her misfortune. Long after the white cat had gone out the window, Rose clung to Fanny and gazed fearfully at the broken window.

"It's all right, Rose," Fanny said. "The cat is gone, there's no more cat."

No one but Fanny paid her any attention. Oliver had gone looking for whoever had thrown the cat into the room. Tipsy women were beginning to lean against the men and hold up their faces to be kissed. They drank more wine and told each other over and over again what the cat had done. Nearly everyone had observed some detail of the cat's wild run down the table that nobody else had seen.

Rose did not like these people. They were Oliver's friends,

every one of them—coarse men and blowsy women he had met in
taverns. None of her people were here—not a parent, not a sister,
not an in-law. She was far from home and alone. In Buckingham-
shire, where Rose came from, she was a famous beauty, with
perfect features and flaxen hair that was so nearly white when seen
in strong light that it was sometimes taken for a wig. In candlelight
it was the color of honey.

Henry Harding, because he was Oliver's best and oldest friend,
had made them a gift of this wedding supper. The twenty guests
had eaten pigeon pie, saddle of mutton and breast of veal, ducks
and sweetbreads and calves' feet and oysters. They had drunk forty
bottles of Canary wine, ten of claret, and two of Nantes brandy. It
was a feast that cost more money than Rose, who came from a
good but impoverished family, had ever seen before in a year. And
now they were laughing at her. Rose burned with resentment.
Who were these low people to have these things when Rose was
the one for whom lovely things were meant and she had never had
them? Who were they to laugh at her at her own wedding supper?
One of them had gathered the hairs that the white cat had left on
the broken glass, rolled them into a ball, and burned them in a
candle flame; the stink, tiny but piercing, made Rose gag. Every-
one else laughed. These people lived for amusement. Before the
wedding they had gone all together to Bedlam, paying twopence
each to look at the lunatics. In church, whispering and giggling as
they waited for the bride to pass down the aisle, they told stories
about a madman who was drilling the birds as they flew overhead
into an army of sparrows and wrens and larks with which he
planned to conquer France. In the month she had spent in London
waiting to be married, she had met no one she liked except Fanny.
No one.

Oliver had come back into the room.

"Cock ale, where is the cock ale?" someone cried. "Oliver must
have cock ale."

"He's never needed it before," said one of the women.

Cock ale, a concoction of beer and spices in which a plucked
rooster had been boiled until it dissolved, was supposed to be an
aphrodisiac and was nearly always drunk at English weddings. A
servant brought in tankards of the stuff. The largest mug, holding
more than a quart, went to Oliver, who drank it off in one long
swallow while his friends shouted cockadoodledoo.

"No sleep for fair Rosie till dawn comes up rosy," somebody
cried, gaping and grinning at Oliver and his bride.

One of the women pulled Oliver to his feet and danced with
him, steering him toward Rose's chair. The woman's breasts quiv-

ered when she moved. She leaned over and whispered to Rose. "Oliver's famous for the size of his dingle, you know," she said. "He *talks* to it. You'll soon be introduced, my dear."

Rose drew away and folded her hands in her lap, and almost for the first time in the month that Fanny had known her, smiled. Because Rose's smile was so secretive, it looked like a bride's smile of triumph. Oliver kissed her while his friends gave three cheers for the wedding night. Then, with his mouth still covering hers, he picked up Rose in his arms and, stumbling, carried her out the door.

Rose was taken by surprise. She heard the others cheering. She tried to scream but Oliver caught the sound in his own mouth and swallowed it. His eyes were laughing. Rose closed her own eyes and tried to breathe through her nose without smelling the food and drink on her bridegroom's breath or the sweat on his body. She failed, and as these strong odors flowed into her head and into her mind, she tore her mouth away and gagged in her effort to expel them. Oliver carried her outside into the street.

"Put me down," Rose said.

But instead of setting her on her feet, Oliver tossed Rose into the air like a child and caught her by the rib cage when she came down. She gasped in pain. Oliver gave her a rough kiss on the mouth, licking the underside of her upper lip. His tongue was as muscular as the rest of him, and to Rose its temperature seemed hotter than was human.

"Stop! Stop kissing me that way," Rose said, but she hadn't the breath to say it loud enough for Oliver to hear. He had drunk too much brandy to hear anything. He threw her up again, very high this time, above his head, and when she came down with her hair shimmering in the amber light from the windows, he caught her in his arms and sank to his knees, covering her face with kisses.

"Ah, Rose, Rosie, my Rose," he moaned, "I love you so."

Rose held her breath and closed her eyes, but she couldn't prevent all her senses from working, so she still heard Oliver's muffled voice and smelled his breath and felt his clumsy hands on her body.

Oliver and Henry, who lived as if they were twins, occupied identical half-timbered houses side by side in Catherine Street near the Strand, so Oliver did not have far to go with Rose in his arms. He threw open the unlocked door and carried her up the stairs. A dozen candles burned in the bedchamber, which smelled of burnt wax and new paint. Having lived in thrift all her life, Rose had hardly ever seen so much light in a house at night. The room had been made ready for her. There was a new bed, the largest she had

ever seen, and a table with a mirror where she could look at herself and brush her hair.

A freshly painted portrait of a flat-faced girl with buttery hair and bone-white skin hung on the wall, and Rose knew that it was supposed to be a picture of herself because she had posed for it for three long weeks. The painter, a rude, scruffy man, had come in the morning at eleven, when the feeble Lenten light was strongest over London. His breath squeaked in his nose when he talked. "Don't move!" he shouted. "Wear the same dress every day!" Rose did sit still, looking into the light until tears came into her eyes, in the hope that her tormentor would capture a flattering likeness. But this hideous thing was what he had done.

"Look, Rose, isn't it a wonderful likeness?" Oliver cried. "It was worth every penny I paid for it."

Rose closed her eyes.

Oliver put her down on the bed. He had been sleeping here before the wedding—this had been his bachelor bedchamber—and Rose smelled not only the living, breathing Oliver—sweat and gas, brandy and smoke—who was fumbling at her buttons and laces but also the scent left by the Oliver who had been here before she came.

Oliver had removed his wig and his cropped graying hair stood up in sweaty peaks. His head looked even bigger with the wig off. He lifted Rose's foot, with the slipper still on it, and murmuring her name over and over again, kissed her ankle through the white stocking that covered it.

Rose twisted her foot and the shoe came off in Oliver's hand. "Give me back my shoe," Rose said. "I want to sleep now."

Oliver did not listen to her. Stocking by stocking, ribbon by ribbon, he undressed her.

"No," Rose said, "no."

But Oliver did not hear her. Rose tried to squirm away but he seized her ankles and, peering along the inside of her left leg with one eye closed as if sighting a musket, gave her a silly grin. Rose did not want what was going to happen to her to happen. Watching Oliver's dazed face, she began to form a plan of escape. She stopped protesting, stopped squirming. She lay on her back, limp and silent, while Oliver removed her garments one by one. At last she was naked.

When Oliver saw Rose for what she really was—the luminous hair, the skin that was pale yet faintly brown like the meat of a pear—he could not believe his eyes.

"Lovely," he cried, tearing off his shirt and breeches. "Lovely!"

The sight of Rose and her generosity in letting him see her naked left Oliver breathless. He had had hundreds of prostitutes

and a good many unfaithful wives, but he had never before seen a nude female body; even with whores, even in the middle of the act, it had always been a matter of groping under shifts and peeking under hems.

"Ah, my friend," Oliver said, "have a look at what Oliver has for you."

He wasn't talking to Rose. She opened her eyes with a start. Had he brought a friend into the room with them? There was no one there.

"Very well, very well," Oliver said, grinning affectionately. "I'll introduce you to the lady."

Rose turned her back, but she could see Oliver's shadow on the wall. Projected by the candlelight, every part of his huge shadow picture was half again as large as Oliver himself. She realized what it was he was talking to. "*He's famous for his dingle, he talks to it,*" the bawd at the wedding feast had said.

"Friend," Oliver said, "meet our wife."

He leaped onto the bed. Rose rolled herself into a ball and looked at Oliver's shadow crouching over her—the tousled head like a dwarf's, the humped shoulders, the paunch, and . . . his friend. Rose peeked over her shoulder at the man himself. His eyes were closed as if the memory of his bride's loveliness would escape from his brain if he opened his lids.

Watching her movements in the shadow picture as if in a mirror, Rose reached out her hand.

"Rose," Oliver whispered, "Rose, Rose, Rose."

The plan was working. He was like a sluggish old fish on the hook. Rose's shadow sat up. Its head, with the long loose hair rippling behind it, bent toward the object. The odor was overpowering.

Rose held her breath, opened her mouth wide, and bit down hard. In the first instant after the pain traveled from the point of injury to Oliver's brain, he did not seem to comprehend what was happening to him. The pain was excruciating, but he could not believe that it was actually coming from the part of his body it seemed to be coming from. Then, realizing the truth, he bellowed in amazement and thrashed so violently on the smelly bed that he nearly pulled Rose's teeth out of her jaw. He seized her skull between his hands, and feeling the strength in his great blunt fingers, she thought that he might crush her skull. She hung on like a rat, tasting salt.

After a moment, Oliver's muscles stopped obeying the commands of his brain. His hands relaxed and he stroked Rose's hair. He spoke her name. Rose opened her eyes and watched his shadow. He gasped. His body arched, twitched, and then went limp.

Rose knew that her plan had worked. He was helpless. But Rose knew, too, that this condition would only last for a moment. She slipped off the bed.

"Jesus, Rose," Oliver said, and coming from him the sound seemed tinier, even, than it was. There was admiration in his voice.

Rose crept stealthily under the bed, tugging the feather bed after her inch by inch. She could still see Oliver's shadow projected by the candlelight upon the wall. It sat up and looked at its wound.

"Sorry, old boy," Oliver said drunkenly. "Had no idea she did such things. Have some brandy."

Oliver's shadow poured brandy onto its wounded part.

"Aaah!" Oliver cried. "Sorry, old boy, very sorry!"

His shadow drank from the bottle and then fell back on the mattress.

Her head filled with the raw aroma of brandy, Rose wrapped herself up in the feather bed and watched the shadow some more in case Oliver should rouse and grope under the bed for her. But he was sore and drunk, and he soon fell asleep, twitching and muttering in his dreams.

Rose heard music. It was coming through the wall of the house, and she realized that she had been hearing it, faint and lovely, all during the time that these awful things had been happening to her. It was Fanny Harding, playing the harpsichord in her own identical house next door.

Rose decided that she would creep away as soon as Oliver fell asleep and slip into bed with Fanny. He wouldn't trouble her there. The brute would never do anything to frighten or injure Fanny, his Fanny-my-love, whom he loved better than anything else in the world.

Cowering naked under the bed with Oliver moaning and drinking brandy and whispering her name just above her, Rose began to think about other things. She remembered the cat squalling down the table, knocking everything over, flying through the window like a stone.

She was sure that the man who had stared at Fanny while she sang was the one who had thrown the cat into the room. He appeared to be rich, even a lord.

"Who *is* he, Fanny?" she whispered, imagining herself warm in bed with her friend. "He said he wanted to eat you up."

"Rose," Oliver bellowed, rousing up. "Rose!"

Rose lay very still, watching his shadow. In a moment he fell back and began to snore. Rose giggled. Men really could not help themselves.

# 2

There were good reasons why Oliver loved Henry Harding's daughter as if she were his own. The two men had been inseparable friends since childhood—so inseparable, in fact, that they had both seen Fanny at the same moment on the day of her birth. Many events in their lives had bound the two men together, but no tie was stronger than Fanny's birth, which took place on February 6, 1685, the day Charles II died and Fanny's mother died too.

Because of the difference in their sizes—Henry in middle age was a small quick-moving man, hardly larger than his daughter, and as a boy he had been even littler—Oliver had believed for nearly forty years that he was protecting his friend from the dangers of the world. In fact the arrangement worked the other way around. At Saint Paul's School, where they met, Henry had done Oliver's Latin and mathematics for him, and by providing him with plausible explanations for his crimes, kept him safe from the masters who wanted to beat him because he was so large and so good-natured. Henry had never been in any physical danger because nobody had ever wanted to hurt him. He had the gift of enthusiasm—everything interested him, new and old, and he had never heard a life story that did not absorb him. His reddish hair grew in curls and he had thick curling eyebrows that he twisted between his thumb and forefinger. He had a wonderful smile that began deep in the dark blue eyes that he had passed on to Fanny and then lit up his whole face with an expression of innocence and eager interest.

There were 153 boys at Saint Paul's, the same number as the fishes brought up from the Sea of Galilee by Jesus and His companions in the miracle of the draught of fishes. At school, Henry formed the three lasting enthusiasms of his life—strangers, books, and Latin. Many of the boys were foreigners, and from them he learned to admire the exotic. He learned to love books and Latin from one of the masters, an ebullient curate named William Peleg Ethelred Graves, who taught Latin by having the boys recite Cicero, Caesar, and especially Horace while hopping on one leg

and talking in the dead language as fast as they could. Graves believed that this combination of physical and mental exercise eliminated shyness and boredom, the two great enemies of learning. However, few scholars could do two things at the same time, as Graves's method required. Henry was one of the rare boys who was both intelligent enough and athletic enough to excel at these strenuous recitations. When Graves discovered that Henry understood everything that he read in English as well as in Latin, he loaned him books. The boy and the man became friends, and every year for the rest of Graves's life, even after the old teacher became arthritic and had to hold on to Henry for support, they would dine together on December 8, the birthday of Quintus Horatius Flaccus (65–8 B.C.), the Roman poet known to the English as Horace, and afterward hop side by side on one leg far into the night, reciting in unison, always ending with the motto of their friendship: *"Omnem crede diem tibi diluxisse supremum/ Grata superveniet quae non sperabitur hora"*—Believe that every day is your last; the hour you don't anticipate will come as a happy surprise.

Henry had been reciting Horace, a small boy hopping up and down in a dim room at Saint Paul's, on the winter day that Oliver had seen him for the first time. He smiled at Oliver in the midst of the Latin for no reason at all. Something about Henry, Oliver never really knew what—the smile, the puppylike quickness of his movements, the ginger hair, the smallness of him—tickled Oliver; he laughed aloud and threw his arm around the other boy. Oliver was just as tickled every time he saw his friend—which was every single day—over the next forty years. Henry brought something into the room with him wherever he went—a childlike lack of fear, a slightly crazy goodness, a generous heart, again Oliver could not name it—that made the other man's whole chest and throat fill up at the sight of him. Henry was the great love of Oliver's life. He felt the same emotion for Fanny, who had her father's smile as well as his eyes, and was as beautiful as Henry was plain.

As for Henry's memories of Oliver, they mostly involved football. Even as a boy Oliver had been the most powerful player in the City of London. He played like a demented giant, knocking grown men down like ninepins and howling at the top of his booming voice. Henry, too, loved the game and was always just behind his friend, sometimes even holding on to his shirt with one hand as he dribbled the ball downfield. Henry was strong for his size and very clever with his feet, and because he was so intelligent he saw what the other side was going to do before they did it.

"Left, Oliver! Right, Oliver!" he would shout, guiding the jug-

gernaut that was pulling him toward the enemy goal. At the end of a game Oliver's face would be covered with blood from the blows he had taken, but Henry would be fresh and unmarked.

Football, as it was played in Britain in the 1600s, was a far bloodier affair than the game the Romans had introduced into the islands in the first century of the Christian era. Usually it was played in the streets with twenty or thirty or even fifty to a side. The only rule was to move the ball across the enemy's goal, and as it might be a mile or more between goals, a proper match commonly lasted from morning to nightfall. The ball usually was an inflated pig's bladder that still smelled of the animal and was sometimes encased in leather. On the great English football day, Shrove Tuesday, the day before Ash Wednesday, nearly every village and parish in the realm had one last match before Lent began. Because these contests were played by sides that had reason to hate each other—countrymen against villagers, merchants against gentlemen, carpenters' guild against masons' guild—they did not so much resemble a sport as a battle between human beings who were so primitive that they had not invented weapons but made war with blows and kicks and strangleholds. The holy day was always marked by cracked skulls and broken shins from one end of the realm to the other, and most English monarchs since Edward the Confessor had tried to suppress the game on grounds that it was noisy, lawless, drunken, and produced so many young cripples that the kingdom was in danger of not having soldiers enough to fight its enemies in real battles. None had succeeded in keeping the English from their sport. When the cry "All fellows to football!" was heard, every able-bodied lad turned out. Oliver and Henry were usually the first on the field.

In the year 1665, when Henry and Oliver were fourteen years old, there was no Shrove Tuesday football match in London. The whole city was in the grip of the Great Plague. The first victims had been diagnosed in December 1664, and by the following summer the disease, which was carried by fleas that lived on the feet of rats, was killing thousands of Londoners every week. Children sang:

> Ring-a-ring o' roses
>   A pocket full o' posies
> A-choo! A-choo!
>   All fall down

The rhyme was a reference to the dreaded tokens, or symptoms, of the disease: fever, rash, cough, and the dark wartlike swellings,

about the size of nutmegs, that appeared on the thighs of the doomed. Bubonic plague was always present in London and other cities of the time and there had been epidemics before, but this one was quickly recognized as being exceptionally dangerous. Parliament was recessed, the king went to Hampton Court, and thousands fled to the countryside, where they were stoned and pelted with manure by country people terrified of infection.

About ten thousand people moved to boats moored in the middle of the Thames. Oliver's family was among the latter, and Henry rowed out nearly every day in a hired boat to talk to his friend across the brown water. Oliver's old father would not let Henry approach nearer than fifty yards because he had come from the pestilential city, and in the event this proved to be wisdom, because of all the Londoners who tried to flee from the plague, the boat people had the highest rate of survival.

In August, the hottest month in memory, Henry's father decided to take his family to Norwood, in the Surrey woods, to drink a potion, concocted by the Gypsies, that was supposed to protect whoever drank it against infection. Many plague remedies, often composed of such ingredients as urine and sulfur, were being sold in the city. The Gypsy brew was supposed to be particularly powerful because it was made from secret forest plants known only to the Gypsies and was accompanied by a magical incantation.

In order to reach Norwood it was necessary to cross the Thames. Oliver arranged to slip away from his parents and meet Henry on the southern bank of the river, so that they walked along the forest trail to the Gypsy encampment together. There were hundreds of people waiting in line to drink the potion, which was dispensed from a single wooden cup that was passed from lip to lip. While the customer drank, after placing a shilling coin in the palm of the Gypsy who held out the cup, another Gypsy—a withered crone who had burning eyes but no chin at all beneath her tattooed lower lip—sang out the magical incantation in shrill Romany.

From the woods beyond came the sound of men and boys shouting and loudly grunting as the wind was knocked out of them.

"That sounds like football," Oliver said. "Are you going to drink that filthy Gypsy muck?"

The boys had not played football since winter; even the school had banned it because there was no place to play except the streets, which were strewn with rotting corpses awaiting burial, and the Anglican clergymen who were in charge at Saint Paul's did not want their boys kicking a ball on such a playing field. "The Lord Jesus forbids it," the masters said, invoking the Savior's name as they always did when denying the boys a pleasure.

"I don't believe the Lord Jesus wants me to drink it," Henry said.

The boys slipped away and joined the match. Henry always remembered it more clearly than any other they had played together. The playing field was a muddy space dotted with saplings whose leaves filtered the morning sunshine into a pale green twilight; in after years Henry always recalled that particular light and the fact that the Gypsies, when they rushed at him, smelled of forest rot and woodsmoke. It was a hard match, with Gypsies on both sides playing treacherously against the English boys, but finally Henry stole the ball and dashed toward the goal. Oliver, who was already bigger and stronger than most grown men, went ahead of him, howling and cursing and knocking Gypsies over left and right. The goal was the stump of an enormous oak, and as the boys approached it, a dozen Gypsies, then twenty, joined arms to keep them out.

"Ninepins!" Oliver shouted.

He seized a sapling in either hand, threw himself back, and then catapulted his body at the Gypsy line. Struck by nearly two hundred pounds of bone and slabby muscle, the Gypsies fell, grunting and shrieking in pain. Henry darted across the goal. Oliver rose up, picked Henry up by the armpits and swung him over his head as if he were no heavier than a child, and shouted "*Oof!*" in imitation of the swarthy fallen enemy.

The potion was all gone by the time Henry and Oliver returned to the encampment.

A week later, Henry's father woke up and discovered that he had developed the tokens of plague. He showed them to Henry, the only boy among his five children.

"This is the fever, touch my head," he said. "This is the rash." He dropped his breeches. "These are the tokens—you see? Dark and something like a nutmeg. Soon I will go out of my head. I'll be unable to look at the light, I'll beg for water. Soon after that I'll be dead. You must know the signs because you'll be alone with your mother and the girls."

He gave Henry a leather sack tied at the mouth with leather laces.

"There's a thousand pounds inside, saved by me in case this happened. Have me buried in the churchyard of Saint Andrew by the Wardrobe. The others, too."

"What others?" Henry said. He was weeping.

"We may all die, Henry. Be a man and try to die last. Make sure they bury us by the church in consecrated ground. Otherwise they'll take your money and dump us into a ditch in Tuttle Fields."

He took off his trousers, folded them carefully, and lay down in the bed.

"Close the shutters, Henry," he said. "The light hurts my eyes."

Henry did as he was asked and then sat down beside the bed.

"If you live, and still have money, go to the Royal Exchange and see a man named Adkins, Praise God Adkins," the old man said. "You can trust him."

In his final hours Henry's father frothed at the mouth and tried to run into the street. Henry struggled with him, looking into his father's delirious eyes as the two of them, both small and wiry, spun around the room like wrestlers. The delirium came and went.

"Tie me to the bed," the dying man said in one of his moments of sanity. Henry did so, and later untied the knots when the dead-cart came around for the corpse.

After that, things happened as Henry's father had predicted. The authorities ordered a red cross painted on the door of the Hardings' house in Shoe Lane and posted guards armed with sharpened halberds at the threshold to keep the victims inside for forty days and nights.

When Henry did not come out onto the river for a whole day, Oliver came ashore to find him. When he saw the red cross on the Hardings' door and the halberdiers standing in front, he went to the nearest tavern and bought a quart of ale and a stack of toast, the Londoner's breakfast. He tapped on the window glass until Henry came.

"Breakfast," he said.

"My father's dead in the night and my sister Henrietta has the tokens," Henry said. "You'd best go away, Oliver."

"If I drink the whole quart of ale I'll be drunk," Oliver said. "Here, have some."

Henry drank, then dipped a slice of toast into the ale, soaked it, and ate it.

"That's better," Oliver said when they had finished. "Where's your dad?"

"Still in his bed. The dead-cart hasn't come around yet."

He told Oliver about his father's wish to be buried in Saint Andrew's churchyard.

"But I can't go with the bastards to make sure," Henry said. "They won't let me out of the house."

The dead-cart was coming through the street, the attendants crying, "Bring out your dead, bring out your dead." Henry watched it with glassy eyes, all traces of his old happiness gone from his face.

"I'll go, then," Oliver said.

Oliver walked behind the dead-cart all the way to the Thames. He kept his eyes on Henry's father, who lay with his eyes open across the lap of a dead girl with a face full of freckles. It seemed strange to see a man Oliver had known so well lying dead on the heap of bodies with other bodies thrown on top of him.

By the Temple Stairs that led down to the river, two boys in rags who were about Oliver's age ran down a big gray tomcat, cornering it by a wall and clubbing it to death. One of them took out a knife and cut off the cat's head.

"Why are you doing that?" asked Oliver, who had been living on his boat for six weeks and knew little of what was new in the city.

"The lord mayor has ordered every cat and dog killed," said the larger boy. "They carry the plague, he says."

He opened a sack he had been carrying and the heads of ten or fifteen dogs and cats rolled out onto the dust, cats' eyes staring, dogs' tongues lolling.

"They pay tuppence each," the boy said.

There were many more corpses in the street now. Mixed in with the waxen men and women and children were hundreds of dead dogs and cats, many of them decapitated. The dead were covered with rats, which had come out by the thousands to feed on the human bodies and on those of their cats and dogs, the rat's natural enemies. The dead-cart men dumped all the corpses onto a stack, kicking rats out of the way to make room.

"Which one was yours?" they asked.

Oliver pointed to Henry's father.

"Twenty guineas."

Oliver showed them the money Henry had given him. "You'll get it when the man is safely in the ground," he said.

They looked at the size of Oliver and did not argue. He saw Henry's father buried in Saint Andrew's churchyard, and then, one after the other, Henry's mother and all four of his sisters. The last to die was Henry's favorite, a six-year-old girl named Pamela who could not bear to look at the light. All the others had suffered when the sun came in at the window, but Pamela, who had been a jolly child, fond of games and full of saucy remarks, was in agony. Even the strip of sunlight in the crack in the shutters made her scream. Henry darkened her room by hanging bedclothes over the window, but on the last day she thrashed about in her bed so that he tied her down and held his hands over her eyes while she died, screaming.

Oliver, waiting outside for the dead-cart, could hear her through

the window, shrieking and sobbing in the final minutes of her life as if she was being whipped.

Henry was now alone in the plague house. Every day, Oliver brought ale and toast in the morning and cheese and eggs in the afternoon, and stood at the window and talked to his friend.

At the end of the forty days, Henry was still alive. The guards pulled the nails out of the door and let him out. Oliver rowed the two of them to the middle of the river. Fires had been lighted all along the embankment of the Thames, on the theory that smoke would disinfect the air. The stink of the dead rotting in the sun came across the brown water. The friends could hear the voices of the dying in their delirium, sounding like savages going about some horrid ritual. It was high noon and the light was strong.

"It hurts them to look at the light," Henry said. "Pamela couldn't bear even a candle at the last. You know, I don't think that the Lord Jesus is or ever was."

And from that day onward, though he lived in an age when men took it for granted that God arranged the smallest events in their lives and multitudes were slaughtered in the name of Christianity and thousands were burned for heresy, Henry Harding did not believe in God. Oliver knew this secret, and he took it, and an even more dangerous secret about Fanny, to the grave with him.

After paying for the burial of the six members of his family who had perished in the house in Shoe Lane, Henry still had eight hundred fifty-six pounds nine shillings and eight pence in the leather sack his father had given to him. When cold weather came and most of the dying stopped, he moved back into the house in Shoe Lane. He had no wish to go back to Saint Paul's: he knew arithmetic and Latin and some Greek, so there was little left to learn that might be useful to him. His father had traded in ships' cargoes, putting up money with others to finance voyages, and then sharing in the profits when the ships came home. Henry decided that he would make his living in the same way.

He put on his father's good suit, which was a size too big for him still, and went down to the Royal Exchange. Inside the hollow stone square filled with bargaining merchants and dickering prostitutes, he found the man his father told him he could trust, Praise God Adkins. He was standing beneath a gallery, watching the bids in an auction by the candle.

"Yes, I know about your father," Praise God said. "You are school friends, I hear, with my nephew Oliver. Sympathy, sympathy."

Praise God Adkins was an old boy of Saint Paul's. It was he who had got Oliver in.

"A great waste," Praise God said. "Oliver is a good-hearted boy but he's only good for football. You must have done his Latin for him."

Henry did not answer. Praise God was looking him up and down, noting the oversize suit, the baggy stockings, the watchful eyes. Praise God's own clothes—stained linen, torn trousers, a baggy coat with papers sticking out of every pocket—were very old. He was a plump man, nearly as short as Henry.

"What do you know about selling by the candle?" he asked.

"I've seen it done," Henry said.

By the rules of selling by the candle, an item was put up for bids at the same time that the stub of a candle was lighted. The last bid entered before the candle went out was the winning one. The trick of winning lay in being able to see the precise moment when the flame would die, and for timing the last bid exactly.

"Would you like to try? They're selling a bale of Moroccan leather."

Henry looked around the circle of men gathered by the auctioneer, at the strange clothes and manners of the dozen kinds of foreigners who were always mixed in with the Englishmen. Pink-faced or swarthy, English or not, they all wore the same wily look, as if each was sure that he was cleverer than the rest.

"How high should I go?" Henry asked.

"How much money do you have?"

"Eight hundred pounds, more or less. But I don't have it with me."

"That's all right. If you win, I'll loan you what you need until you can fetch your money."

Praise God whispered a sum into Henry's ear. Touching an arm here and a shoulder there, Henry moved up to the front of the crowd while Praise God remained in back. The auctioneer described the goods he was offering for sale, then lit the stub of a candle and called for bids. An assistant held up a coat to shield the flame from drafts. Henry moved a little to the left, then a little to the right, adjusting his view of the flame.

Bids came slowly at first, but when the flame began to waver, the tempo increased and the bidding took on a kind of harmony, like a chant with sums of money for words. Henry made no bid. The candle burned up again, very brightly, and there was a silence. Henry swallowed rapidly two or three times, as if clearing his throat to speak. Another man shouted out a bid, and then there were half a dozen quick bids by those who also saw Henry's

Adam's apple moving up and down in his throat. Finally, in his clear tenor voice, Henry made his bid, a pound more than the preceding bid and three pounds less than the figure Praise God had whispered in his ear, and as he spoke, the flame went out.

"Beginner's luck," Henry said half an hour later when he and Praise God were seated at a table in an alehouse around the corner.

"Not luck, I think. How did you know to bid when you did?"

"By watching the candle and the faces. You can see what they're going to do."

Thereafter, rain or shine, Henry went every day to the Royal Exchange to do business. With Praise God's help and his own gift for reading faces and choosing the right moment, he prospered. After he left Saint Paul's at sixteen, Oliver began to go to the Exchange too—at first to play football in the street while he waited for Henry, but later to do business too. Henry loaned him fifty pounds to set him up.

"Are you sure?" Oliver said, weighing the coins in his hand and preparing to pour them into his pocket.

"Quite sure," Henry replied. "It's only a loan. You must pay it back at two percent by the end of Lent."

It was now a week after Shrove Tuesday—Oliver still had open wounds on his face from the football match he had played—so he had more than a month to make good on the loan.

"That's very good of you, Henry."

He started to pocket the money but Henry held out his hand. "Now give it back," he said. "I'll be your banker."

At auctions by the candle and by shrewd choices in quick deals for odd lots, Henry increased Oliver's fifty pounds to seventy-five before Easter. He gave him the whole sum.

"Thank you, Henry."

"What about my fifty-one pounds?"

"What fifty-one pounds?"

"The fifty I lent you and one pound in interest at two percent."

"Interest? Let's spend the odd pound on dinner at Locket's Tavern."

"Your pound, yes. I want *my* pound in the palm of my hand, if you please."

Praise God watched this transaction without expression. In a moment Oliver went away and began talking to a pretty whore; he was friends with all the women who hung about at the Exchange. After speaking a sentence or two, Oliver and the girl, who was no older than he was, walked away toward the door that led into Cornhill.

"Why do you look after Oliver in the way that you do?" Praise God asked. "He has no sense at all, you know."

Henry smiled his radiant smile. "Not much sense, anyway. But there's a great heart inside of him, P.G."

As Henry's fortune grew he conceived the idea of owning a ship. He was never able to find the one he wanted—merchant vessels were so profitable that they were rarely sold. One day a story ran through the Exchange: a Genoese was dying on his ship, which was moored in the Thames. It was thought that he had plague, and there was talk that the ship would be burned with the corpse aboard as soon as the Genoese died.

"What about the crew?" Henry asked.

"They've all deserted," said Oliver, who had gathered all the facts from the whores, who knew everything. "Nobody will ever go aboard her again if she's a plague ship."

The epidemic had been over for four years, but people still died of bubonic plague in London, especially in the rat-infested slums along the river.

The ship was Swedish-built, a fast new kind of two-masted vessel called a brigantine. Next morning early, while the mist was still rising from the Thames, Henry went down to the river and looked across the water at her deep hull and her strange rigging—a square-rigged foremast and a mainmast that carried a trapezoidal fore-and-aft sail.

A man stood on the deck, looking back at Henry. His glance was intense, even appealing; Henry had the feeling that their eyes had met despite the fact that they were too far apart for this to have happened. He went into an alehouse and bought a quart of brown ale and some bread and cheese, and then rowed out to the ship.

The man was still on deck, standing by the rail. Henry shipped his oars and looked up at him. He was only a few years older than Henry, stocky and black-haired with a big Italian nose and a floppy foreign cap on his head.

"Would you like some breakfast?" Henry asked.

"No English," the man said.

Henry asked his question again in Latin and the man on deck answered in the same language.

"There's sickness on this ship," he said.

"So I've heard. But that doesn't mean you shouldn't have a pint of ale when you wake up. May I come aboard?"

"Some say it's plague."

"You don't have plague."

"No, it's my uncle."

"Have you ever seen a man who has plague?"

"No. You can have a look if you like."

Henry climbed the ladder, bringing the ale and bread with him, and followed the other man belowdecks. In the master's cabin, a little round man with the florid face of a wine lover lay in bed. His throat was dry and he could barely speak. Henry told him his name. The other man, struggling to bring the sound up out of a closing throat, introduced himself.

"Giacomo Cerruti. Are you a physician?"

"No, but I have some ale here. Would you like a drink?"

Henry sat down on the bed and held the tankard to Cerruti's lips. The sick man drank but he could not swallow. Henry helped him to a sitting position while he coughed. His body was hot to the touch. After a moment he lost consciousness.

"How long has he had fever?" Henry asked in Latin.

"Three days."

"Has he vomited? Has he had froth on the lips?"

"Both."

"Delirium?"

"It comes and goes."

Henry lifted the covers and examined Cerruti for tokens of the plague. The telltale dark nutmeg swellings on the groin were not present, but there was a fresh wound on his thigh that Henry recognized as a dog bite.

"Can you look at the light?"

"Yes," said Cerruti.

"Then it's not the plague," Henry said. "Have you been bitten by a dog?"

Cerruti was awake now, staring feverishly at Henry. "Last month in the Strand," he said.

Henry knew that the man was going to die of his wound.

At noon, in a corner of the Exchange, Henry told Oliver and Praise God his plan. Cerruti was dying. His ship had no cargo. If he died aboard, the ship would be burned because nobody would be willing to go aboard her. But if Henry bought the ship and then proved that Cerruti had died of rabies instead of the plague, he would have his ship.

"Why would this dago sell you his ship?" Oliver asked. "He can't spend the money where he's going."

"I'll pay the money to his family in Genoa."

"You'll lose everything you have," Praise God said. "No sane sailor will ever go aboard that vessel."

"Then we'll find madmen to sail her," Henry said. "Or Italians."

That afternoon Henry took all the gold he had with him aboard

the ship and made his offer to Cerruti. The Genoese signed the papers that Praise God had drawn up, and then fell into a delirium with the sack of money clutched to his chest.

Cerruti lived for five more days. Henry and the young Italian stayed with him the whole time, learning that there are worse ways to die than the plague.

On Henry's orders the young Italian sewed his uncle's body up in a sail and rowed it to the Temple Stairs, where Henry awaited him with a physician.

"Rabies," the physician said after examining the corpse.

He wrote out a certificate, sealed it, and handed it to Henry in return for a guinea.

"We'll bury your uncle in Saint Andrew's churchyard," Henry said. "I've relatives there."

"In unconsecrated ground, among Protestants?" said the Italian. "No. He must be buried at sea or he'll haunt the ship."

"But we have no crew."

"They'll come aboard again now. Let me have that certificate to show them."

"If they're all Italians, how can they read it?"

"They wouldn't be able to read it in Italian either. They'll look at the seal and think of Italy; *La Purità* is their way home."

"I know the ship's name," Henry said, "but not yours. What are you called?"

"Pietro di Gesù."

"Jesus? Your name is Jesus?" Henry said. "You'd better call yourself something else in England or you'll end up with your neck in a pillory." They decided on Joshua Peters.

"Joshua was the Lord Jesus' true name before the Greeks got hold of it," Henry said. "We'll nail on the Peters for good measure and make a proper Englishman of you."

Not all of the Genoese crew would come back aboard. Some had already sailed in other vessels, and some believed that Cerruti would haunt the ship after dying such a terrible death, no matter where his body was buried.

Nevertheless, enough men came aboard to sail the ship. Joshua Peters, as he was now known, had been the sailing master of his uncle's ship, a high position for a man who was barely twenty-one. Henry wondered what would happen when the moment came to take the ship down the river with a skeleton crew. He sailed with her to see for himself.

Boats were standing by to tug the ship into the Thames channel. Joshua waved them off. He had a weak, almost whispery voice, so he gave orders to the crew through the boatswain, muttering

commands that the louder man bawled out to the seamen in the rigging. Sails were rigged. Backing and filling, Joshua moved the ship sideways away from her moorings, slackened the mizzen, spun on the jib, tightened the mizzen, and took her down the river. She moved along as if guided by Joshua's thoughts.

Even when there was no wind that Henry could perceive, the ship made headway. Sailing steadily among a dozen becalmed vessels in the Downs, a windbound stretch of water between the mouth of the Thames and Dover, Joshua mustered the crew and slid Cerruti's body overboard. While whispering the Latin words of the Catholic service, Joshua kept his eyes fixed on the canvas, interrupting a prayer to mutter an order to the boatswain, who shouted it up to helmsman and crew in Italian.

Finally the body, weighted with a ballast stone, sank into the sea.

Henry had never been sailing before and even in these glassy waters he was seasick, but he knew what sort of seamanship he was witnessing.

"Can you sail this ship as master?" he asked Joshua. The two men—boys, really—were still speaking Latin to each other, and would go on doing so until one of them died.

"Watch me and decide," Joshua replied. He set a course to the Isle of Wight, and when they reached their destination, where a brisk wind was blowing, he sailed the ship around the island, came about, and then circled the island again—backward this time. The maneuver made the sailors laugh with pleasure, and looking into their faces as they peered down from the rigging at Joshua on the quarterdeck, Henry understood that there would be no fear of ghosts or trouble of any other kind on his ship as long as Joshua Peters was aboard.

At dinner in the master's cabin, Henry made his proposition.

"I'll pay you twenty percent of the profits of every voyage of the *Pamela*," Henry said.

"What is the *Pamela*?" Joshua asked.

"This ship—new owner, new captain, new name."

"Done," Joshua whispered.

There were other arrangements. The ship would still sail under the Genoese flag when she wasn't in English waters, and Joshua would still be Pietro di Gesù everywhere but in England. She was a clean new ship, unknown in foreign ports, and with a Genoese captain and a Catholic crew she could sail into any harbor in the world—even trade directly with the French in time of war for claret and brandy and other French goods.

"Twenty percent?" Praise God Adkins said. "You treat that dago better than an Englishman."

"He *is* better than an Englishman," Henry replied. "He can go places no Englishman can go, he can bargain like an Arab, and he'd rather die than do something stupid."

Joshua's first mission, after Henry engaged him, was to deliver the purchase price of the *Pamela* to the dead owner's family in Genoa.

"How can you trust somebody with a name like Pietro de Gesù with everything you own in the world?" Praise God wanted to know.

"It wasn't the Italians who nailed me up in a plague house and put guards with halberds outside the door," Henry replied.

In years to come, with Joshua in command of a Genoese crew who were mostly his cousins, the *Pamela* came home to London three times a year with Canary wine and chocolate from Las Palmas, coffee and leather from Tangier, embroidery and preserved oranges from Cádiz, wine from Madeira, lace from Lisbon, claret from Bordeaux, grape brandy from Nantes, apple brandy from Honfleur, as well as more exotic goods, such as uncut jewels and ivory trinkets from India and Chinese silk, for which there was always a market. Once a year Joshua went back to Italy for three months to recreate himself and his crew, returning to England with Venetian glass, forks, musical instruments, and other Italian inventions. It was he who had brought Fanny her viola d'amore; it had been made at Cremona by a distant relation of Joshua's named Nicolò Amati, and it had the head of a cherub carved at the end of the neck.

The *Pamela* always made a profit. Realizing that he had named the ship, in part, because he had watched Giacomo Cerruti die the same kind of lonely agonized death that his family had died, Henry sent five percent of his profits to Cerruti's family each year. He shared the rest with Oliver and Praise God—each of whom owned a ten-percent share of the ship—and had plenty of money left over for tailors and agreeable girls, silver plate enough for thirty guests to eat off when he had that many to supper, a carriage and six horses to pull it, and everything else of a material nature that he wanted.

Knowing what he knew, Henry never saved a shilling, not even after Fanny was born in circumstances that taught him even more than he knew already about the stealthy ways of death.

# 3

The house in Shoe Lane in which all the Hardings had died was destroyed, like nearly everything else between the Temple and the Tower of London, by the Great Fire of 1666. The fire, coming almost exactly a year after the death of the Hardings, cleansed the city of plague, but it did not end Henry's loneliness. He was seldom alone—Oliver was at his side nearly every waking hour. They always had breakfast and dinner and the evening meal together, visiting a tavern or buying oysters or meat pies from vendors in the streets, and very often they slept in the same brothel at night. Henry made friends easily with both sexes and never lacked for the company of people who lived their lives in public places, but he often felt, even when he was surrounded by merry men and women, even when he was making the jokes that made them laugh, that he was utterly alone in the world.

He built another house in Catherine Street, and one for Oliver next door, and gave parties. He would invite home anyone he took a liking to—merchants and Spaniards with snuff in their mustaches from the Exchange, and ships' masters back from America whom he met along the waterfront.

It seemed wrong to Henry that he should be the only Harding left in the world. Not a day passed that he did not remember every one of the people who had died in the plague house. In his sleep he often met his father and his mother and his sisters again as they had been in life; he would wake up happy and then realize that they were all dead. He took flowers to their graves in Saint Andrew's churchyard on their birthdays, but there was no one to whom he could speak about his family, recalling this peculiarity of his father's or that quality of his mother's, and he knew that they would be forgotten altogether if this silence persisted. He did not, of course, believe that his parents and sisters were looking down on him from heaven; to Henry, the dead were dead, and lived on only so long as they were remembered by the living.

Because of his lack of religious faith, Henry believed even more than most men that the birth of a child was the greatest blessing a

human being could know. Next to a child, the greatest happiness he could imagine was a wife with whom one was in love. Henry wanted to love someone, some pure, calm girl who would give him children who would carry the memory of the Hardings into the future. He took to walking through the residential streets of London in the morning and evening hours when he was most likely to come upon mothers and children together. The sight of a young woman walking for pleasure with a couple of dressed-up girls or boys in the soft light of early day or in the last glow of the afternoon filled him with longing. Would he ever be greeted at the door of his own house by a wife and child? In his reveries he imagined himself lifting up the children, kissing their small faces, asking them questions, and looking over their heads into the grave face of a young woman whose eyes sparkled with love and good humor.

One morning in April, as he walked along a narrow street behind Saint Paul's, he heard music coming from an open window. Though the sun was now shining again, it had been raining and he could smell the stones of the cathedral that had been charred by the Great Fire. He looked into the open window and saw a young girl seated at the harpsichord. The light fell on the place where she was sitting, and the clarity of her image combined with the pure sound of the notes of her music made a very strong impression on Henry. The girl wore a white dress and her dark hair, plaited into a heavy braid, hung down her back and touched the polished bench she sat upon.

When the song she was playing ended, Henry stepped away from the window and knocked at the door. He was greeted by a servant, also a dark young woman, who gave him a suspicious look.

"I was passing by and heard the music," Henry said, "and I wished to compliment the young lady on her playing."

The servant stared at him in silence and closed the door in his face.

Henry came back the next day and the girl was playing again. This time she was singing in French:

    *Quel espoir de guérir*
     *Puis-j'avoir sans mourir*

"What a sad song," Henry said.

The girl turned around and saw Henry standing at the open window, already bareheaded. She had a solemn face with large dark eyes. She did not answer, but she was not startled by the

intrusion of a strange man. Her hands lay quietly in her lap and her whole being seemed to be in a state of repose as she waited to see what Henry would do next.

He smiled. The girl's eyes changed when she saw the smile and she stood up and smiled in return. The same servant who had opened the door for Henry the day before appeared from nowhere, scuttled across the room, and closed the window. But the girl, just behind her, opened it again.

"It's a song about a broken heart," the girl said. "It means, how can I ever get over this without dying?"

"I hope it's only a song."

The girl was smiling now. "It's only a song."

Her name was Genevieve Harris, but because she sang all the time even as a child she was called Fanchon, after the merry girl in the French songs. Her father was a Cavalier, a soldier who had gone into exile in France with Charles II. Fanchon's mother, a Norman woman, had refused to leave France when the king came home from exile, so the child had been raised in Honfleur, the seaport at the mouth of the Seine that had passed back and forth between the French and the English for two hundred years. When Fanchon was fourteen, her mother died and her father brought her to England. She was now sixteen and she spoke English perfectly, but with the softer echo of French in every word.

"Are you a Catholic?" Henry asked.

"Of course. But one is not supposed to say so in England, and there are no real churches. Are you a Protestant?"

"No," Henry said. "But you really shouldn't be telling people who look in at your window that you're a papist."

"God will protect me."

"I shouldn't be surprised," Henry said. "But it's just as well to have friends on earth in case you need them."

Since Queen Elizabeth had promulgated her "Act against Jesuits, seminary priests, and other such like Disobedient Persons" a hundred years before, 311 Roman Catholics had been put to death in England for refusing to renounce their religion. Although the persecution eased under Cromwell, who only executed two papists during his rule, prudent Catholics still practiced their religion in secret rooms and priests went about the country in disguise, hearing confessions in secret and celebrating Mass with lookouts posted at the doors and windows.

Fanchon's father, after he investigated Henry's financial position, raised no objection to the match. Henry and Fanchon were married by a young Jesuit named Philip Evans who came to the ceremony disguised as a barber and afterward played the lute and

sang a song he had written for the occasion. Evans had been confessing Fanchon and her father and the servant, a Norman girl named Antoinette who wept throughout the ceremony, ever since they arrived from France.

"You understand the burden you are assuming in marrying a Catholic girl, especially Fanchon, who has absolutely no guile?" he asked Henry. "We Catholics must live dangerously in England, always hiding, always remembering that we are surrounded by enemies."

"Fanchon will be quite safe with me."

"In body, perhaps, but how can her soul be safe if you do not believe in God?"

"You may satisfy yourself on that point as often as you like. But you'd better have a pretext for coming to my house. Can you really cut hair?"

"Of course."

"Good. Then you can live your disguise by giving me a trim. Then go upstairs and look after my wife's soul."

Marriage transformed Henry. He had never known what it was to sleep with a woman night after night, to eat every meal with her, to make jokes with her, to be kind to her when she was sick, to see love and pleasure and the mirth of passion in her face. Henry was overcome by the sweetness of the arrangement. Fanchon became pregnant almost immediately.

"You see?" she said. "God wants us to be happy."

Henry listened at her stomach, amazed that his child, a Harding coming into a world that the plague had emptied of Hardings, should be growing inside this joyful little person he loved so much.

One afternoon in February, early in the ninth month of the pregnancy, Henry heard his name being called as he and Oliver stood in the New Exchange bargaining over a cargo for his ship. It was Antoinette, the servant, and her face was distorted by fear. She shouted when she spoke English because she thought that the English were stupid; now she shrieked out the words.

"The baby," she cried. "You must hurry, Monsieur Henry. *Sang partout.*"

Henry gripped her by the arms. "*Sang partout?*" he said. "What do you mean, blood everywhere?"

The Exchange was many streets away in the Strand, and Oliver, roaring like a fullback, cleared a way through the crowd as the friends ran home. But by the time Henry reached Catherine Street, Fanchon was dead.

Fanchon lay on the bed on a huge damp bloodstain. The midwife was trying to close her eyes.

"Sometimes they bleed," the midwife said. "She just went to sleep, sir, think of it like that."

Henry looked at her out of uncomprehending eyes.

"Shut up," Oliver said.

He pulled the coverlet over Fanchon's body. Henry kneeled down on the floor beside her and looked into her face. The eyes were still open. Something had happened to the brown in them; it was far paler than before. Her hair was tangled and dull and her skin was sallow, as if the life had gone out of the things that had made Fanchon beautiful before the rest of her died. Henry did not attempt to touch the body; he had seen the dead before, and knew what the flesh felt like, chilly and lax, after the person had gone.

"Sir!" the midwife said, pushing Henry aside and fumbling with the bedclothes as if Henry's rights over Fanchon's body had ceased to exist when the body died.

Henry rose to his feet. Antoinette was sobbing behind him.

The midwife was still fumbling with the coverlet.

"You'll need a wet nurse, sir," she said. "My daughter-in-law is a big healthy girl with lots of milk and I think you can have her for a shilling a week."

"Milk?" Henry said. "What milk?"

The midwife brought a baby out from under the covers. It was asleep.

"The poor lady fed it before she died," the midwife said. "It was the last thing she did."

Antoinette uttered a huge sob. Henry had not realized that the child was alive. He had not seen it, sleeping in its bundle at the side of its dead mother. He could barely see it now because his eyes would not focus; each time he tried to look at something or someone, his mind refused to register the image. Instead, he saw Fanchon as she had been in life.

The midwife opened the swaddling so that he could see the child's parts. It was a girl, wizened but delicate and large-eyed like Fanchon. Henry put his hand on the narrow breast and felt the heart beating inside; the skin was warm and incredibly smooth and already faintly golden. Then Henry's eyes unfocused again and instead of seeing the baby, he saw himself as the child, and his father's hand as his own hand. The child moved, its first sign of life, and opened its lids. She seemed to know her father; Henry had the very strong feeling that Fanchon was speaking to the child, telling her things about him, that she had somehow held some part of herself back from death until her baby and her husband were touching each other for the first time.

Then Fanchon went away forever. Henry felt it strongly. He

held the baby against his face and kissed its powdery skin. His deep love for Fanny began at that moment and never abated.

"Fetch Evans," he said to Antoinette, who was still sobbing. "Quick. Run."

The Jesuit did not live far away. Evans came as usual in disguise, carrying his scissors and razor in his outer pockets and holy water and anointing oil in little flasks concealed in secret pockets. He muttered in Latin and drew crosses in the air.

"Here," Oliver said. "What's this? This creature is a papist."

"Never mind."

"Never mind? But he's baptizing your child."

"Her mother would have done the same."

"A Catholic? In England? How will she live?"

"We'll keep it a secret," Henry said.

Henry named his daughter after her mother, with Antoinette and Oliver as godmother and godfather.

"Genevieve—what a name for an English girl!" Oliver said. "You'd better call her Jenny."

"We'll call her Fanny," Henry said.

Oliver handed the child to Henry, who turned Fanny's small head, which was covered with silky black hair, this way and that. He wore a gold signet ring on his forefinger, large enough and bright enough to reflect the child's whole face. Her eyes were open again, and she seemed to see herself.

It was at this moment that the bells of London began to ring all at once. Evans told them the news. The king had died that day, confessing himself a Roman Catholic on his deathbed. The Jesuit's face glowed with happiness.

"Surely God was in London today," he said.

"Yes," Henry said, and took his child out of the death room.

In fact, neither Henry nor Oliver expected the child to live. The English clay was full of babies. Of Henry's twelve siblings, only four besides himself had lived beyond infancy; Oliver's mother had given birth to eight boys and girls and only Oliver survived. How could Fanny last without a mother?

But she prospered from the first. Antoinette made certain that the wet nurse gave Fanny her share of the milk and didn't favor her own English child, a boy who smothered before he was a year old when his mother rolled onto him in her sleep. He was almost the last child Fanny ever saw. Antoinette kept playmates away because children got sick and made other children sick too, and because English children spoke English. She spoke nothing but French to Fanny.

Evans came as before to hear Antoinette's confession and say

Mass and, later, to catechize Fanny. When Fanny was five Henry had a talk with Evans.

"Fanny needs a tutor. She should know Latin and music and arithmetic."

"And the fundamentals of the true faith," the Jesuit said.

"You've already begun that, so just go on," Henry said. "But leave out the burnings and hangings and cuttings-off of privy parts until she's a bit older. I don't want her in a nunnery."

Henry filled the house in Catherine Street with instruments—a spinet, a harpsichord, violas, lutes. Fanny learned them all; she had the gift. By the age of fourteen she knew a hundred pieces of music by heart, including all the songs her mother had played, and could read music and Latin as easily as English. She also knew a little Greek and a great deal of arithmetic, which came to her as easily as music.

It was the music that pleased her father most. When, in the empty house, Fanny would sing "*Heureux qui peut se plaindre*" or another of Fanchon's songs, the sad music and her young soprano voice that sounded so much like her mother's stirred powerful memories.

While Fanny was still a child, Henry would take her on his lap after she had sung and played and talk to her about her mother.

"There she was, playing the harpsichord in a pool of light and singing in French," he would say. "She had black hair like yours, Fanny, blacker than the hair of any other girl in London."

Henry told Fanny her mother's stories about Honfleur—the plump French ships in the *bassin* sailing off to Canada on the tides that rose and fell twenty or thirty feet, the heaps of fish on the quai, the gray slate houses along the shore, and the beautiful green fields by the river shaded by apple trees. On an eminence above the town there was a cathedral, Saint Catherine's, that was made entirely of wood. It had been built by the shipbuilders, so it was like the inverted hull of a ship; when the prayerful lifted their eyes they saw ribs and planking and the long keel that was the ridge-pole. When the church was full and everyone was whispering it sounded like the sea. Because the Vikings who occupied Normandy had not married the peasant girls they took as wives, Norman surnames were often female Christian names. Antoinette's family was called Marie, and in nearly every generation there was a blond they called *aïeul*, grandfather, even as a child.

Antoinette talked about Honfleur even more than Henry—the food, the wine, the sea air, the good people, the glorious weather.

"Doesn't it ever rain in France?" Fanny asked.

"Certainly it rains in France, but it is lovely rain, the water coming down among the slate houses is so clean that it seems blue like the sky, not brown and filthy as it does in London. And mostly the sun shines in France; God only sends France as much rain as it needs to grow food. He must be trying to drown the English, but they're too wicked to die."

The beauty of Honfleur, a place that Henry only knew from stories and Antoinette had nearly forgotten, was the only matter on which Antoinette agreed with Henry.

"As soon as I saw him in the window I knew he did not believe in God," she said to Fanny. "If only I had driven him away, but if I had, we wouldn't have had you, and then where would we be?"

It was Antoinette who told Fanny, beginning when she was very young, that Fanchon had nursed her even as she died.

"The life ran out of her and you drank at her breast. I thought my heart would break. That's why you're such a sad child and it's why you look just like your mother."

In reality Fanny was not sad except when she was with Antoinette, who lived in a state of melancholy and disappointment. Since puberty she had been trapped in England among Protestants and enemies of France. In all that time she had never had a happy moment, except for the joy that Fanny gave her. She taught the child to speak French, to be a Catholic, and because she was a Catholic, to live like a spy among her father's people. She sewed secret pockets into Fanny's petticoats in which to hide her rosary.

"Don't even tell your father about your holy pocket," Antoinette said. "The Protestants kill Catholics in England, even little girls like you."

"Father is not a Protestant," Fanny said.

"No, he's worse, a man who denies God," Antoinette said. "Of course he would never harm you and you must love him because he's your father, but you will not be together in heaven."

When Evans the Jesuit came secretly to Henry's house and said Mass behind locked shutters, Antoinette felt that she had struck a blow against the Protestants that God would surely notice.

"One day you'll return to France and be happy," Antoinette said. "I feel it in my heart."

When she was small, it seemed to Fanny that they could all be happy in Honfleur.

"You'd be a Catholic then," she said to her father, "and we wouldn't have to have all these secrets."

"That *would* be a miracle," Henry said. "I promise you we'll go one day."

But France and England were always at war, and it was against

the law to take a child out of England without royal permission, so they never went.

Except for his voyage down to the Isle of Wight aboard the *Pamela*, Henry had never been far from London. The city was all the world to him, a great smoky theater that never closed. He loved to show it to Fanny. On their three birthdays—Fanny's, Henry's, and Oliver's—and at Easter and Christmas, and each time the *Pamela* came home, Henry took Fanny out to celebrate. These outings lasted the whole day, and always ended with a feast in a tavern, with Henry's friends calling to him as they came and went and joining him at table for a glass of wine.

"How do you do, madam," they would say to Fanny, bowing solemnly.

Usually she fell asleep before supper was over; Oliver would carry her home through the streets. All her life she would remember waking up with rain or snow falling in the night, to look up into Oliver's massive face and hear the thud of his big feet on the ground.

"Almost there, angel," Oliver would say, smiling and letting out a steamy puff of brandy breath. No matter how small she was, Fanny always had a new dress and hat. Henry had them made for her at a dressmaker's in Watling Street, the same woman who had made Fanchon's clothes. The colors and the cloth—bottle-green velvets, claret silks, deep blue satins that matched Fanny's eyes— were intended for grown women, but they suited Fanny well. Henry would spin her round, laughing with pleasure.

"What a beauty you are, Fanny!"

In winter and spring, when the streets were choked with mud, Henry would ride in the same chair with her, and he and Fanny together weighed no more than a single passenger of ordinary size. Oliver required four chairmen, twice the usual number, to carry him.

Fanny went with Henry and Oliver to Lloyd's Coffeehouse, where she listened to her father do business and watched him take part in auctions by the candle. He was famous now for his ability to judge the dying of the flame.

One winter the Thames froze, and Henry skated among the bonfires with Fanny in his arms.

"We're skating over the place where Oliver and I lived on the water during the plague," he said. "People would come out in boats and sell food and drink."

He made it sound like an idyll of boyhood; listening, Fanny went to sleep watching the flames whirl by and dreamed about this, too,

for years afterward. Henry took Fanny to Saint Paul's in the rain, so that she could smell the Great Fire of London on the scorched stones thirty years after the burning. In the Royal Museum they saw the entire tanned skin of a Moor with the hair still on it, and on a February morning looked down into Fleet Ditch where a drowned man, frozen stiff, stood up in the muck with a dead dog tied to his wrist. All around them people were pointing and making jokes. Henry did not warn Fanny to look away and it never occurred to her to look away; the dead were common in the streets of London, and like everyone else, she was used to them.

From earliest childhood she knew the churchyard at Saint Andrew's, where her mother lay among the other Hardings. They brought flowers on Easter, on birthdays, and on the anniversary of death. All these dates were fixed in Fanny's memories.

"They're not here, of course," Henry said.

"Then why do we come and leave flowers?"

"Because they're here," Henry said, touching his head. "And because you must always have them here." He touched her forehead. "That's where the dead live on, in the thoughts of the living."

Fanny said nothing about souls ascending to heaven. She wasn't sure that she believed that this happened. Although her father had never told her what to believe, and had even paid a priest to instruct her in her faith, the fact that he did not believe had planted doubt in her own mind.

When Henry and Oliver brought Fanny home late at night, or after a long day at Lloyd's Coffeehouse or the Exchange, Antoinette was always waiting at the door with accusation in her eyes. It was no life for a child, Antoinette said, dining at taverns and staying up all night and making friends with bad women and worse men.

"She won't be a child forever," Henry said. "The more she knows of the world, the less unhappy the world can make her."

Fanny loved the *Pamela*, the scent of coffee and chocolate in the holds, the Genoese crew in their striped shirts and tasseled caps, the creak of planking and rigging even when the vessel was lying quietly in the Thames. She wandered through the ship, talking to the sailors or playing hide-and-seek belowdecks with Oliver, while her father and Joshua Peters discussed voyages and cargoes in the master's cabin. Antoinette had been taught that it was bad luck for a virgin to step foot aboard ship. Henry would not listen to her protests, so she spoke directly to Fanny.

"Do you enjoy playing in the ship?" she asked.

"Yes," Fanny answered. "Better than any other place."

"You mustn't go there at night. An old man died of rabies on that ship, and he and the mad dog that bit him are ghosts now. When it gets dark, they walk. You can hear the old man calling for mercy. He wants to go to heaven, but the dog still has his teeth in him and won't let him go. It's horrible."

Giacomo Cerruti, raving for salvation, and the mad dog growling and biting him, entered Fanny's dreams. The next time the *Pamela* came home, Fanny refused to go down to the Thames to visit her.

"Why not?" Henry asked. "Joshua has brought you a present from Italy."

Fanny explained.

"Ah," Henry said. "Ghosts, is it?"

That night, which was moonless, he took Fanny down into the hold, lighting their way by a candle inside a lantern. The cargo was only half-unloaded. In the feeble light of the lantern, the boxes and kegs and sacks took on sinister forms. Henry blew out the candle. He put his arm around Fanny's shoulders in the dark.

"Let's call the ghost," he said. "I'll call the man, you call the dog."

Fanny shrank against him, trembling.

Henry lifted his voice. "*Giacomo Cerruti*," he called, "*Gia-co-mo Cerruti.*"

There was no answer. "Try the dog," Henry said.

Fanny could make no sound.

"Whistle," Henry said.

Fanny pursed her lips, blew, and made no sound. Closing her eyes in case the whistle brought the dog and its master, she whistled a string of notes.

A dog barked in the hollow space behind them. Henry whirled around and called again: "*Giacomo Cerruti . . . Giacomo Cerruti.*"

He was answered by musical notes—the scale played up and down on a spinet.

"What's this?" Henry said. "A ghost that plays the spinet? Come, Fanny, let's find him."

Pulling her along by the hand, he walked toward the sound. Fanny's eyes had adjusted to the darkness now and she could see indistinct shapes all around her. The spinet sounded again, very close now. Fanny saw a chink of candlelight.

"Giacomo, my old friend, is that you?" Henry asked.

"No," said a voice in the dark. The same voice barked like a dog.

Suddenly there was light—another lantern that had been muffled

and was now thrown open. In its light Fanny saw Joshua Peters seated on a stool at the keyboard of a spinet.

"Happy birthday, Fanny," Henry said.

She would be twelve in a week and Joshua had brought her a new spinet from Italy.

"It's the latest thing," Joshua said. "The legs come off and the whole thing fits into a bag for traveling."

"Let me see," Henry said, curious at once.

The two men dismantled the instrument, then set it up again. It was very cleverly made, and the procedure took only minutes.

"Sing '*Heureux qui peut se plaindre,*' " Henry said. "Will you, Fanny darling?"

Fanny struck the first chord. The spinet had a lovely sound.

"Wonderful," Henry said. "We can take this with us when we go to France and have music on the ship, music along the way, music wherever we are."

"It sounds as though I'll be pretty tired by the time we get there," Fanny said.

"Play," Henry said. "Let's see if the dog will howl."

# 4

It was Rose who changed everything. Nobody, not even Henry, thought it possible that Oliver might fall in love and marry at the age of fifty-one, but that is what happened. It happened after a football game on Shrove Tuesday, the best of all possible days from Oliver's point of view.

Oliver had gone up to the village of Chesham in Buckinghamshire to play football. His host was a sporting baronet named Cecil Lockwood. He and Oliver had met fifteen years before, when Sir Cecil passed him on the stairs in the Widow's. Sir Cecil was going up while Oliver was coming down with a squealing girl under each arm and a third riding on his shoulders with her legs wrapped around his neck.

"By God, sir," Sir Cecil said. "If you can do what I think you've just done and have the strength afterward to carry three fat wenches down the stairs, I wonder what you can do with a football."

Oliver's giggling girls were pounding on his body with their soft fists, urging him back up the stairs.

They introduced themselves. Sir Cecil immediately recognized Oliver's name, which was known to everyone in England who loved football.

For fifteen years thereafter, always over a bottle of claret at the Widow's, Sir Cecil tried to persuade Oliver to play in the Shrove Tuesday match at Chesham. Oliver always declined—he had the habit of playing in Saint Andrew's parish and he didn't want a change. But as the years passed, and all the fellows he had played with as a young man grew too old to take the field, Oliver decided that he might as well play one match in Buckinghamshire.

"Just this once, mind," Oliver said. "I'm far too old to be loving mud and blood."

"But you do love it," Sir Cecil said. "I know you do. By God, Chesham is in for a treat."

Sir Cecil himself loved football even more than other Englishmen. "I tell you, sir," he told Oliver, "there would have been no civil war in England if Prince Charlie's father had let him play football. But no. Old James, God rest him, bloody Scotchman that he was, was afraid his boy would break a princely leg. The football field is the one place in England where a man can knock down his betters and not be hanged for it. If the boy had been knocked on his royal arse a few times by some good strong country lads, he'd have had a better idea of where the divine right of kings started and stopped."

Sir Cecil lived for games. He even taught them to his dogs. His mastiffs, beasts bred for size and obedience, had been trained to play a game called Trespasser. When someone wandered onto the grounds of the estate, Sir Cecil would ride out with his mastiffs and hunt him down like a stag. Then the mastiffs, slavering and growling, would tear the clothes off the man without hurting him. "By God, sir, trespassers seldom come back for another game," Sir Cecil told Oliver and Henry in the Widow's. "I have to keep on finding new ones."

Oliver said, "Have you ever tried it on a girl?"

"Once. But she fainted dead away while the dogs were rolling her about on the ground and I couldn't wake her up to fuck her."

Sir Cecil's side, the yokels, won the match that year against the villagers. Oliver scored the only two goals. Sir Cecil, giddy with happiness, wrung his hand at the end. Oliver was so completely covered in mud after more than four hours of play that only his eyes, the white of his teeth, and the bright scarlet patch that was his bloody nose could be seen.

"By heaven," Sir Cecil said, "our side will never lose again. You've put the fear into the rest of them."

Sir Cecil always gave a masked ball on Shrove Tuesday, a holy day known in southern countries as carnival, for the gentry of the county. Oliver, who had a fondness for costume, came dressed as a sultan, with a turban on his head and a scimitar thrust through a broad sash at his waist.

"Splendid costume," Sir Cecil said, reaching up to clap Oliver on the shoulder. He was still overflowing with triumph at winning the match. Sir Cecil himself was dressed as a sorcerer, the costume he wore every year.

It was early still and he and Oliver were the first ones downstairs. No guests had yet arrived. Oliver was tremendously happy, as he always was after playing football, and looking into his battered face, Sir Cecil was seized by an inspiration.

He had a stepdaughter-in-law, the widow of his wife's son, who had just come out of mourning. She was beautiful but penniless, poor material for a match. But Oliver might not care about that once he saw her. His stepson hadn't.

The girl herself wouldn't object. How could she? Oliver looked a lout, but he was a good fellow and he was not badly off at all—owned an interest in a ship, dressed himself up, spent money like water in the Widow's.

A servant came by with a tray of glasses. Sir Cecil took two off the tray and handed one to Oliver.

"You ought to marry, Barebones," Sir Cecil said.

Oliver was startled. Nobody had ever before suggested marriage to him. "Marry? What for?"

"Well, you've got some money to leave behind you, haven't you?" Sir Cecil said. "You ought to have a son to leave it to before you're too old to get one."

"I have a goddaughter who'll serve as heiress if I have anything left when I die," Oliver said. "Besides, I've never seen the point of marriage. It's cheaper the way I do it—a guinea a time for a different girl every time and a brandy wash afterward to keep off the pox."

Sir Cecil hardly listened to Oliver's words. He had seen his opportunity. He was saddled with a young widow who ate too much, burned too many candles, and had no family to go back to.

"Don't say no before you've seen the goods," Sir Cecil said. "I've got a pretty widow for you, yellow hair, lovely tits, nicely broken in by a young stepson of mine before he fell off his horse and killed himself."

"Very kind of you, but I'm happy as I am."

"I say again, don't say no till you've seen the goods," Sir Cecil said. "Ah, here she comes now."

Rose came down the stairs dressed as Salome in a gown made of filmy veils. Her hair was down in a silvery curtain around her face, and her lovely body with its high, wide-apart breasts shimmered inside the translucent cloth as she descended.

Oliver had never seen such a beautiful girl, or one who seemed so untouchable. He could scarcely believe that she was human, much less that she had ever lain on her back and lifted her knees for a husband. The thought of her engaging in that act had a quick effect on Oliver.

Sir Cecil saw what was happening. "What did I tell you?" he said. "Amazing tits, aren't they? And she's very willing, according to my late stepson. Slow-thinking, Robert said, but that's not a bad thing in a beautiful woman. Come, let's get your foot in the stirrup."

Sir Cecil pulled Oliver across the floor and introduced him. Rose looked up at him for a moment, then covered her face with a mask on a stick as her eyes filled up with boredom. Although the music had not started, Oliver asked her for the first dance.

When the dancing began, Oliver claimed his partner. Rose was not a large girl, and she had never been touched by such a strong person. Dancing with Oliver was like dancing with a bear—interesting but impossible, something you would only expect to do in a dream.

After the dance, she could not get rid of him. He brought her drinks, ices, sweets. He sat next to her at supper and watched her in fascination, eating nothing himself, while she sliced up her meat and placed it into her mouth with her slender ringless fingers. She hadn't eaten meat for several days—Sir Cecil kept a thrifty household—and she ate even more greedily than the others at the table. When she was done, her lips, which looked like the lips on a statue of a Greek goddess, shone with grease. It only made her more beautiful. Everything made her more beautiful: the lock of hair that had escaped from her pins and hung along her cheek, the expression of complete indifference to others that made her glow with mystery. She never laughed, never answered when spoken to.

She was the most desirable thing Oliver had ever seen. After the last dance, without even speaking to Sir Cecil—Oliver reckoned that he already had the old man's blessing—he drew Rose into a gallery off the hall and proposed marriage to her.

Rose did not answer this question any more than she had answered any of the others he had put to her in the course of the long evening. Within herself, she was neither surprised nor pleased by

Oliver's proposition. Her husband, Robert, had also asked her to marry him as soon as he saw her. She knew the effect she had on men; she had known since she was twelve. They all wanted her, their faces turned red, they panted like dogs, all the while smiling as if these signs were invisible to her. That this huge stranger in his absurd sultan's costume should fall in love with her the first time he saw her and ask for her hand in marriage even before she had had any supper seemed natural enough.

"I've asked Rose to marry me," Oliver told Sir Cecil as the two of them watched her mount the stairs.

"I thought you might. What did she say?"

"Nothing. She just stepped past me and went away."

"Take that as a good sign," Sir Cecil said. "I'll find out what she thinks."

He did not have to ask. Next day, after breakfast, Rose asked Sir Cecil what he knew about Oliver.

"Respectable family," Sir Cecil said. "Don't you know the name?"

"Yes, but he's the first Barebones I've ever met," Rose said. "Are they all like him?"

Sir Cecil ignored her question. Because he had never had to answer to anyone, his style of conversation was to ask loud questions one after the other until the answers became obvious.

"Do you fancy the man?" he asked.

"Fancy him? He's a dray horse."

"And you're an Arabian mare. Do you think it makes any difference whom you marry as long as the man has money?"

Rose cast down her eyes. She knew what her situation was. Her father, who had no money and three other daughters, all as pretty as Rose but unmarriageable because of their poverty, had told Rose at her husband's grave that he had no place for her at home. Sir Cecil had been saddled with her as a consequence, but he wanted to get the saddle off.

"Do you have money to live on?" he asked.

"You know I am very poor," Rose said, and touched her dry eyes with a handkerchief.

"What a little beggar you are," Sir Cecil said. "Answer me a thing or two. Do you want to stop being alone and poor in this benighted village and live in London wearing fine dresses before your juices dry up? Do you understand that all the eligible men in this county are too lowborn for you or too shy of your looks and Robert's ghost to marry you? Do you know that Oliver Barebones owns a ship, or at least part of one, and a handsome house in the Strand? Do you see that he can't get enough of looking at you and how he bulges and pants while he looks?"

"Yes," said Rose. It was no use refusing to answer Sir Cecil. He would only ask worse questions.

"Then say yes to him. You'll only have to give him what he wants on the wedding night and then once a month for a few years until he's too old to want it any longer. He's fifty or more now. You'll still be a young woman in a town full of young men and you can have anything you want."

"But he's horrible."

"Of course he's horrible. So is being thrown out of this house into the Buckinghamshire weather. Do you know what I am saying to you?"

When, an hour later, Sir Cecil brought Oliver into the room where Rose waited, she accepted the proposal of marriage that had been made to her. The fact that she looked out the window during the whole conversation and never let her eyes rest on Oliver did not trouble Oliver. He thought that it was one of the most charming things he had ever seen a woman do.

# 5

Henry was amazed when Oliver told him that he planned to marry a woman he had met just two days before.

"How old is this country flower?" Henry asked.

"Twenty."

"You're fifty-one."

Oliver was not in the mood for warnings. "If she can't keep up with a man of my experience," he said jovially, "I'll drop by the Widow's for a bit of refreshment. The great thing is to get off on the right foot. That's where you come in, Henry. You're going to bet fifty guineas of my money that it won't rain on my wedding day."

"Why?"

"Because she's made me promise that we won't be married in the rain. Lightning struck the church at her first wedding and she had two dead babies and a husband that broke his neck falling off a horse. It's made her superstitious."

"What if I lose?" Henry asked.

"She'll leave me at the altar. But you never lose."

"That's because I've never wagered that it wouldn't rain in April in London."

"It doesn't have to stop raining everywhere in London. Just in the vicinity of Saint Andrew's—and only for an hour at that."

Despite all the blows that fate had rained on Henry, Oliver believed that he was supernaturally lucky. Hadn't he lived when everyone else died in the plague house? He'd lost his wife and gained the finest girl in London as a daughter. He never lost at auctions by the candle. Money came to him when he needed it: at Lloyd's, where he was admired for his hairbreadth escapes from bankruptcy, they called him Last-Minute Harding.

"Besides," Oliver said, "I've asked Fanny to come along and give us luck."

"Fanny? To this place?"

The two friends were sitting in the Cocoa Tree, a chocolate house in Pall Mall that was famous for attracting customers who would bet on anything, however bizarre. Women, especially innocent girls, ordinarily did not come inside. If they did, they were almost certain to become the objects of insulting bets.

"She shouldn't come here," Henry said.

"Perhaps she won't," Oliver said. "It's raining."

Oliver's mind was elsewhere. He was looking for someone to take Henry's bet; it would have to be a stranger because those who knew about Henry's luck wouldn't bet with him.

"Those fellows will do," Oliver said. He nodded toward a group of men who stood together gazing into the muddy street and drinking chocolate with boiled milk and sugar in it to make it less bitter, a new fashion in London. One of the men was splendidly dressed in silks, with lace cascading from the sleeves of his coat and half a dozen rings on his fingers.

Oliver called a waiter and asked him for the man's name.

"Which one, sir?"

"The one that's dressed like a Gentleman of the Bedchamber on the royal birthday."

"That would be Mr. Alfred Montagu, sir."

"Does he bet?"

"Famous for it, sir."

Oliver strolled over to the window, putting a hand on Montagu's shoulder and smiling to move him aside. Montagu shrugged his hand off and stared pointedly at the place on his shoulder where it had lain, as if looking for a stain. Oliver, a hulking figure in an ill-fitting wig, ignored him.

"Come over here, Henry, and choose your raindrop," he said in a loud voice.

Henry rose from his chair and joined his friend by the window. The glass was beaded with raindrops.

"The other fellow would have to pick his raindrop at the same time," Henry said.

"Yes, of course he would," Oliver said loudly. "Unless there was a handicap."

The chocolate drinkers overheard. "Pick *what*?" asked Montagu.

Oliver looked him coldly up and down and decided to answer even though he did not know him and could not possibly ever know him. "The raindrop," Oliver said. "For the raindrop race. Each man chooses a raindrop and then you see which one wins."

"Which raindrop wins?"

Henry ignored the question with an air that suggested that the man who had asked it was the only one in London who did not know the answer. By now the curiosity of the whole group was piqued: perhaps it wasn't to be a boring afternoon after all.

Montagu spoke. "You mean which one runs down the glass the fastest?"

Oliver answered without looking at him; his eye was fixed on the pane, which was beaded with raindrops. "Yes."

"What sort of handicap were you talking about?" Montagu asked.

"It's obvious, I should have thought. If you choose a drop that has already started down, and my friend here chooses the next one to strike the glass, then he has been handicapped because your raindrop has a head start."

"Your friend would bet so?"

"With suitable odds, yes," Oliver said.

"What if I choose that one?" Montagu pointed to a raindrop that was traveling a rapid zigzag course down the wavy pane. It was about an inch from the top.

"All right," Oliver said. "Two to one. Harding's fifty guineas against your hundred. Neither side can tap the glass or blow on it or interfere with it or the raindrops in any way."

"Done."

"That one," Henry said as a heavy drop struck the pane just below the upper sash.

The race began. Henry's large quivering raindrop stuck on the glass for a moment, then rolled downward. Montagu's raindrop was way ahead. One of Montagu's party placed a side bet of ten guineas on his friend's raindrop. Henry's raindrop began to run rapidly downward. Its weight, and the fact that it had fallen on a

portion of the glass that was less distorted than any other, caused it to fall in a straight line, while Montagu's followed a meandering course. More side bets were placed. A crowd gathered and cheered on the raindrops. Henry's raindrop drew even with Montagu's, and after three or four inches of neck-to-neck progress, overtook it and ran to the bottom sash to win by the breadth of a finger.

Montagu gave Henry his hundred guineas, pouring them into his cupped hands out of a purse so that the last of the coins overflowed and fell to the floor. Oliver bent over and picked them up.

"Most enjoyable," Montagu said. But there was the look in his eyes of a man who hates to lose.

Oliver stood up and gave Henry the coins he had gathered.

"I'll bet you half the hundred that it won't rain on Saint Andrew by the Wardrobe between ten o'clock and noon on the first Tuesday after Easter, then," Oliver said.

"No," Henry said. "You can't choose the day. If it's to be a real bet, I must choose it."

Montagu's back was turned now, but he was silent and it was obvious that he was listening to the conversation between Oliver and Henry.

"Sorry, Henry, you can't," Oliver said. "I met Rose on Shrove Tuesday and I must marry her on the first possible day after Easter. Even that is too long a wait. You don't know what it is to wait for a girl like Rose all during Lent."

Montagu turned his head. He wore a beautifully made wig that was powdered a faint blue. "Have you thought of another bet?" he asked.

"My friend wants to bet that it won't rain on Saint Andrew's between ten and noon on the first Tuesday after Easter."

"What day of the month is that?"

"The seventh of April," Oliver said.

"You want to bet that it won't rain in London on a day in April, do you? Will you say a hundred?"

"All right," Henry said.

"Done," said Montagu. "Let's have them write it down in the betting book."

All during the raindrop race, Henry had been watching Pall Mall through the window for a sign of Fanny. Now she appeared in the door, wearing a sky-blue dress that flattered her eyes and a hat with a plume that trailed over her shoulder.

Montagu saw her first.

"By God," he said. "Look at that, in the blue."

Henry turned around and Fanny smiled at him across the room. Her smile was not so luminous as Henry's. Like Fanchon's, it was

mostly in the eyes, which softened and grew deeper and seemed to open, Henry thought, as if to invite the person she was smiling at to come inside her thoughts and find himself there.

"Is that your piece?" Montagu asked, seeing Fanny's smile. "Where did you find her?"

His long pale face had taken on a peculiar look, the bloodless lips drawn back from the stubbly teeth, the intense gray eyes unblinking, the mouth parted with the tongue moving inside. Fanny was talking to Oliver now and saw none of this.

"She's my daughter," Henry said.

"You're joking."

Henry looked him up and down, then turned away. Montagu took hold of the cloth of his coat to restrain him.

"My mistake," he said. "But daughters who look like that—my God, those eyes!—don't usually live with their fathers."

Henry took hold of Montagu's wrist but the other man resisted, twisting the fabric of Henry's sleeve. His eyes remained fixed on Fanny.

"She's not married?"

Henry didn't answer.

"I'm tempted to make an offer of marriage here and now," Montagu said. "Would you say me no?"

Henry gazed at Montagu without expression. The other man, like most people, was much taller than Henry. He looked down into Henry's upturned face, then patted him on the shoulder.

"I see that you don't fancy me as a son-in-law," he said. "But we still have our bet. Perhaps we can have another one someday soon."

Henry left him and led Fanny out. Oliver was telling her about the raindrop bet, and she was laughing as she listened. She squeezed Henry's hand, proud like Oliver of her father's luck.

At the door, Henry looked back at Montagu and saw that his eyes were still on Fanny. Montagu saw that Henry was watching him; he did not care.

"Shall we have dinner at Locket's Tavern on your winnings?" Fanny asked. It was her favorite place.

"Lobsters," Oliver said.

"Always lobsters," Fanny replied, looking upward into Oliver's grinning face. Henry realized that she had not even noticed Montagu or the look on his face.

# 6

Rose had been tutoring Fanny in the ways of men.

"I had a beautiful sister who drowned," she said, "and when they pulled her poor body from the pond, do you know what they said? 'What a waste of cunny.' Not 'Poor Ella, dead before she'd lived,' not 'How sad.' All they could think about, looking at that poor dead girl, was how she'd denied some man his beastly pleasure. Oh, Fanny, they're horrible, you'll see."

Sir Cecil had brought Rose down to London while she waited for Lent to end and her wedding to Oliver to take place. There was no point in her mooning around Lockwood Hall, he said, if she could be in the city learning to love her husband-to-be. The two of them had arrived unannounced on two pretty horses, a gray Barb for Rose and a big hunter for Sir Cecil, with a couple of countrymen walking along behind pulling Rose's trunk on a cart. The trunk contained everything she owned—one ball dress, two ordinary dresses, a cloak, one pair of slippers, one pair of boots, her petticoats and stockings and ribbons. It was not quite half-full.

"You must get her a horse," Sir Cecil told Oliver. "She's a damn fine horsewoman, has the best seat of any woman in Buckinghamshire. Her father was a horseman, still is, and made her ride all day as a child. Robert never got off a horse except to get on something that wore a skirt, and rain or shine, mud or snow, she rode with him every day."

"What about the horse she's riding?" Oliver said.

"The Barb? Oh, no!"

But before he went back to the country Sir Cecil sold the animal to Oliver for twice what it was worth.

"I must find a horse for myself now," Oliver said, "so that we can go riding together, Rose. By God, you'll turn heads up and down the park!"

Rose paid no attention. She seemed not to hear anything Oliver, or any other man, said. When spoken to she looked away, out a window or into a looking glass or at a point in space, as if she had lost her hearing. In fact Rose had extraordinary hearing. All her

senses were preternaturally sharp. On her first evening in London, after knowing Oliver's friends for no more than three or four hours, Rose had put on a blindfold and told them apart, one after the other, by the way they smelled. It was her only party trick, but it was a wonderful one and it made her instantaneously famous in London.

"By heaven, Oliver," his friends said, "you'd better have a bath before you come home from the Widow's."

"The Widow will never see me again," Oliver replied.

He meant what he said. Rose fascinated him. Her other senses were just as extraordinary. She could sort out words spoken on the other side of the room in the midst of a party, and once at Southend when the Hardings and Oliver took her picnicking by the sea, she saw a ship coming down the estuary of the Thames and described the red lion that was the figurehead on all Dutch ships five minutes before anyone else could even make out the hull.

Oliver heaped presents on her even if it was Lent—buying her trinkets, bringing dressmakers and milliners to the house, hiring the painter to make her portrait. She said, "Thank you for nothing."

For the sake of appearances, she lived in the Hardings' house while waiting for her wedding day. She dreaded its arrival; it meant that she must move next door into Oliver's house.

"I like this house *so* much better than Oliver's," she said.

"But the two houses are exactly alike," Fanny said. "My father and Oliver had them built to be the same."

"They do everything alike. Isn't it boring?"

"I've never thought so."

Rose's face, as she talked about Henry and Oliver, was full of secrecy and scorn. According to the rules she lived by, men were creatures to be outwitted and used. She seemed to think that Fanny was born knowing this because she had been born female and was part of a conspiracy all women belonged to.

"Will you play something for me, Fanny darling? It helps me to sit still."

They were in the music room. The painter was at work on Rose's portrait.

Fanny sat down at her spinet and played some of the simple tinkling airs that Rose liked. She hated anything in French or anything that repeated itself too much. She hated posing, and when the painter left she opened the window to rid it of the hateful smell of turpentine and oils. Antoinette brought in a plate of cakes. Rose, who was very greedy about food, ate three of the four.

"Ah, Fanny," she said with crumbs on her perfect lips, "I never

want to move next door. If only I could go on living here with you."

Rose had been given a bedchamber of her own, but from the very first night she slept with Fanny, creeping into her bed after the rest of the house was asleep.

"You smell so wonderfully different, Fanny," Rose said. "I wish I smelled like you and had your black hair and your black eyes."

"They're blue."

"But such a dark, dark blue, not milky English blue like mine. I wish I looked just like you."

Whispering through the night, she told Fanny about her two stillborn babies, about her husband Robert who had been heir to a thousand acres in Scotland. If one of Rose's babies had been a boy, and lived, she would now be rich and living in Scotland. She believed that all her bad luck had been caused by cats. She had seen a cat before Robert was killed, a cat had appeared in the window on the night she gave birth to her first dead child, a cat had jumped onto the bed on the night that Rose was sure her other was conceived.

"It walked on Robert's back while he was planting his seed," Rose said. "It looked over his shoulder into my eyes with its horrid green eyes. Of course, Robert paid no attention. He was puffing and snorting and dribbling. You'll see what men are, Fanny, poor child."

Nobody had ever spoken to Fanny about the sexual act before. Rose described it in graphic terms—what it felt like, what to do to get it over with as soon as possible. She observed everything, but appeared to feel nothing.

"She's a very strange woman," Fanny said to Henry. "How can Oliver love her?"

"There's no explaining love," Henry said. "Be kind to her."

"Never fear. She leaves one no time for anything else."

Fanny had never played with other children, but living with Rose, she gained an idea of what it must be like. Rose played children's games all day long—card games, singing games, games of pretend. She would pretend that she was the queen and Fanny was a lady-in-waiting.

"What have you brought me?" she would ask in a fluting voice, and then whisper to Fanny, "You say: 'A letter from my Lord Buckingham.' "

"Really, Rose, I can't say that."

"Why ever not? It's a lovely game. My sisters and I played it all the time at home."

"Were you always the queen?"

"We took turns. Do you want to be queen?"

"I want to read."

"*Read?*"

Rose would take down a book and sit by the window staring into it. She never turned the pages. Fanny noticed that she took down books in Latin and Greek as often as she chose those in English.

"What is that book you're reading?" Fanny asked one day.

"One of my favorites."

"What is it called?"

"Come see for yourself," Rose said.

It was a treatise on disease written in Latin.

"Ah," Fanny said, "*Heroic Stanzas.* I didn't know you liked Mr. Dryden's poems."

"They are my favorites," Rose said, and Fanny realized that Rose did not know how to read.

The game Rose liked best was dressing up. Fanny's clothes fit her, and she adored trying them on one after the other and looking at herself in the mirror. One morning shortly before the wedding, she suddenly started talking about witchcraft.

She loved Fanny's mirror, a full-length, very clear one with a carved golden frame that Fanchon had brought from France. She wore a dark blue dress now, with a matching hat.

"Your things are so lovely, Fanny," Rose said. "But the colors are wrong for me." She adjusted the hat. "I wish I had a mirror as big as this one," she said. "Then I could look behind me and see who was who."

"Look behind you, Rose?"

Rose held Fanny's eyes in the glass and smiled without showing her teeth. "I can see *you*, Fanny, but there are some you can't see in a looking glass. Witches don't show in a mirror—they have no reflection."

Fanny didn't believe that Rose really believed in witches; she just had some use for them that would be revealed when she trotted them out in order to get her way about something. "Have you never seen a witch in a mirror, Rose?" Fanny asked.

Rose didn't like the joke; a look of annoyance came and went in her face. She opened another wardrobe and looked inside. Every frock, every petticoat exhilarated her.

"What's *this*?" she cried, unfolding a bottle-green velvet dress. "It can't be yours—it's such a mannish color."

"When I was younger Father sometimes had my dresses made to match his suits, so when we went out together we were a pair," Fanny said.

"You went out together? Where did you go?"

"Everywhere in London. The same places that we go to now."

"How awful for a little girl." Rose was shaking out Fanny's old dresses one after the other and holding them against herself. Each had a hat to go with it. "Weren't you ever frightened to be the only child with all those men?"

"No. And we always had Oliver along."

"Oliver? What did Oliver have to do with anything?"

"Oliver has to do with everything. He's my second father."

Rose uttered a false laugh. "No man is a father to a girl with looks like yours, Fanny. You'll see." She held the velvet dress against her chest and looked at herself.

"Amazing," she said. "You were a little woman, Fanny, not a little girl."

Fanny had learned that Rose liked to do and say the same things over and over again, and never seemed to remember that she had done or said them before. In the weeks that she had stayed with the Hardings, she had tried on Fanny's dresses a dozen times. They were new to her each time.

"Does your French maid keep your things so nicely folded and put away?" Rose asked.

Fanny kept silent; she had answered the question many times before.

Rose shook out one of Fanny's petticoats, then another and another.

"Every one of your petticoats has a little pocket in it right here," Rose said, touching her belly. "Whatever for?"

"Antoinette does that," Fanny says. "The French like pockets for hiding things."

"What things?"

"You could hide money in it, or jewels."

Rose was roguish now. This was the sort of thing she'd never let go of. "What do you hide in yours, Fanny?"

"If I ever have any money or jewels, I'll have a place to hide them."

"I don't think I should like having a French maid," Rose said. "There was a French maid in my husband's family that smuggled a Catholic priest into the house in the night to baptize a newborn baby. They found them in the garret praying in Latin over the child and getting ready to sprinkle it with holy water. He may have taken it back into his priest hole with him, or stolen it for the Jesuits. That's something to remember about the French."

Like most English people, Rose hated Catholics. She thought that they were all involved in secret plots to kill the king, bribe the army, cause riots.

"The plague was caused by the French," Rose said, tying the ribbon of a bonnet beneath her chin. "They sent a Jesuit to smuggle in a Gypsy who had plague, and that's how it all began. The Great Fire was set by the Jesuits, too."

It was Friday, the day that Evans came to hear confessions. Fanny had arranged for Rose to go riding later in the afternoon, but now she tried to change the subject. It was nearly noon. Rose was a clock of appetites—she grew hungry exactly on schedule.

"Are you hungry, Rose?" Fanny asked. "It's past noon."

Rose shook her head. She wanted to talk about Catholics.

"They say King Charles confessed himself a Catholic at his last hour and took the sacraments, and that it was his own brother, King James, who smuggled a priest into the palace," Rose said. "Do you think that's true—that the king himself was a papist?"

"Which king?"

"Both—Charles and James."

"Everyone says so."

"It must have happened to them in France when they were too small to know. Did it happen to your mother too? Was she born in France?"

Fanny pretended not to hear.

Rose went on. "But you were born in England, in this house. Oliver told me so. Which room were you born in?"

"This one. It was my mother's room. Nearly everything in it belonged to her."

"She was so young—as young as me when my girls were born dead," Rose said. "The woman pays, Fanny." Rose shivered as if Fanchon's ghost were present. "The mirror was hers too?"

"The mirror too, Rose." Fanny sighed. "The mirror, the lute, the table, the wardrobe, the picture of my grandfather. I use her comb. My clothes are mine. All the rest was hers."

Suddenly Rose snatched the bonnet off her head and threw it to the floor. She looked at herself in the glass, and at Fanny behind her.

"I don't *want* to be married!" she cried.

# 7

A month later, on the first Tuesday after Easter, as Rose walked out of the windowless waiting room into the nave of the church of Saint Andrew by the Wardrobe, she saw that there was practically no light in the sky over London. Gusts of wind rattled the high narrow windows of the church. An hour before, floating down the Thames through the spring day with Henry and Fanny in a pleasure boat, she had seen no clouds, smelled no rain in the air. The sun shone and the birds flew overhead, instead of chirping in the trees and the eaves as they always did when a shower was approaching. But the weather had changed as soon as the music started for her wedding.

Oliver waited at the altar, dwarfing Henry and the old curate who was going to perform the ceremony. He stood at least a foot higher than Rose's first husband, and he had a bony jaw filled with square yellowish teeth and a great muzzle for a nose. Oliver loved fashion as much as any man with an ideal figure, and he had had new clothes cut for his wedding. His great torso was dressed in a plum-colored silk suit with matching stockings and a ruffled shirt. He wore a curly wig that hung, in the latest fashion, nearly to his waist behind and billowed over his chest in front.

When Oliver saw Rose drifting into the nave in her pale golden dress that was nearly the color of her skin, he gripped Henry Harding's arm as if to keep himself from leaping down to meet her. Ribbons floated round her as she walked. In a pen-and-ink drawing, Rose would have seemed less remarkable than she was in the flesh. It was her color that made everyone look at her—the flaxen hair and the lavender eyes and the voluptuous creamy complexion that were so English. She glowed as she moved through the shadowy church—like an angel, Oliver thought. He expelled his breath in a long heavy sigh. For the whole six weeks of Lent he had daydreamed of nothing but her beauty, imagining her beside him at table, beside him as he read or listened to music, beside him at the theater, beside him in bed.

Rose wore an expression of absent annoyance, as if she had

been awakened from a dream that deeply interested her by some-
one who had no right to touch her. This Saint Andrews was a
replacement for the original church, which had been destroyed in
the Great Fire of London. The gathering storm was clearly visible
through the dusty windows, most of which were glazed with plain
glass while the church waited for gifts of stained glass. The sun had
vanished altogether now. The day grew steadily darker. As yet
there was no rain, just the wind howling high up in the roof beams
and mingling with the tremolo of the choir. A flash of lightning
filled the windows with flickering blue light. Thunder rolled over-
head and the sky opened up in a deluge of rain.

Henry and Oliver exchanged a glance. Rose stopped walking
toward the altar, turned her back on it, and ran back the way she
had come. Fanny, her bridesmaid, stood in the way. Rose pushed
her aside, crushing her bridal bouquet and letting it fall to the
floor. Fanny picked up the bruised flowers and followed Rose
through the narrow door into the waiting room. Oliver started to
do the same, but the curate stopped him, closing his prayer book
with a snap, and himself hurried after the bride. The guests, still
chuckling over the antics of the lunatics at Bedlam, gave each
other looks of delight. They were people who lived for amuse-
ment, but even at Oliver's wedding they hadn't expected to have a
joke instead of a ceremony.

In the musty cubicle at the back of the church, even though it
had no windows, Rose could still hear the wind and the thunder.
The curate came in and took Rose's limp hand between the two of
his and looked with a kindly smile into her numb face.

"You must come back now," he said. "Mr. Barebones and all
the others are waiting."

Rose took her hand away from him. "I won't be married in the
rain," she said.

"God makes the rain," the curate said in a stern voice. "If He
sends it to you on your wedding day, He has a very good reason to
do so."

Rose paid no attention to these words. She turned to Fanny. "I
don't understand why I didn't *smell* the rain," she said.

This remark did not surprise Fanny, who was quite ready to
believe that Rose could smell the rain in the sky before it fell. She
put Rose's bouquet back together and tied the ribbon around the
stems of the flowers.

"We can wait till it stops," Fanny said. "Look, I've brought you
your bouquet."

"There's never before been a thunderstorm so soon after Eas-

ter," Rose said. "Something wrong is happening again. God doesn't want to protect me, Fanny."

The curate gasped. "That is blasphemy. It is superstition, madam. Many have been whipped through the streets of London for less."

The clergyman bowed his head, showing a circle of white hair round a leathery scalp covered with thready brown moles, and intoned a rapid request that the Lord give Rose strength to believe in His goodness and mercy and be spared the lash and the pillory.

On hearing these terms, Rose looked upward, so as not to have to look at the curate's moles, and listened to the storm. She thought that it was growing weaker. Soon the lightning stopped and the wind fell.

"If there is an impediment to the marriage," the curate said, not knowing that the storm was the impediment, "you must confess it now or burn in hell."

"Everything is all right now," Rose said. "I'm ready." She picked up her bouquet and went back into the church.

But all during the ceremony rain scampered across the roof. Rose gave her responses in a parched voice, never looking at the clergyman or the groom. She shrank away when Oliver put the ring on her finger. Then his mouth opened and he caught Rose's lips between his own, which were as big and as rough as a smith's fingers, in a kiss that was like a hard pinch.

At this moment, a snow-white cat trotted down the aisle of the church until it reached the altar. Fanny watched it in fascination. It was a large, well-fed tomcat. It gathered itself and leapt onto the altar, landing with a soft but clearly audible thump among the candlesticks.

Rose heard the sound of the cat's landing while Oliver was still kissing her. She smelled the powder in his wig and the morning's ale and toast on his breath.

It was then, as she tried to shut out the reality of Oliver by holding her breath, that she opened her eyes and saw the cat walking across the altar. It looked directly at Rose out of elongated flickering pupils like candle flames, yawned, and then jumped to the floor with another thump—it was a very heavy, soft animal—and walked slowly away down the aisle. Oliver's raucous friends were delighted again.

Rose tore herself out of Oliver's arms. "Out!" she whispered. "I must get out of here!"

Henry paid the curate for his services and went outside to make sure that the sedan chairs he had hired were waiting for the wedding party. The chairs were all lined up as ordered, with the chairmen standing ankle-deep in the mud. Though the rain had

stopped, the water it had deposited ran down the streets, cutting channels in the grayish soil.

One man was already sitting in a sedan chair on the shoulders of the carriers. It was Montagu, the gambler from the Cocoa Tree. He sat with one emaciated leg crossed over the other, eating nuts and flicking the shells at the front chairman's head with his thumb. When he looked away from the chairman, who squirmed in his rags under Montagu's weight and the sting of the broken nut shells, and rested his eyes on Henry, his expression did not change. If Montagu had spoken the words aloud, he could not have made it plainer that Henry and the chairman were the same low class of creature so far as he was concerned.

"Harding, is it?" Montagu said. "I think you owe me a hundred guineas. I don't suppose you've got it on you."

Henry bowed. "I hardly ever carry that much to a wedding," he said. "But if you need it as badly as all that, you can follow me home if you like."

Henry got into a chair and was carried to the Thames embankment with Montagu coming along behind. There they found a boat to take them up the river to the Temple Stairs. The wedding guests, traveling in a bigger boat, had reached Henry's house before them, and the clatter of conversation spilled out into the street. Montagu remained in his sedan chair until Henry returned with the money. He weighed the sack of coins in his hand.

"They were wrong at the Cocoa Tree," he said. "They all said your ship was late and you'd have no money to pay in case you lost. They also said you never lose."

"They seem to know little about me in the Cocoa Tree," Henry said.

Henry looked upward into the rain, waiting courteously for Montagu to leave. As soon as Montagu had the money, two bodyguards armed with heavy staffs moved a step or two closer to him and looked around suspiciously.

"I rather like your house, Harding," Montagu said. "It has a pleasant situation, so near to the Strand."

"It is very convenient."

Montagu cocked his head as a gale of laughter came through the walls. "Perhaps I'll look in later," he said.

"Whenever you wish."

"It was not, I hope, your daughter who was married?"

"No."

"Good. It would be a pity if she was wasted on the wrong man."

Montagu took some snuff and sneezed three times in rapid

succession. When he looked at Henry again there were tears of pleasure in his eyes.

"She needs a man who knows how to wake a virgin up," he said. "We'll meet again."

# 8

On the morning after Oliver's wedding, he and Henry met at ten o'clock, as they did every day, to drink their morning draft together at the Rose Tavern in Drury Lane. Many of the wedding guests were there already, and as he limped across the floor to join his friend, Oliver was pelted with jokes.

"For some reason I have a thirst this morning," he said, and ordered a second pint. He drank it down, watching Henry over the rim of the tankard.

"Rose was in Fanny's bed when she woke up this morning, talking in her sleep," Henry said.

Oliver put a corner of ale-soaked toast into his mouth and talked while he chewed. "Poor Rose," he said. "She's not used to it. I'll buy her some presents today and she'll be all right."

"Not used to what? I thought she was a widow."

"She's more like a virgin. Very shy, Henry, and needing to be taught."

Oliver spoke these words in a hoarse whisper, a look of great pleasure and affection lighting up his face. His skin was pasty as a result of all the alcohol he had drunk the night before, and his hands trembled slightly as he dipped his toast into his mug of ale.

Henry gave him his second piece of toast and smiled. "It's still love on the morning after, then?"

"Why wouldn't it be?" Oliver asked. "I've been waiting for this girl all my life." He looked right and left, leaned toward Henry, and whispered again. "I tell you, Henry, you can't imagine what she's like. Nobody could."

"Perhaps that's just as well," Henry said.

He paid the bill. Outside, beside the muddy street, the friends waited in the doorway of the tavern for sedan chairs to carry them over the mud to the Thames, a few hundred yards away.

"Rose's rain has ruined the streets," Henry said, "besides costing me a hundred guineas."

"Montagu was right," Oliver said. "Only a fool would bet against the rain in April."

They hailed a couple of chairs, the chairmen grunting as they lifted Oliver to their shoulders and moved off down the Strand.

The storm had roiled the river, and the water was even browner than usual. The weak springtime sun had not yet burned away the fog, but the air was fresh, and the dingy gulls, flashing in the sunlight and then vanishing into the mist, sounded unusually loud. Seeing Henry and Oliver approaching the embankment, the crowd of boatmen waiting for passengers at the end of Strand Bridge Lane began shouting the customary "Oars! Oars! Anyone for oars?"

Oliver, who always made such arrangements for the two of them, selected a man he knew and gestured Henry into the bow.

"London Bridge," Oliver said.

"Would the gentlemen want to row on to the Tower first, to see the faces looking out the windows?" the boatman asked.

"No."

"I don't blame you, sir," the boatman said, grunting as he pulled on his oars. "Really I don't. There hasn't been a new face looking out the windows of the Tower that you'd know or care to see since the Duke of Monmouth was inside, and that was fifteen years ago. You remember the noble duke, sir. The ax was dull and he had to tell the headsman to sharpen it after the first stroke barely nicked his neck. The duke's words were sharper than the ax, is what I always say. The second chop didn't kill him either, and the headsman had to finish him off with a knife. Horrible it was, sir. Now *that* would have been worth seeing."

Oliver said, "Row, will you? We don't want any damned river wit."

The boatman raised his voice so that it carried over the water to the dozens of other boats around them. "Want to be alone with your thoughts on the day after your wedding, sir? Of course you do. You may wonder, sir, how I know about your happiness. You *do* wonder, I see that, so I'll tell you and put an end to your curiosity. I saw you yesterday, going down the river to the church and then coming back again. That's a lovely bride you've got, sir. Boats were turning over right and left in admiration as that lovely lady floated by, but of course you were too happy to notice the drowning men. Every man died happy himself, sir, having drunk in your bride's beauty before he drank the Thames."

The boatman pulled harder on the oars and overtook a boat

loaded with fashionably dressed people who were laughing at his jokes.

"Bridegroom aboard!" the riverman cried. "Married just yesterday and this morning he already needs 'ores! 'Ores, 'ores, he needs 'ores!"

Oliver paid no attention to this rude joke. But when they debarked, Henry gave the man an extra sixpence for it.

At the end of London Bridge, a chairman looked Oliver up and down and said, "Sorry, sir, I can't risk it in this mud when the hill's so steep."

"You've done it before," Oliver said. "Why should I have mud on my boots because God made me big? Use four men. Use six if you want to."

"Even so, it won't do, sir. Two men have fallen under heavy loads in this mud and broke their legs. If I have no legs I have no food."

"Blast! Nobody wants to work in England anymore."

"Come," Henry said. "I'll walk with you."

"No. Up, up!"

Oliver strode through the knee-deep mud in Fish Street Hill. It was clear that it was painful going for him, and Henry, smiling at his back, wondered how he had injured himself. As a young man Oliver had often fallen out of bed at the Widow's, taking the girl with him; the other clients, hearing the crash above their heads, would cry "Barebones!" and give him a cheer.

The chairmen, stepping into Oliver's footprints, followed with Henry's sedan chair on their shoulders. They threaded their way through a traffic jam of mired carriages and floundering horses. Oliver lost one of his boots in the muck and stood on one leg, leaning on Henry's chair while he put it back on.

The two men were on familiar ground in this neighborhood, and as they turned into Lombard Street they began to see their friends. The street was full of ships' owners and ships' masters on their way to Lloyd's Coffeehouse.

As he did every day, Praise God Adkins awaited his partners at the table that was their center of business. An auction by the candle was in progress as usual.

"What are they selling?" Henry asked.

"A cargo of coffee waiting in a French ship at Honfleur," Praise God whispered. "Will the *Pamela* stop there on this voyage?"

"Joshua said so. We have an order for ten barrels of Normandy applejack."

"But he's overdue. He may sail on to London."

"He's often overdue. He always fills his orders."

"The *Pamela* is overdue?" Oliver asked. This was the first he knew of it, and a look of anxiety came into his face. "Does that mean there'll be no money?"

"That's what it always means," Henry said. "Why, are you short?"

Oliver laughed and his eyes wavered, a mannerism new to Henry.

"I'm a married man now," he said. "Worrying about money is part of the husband's job."

Henry examined his friend's expression for a moment. He looked as if he really was worried. This, too, was new.

"I'll see what I can find out," Oliver said, and limped away into the crowd of men—Englishmen and foreigners of all kinds—who hung about at Lloyd's for shipping news and gossip.

Because the *Pamela* sailed under two flags and this was a risky practice, Henry kept her destinations and her cargoes in his head, telling his partners only what they needed to know.

Henry joined the auction and won the cargo of coffee at the excellent price of sixty-five pounds, ten shillings—the ten shillings being his final bid. He went back to the table. Oliver was already sitting there with another mug of ale before him.

"No useful news of the *Pamela*," he said. "There's a dago master over there who saw her loading chocolate in Tangier eight weeks ago, but no one has seen her since, in port or at sea. The dago said there was a storm in the Bay of Biscay three weeks ago that nearly sank his own ship."

"Which dago?" Henry asked.

"There," Oliver said. "The one talking to Montagu."

Montagu stood in the middle of the room in his gaudy clothes, talking to a burly Portuguese dressed in black.

"The parrot and the crow," Henry said. "What's Montagu doing here? I don't like that man, P.G."

"You're right not to like him, Henry. He's the rottenest man in London."

Henry looked at Praise God in surprise. The old man hardly ever spoke a bad word of anyone. London, and especially Lloyd's, was full of men who made you want to count your fingers after you shook hands, but Praise God ordinarily made no moral judgments. He was only interested in business. Did they keep their word? Did they pay their debts? Nothing else interested him.

"Rotten how?" Henry asked.

"Cheats people," Praise God said. "Goes round behind their backs and takes what's theirs. Uses toughs and bullies to get what he wants. Doesn't give a damn about the law. He'll steal your eyes

and diddle your wife while you're screaming from the pain, that's what they say about Montagu."

Montagu was through with the Portuguese. He walked across the room to Henry's table.

"Ah, Harding," Montagu said. "You again. I admired your bidding by the candle just now. Never saw a man who could do as many tricks as you."

"Really? I thought everyone was tricky in the Cocoa Tree."

Montagu did not answer for a moment. Then he said, "I've been asking for news about your ship—the *Pamela*, is it? They say she's overdue."

"Ships are often late—winds, tides, slow work in foreign ports."

"And pirates and shipwreck, I suppose," Montagu said. "They say your captain is a dago. I shouldn't be happy if I had a dago for a captain and my ship was late."

"Perhaps it's just as well you're in some other business than shipowning, then. I've never seen you here before."

"I've never had a reason to be here."

Montagu turned to Oliver. "Sorry it rained on your bride," he said. "She's certainly a beauty. Not in the same class with that musical daughter of Harding's, of course. Fanny, is it? My favorite name. Amazing skin—and that dago hair! I congratulate you, Harding, you've trained her up to be a paragon as well as a beauty. She'll make some lucky man a fabulous wife."

Montagu turned to Henry and smiled flirtatiously, almost as if he were smiling at a woman.

"On that subject, my offer stands," he said. "Assuming, naturally, that the dowry is adequate. That seems rather chancy. What if your ship has sunk?"

Montagu turned and left.

"What offer?" Oliver said. "What dowry?"

"He says he wants to marry Fanny."

"Marry Fanny!"

Oliver rose to his feet, blood running into his face, fists doubled, and knocked over a chair.

"Sit down," Henry said. "He's not the man for her."

"Not the man for her?" Oliver said. "I'll stick the bastard into the muck by his head."

Henry turned to Praise God. "Tell me more about Montagu," he said.

"How can you not know? Everybody else avoids him like the plague. Montagu builds houses, whole streets of them, and sells them to people who want to make a show. He's famous for taking what he wants—money, property, women. I heard of a man who

wouldn't sell Montagu a house he wanted, so Montagu came in the night and pulled it down around his head. Half of London is suing him."

"Oh," Henry said. "*That* Montagu. I thought this one was a connection of Mountagu, the Earl of Sandwich."

"He wants you to think that. Montagu is not even his name. He just calls himself that."

Oliver had been drinking ale rapidly to cool himself off. As he drank, he listened, and a look of curiosity had come into his eyes. He leaned toward Praise God and asked a question. "Is he rich?"

"Sometimes, when he isn't bankrupt. How do you two know him?"

"We saw him in the Cocoa Tree a few weeks ago and made a bet with him."

"You won?"

"There were two bets, actually. I won the first and lost the second. He called on me to collect the money. Maybe Montagu's in one of his bankrupt periods."

"That's when he's dangerous," Adkins said. "But as it happens, he's far from bankrupt just now. He's been lending money all over London."

"Damn!" Oliver said, remembering his anger. He rose to his feet and thumped across the room, pushing men aside and muttering as he went.

"Oliver," Henry called. "Come back, forget the man."

But Oliver was already outside in Lombard Street. He saw Montagu far down the hill in his bright clothes, being carried away on a sedan chair. He shouted his name, and then set off in pursuit, floundering in the mud.

Henry, watching from the door of the coffeehouse, shook his head and went back inside.

# 9

All morning long, Rose had been whispering to Fanny about marriage. Her first husband, Robert, had had Rose whenever he pleased for three entire years, day or night, standing up, lying down, sitting on his lap, bent over a wall in the rain while the

horses watched. He had always stripped her naked, no matter what the place or the weather, crying, "Skin! I must have skin!"

"His belt buckle dug into my poor stomach, I'd be lying on slimy wet stones or on the grass, itching terribly, he didn't care," Rose said. "All he could think about was spending, and then he'd want to spend again. In a way the belt buckle and the grass and the stones were a blessing because I could think about those things and not about what Robert was doing."

Rose had never experienced sexual desire, not even in her sleep; she did not believe that it existed in women. In men it seemed to be a sickness; they had a swelling, their faces twisted in what looked like pain but evidently was ecstasy, and then they went to sleep. The woman lived with shame for an hour afterward and with fear for a month.

"The consolation is that you forget what it was like between-times," Rose said. "After it stops hurting, it's as if nothing has happened until it happens again."

"What about Oliver?" Fanny asked.

"What about him?" Rose replied. "Let him go to the Widow's."

She got out of bed, opened Fanny's trunks and wardrobes, and began trying on clothes. Fanny watched her from beneath the covers. She knew what the sexual act involved; it happened in the streets between animals, and even between men and women, and she had often seen it. No woman had ever described it to her before, sparing no detail. As usual, Rose seemed to have no memory of what she had said five minutes after she had said it. She was smiling at herself in Fanchon's looking glass.

"I love your mirror so, Fanny," she said. "May I borrow it, take it next door? There's not a decent glass in that house. I *hate* it there."

"Ask Oliver to buy you one. He's always buying you things."

"And now you know why. Can I borrow this one until he finds me another? I *need* a glass, Fanny. I must have one tonight."

Fanny did not want to let her take the mirror, but lending it was better than being coaxed.

"All right. I'll fetch Antoinette. She'll carry it."

"But I don't want to go yet," Rose said. "Can you play for me? I could hear you playing last night all the while Oliver was at me. I should have gone mad if I hadn't heard you."

Rose remained with Fanny until evening, and when at last she came inside her own house, with Antoinette and the mirror following behind, she found Oliver waiting beside a table piled high with presents.

Rose took down a portrait of Oliver's mother, who was a female version of her son, and stood it against the wall.

"Hang the glass here," she said.

Oliver obeyed.

"That's Fanny's glass," he said, looking at Rose's reflection behind him as he spoke.

"I've borrowed it," Rose said. "Can you see me in the glass?"

"Yes. Beautiful."

"Fanny says you must buy me another glass very soon so that she can have this one back again. It belonged to her mother. Was she as pretty as her picture?"

"Prettier, but not so pretty as Fanny. Or you."

Oliver grinned as he talked, delighted to have Rose speaking to him so calmly. He had expected anger, tears, reproaches. That was why he had come home armed for the problems of matrimony.

"Look, Rose," he said, handing her a box.

He waited for her to open it, but she did not. There were a dozen or more boxes, all different sizes, piled on the table in the hall. He had brought her hats, cloth for dresses, two silk scarves, three different boxes of sweetmeats, and a little jointed wooden doll that danced on a string.

Rose's mood changed as soon as she saw the gifts. She wouldn't touch them or even look at them. Oliver opened the boxes one by one and offered them to her.

"Look, Rose! Let's have a smile."

She turned her unsmiling, wounded face away, as if nothing he could give her could interest her—much less make him worthy of her.

Oliver thought she was teasing him. He'd never known a girl who didn't like presents. "Come, Rose, try to be happy," he said. "These aren't dead rats I'm offering you."

"I shouldn't be surprised if they were," Rose murmured. "I remember my wedding night even if you don't, you drunken beast."

"I may have had a bit too much," Oliver said, "but a man only gets married once. Here, have a sweetmeat."

Rose turned her face away, squeezing her eyes shut as if he really had offered her a rodent. She sat in a chair with her hands folded in her lap. Oliver was sprawled on another chair between her and the door that led into the hall. He was in a husbandly state; Sir Cecil had been right, it happened to Oliver just by looking at her.

"Ah, Rose," he said, grinning and trembling. "You're the most beautiful thing I've ever seen."

To his surprise, Rose stood up and walked toward him, lifting

her skirt to her boot tops and holding out her hand, as if she meant to take the sweetmeat after all. Oliver's face lit up with happiness and he reached out a hand to her.

Rose looked downward. His wounded friend. Wounded or not, it was engorged and old and disgusting. She whirled, just beyond Oliver's reach, and ran up the stairs.

Oliver liked games before bed, and he still thought that this must be a game that Rose was playing. He pushed the sweet into his own mouth and chewed it as he thundered after her. Sore as his bitten flesh was, he wanted Rose more than ever. He imagined her on the bed, glorious, as he had seen her the night before.

"By God, I don't know how you're going to do it in your condition," Oliver said aloud to his bitten part, giving it an affectionate squeeze as he bounded up the stairs. "But do it you shall."

Rose's door was locked from the inside. Oliver called through the wood to her, but she was silent. It was a very heavy door, closely fitted except for a space about an inch high at the bottom. The room might have been empty, it was so quiet, but he knew that Rose, with her extraordinary ears, could probably hear him breathing.

"Rose, come out," Oliver said. "I have something more for you. It's a truly beautiful thing—more beautiful than all the other things together."

"I don't want to see it."

"You'll be sorry if you don't."

There was a long silence. Then Rose's voice, surprisingly clear, said, "How big is it?"

"As big as a plover's egg."

"What color is it?"

"Something like a strawberry. No, redder than that."

"I don't like red. But put it under the door."

"I won't, Rose. You must come out if you want to see what it is. It's a beautiful thing."

"Put it under the door if it's so wonderful and then we'll see."

"No. I don't trust you."

"Then give whatever it is to somebody else. I'm sure I don't want it."

Oliver took a ring out of his pocket and looked at it. Even in the dim evening light that filtered into the upstairs passageway, the stone, a huge ruby surrounded by a circle of sapphires, shone brilliantly. It was the largest jewel Oliver had ever seen except on the finger of the queen in a royal portrait. Only that day, he had mortgaged everything he owned in order to buy it.

Oliver wrapped the ring in a scrap of silk and slid it under the

door. Hearing Rose gasp, he smiled: let her resist a ruby as big as a plover's egg! No human being could. Oliver imagined her slipping the ring onto her finger. He imagined her with her hair floating around her, wearing the ring, and only the ring. He called to her. Still Rose didn't answer or open the door. Oliver thought of battering it down, but he was afraid that she would go out the window before he could knock the hinges off.

Much later, after he had drunk a whole bottle of French brandy, Oliver went to sleep on the floor outside the bedchamber door. A cold supper had been laid out by the maid on the table in the hall downstairs. Even Rose had to eat and drink in order to live, and she would have to step over his body to go to the food. That was her weakness: he would capture her when she came out.

When Oliver woke up, Rose's door was open. He lurched to his feet and looked inside the empty bedchamber, even searching under the bed before he heard the rattle of crockery below. He went down the stairs in his stocking feet and cautiously opened the door into the hall. Rose sat at the table alone with six candles burning in a silver candelabrum that had come from Spain in the *Pamela*. Oliver was amazed to see her. She was eating a chicken leg and watching herself in Fanchon's mirror. When Rose saw Oliver, she smiled, the first time she had ever done so. Sour as his stomach was after all the brandy, his heart lifted.

"Have you eaten?" she asked.

Oliver shook his head. Rose, all of a sudden wifely and mild, filled a plate with cold meat and cheese and poured him some ale. Oliver sat down on the other side of the table. Needing food to absorb the brandy he had drunk, he ate as quickly as he could, cutting chicken and mutton off the bone with one hand and stuffing it into his mouth with the other.

Rose smiled again and licked her fingers with her pink tongue. Her lips shone with fat from the chicken leg. She wore a robe that was belted very high under the bosom, an exciting fashion to Oliver, as everything about Rose was exciting. When Rose lifted her goblet to drink, Oliver saw that she wore the ruby on the index finger of her right hand. She was, Oliver thought, like a shy nymph with her huge tremulous eyes. Any sound or sudden movement would frighten her away.

Rose neither moved nor spoke. Smiling, Oliver went around the table and knelt beside her. Cautiously he moved the candelabrum closer. He looked at her for a long time. He touched her hair, then stroked her cheek with the back of his hand. Rose didn't resist; she seemed not even to notice what he was doing. Oliver had never

touched such skin. It brought back what he had seen and felt when he had been with her the night before. He untied her gown and spread it apart. Inside the airy cloth Rose's body sat, the pretty breasts standing up, the legs slightly parted, with flaxen hair between them that was the exact color of the shimmering hair on her head. Very carefully, as if he were capturing two wild birds, Oliver took one firm breast in each hand, then ran his palms along the ribs, over the silky pelt, down to the thighs. He pushed the legs apart a little more and kissed the inside of each knee.

Rose stirred for the first time and pressed her thighs together. "Sshhh," she whispered. "What's that?"

Oliver's face was buried between Rose's breasts. Her arms hung lax at her sides. She was breathing normally. She had a very slow heartbeat; Oliver could hear it through her ribs.

"Listen," Rose said. "It's music."

Oliver didn't lift his face. Holding Rose's waist with one hand in case she should try to slip away, he worked free of his breeches with the other.

"Fanny's playing her spinet," Rose said. "I can hear it through the walls. I can't bear it to be so loud. Go tell Fanny to be quiet."

"For God's sake, Rose. I can't hear music. How can I go next door in the state I'm in? Feel."

Her guided her hand, expecting her to flinch. The first touch was always a surprise to girls. Of course she had touched it the night before, in a way, but Oliver supposed she did not remember that. She must have been hysterical to do what she had done. The wound throbbed even now. But slowly, like a face swimming toward him in a dream, Rose's face drew closer until it touched his own. She kissed him chastely on the lips, then drew back just as slowly, smiling, still holding his distended part lightly between her fingertips.

"It's the music that disturbs me," she said. "You can see that, Oliver. Go and tell Fanny to stop. And when you come back I'll thank you very nicely for my ruby ring. Really I will."

Oliver listened for the music. Still he could hear nothing. Clumsily he stood up and tried to pull up his breeches.

Rose watched the struggle.

"You great rogue," she said with a smile, her robe open, the ring glowing on her finger. Then she stood up too, and led Oliver toward the mirror. They stood in front of it together for a moment.

"I thought so," Rose said.

She turned to Oliver—to Oliver himself, not to his reflection—with a look of such triumph that he mistook it for love.

"Thought what?" Oliver said.

"Never mind," she said. "Go now. Fanny won't mind your telling her to stop."

The watchman, an old man carrying a lantern and a cudgel, was all alone in Catherine Street, calling out one o'clock. He flinched when Oliver burst out of the door and threw his cudgel away to show that he meant no one any harm.

"Have you heard music from that house?" Oliver asked the watchman. There were no lights in the Hardings' windows.

"It's been dark at Mr. Harding's since ten o'clock," the watchman answered. "The little girl never plays after eight o'clock unless there are guests in the house."

Oliver went back inside his own house. Rose was gone. What was left of the food, Rose's neatly stripped chicken bones and some crumbs of cheese, was still on the table in the hall. The door to Rose's room was locked tight. Oliver pounded on it.

"By God," he said hoarsely, speaking to his member and giving it a companionable squeeze, "she has no mercy. None at all."

Rose whispered to him under the door. Her voice was hoarse. "Olly Olly Oliver," she said, "I couldn't see you in the mirror."

"For God's sake, Rose, leave off this nonsense. I'm dying for you."

"And I know why. You can't come in—not for rubies. Not even for pearls and diamonds. I know what you are now."

"Know what I am?" Oliver cried. "What am I?"

"Talk to the cat," Rose whispered through the door. "She'll remind you that a witch is always a witch."

# 10

A week later the *Pamela* still had not come home.

"She must come soon," Oliver said. "Bloody dago, always late."

"Yes, always," Henry said. "And he always makes money for us. What's wrong with you, Oliver?"

They were seated with Praise God Adkins at their usual table in Lloyd's Coffeehouse.

"I think I know what's wrong," Praise God said.

He took a rolled document out of an inside pocket and handed it

over to Oliver. The big man read it, then rolled it up again. He closed his eyes.

"Is your signature on the original of this paper, Oliver?" Praise God asked.

Oliver nodded. Adkins leaned forward and looked around him for eavesdroppers before he spoke. When at last he did speak, he whispered. "This is a copy of a demand note, my friends, for two thousand guineas." He paused. "Yes, two thousand guineas. The loan is secured by the entire cargo of the *Pamela*—not just Oliver's one-tenth share—and by the deed to Oliver Barebones' house in Catherine Street near the Strand. The note is held by Alfred Montagu, Esquire."

Henry picked up the note and examined it.

"Two thousand guineas is more than you and Henry will have between you after you sell the *Pamela*'s cargo and settle your debts," Praise God said. "What did you need with so much money, Oliver? And to borrow it from Montagu, of all the thieves in England!"

"Nobody else was willing to lend it to me," Oliver said.

"There was a reason for that," Praise God said. "He wants your house. And not just yours. Henry's too. You've given him a way to get them."

"He wants our houses?" Henry said "What for?."

"Who knows? Usually when Montagu wants houses it's because he wants to pull them down and put up bigger ones for the gentry."

"Well, he can't have them. I'll find the money."

"He doesn't want the money. He wants the houses."

"We'll refuse."

"Then he'll pull them down around your heads before the matter comes before a judge and argue afterward. He's done it before."

"He won't do it this time."

"No? You don't know the rest," Praise God said. "He's buying up your debts, Henry, offering a guinea for each pound you owe. I wouldn't sell, but with the *Pamela* long overdue, you can be sure that others will. Once he owns your debts, Montagu can do as he likes with you. In the past, it has amused him to send people to debtors' prison."

"What debts of mine has he bought up?" Henry said.

Praise God handed him a list.

"These are the ones I know about. There may be more."

Henry read the list. "He has them all," he said. "Except my tailor."

Praise God rose to his feet, tucking account books and rolls of paper into the pockets of his coat and under his armpits.

"You may very well be ruined this time, Oliver, and Henry with you," he said. "I say that very sadly, nephew, very sadly indeed."

Henry had been sitting quietly, reading over the list of debts. Praise God had totaled them. They added up to about four thousand pounds, or more than the value of the *Pamela*. Clearly Montagu intended to take the ship too.

"Well," Henry said. "This will take some thought." He handed Oliver his hat. "Come along, we'll fetch Fanny and take her to Locket's for supper," he said. "We can't think on an empty stomach."

"Not I," Praise God said. "I couldn't keep food down."

At Locket's Tavern, Henry and Oliver ate a boiled haddock with vegetables and half a breast of veal off the spit, finishing with a dozen oysters each and a marrow bone before they ate their pudding and cheese. They drank four bottles of claret and a pint of ale with the oysters before settling down with their brandy.

Fanny had a lobster and a glass of Canary wine. Her eyes were on Oliver. He had not spoken through the whole meal. At the next table, a man they had never seen before was kissing a woman called Kate and running his hands inside her dress.

"That tickles Kate," the woman said, laughing. "Locket's front room is no place for tickling, sir."

Fanny remembered what Rose had told her, every word of it. Were matters between men and women really the way she said they were?

"Smile, Oliver," Henry said. "The *Pamela*'s sailing home. We'll hold this man Montagu off with lawyers, and if that doesn't work, you can break his neck for him. So look a little happier."

"Montagu?" Fanny said. "Who's that?"

"The man who was looking at you while you played the other night."

"You mean the man who threw the cat on the table."

"Was it him? You saw him?"

"Through the window. He had a man waiting in the street with it. He went outside and took it from the man, then came back into the house and let it go."

"Bastard," Oliver said. He was wearing the new curly wig that he had bought for his wedding and he was quite drunk. His face was flushed and his speech was slurred.

"I've lost everything," Oliver said.

Henry smiled again. "I don't think so. The ship will be all right. So will we."

Fanny looked from one man to the other. "What's this?" she said.

Oliver covered his face with his hands. "I borrowed two thousand guineas from Montagu," he said.

"Two thousand guineas? What for?"

"I bought a ruby ring for Rose," he said.

"You paid all that for a ring?" Fanny said.

Oliver's hands, bony and veined, still covered his face. "There was a necklace too, but I held that back."

"Then we can sell it."

"I tried. Even the man I bought it from would only offer five hundred."

"I saw the ring," Fanny said. "It's beautiful."

"For all the good it did, I might as well have thrown the money into the Thames," Oliver said. "Rose won't let me be a husband to her. She says she can't see me in the mirror."

"Can't see you in the mirror?"

"She says I'm bewitched and if we're man and wife we'll both turn into white cats."

Tears ran down Oliver's cheeks.

Henry looked at his friend for a long moment, then gave his arm a squeeze.

"Witches and white cats, is it?" he said. "I think we'd best go visit the Gypsies."

# 11

In their cold-eyed contempt for anyone who was not exactly like them, the Gypsies who lived in the Great North Woods of Surrey were like peers of the realm, lawyers, and pickpockets. Henry brought Rose Barebones to them because she resembled them, being proud, vain, superstitious, and able to understand only the simplest facts. If Rose mistook nonsense for wisdom in her own world, Henry reasoned, she might do the same among the Gypsies and be cured by them of her stupidity—or her madness, if

that was what the matter was. He saw little difference between the two conditions.

The forest had been thinned by centuries of woodcutting, and the great trees that had given highwaymen and other desperadoes a hiding place were gone. Even so, it was not safe to travel through the forest without an escort even in daylight, and Henry had sent word of their coming. Four male Gypsies waited with ponies on the south bank of the Thames when Henry and Oliver and Rose and Fanny were rowed ashore. It was Sunday. The sun was near the equinox, and it burned round and white in a cloudless blue sky.

The ponies wore no saddles, so Fanny rode astride with her sky-blue dress billowing around her ("Your eyes!" Rose cried) and her slim calves in their white stockings gripping the animal's ribs. Rose mounted sidewise, and rode easily even without a saddle. In moments they were deep in the forest among slender young trees that filtered the watery April light.

Henry rode beside Fanny and talked about Fanchon. "When your mother and I were engaged to be married, I brought her out to visit the Gypsies," he said. "She was amazed by the trees, enormous oaks with trunks eight or ten feet thick. But not many were left even then. They cut them down by the thousands to build the Royal Navy."

"Where is the *Pamela*? Do you know?"

Henry looked around him to see if anyone was listening. "She'll soon be in Honfleur," he said. "Perhaps we'll go there at last."

"To escape from this man Montagu?"

Henry always called him that: this man Montagu. He knew that Fanny was teasing him and smiled.

"To beat him at his own game. He thinks he can get my ship. But we'll sail the *Pamela* to Portsmouth instead of London, transfer her cargo to another ship that will be waiting, and send that ship to London. We'll sell the cargo, pay off our debts, put horns on Montagu, and spend whatever's left on pigeon pie and lobster in Locket's Tavern."

"Where will you find a second ship?" Fanny asked.

"Practical Fanny. It's all arranged. No one knows but you and me. Not Oliver, not even Praise God."

"When will you go to Honfleur?"

Henry pointed to Rose, riding down the path ahead of them. "As soon as the Gypsies chase Rose's witch away," he said.

"And I'll go too?"

"Oh, yes. It's you that Montagu wants."

"Wants me?" Fanny said. "What for?"

"You're a beautiful girl, Fanny. But don't worry. He won't have you."

Have me? Fanny thought, remembering the things that Rose had told her. Henry was smiling his sunny smile again.

"Think," he said. "We're going to Honfleur at last to see the slate houses and the cathedral that's like a boat upside down, and then we'll sail to Portsmouth on the *Pamela*. Not a bad chap, Montagu, to make all that possible."

But Fanny saw the worry in his eyes. It was more than worry; she thought that it might be fear. She wanted to ask him more questions. How did he know that Montagu wanted her? What did that mean? How great was the danger?

Just then Rose's pony stumbled and they caught a glimpse of her anxious face. Rose feared the forest. The day before, while she tried on dresses to see how they went with her ruby ring, Rose had told Fanny stories of rich travelers being robbed in Norwood and tied to trees and left to starve, and of innocent girls being kidnapped by the Gypsies.

"They'll make any English girl they can steal wife to the whole tribe, Fanny," she had said. "At night you belong to anyone. They sell your children to people who have an evil use for them because their own children are too ugly and black to bring a good price."

Fanny knew that Rose was a fool. She had never imagined, when she imagined marriage, that she could ever feel toward a husband as Rose felt toward both of hers. But suppose the husband was a man like Montagu?

Henry seemed to read her thoughts. He reached across and touched her cheek.

"I shouldn't have told you these things," he said. "But you know no harm will come to you while I'm alive."

"I know. But what about poor Oliver?"

Henry winked. "The Gypsies will cure his troubles."

At the Gypsy encampment, Henry opened the bottle of excellent Nantes brandy he had brought for the head Gypsy and poured out two cups. They drank and talked.

"My friend is having a bit of unhappiness with his bride," Henry said.

The Gypsy immediately put on a solemn look. "Trouble of the spirit or trouble of the blood?" he asked.

"She won't do it for him."

"Then he should beat her on the bottom until she's wet and stick it in."

"He doesn't think that would change her mind." Henry told him

about Rose's fear of witches. "She thinks they get in through the cunny."

"Sometimes they do," the Gypsy said. "But usually they get in by the mouth. Where does she think they come from?"

"Out of her husband's dingus. She believes that he was bewitched by a cat."

"By a witch that had turned itself into a cat, you mean."

"Is that the way it usually goes?"

"Yes. Then the cat would have turned into a woman in order to steal his seed, because witches have no seed, then turned into her husband in order to put the seed into the victim."

"I see it is a complicated case."

"What color was the cat?" asked the Gypsy. He studied Henry closely as he answered, as if to give him a silent warning that Gypsy magic would not work unless he told him the absolute truth.

"It was a white cat."

"Then something strong will be needed."

"Not too strong. She's a nervous woman."

The Gypsy looked down into his brandy for a moment. "Two pounds, then," he said. "Including food and music."

Somehow the rest of the gypsies knew that the bargain was struck. The women came out of the tents and began to cook and sing while the men played instruments.

Nearly forty years after the Hardings had come to this encampment to drink the potion against the plague, the Gypsies still smelled of woodsmoke. Like very few other people in England, where there was hardly any firewood left after centuries of cutting, they could burn as much wood as they could poach. In London it was a rare sight even in midwinter to see a log burning in the andirons.

Fanny liked it here. The aroma of a young pig cooking on the spit mingled with the damp ferny scent of the forest in spring. A Gypsy girl came out with a basket full of plucked larks, twenty or more of them, and showed them to Fanny with a wide smile before she arranged them on a grill beneath the spit. By signs she explained that the pork drippings would baste the larks and they would be delicious as a result.

After the meal, the head Gypsy made a sign and an old crone was brought out. She was chinless like the crone who had mixed the potion for the Hardings, but it seemed impossible that she could be the same woman. Whoever she was, she was ancient. Four young Gypsies carried her from her caravan to the fire like a bundle wrapped in a long black dress that was covered with glass

beads and white buttons. Her face, brown as ale and hatched with wrinkles, peeped out of her head scarf.

The young men lowered her feet to the ground and held her steady, asking anxious questions in Romany, until she found her balance. Clearly she was held in great reverence. Standing upright, swaying slightly, she was no more than four feet tall. She stared fixedly at the English visitors with the glittering green eyes that gave her her powers.

In a surprisingly loud voice the crone said something in Romany. The head Gypsy explained, "She will cure the woman. But the men must go away."

"Have you got a football?" Henry asked.

The man nodded.

"All fellows to football, then!" Henry cried.

While Fanny waited for the fortune-telling to begin, she listened to the men shouting in the meadow beyond the trees. They sounded like hounds, a mixture of baritones and tenors with Oliver's deep bass belling beneath the pack.

She heard her father calling for the ball, every word distinct: "To me, Oliver, to me!" And then a loud grunt as if someone had the wind knocked out of him.

The crone had gone into a trance. She was quiet for such a long time that Fanny thought that she might not wake up again, but at last the old woman opened her green eyes and asked for Rose's hand.

"What for?" Rose asked.

"She wants to read your future," Fanny said. "It's all right."

The crone traced a line on Rose's palm. "I see a ship," she said. "And a great storm. The lady will see monsters. She will see death by steel and death by fire, death by drowning and death by ice."

"Where does she see these things, Fanny?"

"In the lines in your hand."

"But she's in a trance, Fanny. Look at her."

"Riches, I see great riches," the crone said. "A rich man will marry the lady. But before that, war. I see a child that is not the rich man's child."

"But I'm already married."

"Nevertheless, I see a rich husband," the crone said.

"A new husband?"

The crone lifted her glittering eyes. "Perhaps. Or a husband who becomes rich. I cannot see which."

The rest of the Gypsy women crouched on the damp ground behind the crone, giving each other wise sidelong looks at each

prediction. They all wore the same expression and uttered the same gasps at the same time, as if they shared a single mind among their twenty bodies. Their swarthy faces shone. Rose wondered if they rubbed some sort of secret Gypsy grease on their skin. The sour smell of old woodsmoke coming from their clothes and hair was overpowering, and Rose covered her nose with a handkerchief.

The crone, still holding Rose's hand, seemed to go to sleep.

"What does she mean, I'll see monsters and death by drowning?" Rose said.

Fanny had had her hand read by the Gypsies many times. "I've never heard that before," Fanny said. "The rich man and the baby are usually part of it, though."

The crone stirred and looked at Rose's right hand again.

"I see a bear, very big and dark," the crone said. "The lady's child will be a daughter, and the bear will be its father."

The crone looked at Fanny as she told Rose's fortune, as if she thought that Rose was too stupid to understand or remember it. "She will try to escape from this bear," she said. "I see many voyages over water and land. She can go wherever she likes, it won't matter. She cannot hide from him. The bear will find her. She owes him this child from another life and he will make her give it to him."

"A bear?" Rose said. "She must mean Oliver."

"It is no one she has ever seen," the crone told Fanny. "But she'll know him when the time comes. He will smell like a bear, a very strong smell. There is more, but I can't quite see it. There is a veil of white in between. Like smoke, but it isn't smoke."

Rose was not interested in the bear. She tapped the palm of her hand. "What about witches?" she said. "Do you see witches?"

"No witches," the crone said.

"But there must be witches. Look for a white cat."

The crone put Rose's hand back in her lap. "I only see what I see," she said.

"What a fool," Rose said.

The crone gestured Franny closer and lifted her left hand in her own gnarled blue one. She examined the palm for a long moment, then looked at the right hand. She gave Fanny a look filled with sharp surprise, spoke a single word in Romany, and let go of her hand. All the Gypsy women's faces lost expression at once.

"What does she see?" Fanny said.

No one answered. The Gypsy women looked at the ground, then moved quickly forward to help the crone rise to her feet. She had closed her eyes again. They picked her up, cushion and all, and carried her away toward her tent.

"What did the old woman say about you? Why are they taking her away?" Rose asked.

"I don't know."

"Then ask. I want to know."

"There's no one to ask, Rose. They've all gone into the tents."

"What did she see in your hand?"

"I don't know."

Rose stood up and shook out the folds in her dress. "Maybe it was another bear," she said, giggling. "Don't be afraid, Fanny. There are no bears in England."

With the women gone, the silence in the encampment was disturbed only by the faint crackle of the fire and the voices of the men coming from the meadow. Rose's face was sullen.

"Let's go watch the football," Fanny said.

"I hate football."

Fanny did not coax her. She lifted her skirt and walked rapidly into the fringe of the woods, leaving Rose behind. By the time Rose noticed and began to call Fanny's name, she had vanished into the trees.

Oliver's wig lay inside his upturned hat on the grass beside the playing field. Most of the players, woodcutters and swine drovers and poachers who lived in the forest, were dressed in rags. They were gaunt and unwashed, and they played football hard.

Players not only sounded like hounds to Fanny, they behaved like a hunting pack, merging into each other so that each team became a single creature bent on a single idea, to drive the ball through the goal. Fanny never watched men playing the game that she did not feel the same deep feminine amusement. When they were like this, men were as they were meant to be. That was why football made them so happy. She watched Henry especially, a ginger-haired figure smaller than the rest running down the field behind Oliver, throwing his thin body this way and that as he kicked the ball ahead of him. Henry was far too old to be doing this, but he glowed with enjoyment like a boy.

Oliver and Henry ran down the field, Oliver smashing everyone before him, Henry dodging along in his shadow and keeping a lookout for an opening to the goal. The players were breathing hard now, and the game was played in silence except for grunts and curses as men were trampled under Oliver's downfield charge.

Fanny heard Rose's voice behind her. She was whimpering a little as she walked because the hem of her dress had been muddied.

"They're still playing," Rose said. "Tell them to stop, Fanny."

"It's almost over, Rose."

"They *must* stop," Rose said. "I'm catching a chill. I hate it here."

"Oh, Rose, think of somebody besides yourself for a moment," Fanny said. "Let Oliver have something to enjoy."

Rose flushed with anger. Fanny hadn't known that she was capable of such feeling.

"I hate you," Rose said. "You and your father and his filthy black-haired Gypsies."

"Hate us? Do you, Rose? How sad, when we're so very fond of you."

But Rose was already running out onto the field toward the sweating, cursing knot of players. She was shrieking Oliver's name at the top of her voice.

Oliver stopped in his tracks and looked away from the game. Behind him, Henry swerved to avoid running into him. One of the woodmen, a man nearly as tall as Oliver whose cheeks were covered with a rough beard, tackled Henry.

The ball squirted into the air. Henry's head snapped backward and he uttered a loud, comical "*Oof!*" and fell to the ground.

Oliver had not moved. He seemed to be transfixed between Rose, who stood upright with a look of anger on her face, and Henry, who lay on his side in the mud with his left arm twisted behind his back.

Oliver was trying to touch Rose, to cure her anger, but she wouldn't let him near.

The game went on, with the other team pushing the ball up the field. The tall woodman, who had been crouching beside Henry's inert figure, rose to his feet and trotted down the field as if to join his teammates at the goal, but then he swerved, ran faster, and vanished into the woods.

Fanny ran out onto the field and knelt beside Henry in the cold mud. His eyes were open. There were beads of sweat on his face. He was dead.

# 12

Fanny could barely remember the old man, but she recalled his story vividly. She was a child when she heard it.

"This is Captain John Pennock, my uncle," Oliver had said, holding Fanny in his arms so that she looked straight into the fierce bearded face of the old man, whose visible skin, from the bridge of his nose to the top of his forehead, was covered with scars—saber cuts, bullet holes, burns.

"He's come from America," Oliver said.

Oliver put Fanny down on the floor and she found herself standing in front of two dark, silent children about twice her own age—a Nipmuck Indian (she remembered the tribe) named Magpie and a Negro called Coffee. Both were slaves. They sat under the table during supper, taking scraps of food from Captain Pennock's hand.

As a reward for Captain Pennock's loyalty to the Protestant cause and for the wounds he had suffered in nearly thirty years of war against the pope, King William of England had granted him a tract of ten thousand acres along a river in the colony of Massachusetts, but far to the west of Boston.

"The river is called the Connecticut by the Indians," Captain Pennock said, pronouncing the word syllable by syllable, "and on its banks I built a city in the wilderness as God had ordained I should do. You're a very pretty child."

The old man looked at Fanny, and no one else, as he talked, speaking very simply. From time to time he paused and smiled, seemingly anxious that the child should understand everything he said.

Fanny squirmed in embarrassment and Oliver whispered in her ear. "He's taken a liking to you because his own little girl was captured by the Indians and he can't find her," he said.

Captain John Pennock was not Oliver's blood uncle, but had married Hope Barebones, Oliver's father's sister, late in life. She had been murdered by wild Indians who had been incited by the papists in Canada to attack Pennock's city in the wilderness.

"The savages tore the son my wife was suckling from her arms and dashed out his brains against a tree," Captain Pennock said. "Then they killed the grieving mother with a hatchet and stole my daughter."

Pennock had gone from village to village among the Indians, searching for his daughter, but had never found a trace of her.

"Everybody say she dead, hung up in a tree because she worth nothing," said Magpie, the Indian girl, from beneath the table. She had traveled with Pennock as his interpreter.

"If she is dead, it is God's will," Pennock said. "But I think she is alive, hidden in some village. She had red hair and freckles like all the Pennocks, and a birthmark like this one under her hair, so they will never be able to say that she is a savage, as is their habit when speaking of English people they have stolen."

He brushed back his white hair, which was slightly pink even at his age, and held up a candle to show Fanny a red birthmark on his scalp. It was round, like a wax seal. Fanny saw that even before Pennock pointed it out to her.

"It is the Pennock seal," he said. "If you ever see a girl with this mark on her scalp, you'll know that you've found Thoughtful Pennock."

Despite the tragedy that had befallen him, Pennock believed that America was a paradise set aside by God for the English. That night at supper, the only time Fanny ever saw him, he had described streams so full of salmon and alewives that the fish crowded each other out of the water and onto the banks and drowned in the air. He told of strawberries and blackberries growing wild in the forest and the meadows, and about a wonderful kind of winter deer with flattened antlers that was as large as a horse and so brainless that it would stand still and let itself be killed while gazing like a martyr into the hunter's eyes. From the windows of his manor house, which had been rebuilt from the ashes after the Indians burned it, Pennock said that he could see for twenty miles in all directions on a clear day and never see anything that had been touched by any other hand than God's.

The old man died after returning to America. As a young man, Captain Pennock had ridden beside Oliver Cromwell in the English Civil War and in Ireland, and because Oliver's full name was Oliver Cromwell Barebones, and because Oliver was Hope Barebones' nephew, Pennock left his lands and all his other property in America to him.

When, on the day after Henry's death, Alfred Montagu came to the house in Catherine Street to pay his respects, he mentioned this inheritance to Oliver.

"It sounds a handsome place," Montagu said. "I suppose it has a lot of trees that could be cut down and sawn into planks and timbers and shipped back to England—if one had a ship."

Henry's body, dressed in a black silk suit and a white shirt, lay on its back on the hall table. The shutters were drawn. Candles burned at all four corners of the table, throwing Henry's face into shadow but clearly revealing the portrait of Fanchon that hung on the wall above his head.

While he spoke to Oliver, Montagu's eyes were fixed on Fanny, who sat by her father's head on the other side of the table. Montagu took some snuff, shifting his gaze to the portrait while he sniffed and then sneezed.

"Is that the mother?" he asked.

Oliver looked at him dumbly. Montagu behaved as though he had received a long and detailed answer to his question.

"I thought so when I first saw the picture," he said. "The resemblance is striking, except, of course, that the daughter has a much fresher beauty. It must be the eyes. Because they are such a remarkable blue they set off the skin, making it appear even more golden than it is by nature. You see how even a little light illuminates her face? Even in black she is astonishing."

"Get out," Oliver said.

"Ah," Montagu said. "You are disturbed. Of course. It was wrong of me to speak of our affairs in the presence of your dead friend. But I only meant to reassure. The rubies you offered will not satisfy your debts, or those of this orphan. . . ."

"Orphan?" Oliver said. "What orphan?"

"Young Missis Harding there. She is now alone in the world, and as her father's heiress, inherits his debts."

"She is not alone. I am her godfather."

"Then she is doubly unfortunate. She acquires your debts as well. I was only going to suggest an arrangement with you that might make her situation less painful."

"And what would that be?"

Oliver had been advancing on Montagu as he spoke and had herded him to the head of the bier. Dressed in pink silk, with the usual cascading lace and a wig tinted pink (it was this that made Fanny remember the pink in Captain Pennock's hair over a distance of years), Montagu stood directly behind Henry's head. He looked down into the dead man's face and then gave Fanny another long look.

"I had discussed this matter with poor Harding," he said. "Fanny cannot be unaware of it."

"What matter?"

Montagu waited a long moment with his eyes averted, as if expecting to sneeze, but no sneeze came.

"I am planning to pull down this whole street of houses," he said just as the sneeze did come. He smiled. "A dividend from the snuff," he said. "They say that sneezing is the second greatest of the pleasures. Do you agree with that, Barebones?"

Oliver took hold of him. Montagu reached for his sword, but Oliver seized his wrist.

"Let me go or I shall call in my men," Montagu said. "Surely we don't want that to happen in a room where a dead man is lying."

Fanny was standing now. She had been concealing her rosary in her hand, but now Montagu saw the beads. He smiled very broadly and inclined his body toward her as gallantly as he could while Oliver still held him.

"What a lot of secrets your family has, Fanny," he said. "Mysterious ships, lands in the colonies, and now those pretty papist beads."

Oliver's body was trembling. Fanny thought he might kill the man.

"Let go of him," she said.

Oliver did so. Montagu shrugged and wriggled his body back into place inside his elegant costume. His hat, decorated with a plume, had fallen to the floor.

"My hat, if you please," he said.

Fanny said, "What do you mean, you're going to pull down this whole street?"

"I mean I am going to remove the houses that now stand along Catherine Street—just the ones at this end by the Strand, actually; I exaggerated when I said the whole street."

He was smiling again and examining Fanny's face and figure. His eyes kept straying to the rosary. It had been Fanchon's and it was very fine, with a silver crucifix and ivory beads; Henry had had it made in Italy.

"Remove the houses?" she said. "How can you? What for?"

"I can remove them because they are my property, and I shall do so. And then, to answer your second question, I shall put up a stand of far better houses and sell them to a somewhat better class of people. Everyone profits."

"But you don't own this house or Oliver's."

"For your sake, my dear, I wish that that were true. But it is not. I own your father's debts. He cannot pay them. Therefore I own whatever he owned and can do as I like with it."

"Even pull down his house while his dead body is lying inside it? The law will not permit it."

"There are quicker things than the law."

Montagu had moved closer to Fanny while she spoke. Now, with a fingertip, he touched the back of her hand, the one that held the rosary. She moved away.

"And there are alternatives," he said. "If this house comes down, and Barebones' house too, you'll have no roof above your head. I should be very sad about that."

He had placed the bier between himself and Oliver, and now he spoke to him across it.

"I would accept the ten thousand acres in America as a dowry," he said. "Of course, your goddaughter would have to renounce the popish religion. But that's a small enough thing, considering what faces her in other circumstances."

Oliver's mouth was agape. Fanny had read about this gesture but she had never seen it in real life.

Montagu watched Oliver's face in open enjoyment.

"You are astonished," he said. "I realize that the match seems wrong—your goddaughter has no fortune, no family, no rank. But I am entranced by her beauty, sir, and have been from the moment I saw her."

Oliver bent down and picked up Montagu's hat. When Montagu reached for it, Oliver seized him, lifted him into the air, and shook him. Resistance was impossible. Montagu seized his wig with both hands to keep it from flying off his head and tried to shout for help: the toughs who went everywhere with him were waiting outside the door. But his voice came out of his mouth in a shrill gargle. His sword shot out of his scabbard and spun across the floor.

Still shaking, and growling all the while like a big dog killing a smaller one, Oliver carried Montagu out of the hall and threw him out the door into the mud. His toughs rushed across the street to rescue him.

"Kill the bastard," Montagu squeaked. But seeing what was in Oliver's eyes, they did not advance.

Montagu shook his jeweled fist, "Tomorrow," he said. "Tomorrow!"

Inside the house, Fanny had thrown her body across Henry's to protect it from violence, and touching it for the first time since the warmth went out of it, she knew that whatever had made her father what he was had gone away.

Feeling the cold face of the corpse, she understood that everything had changed. She was alone, as Henry had been alone, and she knew that that was one thing that remained the same forever.

# 13

As she woke from a dream about the *Pamela,* Fanny imagined that she heard all around her the creaking of a ship under sail in a storm. Then, wide-awake and sitting up in bed, she recognized the sound for what it was—the shriek of nails being pulled from timbers. Rose was asleep beside her. She remembered that her father was lying dead downstairs.

The glass in the window shattered with a loud report. Rose woke up with a scream. A hole opened in the side of the house, letting in a shaft of light filled with swirling dust. Fanny got out of bed and looked through the gap. On the ground below, a man whipped a span of eight red oxen so hard that his hat fell off. The animals bellowed and shat, terrified by the crash of the huge lump of masonry and slate and splintered beams—Fanny's bedroom wall and part of the roof—that cartwheeled behind them, spewing bricks, at the end of a whipping chain.

Outside in the smoky London morning, a crowd of Alfred Montagu's friends had gathered to watch while he pulled Henry Harding's house down around his daughter's head. Montagu and his friends had come from a party; the men were dressed in silk and the women wore ball gowns and jewels. They were all seated in sedan chairs to keep them out of the mud, drinking wine and eating cakes and making the giddy gestures that people make when they have been up all night. Montagu had brought extra thugs; at least twenty men surrounded him as he sat with his left ankle crossed over his right knee, chatting with a pretty woman who was dressed nearly as magnificently as he was. The oxen had already been hitched to a second roof beam, and Montagu raised a finger to warn the woman that something was going to happen. The oxen threw themselves into their yokes and tore another gobbet from the body of the house. The spectators applauded and cheered. Montagu gave a slight bow and held out his glass to be refilled.

Some of the Hardings' possessions had been carried outside—a spinet, a few of Henry's books, a heap of silver plate, casks of wine, the painting of Fanchon. Antoinette stood guard over them.

Among the crowd, chatting with one another and calling out witticisms to Montagu, were people who had dined in this house. One of them, a tall man with a whore on his arm, struck a note or two on the spinet. A silver box full of dried rose petals rested on top of the instrument. The man picked up the box and sniffed the rose petals. He offered the tart a smell. She took the box from his hand, snapped it shut, and dropped it into a pocket among the fringes on her skirt. When Antoinette protested, the woman laughed and dropped the box into the mud.

The house, torn lumber howling, shifted under Fanny's bare feet as it swayed on its foundation. Fanchon's mirror toppled and broke. The bed slid across the tilting floor and came to rest against what was left of the wall. Fanny seized a jagged piece of wood and pulled herself back into the room. Rose began to scream. She was pressed against the wall in her nightclothes, hands fluttering over the plaster as she searched for something to hold on to. She lost her balance and lurched toward the gap in the wall.

Fanny caught her in her arms and they staggered together across the steep floor. Like a drowning person, Rose clawed at Fanny's face and pummeled her chest. Fanny seized Rose by the hair. She pulled it violently, first one way and then the other, until Rose stopped screaming and instead howled from the pain.

Fanny had never hurt anyone before, but she felt nothing for Rose, who sank to her knees shrieking from the pain.

"Where's Oliver?" Fanny asked.

Rose was sobbing. Her nose ran. Fanny pulled her hair again, gently.

"Rose, tell me."

Rose found her voice. "What is happening to me?"

"Never mind that. Tell me where Oliver is."

"Drunk. Gone. I don't know."

"Then you'll have to help me," Fanny said.

The house shuddered as the oxen pulled off another chunk of the roof. Rose screamed. Fanny tried the door. It was jammed into its frame, but she managed to pull it open a few inches. She forced her body through the crack.

"Squeeze through, Rose!"

Rose crossed her hands over her breasts.

"I can't, Fanny. No one could. "

They could hear the crowd outside, cheering and laughing. Someone played a scale on the spinet, badly. Fanny looked through the door at Rose. She beckoned.

"I'll help you," she said.

She showed Rose how to stand sideways to the door and, prying

her hand from her breast, helped her to fit the soft flesh through the narrow gap.

"Now the other one," Fanny said. "Gently. Turn your body."

But just then, with Rose halfway through the crack, the house shuddered again.

"Oh, God, Fanny, I can't move," Rose said. "It's going to cut me in half."

Fanny seized her by the hair and pulled as hard as she could. Screaming in pain, Rose spun free.

Leading Rose by the hand, Fanny ran down the stairs. The door to the street was ajar. Montagu had moved closer in his sedan chair, and they could see him just outside in his silks and laces. Rose ran toward the door.

"No," Fanny said. "Into the hall."

Rose realized what Fanny wanted. "I can't," she said. "Fanny, I can't. There are men outside. They'll help you."

She screamed and tried to get away, but Fanny held on to her hair and pulled her after her.

Henry's body lay on the table. The air, filled with dust and the light, was dappled and dim, like the light in a wood.

"Take his feet," Fanny said.

Rose fell to the floor and rolled herself into a ball. The house shook around them. The dust grew thicker. Rose's face was black with it. They were both coughing violently.

"You'll help or you'll be buried with him, Rose," Fanny said. "I won't leave my father here to be crushed by his own house and dug out by strangers."

Rose took hold of Henry's feet while Fanny seized his shoulders. They slid him off the table. Henry's small corpse was far heavier than either of them expected it to be and it thumped on the floor. Gas moved inside the body and made a sound like a voice. Rose shrieked again.

"*Up,*" Fanny said. "Lift him up."

They staggered toward the door. The body was stiff, but Henry's head moved about loosely on its broken neck like a hanged man's.

Outside, Fanny laid her father down gently in the mud of the street and straightened his head. Montagu stood over her. He wore a bright green cape trimmed in fur and a hat with an ostrich plume pinned to it.

"My dear child," he said. "I had no idea. The fools have pulled down the wrong house."

Montagu covered Henry's corpse with his cape and helped Fanny into a sedan chair. He swept off his hat, and with a charming smile lifted Fanny's bare foot to his lips and kissed it.

# 14

Very early in the morning on the third Wednesday after Easter, Fanny buried her father in Saint Andrew's churchyard. A fine windblown rain darkened the stones that marked the graves of Fanchon and the rest of the Hardings and soaked the mourners in their black clothes. There were only five of them. Antoinette and Oliver stood on either side of Fanny. Both were weeping. Nobody else was there except Rose and Praise God Adkins. Fanny had told none of Henry's friends about the funeral; she did not want to be comforted by people who would make jokes about it afterward in the Rose Tavern.

The old bald curate looked at Oliver. "Is the shroud made of wool as the law requires?" he asked.

Oliver stared back with uncomprehending eyes.

"Yes," Fanny replied.

The clergyman nodded, his duty to the wool trade done, and read the burial service very rapidly in a shivering voice, coughing into the prayer book as he went. He wore a petulant look—it was barely six o'clock and he was awake before the city for the first time in many years. Fanny gazed down into the grave at the raw lumber box in which her father lay. Oliver began to sob deep in his chest. He was trembling all through his great frame. The clergyman read on in a louder voice. Fanny took Oliver's hand and warmed it against her body, but he could not stop sobbing. This was a place where corpses had been buried on top of one another for a long time, and there were old bones in the walls of the grave. Rose, bundled up in a cloak trimmed with fur, held a cloth over her nose and looked at the minister out of her unblinking eyes as if trying to remember who he was.

Rain drummed on the coffin. River water had already seeped into the grave. Smelling it, Fanny realized that it would rise into the coffin after the hole was filled. On visiting his father's grave, Henry had always patted the stone and said, "Sorry about the damp, Papa." The old man, in his delirium before he died of the plague, had kept crying out that he did not want to be buried in a

watery grave, and Henry would have dug him up and reinterred him elsewhere if the law permitted.

Fanny knew that Henry would not have been troubled by the wet: the dead were dead, there was nothing afterward, there was no return and no reunion.

Fanny could hear the first muted morning noises of the river—men joking and the thump of wood against wood as oars were dropped into their pins. She closed her eyes again. The curate, as he sped through the last hopeful phrases of the Order for the Burial of the Dead, spoke in a very loud voice, as if a congregation of hundreds was trying to hear him over the hubbub of London instead of the little knot of mourners who were actually present in the still of the morning. When the time came for the Lord's Prayer, Fanny did not attempt to repeat the words.

She heard a cough and opened her eyes. The curate was offering her a trowel full of mud. She threw it down into the grave. It thudded on the coffin.

"Your father is in heaven with God and His angels," the curate said to Fanny, shuddering from the cold. He gave Antoinette a look of deep sympathy. "Your mother, here, will look after you now."

Antoinette made the sign of the cross on her bosom and slapped Fanny's hand to remind her to do the same. Fanny ignored her. The curate's eyes widened at this popish behavior and he hurried away into the church, tripping over the muddied hem of his surplice.

Fanny put some of Henry's flowers on Fanchon's grave and closed her eyes, trying to imagine her parents' faces. She saw the Fanchon of the portrait clearly enough in her mind's eye, but she could not picture Henry: when she attempted to see his face she saw the oxen, the crowd in Catherine Street, the dust exploding from the shattered walls.

She felt a kiss on her cheek. It was Oliver.

"I must go straight back and guard the house in case Montagu comes again," he said. "Praise God will look after you until tomorrow. Then we'll decide what's to be done with you, Fanny."

"What?" Fanny said. Her voice was so harsh that Oliver started and looked to the right and left of her as if he thought that it came from somebody else. Rainwater ran off his hat brim in a thin sheet. His eyes wandered. Fanny realized that Oliver and Praise God and Antoinette—everyone but Rose, who was whimpering and sucking in her breath in the cold rain—were all looking around the churchyard for the patch of gaudy color that would be Montagu.

\* \* \*

Praise God Adkins took Fanny and Antoinette to his own house, a shuttered narrow structure at the end of a muddy narrow street near Lloyd's Coffeehouse. They walked up from the river because there were no chairmen out in the rain, and by the time they reached the door Fanny's skirt was heavy with mud. No fire burned in the grate. The hall was draughty and damp, with rain blowing against the windows and people trudging by outside as slowly as sleepwalkers.

"We will die of a chill," Antoinette said, shouting because Praise God was an Englishman. "Someone must make a fire."

Praise God was surprised by Antoinette's vehemence. Fanny could see that he thought that it was wrong to speak so loudly so soon after Henry had been buried.

"I don't know if there's anything to burn," he said. "Go find Royce. He'll know."

Antoinette took Fanny's dripping cloak and disappeared toward the back of the house. She returned with Royce, Praise God's aged servant, who carried two cups of brandy and hot water on a tray that trembled in his hands. Antoinette had found a few faggots of wood, and she kneeled down in her black dress to place them in the fireplace.

"*Poussière!*" she cried in disbelief, flailing with one of the sticks of wood at the dust kittens that had accumulated between the andirons.

Praise God, oblivious, handed Royce his dripping cloak and hat and the servant gave him a nightcap, which Praise God placed on his bald head.

Suddenly Fanny was able to imagine her father as he had looked in life, grinning and quick to tell a story. Praise God had not worn a wig since the year of the Great Plague. Because Henry had often told her the story, Fanny knew why. A man had tried to borrow money from Praise God to finance a scheme to make wigs from the hair of the dead.

"There's lovely hair just lying about all over London for the taking," the man had said. "It's a chance from heaven."

Henry had called the wigmaker the hairy wretch. Drinking her rum and hot water, Fanny began to smile. Then other pictures came into her mind—her father lying in the mud on the football field, lying in the mud at Montagu's feet in the street outside his ruined house, and now lying under the mud in Saint Andrew's churchyard.

Fanny realized that Praise God was speaking to her. Huddled in front of the tiny fire that Antoinette had lighted, he drank his grog and looked at Fanny with sad eyes.

"We must find a better place for you," he said "Greenwich, perhaps, or some town even farther off. Oliver's house isn't safe."

"To hide myself from Montagu? What more can he do?"

Praise God gave her a severe look. "Remember what has happened. Remember the kiss, Fanny."

Fanny did remember it—the lips wet with wine, the ringed fingers with their yellow nails sliding up her calf.

"You've no one to protect you," Praise God said.

"I have Oliver."

"Oliver? Of course, Oliver. He would gladly die for you, you're everything in the world to him and always have been."

Praise God shook his head. "But this is not a case for Oliver. Oliver is a strong fellow, but he's muscle only, Fanny. It's not enough. What's needed against Montagu is brains."

My father wouldn't have hidden me away from the likes of Montagu."

"Perhaps not. But none of us is Henry. We don't have what he had to fight with. Not the cleverness, not the friends, not the *Pamela*."

Fanny waited for a moment. Then she said, "But we still have the *Pamela*."

Praise God sighed. "I fear not. Montagu will have the *Pamela* and her cargo seized at the docks."

Fanny's voice did not rise, but she learned forward a little in her chair to be certain that Adkins heard her words. "I'll burn her first," she said.

"Burn the *Pamela,* Fanny? Come, come."

He gave her a melancholy look. The girl was distressed by her father's death, but why could she not accept the good advice she was being given? She did not know what lay in store for her otherwise. Montagu would steal her, debauch her, let his friends use her, and then throw her into the streets. Praise God closed his eyes against these thoughts and the images they conjured.

Fanny spoke to him. "How much ready money did my father leave?" she asked.

"Ready money?" Praise God said. "Whatever was in his pocket. Your father lived on moneylenders, Fanny. He borrowed to buy you dresses, he borrowed to loan money to Oliver, he borrowed to give him a wedding feast. He was going to borrow another fifty guineas from me yesterday. He owed six hundred pounds against the *Pamela*'s next cargo. That is more than enough to buy another house just like the one Montagu . . . the one in Catherine Street."

"Oliver?"

Praise God shrugged. "Oliver owes Montagu two thousand pounds

and he owed your father a thousand. He has his house as long as Montagu lets it stand and his wife's new ring, worth half what he paid for it if he's lucky. He inherited a wilderness in America when his uncle died. Even Montagu can't want that."

"Don't be so sure," Fanny said.

Praise God reached across the mounds of paper to squeeze Fanny's hand. But she moved it away before he could touch it. Her face was calm.

"What if the *Pamela* never comes home?" she asked.

"Not come home?" Praise God said. "What nonsense. She has a cargo and crew, Fanny. She must come home."

"Yes," Fanny said. "But what if she sailed not to London but to another port in England? Could the cargo be sold there without Montagu finding out?"

"It's possible," Praise God said. "But how can we arrange such a thing? We don't know where the *Pamela* is, do we?"

"What if we do know?"

Suddenly Praise God's eyes were not wounded but interested. "Are you saying that your father told you where his ship is?"

Fanny did not answer his question.

Praise God leaned forward. "Where is the *Pamela*?" he asked.

Fanny kept silent. If she was alone, whom could she trust? She was counting days in her mind. She knew how long it took to go to Honfleur in good weather: a day to Dover, a day to Calais by packet boat, a long day from there down the Channel. Then two or three days from the coast of France to an English port.

"What if the *Pamela* came into Portsmouth?" she asked. "Could we sell her cargo there? Is that far enough away from Montagu?"

"Yes. But you'd have to be quick."

"Will you loan me fifty guineas?"

"What for?"

"In case I need it."

Fanny had watched her father deal with Praise God Adkins a hundred times. That was what Henry had always said when asked why he wanted to borrow money: "In case I need it."

Any proposition that mixed profit with friendship was irresistible to Praise God. He got out his purse and counted out the coins in ten stacks of five each. He still believed in the Harding luck.

"When will I get my money back?" he asked.

Fanny paused, as if she had to do the mental arithmetic she had already done.

"Today is the sixth of May," she said. "You'll have your fifty guineas, and every shilling my father owes you, in Portsmouth on the fifteenth of the month."

# 15

"Honfleur, Fanny!" Antoinette said as the town with its steep roofs and slender steeples came into sight across the estuary of the Seine. Even in the steely light of afternoon, the town had more color than Henry had said. The gray slate houses stood along the waterfront just as he had described them, but he had left out the stone castle and the big royal flags in front of the Lieutenance and the yellowish thatched cottages marching up the hillside beyond the town. White cows grazed in green fields along the riverbank and pale blue fishing boats bobbed on the rising tide.

"Does it look the way you thought it would?"

Because Antoinette was speaking French, her voice was gentle and happy. She was dressed in black and so was Fanny. They were heavily veiled, and on the packet boats that had carried them across the Channel and then down the coast of Normandy to Honfleur, Antoinette had said that Fanny was a French girl called home by a death in the family. At night Antoinette had barred the doors and sat up in a chair to guard Fanny against Montagu. In the holy pocket of her petticoat, along with her religious objects and the two hundred gold sovereigns she had saved in her twenty years in England, she carried a dagger.

"If he finds us he will turn his back on me in order to feast his eyes on you," Antoinette said. "And then!"

Now, however, Honfleur had captured Antoinette's whole attention. Puffing a little in her happiness, repeating herself for the hundredth time, she told Fanny her plans. She was going to live in her sister's house in the rue aux Chats. She had never seen her nieces and nephews. She would give them their presents and speak English for them. She could hardly wait to see the looks on their faces. Perhaps she would invest her savings in a tavern. She might even marry—a widower by preference because he would be a steady help at the tavern and, besides, she hated the jealousy of young men. She was only a bit more than thirty, young enough still to have a child. She had her virginity; she had a certain mystery. And, after all, she was not poor.

She looked at the town again, making a gesture that seemed to say that she gave it as a gift to Fanny.

"Well, is it not just as I said?" she said.

"No," Fanny said. "It's different from the stories."

"Certainly it is different," said Antoinette triumphantly. "It is even better than you imagined. One cannot describe France, so near to England and yet so much more beautiful."

Antoinette's round bosom rose and fell as she breathed in the damp air of France. Fanny smiled, her first smile in days, and hugged her. A tear ran down Antoinette's cheek. How French Fanny was; no French person on the packet boat had suspected that she had a drop of English blood in her veins. She was so pretty and good. What English girl could possibly be like Fanny? See how she drank in the sight of France, her eyes sparkling! Antoinette stroked her gloved hand.

"*Notre chèrie France,*" she said. Our darling France.

Fanny threw back her veil. There was pallor beneath the gold of her cheeks and her eyes were tired. Sadness made her prettier, Antoinette thought. She murmured a prayer of thanks that they were safe in France.

"Look, Fanny, you can see the spire of Saint Catherine's."

But Fanny's eyes were elsewhere. She was looking for the *Pamela,* and as the packet boat tacked around the end of the breakwater she saw her, her silhouette unmistakable among the bulbous square-rigged French naval vessels moored all around her. She rode low in the water, a heavy cargo obviously still aboard.

The packet boat sailed so close that Fanny could hear the hiss of its passage echoing off the *Pamela*'s planking and see the faces of the men on board.

Joshua Peters stood on the quarterdeck talking to two Frenchmen. One of them, younger and more plainly dressed than the other, turned and watched the packet as it sailed by. He looked like a soldier—dark blue coat neatly buttoned, plain sword, hat square on his head, watchful eyes. His eyes met Fanny's. His windburned, beardless face was utterly without expression.

Then, just before the view was obscured by the hull and masts of the next moored vessel, Fanny saw a fourth man aboard the *Pamela*—a tall, thin figure dressed in a bright yellow coat and hat with a white plume that rippled in the offshore wind.

"Look," Fanny said. "Montagu."

Antoinette gasped and looked. She pulled down Fanny's veil.

"It can't be," she said, "God wouldn't permit such a thing."

There were no formalities at the pier. Fanny simply stepped ashore and watched while Antoinette bustled about, casting fearful

glances over the water at the *Pamela* and finding men to carry the baggage. The pleasure of being back in her own country, speaking a language in which she could say exactly what she meant and have it perfectly understood, very nearly overcame Antoinette's terror of Montagu. Crossing the Channel, Antoinette had searched the boat over and over again, looking into every passageway and into every face in case he should have disguised himself and crept secretly aboard. Now, just when they should have been safe, just when Antoinette should have been beginning her own life at last, he had reappeared.

Fanny read the mixture of fear and anger and resentment in Antoinette's face. When all the baggage had been piled up and Antoinette had stopped bustling about, Fanny touched her arm.

"There's nothing to be afraid of," Fanny said. "He has no power in France."

"He had no power in England except lies and thievery," Antoinette replied, "and he pulled down the house while we slept."

The porters stood nearby with the luggage already balanced on their shoulders.

"Come," Antoinette said. "We must hurry."

Looking into this sharp-nosed face that she had known better than any other except her father's, Fanny could only think of the *Pamela*.

"I must go out to the ship," she said.

"Go out to the ship? That monster is aboard the ship."

Fanny still had her hand on Antoinette's arm, and she squeezed the plump flesh.

"You've done all that you can for me," Fanny said. "It's enough. Go to your sister's. I'll be along soon."

Across the harbor, the two Frenchmen in their uniforms and Montagu in his brilliant coat climbed down the ladder of the *Pamela* and settled themselves into a boat.

"You'll be captured like a fly," Antoinette said. "Come. You will hide for a few days—he'll never find you in the rue aux Chats, nobody will speak a word of truth to him—and then he'll go away. After that, you can be happy again."

Fanny put her veil down. The thick lace concealed her features entirely and even muffled her voice.

"I didn't come to Honfleur to be happy," Fanny said. "I came to find my ship and sail her back to England."

The boat from the *Pamela*, rowed by four French sailors in striped shirts, was moving rapidly on the tide toward the dock. Montagu lolled in the stern beside the older Frenchman, who was also splendidly dressed, while the young man stood up in the bow.

"Fanny, please," Antoinette said.

"Go," Fanny said. "If Montagu sees that we have baggage he'll know that we came on the packet boat. He'll ask questions. We will be discovered."

Antoinette hesitated, sighing. She wanted to see her sister; she never wanted to see another English person.

"You've given me years and years that really belonged to you," Fanny said. "Go. Peters is aboard the *Pamela*. I saw him. I only have to go out to the ship to be safe."

Through the veil, she could see the look of temptation on Antoinette's face.

"Go, you've done enough," Fanny said.

"You have no sense," Antoinette said. "You're like your father, not French at all. I've always known it when nobody else could see it."

She lifted Fanny's veil and kissed her on both cheeks, rubbing her tears onto the skin.

"Before they dry," she said, "you will have forgotten me."

"No," Fanny said. "Never."

Antoinette shook her head emphatically. "Oh, yes," she said. "I know the English."

Fanny smiled at her and for an instant the pallor and exhaustion left her face.

"Put down your veil," Antoinette said. "Speak only French. If you need help, tell anyone the rue aux Chats, the family Marie. Remember, the French help the French."

Antoinette put down her own veil in case Montagu, by some trickery, should intercept her. She ordered one of the porters to bring Fanny's small bag to her. Then she led the men into the twisted streets that she remembered from her girlhood, and disappeared.

Fanny walked out onto the pier. Montagu's boat was quite close now. The fishermen who had come in with the tide were selling their catch and the air was raucous with their cries and saturated with the odor of chilly mackerel and flounder and cod.

The boat came into the dock with a flourish and the oarsmen leaped ashore and helped the older Frenchman to debark. He wore an elaborate uniform; clearly he was a personage. The fishermen took off their hats and bowed as he passed by and called him *monseigneur,* the form of address used for a prince or a cardinal. Striding across the pier among the gleaming heaps of fish, he held his body as if it were a house or a jewel or a beautiful wife, a possession in which his rights could not be challenged. Montagu,

following along behind, seemed tawdry by comparison. He had lost his scornful smile.

The older Frenchman stared at Fanny. Inside the veil, she did not lower her eyes. He stopped and asked a question in a low voice.

Fanny did not hear him—did not understand him. Apart from the people on the boat who had said good morning to her and how-do-you-do, she had never heard anyone except Antoinette speak French.

The soldier came a step closer to Fanny and bowed slightly.

"Mademoiselle, listen," he said. "The Count of Vallier asked if you have suffered the loss of a relative."

He stood quietly in his neat clothes, heels together, boots polished, sword held firmly in the left hand, right hand behind his back. Fanny had never seen such a quiet man so near her own age. He was no more than twenty-two or twenty-three. He spoke in a boyish voice, forming each syllable very precisely, and this went oddly with his solemn demeanor.

Fanny understood every word. But she did not wish to reply in case her voice should be recognized. Montagu stood a few paces away, gazing at Fanny in her black clothes with elaborate disinterest.

She nodded her head. The young Frenchman gazed into the folds of her veil as earnestly as he might have done had he been looking into a face.

"A parent?" he asked.

Fanny nodded again.

"Your mother?"

Fanny shook her head no.

"Your father, then. Our condolences."

The older Frenchman spoke again. This time Fanny understood him without difficulty.

"Why is she wandering about the town alone if she's in mourning?" he asked.

The younger man lifted his eyebrows, waiting for an answer to the other man's question. A glint of amusement had entered his eyes.

Fanny whispered. "I wanted some air."

"She wanted some air, Count."

Montagu, who evidently could not understand French, had lost interest in this encounter.

"Look," he said in English. "I wonder if we could discuss my ship."

The older Frenchman looked up at the sky.

"Tell him I have not yet made my decision," he said.

The young man repeated these words in English. Evidently he had the job of talking to people whose station was too low to entitle them to be addressed directly by the older man.

Montagu shook his head. "Why not now? What if that dago sails on the tide? I should, if I were he."

"The court will make his decision tomorrow at ten," the young man said firmly.

Montagu drew in a long exasperated breath through his nose and blew it out between fluttering lips.

"Very well, but if she's stolen in the night, someone will pay!"

He strode away, ignoring Fanny, an uninteresting local swathed in black.

In his bright coat he cut a strange, agitated figure among the placid fishermen in their blue clothes and the grim slate houses. It seemed odd, too, to see him alone; he must not take his bullies with him when he traveled.

The young Frechman was speaking to Fanny again. "The count asks if he may see your face," he said.

Fanny lifted her veil. The young man's eyes, which were deep blue like her own, widened slightly. Now that she could see him clearly, she noticed that he had a fresh scar on his jaw. She thought it was a saber cut and wondered if he had killed the enemy who gave it to him. Probably. He was one of the Viking Normans— fair, and tall for a Frenchman, with dark blond hair tied up at the nape of his neck, military style, by leather thongs. She saw that he recognized her.

"You came in on the packet boat from Calais," the young man said. "I saw you on deck."

Fanny lifted her eyes again. "I remember," she said. "You were standing on the deck of my ship."

The Frenchman drew back his head in puzzled surprise, as if he had expected her to speak to him in a different voice, even in a different language.

"*Your* ship?" he said. "Which ship is that?"

"The one you just left. The *Pamela*."

"That ship seems to have a great many owners—another one just walked away in that yellow coat."

"That man has nothing to do with the *Pamela*."

"You know him?"

"Yes."

"But he's an Englishman. I haven't seen you before in Honfleur."

"As you said, I've only just arrived."

"From England?"

Fanny nodded.

He asked her name and the nature of her claim on the *Pamela.* Fanny answered with the bare details.

"Who is that man?" she asked, nodding at the older Frenchman, who stood a few paces away, taking snuff out of a silver box.

"The Count of Vallier. He is the king's lieutenant in Honfleur."

"And you?"

"His aide-de-camp."

The other man sneezed and touched his blinking eyes with the knuckle of his middle finger.

"Philippe," he said.

"Philippe," Fanny repeated in a whisper. She didn't know why. As a child, obliged to recite the names of the kings of France for Antoinette, she had always like the Philippes. They were a relief, popping up among all those Louis's and Charleses.

This Philippe went over to his superior and reported in a low voice. While he listened, the older man stared at Fanny with a boldness that reminded her of Montagu.

"Who is she?"

"An English girl. She says she owns the *Pamela.*"

"I wonder how she got it," the count said.

"Her father died."

"In England? And she's come here alone?"

"Evidently."

"Bold girl," the count said. "Look. That hair, those eyes, that figure. Can you imagine her at Versailles?"

He made no effort to lower his voice, so Fanny could hear him quite clearly. She lowered her veil. Both men were looking at her now.

Philippe, the young man, spoke to her in his beautiful, simple French. He had a clear baritone voice, but it lacked timbre and Fanny did not think that he would be able to sing very well. It was a voice for talking to soldiers.

"The count asks if you have any means of verifying your claim to own this ship."

"The master of the *Pamela* will tell you who I am."

"Row her out to the ship," the count said. "Find out if she's what she says she is."

Philippe looked at Fanny. "Is that agreeable?"

She said, "Perfectly, monsieur. In fact, I will stay aboard."

"As you wish."

The count turned to Philippe. " 'Perfectly, monsieur,' " he repeated, reproducing Fanny's accent in a French quite different from his own. "Have you ever heard such French coming out of an angel's mouth?"

He walked away.

"The boat is just there," Philippe said.

He got in before her and lifted her down from the quay. His strength, running like a current through his compact body, surprised Fanny. She did not think about it very long. She was wondering what was wrong with her French, as earlier she had thought of the color of her own eyes when she saw Philippe's. She realized, as the boat slipped through the water with a groan of oars against pins, that she had been thinking about herself, wondering about how she looked and how she sounded, for the first time in her life.

Philippe, seated beside her in the stern, closed his eyes as if to rest himself from a tiring duty, and said nothing. Fanny closed her eyes too, and tried to make her mind a blank.

After a few minutes, one of the oarsmen hailed the *Pamela* and Fanny looked up to see Joshua standing at the rail. She lifted her veil.

On deck, Joshua kissed her.

"It's true, then," he said in English.

Fanny nodded.

"I didn't believe it when that man came aboard with Grestain and your young friend, there, and told me."

"Who is Grestain?"

Philippe was still in the boat, giving orders to the oarsmen. Nevertheless, Joshua lowered his voice.

"The man you talked to on the pier, Armand de Grestain, Count of Vallier. He's taking over the army of New France."

"I thought he was the king's lieutenant in Honfleur."

"He is, but he's leaving. Grestain wanted to know if I thought it was possible to sail across the Atlantic by the northern route so early in May."

"What did you say?"

"That it was possible but there would be icebergs."

Joshua had sailed in nearly every ocean. He had told Fanny tales of icebergs as big as Saint Paul's Cathedral floating in the black northern water. As he told it, the icebergs were always covered with birds that rose into the air like a cloud when a ship came near, or by fearless seals that swam around the vessel like saucy boys.

It was late afternoon, and a sharp breeze was beginning to blow across the harbor. Fanny shivered and drew her cloak more tightly around her shoulders.

"Come below," Joshua said. "I have hot chocolate if you still like it."

"I still like it."

Inside the cabin, Fanny took Joshua's hand in both of hers and looked at him closely. His fingers, his whole square body, was twisted by old fractures, and now that he was past fifty he groaned when he sat down and limped when he got up. His grizzled hair was cut short like a monk's, and he had eyes that were so sympathetic and intelligent that they seemed out of place in his brown Mediterranean face covered with sun-cooked sailor's skin.

Fanny told Joshua what had happened.

"The neck was broken? Then there was no time."

He meant that Henry had had no time to repent of his sins.

"No," Fanny said. "I think he was dead before he knew he was dying."

When the *Pamela* was in Catholic waters, Joshua kept a crucifix on the wall of his cabin. He looked at it while he spoke.

"Your father thought that there is no heaven," he said. "But we know that he is there."

"If so, he will be very surprised," Fanny said.

"What Henry said and what he believed in his heart might not be the same. I don't know how a man could be so good without the help of God. He had you baptized a Catholic, after all."

Fanny had taken off her hat and cloak. There was little color in her lips and Joshua saw faint dark bruises under her eyes. She was tense, as if she had not slept in a long time.

"Have you cried yet?" Joshua asked.

"No."

"You must, you know."

Fanny shook her head. "First, you must know about Montagu."

"He says he owns the *Pamela*."

"That's not all."

Joshua listened, his face working, while Fanny told him what had happened in England.

"He wants everything," she said.

The cook brought the hot chocolate. Fanny's hands trembled slightly when she lifted the cup. Joshua wondered how she could be so calm, telling him the things she had been telling him.

"What now?" Joshua said.

"How long does it take to sail to Plymouth from here?"

"Two days when it's calm. Longer in a storm. I think a little storm is making up between here and England."

"Then we'd better sail on the tide," Fanny said.

A boat thumped against the side of the ship. After a moment they heard boots clumping across the deck above their heads, and

then the sound of men coming down the ladder that led from the deck to the master's cabin.

Fanny, drinking her chocolate, looked up inquiringly.

Joshua shrugged. "The French are always coming aboard," he said. "The *Pamela* is well-known here."

Behind him, the door of the cabin opened. Philippe stood there, his three-cornered hat with its cockade set squarely on his head as before and his sword in its dull steel scabbard gripped in his hand. Montagu stood behind him. He had changed into a lavender coat and he wore the pink wig that Fanny had seen before.

"Ah, Fanny," Montagu said. "How good of you to come all this way to join me." He turned to Philippe. "This lady is betrothed to me."

"Betrothed?" Joshua said.

"Actually not quite, quite betrothed," Montagu said. "Her father and I were on the point of an agreement, but there have been . . . unfortunate events."

Fanny spoke to Philippe. "Did you bring this man here?"

Philippe did not reply. Fanny was still seated. She looked up at the three men standing over her.

"He must get off the ship at once," she said.

"I'm afraid I can't do that," Montagu said in English. "Ask the frog."

Fanny turned to Philippe, meaning to interpret, but then she remembered that he understood English. The signs of it were on his face, which up to now had been so calm. His skin was flushed around the fresh scar on his cheek and he looked very slightly nauseated.

"What he says is true," he said. "The count has placed all of you under arrest aboard this ship. I, too, will stay aboard, and in the morning the count will hold an inquiry in this cabin as to the facts."

Even before she woke in the cabin where Giacomo Cerruti had died, Fanny knew that she could not possibly be dreaming. She really was suffocating. Someone had stuffed a gag into her mouth. She sat up in bed and tried to snatch it out but she could not move her arm. Someone had tied them together behind her back.

Fanny heard someone breathing. In the nervous half-light that came in the stern windows, she saw the man standing over her. He was tall and thin; his face was turned away. He seemed to be listening for something, but the ship was silent. Joshua Peters was sleeping outside the cabin door; Philippe and his French sailors were standing watch on deck. The man in the cabin turned his

head and his skull came into the weak light. He wore a knitted cap instead of a wig. Fanny could not see his face.

She tried to cry out, but the gag muffled her voice. As soon as she uttered this small sound the man whirled, lifted his arm, and brought it down. A cane whistled as it cut the air, then struck her buttocks. Fanny had never felt such an excruciating pain. It spurted through her body, burning and jagged, and forced the air out of her lungs in a scream. Stifled by the gag, the sound came out as a whimper. When the man heard this sound he hit her again.

He went down on one knee and took her by the hair, pulling her face into the light.

"Did you like that?" he whispered.

Fanny saw that the man was Montagu.

"You're crying," he whispered. "That's good. I like a wet girl."

He stood up and caned her again, just as hard as before. This time, because she knew what to expect and sensed that he would not stop as long as she made noise, Fanny gasped but did not cry out.

Montagu whispered into her ears. "Good," he said. "You learn fast. I like that too."

He stroked Fanny's hair, then yanked it hard, twisting her face close to his.

"Poor Fanny is crying," he said. "Let me help."

He licked the tears from her cheek. Then he straightened up, his tongue flickering.

"Delicious," he whispered.

Fanny was still immobilized by the pain inflicted by the cane. She wore only a nightdress, so that her skin was protected by a single layer of fine wool. Montagu was tugging at the hem, pulling the nightdress up over her legs. He drew a finger along the welts he had made. They smarted like burns. Montagu pressed the cane against her nose, forcing her head back.

"I want to have a look at you," he said in his shrill whisper. "Come quietly unless you want another stroke."

He seized her hair and pulled her to her feet, hauling her across the cabin to the windows that ran across the stern bulkhead. One of these was a Dutch door that opened onto a narrow gallery over the water. The door stood open and a rope dangled outside. Fanny realized that Montagu had climbed down from the deck, opened the door, and come into the cabin that way.

Montagu turned her around with her back to the open window and bent her over. He lifted her skirt and ran his fingers along the welts again. Now he could see them as well as feel them. He was breathing noisily. His hands trembled.

"Ah, very pretty marks," he said. "I wish you could see them."

He let go of her hair and turned her around. She was standing directly in front of the open window. For an instant, before Montagu pulled the skirt of her nightdress above her head, she could see the town in the starlight and, much nearer, Montagu's face. It looked quite different now—lax-muscled and eager, with the eyes loose in their sockets instead of being contemptuous and cold. She wondered why he was wearing a cap. The tassel hung down beside his cheek.

Fanny felt Montagu's hands on her body and his breath on her skin. She waited. When his hands were on her thighs and his breath was on her stomach, she drove her knee into his face. She felt Montagu's nose, cartilage and flesh, collapse under the blow. He cried out in pain.

Fanny stepped backward. The nightdress slid down of its own weight and she could see Montagu kneeling on the deck with his hand gripping his nose. She lifted her right leg and kicked him in the face with all her strength. He uttered a piercing grunt, tried to get to his feet, and fell onto his hip with his hands covering his face.

"Bloody bitch," he hissed.

Fanny hurled herself toward the open window, stepping on Montagu's prone body to reach it, and threw herself through it. Montagu seized her ankle as she went, but he was weak, and when, hanging upside down above the water, she kicked him hard with her free foot, he let go.

Fanny, tumbling as she fell, struck the water with a loud splash. Her nightdress was tangled around her face, so a moment passed before the water enveloped her head. It soaked the gag, and salt water that tasted like slops dribbled into her mouth. Fanny closed her throat to keep the air in her lungs and tried to push the gag out of her mouth with her tongue, but the water kept coming in. She struggled with her bound hands, but she could not free them.

She kicked her legs and climbed the ladder toward the surface as Henry had taught her to do long ago when he took her swimming in the Thames. Her head broke the surface and she snorted air into her lungs. The water made her cough. She could see nothing because her head was swathed in the nightdress. She thought that she heard voices shouting and another splash. These noises did not matter to her.

Pushing with her tongue, she tried to force the gag forward between her teeth and lips. It would not move. She took in another lungful of air through her nostrils and went under the surface again.

Water rushed into the soaked gag and went up into her nose. Fanny knew that she was drowning, that she could not possibly save herself. In her mind's eye she saw Montagu's flickering tongue, narrow and coated with something white, as it had been when he licked the tears off her face.

No, she thought, driving the image out, I won't think of that as I die.

She thought, instead, of swimming with her father. As a boy he had swum across the Thames on a pig's bladder, the same one he and Oliver used to play football on the other bank. When Fanny was small, Henry had hired a punt at Oxford, where the green water was clean and fragrant, and poled the boat to a hidden place. There they stripped and lowered themselves over the side.

"Go gently," her father had said, "imagine you're safe in bed. Let the water hold you up and carry you."

She had lain on her back, naked in the August sun, and gradually the chilly Thames had grown warmer and carried her dreamily along on its gentle current.

Now, suspended beneath the surface of the harbor, Fanny felt the same thing happening. The water was warmer. It was carrying her away. She stopped struggling. The water took hold of her. As if from a distance, she saw her white nightgown, her pale legs, her long black hair swirling lazily in the water and mistook the drowning girl to whom these things belonged for Fanchon. Fanny realized that she was weeping as she drowned.

Something very strong took hold of her. Fanny struggled against it with the last of her strength but she was helpless in its grasp. She began to move much more rapidly and it seemed to her that her body was rising through the water. She wondered if she would see light at the top, green light like the light within the Thames, and opened her eyes.

Her head broke the surface and she tried to breathe. Seawater ran into her throat from the soaked gag and she coughed, expelling water though her nostrils. Whatever had hold of her held her up, It, too, was being swept along by the current.

A man was looking worriedly into her face. His concern was so great that Fanny mistook it for love before she recognized her rescuer. It was the French soldier Philippe. His hair was plastered to his skull and was darker than she remembered, but the Viking eyes were the same.

Fanny was choking, drowning in the open air on the water in Montagu's gag.

"Good God," Philippe said.

He pulled the gag out of Fanny's mouth. She gasped and coughed,

her lungs full of water. Philippe turned her body in the water, put his arms around her chest, and squeezed her chest. Water spurted out of her mouth.

The two of them sank beneath the surface. Once again Fanny could see him in front of her. His eyes were open, his hair stood out around his head, the sleeves of his white shirt ballooned around his arms. He swam upward, striving with his body arched, pulling Fanny with him. He was tremendously strong.

Their heads broke the surface. Fanny coughed again, but she could breathe now. Philippe held her up.

"Kick," he said. "Help me. Kick."

Fanny rolled over onto her back and began to kick. The nightgown flowed in the water. There were ships all around, every one of them sailing away from her. In a moment she realized that she was the one who was moving, not the ships. The tide was carrying her and Philippe out into the Channel. They were being swept straight toward the hull of an anchored vessel.

"Now," Philippe said. "Hold on."

He seized the anchor cable and the two of them swung around it.

"Take hold," he said.

"I can't," Fanny said calmly. "My hands are tied."

She was surprised that she was able to speak. Until she did, she was not sure that she was alive. But now she felt Philippe untying the knots. Her hands were free. She seized the cable.

Philippe swung himself around so that he could look into Fanny's face. His scar was not so vivid in this light. His face, glistening with seawater, was grim.

"Were you harmed?" he asked.

Fanny shook her head. Philippe looked deep into her eyes to make sure of the truth, then looked away. Now that he had saved her life, he was remembering her modesty.

"The boat is coming," he said. "Hold on."

Philippe's boat, rowed by the sailors in their striped shirts, moved toward them very fast on the tide.

Fanny looked back at the *Pamela*. She was easy to find because there were lights burning in all her portholes and men were shouting and running up and down the deck and looking over the side.

The boat thudded against the stern of the anchored ship.

"I'll get in first," Philippe said.

He did so, then helped Fanny aboard. The nightdress clung to her body. She shuddered with cold. Philippe's men had brought his cloak. He draped it around her shoulders and she hunched inside it, water running over her face. Now that her body was covered,

Philippe was looking at her again. Fanny looked him straight in the eyes.

He did not waver, but held her gaze all the way back to the *Pamela*. The row back to the ship took a long time because the sailors were pulling against the tide.

On deck, Joshua Peters embraced her.

"Where is the Englishman?" Philippe asked.

With Fanny still in his arms, Joshua made a gesture with his head. "Overboard."

"You saw him go?"

"Yes. If the tide took him, he's halfway to England by now."

"Or on the bottom. I must report to the count."

Philippe lifted his hand. Fanny saw that he had saved the gag and another rag that had been used to tie her hands. Evidence. Fanny tried to speak, but coughed up water instead. After a moment she was able to talk again.

"We must sail on this tide," she said.

Philippe was looking into her eyes again with the same expression he had worn when they were in the water together, as if he could not make himself believe that she was alive.

"If the man who attacked you is in France," he said, "he will be brought to justice. Now I must go ashore."

"Do we have permission to sail?"

"I am not empowered to give you permission."

A sailor stood waiting with Philippe's hat and coat and boots and sword clutched against his chest.

"Your cloak," Fanny said.

"You can give it back tomorrow," Philippe said. "That will be time enough."

As soon as Philippe's boat reached the quay, Joshua gave orders to the crew to haul anchor and make sail. The noise this made—the boatswain shouting, the windlass shrieking, the ship groaning—must have carried clearly over the water, but Philippe did not look back.

Hugging his cloak about her, Fanny watched him through the broad stern windows of the master's cabin as he marched away into the town.

# 16

The *Pamela*, sailing for England in a four-foot sea, creaked exactly as she had done in Fanny's dream before Montagu pulled down the house in Catherine Street. Fanny fought against sleep as she tried to finish her supper, dry biscuits and a cold cod whose white flesh peeled away in big firm flakes. She had no appetite. A lantern swung overhead and the pewter trencher slid back and forth on the table.

Fanny was dressed now in her warmest clothes and wrapped up again in Philippe's thick cloak, but still she trembled with the cold. The sea washed against the glass door in the stern through which Montagu had come the night before. Fanny watched it, shuddered, and turned her face away.

"Are you seasick?" Joshua asked.

"No, not seasick."

"Don't worry about the weather," Joshua said, chewing his food. "The *Pamela* is happy in seas ten times worse than this."

"I know."

Her mind was elsewhere. Joshua had asked her no questions; he did not want to know what had happened to her in this cabin while he slept outside the door.

"Now that you own this ship," he said, "you should know her particulars. She's one of a kind, built in Sweden to my Uncle Giacomo's plans. He wanted a ship that was faster and handier than a brig, which has two square-rigged masts. The *Pamela* has only one set of square sails, on the foremast. The mainmast carries a fore-and-aft sail. It can be hauled up without climbing the rigging, so we can handle the ship with a smaller crew. The *Pamela* has a keel length of eighty feet and a width of thirty. She has a steering wheel instead of a whipstaff, which means that you can steer the ship, if things are right for it, without trimming the sails. I wouldn't hesitate to sail her among icebergs."

Fanny listened dully. Joshua's voice seemed far away.

He stopped talking and reached across the table and put his

hand, crooked with old fractures, on her forehead. Her skin was hot to the touch.

"When was the last time you slept?" he asked.

"I don't know. Not since London."

"Get into the bunk, Fanny. I'll get you something hot to drink. We've got some special honey to put in it."

He went out. Fanny shivered and hugged herself for warmth. She pulled the chair away from the table and got out her comb and hand mirror and started to braid her hair for the night. Halfway through, her brain stopped telling her fingers what to do and she had to start over again. She got into the bunk, covered up, and drew up her knees. The heavy blankets rubbed against her face like an unshaven cheek.

Joshua returned with the drink, honey and brandy mixed with hot water. Fanny took a sip and made a face when she tasted the brandy.

"Drink more," Joshua said. "The honey is from Seville. The bees make it from orange blossoms. Can you taste it?"

Fanny nodded to please him. But she did not taste the orange in the honey. She closed her eyes.

She said, "Is this the bunk your uncle died in?"

Joshua tapped the back of her hand where it held the cup. "Have some more toddy."

Fanny opened her eyes. "Did he die in this cabin?"

"Yes, but there are no ghosts aboard this ship. You know that. And no Englishmen either."

"Do you think that Montagu drowned?" Fanny asked.

Joshua adjusted the covers around her face and took the glass from her hand.

"Maybe," he said. "Men like Montagu are hard to kill. The devil has his hand on them."

"But he did go overboard."

"I saw him go. He jumped through that hatch when I came into the room."

"Jumped? Why?"

"I fired a pistol at him."

"And missed?"

"Yes, but I had another one. I saw him in the water with my own eyes, Fanny. The tide was taking him out into the Channel."

Fanny stopped trembling and closed her eyes.

"Go to sleep," Joshua said.

Her breath came very quickly. After a moment Joshua spoke her name, but she did not stir. She turned over onto her side and he felt her forehead again while he listened to her breathe. She

flinched at his touch. Joshua drank what was left of Fanny's drink, then blew out the lamp and lay down on the floor against the door, covering himself with his cloak. Fanny coughed in her sleep, a long string of sharp barks that sounded angry in the dark.

# 17

Not knowing where else to turn, Oliver sent Rose to Sir Cecil Lockwood to ask for help. It was a journey of twenty-five miles by coach to Chesham, and by the time Rose arrived she was nauseated by fatigue and sore in every muscle.

Sir Cecil Lockwood, interrupted at his supper, was full of ale and not glad to see her.

Sir Cecil was a rapid feeder. "Back from London in the middle of the night, madam?" he said with his mouth full. "What damn nonsense is this?"

It was a cold night with the usual rain glistening on the stones of Lockwood Hall, and Sir Cecil was dining alone with his dogs in a small upstairs room. They were big drooling dogs, mastiffs mostly, and there were about half a dozen of them. There was no fire; Sir Cecil relied on the heat radiating from the dogs' bodies to take the chill from the air. One candle burned in the candelabrum. Sir Cecil left Rose standing by the table as he hacked meat off a cold leg of mutton with a sharp knife and stuffed it into his mouth with greasy fingers. When he wanted a drink of ale he wiped his fingers on the fur of one of his dogs before picking up the mug.

"I've brought you a letter from my husband," Rose said.

"What? Sending you back for poor behavior? I won't have you, missis. Do you think I can afford to feed another mouth? Well, I cannot."

Rose put Oliver's letter on the table. She was giddy from hunger, and the fatty aroma of the mutton made her close her eyes. While Sir Cecil looked at Oliver's letter, turning it over with the point of his knife to examine the seal while he went on chewing his mutton, Rose slipped into a chair, giving one of the mastiffs a sharp kick in the ribs to move it out of the way. The joint of mutton lay under her nose. Sir Cecil had the only knife. Without

asking permission, Rose tore a strip of the bloodless cold meat off the joint and put it into her mouth. Chewing his own mouthful, Sir Cecil glowered at her, but she hadn't eaten since morning, and the food made her feel so much better that she tore off another piece before she had swallowed the first.

"If Barebones hasn't put you out," Sir Cecil said, "then what *does* he want? Money? Because he won't get any."

"It's in the letter."

Sir Cecil moved the joint away from Rose to the other side of his place and went on carving it and eating it, throwing bits of skin and fat to the dogs. When he finished, he rang for a servant.

"Take this up to her ladyship and her clergyman," he said, handing the haggled joint to the footman who answered the bell. Rose uttered a tiny sound of protest.

"Wait," Sir Cecil said. He sliced off a long sliver of meat, stabbed it, and handed it to Rose. "More ale for me," he said to the footman. "And bring this lady from London something to drink too, before she goes back to her husband."

Sir Cecil called one of the dogs and wiped both hands thoroughly in its fur. Then he read Oliver's letter.

"You mean to say this man pulled Harding's house down around his corpse and is now going to do the same to Barebones?" he said.

"He's a terrible villain. I was asleep in the house when he came with his oxen—"

"Asleep in Harding's house? Don't you sleep with your husband?"

"Fanny is only a girl. She could hardly be left alone with her father lying downstairs dead in the hall."

"Yes, yes, yes." Sir Cecil wasn't interested in the details. "What killed Harding?" he asked. "Something fall on him?"

"No. As I said, he was already dead when the house was pulled down."

"Already dead? What killed him?"

"He broke his neck playing football."

"Playing football? Where was Barebones when all this was happening?"

"He was playing too."

"And he let Harding get his neck broken? Doesn't sound like Barebones."

Rose ground the tough mutton between her back teeth and drank come cider from the cup the footman placed in front of her. "At the time my husband was . . . distracted," she said.

"Who *is* this bloody man Mountagu? Is he one of the real Mountagus?"

"No. My husband says Montagu just took the name to make himself grand."

"You're sure he's not from the wrong side of the old earl's blanket? What did Harding say?"

Sir Cecil was paying close attention now. He did not want to take sides against anyone who was related, however illegitimately, to the Mountagus who were the Earls of Sandwich.

"Henry said the same as my husband."

"Then it must be so. Harding knew what was what."

Sir Cecil finished his ale and went outside onto a balcony and urinated over the railing. When he came back inside he moved the dogs around, calling first one and then the other and commanding them to lie down. Soon they were all panting in a circle around a deerhide rug on the floor. Sir Cecil lay down on its hairy surface, his usual napping place, and called the two largest mastiffs closer with smacks of his lips.

Before he closed his eyes he looked at Rose, who was still sitting quietly in her chair.

"Find a bed, Rose," he said. "Tomorrow we'll see about Barebones."

Next morning at breakfast, when Rose looked out the window, she saw two dozen strong young men standing in the park with their caps in their hands, looking up at Sir Cecil, who was talking to them from the back of a gray horse. All the dogs were with him too, as usual. Rose helped herself to breakfast, the only meal of the day that was eaten in the hall because Lady Lockwood came down for it.

Sir Cecil's silent wife was at the table now in her peignoir and nightcap. A thin silent clergyman was seated beside her. He had fine features and the ashen complexion and wild look of a man whose heart has recently been broken. Though he could not have been more than thirty-five, his hair was mousy gray. Rose gazed at him in fascination. He was like the ghost of a young poet.

Sir Cecil came in through the French windows, leaving the mastiffs barking outside in their uncertain throaty voices. He saw Rose's look of fascination.

"Gray sort of little man, isn't he?" he said. "Wait till you hear his name. Introduce them, Lucy, go on."

"Missis Barebones of London, may I present Mr. Edward Ash, late of Trinity College, Cambridge," Lady Lockwood said.

"Later of the king's whipping post," Sir Cecil said, shoveling eggs and kidneys onto a plate. "Ash. Suits the little gray sufferer."

Ash ignored him. "Barebones," he said. "Is that the Parliament fellow, Praise God Barebones, Oliver Cromwell's friend?"

"A relation, I believe," Rose said.

"He was her husband's great-uncle," Sir Cecil said. "Old Praise God had two brothers. The first was called Christ-came-into-the-world-to-save Barebones and the other was called If-Christ-had-not-died-thou-hadst-been-damned Barebones. They couldn't very well call them both Christ, so they called one World and the other Damned. It was Damned Barebones who was Oliver's grandfather. Oliver's named for Oliver Cromwell, poor chap. Very pious Puritan family, the Bareboneses, but you wouldn't know it to see Oliver in a sporting mood, eh, Rose?"

"Ah," Ash said. He looked very directly at Rose, and for a longer time than was usual. Even though there was nothing male in his examination, she flushed.

Sir Cecil began to speak to Rose, but Ash did not remove his eyes from her.

"I'm sending you back to London with twenty lads that played football with Barebones," Sir Cecil was saying. "They'll do as Oliver tells them, as they think he's one of King Arthur's knights, but they must do it quick and get back here to plant my crops."

Rose felt Ash's eyes on her, like two spots of heat on the skin of her cheek. "Yes," she said to Sir Cecil. "But I should like to stay here until it's over."

"Oh, no, madam," Sir Cecil said. "None of that. It's back to London and husband for you. Take Ash with you. You'll need the help of heaven, and Ash knows what it is to suffer the scorn of the lash."

"The lash of scorn," Ash said.

"Is that what it's called? You can show Rose your poor whipped back along the way, Ash. But remember, she's a virtuous married woman and you're the property of the Redeemer."

Ash turned his steady blue stare on Sir Cecil. "Your Redeemer hears you," he said.

Sir Cecil, washing down fried kidneys with a quart of ale and calling for bread and cheese, ignored him. Seeing Ash in profile, Rose realized that he was like a head carved on a coin, more perfect than flesh could be.

"Cecil," Rose said.

Sir Cecil lifted his head. Rose had never dared to call him by his name before.

"May we borrow horses for the journey to London? The coach is unbearable."

"Borrow twenty-two horses? Are you mad?"

"Not twenty-two, Cecil. Just two. The men can walk."

Sir Cecil ate another fried kidney. "All right," he said. "It'll

make the men walk faster and at least you won't fall off. You can rescue this idle curate if his horse runs away with him."

Before he rose from the table Ash said a prayer. He had a melodious voice, but even in ordinary conversation it was so loud and had such an edge to it that it hurt Rose's ears.

Rose watched him as he prayed. His face was turned toward her and he seemed to be staring at her even with his eyes closed.

# 18

Rose Barebones and Edward Ash rode side by side down the road to London, Rose on a handsome hunter that had belonged to Robert, Ash on a shaggy beast that was a walking insult. He sat with one long thin leg crossed over the scrub's withers, reading a small thick book bound in black cloth. He winced from time to time as the broad-joking Buckinghamshire voices of the yokels, who were skylarking along behind them, carried to their ears.

Rose watched him intently as he read his book. Then she said, "I beg your pardon, Mr. Ash."

Ash marked his place with his index finger and looked at her without interest. She had never seen that expression on a man's face before.

Rose smiled. "I was going to ask if you would mind reading aloud."

"I doubt that you would enjoy it. I am reading a work of philosophy, or so-called philosophy, by Mr. Thomas Hobbes."

"You have no Bible? I love to hear the Bible."

"I have one in my bag, but I do not wish to read it now."

"Is Mr. Hobbes's philosophy like the Bible in any way?"

"No. In fact it may be the work of Satan."

Rose's interest was immediately aroused. "Is it about witches?" she asked.

"No. It is about the king, Mr. Hobbes was tutor to Charles II when he was crown prince. His view, therefore, has been more than usually influential at court. It is Mr. Hobbes's thesis that the powers of the sovereign are unlimited because God gave those powers to him and that the obedience of his subjects must there-

fore be unconditional. There is only one limitation on his power. An Englishman may defend himself even against the king. The right of self-defense is absolute. Even a poor clergyman who has been deprived of his living by the Act of Uniformity, and stripped of his right of movement by the Five Mile Act, and denied his right of conscience by the Test Act, at least retains the right of self-defense. Or so Mr. Hobbes says. The king does not think so. 'My power is absolute,' says the king. 'Whip the man who says otherwise. That will prove it.' "

As soon as he finished speaking, Ash opened his book again and raised it to his face. Evidently he was shortsighted. Rose wanted to hear him speak again.

She said, "Is it because of Mr. Hobbes and his Acts that you were whipped, may one ask?"

Ash marked his place again and looked into her face with that peculiar intensity of his. "The Acts were not Mr. Hobbes's but the king's. I was whipped for writing a book that attacked Mr. Hobbes's doctrine of passive obedience. I wrote that a Christian must, in certain circumstances, resist the king."

Though Ash spoke no less loudly when he uttered these words, he spoke very calmly. Rose did not know how he could. She had never heard such madness spoken aloud.

"Resist the king?" Rose said, barely able to get the words out. "That's treason. They'll put you in the Tower."

Always before, men had said things to Rose that they imagined she wanted to hear. Ash seemed to care nothing about that.

"You needn't worry," he said. "You're in no danger of having your head cut off as a result of hearing my treasonous words. It was King James, not the present king, who had me whipped."

King James had fled to France at least ten years ago. Ash must be older than he looked.

"What a terrible punishment," Rose said.

Ash did not respond to her sympathy. "I will give you the details," he said. "My book was burned by the public hangman. I was ordered to pay a fine equal to my entire inheritance so that I should be impoverished forever. I was sentenced to stand in the pillory at Westminster, Charing Cross, and the Royal Exchange. And I was whipped from Newgate to Tyburn."

Ash would have gone back to his reading again, but Rose was now enthralled. "How far is that?" she asked.

Ash was startled by the question. "How far is what?" he said.

"How far were you whipped when you were whipped from Newgate to Tyburn? I do not know London well."

"It is about fifteen furlongs."

"You walked?"

"No. They tie you up on a frame in a cart drawn by oxen and as it rolls slowly through the streets, you are whipped. The crowd cheers."

Rose was very moved. Hunting with Robert and Sir Cecil, she had often seen a stag brought down by the hounds, its hide bitten to ribbons. It must have looked and sounded like that when Edward Ash was whipped across London. What must his scars be like?

"How could you bear it?" she asked.

Ash was reading his book again. He answered without putting it down. "With fortitude," he said. "God made it possible for me to pray harder than the brute could whip, and louder than the mob could howl."

# 19

Montagu was back in London. Praise God had seen him in Lloyd's Coffeehouse and had himself carried to Catherine Street to warn Oliver.

"Thank you," Oliver said. "I'm ready for him."

He sat at the table in the hall with four loaded pistols before him and a stout cudgel on the floor beside him. His eyes were rimmed with red and his face was colorless. He had not slept for days, except to nod off at his post and then wake up with a guilty start.

Waiting for Montagu to come, Oliver thought about America. He had thought about very little else since Henry's death. Even Rose did not tempt him. Oliver had not had a sexual thought since the moment on the field of play when he had heard the snicker of Henry's neck breaking like a joint being twisted apart in a cold roast of mutton. Of course he had heard no such sound; it was the look of Henry's neck as he lay dead and the expression on Fanny's face as she knelt by the corpse, the color and the life draining out of her own features in an imitation of death, that made Oliver imagine that he had heard it. He had not been able to touch his friend's body or look at it. The Gypsies carried it to the river while Oliver helped Rose along the path and Fanny rode on ahead

with the corpse, one hand touching it and her own face as blank as Henry's. When Fanny took Oliver's hand and held it against her body at the grave, Oliver had wondered if Henry was using his daughter's hands to touch him for the last time. When Praise God Adkins told him that Fanny had gone to France to find the *Pamela*, a farther distance than Oliver himself had ever traveled, he merely nodded, as though his goddaughter had gone to Greenwich on a day's outing.

Oliver had begun to think about America as a means of not thinking about Henry. He imagined himself in the wilderness with Rose beside him. In his mind he saw the tall pines, twenty feet around at the base, that his Uncle John Pennock had described, and wooden houses with shingle roofs standing in a valley beside a wide sparkling river. Deer drank from the river. Flights of ducks and partridges obscured the sun like clouds.

Oliver, like most people who had grown up among Puritans, believed in predestination. "God would, by things that are not, bring to naught things that are . . . and God did," said Oliver Cromwell after he destroyed King Charles's infantry and scattered his horse at the Battle of Naseby on the fourteenth of June 1645. John Pennock had ridden at Cromwell's side at Naseby, had actually heard him speak these words; they became the motto of Pennock's life and gave him hope that events he could not foresee would drive the Stuarts off the English throne again and replace them with a man who derived his idea of God directly from the Scriptures. That man was William of Orange, who granted Pennock his lands in America. What clearer proof of God's intentions could there be?

Gradually, as he thought about America, Oliver, too, began to believe that fate was calling him there. Everything that had happened since Shrove Tuesday—his sudden irresistible passion for Rose, her coldness to him, the bets with Montagu, the trouble with money, the ruby ring and necklace, Henry's death, Fanny's flight to France—had been ordained by destiny.

He said so to Praise God Adkins.

Praise God was taken aback. "You mean you think that Henry's death, financial ruin, this lust you can't satisfy—that all these misfortunes are messages from the Almighty?" he asked.

"Why shouldn't I think so?" Oliver asked. "God has the power to make His plan come true in every man's life. Otherwise, it all means nothing."

"I wish Henry were here to hear this. What do you think you're being told by heaven?"

"To go to America."

"What?"

"*America.* It's quite clear. I'm being told to go to America."

Praise God was dumbfounded. "America," he said. "But people like you, people like Rose, don't go to America."

"Everyone told my uncle the same thing. He went anyway."

"And had his wife and child killed by savages."

"Savages, you say? What do you call Montagu and his kind? Henry was killed right here in England."

"Oliver, my dear fellow. Friends die. Life goes on."

"Yes, P.G., that's what I'm saying to you. For me, life will go on in America. It's meant to be."

Oliver's inheritance in the wilderness had always been a joke to his friends. Henry had called him the Earl of Massachusetts after the place where his ten thousand acres were located. "You may laugh," Henry would tell the crowd in the Rose Tavern or the misses at the Widow's, "but Oliver owns a river bigger than the Thames and more trees and deer than his majesty the king—and also an Indian maiden who owns a slave."

This was perfectly true. John Pennock had bequeathed Oliver, besides the ten thousand acres of meadow and forest, including a stand of six hundred pines large enough to be cut as masts for men-o'-war, the Nipmuck slave girl, Magpie. She was by this time grown up and married to the Negro Coffee. In his will Pennock left Coffee to Magpie, an eccentric bequest, and one of dubious legality, because a slave, who had no right to own anything, had never owned another slave, as far as anyone in New England knew.

In his will Pennock spoke of Oliver's "quick wit and merry heart." But it was Henry, with his love of stories, who had got the old soldier to tell him and Oliver about America. Praise God believed that Pennock must have mixed up the two boys as his memory failed, and believed that Henry was Oliver.

# 20

As Montagu and his toughs marched into Catherine Street, twilight was beginning to fall; the men were shouting and beating their picks and sledgehammers together to make a din. They sounded like a hundred, but in fact there were no more than twenty of them, poor men with dirty skin showing through their rags. Leaving his pistols on the table, Oliver ran up the stairs and flung open the window of Rose's bedchamber to get a better look at them.

Montagu, seated in his sedan chair, saw Oliver immediately his face appeared in the window. Just as immediately, as if Oliver was the last object in the world that could be of interest to him, Montagu turned away to exchange a word with a woman he had brought along to watch the sport. Oliver recognized her; she came from the Widow's. The sound of yoke bells made the men shout louder. A span of six oxen, driven by the same man in the red cap who had pulled down Henry's house, plodded into view. Montagu's men, each carrying a sack over his shoulder, stood in a double rank in the mud. Montagu made an indolent gesture and spoke a word. The men dropped their sacks at their feet and spread open the tops. There were bricks inside. Like soldiers responding to a command, each man picked up a brick, set his feet, and threw it at Oliver.

Oliver followed the dreamy flight of the bricks through the air and then heard them thud against the side of his house. It seemed to him that they all arrived at once. Windows shattered. Three bricks struck Oliver one after the other like a flurry of punches, the first hitting his left elbow and causing excruciating pain, the second bouncing off his chest, and the third opening a cut on his scalp and knocking him unconscious for a moment. When he woke up he was sitting on the floor while bricks cannonaded through the open window, smashing Rose's new mirror and the scent bottles on the dresser. The air smelled overpoweringly of Rose. Her pale wafting dresses hung all around him on hooks. Oliver looked into

the broken mirror and saw that his face was covered with blood from the gushing scalp wound.

Outside, men were shouting, a shrill beastlike roar. Captain John Pennock had said that the Abenaki Indians had yipped like dogs that had just been kicked away from a fight. Montagu's bullies sounded the same. Oliver no longer thought about the destruction of his house or the loss of his ship. Nothing in England mattered. In his mind, he was already living in Massachusetts, and even now, with a mob howling at the door, his thoughts were of his estate in America—its broad river, its majestic trees, its fertile meadows, its woods in which bears grazed on sweet wild berries. Eden!

The howling toughs in the street were as strange to Oliver as wild Indians. Except when playing football, he had never taken joy in his strength. After he discovered, when he was still a boy, that he could break the bones of playmates without meaning to do so, Oliver had always been reluctant to injure other people. He would use his strength to defend others, as he had always protected Henry. But when he himself was threatened, Oliver often yielded to weaker men—after all, how could they hurt him?—rather than inflict pain and humiliation on them. He was tempted to yield now. He was not afraid; he had never been frightened. It did not trouble him that he was alone. Oliver had never expected rescue or help of any kind. Sending to Sir Cecil Lockwood for football players had been Praise God's idea. Oliver had seized on it as a means of getting Rose safely away from danger yet not losing her, but he pinned no hopes on Rose's mission. Chesham was far away. Nobody in London would lift a hand to help. Montagu had made Henry ridiculous even in death, and now he had made Oliver ridiculous too; Oliver knew that no one in London would befriend or defend the laughable. Even Montagu's whore, whom Oliver had made squeal and sweat for her guinea no more than a month before at the Widow's, could laugh at him.

In Rose's bedchamber, Oliver was blinded by his own blood; it was beginning to congeal, sticking his eyelashes together. This had happened to him before, and he knew his scalp wound wasn't serious. He snatched one of Rose's dresses off a hook and scrubbed his eyes with it, then tore the filmy cloth into strips and bandaged his head with it. In Rose's mirror it looked like the sultan's turban he had worn at Sir Cecil's masked ball. Going down the stairs to get his pistols, Oliver remembered every detail of the carnival ball, the Buckinghamshire gentry in their countrified costumes, the awful half-cooked supper, Sir Cecil's sly look when he talked about Rose's breasts and what her dead husband had taught

her in the marriage bed, and then the inconceivable reality of Rose herself.

Why did his mind keep wandering? Oliver shook his head violently to clear it. He was surprised to see that he held a dueling pistol in each hand and had two more thrust into the waist of his breeches. Outside, Montagu's savages went on screeching. In another dreamlike moment, Oliver saw Rose walking in flaxen nudity through the crowd; she was smiling, they fell silent. Oliver pulled himself back to the present. His ears rang; objects seemed far away and insubstantial; all movement was very slow; every face seemed ready to break into a derisive smile; everyone except Oliver appeared to know some secret joke. Sometimes when he was muddled by too much drink, Oliver had asked whatever woman he was with to slap him hard across the face to unstop his mind. Now he felt that he could come back from wherever he was—unconsciousness? sleep? death?—if only someone could hit him hard enough on the face. Oliver knew that a blow on the head had done this to him, but just the same he thought it very odd that his mind should be elsewhere, in America, when so much was happening to him in the here and now.

He threw open the door. The sight of him—massive, hairy, naked to the waist, head bound in blood-soaked gauze, two maddened eyes glittering in a mask of blood, pistols at the ready—hushed Montagu's men. The oxen were already hitched to a roof beam and the man who had climbed up to attach the chain was still at the top of the tall ladder. Seeing the oxen and the man standing thirty feet up as if suspended in air, Oliver realized that he had had a plan all along. Grinning through his mask of blood, he thrust his pistols under his armpits and tipped the ladder over. The climber swept across the sky, clinging to the top rung as he fell. He howled at the last moment, just before his body struck the mud, and uttered the same loud "*Oof!*" as Henry had done when his neck broke. But this man was still alive, rolling and groaning in pain.

Gripping his pistols, Oliver took three more long paces to where the span of oxen waited. The driver stepped between Oliver and the animals and menaced him with his whip. Oliver picked up the ox driver by the crotch and heaved him into the rubble of Henry Harding's house. Then he raised the pistol in his right hand, cocked it, placed the muzzle against the forehead of the near lead ox, a big red animal with a curly Devon fringe between its sweeping horns, and shot it dead. It fell as if decapitated, and the weight of its limp carcass pulled the animal yoked to it down too. The unwounded ox, its neck twisted in the yoke, bellowed and thrashed. With the pistol in his left hand, Oliver shot the off ox in the second

yoke. It, too, slumped to the ground, pulling its mate down with it. The four living oxen, eyes frantic, bells ringing, tried to stampede, but their yokes held them fast to the two dead ones. In death, the oxen Oliver had slaughtered looked quite human with their dazed expressions and their pink curls on their foreheads.

A gasp of horror rose from the onlookers. They shook their fists at Oliver for his cruelty in killing innocent defenseless animals. "Here now!" they shouted, and "Bloody bastard!" All the while, Montagu sat where he was in his sedan chair, an amused smile playing over his lips. His lackey was running among the ragged bullies, shouting orders. They began to throw bricks at Oliver again. Two or three of the missiles struck him. He uttered a loud grunt after each impact but stood his ground. Suddenly, amid the milling bullies, Oliver saw the slack-jawed woodman with the black hair who had killed Henry in the Gypsy football game and then run away into the wood. With a roar, Oliver ran straight for him. Bricks filled the air, the melee shifted in front of Oliver's eyes, the man disappeared.

Oliver knew that these men would kill him if he let them go on throwing bricks at him. The woodman reappeared, flinging bricks with a whippy motion of his arm. His hair hung down over his unshaven face. He was missing all his front teeth, so that he had a black mouth in the middle of a black beard. Was he the same man? He vanished again.

Oliver drew the other two pistols and aimed them at his enemies. Over the gleaming blue barrels of the weapons he glimpsed terrified faces, oxlike faces with glazed eyes. The bullies scattered, looking back fearfully over their shoulders. Oliver saw everything that happened around him. Montagu said something to his lackey. "Surround him, you fools!" the lackey shouted. "Come at him from the back!" Two or three bricks struck Oliver in the kidneys. He hunched his back against the pain and fired one of the pistols. Somebody howled. The rest fell back. Oliver lowered his pistols and looked at the crowd of onlookers. They were watching the oxen rather than the men. One of the animals had broken its neck trying to escape from its yoke and the other three looked as though they might do the same. Oliver's chest heaved; half-strangled by pain and rage, he drew in his breath in rasping gulps.

To Rose, riding around the end of Catherine Street with Edward Ash beside her, Oliver looked like a bear. Other men were circling around him, baying like hounds. What else could Oliver be if he were not a bear? How could there be any mistake about it? Suddenly Rose saw the oxen, feebly thrashing and lowing beyond Oliver's embattled figure.

"Look!" she said.

Ash glanced up from his Hobbes, marking the place with a finger as usual. He said, "That is your husband." It was not a question, but Rose answered it anyway in her absent tone of voice.

"Yes," she said. She bit her gloved fist. "But, oh, the poor oxen!"

"Oxen, madam? Oxen? Your husband is bleeding in the public street."

While they rode across Buckinghamshire, Rose had told Ash the whole story of Henry's house being pulled down. At the time, he did not seem to be listening, but now he appeared to know every detail.

"That is what's left of Harding's house?" he asked. "And that person in blue is Montagu?"

Rose nodded. Montagu wore pale blue silk today. Coat, breeches, shirt, hat, matched beautifully, making the lace on his cuffs and collar seem whiter than it really was. His hat and stockings were a paler, matched blue. Even his boots were blue. He was wearing a magnificent wig that also seemed faintly blue.

Lolling in his sedan chair, Montagu was eating another walnut; the mud around him was littered with broken shells. The woman from the Widow's, seated beside him in a second sedan chair, drank wine greedily from a glass goblet while watching Oliver and his tormentors over the rim.

"You, there," Ash said in his mighty voice.

Montagu gave no sign that he heard. Who in this rabble had the right to address him?

But Ash's voice had an effect on everyone else. Even Oliver heard it. It penetrated the muffling cloud produced by his concussion and caused the buzzing in his ears to stop. Oliver thought it was miraculous.

"You, on the sedan chair, in the blue wig," Ash said.

Montagu looked for the owner of the voice. His eyes sparkled when he saw Edward Ash seated on his ridiculous off-color horse, gray-haired and gray-faced, wearing plain black cloth and a round hat without a band and twisted stockings instead of boots.

"What did you say, you silly weed?" Montagu said. As he spoke, his gaze was on Rose, who sat her horse easily a few steps beyond Ash.

"Answer me, weed," Montagu said, looking Rose up and down.

Ash put his book into the pocket of his baggy coat, which was so old that its black dye was fading into dull green.

"If you wish it, sir, I will come closer, so that you will hear me," he said.

The crowd laughed—not at Ash's words, but at the novelty of his voice. He could have been heard on the other side of the Thames.

While they laughed, Ash clapped his heels into the ribs of his horse and spoke to it. The astonished beast, which had walked all the way from Chesham with a man reading a book in the saddle, suddenly found that it had a cavalryman on its back. Hands gripping the reins squarely in front of his belt buckle, back straight, heels down, Edward Ash drove the old hammerhead through the bullies and straight for Montagu's sedan chair. Sir Cecil Lockwood's mastiffs, footsore after their long walk but excited by the noise and the smell of ox blood, bounded after the horse with phlegmy barks.

The crowd scattered. Montagu's chairmen tried to get out of the carrying poles, but the mud was too sticky for fast movement. Ash turned the pony at the last instant so that its shoulder struck the sedan chair, then pulled his wild-eyed mount to a halt with its haunches in the muck.

Far away beyond the mob of bullies, Rose shrieked. Montagu sprawled into the mud in his silk suit, taking the woman from the Widow's down with him in a tangle of skirt and sword. His wig fell off, revealing a bald crown surrounded by a long fringe of wispy white hair. For the first time, Rose noticed that Montagu was not a young man. He could not get up without assistance, but lay in the mud, struggling to sit up, tugging at the hilt of his sword, which was pinned beneath the whore. He slapped the woman on the side of the head and tried to push her away.

The mastiffs, four of them, leaped on Montagu and the woman. The weight of the dogs knocked Montagu backward into the mud again. A brindle animal growled and snuffled Montagu's face. The others seized the skirt of his coat and dragged him a few feet over the slimy ground while the first dog licked his face. The blue silk ripped in their teeth. Then they bounded onto him again, growling and drooling and woofing happily as their teeth shredded Montagu's clothes. One of the mastiffs snatched the big puff of lace from Montagu's neck, revealing a dark brown mole the size of a small plum, and gamboled over the mud with the lace, shaking his blunt head and growling like a puppy. Another rolled Montagu in the mud and stripped off his shirt, leaving him with nothing but the sleeves. The mastiffs growled and frisked as they worked. They weren't angry or dangerous; they were playing Trespassers.

Suddenly Ash called them off. Although they had never heard his voice before, they obeyed it. They sat all in a row between

Montagu and Ash's horse, which watched the scene with lowered head and pricked ears.

Ash looked down on Montagu's prostrate figure. Montagu was practically naked. His chest and back were covered with large brown moles, and others were forming beneath the skin. Some had been sliced off by a quack and were suppurating. A look of pity came over Ash's face.

"Give this man a cloak to cover himself," Ash said.

Montagu's lackey handed him his own cloak. Still sitting on the ground, Montagu hid himself inside it, but when the woman from the Widow's crawled across the mud and offered him his wig, he dashed it into the mud.

"You bloody bastard," Montagu said. "You'd put the dogs on me?"

Montagu was on his feet now, frizzy-haired and smeared with mud, blue silk hanging in tatters from his emaciated arms and legs. The woman from the Widow's sprawled in the mud with her skirts thrown up and two plump legs spread out in white stockings. She began to sob hysterically. Montagu, struggling to find his sword beneath his cloak, kicked her hard in the ribs; she sobbed louder and lay where she was.

Finally Montagu got his sword out of its scabbard.

"Put that weapon down," Ash said.

"I'll put it down your fucking throat," Montagu said. He flogged the chairmen onto their feet with the flat of the sword and got back into the sedan chair. Shoulder-high again, he lifted the sword above his head and shouted to the bullies.

"Pull this noisy bastard off his horse and bring him to me," he said.

"Do not attempt it!" Ash said.

"Attempt it?" Montagu said. "I won't attempt it, I'll do it. You'll learn to get out of the way when I pass by—by God you will!"

Ash was completely unruffled. "You won't pass by very much longer, friend," he said. The words clanged down the street. "I forewarn you of your end. The tokens are all over your body."

"*What?*"

"Friend, believe the danger. Do not put off your preparation for your end."

"What the hell are you?" Montagu tried to laugh.

"God has arranged that we meet. I am very sorry to say it, friend, but you are dying. Any physician will tell you so after a single look at those brown growths you are having treated by a fool."

"Dying, am I?" Montagu said, his voice sounding thin coming after Ash's. "Not before you do, friend. Seize this madman!"

The bullies hesitated for a moment. Then, led by the lank-haired woodman from Norwood, they surged forward. Oliver seized the woodman, who squirmed in his grasp with his toothless mouth open like a carp's. "I know you!" Oliver cried. "I know everything!" The woodman pulled a knife—a homemade knife with a broken blade tied with thongs into a piece of split sapling—and stabbed Oliver in the biceps. Blood spurted. Oliver released the man, who ran away waving his bloody knife and bowling people over in the crowd.

"An artery!" Ash cried. "Help him!"

Oliver, swaying, looked at his gushing wound.

But Sir Cecil's yokels hung back. This was not the jolly, rough, ale-drinking Oliver Barebones they knew. Things in London were not as they had imagined they would be. They had not expected to see murder. They were shocked by the suffering of the oxen, who were still thrashing around and bellowing piteously. Not one of them had ever been more than five miles from home. They had never heard so much noise before. What did Sir Cecil want them to do?

While they pondered this question, Montagu's bullies knocked Oliver to the ground and bore down on Ash. Montagu stood up in his sedan chair and waved his sword.

"All fellows to football!" Ash thundered, and plunged his horse into the onrushing knot of toughs.

Several of them fell. Others grasped at Ash's leg and he reared his mount to shake them off. With a cheer, the yokels burst into motion at last and began to knock down Montagu's men. The crowd fled, with the woman from the Widow's swaying among them in her ruined clothes.

Oliver was on his knees with his undischarged pistol still dangling from his hands, staring dumbly at the blood spraying from the wound in his arm.

Ash leaped off the horse, seized the pistol, and fired it into the air. Behind him the yokels and the bullies were fighting so hard that they did not hear it go off. Oliver did not question Ash's action. He was feeling very faint and sick at his stomach. There was a roaring in his ears that even Ash's voice could not pierce.

Ash pulled the turban from Oliver's head, tore off a strip of cloth, wound it around the bleeding arm above the knife puncture, tied a knot, inserted the barrel of the pistol into the knot, and twisted.

Oliver said, "The blood stopped."

Ash nodded in satisfaction. "Yes. It is a method invented by the French, though some say it was originated by the Red Indians of America," he said in what was, for him, a conversational tone. "Pinch the artery between the wound and the heart and the bleeding stops."

"Wonderful," Oliver said. "The Indians, you say? I am going to America soon."

"Then you can thank your benefactors in person. Now, Mr. Barebones, on your feet, if you please. We must sew up this artery before the flesh mortifies."

Rose had not moved. Mounted sidesaddle on her beautiful chestnut, her profile prettily displayed under her favorite bonnet, she watched the fight with fascination. Two of the yokels had captured Montagu's chair and they were dashing up and down the street with it while he slashed ineffectually at them with his sword.

Ash spoke to her. "Off your horse, if you please, madam," he said. "Your husband needs doctoring."

To her own surprise, Rose dismounted instantly and walked obediently to where Oliver kneeled, soupy muck splashing over her boots and hems. She took Oliver by his unwounded arm.

"Come, husband," she said.

It was the first time she had touched him of her own accord. Oliver felt love in his heart again and desire coursing through his wounded body. He imagined Rose beside him in the lovely soft light of the American forest.

"Lay him in his bed and stay by him," Ash said. "I must fetch my box."

Sir Cecil's men had pushed the baggage down to London on a little cart. Ash strode toward it through what remained of the battle. Montagu's men, Rose's enemies, lay groaning all over the ground. Like any general whose mind was elsewhere, Ash paid them no heed. Yet he was tremendously alert, and he rode better than Robert.

Who was this Edward Ash? What was he? Rose had to think in order to breathe; the air burned in her chest. London seemed very strange, like a place she had never seen before but only heard about, which was filling up a space that had been saved for it in her mind.

"Rose," Oliver said.

Why didn't Ash speak to her in his wonderful voice? Rose did not realize it, but she was feeling the same things that Oliver was feeling as he stumbled along beside her, dreaming from his wounds and murmuring her name.

# 21

The condition that Edward Ash observed in Montagu, consisting of the formation of a large number of malignant moles or tumors on and under the skin, was one he had seen before. It was a form of cancer that appeared suddenly and killed very quickly.

In addition to being a minister of God, Ash was a physician and surgeon. This had come about, Ash knew, through God's intention. Ash had been created as a man of powerful sexual instincts—so strong, in fact, that he knew from an early age that only marriage could contain them. He had married at the age of twenty, as soon as he was ordained. His bride, a fifteen-year-old Chesham girl named Betsy, was pretty and mild and possessed of a radiant smile. Betsy had borne him a child every ten months, including a set of mixed twins, so that by the time Ash was whipped and impoverished and cast out of London, he was the father of six living children.

After the whipping, Ash returned with his wife and children to Buckinghamshire and lived in a cottage on his family's property. His people were minor landowners, more than yeomen but not quite gentry, who had always been puzzled by their son's religious zeal. While Ash's back healed, he prayed, locking himself into a room for five or six hours a day, and sometimes praying all night too, so that Betsy would find him unconscious—not asleep—on the floor in the morning. His muffled voice, locked up in the room with him, made the atmosphere in the cottage tremble like the skin of a drum. Ash knew that he could not have suffered so greatly in the absence of a purpose. In his prayers, he asked God for a sign that would reveal His plan for the remainder of His servant's life.

Sickness struck. All six of Ash's children died of meningitis in rapid succession. Like less horrible illnesses, the disease began with a low fever and loss of appetite. This was followed by intense headache and by constipation and retention of the urine so that the stomach became distended and the skin turned yellow. In the final stage, the neck arched backward toward the heels as if the body was seeking to form itself into a circle, causing indescribable ag-

ony. As in the plague, the victim could not bear to look at the light. Noise also caused pain, and the dying children shrieked at their father to stop praying. He could not do so.

The physician called by Ash subscribed to the dominant medical theory of the day, which held that all illnesses were caused by distempers of the four humors that ruled the body—blood, phlegm, yellow bile, and black bile. Meningitis, the doctor explained, was caused by an excess of phlegm, or pituita, dripping down from the pituitary gland at the base of the brain. To drive out the excessive phlegm, he prescribed expectorants, which the children could not swallow because they were screaming. The doctrine of contraries, recorded by the Greek physician Galen in the second century after Christ, stated that the body was ruled by the four elements, heat, cold, wet, and dry, and each part should be treated by its opposite element. The stomach was cold. Therefore the physician prescribed hot drinks and hot compresses. Forcing liquids into children who could not void may have been a merciful treatment in the end, in the sense that it hastened their deaths if it did not make them easier.

Betsy was unable to bear these blows. She had a morbid fear of meningitis, a disease that had killed all of her own sisters. Terrified of infection, she sat all day on the floor behind the bed, refusing to touch her children while they died. At this time she herself was only twenty-one years old. When the last child died, Betsy stopped speaking. Ash found it impossible to comfort her. She would not utter a word, even in prayer, and would cover her ears when Ash prayed; sometimes Ash thought that Betsy believed in her heart that his praying had killed the children because it had agonized them so.

Like everyone else, Ash understood that most children in England died before they grew up; as a minister he had buried nearly as many as he had christened. He accepted God's will in this matter. He realized that excessive grief was impious. But as he watched the small bodies of his children, which had been so perfect and so beautiful, twist in pain and waste away, he could not accept his helplessness.

Ash locked himself into a room and fasted, taking in nothing but water for two weeks, and prayed aloud day and night. One morning as he lay on the floor whose rough boards glistened with his tears, he realized that God intended him to become a physician, so as to unite healer and minister in the same person. Taking Betsy with him, he walked to London and apprenticed himself to a practitioner of medicine called Thomas Sydenham.

It was Sydenham who introduced scientific diagnosis and specific treatment into medical practice. He discovered new and gentler methods for treating fever. Though he was not the first to do so, he cured malaria, which had long ravaged Europe, with a potion of "Jesuit's bark"—actually the bark of the cinchona, a tree that grew in Peru. Quinine was the first great specific; it cured malaria, and little else, though it was tried on nearly every other malady after a quack named Robert Talbor cured Charles II of malaria with it. Sydenham described scarlet fever, St. Vitus' dance (Sydenham's chorea), hysteria, smallpox, gout, and many other diseases and conditions, including malaria.

Ash was breaking the law by setting foot in London. He had been banned from the city for life, and the Five Mile Act made it illegal for a dismissed clergyman to come within five miles of a corporate body. Sydenham knew this; Ash's case was a famous one. But Sydenham had been a physician to Cromwell's troops in the Civil War, and he was sympathetic to a young man who had been whipped for defying the king. Charles I, after all, had been beheaded for insisting too much on the divine right of kingship, and Sydenham admired a man who would stand up to his monarch.

Sydenham, like his younger friend John Locke, was a writer as well as a physician. He received Ash in Will's Coffeehouse in Covent Garden, a hangout for authors and wits. Bowls of coffee sweetened with sugar were set before them, but Ash let his go cold.

Sydenham asked him why: "Don't you like politician's porridge?"

"I like it very much," Ash said. "But I have been fasting for two weeks and I fear that a stimulant will make me giddy."

"Fasting? Why?"

"It brings one closer to God."

"It deprives the body of sugar and causes hallucinations."

Though Sydenham was already old, he had the clear eyes, the firm chin, and the steady hands of a man of forty. As Ash observed these qualities, Sydenham observed Ash. Then, with minute attention to detail, he took his history.

"What did you read at Cambridge besides theology?" he asked as his fiftieth question. Sydenham enunciated the word "Cambridge" daintily; he himself had been educated at Oxford.

"Greek and Latin, French and German," Ash replied. "Mathematics. A certain amount of philosophy. Chemistry."

Sydenham gave him a keen look. "Chemistry, eh?" he said. "What do you know about the circulation of the blood?"

"Little is understood. The ancients supposed that the arteries carried air to the body, and thus their name for them, *arteria*, or

'windpipe,' " Ash said. "But Galen, while dissecting an ape, established that the arteries carried not air but blood. In our own time, William Harvey of London, in his great work *Exercitatio Anatomica de motu cordis et sanguinis*, told us that the heart is a pump which drives the blood into the arteries and thence into the tissues through smaller blood vessels, which return it to the veins after the flesh has been nourished. The veins carry it back to the heart, which pumps it out again."

"You say that Harvey's theory is a great work. But it has been violently attacked by dogmatists as being wrong."

"Dogma does not matter in medicine. It is the observed and proven fact that matters. Blood moves through the body according to God's design."

"You are aware, I know, that Galen was Marcus Aurelius' physician and a very fashionable doctor at Rome," Sydenham said. "Do you know what his admirers called him?"

"Paradoxopoeus—the wonder worker," Ash said. "It created jealousy."

"Do you believe in wonders?"

"Only in God's wonders, of which the human body is surely among the greatest."

Sydenham studied Ash. It did not take a great diagnostician to see that this poverty-stricken young man was a mystic who had very recently undergone great trials. Ash was emaciated, unsteady, pale; his eyes, which shone with intelligence, were red-rimmed from weeping. Sydenham was not troubled that he was a little mad. Many, if not most, gifted physicians were.

"Are you married?" he asked.

"Yes."

"Your wife has been a servant, I suppose."

"An undercook."

Whatever their own origins, ministers in Ash's day were not encouraged to marry into the gentry, much less the aristocracy, but were expected to find their mates among the servant class. Clerical conjugality was a national joke. Hardly a popular play was performed anywhere in Britain in the seventeenth century that did not number among its characters a curaté who married a cook after a laughable courtship.

"I do not need an apprentice, but I do need a maid of all work," Sydenham said. "I'll take you into the bargain. The course in physick normally lasts four years, but I no longer promise myself that far ahead. Two years should be enough for you. You will be entirely at my disposal all day, every day, except for two hours on Sunday. You and your wife will be given rooms at the top of my

house, healthy food, and a stipend of two hundred pounds—half now and half at the end of your apprenticeship. Your wife will be paid an additional ten shillings per month. Is that satisfactory?"

"Yes. But I must have time to pray."

In his relief at having interpreted God's intentions correctly by coming to a man who accepted him so readily, Ash shouted out these words. He surprised even himself with their loudness. Sydenham leapt a little at the force with which they split the air. He handed Ash his bowl of cold coffee.

"There is one condition," he said as Ash drank at last. "You must not pray in that amazing voice in my house. Talk to the Lord elsewhere, Mr. Ash."

In Sydenham's London, the three classes of specialist—physicians, apothecaries, and surgeons—were strictly separated, and in theory no man could practice more than one specialty. In practice, however, Sydenham himself, like many other practitioners, was both physician and apothecary. To these two skills, Ash added surgery after he had completed his studies with Sydenham. The old physician didn't believe in it.

"You will hear them scream," he told Ash. "They will never forget the pain and the fear, or forgive you for inflicting it upon them."

Ash had found that Sydenham was right about this, as he was about so many other things. After observing the effects of operations for kidney and bladder stones and the trepanning of the brain, Ash decided that he would operate only to repair wounds. In such cases, shock sometimes masked or overcame the pain of surgery if it was undertaken quickly enough. That was why he had rushed Oliver into the house so quickly after he was stabbed by the woodman.

Even so, Ash worried about inflicting suffering. He experimented with ways to divert the patient's attention until he was overcome, as he almost always was, by unconsciousness. While he tied Oliver Barebones to the table to prevent his doing violence to himself or his surgeon, Ash described the currently fashionable iatrophysical school of medicine, which argued that the body was a machine.

"Iatrophysiology is a relatively new theory, described by the Italian, Borelli, in his posthumons treatise *De motu animalium*," Ash said. However it may have seemed to others, Ash's voice did not sound particularly loud in his own ears, so he spoke to Oliver a little more distinctly than usual. "Borelli explains the functions of the body on mechanical principles. The bones are levers, the muscles are pulleys, the digestive system is a threshing machine,

secretions are controlled by the tensions of the vessels, the blood circulates under pressure generated by the compression of the heart, and . . . *Ah!*"

Ash had located the wound in the brachial artery inside Oliver's left biceps. Oliver lay on the table in the hall, his wrists and ankles tied to its legs. Though he was pale and his breathing was rapid, he did not cry out or try to twist away from the knife.

Ash had to work very fast because of the danger involved in depriving the arm of blood. He was a skillful and gentle surgeon who used only the sharpest instruments and cut as little as possible. Surgery on Oliver's body was made more difficult than usual by the size and development of his muscles. Cutting delicately, Ash had enlarged the puncture wound. The artery was not completely severed. Holding the mouth of the wound open with his left hand, Ash tied off the upper end of the artery with a loop of silk thread with his right hand and stitched up the cut. Then he removed the ligature and watched the artery fill up with blood. It did not leak.

Now he fitted the fingers of his left hand into the incision, gazing intently into Oliver's face for the first signs of the pain that he knew to be inevitable. Oliver ground his teeth but kept his eyes open.

"The muscles have been pierced by the knife," Ash said, "but they have not been severed. The nerve is intact. The wound will heal satisfactorily, barring suppuration, and we will prevent that."

Some physicians were pleased to see suppuration or "laudable pus" appear in a wound, but Ash did not subscribe to the theory that pus was a sign of good healing. He tried to prevent it, as Sydenham had taught, by leaving a clean incision and letting the wound drain.

Ash removed his bloody fingers from Oliver's wound and gestured with them to Rose. The blood did not disturb her. Nothing about Ash disturbed her. She stood against the wall, next to a burning fire in the grate, watching him work. To Rose, of course, the odor of blood was very strong in the hot, airless room. She did not think about it; she thought about the questions she wanted to ask Ash about witches when the occasion arose. He would be able to tell her exactly what she wanted to know.

"Bring me two basins of hot water and towels," Ash said brusquely.

Rose did so, dipping the boiling water out of a kettle that had been heating over the fireplace. Ash washed his hands in one bowl, and then scrubbed the area around the wound, using a lot of soap.

"Will you not sew it up?" Oliver asked.

"No. The knife was dirty. The wound must drain. Otherwise the animacules will do mischief."

"Anima . . ." Oliver nodded sleepily. He did not understand a word.

Animacules were one of Ash's great interests. He was one of the few men who knew that God had made complex creatures that were too small to be seen by the eye, and that these creatures were everywhere. He had spent half of the first hundred pounds Sydenham had given him on a microscope. It was an excellent device, made in Delft by a Dutchman named Anton van Leeuwenhoek, that could magnify an object five hundred times. Under Leeuwenhoek's instrument, Ash studied muscle fiber and nerve tissue, and, above all, the animacules that lived as parasites on everything. He became convinced, watching these minute creatures wriggle under the lens, that animacules migrated from body to body, and even over the oceans from continent to continent, on the skin and clothes of travelers, carrying disease with them. In this fashion, syphilis, previously unknown in Europe, had come from America, while smallpox had traveled in the other direction. Ash had observed, by treating the animacules with a soapy solution while they were under the lens, that soap sometimes killed them.

Rose took away the basins and poured the pinkish water they contained out the window. Nothing was left to be seen of Montagu and his bullies—not even the dead oxen, which had been dragged away to be sold as beef. The yokels and Sir Cecil's horses and mastiffs were gone. Someone had scavenged the shreds of Montagu's silk costume out of the mud where the dogs had left it.

Ash's voice began. Turning around, Rose saw that he had fallen to his knees beside the table, clasped his hands together, and started to pray. He continued for about an hour, never pausing, never searching for a word. Like a baby being sung to, Oliver fell asleep. From time to time, though he never stopped praying, Ash unclasped his hands and examined his patient, taking Oliver's pulse, feeling his brow for signs of fever, rolling back his eyelid, touching the skin around the bruised lips of his wound.

Oliver woke and tried to sit up, but he was still tied to the table. Ash untied him. The two men seemed to like each other tremendously. Ash was tender with his patient. Oliver accepted whatever Ash did. Their sudden friendship mystified Rose. How could they behave with such trust, when they had only just met?

Ash made a gesture, and Rose helped him to walk Oliver up the stairs. In Rose's bedchamber they removed what few clothes Oliver still had on, his breeches and stockings, and drew his nightclothes over his head. Rose stood over the bed. She had never

before seen Oliver from above when he was lying down; always before he had been crouching over her, moaning her name. He looked quite shrunken in his nightcap, under the puffy feather bed, with his wounded arm lying useless on the coverlet.

On the table by the window, Ash mixed a prescription, depositing small quantities of half a dozen powders and herbs into a cup and mixing them together with water. He held the cup to Oliver's lips.

"What I want is brandy," Oliver said again.

"You shall have it," Ash said.

Rose fetched a bottle of Nantes brandy. It burned Oliver's throat, and when he spoke, his voice was hoarse and thin. His gaze was fixed on Ash.

"Montagu," Oliver said. "Will he die?"

"Oh, yes," Ash said. "And soon—in a week, perhaps two."

"Poor man, to be such a bastard."

"You must sleep," Ash said.

While Oliver did so, Ash prayed again, much more quietly. A listener might have thought, as Ash certainly did, that God was in the room hearing every word and judging it, like a kindly but exacting schoolmaster. Rose went to sleep listening to Ash's voice.

When Rose woke up, Ash was still seated by Oliver's bed. Oliver was asleep, breathing deeply and snoring a little, his face unshaven and dumb as a dog's. Ash had covered Rose with her fur-trimmed cloak as she slept. She stroked the collar and watched him.

Ash was reading Hobbes by the light of the fire. He was deathly gray again. She realized that he had looked different—brighter, more ruddy, soldierly, even—while he confronted Montagu and doctored Oliver.

"Mr. Ash?"

Ash marked his place and looked at her, waiting for whatever it was she was going to say. When the question came, he seemed surprised.

Rose asked, "Can witches take the form of cats?"

"Witches? Yes, of course they can."

Ash was clearly anxious to return to his book. But Rose wanted to know more.

"And can they travel from one person's body into the body of another?"

"By what means?"

Rose took a breath. "By way of the natural entrances."

"Of course. 'Now the works of the flesh are manifest, which are

these; adultery, fornication, uncleanness, lasciviousness, idolatry, witchcraft . . .' Galatians, fifth chapter."

"Then witches do exist?"

"Certainly they exist. We are told that they live in Exodus: 'Thou shalt not suffer a witch to live.' "

"And one must resist, no matter whose body the witch may use as a hiding place?"

"Certainly. Leviticus is quite clear on the point: 'And the soul that turneth after such as have familiar spirits, and after wizards, to go a-whoring after them, I will even set my face against that soul, and will cut him off from among his people.' "

As Ash recited flawlessly from the Bible—he must have the whole of the Scriptures committed to memory—Rose's face glowed. She had never been in the presence of such a powerful mind. It enveloped her and made her want to draw closer to it, like the aura of kingship or great wealth or fame. Or even beauty. For the first time, Ash noted some sign of sensibility in this woman. Until now he had only seen her beauty, and it was not his experience or his belief that beautiful women, imprisoned in their vanity, were interested in the nature of God.

"Witches exist because Satan exists," Ash said. "And Satan exists because God exists. Therefore, if you believe in God and in His works, you must believe in Satan and in his works, and among the latter are witches."

Ash had no difficulty in understanding the germ theory of disease, and at the same time in believing in witches. He examined Rose to see if she understood. He was sure that she did not, but it was clear that his answers had made her very happy. There was adoration in her eyes rather than intelligence.

Rose went to sleep again. Men's voices, one voice whispering and two others shouting, woke her at dawn. She did not understand at first what she was doing on the floor, or what Praise God Adkins was doing in her bedchamber, but as soon as she saw Ash, she remembered everything.

Praise God's clothes were covered with dust and his face was drawn by fatigue. Rose knew that he had gone to Portsmouth on business. She had thought it very cowardly of him to leave Oliver to face Montagu and his bullies alone. What had he found in Portsmouth that sent him flying back to London? He must have come all the way without stopping to rest.

Oliver appeared to be alive. In fact he was sitting up in bed. He had raised himself onto his good elbow and was clearing his throat and coughing and repeating Fanny's name over and over again.

"Fanny?" Oliver said. "Not Fanny. I must go to Portsmouth at once."

"You cannot be moved," Ash said.

"Then I'll move myself," Oliver said. "Didn't you hear what Praise God said? That beast Montagu tried to have her in the night. She jumped into the sea to save herself. I must go to her."

"You have cut an artery," Ash said. "It has not healed. If you go by coach to Portsmouth the jouncing will open the wound and you'll bleed to death."

"Then I'll ride a horse and you will come with me to sew me up again, friend," Oliver said. "You can save Fanny as you saved me."

Moving ponderously, Oliver got to his feet. He was weaker than he thought, and he held on to Ash, head swimming, coughing violently.

"We must leave at once," he said. "P.G. will mind the house, won't you, P.G.?"

"Yes, of course," Praise God said. "But what about the *Pamela*'s cargo?"

Oliver, staggering on one leg as he tried to put on his trousers, fell to the floor with a crash.

"I've decided to take it to America with me and sell it there," he said.

Sitting on the floor, Oliver held out his hand for assistance. Ash grasped it with surprising strength—Oliver looked up at him with a flicker of admiration when he felt his wiry grip—and pulled him to his feet.

"America?" Praise God said. "What do you mean, sell the cargo in America?"

Rose was fully awake now. She thought Oliver must be delirious. She tried to get Ash's attention in order to ask him to explain what was making Oliver think that he was going to America, but Ash's full attention was focused on Oliver.

"I made up my mind while you were in Portsmouth, P.G.," Oliver said. "It's America for me. Henry always said I should go there, and now I'm sure he was right. Henry's gone, London's done. I want to get right away."

Rose turned away and looked at herself in the broken mirror to make certain that what was happening was real. All three men appeared in the glass, Oliver too. In her fright, Rose had forgotten that he wasn't supposed to have a reflection. America! Sea monsters, painted savages, wild beasts, homespun cloth—the wilderness.

"Not America," Rose said.

Oliver lurched toward her, nearly losing his balance again. His face was the same foolish moonstruck mask. He must think that she would love him if he carried her across the ocean.

"We have ten thousand acres there and a whole town full of people that belong to us," Oliver said. "Henry always said I'd be the Earl of Massachusetts. You'll be a countess, Rose."

"The earl of what?" Rose said. "Of *what*? You're mad. I've married a madman. Marriage can be annulled if the husband is mad—isn't that so, Mr. Ash?"

Ash paid no attention to her question.

"When would you sail?" he asked Oliver.

"As soon as Fanny's well. How long will that take you—to cure her?"

"That is impossible to say, but she can be treated at sea as well as in port," Ash said. "There need be no delay."

"No delay? You mean you would sail with us?"

"Perhaps. What made you decide to go to America?"

"It just came over me after Henry died that it was the only thing to do."

"You are describing the voice of God."

"Is that so?"

Ash gave him a radiant smile. "Yes, it is so. Clearly it is God's will that you should go, and it is His will that I should go with you or he would not have arranged our meeting in so unmistakable a fashion."

"God arranged our meeting?"

"Of course He did—and all that came before it," Ash said. "All my trials, all my losses, were a prelude to this moment. It is quite clear to me now. I see His purpose. There is work for me in America. Yes—I will go with you!"

Oliver's face, ravaged by grief and the pain of his wound, broke into a grin of delight. "Splendid," he said. "Mr. Ash will come with us. Do you hear that, Rose?"

Rose looked straight ahead, her expression unchanged. Her slow brain had not had time to absorb this new information and signal new instructions to the muscles of her face. Ash go to America? Perhaps this was a joke—Robert and his friends had often played jokes on her, telling her that the house was on fire, leading a stallion into her bedroom while she was asleep. They had thought that she was funny because she could never see a joke. Now Oliver and Ash were calmly discussing arrangements for a voyage from which none of them could ever hope to return; Rose had never heard of anyone except Captain John Pennock who had ever come back from America, and she did not know whether Pennock was a real person or just another joke.

"My wife can travel down to Portsmouth with Missis Barebones," Ash said. "I'll have her fetched from the country."

"Of course," Oliver said. "They can bring Fanny's instruments and music—she'll want those as soon as she's well—and the few things my wife and I will wish to take with us to America."

America? Rose realized that this was no joke. Ash would never joke about God's will. She must escape from this lunacy.

"Annulment," she said, barely able to get the words out because she was so short of breath. "Mr. Ash, can my annulment be arranged?"

"Too late, ma'am," Ash said absently. "You are married in the sight of God."

"God knows it is *not* too late," Rose said.

"Then, you must learn to obey your husband," Ash thundered. "Pack up, woman, and accept the fate that God has prepared for you!"

All during this conversation, Oliver had been struggling to put on his clothes. Praise God, kneeling with difficulty, helped him into his boots.

"Put Rose on a horse and Ash's wife in a carriage," Oliver said. "Don't forget Fanny's instruments—especially the spinet that came from Italy. It folds up very neatly."

"What about the house?"

"Pull it down after you empty it out, or let Montagu die in it and be the ghost of Catherine Street."

"You won't mind if I just keep it for you in case you want to come home?"

"I'll never come home, P.G. My life is in America."

Praise God seemed to accept Oliver's ravings without question. So did Ash, for all his genius. Rose could not believe these things were happening. How could it be that they all took leave of their senses at once? Witchcraft was the only explanation. They were all under a spell.

Rose sank to the floor, hugging her fur-trimmed cape as if there were a beloved body inside it. She wore her ruby ring on her index finger.

Her movements attracted Ash's attention. He held out his hand. "Let me have that stone," he said. "It won't be safe on your finger on the road to Portsmouth."

Without hesitation, as if she were under a spell herself, Rose handed it over. Reaching behind himself, Ash handed the ring to Oliver.

"Obedience," Ash said. "As the Apostle Paul wrote in his epistle to Titus, 'To be discreet, chaste, keepers at home, good, obedient to their own husbands, that the word of God be not blasphemed.' There is joy in obedience, I promise you, madam."

# II

# AMERICA

# 1

Always afterward, the smell of vinegar reminded Ash of the circumstances in which his passion for Fanny began, and of all the torment that his desire for her brought into his life. But at the first moment, in the cabin of the *Pamela*, he only saw a young girl shuddering under a load of covers with the chills of a fever. He examined her. The face, with its golden complexion, was without active color; even the lips were drained. The eyes were as expressionless as coins behind fluttering lids. The hands were too weak to grip the physician's forefingers with sufficient strength to keep him from easily pulling them free. Fanny coughed constantly, a spitty little bark. Ash knew at once that she had an advanced case of pneumonia, and that her chances of survival were no greater than one in three.

Ash pulled down the covers. Fanny's nightdress was dry. There was no smell of sweat.

"Have you sweated?" he asked.

"No." Fanny's teeth were chattering; she spoke even this one word with difficulty.

"How long have you been chilling in this way?"

"I'm not sure. I sleep and wake up."

Her speech was slow and slurred. Ash touched her face again and then reached inside the back of her nightdress and felt her armpit. It was dry and very hot. He felt the glands in her neck.

"Tell me how your chest feels," he said in the loudest voice Fanny had ever heard.

The cabin was dark. Fanny had no idea who this man was who was running his hands over her body. She knew that she wasn't dreaming, but he behaved like a figure in a dream. She wanted to go back to sleep.

"My chest hurts," she said.

"Describe the pain."

Fanny touched her ribs, then her breastbone. "It feels like glass, moving from here to here."

"Have your bowels moved since you've been sick?"

141

"I don't think so. No."

Ash gripped Fanny's wrist and held it for a full minute, forefinger pressed against her pulse. Fanny was looking straight up at his face. Everything about him was gray. His chin was covered with gray stubble. His nostrils, set in a big arched Norman nose, were clean and pink, but the hairs in them were gray. Most men wore gray wigs and had eyebrows and whiskers of another color. Ash wore no wig. A lick of coarse gray hair, escaping from the club into which it had been pulled, fell over his forehead. Yet he was not old. Fanny had the strange thought that his hair had always been gray, that it had never been black or brown or blond even when he was a child. What made her think such a thing? She stopped wondering about it as another fit of coughing doubled her up.

While she coughed, Ash held a clean handkerchief to her lips. The sputum was the color of rust. He pushed back his hair, closed his eyes, and laid his ear against Fanny's chest.

"Sit up, please."

Ash tapped her back and listened. The congestion in her lungs was clearly audible. He laid Fanny down and covered her up.

"We must do something to bring the fever down," he said. "I can give you nothing for the pain in your chest. Opium would immobilize the mechanism of the lungs, and you must cough up the phlegm. We will apply compresses."

Fanny heard Ash's voice distinctly, but from a long way off, as if she were a swimmer and it was coming over the water. How could this be, when he had such a loud voice? What was wrong? Ash was sitting on the bunk beside her. Bright sun came through the windows behind him and threw his face into shadow. The *Pamela*'s deck was motionless and the ship was silent. Fanny heard her own breathing, growing quicker. She was not getting enough air. She really was underwater. Gasping, she strained upward like a swimmer trying to reach the surface.

Ash saw her difficulty. Moving swiftly, he opened the door onto the gallery, pulled down the covers, and picked her up in his arms. He carried her into the open air.

"Lie back," he said. "Let your head fall back. It's all right—I'm holding you."

Fanny felt the bone of his forearm behind her neck. She could hear her own breath, thin and squeaky, and the double beat of her heart. She heard nothing else; again, she had the illusion that she was underwater. Hanging in Ash's arms, she saw everything upside down—her black hair hanging downward in a plait, the masts and spars of other ships reflected in smooth water in which trash and

drowned vermin were floating, a row of houses on a shore. Portsmouth harbor, Fanny thought. We're in England again.

Boats were coming in with heaps of fish gleaming on their decks. It must be afternoon. One boat passed quite close and the truculent red country faces aboard her stared curiously at the man with the girl in his arms. Fanny thought of Honfleur—the cod, the *Pamela* at anchor where Henry had said she would be, the hushed young soldier buttoned up inside his blue tunic. Why was he so quiet?

"*Pourquoi si silencieux?*" she whispered.

"What?" Ash said.

But Fanny was coughing again. Ash turned her over with her face to the water. Sputum fell lazily into the oily water. After that, Fanny breathed easier. Ash was speaking to her but she hadn't the energy or the breath to respond. She saw her hand dangling, and below it, something large moving in the water. It was a shark, following the fishing boat as it sailed into the harbor, dripping blood. Fanny knew it was a shark—the broad snout, the diamond fins, the slim supple tail—from Henry's stories and from pictures she had seen. It was fifteen feet long, moving at precisely the same speed as the fishing boat, with only the smallest movement of its sinuous tail.

Ash did not see the fish. He was looking at Fanny with blazing eyes. "Breathe through your mouth," he said. "Try to breathe more slowly and deeply. Do not breathe naturally. *Think* about each breath. Command your body to obey your mind."

The man, whoever he was, was shouting; he appeared to be angry. This puzzled Fanny; she had never before seen anger in a male face. She tried to ask Ash what the matter was, but she hadn't the voice to do it. She tried to slow her breathing. The air going into her lungs did feel like shards of glass shredding the membranes. She remembered the window exploding when the oxen pulled the first chunk out of her father's house.

Joshua and Oliver were in the cabin when Ash carried Fanny back inside. Oliver closed the door behind them.

"No!" Ash cried. "She must have air!"

"What is it?"

"Inflammation of the lungs. *Pneumonia* is the Greek word for it. Her fever is dangerously high. I fear convulsions. She is coughing blood."

Fanny heard every word, but not the meaning of what Ash said. Oliver's arm was in a sling. He wore no wig either, and in all the years that she had known him, Fanny had never seen him in his own hair except when he played football.

Oliver said, "But you can cure her." His voice was weak. He and Ash had ridden the seventy miles from London to Portsmouth in a night and a day, stopping only to change horses and eat some meat and bread in a tavern at Guildford, and to change Oliver's bandage.

"We shall see," Ash said. "The fever must be broken. The girl must be bathed in a tepid solution. We must have a woman."

"A woman?" Joshua said. "There is no woman aboard this ship."

"We'll take her ashore," Oliver said.

"No!" Ash cried. "It must be done at once. Have you vinegar?"

"Barrels of it."

Ash was stripping off his coat. He threw it into a corner and kneeled beside Fanny's bunk. There was a tin hip tub underneath the bunk. He dragged it into sight. It was shallow and just large enough to accommodate the buttocks of an average-size man. Joshua kept his crucifix in the tub when he was in a Protestant harbor. So that he would not have to touch this object, Ash picked up the whole tub and held it out to Joshua, who picked up the crucifix and automatically dusted it on the sleeve of his coat.

"Bring me clean cloths, a pint of vinegar, and fresh water—three buckets of cool and one of boiling water," Ash said.

Joshua nodded and started to go.

"Wait," Ash said. "If there are any more idolatrous objects in this room, they must be removed."

Joshua opened the lid of his desk and removed some beads and medals. He opened his hand to show them to Ash, who turned his head away.

Ash had given orders as soon as he came aboard the *Pamela* that water must be boiled, and in moments Joshua was back with two Italian sailors carrying buckets. They found Ash praying over Fanny with tremendous strength. He stopped when they came in.

"Dump the cool water into the tub," he said. "Leave the boiling water in the bucket. She must have nourishing food that she can swallow. Kill a chicken. Have your cook boil it with all the fat into a soup."

As he spoke, Ash herded Joshua and the sailors toward the door and pushed them outside. "I'll call from the gallery if you're needed," he said. "Do not come back otherwise."

Ash mixed the water in the tub to make a tepid solution, and added a cup of vinegar.

"Fanny," he said, "wake up."

Fanny had not been fully asleep. She was surprised that Ash called her by name. She felt very cold.

"You must have a cool bath now, to break your fever," Ash said. He pulled the covers off Fanny and sat her up. "You must take off your clothes and get into the tub."

Fanny nodded but stayed as she was. She had stopped shuddering, but her eyes were duller. Ash saw that she did not understand his words. He picked up her feet and put them on the floor. He could feel her heated skin through her thick woolen stockings. He gripped the stockings by the toes and pulled them off.

"Stand up, Fanny."

Fanny began to shudder again, teeth chattering, limbs jerking. "*Peux pas, peux pas, j'ai froid*," she said.

"French?" Ash said. He began to speak to Fanny in this language. "Who taught you to speak French?" he asked.

"Antoinette."

"A servant?" Ash said. "You speak it like a servant."

She spoke French like a servant? *That* was why the young soldier in Honfleur had looked at her so strangely.

Suddenly she began to shudder again. Every muscle of her body seemed to be involved. She gagged. Waves of darkness engulfed her. She tried to resist fear, and as she lost consciousness, she tried to identify what it was that she was afraid of. What was Ash doing to her? She couldn't hear his voice any longer. In the very last instant she tasted blood as she bit her tongue.

Ash saw the convulsion coming on, and knew what the paroxysms of the muscles meant. Fanny's fever had risen so high that it had attacked her brain. He forced open her clenched jaws and wedged a knotted handkerchief between her teeth. The tongue was lacerated and bleeding but he did not pause to deal with that. He stood Fanny on her feet, seized her nightdress by the hem, and pulled it over her head. Then he carried her twitching body to the tub and plunged it into the tepid water.

The involuntary movements of Fanny's body were so violent that Ash feared that she would injure herself. She lay with her buttocks in the tub, one leg to either side, arms flung out. All four limbs were thrashing. Ash brought her legs together and pinned them between his own. Cradling her head in his left arm, he was able to grasp both her wrists, which were very fine, in his left hand. With his right hand he dipped a cloth into the water and bathed her head, neck, and chest, dipping the rag and squeezing it over and over. After a moment or two, Fanny's body quieted enough so that he was able to stop touching it and release her legs and wrists. By then his clothes were soaked with the vinegary water and he was shivering himself. He crouched by the tub and went on sponging Fanny's face and body.

On the road from London, Oliver had spoken about Fanny as if she were an angel instead of a girl, describing her music, her intelligence, her kindness, her calm heart, her loyalty, her love for her father. He told Ash how she had saved Rose's life and carried her father's corpse out of his ruined house. Listening to Oliver, Ash had got the idea that Fanny was still a child. Lying under the blankets, so slight and quiet, with her feverish face peeping out, she had looked like a child.

Unclothed, she was no child. As Ash watched the hectic flush fade from her skin as the fever receded, he fought against the involuntary reaction of his own body. He had feared that this might happen. Betsy had permitted him her body, but she had not been wife to him since their children died. He could never turn away from Christian marriage to another woman. But the temptation of the flesh was a constant torment, even when he was asleep. He resisted the women who came to him in dreams, turning away, commanding his body to hold back, rising from bed to pray. He began to pray now.

" 'Walk in the Spirit,' " he cried, " 'and ye shall not fulfill the lust of the flesh.' "

Fanny heard Ash's voice long before she opened her eyes. He was kneeling on the deck with his back turned to her. She was not surprised to find herself naked. She knew that she had not been molested; the bath had been some sort of medical treatment. Exposure to a man's eyes was the last thing that worried her; she supposed, without resentment, that she was dying. She was too weak to stand up, and she did not wish to embarrass Ash by asking him to help her, so she crawled to the bunk on her hands and knees, coughing so violently that her ears rang, and put on her nightdress without help.

Ash seemed to be waiting for that. He tucked the blankets around her and went to the table where his medicines were arranged. Fanny heard him mixing a potion. He gave her something bitter to drink from a spoon. Fanny stopped coughing, and as she drifted into a kind of light sleep in which everything was sharply drawn and clearly understood, she dreamed that she was her mother on the night when she, Fanny, was born, and that she was watching while Ash baptized Rose Barebones; Ash wore a stole like the Jesuits' and petted a white cat with his left hand while he sprinkled water on Rose's brilliant hair with his right hand. Henry asked Fanchon to play "Tell me no more you love." Nobody was dead. While Fanny dreamed, she heard a loud sound like a cat purring and realized that she was hearing Ash's voice as he prayed.

# 2

Carrying Rose's fur-trimmed cloak over his shoulder, Oliver came into the cabin shouting with his old exuberance. His sling was gone. He wrapped Fanny in the cloak and picked her up in his arms as if he'd never been wounded.

"Come, Fanny-my-love," he cried. "There's something marvelous to see up top."

He carried her out the door and up the ladder to the deck. Porpoises, dozens of them, gleaming and jolly, were playing around the ship. They seemed to be flying as they rose effortlessly out of the sea, turning twinkling faces toward the people on deck.

It was the first time Fanny had been on deck since her illness began. The *Pamela* was halfway to America, four weeks out of Portsmouth. She had been at sea for a week before Fanny knew that she had left England, and even then she had not understood why she felt the ship in motion, or if she really did. She dreamt almost constantly. Ash had treated her pneumonia with opium. It stopped her coughing, but because it was a respiratory depressant, it made breathing very difficult. When she gasped for air, as often happened, Ash carried her outside, and as she looked down from the gallery at the wake of the ship, she heard his voice commanding her over and over again, "Breathe! Think! Breathe!"

Now it was Oliver who hoisted Fanny up on his shoulder so that she could see the porpoises. Ash had cured her. Her head was clear and she was breathing easily again.

"Maybe one will fly onto the deck, Fanny," Oliver said. "Other fishes have jumped aboard while you've been sleeping. The sea is filled with amazing things."

They were standing on the quarterdeck, well aft of the mainmast. Oliver grinned up at Fanny and squeezed her hand. Her face, inside the fur-trimmed hood, was thinner than before, but her color had begun to come back.

Spray was breaking over the beak of the ship. The *Pamela* was sailing before the wind through a soapy six-foot sea. All her sails were up and filled. Though it was a bright June day, the sun gave

off very little warmth. Even wrapped up in the cloak, Fanny felt a slight chill.

One of the sailors, a London boy from the sound of him as he shouted to other members of the crew, was climbing into the rigging with a harpoon in his hand.

"Fresh meat for supper," Oliver said. "The sailors say that we'll have a storm—it's one of their sayings that porpoises are a sign that there'll be wind."

The young sailor, tied to a spar by a line around his chest, toes gripping the shrouds, hung out over the frolicking porpoises. He cast the harpoon and missed, hauled it in, and cast it again. This time he speared one of the animals. It leaped into the air and turned completely over, wrapping a loop of the harpoon line around its body. Other sailors hauled it aboard.

"By God, Fanny, what a fish!" Oliver cried. "Watch him twist and flop!"

The wounded porpoise skittered across the deck, leaving a broad smear of blood on the scrubbed blond planking and emitting a high-pitched whistle of distress. While this first porpoise suffered, the young sailor harpooned another, and then another, and they, too, were hauled aboard.

There were now half a dozen dying porpoises floundering on the deck. Barefoot sailors dodged among them, skylarking, slipping in the blood and smearing it on one another's faces. The young harpoonist came down from the rigging. The first porpoise he had speared was nearly dead, its flippers quivering weakly, its voice gone. The sailor drew a knife. It seemed to Fanny that the porpoise was watching the man out of its small round eye. The sailor plunged his knife into the porpoise's belly and sliced down the length of it, first exposing a layer of white fat, then a long running stitch of blood, then amber blubber, and finally cascades of blood. The creature's eye widened in pain and terror—Fanny would have called it amazement if a man instead of an animal had been dying—and then, an instant later, the light went out of it.

Blue guts spilled onto the deck. Ash ran to the dying porpoise and examined the offal. He snatched the sailor's knife from his hand and with a few deft strokes completed the job of disemboweling the porpoise. While he worked, he beckoned to Oliver.

"There are the intestines, the stomach, the spleen, the lungs, the heart, the liver, exactly as in the other mammals," he said. "Look, it is for all the world like a swine that swims. It is extraordinary what God has made to swim in His sea!"

Oliver nodded. He was not really interested. The young harpoonist,

giddy from the slaughter, dipped his thumbs in blood and drew two crimson lines on his own face.

Ash insisted that Fanny eat as much porpoise liver as she could while it was fresh. It tasted like sheep's liver, but saltier and slightly fishy. Fanny was nauseated by it, but Ash would not let her refuse it. To encourage her, he tried it himself and found that it had been soused in vinegar. His face contorted, he opened the window and threw it into the sea. He shouted for the cook.

"No vinegar!" he ordered. "Slice it thin and cook it plain with a little fat in a frying pan.

"It will build up your blood," he said to Fanny. "You are suffering from anemia. Do you know what the Greek word means?"

"*An*—not, *emia—haima*? Blood?" Fanny replied. "I have no blood."

"You have plenty of blood. But it's weak. You mustn't miss a single day of liver."

Ash had discovered that Fanny knew Latin and a little Greek. It was strange to find such knowledge in a girl of seventeen. He asked who had taught her; keeping Evans the Jesuit a secret, she avoided the question.

Ash asked Oliver for more information.

"Her father talked Latin for pleasure. Maybe she learned from him."

"Was her father Welsh?"

"Of course not."

"Fanny speaks Latin and Greek with a Welsh accent, so a Welshman must have taught her, just as a French peasant taught her to speak French like a kitchen maid," Ash said. "She has an extraordinary ear."

"It must be her gift for music," Oliver said. "She had a tutor for that—and come to think of it, he did teach her Latin and Greek, and he *was* a Welshman."

"Tell me about this Welshman," Ash said to Fanny a little later. "What was his name? Was he old? Young? Was he educated at Oxford? Cambridge?"

"I hardly remember," Fanny said. "He had a very good singing voice."

Ash pressed her for details. Fanny pretended not to remember. He talked to her in the ancient languages, as well as in French, to divert her mind from her sickness and to divert his own mind from his constant thoughts of her. Ash's French was heavily accented, but perfectly grammatical, and exact also from the point of view of etiquette. He had learned it at Trinity College from a man who had gone to France as a child with the retinue of Charles II and

lived at court. It was this French, formal and roundabout but clearly articulated, that Ash was attempting to teach to Fanny while she convalesced. With allowances for Ash's English intonations, it sounded somewhat like the French the old count and the young soldier had spoken to her in Honfleur. Fanny began to sound like Ash when she spoke French, but she tried to remember how the two men in Honfleur had spoken so that she could sound like them.

Betsy was aboard now, and she sat in the cabin with them while they talked, sewing and looking out the window. When Fanny needed nursing, she provided it, giving her sad looks and feeding her chicken soup while the chickens lasted and porpoise soup after that. Ash said that the fat of the porpoise tasted like fresh pork and the lean like beef or veal, but it made Fanny gag. Of course Betsy knew no foreign languages, and she never spoke even in English. When Ash prayed, she went outside, rising quickly out of her chair and leaving as quickly as she could.

Like Philip Evans before him, Ash had discovered that Fanny was a natural student, and he enjoyed teaching her for the sake of observing the quickness of her mind. He began to teach her medicine as a means of improving her Latin and Greek. She learned with astonishing rapidity. Ash explained and asked questions. Fanny never asked questions; she answered Ash's and conversed with him about his cases and Sydenham's. She learned symptoms, treatments, medicines, herbs. She was eager to learn. For all her intelligence, she was a mild girl. She never argued, never disputed, even when he felt strongly that she disagreed. It occurred to Ash that he could keep her by his side indefinitely by imparting knowledge to her. He could teach her medicine and surgery, actually apprentice her to himself as Sydenham had apprenticed him. It did not matter that she was so young. It did not matter that she was female—she could call herself nurse or midwife, or nothing. She need not practice. She could learn for the sake of learning.

Now that Fanny was better, Ash spent his nights in another cabin with Betsy. Oliver and Rose slept in an adjoining cabin. Sometimes he heard Rose's voice as she berated her husband. In spite of Ash's teaching, Rose hated the very idea of America. She only spoke to Oliver at night when they were alone, never in daylight in the company of others. But then she talked without ceasing, weeping and begging Oliver to turn the *Pamela* around and sail back to England, murmuring from bedtime till dawn.

Betsy had begun talking to Ash again—but also in the dark. She was pregnant, and she was obsessed by a fear that the child she carried would be captured by the Indians and be lost to her.

"What if the Indians take my child?" she whispered. "He'll never come back and then I'll have no one. There'll be nothing left."

"You will have God and a husband," Ash replied.

But he knew that his answer was nonsense; Betsy had neither and wanted neither. She stopped talking to him.

Her silence was not enough to drive images of Fanny out of Ash's mind.

Neither was prayer. For the first time in Ash's religious life, he could not concentrate on God. He hardly ever wept anymore as he prayed. His voice would stop in the middle of a phrase; his mind would go blank. Sometimes he even fell asleep while he was at prayer and woke up a long time later, stunned by guilt. Sometimes he thought he could not pray at all, could not begin. But always, in the end, the habit of worship overcame his weakness and his voice came back. But Ash was changing; even as he prayed, he doubted that prayer would cure him.

Once, after a long silence, he put a hand on Betsy in the dark. Betsy shook her head and took Ash's hand off her body. Watching Ash's face transform itself into a mask of carnality when he turned away from Fanny after one of their polite conversations, she knew well enough that it was Fanny, not his wife, that he was thinking about when he wanted her body. Fanny's body was all he could think about.

A day or two after the porpoise hunt, a storm blew up just as the sailors had predicted. Sails reefed, the *Pamela* was driven through thirty-foot seas on a long counterclockwise track that pushed her eastward and then many miles to the north. Oliver lashed Rose into her bunk so that she wouldn't be thrown onto the deck and injured by the violent motions of the ship. He himself lay on the floor, violently sick, vomiting into a sloshing basin. The stink was maddening.

The Bareboneses' tiny cabin was located between the one occupied by the Ashes and the forecastle. Through one wall Rose could hear Ash's mighty prayers; through the other she heard the sailors shouting obscenities and singing bawdy songs at the top of their voices.

They could hear Ash, too, and like most sailors of the time they believed that prayer only made storms worse; they all knew stories about ships that had sunk because some fool had prayed aboard them in a tempest. "Shut up, you bastard!" the sailors shouted through the walls at Ash, and when he went on praying, they lowed like cattle, baaed like sheep, barked like dogs in an

effort to drown him out. They nailed horseshoes to the mast and cast what remained of the porpoise meat overboard.

After four days the winds died. The *Pamela* drifted in a fog, and after the tumult of the storm, quiet fell over the ship. Sailors worked quietly, whispering as they repaired the storm damage. Even Ash kept still for a time, but then, lying awake in the sour air of the cabin with Oliver asleep on the deck at her feet, Rose heard him praying on deck. Wrapped in a black cloak, a black hood covering her hair, she went up on deck to listen.

At first she could not find him. Then she saw a shrouded figure hunched in the bow, and realized that Ash had covered himself with a sail as protection against the cold. The canvas muffled his words and even for Rose it was difficult to make them out. A person with ordinary hearing might not have been able to catch the words at all. But Rose did, and she understood at once that Ash was struggling with temptation.

" 'Whoso committeth adultery with a woman . . . destroyeth his own soul,' " he shouted. " 'A wound and a dishonor shall he get, and his reproach shall not be wiped away. For jealousy is the rage of a man.' "

Rose listened, fascinated; whom else could he love but her?

" 'Ye shall stone them with stones that they die,' " Ash bellowed inside his sail.

Sailors, posted as lookouts in the rigging, barked and mooed and whinnied.

The *Pamela* was far to the north of her intended course. It was very cold. The fog glowed with pink morning light, and as the *Pamela* drifted through it and Ash's voice rolled out over the glassy water, Rose heard the sound of many birds. For a moment she did not believe that she was hearing what she heard. How could birds be singing in the middle of the ocean? Then, out of the fog, an iceberg appeared. Hundreds of birds, large and small, clung to its craggy surface.

The lookouts, shouting frantically to one another, clambered higher into the rigging to trim the sails. On the quarterdeck, Joshua and another seaman hauled desperately on the helm. The ship groaned. Rose sensed no danger. The *Pamela* turned dreamily to port and the blue-white floating mountain, ten times as big as the ship, wreathed in mist and covered with squawking birds, drifted back into the sunshot fog.

Ash, silenced, watched this spectacle from his knees. Rose pushed the hood off her hair, concentrating her mind to make him look at her. But Ash went on staring at the iceberg as if he had witnessed a miracle. The birds could be heard for a long time after it vanished.

# 3

Oliver, electrified by the idea of living like an earl in the wilderness of Massachusetts, had hardly been able to wait to sail away from England. The *Pamela* had remained in Portsmouth for less than two weeks. Part of her cargo had been offloaded into the ship Henry had arranged to meet her there. Then provisions and water had been brought aboard and the *Pamela* had put to sea.

After the storm, as soon as Ash would let him, Oliver came to Fanny's cabin to tell her why he had been in such a hurry to depart. The Atlantic was rough that day: hillocks of seawater with plumes of spray snapping off their crests formed and disappeared in the stern windows. The *Pamela* groaned and creaked happily as she plunged through the waves; Fanny, who heard musical notes in nearly everything, had been surprised to discover how many peculiar voices oak and rope and sail could produce, according to the strength of the wind and the movement of the sea.

Oliver held on to the table while he described the conviction that had come over him while he waited for Montagu to come.

"It was like a voice I couldn't quite hear, telling me that England was finished for me and I must go to America," he said. "Anyway, I knew I had to go. Ash says it was God's work."

"And was it God's work?"

"I wasn't praying, I was drinking French brandy," Oliver said.

Fanny sat up in her bunk, wrapped in a cloak, with her legs folded under her skirt and her back against the sea-rocked wall, waiting for Oliver to go on. She would not have been surprised if Ash had turned out to be right. Worse sinners than Oliver were always being changed and driven into strange adventures by religious experience; one heard stories about it every day.

"At the time, of course, I didn't know that Montagu was going to die," Oliver said.

"Montagu died?"

Oliver told her the details of Montagu's disease—the horrible brown moles growing all over his emaciated body. "Praise God heard that he'd locked himself up in his house in Pall Mall. Stran-

gers hear him screaming as they go by in the street. Let the bastard scream."

The ship creaked.

"Forget Montagu," Oliver said. "We're partners in the *Pamela* now, and we've got debts to settle and matters to discuss."

The silk, the coffee, the chocolate, the leather, and all the fine wine—enough value of goods to cover Praise God's share of the cargo and pay all the partners' debts to Montagu—had been transferred from the *Pamela* to the other vessel. Oliver proposed to sell the rest of the wine and spirits in Boston for ready cash, and for a new cargo of American goods that were in demand in England—shingles, spars, smoked and salted fish, and sassafras, a New World medicinal plant that was used in England to treat syphilis and other diseases, including plague. Pennock had said that sassafras grew abundantly on his estates. Ash said it was useless as a specific against anything more serious than stomachache; Oliver believed that it was just one of many things growing on his land that would make them a great deal of money. The *Pamela* would make a voyage to America every two years, to bring Oliver and Fanny their share of the profits, but otherwise she would call at her usual ports.

"The partnership's divided just as it always was," Oliver told Fanny. "Peters at sea getting twenty percent, Praise God in London taking ten percent, and me in America getting ten. All the rest belongs to you. You're a rich woman, Fanny."

Oliver reached inside his coat and brought out the ruby necklace. It was a necklace for a princess. Each of the rubies, set among pearls and sapphires along a woven gold chain, was as large as the stone in Rose's ring. There were six of them. Oliver hung the necklace around Fanny's neck and held up a small mirror so that she could see the gems against her skin.

"This is not mine," Fanny said. "It's the necklace you bought for Rose."

"How do you know that?"

"How could I not know? Everyone in London knows. I don't want it. Give it to Rose."

These words wounded Oliver. His dull puzzled eyes grew moist. Fanny was trying to take the necklace off, but she couldn't unfasten it. She tugged at it with all her strength, hoping to break the chain, but she only hurt the skin on her neck.

Oliver recovered his voice. "What difference does it make?" he asked. "It's just rubies and gold and it's worth a thousand guineas. You don't have to wear the bloody thing, Fanny—just keep it. You may need it someday."

"I'll never need it. Get it off me."

"Do you think I don't know I killed your father with my stupidity, Fanny?" Oliver said. "Don't you be stupid too—Henry wouldn't like it. You can throw the necklace into the sea if you want. But it's the only thing of value I have to give you. I don't know what we'll find in America, but like it or not, I'm all you have, and we both know that if I die as quick as Henry did . . ."

He unhooked the necklace and handed it to Fanny, pouring it out of his big hand into her small one. The weight of the stones pulled the gold chain after them into a little heap of glitter in her palm. Oliver's eyes glistened. Closing Fanny's fingers over the jewels, he pursed his lips and made a slight movement of his head. Large as he was, sad as he had become, different from Henry as he had always been in every way, he fleetingly reminded Fanny of her father. He had often done so, just as Henry sometimes made her think of Oliver. She had seen them together all her life. They had been together so much, and for such a long time, that they had acquired each other's gestures and mannerisms, and like brothers who took after different parents, they resembled each other even though they did not look alike.

Fanny kissed her godfather and closed her hand on the ruby necklace.

# 4

Rose Barebones could not bear the heat of America. She began to feel it, like the weight of a man's body, while the *Pamela* was still miles offshore. By the time the ship sailed into Boston Bay on the first Sunday in August, the heat had actually become visible; worms of superheated air danced around the blurry masts and hulls of anchored ships, the docks, the low houses of the mean little town. With nearly seven thousand inhabitants, Boston was by far the largest English settlement in North America, but it was smaller than Chesham and ruder than any place Rose had ever imagined— little skewed houses built of raw unpainted lumber, a low bald shore without a single tree or lawn, the smell of a slaughterhouse on the offshore wind. On first seeing the settlement, Rose thought

that it must be the place where the Indians lived, and that they would sail on to the English town. But then the sound of church bells came rolling out over the water and she knew that this dreadful slum was Boston.

"Oh, Fanny, it's cruel, cruel," Rose said. "What have I ever done to be punished so?"

These were very nearly the first words Rose had spoken in Fanny's presence since sailing from England. She did not look at Fanny as she spoke. Her eyes were on Edward Ash, as if she expected he would answer. But Ash was absorbed in the view of the harbor and paid no attention to her. Betsy stood beside him.

"Look, wife, America," he said in a voice that reverberated through the ship. "Look how it sleeps, waiting for the coming of the Word."

"How true," Rose said loudly, as though Ash had addressed his remark to her. "The country *is* asleep. You can feel it."

Ash took no notice of her. As the *Pamela* drifted toward her anchorage in the brutal heat, Rose was wearing a white dress and a white hat decorated with red cloth roses. She was pale, with blue shadows under her eyes, and she was a little thinner than she had been in England, so that her body appeared to inhabit her clothes without actually touching the fabric. Her lips were somewhat swollen. She looked like a bride who had been making love all the way across the ocean.

Apart from the church bells, there was no sound at all outside the tiny capsule of noise that was their English ship. The bells were very feeble, not tuneful like English bells. Then even the bells stopped.

In the quiet that followed, Fanny understood that she had crossed the ocean, that she was about to set foot on a different world, that she would never go back. America was as silent as the grave. Fanny had never been in such a silent place, and she realized that she was only at the edge of it. How far could the bells be heard when they were rung on Sunday—a mile, two miles if the wind was right? Beyond that point, Fanny thought, it must be just as silent as it had been before the English came. We are at the edge of an enormous place, the largest, emptiest place left on earth, and there is nothing in it but silence. It is to the ear what darkness is to the eye.

Fanny breathed in and out very deeply. She was dressed in black from head to foot, black hair framing her golden face that had not smiled since Henry died. She turned her back to the shore and found Ash staring at her. Rose was still waiting for Ash to respond to her own remark.

"Did you hear what Mr. Ash said?" Rose asked in a hostess's voice. "Don't you think he's right, Fanny, to say that the country is *asleep*?"

"Not asleep," Fanny said. "Waiting."

# 5

Joshua Peters disposed of the *Pamela*'s cargo without difficulty and for good prices; the demand for alcohol was as great in New England as anywhere else. There were far fewer drunken women and children to be seen in public here than in London, and no gangs of youths robbing in the streets. No one was permitted to drink more than a quart of ale outside of mealtimes, and the drinking of healths was punishable by a fine of twelve shillings, but these prohibitions were largely disregarded. A quart of ale cost a penny. Puritans liked strong drink and believed that it was a friend to man.

The local taste surprised Joshua and taught him a lesson about future cargoes. Canary wine sold for more money than claret because it was better known to the Bostonians. Nantes brandy was prized for medicine and for drinking healths. The apple brandy from Calvados set the Puritan merchants thinking—cider was the drink of the poor in America.

"Bring us no more of this," one man said, eyes watering from drinking the fiery stuff. "If the laboring class develops a taste for it, the colony will cease to exist."

On the first day, Joshua and Oliver saw a red-faced man standing in the stocks with a scarlet D hung around his neck to mark him as a drunkard.

Oliver's plan to load up the *Pamela* with shingles and spars came to nothing. The Indians had cut down the forests near Boston; from the beginning, the English had had to cut firewood on islands in the harbor. Oliver was tremendously disappointed. He had imagined majestic trees, an inexhaustible supply of them, growing down to the water's edge, and shiploads of masts and spars and shingles making him rich.

The Bareboneses and Fanny and the Ashes were invited to

dinner by the Boston lawyer who was in charge of John Pennock's affairs in America. His name was Lebbaeus Williams.

Williams was a nearsighted rotund man with a deep bass voice and a cordial nature. He had a mannerism that would have delighted Henry Harding: when he answered a question, he gripped the edge of the table with both hands, half-rose from his chair, leaned forward, and shouted, rather than spoke, the key phrases. Oliver asked him for his opinion about the timber business.

"*Opinion*, Mr. Barebones?" Williams replied. "The country is *too young* for opinions to have formed, and I am already *too old* to express them. All I have to give you, in exchange for the fee you will pay me, is *facts*."

"Then give me facts," Oliver said. "Where are the American trees we hear so much about in England?"

"There are trees aplenty," Williams said, sipping the excellent claret Oliver had brought as a gift. "Trees to the west of us, trees to the south and north of us. Enormous trees, Mr. Barebones, infinite numbers of them, giants of the forest standing a hundred feet high, oaks and firs and elms and maples as well as other kinds, both hard and soft, that are unknown in Europe. But you see, Mr. Barebones, there are no roads between Boston and these trees, and no rivers flowing eastward to float them in, and the Indians will not let themselves be hired or enslaved to carry masts for his majesty's navy over a hundred miles or more of swift rivers and steep hills and treacherous bogs, so the idea of shipping wood from here to England has never come to reality."

"What if a road were built?" Oliver asked.

"A road? That would require the labor of a thousand Englishmen, sir, and there are not that many idle in the whole colony. That is a difficulty. If you overcame that, the Indians would doubtless attack you as you started carrying trees out of the forest, because this involves the most peculiar fact of all. Yes, very peculiar, Mr. Barebones. Would you like to know what it is?"

"Very much, Mr. Williams."

"Then I will tell you," Williams said. "The Indians believe that the English have come to America *to steal the trees*. They all believe it. King Philip believed it when he waged his bloody war against us. They have guessed that we have cut down all our own forests and there are not enough trees in Europe."

"What an amazing idea," Rose said.

"Indians are amazing altogether," Williams said. "Take the case of Magpie, the Nipmuck woman bequeathed to you by Captain Pennock. Pennock had her educated, you know—she reads and writes and even plays the spinet a little. When he died, he left her

the Negro slave Coffee in her own right. And she immediately sold him."

"Sold him?" This was the first Oliver had heard about this transaction.

"Sold him down the islands, as they say. Poor Coffee was transported to the island of Nevis in chains. Magpie realized two hundred pounds for him."

"But he was her husband."

"Nevertheless, she sold him."

"But why?"

"Magpie did not explain. Indians never do."

Williams chuckled, drank more claret, hacked a piece of meat off the neck of mutton that lay in the pewter trencher in the center of the table, and chewed it off the bone without using a knife. Williams kept a fine house for Boston, but there were no plates, no glasses. Everyone ate out of the trencher. The Bostonians' grandfathers, simple unknown people to begin with, had brought their manners over from England three generations before, and these were the manners that were still in use. Their houses and furniture and clothes were the same. The rooms were too small, the ceilings were too low, the roofs were too steep, the chairs and tables were the wrong size, the wood had not been properly finished. Nothing was beautiful.

Rose, smiling faintly, ate nothing and wondered how soon she would go mad. She had nearly died of boredom in Buckinghamshire. What would happen to her here? She wore one of her floating dresses, pale yellow, but modest. Rose had already noticed, in her one walk through the town, that breasts were not displayed in America, so she had covered hers with a shawl. This made the heat even more oppressive, and the sweat dripped down the furrow of her back. The room smelled strongly of food, sweat, dust, tallow, and Americans. The people here had a very plain odor—no wig powder, no hyacinth or heliotrope perfume, no lingering aroma of the milk bath on the women's skin; and like the Gypsies in Norwood, Americans smelled strongly of woodsmoke.

Dinner began at noon, a little later than it would have done outside of Boston, where the principal meal was consumed as early as ten-thirty in the morning. They had begun with a pudding— begun with a pudding!—made of Indian corn, molasses, and butter. Rose had tried this, dipping her spoon into the yellow quivering heap of it along with everyone else, but it was too sticky to eat.

Williams' stout wife and lank daughters all wore Puritan bibs and caps and chewed with their eyes down, saying nothing. They drank water fearlessly from large white cups and helped them-

selves to more from a pitcher, something that Rose, coming from England, where only animals drank water, had never seen before. Speechless though they were, the Williams females were fascinated by their visitors. Rose supposed that they had never seen such clothes, such elegance. She spread her hand on her bosom so that they could admire her ruby ring.

Williams, at least, was transfixed by Rose's dazzling appearance. He could not take his eyes off her. He had never seen a woman dressed in such bright colors. Though his remarks were always addressed to Oliver, his eyes only darted to him at the beginning and end of every sentence. Otherwise, he watched Rose.

"Will you not have a potato, mistress?" he said, enunciating all the letters of a word that had been pronounced "missis" in England for at least a lifetime. "It is not, I assure you, in the least . . . gallant."

Even in London, this would have been a daring remark to make to the beautiful wife of another man; the potato, called the gallant root, was regarded as being exciting to the senses; even Oliver had only eaten it in brothels.

Oliver did not take offense; knowing how much this guileless, talkative American would have amused Henry Harding, he himself liked Williams tremendously. Besides, Oliver had begun to see the comic side of Rose's vanity.

"Maybe you should have some potato, my dear," he said.

Rose's smile did not change, nor did she answer. The maidservant, a gawky staring girl whose boots clumped like a soldier's on the squeaking floor, brought in a platter of baked birds, dozens of them lying on their backs with their skin glistening with bacon fat.

"Pigeons," Williams explained. "The season is nearly over. In June and July, when they are flying over us in their migrations, strangers may think on looking up that the sky is black with pigeons. But they are growing very scarce. I can't think why. As a boy I once netted five thousand in a single morning."

"Netted?" Ash said.

"You catch them like fish, sir. Hang nets between the trees and the blind foolish things fly into them."

"How did you eat five thousand pigeons, sir?"

"Eating them was not the object. Even the Indians, who are very frugal, sir, far more frugal than Englishmen, caught them to watch them flutter. They are so brainless that it is impossible to have pity for them."

When dinner was over, Oliver and Williams retired to Williams' office, a low narrow room under the rafters that was as bare and as

stifling as all the other rooms in the house. All the windows were
shut. Oliver wore the plum-colored suit and the long curly wig that
he had had made for his wedding. These garments—the wig was
like a thick wool hat, good for keeping off the English rain—were
not suitable for the humid weather, and Oliver's body steamed
inside them.

The walls were lined with shelves filled with wooden boxes.
Williams got one of the boxes down, and wearing a delighted
smile, sat himself and Oliver down, knee to knee, in a pair of
straight chairs. He rapped sharply on the box and held up a key.

"Captain John Pennock's box," he said. "All the particulars of
your situation are locked safely inside."

"I must say," Oliver said, "that the particular about Magpie and
Coffee is very shocking."

"Yes, I can see that," Williams said. "You will find, sir, that
Indians do shocking things. But what they do is not always what it
seems. I will leave it at that."

"But poor Coffee."

"Indeed. But it may not be as bad as it seems. Nevis is a place
for the breeding of slaves. There are worse lives, sir, than the life
of a prize bull."

Williams opened the lid of Pennock's box and extracted a paper.
He held it out so that Oliver could see the seal and read the
superscription, written in Pennock's own hand: "A Description of
my Nephew Oliver Cromwell Barebones, Gent." The seal was
Pennock's, a lion with an owl's head; Oliver had seen the ring on
the old man's finger and the seal in wax many times before.
Williams broke the seal, unfolded the paper, and read rapidly,
moving his lips and pausing after every sentence or two to look
sharply at Oliver.

"Yes," he said at last. "You appear to be Oliver Cromwell
Barebones. Captain Pennock's description is precise."

"So much for Praise God and his theories on mistaken identi-
ties," Oliver muttered.

"What?"

Oliver waved the question aside. Williams folded up the paper.
"Everything is in order," he said. "May you prosper here in ways
that will please the Lord."

"One always hopes to do so," Oliver said. "Thank you very
much. What is the condition of the estate?"

"That," Williams said, "is a matter you must judge and manage
for yourself on your arrival. There is one complication of which
you may not be aware."

"Complication?" Oliver said. "What complication?"

"It concerns Captain Pennock's lost daughter, Thoughtful. It appears that she is no longer lost. One year ago she was discovered among the Abenaki Indians in Canada. A ransom was paid—Captain Pennock had provided for this by leaving a sum of money in my care—and she returned to Alamoth. She lives there now, in her father's house."

Sitting in his chair in his sweat-soaked suit, legs apart in plum-colored stockings, Oliver could think of nothing to say for the moment. He was glad that his cousin Thoughtful had been rescued from the Indians, but he realized that not even an American Christian would be likely to believe that.

"Thoughtful is what age now?" he asked.

"She appears to be the correct age—about fourteen."

"There is no doubt?"

"None. She resembles her father very strongly—red hair that frizzes, eyes, freckles, long jaw. Everyone remarks that the expression is remarkably like the parent's. Also, there is a birthmark on the scalp at the back of the head. Thoughtful Pennock's rescuer, a man named Gustavus Hawkes, shaved her head in order to examine it."

Oliver's head itched furiously. "Then everything belongs to her," he said. Then he took off his wig, gave Williams an apologetic smile, and scratched his scalp furiously.

"Ah!" Williams said, astonished but alert. He waited until Oliver was done scratching before he spoke again. Then he said, "In terms of the law, you understand, the discovery that she is alive alters nothing. A disinherited child, especially a female, has no claim on a parent's estate. You remain the heir."

"Still, she is her father's daughter and my cousin."

"Exactly. And you will, of course, remember that Captain Pennock specifically charges you in his will to provide for his daughter in case she returns to British territory alive and of her own free will."

"I shall do so with pleasure."

"Of course you will, Mr. Barebones. But there are peculiar facts about your cousin. She is not an English Christian. She does not wish to live among her own people."

Oliver was startled. A picture of Thoughtful had already begun to form in his mind, and in the picture she was overjoyed to be at home, with Oliver for a benefactor and Fanny for a friend. He said, "What do you mean, she doesn't want to live among her own people?"

"She thinks of herself as an Abenaki Indian. She misses the . . . license of savage life."

"The license, you say? Then why did she come back?"

Williams was no longer smiling, but there was amusement in his expression; he knew things that no Englishman freshly in America could possibly guess. "She was rescued by force," Williams said.

"Rescued by what?" said Oliver.

"By force. She did not wish to leave the Indians. It is often the case with captives. Her rescuer bound her with thongs and carried her on his back through the forest."

"But why, if she didn't want to come?"

"A reward was involved, a considerable reward, in fact, one hundred pounds. It was Gustavus Hawkes who brought Thoughtful Pennock back to us. I paid him the reward, as Captain Pennock had provided. For me, the matter ends there."

The curly wig dangled from Oliver's hand. He shifted his weight and the chair squeaked beneath him.

"How can you ransom somebody who doesn't want to be ransomed?" he asked.

"An excellent question," said Williams, "and one that you may, or may not, seek to answer as Thoughtful Pennock's guardian. There is one more thing."

Oliver waited. Williams lifted his eyebrows.

"Hawkes wishes to marry the Pennock girl. In such a case, he would control the property as he controlled the wife."

"What does Thoughtful have to say about that?"

"She is ignorant of his passion. 'She ain't used to me yet,' Hawkes says. You will soon see why."

# 6

While they waited for Gustavus Hawkes, Thoughtful Pennock's rescuer, to come for them through the forest that separated Boston from the Connecticut River, Fanny and the Bareboneses and the Ashes moved ashore, into Lebbaeus Williams' house. The charge for room and board for all five of them, including ale twice a day but no wine or spirits, was a pound a week. Williams moved his own family into the attic to make room for them, but still the house was crowded. Once again Fanny shared a bedchamber with Rose.

"It is more convenient," Rose said to Oliver. "Fanny can hardly sleep alone in a strange house, or with one of these American girls with their cow eyes and their big feet. I'm sure they must kick people in their sleep."

Rose found the Williams females comical. She found all the Americans comical: everything they did was so unfashionable. She liked to dress up in her most splendid afternoon clothes and take walks up and down the twisting Boston streets—cow paths, really—with the drab Williamses scurrying along behind and a hired boy or two going before to drive the pigs away. Boston was full of loose pigs; they ate the gardens and the crops and fought with the dogs for the garbage that the Bostonians threw out the windows into their dooryards. The pigs chased down chickens and ducks and ate them, feathers and all. The Williams girls, who never joked because they had never heard a joke, said that pigs sometimes ate the smaller children of the poor when their parents were too drunk to drive the animals away.

Faces looked out the windows at Rose as she passed. She suspected that everyone in Boston thought that she was a member of the English nobility who had come to America incognito in order to have an adventure.

"I wonder what they think *you* are, Fanny," she would say. "Or Oliver; even they would suppose that he can't possibly be my real husband."

At supper in the Williamses' plain dining room, Rose wore low-cut gowns and pasted beauty spots on the swell of her left breast one night and on the swell of the right the next. Williams looked on the wrong side. "Mr. Williams is confused again," she would whisper to Fanny.

Edward Ash never looked at Rose's bosom; he was always gazing sadly at Fanny, as if he knew that her shipboard illness was not really cured and she was going to die.

Although she herself had first eaten with a fork and a round-ended knife while staying at the Hardings', Rose lectured the Williamses at table on the technique of spearing food with a fork held in the left hand, cutting the food with the edge of the knife held in the right hand, and then pushing the severed morsel securely onto the tines with the tip of the knife and lifting the fork bearing the food to the mouth, still with the left hand.

"That," she would explain, "is how it is done nowadays in England—not everywhere, you understand, but in the better houses, such as Lockwood Hall in Buckinghamshire, the home of my late first husband, the Honorable Robert Pomeroy."

After hacking off a bit of mutton or beef from the trencher and

eating it from her hand, Rose would give a tiny shudder and hold her greasy fingers suspended limply in the air. Antoinette had packed a few Italian forks into Fanny's baggage, but when Rose got them out to give the Williams girls lessons, the experiment failed because the Williamses only had old-fashioned pointed knives. It was impossible to push the food onto the forks with these implements, so the Williams girls would spear their food, cut it, then put down the knife, transfer the fork to the right hand, lift the morsel to their mouths, and chew. By the time knives with round ends finally reached America, this roundabout style of eating had become good manners in the New World. It made Rose laugh out loud.

Fanny's musical instruments, brought down from London with Rose's things, had been carried ashore. In the evening at the Williamses', she played and sang, but never in French. Because Lebbaeus Williams was even more reluctant to see candles burning than Sir Cecil Lockwood, she often played in the dark. This added to the conviviality: the bashful Williams girls would only sing if no one could see them. The songs they knew were like their manners and their speech, nearly a hundred years old, but by singing in the dark they learned new airs from Fanny: "Lady if you so spite me," "Awake, sweet love," "Now, oh now I needs must part," and a song from the works of Philip Evans, "I had imagined this place."

To the Protestant ear, this Jesuit dirge, so full of secret meanings—every member of the Society of Jesus sent into England was required to imagine, as a spiritual exercise, the gory details of his own torture and execution at the hands of the Protestants—sounded like a love song.

Ash sang nothing but hymns, and when he sang, nobody else could be heard above him. After the first week or so, Fanny stopped playing hymns. She began to hear a fine contralto among the voices. It was Betsy Ash. She would come close to the spinet in the dark and sing counterpoint. Betsy made mistakes because she had no musical education, but she had perfect pitch and a sweet and limpid voice. One night, at the end of some lighthearted country song, she suddenly sang a whole-note scale of such purity that Fanny's hand froze on the keyboard. This brilliant singing was the only sound Fanny had ever heard come out of Betsy, who never looked at Fanny in daylight and never spoke to anyone at any time.

# 7

Joshua Peters, in his search for a cargo to take back to England, had made the acquaintance of half of Boston. The Americans amused him, too, but for different reasons.

He said, "They tell you some tale of American wonders and then they look you in the eye and say, 'Of course, you haven't seen whatever-it-is, and so you may not think I'm telling you the truth, but it is the real truth.' And usually it is."

Among the wonders Joshua had heard about was the teeming shore of Cape Cod—the transparent shallow water crowded with cod and haddock that swam among enormous oysters, huge clam beds, and whole nations of lobsters rolling in the tide.

"I don't believe it, nobody could," Joshua said, "but if it's half what they say it is, then it's worth looking at. Besides, we've got to have a partners' meeting somewhere away from all these strangers."

Oliver and Fanny and Joshua left Boston harbor at first light in the *Pamela*'s boat with one old sailor as crew. By late morning they were ashore in their bare feet on a curving white beach. Coarse grass and stunted pine trees grew thickly on the dunes. There were countless thousands of birds. Gulls had followed the boat down the coast in large numbers, but the canopy of bleached northern sky above the beach contained more birds, all calling and flapping, than Fanny had seen in her whole life up till that day. Birds snatched shellfish from the combers, climbed upward, and dropped their prey, diving after it to eat the meat after the impact smashed the shell. Ospreys crashed into the water and emerged with fish in their talons. Some birds seemed to exist by stealing from others.

"By God, these birds seem to know how lucky they are," Oliver said, watching the thousands of gulls and terns, falcons and herons, as they dove on the millions of other creatures that waited, as dumb and helpless as plants, to be eaten.

The sailor from the *Pamela*, a stumpy man from Kilkenny named Dick Condon, was as excited as the birds. He pulled off his boots and ran over the sand. There were so many squirting clams under

the surface that it was like running through a mechanical water joke, and he came back soaked, with twenty or thirty big sandy shells cradled in his arms. Condon grinned a sideways grin and shuffled sidewise over the sand, bent over in a posture of submission. He had learned manners as a prisoner of the French; captured off a sinking British frigate in the Mediterranean, he had spent five years as one of 462 galley slaves in Louis XIV's great rowing ship *La Reale*. Now, bowing and moaning like a slave, he opened the biggest clam with his knife and handed it to Fanny. The meat, pink and yellow, was as large as a plum. Condon touched the quivery frilled edge with the point of his knife.

"It's alive, girl," he said with a wink, and watched her like a monkey while she chewed, all his obsequiousness gone.

The old sailor handed her another opened clam and then trotted away toward the dunes, looking for a suitable spot for a fire. Fanny followed and helped him dig a pit in the sand. Condon gathered the dead lower branches of pitch pine, breaking the twigs over his knee and lying on his belly to reach into the pit as he arranged them into an inverted cone. On top of this wood he arranged larger driftwood, looking up at Fanny and grunting after each step to see if she understood what he was doing. When the fire was laid, he opened six more clams and arranged them on the sand for Fanny, and then ran down to the boat.

He came back with a musket and a powder horn. He sprinkled a little powder onto the pitch pine at the bottom of his stack of wood, cocked the musket, and fired it into the wood. The fire started with a whoosh.

"Now for the food," Condon said. He had a hoarse Irish voice, burnt by brandy, arrack, whisky, and anything else that had alcohol in it.

While the fire burned, they gathered food from the surf. Fanny took off her stockings and waded into the bubbly water. Green lobsters rolled in the combers. Condon threw a dozen of them up on shore, losing them to the birds as soon as they hit the sand. The same thing happened with oysters and mussels, until finally Condon stationed Oliver as a guard and used Fanny as a runner to carry the shellfish to him. Oliver stood over the growing heap, waving his arms and crying "Shoo!" at the whirling birds while he opened oysters that were so large that he had to tear them in fourths in order to chew them.

The driftwood fire in the sand pit burned down to a bed of coals. Condon laid a dozen big clacking lobsters on the coals, covered them with seaweed, and then dumped a mixture of oysters and mussels and clams on top of these. While the shellfish cooked, he

crawled under a pitch pine, chosen to be out of earshot, and went to sleep.

"We must talk business," Joshua said.

Oliver's expectations of a rich American trade had not materialized. Joshua had sold the wines and spirits for more than a thousand pounds and could have sold more. He thought that coffee and chocolate could be sold in Boston.

"These people may be prayerful, but they like stimulants as much as the rest of the English," Joshua said. "But they've little to trade back. Even in Boston, the Americans aren't artisans, they're farmers. That's what they were before they came, and that's what they've remained. Look at their houses—there's no upper class, no one who knows how things ought to be, no one to demand good work. They make very little beyond what they need in order to live, and what they do make, no European would want. The harvest isn't in, and even if it were, they might not have anything left over beyond what they need to get through the winter. It's the wrong time for salting fish, it's too late or too early for furs, and if what Lebbaeus Williams says can be relied upon, there's no prospect of taking back a cargo of wood as you had hoped, Oliver."

Fanny had never heard Joshua make such a long statement. His brown face was expressionless. "You're saying that the *Pamela* can't trade in America?" she asked.

"I don't know if she can or if she can't in the future," Joshua replied. "But all I've managed to lay hands on this time is a hundred barrels of molasses. Other than that, it looks like we'll have to sail her home empty."

"That can't be," Oliver said.

"No? Well, all suggestions are welcome."

Condon woke up and raked the seaweed off the cooked shellfish with a piece of driftwood. Fanny thought constantly of her father. What a story this would make: the giant oysters, the clams nearly as large, the plump orange mussels, the lobsters as big as sea monsters that turned from green to red when cooked and had claws full of delicious rubbery meat.

"Why not oysters and clams?" Oliver said. "Or lobsters, at least—how long will a lobster live out of the sea if you keep him in seawater?"

"Forever, I suppose," Joshua said. "But we don't know how to keep them alive."

"I'll talk to Ash," Oliver said. "He'll know."

"As long as he doesn't want to pray over them," Joshua said.

\* \* \*

When Oliver explained his plan—to transport Cape Cod lobsters across three thousand miles of ocean and sell them in London—Ash did not dismiss it as impractical. He asked to be taken to Cape Cod. He studied lobsters in the wild, kept them alive in tubs in darkness and in light, dissected half a dozen, and delivered an opinion.

"It can be done—possibly," he said. "But we must build an apparatus that will cost a great deal of money."

Ash's idea was a simple one—build tanks in the hold of the *Pamela*, fill them with seawater, and pump the water out so as to replace it constantly with new water all the way across the Atlantic. He proposed to do this by attaching the pump to a windmill on the stern of the ship.

"She will not steer with a windmill on her stern," Joshua objected.

"Then the plan will not work," Ash said. "The lobsters must live for eight weeks in an artificial sea."

"Four weeks," Joshua said. "Less. We have wind and current with us on the return voyage."

"Can the men pump by hand, then? The lobsters require seawater that moves like the waves, they require water that is alive."

"The men won't like it, but they'll prefer it to a windmill."

Ash studied the problem of feeding. He kept different lobsters in different tubs, feeding them meat and fish, salted and fresh, newly caught and rotted. In the end he had a fair idea of what the creatures would eat—fish, oysters, mussels. These things, too, would be put into the tubs.

Ash worked in secret in a barn behind the Williams house. Joshua was worried by Ash's participation in the work. "If the men find out these orders come from him," he told Fanny, "they won't carry them out. They think Ash is mad and brings bad luck."

"Then don't tell them," Fanny said.

"I think he's mad myself. This idea is mad. We'll have a hold full of dead lobsters."

"Maybe. But if it works, Oliver will be very happy. What we need is another cargo, for insurance. What about smoked oysters?"

Joshua gave her a sharp look. "Mussels too. You're Henry's daughter in more ways than one," he said.

He put Condon and two or three young sailors on the beach, gathering oysters and mussels and smoking them over pitch-pine fires. They had a tarry taste that Oliver thought would create a sensation at Rose Tavern.

Lebbaeus Williams, intrigued by the idea of making money out of something like the lobster that simply occurred in nature, helped enthusiastically. "It is a gift from God, like the New World itself,"

he said. He found coopers to make watertight tanks that would fit into the hold of the *Pamela*. Fanny went with Williams to the cooperage and watched the tanks taking shape. It was intensely satisfying to see the staves shaved and shaped, then fitted together and bound with iron, then put to soak to swell the joints and plug the natural leaks.

By the first of September, the lobster vats and the pumps were ready to be fitted. Joshua sailed the *Pamela* to the beach and for a week the whole crew caught lobsters in long-handled nets that Ash had designed for the purpose. Fanny counted them as they came aboard, throwing all but the largest back into the sea, and calling a halt to the fishing when there were two thousand lobsters in the vats.

"If half of them live, and you can sell them for a shilling each," Fanny said, "we'll be five hundred pounds richer."

Joshua made a Genoese shrug. "The tanks cost us two hundred."

"If they all die, sell the tanks," Oliver said.

"I'm sure there'll be a tremendous market for them," Joshua said.

The *Pamela* would sail on the tide, leaving Fanny and the others behind. Fanny had no real hope of ever seeing England again. She took Joshua by the arm and walked him far down the beach. When they were far enough away, she talked to him.

"You don't have much faith in this cargo, do you?"

Joshua shrugged again. "The men don't like pumping water into the ship, it isn't natural," he said. "But for me, it's not the cargo, it's this Ash. They think he's bad luck."

He and Fanny were standing on a smashed pavement of mother-of-pearl left by the hunting birds. Joshua reached into his pocket and brought out a rosary with a silver cross. It had belonged to Fanchon, and Fanny had carried it in the secret pocket of her petticoat since taking her First Communion. She hadn't seen it since she left France.

"Ash found it on the floor of the cabin while you were sick," Joshua said. "Naturally he thought it was mine."

Far down the beach, Ash was watching them. He saw Fanny looking back at him and turned away. She lifted her skirt, unbuttoned the pocket in her petticoat, and put the rosary inside. The ruby necklace was already there, wrapped in a piece of linen.

A strand of Fanny's hair had blown across her face. Joshua lifted it and put it back in place.

"You're a lovely girl, Fanny," he said. "Don't stay here. This place is empty."

"Empty? With all these birds and lobsters?"

"You can't talk to birds and fish, or marry them," Joshua said. "Come back to England. You should find a husband and have a son who'll grow up to be like your father. Henry didn't bring you up to be alone all your life in a place like this."

"I wouldn't be alone in England?"

"At least you'd be a long way away from this man Ash."

Joshua was looking over her shoulder as he spoke. Fanny turned around and looked too. Still far away, but coming steadily on, was Ash. He waved and shouted; they heard him perfectly despite the racket made by a sky full of birds and the pounding of the surf.

"Look at him," Joshua said.

Ash broke into a run, his gray hair feathering as he moved; he was remarkably athletic and this muscularity was always a surprise because it was the last thing one expected to see in him.

"See how he runs to you," Joshua said.

Ash? Fanny laughed and called Joshua by his real name. "Oh, Pietro . . ."

"Don't laugh, Fanny. He's after you. Come back to England on the *Pamela*. I ask you as your father's friend."

Ash was much closer now. He looked as if he had happy news. It was impossible to talk. Moved by Joshua's affection for her, knowing that she would probably never again see this wrinkled brown Italian who had always been so good to her, Fanny kissed him—threw her arms around him and kissed him on the lips and then gazed into his eyes for a long moment and patted his cheek.

Ash was very close when this happened. When Fanny took her eyes off Joshua and looked at Ash, she saw that his face was drained of expression. He stared at Joshua, then at Fanny, then at the sea.

"What is it?" Fanny asked.

Ash, who spoke as easily as he breathed, had to clear his throat before he could reply.

"Williams has sent a message," he said. "Hawkes, the guide, has arrived in Boston and we must leave for the west tomorrow."

Joshua held on to Fanny's hand. "Will you go, too?" he asked.

"I must," Fanny said.

"Then I'll bring your ship back to Boston," Joshua said, "in case you need her."

# 8

John Pennock had been possessed of the religious temperament. While praying at the age of sixteen, he was seized by the belief that he must devote his life, the only thing that was truly his—as opposed to the estate on the Scottish border that he would inherit when his father died—to the defense of Jesus Christ against His chief earthly enemy, the pope of Rome. Just then there was no religious war in England (though Pennock thought there ought to be because of young King Charles's marriage to the Catholic sister of Louis XIII of France), but the possibility of killing papists existed on the Continent.

Pennock went to Germany to fight in the protracted conflict between the Holy Roman Emperor and a shifting coalition of Protestant and Catholic enemies that was afterward called the Thirty Years War. He seldom came home to England after that. Catholics and Protestants were never at peace with one another everywhere in Europe for a single day during his lifetime. During his first years as a soldier, Pennock served under Gustavus Adolphus, Protestant king of Sweden. Though Gustavus' troops were, for their time, highly disciplined and well-behaved, Pennock nevertheless saw entire towns massacred and whole provinces laid waste by what both sides believed was the providence of God. Gustavus, the greatest military genius of the age, invented the practice of infantry firing their muskets in unison, or "in salvo" as he called it, as they advanced, and insisted that cavalry must charge right into the enemy and fight with the saber. Pennock believed in Gustavus' principles of warfare nearly as strongly as he believed in the truth of the Scriptures, and was as willing to die for them.

After Charles I of England was beheaded in 1649, Pennock fought with Oliver Cromwell in Ireland, taking part in the massacres at Drogheda and Wexford, in which the Catholic defenders were put to the sword to the last man after they surrendered to Cromwell's army. At Wexford, Pennock saved the lives of three Irish wolf dogs, enormous beasts with dejected whiskery faces, that were about to be shot by archers because they were ferociously

defending their wounded master against the English who wanted to kill him.

"There's no hope for you, but there's no need for the dogs to die; I'll look after them," Pennock had said to the dying man.

"Very well," the papist replied, and called off the dogs.

"Magnificent animals, biggest dogs I've ever seen," Pennock said to his enemy as he took away his sword. "What are they for?"

"Wolf dogs," the other said as he sank to his knees, making the sign of the cross. "That big chap ran a wolf for fourteen hours only last year—ran it right back to me and the other dogs and then killed it."

"Fourteen hours!"

The doomed man called his dogs over and pounded them affectionately on the ribs. Then he told them to lie down; they did so obediently, watching him and whimpering low in their throats as he prayed. When he was finished, he opened his eyes and nodded. Pennock gave the order and the archers killed him; the dogs howled in anguish when they smelled his blood. True to his word and impressed by the wolf dogs' obedience, Pennock took them back to England with him. As there were no wolves on the Scottish border, he used the dogs to run stags, and found that their dead master had not exaggerated their endurance or courage. He gave instructions that they should only be bred to each other, never crossed with another breed.

After Cromwell died and Charles II was restored to the throne, Pennock returned to the Continent and joined the great Dutch Protestant William, Prince of Orange, in his battles against Louis XIV. When, in 1688, William of Orange invaded England at the invitation of a group of English noblemen, Pennock rode with him.

By then Pennock's work in England was done. He had always been rich and his faithful service under William now made him richer. During the winter, while at morning prayer among the strangers who were his servants, Pennock underwent a second religious experience. It was just as forceful, and just as irresistible, as the one half a century before. While listening to the reading of the Forty-sixth Psalm, he was seized with such a strenuous desire to leave England and go to the colonies that he could only believe that the idea was an instruction from God. "There is a river," read the psalm, "the streams whereof shall make glad the city of God . . ."

Pennock decided to build a city in the wilderness where he and all who followed him would live in harmony with God and nature, out of reach of Catholics. "A quiet place on the banks of a river,"

he told his servants, explaining that he intended to take them with him. "A godly place without argument or discord."

He located a river, the Connecticut, on a map of New England and applied to King William for a royal grant of land. This was soon approved by the king, as foretold in the psalm. In the ensuing three months, Pennock sold everything he owned in England. He had never married. Requiring a wife to go into the wilderness with him, Pennock married Oliver's spinster aunt, Hope Barebones, who was kindly and clever like her Adkins mother and tall, broad-shouldered, and plain-minded like the Barboneses. On the four-teenth of June, the anniversary of the Battle of Naseby, Pennock sailed for the New World in two ships—a little one for the farmers and craftsmen who were going with him and a larger one for livestock, tools, and supplies. Besides his bride, Pennock took along an entire community of people—farmers with all the neces-sary breeding animals and seeds, carpenters, masons, tanners, and weavers and their tools, a miller, a brewer, a tavernkeeper, a sergeant named Amos Hawkes who had fought with Pennock in Ireland and in the Low Countries, and others.

By the time Pennock came back to England and told Oliver and Henry his stories, he had built his city in the wilderness—a church and other necessary buildings, a big house for himself, and thirty small ones for his colonists, on a hillside above the Connecticut River. The settlement was protected from savages by a log stock-ade fifteen feet high with watchtowers at each corner. Pennock called it Alamoth because the Forty-sixth Psalm was described in the Bible as "A Song upon Alamoth" and he assumed that that was the name of the city of God. Ash explained, when he heard the name of the place years afterward, that *alamoth* was a Hebrew word meaning "soprano"—from *almah*, "a virgin."

Alamoth's natural setting was a place of remarkable beauty. The Connecticut at this point was as wide as the Thames at London, but more meandering. Natural meadows lying in bends shaped like oxbows were fertilized by annual floods that covered them with rich silt. Pennock's border farmers planted these oxbows with wheat, rye, Indian corn, beans, hay, and other crops, and set out apple trees and other English fruits on the hillside. Deer came down from the encircling forest and grazed peacefully in the pas-tures among the Devon cattle and Shropshire sheep and Berkshire hogs that had crossed the Atlantic in Pennock's cattle boat.

There were fiercer beasts, too, and in a letter to her family Hope described hearing what she thought was a baby crying in the forest. But it was a lion. "The Indians sometimes imitate this beast, as well as the calls of other animals, in order to approach closer to

their enemies," Hope wrote. "They regard the English as enemies, but my husband has brought along a goodly supply of muskets and pikes and already he and Sergeant Hawkes are drilling the other men to be soldiers. I am with child." Hope bore Pennock two children, a girl named Thoughtful, and a boy, born a year later, who was also called Oliver after Pennock's hero, Cromwell. Pennock was seventy-five years old when his son was conceived.

During the fourth summer of Alamoth's existence, a band of Abenaki Indians, a tribe from the north, attacked the village. The war party, gaunt painted men with stringy limbs who yipped like terriers as they fought, came down from the forest before dawn, killed the English sentinels in their watchtowers, and set the church and some of the houses afire. Pennock tried to rally the men he and Sergeant Hawkes had trained and armed with muskets and pikes, but the tactics that had driven King Charles from the field at Naseby and overcome the Catholics at Lützen and Wexford were useless against the savages. The Abenakis simply ran ahead of the amateur troops as they marched stolidly across a meadow. There was no cavalry to cover them except Pennock and his old sergeant. When the English fired their muskets in a salvo, so that they all had to reload at once, the Indians dashed closer, killed half of them with bows and arrows and hatchets, and captured the rest. Pennock killed one Indian and wounded another with his saber before the Abenakis hamstrung his horse and dragged him, slashing and cursing, off its back.

As Alamoth was twenty miles from the nearest English settlement, there was no possibility of rescue. The Indians stripped off Pennock's boots—he was the only man along this part of the river with sufficient wealth to be entitled by law to wear full-length boots that came up to his thighs—and locked him in the pillory. The Abenakis then built a fire under him and left him to burn to death while they finished with the killing. Twenty of the sixty villagers were killed, including Hope's small son, Oliver, who had his brains dashed out by a savage who swung him by the heels, cracked his head against a tree, and then threw his small body into the burning church. Hope was hatcheted to death by the same Indian when she tried to save her child. There was so much murder, clumsily accomplished with the only tools the Indians had, badly sharpened knives and hatchets and the saber they had captured from Pennock, that the small brook that ran through the village turned pink with English blood.

While the massacre progressed, Pennock was doing a mad dance as he tried to escape the fire. His head and wrists were trapped in the stocks, but his feet were free, so he kicked away the burning

brands with his bare feet. Four of his toes were burned off,
together with his clothes and his beard and all the hair on his body.
When the old man told this story to Henry and Oliver, he said that
what he feared most was that his dangling parts would be burned
off. The Indians seemed to realize this. About half of them mo-
mentarily forgot about the slaughter and gathered around the
pillory to watch, clutching their own privy parts and pointing
merrily at Pennock's, which swung between his legs as he per-
formed his frantic dance. Pennock felt no resentment toward the
Indians. However primitive, this was war; he had seen worse
things happen in Germany. Nor was he surprised that the pain of
being burnt at the stake was so excruciating. Marching through
Bavaria with Gustavus Adolphus, he had seen as many as a hun-
dred witches burned in a single captured town. The Forty-sixth
Psalm, which Pennock, who knew it by heart, had been repeating
in his mind in order to prevent himself from screaming, said,
"Come, behold the works of the Lord, what desolations he hath
made in the earth."

As soon as the Abenakis departed, the Nipmuck girl, Magpie,
released Pennock from the pillory, then held his head above the
water when he lay down in the brook to cool his burns. Little
ribbons of charred flesh fluttered in the current. The Indians
carried all the children away with them, including Pennock's small
daughter, Thoughtful, and Sergeant Hawkes's ten-year-old son,
named Gustavus after the great Swede. The boy escaped almost
immediately and ran all the way to Deerfield, twenty miles away,
to summon help. A column of soldiers marched after the Indians,
but the Abenakis split up into small groups and escaped into
Canada.

Most of the Indians of New England and eastern Canada spoke
some form of the Algonquian language, and they all conversed
fluently in a universal sign language, so that they generally under-
stood each other in a rudimentary way. Pennock realized that
Magpie, whom he had taught to speak and write English, gave him
the means of asking the Indians about the fate of his child.

"God has now revealed his purpose in causing me to teach you
the English tongue," he told Magpie.

For a whole year, Pennock traveled among the Indian villages
with his small slave, inquiring about Thoughtful. Magpie was reluc-
tant to accompany him, because he had also caused her to learn to
sew and she feared that she would be captured herself if this secret
became known to the Abenakis. She confided her fears to Pennock.

"Nonsense," Pennock said. "Why should Indians want a seam-
stress when they wear leather clothes?"

Magpie did not tell him that her own father had kept an Englishwoman he had captured during King Philip's War hidden in his village for fifteen years. The Englishwoman sewed the whole time, cutting up the same few pieces of cloth over and over again and sewing them into fanciful garments for her captor and his wife. Magpie's father would not let the woman eat or drink while she was sewing, for fear that she would stop before she had finished. Her reward for a shirt or a pair of trousers was a handful of no-cake and gourd filled with water. When the English came, usually to pray and sing hymns and explain to the Nipmucks about Jesus Christ, Magpie's family would force the seamstress to climb high up in a pine tree, where she would be gagged and bound to the trunk until the visitors went away. In the end the woman went mad and one of Magpie's brothers had to kill her with a club.

Magpie believed that Pennock's daughter was almost certainly dead, hung up in a tree to starve, because she had no value. Other Indians agreed. They had found other English bones along the line of the Abenaki retreat, but not the skeleton of such a small child.

"What do they say?" Pennock would ask at the end of a long dialogue in Algonquian and signs.

"They have not seen her, but they will look for her."

"Then they think she is alive?"

Magpie would look at him in silence, unable to tell him that the Indians were only being polite.

"It's been a long time," Magpie would say. "But they will ask."

She did not explain that it was the birds who would be asked.

"The birds have probably forgotten," said a Cowasuck, speaking directly to Pennock in Algonquian because he felt sorry for him. "But when they come back in the spring, we will ask them."

Pennock did not accept these speculations. He believed that Thoughtful might have been taken to Canada by the Abenakis and sold to the Jesuits, who were said to purchase English souls from the Indians with beads and mirrors and hatchets in the same way that the English in New York commonly bought French and Indian scalps. With Magpie on the crupper, he rode his horse into the forest summer after summer, and finally, in an interval of cease-fire between the English and the French, took ship to Canada. He died unsatisfied.

When the news of Pennock's death and the details of his will reached England, the Barebones family assumed that the old man had left what he owned to Oliver because his wife's nephew had the same Christian name and the same curly reddish hair as the old soldier's only son, who had been killed by the Abenakis. In any case Pennock never described the murder without speaking of the

child's curls and how his boy's skull had burst so that when the Indian flung him toward the fire and his little body tumbled through the air head over heels and heels over head, as Pennock said, it sprinkled blood onto the upturned faces of the English.

# 9

John Pennock left everything he owned in America to Oliver Barebones except his Irish wolf dogs. These he bequeathed to Gustavus Hawkes as a reward for the boy's bravery in escaping from the Abenakis and making his long run through the forest to Deerfield. In his will he had specified again that the wolf dogs must be kept pure and never bred to any other kind of dog.

Now Hawkes stood before Oliver and the rest of the English people in the front yard of Lebbaeus Williams' house. They had all come out to see him, even the Williamses, who seemed to find him as exotic as the newcomers did.

"He's called Gustavus Adolphus Hawkes," Williams said, making the introductions. "He and his dogs are the terror of the Indians. They think that Gus and his dogs are ghosts. Isn't that so, Hawkes?"

Hawkes did not reply. His hands were folded over the muzzle of his musket and his chin rested on his hands. Fanny had never seen anyone who looked remotely like him. He was a big, dull-eyed young man, almost as large as Oliver, but with a different sort of body. Whereas Oliver was bony and rangy, with long shanks and sharp joints, Gustavus was stout, like a man made out of hams that had been strung together and stuffed into a suit of clothes. He was so thick in all his parts that he seemed at first glance to be obese. But then Fanny saw that what looked like layers of fat were slabs of muscle. Standing apart from Oliver, he seemed to be a foot shorter; side by side, their height was almost the same. Gustavus was dressed in Indian moccasins that laced up to his knees, brownish homespun breeches, a loose shirt, and a round Puritan hat with a hawk's feather stuck into the buckle. He wore a necklace made from the teeth and claws of a bear. Besides the musket he was armed with a hatchet and a large knife.

Hawkes was accompanied by a pack of dogs—four or five mongrels that dashed around the Williamses' yard, sniffing and scratching in search of food, and three enormous, sluggish animals that sat in a row with their eyes fixed on Hawkes. Oliver had thought that Sir Cecil's mastiffs were large, but he had never seen such dogs as these—sitting down, they were at least three and a half feet high from paws to ears.

"Are those the Irish wolf dogs?" Oliver asked.

Hawkes gave him a long suspicious look before he answered. "They're mine," he said. "Captain Pennock willed them to me."

"That is not in dispute, Gus," Williams said. "Mr. Barebones is quite aware of the terms of Captain Pennock's will."

Rose and Ash came out of the house. Hawkes looked at them with the same wary expression on his round face.

"He smells like his dogs," Rose said, whispering into Fanny's ear.

Fanny ignored her. "May I ask you a question?" she said to Hawkes. He looked at her but made no other sign that he had heard her. "What is your necklace made of?"

Hawkes looked down at his breast as though to make certain that he was actually wearing the necklace. "Teeth and claws," he said.

"From what animal?"

"Bear."

Rose drew in her breath and examined Hawkes more closely. He *looked* like a bear: slow, humped, shambling.

One of the Irish wolf dogs got up and walked with a peculiar swiveling gait toward Fanny; the animal appeared to be taller in its hips than in its shoulders. Hawkes called it back. It wagged its tail and whined, looking back over its odd body at Hawkes.

"Let him come if he wants to," Fanny said. She chirped at the dog. It trotted over to her and sniffed her hand. "Yes," Fanny said, "yes, dog, yes." She did not touch the animal. It pushed its muzzle under Fanny's hand and with a flip of its neck tossed the hand onto its back. Fanny patted him vigorously. The dog sidled against her, knocking her back a step before she laughed and caught her balance.

"You've made a friend, Fanny," Oliver said.

Hawkes called the animal again. Fanny instantly stopped petting it, and after whining and licking its chops, it went back and sat down with the other dogs.

"They say you own a ship," Hawkes said. "Before it sails, tell the master to bring me a wolf-dog bitch on his next voyage to Boston—two bitches and a dog. I'll pay up to ten pounds each."

"The ship has already sailed."

"Sailed? Shit!"

Hawkes banged the butt of his tall musket on the stone path. The Williams daughters, standing together in the doorway to watch Oliver and Hawkes, jumped twice, first at the rude word and then at the clatter of the musket butt.

Ash broke the silence that followed. "Tell me," he said, causing the wolf dogs to look around for him in a startled way, "having all these dogs, why do you want another?"

Hawkes considered the question for such a long time that Ash and the other English people thought that he had not heard it even though it was Ash who had asked it. But finally the American spoke.

"These are all males," he said. "They'll die out if they don't breed."

"Ah. But you have other dogs."

"They do the tracking. The wolf dogs hunt by sight and hearing. They've got no nose at all."

"Why so many small dogs?"

"The big ones run 'em to death. They'll go for days, until they run down whatever they're after."

"Like stag hounds," Ash said. "I should think they'd be useful in a country where there are so many deer."

Hawkes grinned. Occurring on such a broad, uninterested face, it was a surprising smile, full of charm and eager response. Clearly Ash had stumbled onto a line of thought that interested Hawkes.

"They are useful," Hawkes said, rattling his necklace. "They killed this bear. They'll fight anything. But the game I hunt is what they hunt best."

"What would that be? Bear?"

"No, not a bear."

He grunted. A sly smile played over his face.

# 10

The walk from Boston to the Connecticut required five days, and at first the wilderness was not what Fanny had expected. For one whole day there was no forest at all. They left Boston at sunrise— six people, five horses, and Hawkes's dogs— and for all the first day walked westward through rolling country. The paths, worn into the earth by the footsteps of animals and Indians, followed the contours of the hills. From the hilltops they could see thousands upon thousands of acres of open grassland, watered by ponds and brooks. Sometimes they came upon a stand of willows by a stream, but the big trees that Oliver had imagined were nowhere to be seen.

As there were no roads, there could be no wagons. Ordinary baggage—Rose's trunks, Henry's books, a crate of muskets Oliver had discovered in the hold of the *Pamela*—were lashed to litters, crude stretcherlike devices made of oozing green saplings. One end of each litter was hitched to a horse like the shafts of a wagon, while the other end dragged on the ground. Fragile items were slung over the horses' backs in saddlebags made of old sails, an invention of Ash's. Fanny's spinet was transported in this way, wrapped in quilts, with the legs removed. Ash carried his microscope and his pharmacopoeia in a pack on his back.

Fanny walked behind Hawkes, far ahead of the others, so that she would not have to listen to Rose.

As she stumbled over the tussocky ground, Rose kept poking Oliver with her walking stick and crying, "Did you *ask* for a horse for me? Did you *ask* for a horse for me?"

Rose had pictured herself riding on horseback through the wilderness, and she was angry because she had to walk.

Oliver, leaping aside to avoid the point of Rose's stick, tried to placate her by picking strawberries as he went and giving her great handfuls to eat. The hands and lips of all the travelers were stained red with their juice.

In some places the berries, as large as the end of a woman's thumb, grew so thickly in the grass that it was impossible to avoid

stepping on them. The pulp and juice of the crushed berries, heated by the sun, made the air smell like strawberry jam.

Fanny ran ahead, passing Hawkes by, in order to get out of earshot. Huge flights of birds—more, even, than they had seen on Cape Cod—also fed on the berries, flocking and circling to form funnels and wedges that cast dense shadows on the ground, and then rising in their thousands with scarlet berries gripped in their beaks.

Fanny saw no homely English birds such as sparrows or starlings or wrens. She recognized the swallows for what they were, but asked Hawkes, who had caught up with her while she stood in one place gazing at the teeming sky, to identify others: a plump bird that bobbed along at knee height, showing a white backside and a yellow spot on the back of its head, a blackbird with a lozenge of red and a yellow stripe on the base of its wings, and a small yellow bird with black wings that had an undulating flight.

"Bobolinks, red-winged blackbird, and they call the yellow ones yellow birds," Hawkes said, surprised that Fanny should not know what everyone knew. He imitated the calls of each, whistling through his teeth.

"What do the Indians call them?"

"The Indians won't give names to things that be alive," he said. "They say it steals their spirit."

He whistled the bobolink's three-note call again, and the birds answered from all around.

He looked back at the horses, tall docile animals stepping slowly through the grass pulling their top-heavy loads. Litters were a bumpy means of transport, and from time to time something would fall off.

As Fanny watched, Rose's trunk tumbled to the ground. The latch gave way and clothes spilled over the ground. Rose shrieked. Betsy and Oliver helped her to repack.

"The berries! Be careful or everything will stain!" Rose cried. "Oh, what a savage place."

She liked the sound of that phrase and repeated it several times, watching Ash to see if he heard and admired her choice of words. But his eyes were fixed, as usual, on Fanny. She had turned her back to the scene and was looking at the far horizon. A breeze had risen, causing the grass to sway, and she put her face into the moving air. It lifted her hair and filled her skirt.

When she turned around, she saw that Ash was watching her with a look of hopeless longing on his face. She moved her eyes away from him as if she had not seen. By now she knew that Joshua Peters had been correct: Ash *was* obsessed by her. She

stared at him. Suddenly filled with purpose, he whirled around and began to help Oliver repack the litter.

The two men were tremendously companionable as a result of the surgery in London and all that had happened since, and they worked easily together, smiling and nodding in agreement and sometimes pounding each other on the back and shoulders when they had reason for praise or agreement or congratulation.

Fanny could see that the things they were lashing to the litter would almost certainly fall off again. Hawkes watched impassively, offering no advice and no help.

"Is that the best way to load the litter?" Fanny asked.

"There's no best way. Everything falls off because of the bumps."

"But they've never done it before."

"I'm hired to guide," Hawkes said. "The woods is no place for baggages."

He shouldered his musket and plodded on. Fanny followed. Hawkes's dogs scouted ahead, galloping in a pack over the ridge lines of the rising country, and every now and then pausing to play some sort of game in which they formed a circle with their heads pointed inward, tails wagging. Hawkes paid no attention to them. After a while the dogs came back and walked with the people.

The big wolf dog that had taken a liking to Fanny walked close beside her, nosing her hand onto his head so that she would pet him. Suddenly the dog saw something in the grass and exploded into motion. The other two wolf dogs were beside him instantaneously, followed by the slower mongrels. Fanny followed the dogs into the tall grass. They had surrounded a brown roly-poly animal that looked like a huge good-natured rat except that it had no tail. The animal darted this way and that, trying to escape from the circle of dogs. Wagging their tails, the wolf dogs panted and woofed and gave each other jovial looks, like old human friends having a joke together. And then, so quickly that Fanny's eye could not follow, they killed the animal. One dog feinted an attack from the side, a second seized the terrified prey by the hindquarters, and before it could twist its body to bite this attacker, the third sank its teeth into its neck. With amazing efficiency, the dogs tore the creature apart. What had been fur and whiskers, teeth and eyes, became lumps of raw shredded meat.

The big wolf dog, its breath reeking from the kill, rejoined Fanny and trotted along beside her, grazing on strawberries. Every few hundred yards, Fanny heard the buzzing of flies. Investigating, she found the evidence of a dozen other wolf-dog kills—scraps of hide, smears of blood, crunched bones—on which swarms of big purple flies were feeding. Fanny caught up to Hawkes again.

"What are these things that the dogs are killing?"

"Groundhogs. Look."

He gave a shrill whistle. Dozens of the animals sat up by their dens in the grass, as if responding to his signal. He showed her the burrows in which they lived, kicking the dirt around the holes.

"Do they have a back door in case something comes in the front?" Fanny asked.

"How'd you know that?"

Hawkes gave Fanny another long look, but there was less puzzlement in it than before. He was getting used to her. He had never seen an English person who looked like Fanny; from a distance, if you didn't see her face, you might think she was an Indian. In his eyes, she wasn't pretty—he liked nothing that resembled an Indian. But she had sharp eyes and ears, things that most English people did not have. She had learned to find the dogs' kills by listening for the flies—he'd seen her doing it. If the Abenakis captured her, Hawkes thought, she'd never want to come back. But the dogs liked her.

They did not stop to rest or eat until they reached the edge of the forest. They crossed a river, Oliver lifting the end of each litter above his head and wading the stream behind the horses. Fanny watched from the side of a hill, and then climbed to the top. Hawkes was already there, leaning on his musket as before. The sun was setting behind a formation of long dark clouds. Shafts of light radiated from the horizon, whitening the bellies of the clouds, and then the whole disk of the sun became visible as the sky all around it glowed in tints of rose and violet.

There was not enough light in England to make a sunset like this. Fanny wished once again that Henry could be beside her as she discovered these wonders. Because of the change in the light, the forest seemed very close. The trees were huge. She heard the wind moving through them and saw their filigreed tops tossing gently in the evening breeze, silvering and unsilvering as the leaves turned on their stems.

The others came up with the horses. By then the splendor of the sunset had faded and twilight was falling. They went down together, following a faint path along the contours of the hill, and entered the forest. Big trees stood all around in the dusk, and when Fanny looked toward the remnants of the sunset she saw curtains of dusty light among the trunks of the oaks and chestnuts. Birds sang in their thousands, hidden in the leafy canopy far overhead. There was no undergrowth. The springy floor of the forest, covered with moss and wiry grass and a few fallen leaves,

was like the ground in an English park. An army could have marched through without breaking ranks.

"What are these trees?"

"Chestnut, oaks," Hawkes said. "Farther west you'll see pine and maple and lots of spruce."

"As big as these?"

He had already turned away. They had arrived at a camping place. It was surrounded by high black rocks. A spring bubbled out of the rocks. Hawkes lay down on his stomach and sucked up water. When he was finished, Fanny kneeled beside the spring and plunged her hand into it. The water was icy cold. She drank and then washed her face, which was dirty and sunburnt after the long walk. The water, utterly free of dirt, tasted of the rocks. Fanny could hear water running over stones.

A big fire—the logs crisscrossed waist-high—had already been laid inside a circle of stones. Hawkes fell to his knees, struck sparks from a flint and steel onto a bit of birchbark tinder, blew the tinder into flame, and placed it carefully at the center of the fire. Soon the whole wigwam of wood was ablaze in the hot evening, and the travelers moved away from it.

Ash unhitched the litters from the horses and laid them side by side on the ground. Rose opened one of her trunks and rummaged through it. Hawkes sat down near her on the moss and began to eat, dipping two fingers and a thumb into a sack and stuffing whatever was inside rapidly into his mouth. Then he chewed, very deliberately, for a long time.

Betsy put a pot on the coals and stirred it with a wooden spoon. She had carried porridge all the way across the grassland. The flames made a lot of red light in the dark woods, reflecting from the trees to create the illusion that they were in a cave.

"What is this stuff?" Ash asked.

"Nocake," Hawkes said. He turned his slow eyes to Fanny. He reached into the sack with his eating fingers, pulled out a big pinch of nocake, and offered it to her.

She put it into her mouth and chewed. It was tasteless and so dry that Fanny wondered how it would be possible to swallow it.

"What's it made of?" Oliver asked.

"Indian corn," Hawkes said, watching Fanny as she chewed. "It swells up inside you if you drink water before and after. Keeps hunger away."

"It's too dry to swallow," Fanny mumbled.

"Work some spit into it," Hawkes said. "It'll go down all right."

Fanny chewed, forcing saliva out of the roof of her mouth. The nocake, made of parched kernels of maize that had been pounded

in a stone mortar and mixed with salt and molasses, doubled and trebled in mass as it absorbed saliva and became chewy and even pleasant to the taste. Hawkes watched, nodding in approval.

Fanny swallowed.

"Have some water," Hawkes said. "Now you know how to do it in case you're captured by the Indians."

Hawkes tied up his sack of nocake, put it back into the big pocket in his homespun shirt, and lay down at the spring to drink. When he rose to his feet, he went off into the darkness without a word, followed by his dogs. He didn't come back that night.

One by one, the party stretched out on the moss and went to sleep. Fanny thought that she might never fall asleep. Rose, wrapped in her cloak, lay beside her on the moss groaning with a stomach-ache. She had eaten too many strawberries. Every few minutes she would jump to her feet, grasp Fanny's hand, and pull her along with her as she ran into the forest.

"Ah, Fanny, my poor, poor stomach," she moaned, holding her skirts under her arms and looking fearfully into the darkness. "Even the strawberries are poison in this horrible place."

Finally Rose fell asleep, whimpering in her dreams. She was afraid of Indians; they all were. Betsy gasped with fear even in her sleep. Ash sat with his back against a tree and Fanny could not tell if he was asleep or if he was watching her again. Oliver had brought his pistols and he slept with them crossed on his chest. The fire shifted, sending sparks crackling upward. They died long before they reached the roof of the forest, and soon the fire died down to a dull red glow.

A half-moon hung in the sky, suffusing the woods with a skimmed light that was strong enough to silhouette the boles of the ancient oaks and chestnuts and maples for several hundred feet in all directions. An owl hooted.

Fanny got up and walked away from the camp, looking over her shoulder as she went to make sure that she could still see the glow of the coals behind her. Ash sat against his tree like a dead man, sound asleep.

Fireflies blinked among the shadowy trees. Watching them, Fanny stumbled into a brook, the continuation of the stream that flowed out of the spring, and fell to her knees in the shallow water. She climbed out, removed her shoes and stockings, and wrung the water from her soaked skirt. She walked on with the wet cloth slapping against her bare legs. This made her calves itch. There seemed to be a place ahead where there was more light. She walked on and came to a small meadow. It was filled with deer, fifteen or twenty animals, some with antlers in velvet. All the

heads were up, rounded ears quivering, eyes glimmering like gilt. Hundreds of fireflies flickered among the deer. When Fanny appeared at the edge of the wood, the deer froze for a moment, and then they bolted all together, bounding away into the darkness with the fireflies swirling behind them and their white tails and rumps flagging as they went.

It was a spectacle of almost unbearable beauty, and Fanny, who had not cried since Henry died, began to sob. What if Henry was looking down on this scene from heaven, instead of rotting by the Thames in a grave full of filthy water?

She had seen herself only once, while drowning in the harbor at Honfleur. Even now she could summon the picture of herself, or Fanchon, whichever girl it had been, and the swirl of hair and cloth and limbs and escaping breath. Had her father seen her as she drew close?

She had been ready to die. Perhaps she *had* died and America was the other world. Since coming here she had thought of nothing but the dead, and had lived only among the dead: Oliver, who died with Henry; Rose, who had never been alive in the first place; Betsy, who had lost every power except grief; Ash, who cared nothing for life on earth; the Americans, who had no past.

Biting her lips, Fanny leaned back against a tree, crushing her head and body into its rough bark.

In the delirium aboard the *Pamela* she had often been under the water with Philippe. He seized the drowning girl, who was amazed by his strength, he drew her up into the air, he let her breathe again, he drove the water out of her lungs with an embrace, he looked at her with love. He had feared her death. In those dreams, he never spoke.

"Why so silent?" she whispered now.

She knew that she would never see him again. She gazed at the field where the deer had been, barely able to believe that they had ever existed.

# 11

When Betsy Ash woke on the first morning in the forest and saw the Indians, she did not scream or try to run away. She was very calm; her mind worked its way from one possibility to the next. She wondered why Hawkes's dogs weren't barking, and then remembered that Hawkes had gone away.

The men were asleep. The camp was defenseless. Had death come for her, or did her foreboding about kidnapping mean that the Indians were going to capture her and her unborn child with her? Seeing the Indians standing on the rocks above the camp in the vaporous light of early dawn, three squat figures with brown faces and wrinkled brown paunches, she realized that they could easily have killed everyone in the camp in their sleep. Yet they had not done so. This was an important fact. Betsy found herself thinking very clearly. Perhaps Indians did not kill people while they were asleep. They had strange religious beliefs, and this could be one of them.

The Indians were incredibly alert. They had known at once that Betsy was awake. The tiny movement of her eyelids, the small change in her breathing, were enough to warn them. The instant her eyes opened, they stared at her, ignoring everything and everyone else. They were still staring at her. Transfixed, she stared back. Betsy, who had imagined this scene so many times before it became reality, felt a deep calm take hold of her mind and body.

One of the Indians held something in his hand, half-hidden behind his back. The light was not strong enough to see exactly what it was. As abruptly as they had begun, the Indians had stopped looking at Betsy. They just lost interest in her, and turned their six black eyes on Ash, who was sound asleep with his back against the tree and his chin on his chest. The light was growing brighter, but because it was behind the Indians, Betsy could not see them very well. She became aware of movement elsewhere in the camp. Out of the corner of her eye she saw that Fanny was awake and sitting up. Rose was still asleep beside her with her

flaxen hair half in and half out of the cloak in which she had wrapped herself.

Fanny did not see the Indians. Betsy did not warn her or make any sign that she herself was awake. She lay absolutely still and watched. The Indians were going to do something. They did not speak to each other or even move, but some sort of current passed among them. Betsy sensed it.

The Indian in the middle stepped forward until he was at the very edge of the high rock. He still held the long object in his hands. Stiff-armed, he held it well away from his body. Was it a bow, a spear, some other kind of Indian weapon? Would they fire arrows into the sleeping men? Betsy could not make it out; the light was still too dim. The Indian leaned forward again, peering at Ash. He seemed to be judging the distance between himself and the sleeping Englishman.

Suddenly the Indian rocked back on his heels, swung the object around his head like a sling half a dozen times, and threw it at Ash. It made a whirring sound as it passed through the air. Betsy watched its blurry flight with interest. The Indians were watching too, leaning forward and looking up at the flying object as if they wanted to memorize its every detail. It never occurred to Betsy to warn her husband or to interfere in any other way. Whatever happened was meant to happen.

The Indians paid no attention to her. Ash woke up. The black-snake the Indian had thrown at him landed on his shoulder and wrapped itself around his neck. It was at least six feet long and as big around as Ash's forearm. The blacksnake, a placid eater of rodents, is perfectly harmless. Ash did not know that. He did not see the Indians; he thought the snake must have dropped from the trees and he looked up in terror, thinking that the whole canopy of branches might be alive with them, that it might start raining snakes. How could there be just one snake in a place where wild things always came in thousands? Ash ceased to be one of the most learned men of his time and became, in an instant, the first man seeing the first snake.

He leaped to his feet, shrieking in his extraordinary voice. The Indians hopped up and down when they heard him and whooped in reply. Everyone who was still asleep woke up at once. Ash whirled about in a mad dance and fell over Oliver. The snake was still cold after the long night, so it was very sluggish in addition to being confused by being whirled around the Indian's head and thrown fifty feet through the air. It tried to get away, undulating its thick body.

Ash thought that it was trying to coil itself around his neck. He

was gripping it about midway down its body. As the serpent squirmed in its frantic effort to escape, it slipped through Ash's sweaty hands, growing ever longer, as if it had the power to slither upward on thin air. Three feet, then four feet of snake protruded from his fists. Ash stared in horror at its flat head with its eyes like yellow seeds and its flickering vermilion forked tongue.

The portion of the snake that waved in the air in front of Ash's face was now longer than Ash's arms. It could bite him whenever it wished. Ash was certain that he was going to die, but he could not let go. He ran through the dead fire, struggling with the snake. Oliver saw that Ash must have help; he knew that he, Oliver, was strong enough to control the snake, even kill it, if he could get his hands on it. He ran after Ash, shouting, and when Ash stopped in his tracks, he crashed into him. The two men and the snake fell down together in a powdery explosion of wood ashes. By now Ash was holding the snake by the last foot or so of its tail. It escaped at last and wriggled away toward the rocks.

"Kill it!" Ash cried. "Kill it!"

He scrambled toward Oliver's pistols, lying a few feet away. But the snake disappeared into a fissure in the rocks.

On top of the rock, the three Indians danced up and down, laughing uproariously and slapping each other loudly on the bare skin.

Hawkes had come back. He was laughing too.

"Nipmucks," he said, looking up at the giggling Indians. "Silly bastards. But they sure woke Ash up in a hurry."

Now Oliver saw the point and began to laugh. He looked at Ash to share the joke, but Ash was still breathing hard and staring wildly at the crack in the ledge into which the blacksnake had fled. Dusted with ashes, he was grayer than ever.

# 12

The most intense sexual memories often involve uncompleted acts. So it was with Edward Ash when he recalled his moments with Fanny in the cabin of the *Pamela*. His mind insisted on reliving this scene. It had stored every detail: the violent trembling

of Fanny's limbs, the lips cracked by fever, the eyes brightened by it, the heavy damp hair, the water running out of the twisted cloth over the little golden breasts with their dark foreign areolas, the parted knees, the odor of vinegar. After the bath, Fanny stood up again, too innocent to understand shame, and lifted her arms over her head, but this time . . .

He had prayed in order to overcome his sexual obsession for Fanny, but praying to be freed of the haunting image of her feverish body lying in the bath aboard the *Pamela* only made the image form again, even more vividly, in his mind, so that his flesh overcame his spirit even as he prayed to be vouchsafed the opposite effect. As he walked westward through the great wood, Ash repeated, in time with his footsteps, the same silent phrase over and over again: *Turn from that girl your lustful thoughts. . . . Turn from that girl your lustful eyes. . . .*

This was, of course, a form of prayer, though by now Ash had otherwise ceased praying altogether. His voice had not been heard in the night at the Williamses'; it was not heard in the forest. What had been difficult for him aboard ship became impossible as soon as he set foot in America, as though crossing the water had separated him from the man he had been in England, creating a new, diminished version of himself.

He did not doubt that this new Ash was destined to be tested in some unexpected way in the wilderness, and that his passion for Fanny was part of the test. Accordingly, Ash accepted his new status as a mute, as he had accepted his old powerful gift for prayer, as an example of God's work. By these baffling signs the Lord must be instructing him to leave off praying for a while and occupy his mind with other interests. That is what Ash's reason told him. But he knew very well that he was putting his immortal soul in hazard by continuing to prefer the memory of a girl's body to the image of Christ. That the two were very much alike did not occur to him.

Ash reverted to the remedies of adolescence. He took cold baths, he exercised, he talked about football with Oliver and discussed witchcraft with Rose. In his struggle with his own lust for Fanny, he was blind to Rose's passion for him. There was something soothing about Rose's stupidity; her clumsy questions exasperated him, and when he was exasperated he could think of nothing else, not even sex. Rose mistook his exasperation for interest, so he avoided her as much as possible. Nevertheless she would find him and he would hear her voice behind him.

"What does God say about magic?"

Sometimes, while he was quoting the inventory of the black arts

from Deuteronomy ("There shalt not be found among you anyone that maketh his son or his daughter to pass through the fire, or that useth divination, or an observer of the times, or an enchanter, or a witch, or a charmer, or a consulter with familiar spirits, or a wizard, or a necromancer") or explaining how evil existed by God's design in order to strengthen the good, Fanny would appear with her dark hair rippling around her slender form, and Ash's eyes would snap away from Rose's spellbound face.

At such moments, he would talk all the louder for a moment in an unconscious effort to drown out his thoughts as an agonized look came over his face, and then he would stop speaking and turn away. Rose thought that he was affected, as Oliver and so many other men had been, by her own beauty. Afterward, Ash would be silent and withdrawn, marching along through the filtered light with a stern, composed expression that made him look, Rose thought, more like a Roman than ever.

Ash did not suffer all the time. He found moments of peace—usually in the form of a religious idea. Ash was, of course, exceptionally susceptible to such ideas. Even his passion for Fanny was a religious idea: self-denial. In the Nipmuck Indians, Ash found an unexpected opportunity for philosophical speculation. Almost from his first moments in America, he was deeply interested in Indians. He had not expected this to happen; savages had never before played any part in the life of his mind. He regarded them as falling somewhere below the Jews and the Mohammedans in the order of beings that existed between Christians and the animals. Those who did not know Christ, and know Him truly, as He was portrayed in the Scriptures, were of little interest to Ash. Yet on the mountain in Galilee, Jesus had said to His disciples, "Go ye therefore, and teach all nations, baptizing them."

Were the Indians a nation, and if they were, was that somehow the reason for Ash's painful journey to America? Did it explain the temptation that had drawn him here? Was it possible that his lust for Fanny was a sign from heaven that some great work—even the conversion of the savages—awaited him here? Was this torment of the body the means by which God wished him to understand His will, by overcoming it?

Lebbaeus Williams, who was fond of quoting the Boston divine Cotton Mather, who was an in-law of the Williamses', had told Ash that Mather believed that the great epidemic that ravaged the Indians a year or two before the Pilgrims arrived had been a sign of God's plan to prune the wilderness of inferior growth in order to make room for a hardier one—the English Christians who were then getting ready to sail for New England.

What epidemic? asked Ash. What were the victims' symptoms? Williams had not known the details.

Now, in the forest, the three Nipmucks who had tossed the blacksnake at Ash stood near the fire, chewing bacon. Ash had quickly forgiven them, and then made friends with them by chirping them close, as if they were strange dogs, and rewarding them with bits of food when they approached. He discovered that they loved fat and salt, and every night now they turned up by the campfire to be fed. By day they drifted among the trees, just within sight of the English, keeping pace without actually making contact.

Ash asked Gustavus Hawkes what he knew about the epidemic.

"The Indians say that whole villages died along the coast," he told Ash. "It wasn't as bad with freshwater Indians like the Nipmucks. They lost maybe one in ten."

"What were the symptoms?"

Hawkes talked to the Nipmucks, partly in their throaty language, partly in signs, and they replied in the same way. Ash could not make out their meaning, but it appeared to be perfectly understandable to Hawkes.

"They say the sick ones had fever," Hawkes said. "Then they turned yellow just before they died."

"Turned yellow? It must have been a disease that produced jaundice. Had they ever seen these symptoms before?"

"No. They say that the English gave it to them so they would all die and then we could cut down the trees and take them back to England."

"But there were no English here then."

"Yes, there were—white people anyway. There were fishermen on the coast a hundred years ago. They've been seeing ships for a long time."

While Ash and Hawkes talked, the Nipmucks masticated rapidly and swallowed convulsively. They asked for more bacon, imitating Ash's chirping noises.

"Why do they do that?" Ash asked.

"They always imitate the way things sound."

"You mean they think it's a language?"

"Indians don't think," Hawkes replied. "But they can sound like they're talking English when they want to, just like they can sound like a crow or a duck. They get all the sounds right, there just aren't any words."

The Indians were very interested in Ash, too, because of his gray skin and hair and his voice. They had thought that he must be a ghost.

"That's why they threw the snake at you," Hawkes said. "Everybody's afraid of snakes, but the dead ain't afraid of nothing."

"They wanted to find out if I was dead?" Ash said.

"That's right. What made them laugh was that you was scared of a blacksnake. Everybody knows it can't hurt you."

"But I didn't know the snake was harmless," Ash said. "Tell them that."

"They wouldn't understand," Hawkes said. "They think everybody is born knowing that blacksnakes ain't poisonous. Indians don't know a hell of a lot, but they all know the same things."

"You mean they have no concept of ignorance?"

Hawkes did not understand Ash's question. He often had trouble knowing what this man meant.

But Ash was excited by a new thought. Was it possible that the Indians were in a state of innocence? Of course they sinned. But was sin really possible in the absence of belief? As nearly as Ash could make out, the Indians had no sense of doing wrong even when they committed murder, and no guilt afterward. He asked Hawkes about this.

"Guilt?" Hawkes said. "They think everything's funny. If they could have flung a rattlesnake at you and watched it bite you they would have had an even bigger laugh."

"But that would have been murder."

"The way they look at it, the snake would've killed you, not them, and even the snake couldn't help it. It's a *snake,* so you have to expect it to bite."

Hawkes's taciturnity disappeared when the subject was Indians. He had stores of information about them and could tell them apart by tribe and even by the many subtribes into which they were divided. The Nipmucks who threw the blacksnake at Ash, for example, were Hassamaniscos from one of the easternmost of the Nipmuck settlements. Magpie, the slave girl who had come to London with John Pennock, was a Quabaug Nipmuck and came from a village farther west.

"How many Indians are there?" Ash asked.

"Nobody ever counted 'em," Hawkes replied. "But I'd say twenty, thirty thousand in the Bay Colony. They's maybe four or five thousand Narragansets and Wampanoags down east of Boston, and quite a few Mohegans south of where we are now. The Pawtuckets and Massachusetts live up north, Nipmucks around here, Pocumtucks along the river, Mahicans in the mountains to the west, couple of thousand each."

According to Hawkes, it was the Indians who had created the open forest with its columns of light and its leafy naves along the

oaks and chestnuts. Every spring they set the ground afire. The flames consumed the leaves that had fallen the previous autumn, killed seedlings that would not have survived in any case, and fertilized the damp soil so that grass and other browse prospered. The low fire, creeping among the roots of the big hardwoods, was not large enough to harm the trees. These burnings, combined with natural forest fires caused by lightning, kept the woods healthy and huntable.

"They's always plenty for the deer to eat," Hawkes explained, "and no small trees to stop an arrow when an Indian wants to shoot a deer—or shoot another Indian, or you or me."

The Nipmucks stayed with them for three days and nights. It wasn't only the bacon and Ash's appearance that kept them. They were intrigued by one of the horses, and would walk along beside it, sometimes pressing their ears to its jouncing load. The horse carried Fanny's spinet, and each time it took a step the instrument, muffled in quilts and blankets, emitted a twanging accidental chord. Ash noticed that the Nipmucks tried to be near the spinet and guessed the reason. He and Oliver unpacked it, fitted the legs back onto it, and set it up on a level slab of rock among the trees. Hawkes's dogs sniffed at it, wagging their tails.

Playing reminded Fanny of her father, but it was easier to play than to explain her reasons for not doing so. She played the scales. The spinet was out of tune as a result of its journey, but Fanny went on. Instead of playing Henry's songs, she chose hymns—two new ones she had learned by listening to the music at Rose's wedding, "Hear my prayer" and "O Lord, rebuke me not," to which nobody present knew the words. Then she struck up Henry Purcell's old Anglican favorite, "My song shall be alway," and everyone sang, voices drifting away among the tree trunks until the Nipmucks, who knew all the sounds if not their meaning, joined in with Ash on the bass coloratura and made the air ring. Every note was flat; every verse was gibberish. Ash was filled with Christian delight. "Miraculous!" he cried during a rest between verses. Oliver's right eye closed in a slow wink and he twisted his eyebrows. Fanny looked away and bit her lips. The memory of her father, which had made her weep the night before, was now making her laugh.

As Hawkes later explained, the Nipmucks came from a praying village, one of many Indian encampments in Massachusetts that had been converted to Christianity. Surely, Ash thought, God had rescued Fanny's spinet from Henry Harding's wrecked house, brought it safely across the ocean, and caused it to be played in this desolate place in order to remind them all that He was every-

where. Even Fanny, who until now had seemed to have no heart for religion, was so deeply moved that she rose from the keyboard and ran off alone into the forest. She wore a pale dress and a white ribbon in her hair, so that she was visible for a long time in the moonlight, swaying as she ran over the mossy ground.

Ash made himself look away. When he did, he found himself examining the Nipmucks' faces. Now that the music had stopped, their features were once again as blank as those of Hawkes's dogs, which were also gathered round the spinet. Were these Indians truly saved? Ash's doubts came back in a rush, and he thought that it was far likelier that the Nipmucks simply enjoyed music than that they understood the idea of Christian salvation. These were men who believed that the dead feared nothing and threw snakes on sleeping Englishmen to test the theory. How could they be saved if they did not understand that real fear, the fear of hell, began with death?

Fanny returned. She carried the white ribbon in her hand and her hair was loose like a bride's. Rose asked her to play again; Oliver, speaking for her, said she was too tired. The English people were all looking at Fanny. Only the Nipmucks watched Ash, and when they saw the look of longing on his face they burst into explosive chuckles and spanked one another rhythmically on the bare skin, as they had done on the first morning while watching him struggle with the snake.

# 13

Alamoth looked almost exactly as Captain John Pennock had described it—the big wooden house, scorched by fire, that Hawkes called the Manor, the cottages on the hillside, the homely English animals in the common paddocks, the young orchards heavy with English fruit, the fields of brown stubble in the oxbows beside the river. It was late afternoon when Fanny and the others first glimpsed the settlement from the top of the ridge. They were looking west. Rain was coming. In the dull light, the river, low and sluggish, was the color of tin. Across the broad valley, beyond the river, thun-

derheads were forming. Chain lightning flickered inside them. After several minutes they heard faint claps of thunder.

Lightning probed the ground beneath the clouds as the storm moved eastward.

A bolt of lightning hit a big green tree and set it on fire. Fanny could see the flames, burning furiously in a driving rain. Like so much else in America, this defied every law of nature she had ever been taught.

This country looked like England—but like England in a dream. Nothing was as it should be. Everything was too large, too sudden, too violent—the birds, the strawberries, the forest, this storm the size of London, filled with lightning that set the trees on fire. Walking through the American wilderness was like walking across a giant's body in a nursery tale. When would the monster feel their footsteps on his hide and stuff them into his mouth?

The storm was much closer now. The thunder was deafening even at a distance of two or three miles. Alamoth, which had been lying in mellow sunlight ten minutes before, was now engulfed in shadow. Sheets of rain approached the river behind a wind that twisted the trees and sent leaves and twigs swirling through the air. The horses nickered and backed away.

"We'd best get out from under this tree," Hawkes said.

They were standing beneath a dead trunk thirty feet high, the lightning-blasted remains of one of the gigantic yellow pines that Pennock had called firs. The bole, stripped of its bark, was five feet thick at the base.

Oliver seized Fanny's arm.

"Fanny, look!" he said. "It's a mast for the greatest ship ever built!"

There was hope in his eyes again—perhaps there *was* some way to fell this monster and carry it to England.

"We'll *float* it across the ocean," Oliver said.

Hawkes led them back into the woods through a worsening darkness. They could hear the wind coming, but the place where they were was calm. The forest had been changing as they approached the river. The Nipmucks had left them the day before; when the party reached an outcropping of gray schist that was layered like a pastry, the Indians just stopped in their tracks and stood where they were, watching until the English disappeared.

"Pocumtuck country begins here," Hawkes had explained.

After this, the chestnuts and oaks were fewer. They began to see groves of birches and maples, and there were many more conifers, dark stands of hemlock and smaller pines as well as the big firs, and a great many ferns and low bushes. These uplands were as full of

berries as the grasslands had been—black and red raspberries growing on breast-high bushes among the hardwood trees, and a round dusty-blue berry, about the size of a gooseberry but unknown in England, that grew in stands of hundreds of bushes. It had a very sweet taste.

There was an uproar of birdsong in expectation of the rain. Suddenly the wind began to blow, howling through the treetops and causing the blueberry bushes to twist on their roots. This made a loud swishing noise. The horses shied, eyes rolling, and Rose and the men had to whip them to get them to move through the bushes. In a moment, the animals were jogging forward along an invisible path among the blueberries, gobbling and kicking as they went. Big isolated drops of rain fell out of the sky. Fanny's spinet twanged as it thumped against the horse's back.

Beyond the blueberry field, Hawkes led them under the shelter of a large flat rock that jutted out of a steep hillside. There was room enough beneath it for ten or twelve people to stand up. The men tied the horses to trees and pulled their loads under the shelter of the rock. As the first big raindrops pelted the horses, they laid back their ears and crowded together. Hawkes's dogs ran to the back of the shelter and lay down together, muzzles on paws, eyes shut.

Then the storm broke in earnest. Rain poured off the edge of the rock, spurting two or three feet straight out and then splattering on the brown forest dirt to form a brook. Lightning blinked among the rain-blackened trunks, thunder crashed overhead, the air smelled like burned copper. Fanny drew a deep breath. This was wonderful. The storm at Rose's wedding had been nothing compared to this.

Fanny felt herself being pulled backward, deeper under the rock. Rose had her arms around her.

"Oh, please, Fanny," she cried. "Come away from the harm."

Fanny resisted. Rose kept on tugging, a look of supplication on her face.

"Oh, Lord," Rose said. "What a fearful place! We must hold each other!"

Fanny let herself be drawn back into the dimness. The storm was directly overhead now. A dozen brilliant flashes of lightning lit up the cave and Rose's hair turned gold in the sulfurous light. She trembled and whimpered, grinding her skull into the soft flesh of Fanny's chest. Fanny shifted her body, trying to draw away. Rose pushed against her harder.

Fanny turned her head away. She thought that she had glimpsed something in the shadows deeper in the shelter. She looked again

and saw nothing. Still, she felt that something was present. On the night they had gone looking for the ghost aboard the *Pamela,* Henry had taught her to see in the dark by looking to the left and right of an object that seemed to be invisible.

Fanny tried the trick again. It wasn't really dark beneath the rock, just dim and confused because of the storm. Looking slightly to the right of what she thought she had seen, she now saw it clearly. A girl stood, absolutely still, against the rock wall. Even the dogs had not noticed her.

She was tall and very thin, with sharp bones outlined under the scratchy wool of a long butternut dress that was much too large for her. Her red curly hair, growing in a mop, was confined by a beaded headband. Beneath the headband, two long green eyes looked steadily at Fanny with a complete absence of fear. The eyes made no inquiries; the girl seemed to know exactly who Fanny and the others were. Her face was covered with freckles. When the lightning flashed, her skin looked so pale that it was faintly blue. A wooden bucket filled to the rim with blueberries stood on the ground beside her.

The air was very cool now and drenched with the smell of mud and vegetation. Rain misted into the shelter. Rose muttered a complaint. Fanny covered her hair with her shawl and said, "Ssssh." Instinct told Fanny that the red-haired girl did not want to be seen. If Rose opened her eyes she would certainly see her, no matter how still she stood. Fanny pulled up the shawl until it covered Rose's whole head. The other girl watched, and Fanny had the feeling, without any need for words, that she understood what Fanny was doing, and why.

The girl was Thoughtful Pennock. Fanny was so sure of this that she nearly whispered her name.

Fanny was sure that this would be a mistake. So, hiding Rose's face against her breast, she looked away from her and watched the rain beating down on the horses, which stood with their legs splayed and their noses between their front hooves.

# 14

When the storm was over, Rose insisted on having her sidesaddle strapped onto one of the horses so that she could appear before the people of Alamoth on horseback the first time they saw her.

While this was being done, Rose retired into the woods and changed into one of her London riding habits.

"You should be mounted too, husband, and properly dressed," Rose said to Oliver as he tried to force the bit through the teeth of a bay gelding.

"I've walked this far," Oliver said. "I'll walk the rest of the way."

"Very well. But it makes the wrong picture."

Rose, who always seemed to lose half her weight when she got on a horse, put her foot in Oliver's hand and sprang nimbly into the saddle.

Riding beautifully, Rose Barebones emerged from the forest and proceeded at a walk down the muddy slope above Alamoth, her pleated skirt hanging in a perfect arc from her upraised right knee to the stirrup that contained her left boot. The storm had knocked many apples off the trees, and by the time Fanny and the others reached the orchard, most of the women and female children were crawling through the wet grass, picking up the fruit and putting it into baskets. The apples were about two-thirds the size of English apples, the first living things Fanny had seen in America that were smaller than the home version. The women and girls, all dressed alike in butternut homespun dresses and bonnets that hid their hair, stood up in their sopping skirts and stared as Rose and the others passed by. Then they hoisted their baskets of apples and chased after the newcomers.

A hearty young woman with big jouncing breasts fell into step with Fanny. She gripped one handle of a basket, dragging along a little girl by the other handle. For several paces she walked along backward, staring into Fanny's face. All the while, the woman and the child kept up a running conversation in a language or dialect Fanny could not identify.

Then the woman began to speak to Fanny in a loud voice, grinning amiably while she looked her up and down. Fanny couldn't understand a word. The woman would ask what seemed to be a question, wait for an answer, then ask it again in an even louder shout. After each burst of speech, she and the little girl exchanged looks filled with fun and country cunning.

"I'm very sorry," Fanny said, "but I don't understand what you say."

The woman put her face close to Fanny's and raised her voice again, shouting nonsense in which an occasional English syllable could be detected. The little girl giggled shrilly. Fanny thought the woman might be a simpleton or harmlessly mad. There had been a crazed female beggar in London who had done well at her trade by cornering people in the Strand and shrieking at them until they gave her money.

Ash saw Fanny's difficulty and hurried forward. By now the woman was red in the face and the child was in a fit of giggling. Tears ran down her cheeks. Ash gave her a hard pinch on the arm and she stopped. His walloping voice sobered the young woman, and she began to explain something to him.

"You understand her?" Fanny said.

"So can you, if you listen," Ash replied. "It's only north-country speech."

Fanny had no trouble understanding the young woman now. Then, suddenly she became shy, as if she spoke Fanny's language too badly to be understood, and would only answer Fanny's questions through Ash.

"Why was she shouting at me?" Fanny asked.

"Why were you shouting at this young lady?" Ash interpreted.

"We always yell like that the first time at strangers," the young woman said, holding a muddy hand over the mouth of the child, who had started to giggle again. "It makes us laugh."

"Ah," said Ash, smiling fondly. "It's the village joke." He turned to the woman. "Do you do this to your neighbors too—shout at them in that ghastly burr?" The other towns in the valley had mostly been settled by people from East Anglia, Sussex, and Kent.

"When they come. But they don't."

The young woman's name was Hepzibah Clum. The child was called Totsie, and she was Hepzibah's sister, not her daughter.

"Why 'Totsie'?" Ash asked.

"Because Dadda gave her tots and she got drunk on cider when she was just walking."

Ash was amused, laughing, a new condition in Fanny's experi-

ence of him. He liked country people. As a young undergraduate, the summer before he had taken holy orders, he had walked through Yorkshire all the way to the Scottish border, getting lost on the moors and preaching from stiles to little bunches of yokels. He had preached a sermon in Latin from Hadrian's Wall to a couple of shepherds who congratulated him afterward: "Finest English we've ever heard, sir." Ash thought the joke was on the shepherds until he'd walked along thinking for a couple of miles.

Now, as they sauntered into Alamoth, Ash asked Hepzibah Clum question after question. Yes, that was the same pillory where the Abenakis had set fire to Captain Pennock. . . . Yes, that was Pink Brook that had run red with English blood. . . . The church was new, but look—they nailed some of the charred clapboards back on when they rebuilt is as a reminder of the day the Lord took His vengeance. Hepzibah answered Ash's questions about the Indian attack in monosyllables, eyes downcast.

Nothing in Alamoth was painted. All the houses were made of overlapped whipsawed hemlock boards nailed to rock-maple beams. The ages of the houses and sheds could be told by their color. New structures were as white as fat in a butcher shop. Then, year by year, the clapboards grew darker until they became silvery gray when they were old. There were few such gray buildings in Alamoth—the tavern, which the Abenakis had spared, two walls of the Manor, a few cottages and barns, the rail fences around the common.

The working day was coming to an end. People and animals were all mixed up together inside and out. Inside cottage doors, girls were milking red Devon cows and smelling the milk to see if it was sour after the thunderstorm. Chickens perched in the window-sills. Pigs rooted and rolled in the wallows left by the rain. Alamoth seemed to be a very industrious place. Smiths, carpenters, masons, coopers, tanners, and half a dozen other trades worked busily in shops along the single street. A breeze came off the river and a tavern sign squeaked overhead.

Rose rode through the scene with her head in the air. The village women shuffled their feet and picked up the corners of their aprons and the men took off their hats as she passed.

The Manor, Captain John Pennock's house, placed in such a way that it was visible from every point in the village, stood on a knoll in a grove of ancient trees. It was a plain rectangular building with chimneys at either end, seven upstairs windows on the long side of the rectangle, and a doorway that was somewhat too tall for its width, like a gravestone. The lintel was carved like a grave-stone, with cherubs holding an orb on which, as the Manor's new

residents already knew, John Pennock's Cromwellian motto had been chiseled.

"That there's the Manor," Hepzibah Clum said in a solemn voice. "Captain Pennock died there all alone. We could hear him yelling all night long, giving orders to soldiers. Nobody's seen inside since then except Magpie and her nigger, before she sold him."

Hepzibah's eyes were round with reverence. Rose overheard her words.

"We do not call it that," she said to Hepzibah.

"Don't call it the Manor?" Hepzibah said. "What do your ladyship call it, then?"

Rose had not decided what to call the house now that it was hers; she had decided to rename it just the moment before. Hepzibah, jogging along beside the horse, breasts bouncing, clearly expected an answer. Rose rode on in silence, her eyes fixed on the Manor. A kind of washed light suffused the landscape after the rain so that it looked like a painting of itself. In Rose's eye, the Manor was a mellower color than the other buildings. Perhaps, she thought, it had been made of rarer woods.

Rose had been prepared to be disappointed by her new house. How could it be anything at all if it was in America? But she was not disappointed. The Manor was not Whitehall Palace, or even Lockwood Hall, but it was five times as large as any other building in Alamoth, and at least double the size of any house in Boston. And Rose, who had been made to have babies she didn't want, Rose, who had been forbidden to light candles in Lockwood Hall, Rose, who had been made to stay upstairs in her tiny bedchamber except when Sir Cecil wanted to show her off like an Arabian mare to people like Oliver Barebones—Rose was mistress of this house.

"Not 'the Manor,' " she said to Hepzibah. "*Rose* Manor. That is the name by which my husband wishes the house to be called from now on."

Magpie awaited them at the gates. Rose had expected her to be dressed as an Indian, but she wore ordinary clothes.

"Ah," Rose said. "The Indian slave. Is is true that you sold your husband in the Indies?"

Magpie was silent.

"No reply?" Rose said. "Very well. We have a long time before us."

She gazed down haughtily on the stunted Indian girl. Magpie walked ahead of them as they passed down the avenue of trees that led to the Manor. She unlocked the double door with a large key, lifted the latch, and threw the doors wide open. Magpie was not as

Oliver had described her or as Fanny remembered her. She had been a memorably bright and comical child, but now she was withdrawn and unsmiling. Oliver supposed that she must be in her twenties by now, but she did not look like a young woman. She had a hen's torso and spindly legs and arms, like an old woman who had always drunk too much.

Oliver wanted to talk to her, to tell her who he was and ask her if she remembered Fanny, but he was interrupted by a shriek from Rose.

"Husband!" she cried.

# 15

The Manor was full of cats. The poisonous stink of their droppings, stronger than that of any other animal, spilled through the door. Rose yanked on the bit and her horse neighed and backed rapidly away, then wheeled and galloped up the street, scattering pigs and dogs and splashing mud on Hepzibah Clum and the others who had followed Rose home.

Holding the plunging horse, Rose pointed her whip at Oliver. "Cats!" she cried, her voice breaking with anger and accusation. "I won't have cats!"

Oliver followed Magpie inside the Manor. Cats scampered away in every direction, paws thumping softly on the bare wooden floors.

Magpie watched them calmly.

"Captain Pennock said someday we'd need the cats," she said. "He said someday there will be rats, they'll come over on ships with the people because there is one rat for every person. It was not natural, he said, that there weren't any rats in America."

"Captain Pennock said that?" Oliver replied, glad of the chance to speak to Magpie alone. "Do you know who I am?"

Magpie looked into his face. "You are the same."

"Not you."

The smell of excrement and urine was overpowering. Oliver had never experienced anything like it.

"Your mistress will faint if she smells this," he said. "Open all the windows."

Oliver opened the first one himself and stuck his head out to get some fresh air. He could hear the windows being put up all over the downstairs, and then the patter of dozens of paws as Magpie went upstairs. Cats poured down the staircase but stopped when they saw Oliver and gathered into a furry mass before they scampered back up the stairs.

Oliver had always liked cats. He tried to count the ones he could see, or at least estimate their numbers, but there were far too many of them. A dozen or so leaped out the open windows.

"Well done," Oliver said to Magpie. "Now chase out the rest."

Magpie looked around at the multitude of cats. "How?" she asked.

Oliver looked out the window. Rose was still seated on her horse at the other end of the village. Even at a distance of a hundred yards or so, Oliver could see how angry the cats had made her by spoiling her arrival at the Manor. Even Rose would never get rid of them all. Oliver grinned, imagining the war to come between Rose and John Pennock's cats.

"I don't care how you do it," Oliver said. "Go find someone to help you."

Magpie left. Oliver, staying near the window for the sake of the fresh air, watched her as she trotted down the sloping Manor path toward Rose and the crowd that had gathered around her. Rose was talking very rapidly, spitting words downward from the back of her horse at Gustavus Hawkes, who stood at her stirrup with his musket cradled in his arms. As Hawkes listened, a smile broke over his face. His movements became brisk. He slapped Rose's horse on the rump as though he were giving Rose herself a companionable swat on the backside, and strode toward the house, whistling up his dogs. The big placid wolf dogs and the small noisy ones frisked around him.

What happened next took Oliver by surprise, and it happened so quickly and produced such a racket that he could not have interfered even if he had wished to do so. Hawkes led the dogs straight into the Manor. They paused and whimpered when they smelled the ammonia and digested meat of cat droppings. Hawkes made several loud kissing noises. The dogs looked up at him with loving eyes.

"Cats," Hawkes said. "Cats! *Sssssic 'em!*"

The dogs burst into motion, knocking over chairs and tables as they coursed through the house.

The few cats left downstairs shot yowling out the windows, as if

(Oliver thought) they had been kicked through a set of goalposts. It brought back vivid memories of the white cat going through Henry's window at the wedding feast, and Oliver laughed out loud, thinking, as he often did, how Henry would have enjoyed this scene. The dogs, barking hysterically, galloped up the staircase; the sound of their toenails skidding over the board floors came through the ceiling. So did the padded scurrying whisper of dozens of cats' feet. Cats poured down the stairs and out the open windows.

Pennock had built the Manor in a grove of ancient white oaks. The trunks of these huge trees were some distance from the house, but their branches were themselves as big around as ordinary trees, and extended twenty or thirty feet outward from the trunks. As the dogs chased them through the upstairs, the cats began to leap out the upper-story windows into the trees. From outdoors, where Fanny and most of the village were standing, it was a dreamlike sight. The house seemed to be sneezing cats. They would fill up a windowsill, black ones with white faces and boots, striped yellow ones, and tabbies, every one of them descended from Pennock's original three cats. Then all would spray outward like globules of fur, and float downward toward the leafy sanctuary of the oaks. Most landed in the trees, but some fell out, clawing frantically, and others missed altogether. The ones who hit the ground mostly ran straight back into the Manor, to be chased out again by the dogs. But the rest stayed in the trees, stalking with arched backs up and down the branches and yowling at the wolf dogs, whose good-natured tufted faces and lolling red tongues appeared every now and then in a window frame.

Rose, seated on her plunging horse, watched this scene in fascination. Why hadn't the Gypsy crone foreseen this plague of cats? How could any fortune-teller not predict such an event? Rose had already all but stopped believing in the bear that was supposed to control her fate.

Her anger subsided. She realized that the cats had made it impossible for anyone in Alamoth ever to forget the day she arrived. If gossip traveled in America at the same speed as in England, they'd know about this in Boston next week. Rose had driven out the cats. She could never have done it, she knew, without Edward Ash, who had explained so much to her about God's purposes. That was why she had known what Hawkes and his dogs were really for.

Never in her life had she felt so calm or so powerful; she thought that anyone in America, except Ash, of course, would do whatever she told him to do. She kicked her horse into motion and rode toward the house. Hepzibah Clum stood next to Fanny, looking

upward openmouthed at the cats in the oak trees. Rose knew that she would need servants to clean up the manor.

"You," Rose said, poking Hepzibah with the green switch she was using as a riding whip. "What's your name?"

Hepzibah told her.

"I've never heard that name. I need you and two more like you. Find them and bring them back here."

Rose caught Fanny's eye and gave her a long look, rolling her own eyes upward at the cats. She mouthed a silent word: "*Witches.*" Then she started shouting at Oliver to close the windows so that the cats could not get back inside.

When Rose dismounted at last, the villagers hung back, gazing at her. They had, Rose knew, never imagined that such a person as herself existed. She handed the reins of her horse to a young boy, as if he had been born to serve as her groom, and strode into the Manor, shutting the door behind her. Hawkes's dogs had killed a certain number of cats. Rose regarded the shredded remains with satisfaction.

Only a few kittens remained alive, hidden in nests in the attic and cellar. The dogs sniffed them out and Hawkes gathered them up, dropping them into a porous sack. When the sack was full, he left with his dogs frisking around him.

Twilight was falling. The cats were beginning to climb down out of the trees. Fanny did not want to go inside; she had already heard too much noise. She walked away by herself beyond the end of the village. Halfway up a steep hill behind the Manor, she found the source of the brook that ran through Alamoth, a spring gushing out of a wall of rock.

She drank and washed her face and hands and wished for a bath, then followed the brook down toward the village. It grew larger as it descended, with knee-deep pools of clear water lying under grassy banks. Fanny paused by one of these, behind a screen of willows, and thought again about a bath. Her body was sore in its creases for having gone unwashed for such a long time.

Fanny heard cats mewing. The sound was loud, yet not loud. She had never heard anything like it. She listened intently, trying to discover where it was coming from.

Making no noise at all, Thoughtful Pennock stepped out from behind the willows. She lifted her skirt and tied it around her waist. She wore no petticoats and her legs were bare. She waded into the pool and pointed downward. The mewing was coming out of the water. Hawkes's gunnysack was full of kittens, swimming up into pockets of air and crying as they drowned.

"Help me," Thoughtful said in French. "He's filled the sack with rocks."

Fanny waded into the pool and the two girls dragged the heavy sack onto the bank and opened the neck. Many of the kittens were dead, but some were still living. Thoughtful picked up one of the little animals. Its fur was soaked and it shivered in her hand. She put it inside the bosom of her dress to warm it.

"*Pauvres petits*," Fanny said.

Thoughtful peered into Fanny's face. "*Tu parles français?*" she said. "Good. Now I can find out who all you people are."

# 16

" 'Thoughtful,' " Thoughtful said. "What name is that in French?"

"Pensive," Fanny replied.

"Pensive? That's not a name, it's an adjective."

"In English it's a proper name."

"Is it normal for the English to give a child an adjective for a name? Are there Jolies and Petits and Rouges?"

"Not yet," Fanny said. "Thoughtful is a name used by the Puritans. They often name their children for the virtues."

"Puritan? You mean Protestant?"

"The most Protestant of all Protestants."

"*Oh la-la!*" Thoughtful crossed herself. "What next?"

"What do you want to know?"

"Your story. Who are your people, where do you come from? Who are the ones who came with you?"

"Nobody told you?"

"Magpie told me in signs, but she's afraid of you. She thinks you'll find out she can sew and take her back to London and sell her. That's why my dresses don't fit me. They belonged to Strong Woman."

"Belonged to whom?"

"The Englishwoman who was my mother before I was an Abenaki."

"Hope Barebones, the wife of Captain John Pennock. She *was* your mother."

"I know. It's in my story. I am as tall as she was, but she was stronger. Magpie won't make the dresses smaller because then you'd know she can sew. Now tell me *all* the names."

Fanny told her about John Pennock's will, about Magpie's visit to London, about London, about her father and mother, about Oliver and Rose. Thoughtful listened politely.

"Is that all?" she said. "There must be more names. What are the names of the rest of the family—all of them? What are they famous for?"

"They're all famous for their names. Your maternal great-grandfather was called If-Christ-had-not-died-thou-hadst-been-damned Barebones. You have a first cousin once removed called Praise God Adkins."

"More Protestants. What are you? Fanny isn't a French name."

'I was taught by a Jesuit. My real name is Genevieve."

"A Jesuit? Really? The Ursulines taught me. I'll still call you Fanny." Thoughtful pronounced it Fan-*ny*.

"What are you called?"

"My saint's name is Catherine," Thoughtful said, "but to my people I am Arosen Aongotee, which means Squirrel who became an Abenaki, daughter of Thorakweneken, Two Suns, and of his wife, Tewatewiseree, Thin Ice, who love me well," Thoughtful said. "All the Abenakis love me well, and would sooner part with their hearts than part with me. Also, I am sister to the red squirrel who was the first to tell that I am the daughter of Two Sons."

Thoughtful had a surprisingly deep voice, almost a baritone, and she recited these words in a throaty singsong.

"That's how my story begins," she said. "It sounds quite nice when you sing it in Abenaki, but less so in French because there are no echoes in French words."

Thoughtful told Fanny these things in the matter-of-fact tones of one who is recounting facts that are obvious and well-known. The two girls sat facing each other among the willows with the crickets singing all around them. Thoughtful had the pleased but faintly mystified eyes of someone who has just awakened from a long sleep. She had pulled her skirt up through her belt before wading into the brook for the kittens and now she wound one bare shin around the other, gripping her feet and rocking slightly in rhythm with her speech. As she had said, the dress she wore was much too large for her, and her slight, agile frame was not so much clothed as veiled by it; she moved around inside the cloth like a mouse in a glove. Her freckles and her wild red hair gave her a vitality that made Fanny want to smile at everything she said and did.

"I think we are sisters," Thoughtful said. "My family knows

these things, as you will see when I tell you about my father, Two Suns. Now I will tell you my story."

The first thing any two Abenakis did on meeting for the first time, Thoughtful explained, was to tell each other the names of all their ancestors back to the creation of the tribe; then they recounted the events of their own lives. This ritual made it possible for every Abenaki to know exactly where every other Abenaki fitted into the history and genealogy of the tribe—an important matter for a people that was divided up into scores of independent villages and bands scattered over hundreds of square miles of forest in Maine and southern Quebec.

"I'll leave out all the names of Two Suns's and Thin Ice's ancestors and everything they did," Thoughtful said. "It takes a long time to tell about them all."

Although Thoughtful had only recently learned her English name and those of her parents, she had always known who she was. The Abenakis realized—Thoughtful did not know how, they simply knew—that the leader of the English they had massacred at Alamoth was her natural father. They called him Takesinontee, Flying Leg, because of his dance in the fire by the pillory. Her mother was called Strong Woman because she had nearly killed an Abenaki warrior with her bare hands. Thoughtful's life story was the very first thing she had learned in the Abenaki language, and she had heard the story told, and had told it herself, hundreds of times.

"I come into it," Thoughtful said, "when the ducks tell Two Suns about me. This happened in the summer that Two Suns helped kill the drunken bear and was bitten by the big ghosts that came as dogs."

Although he was not asleep, Two Suns was dreaming about ducks landing on Lake Champlain when the French came to his village on the Saint Francis River and asked for men to go down the Connecticut with them to fight the English. Two Suns tried to go on dreaming because the ducks were trying to tell him something— birds often talked to Two Suns in his dreams, though other animals seldom did—but he had to stop in order to listen to the French. He liked the French; everybody liked the French, who never lied to the Abenakis or cheated them.

Ordinarily the Abenakis were glad enough to raid the English. But on this occasion they weren't sure they wanted to go. After they had talked and thought for a day or so, they looked at each other and told the French *jaghte oghte*, maybe not, which is the strongest negative in the Abenaki language.

It was July. The fish were asleep in the rivers, the deer's antlers

were in velvet, the ducks had not come back, the berries had not yet come onto the bushes.

The Abenakis said: Summer is the wrong time of year for war.

The French said they knew this. But they had learned that a new English village had been built on the Connecticut River above Deerfield, and they had decided to send a scouting party led by a French officer to spy it out, kill some of the English, slaughter all their animals, and burn their crops. The French would give each Abenaki who went one knife, one hatchet, one horn of gunpowder and fifty lead balls, one pound of salt, one small pig, and one rosary. This was much more than usual. In addition, each Abenaki could bring one English captive back to the village with him; any extra captives would be offered to the English for ransom by the governor of New France, and the money would be evenly divided between the Abenakis and the governor's treasury.

That night, the ducks in Two Suns's dream told him that he had better go with the French; the ducks had been talking to some squirrels in an oak forest along the Connecticut River, and they had told about a female child that had red hair like a squirrel. The child already knew Two Suns by name; her own name was Squirrel.

Two Suns told his wife, Thin Ice, about the dream. "I think this Squirrel must be our lost daughter," Thin Ice said.

Two Suns and Thin Ice had had two sons, named Hair and Talks in His Dreams, and they loved them both, but they had never had a daughter. Each time she was pregnant, Thin Ice thought that the girl was coming, but it was always a boy instead. Their daughter was lost somewhere. Now, thanks to the ducks, they knew where she had been.

"You'd better go with the French and bring her home," Thin Ice said. "If she's very nice, steal another girl to give to the Ursulines." Thin Ice thought that the ducks might not deserve all the credit for locating Squirrel; she had been praying for a daughter with the Ursulines for many years.

"We've already told the French maybe not," Two Suns said. "It's hard to change after that."

"The others will change if you tell them what the ducks told you about our daughter."

When the Abenakis sent a runner to the French to tell them they had changed their minds, the French were surprised. Always before, the Abenakis had meant "never" when they said maybe not. But the French asked no questions; that was another thing the Abenakis liked about them. They realized that the Abenakis understood certain things that a Frenchman could not understand.

The war party consisted of twenty Abenakis armed with bows

and muskets, one Jesuit priest, and one very young French officer.
The journey south, a distance of nearly three hundred miles, took
sixteen days, traveling at night by canoe and portaging the long
distances between the Saint Francis and the Connecticut Lakes,
where the rivers begin to run south to Long Island Sound instead
of north to the Saint Lawrence River. The Abenakis caught some
pickerel and bass in the lakes and ate them, but while traveling the
party lived on parched corn and water and some dried beans and
dried salmon they found in an Indian barn near the junction of the
Connecticut and the Ompompanoosuc rivers in central Vermont.

"Indian barns?" Fanny said.

Thoughtful blinked, surprised by the other girl's bad manners.

"All Indians dig holes and line them with stone and hide corn
and beans in them for the winter," Thoughtful said. "But that's
not part of the story. Ask questions afterward."

The Abenakis made up a song about how angry the Cowasucks,
the tribe to whom the barn belonged, were going to be when they
found it had been looted. They sang it while they paddled to show
their contempt for the Cowasucks:

The Abenakis stole our beans and fish.
    What bird told them where we buried food?
We'll kill that bird and break its eggs.
    Cowasucks are not afraid of birds, ho-ho.

The Abenakis warned the young French officer and the Jesuit
that there was a big falls a few miles north of Alamoth and
recommended leaving the canoes and walking the rest of the way.
The officer, who had never before been down the Connecticut,
decided to scout the falls at night in a canoe. No Abenaki would go
with him, so he went alone. His canoe overturned in the rapids
above the falls and he hit his head on a rock. Two Suns and
another Abenaki found his body below the falls in the morning and
stood it up and punched it in the stomach and bent it over to make
it spit out the water it had swallowed, but it would not wake up
even after they held it over a fire to warm it up.

The Jesuit arrived at this point and administered the last rites of
the church. A young man called Bear, who was very strong,
carried the dead Frenchman piggyback up onto the ridge and into
a grove of stately pines. Two Suns climbed up into the branches
and tied the body tightly to the trunk with rawhide thongs, so that
the bones would not fall down after the porcupines and the birds
and insects had eaten the flesh. The drowned Frenchman wore a
beautiful silver cross around his neck.

Because Two Suns had tried to make the dead man breathe again, and had then tied his body to the pine, the Jesuit gave him his blue coat and three-cornered hat. Two Suns put these things on and began to dream about his daughter as he walked along. A sentinel crow, sitting on top of a tree that had been blasted by lightning, told Two Suns that he was going to be bitten by a big dog that hated Frenchmen, so he took off the coat and hat and hid them under some rocks. The Abenakis were only hours away from Alamoth now. They continued south, traveling in the forest along the ridgeline. It was blackberry time in Massachusetts—the seasons came earlier this far south—and they stopped to eat from time to time.

In a grassy meadow the Abenakis saw a drunken black bear staggering about, swatting the air and uttering loud growls. The berries on which the animal had gorged itself in preparation for its winter hibernation had fermented into alcohol in its slow-working digestive track. The Indians were too close to Alamoth to risk shooting it with their muskets, so they followed the bear, which did not notice them. The bear kept falling down as it crashed through the woods until finally it came to a spring. There it fell down again and drank thirstily.

While it was drinking, Two Suns fired an arrow into its side. The bear roared, swatted idly at the arrow, and went on drinking. Nobody had ever seen such a thirsty bear. It could not stop drinking even to die. The Abenakis surrounded it and killed it with the French knives that fitted onto the barrels of their muskets.

They butchered the bear in the shelter under the hanging rock, eating the liver raw and cooking the flesh and packing the surplus fat into the bear's intestines, along with the sugary half-digested blackberries they found in its stomach, as provisions for the journey back to Canada. Because they had eaten the entire bear, except for the skin and bones and the fat they had saved, the Abenakis had to sleep for a day and a night in order to digest their meal before attacking Alamoth. During this time, Two Suns had his dream about the ducks again.

They decided to slip down the hillside in the dark and attack at first light. While waiting for night to fall, they crept to the edge of the forest and examined the peaceful scene below—the fields full of ripening corn and wheat, the cattle and sheep with deer grazing tamely among them, the town itself, dozing inside its palisade of sharpened posts.

Two Suns and all the other Abenakis were devout Catholics. On the night before the attack, the Jesuit heard their confessions, served Communion, and gave them absolution. Then, after rub-

bing bear grease on their bodies and painting their faces, they slithered over the lip of the ridge, calling to each other in the voices of whippoorwills and frogs and owls, and descended through the meadows on the sleeping Protestants. The Jesuit, dressed in black robes and carrying a cross on a staff instead of a musket or spear, went with them. On their way the Abenakis hamstrung every cow they encountered; the animals just sat down with a grunt of puzzlement when their legs were cut from under them, and then fell over in the dark and lay still and quiet, as if they believed themselves dead.

In Alamoth itself, the Abenakis achieved complete surprise. The Abenaki account of the battle that killed Thoughtful's brother and mother was remarkably like the report of Captain John Pennock, except that it contained details that only the Indians could have known. The Indians had brought several springy birch saplings with them, each about ten feet long. Two Suns balanced himself on one of these while his sons Hair and Talks in His Dreams lifted him shoulder-high, flexed the sapling, and tossed him over the twelve-foot-high stockade.

Two Suns landed on his feet with a loud grunt and found himself face-to-face with an English sentry. The man stood frozen in his tracks. He did not seem to see the Indian, and as this was clearly impossible, Two Suns whooped, "Thank you, ducks, thank you, crow," and darted around behind his enemy. The Englishman still did not move but kept looking straight ahead as if nothing had happened. Two Suns severed his spinal cord with a tomahawk blow at the base of the neck and he fell in a heap, even dumber than the hamstrung cows.

Half the population was outside doing morning chores and the rest were just rising. Hair and Talks in His Dreams crept up on two chattering girls as they milked cows. The Abenakis reached under the cows, snatched the milk pails from between the girls' knees, and then popped their heads above the cows' backs. The girls shrieked when they saw the paint and feathers, so Hair and Talks in His Dreams hit them lightly on the head and dragged them outside to look at them while they drank the milk. Hair's girl had bigger breasts than Talks in His Dreams's, but the other girl was pregnant, a stroke of good luck. Hair and Talks in His Dreams tied up the girls and streaked their faces with paint to show whom they belonged to, and set the barn on fire. Then they ran toward the fight in the center of the village.

By now John Pennock's troops had fallen out and were marching across the common all in a row, holding their muskets across their chests. A boy was beating a drum. Pennock was mounted on a big

wild-eyed horse. The Abenakis, all drawn up into a knot, watched transfixed. They had never seen men fight like this, but the Jesuit had. He ran out onto the common and shouted to the Indians to scatter out of musket range and then come at the soldiers from all sides after they fired. At that instant, Pennock gave the order to fire. The crashing volley startled the Abenakis and killed the Jesuit, who stood directly in front of the troops with his cross held out before him, and wounded three or four English people who happened to be in the line of fire.

Two Suns ran to within ten feet of John Pennock, who was kicking his horse into a gallop while whirling a saber around his head, and fired at him with the French officer's musket. The shot went wide, as musket shots often did, so Two Suns fell to the ground and thrust the barrel of his musket between the legs of Pennock's horse as it galloped by. The horse tore the musket from Two Suns's grasp, nearly dislocating his wrists and elbows. The horse somersaulted, falling on top of Pennock. Hair and the big man called Bear jumped on Pennock, meaning to capture him, but the old man hit Hair in the face with the pommel of his saber, scrambled to his feet, and sliced off Bear's left ear. Bear got down on his knees and looked for his missing ear while three or four other Abenakis captured Pennock. He never found it.

After that, Bear was called Used to be Bear. Obviously he was not the same person if he had lost one of his parts, and that was why he was looking for his ear. If he had found it, he could have worn it in a bag around his neck and would still have been called Bear.

Even though he was very old and had just been rolled on by a horse, John Pennock put up a terrific fight. Besides breaking Hair's nose and cutting off Bear's ear, he killed one Abenaki by kneeling on his back, grasping his chin with both hands, and jerking his head backward until the neck broke. He drew blood from two others, also with his bare hands, before Two Suns darted in and cracked him on the head with a war club made from a stone with a hole in it that he had found a long time ago inside a curious circle of rocks when he had gone looking for mussels by the sea. It was then, after Two Suns had knocked the old man unconscious, that he and the other Abenakis locked Pennock in the pillory and lit the fire under him as a compliment to his bravery and strength.

The fire woke up Pennock almost immediately. His clothes caught fire. Two Suns ripped away the burning cloth with the tip of a spear so that the old man would not die too quickly. Pennock was already dancing, arms and legs jerking, hair afire.

The English were trying to fight, but everyone on both sides

knew that the battle was over as soon as Pennock was subdued. It was a curiously silent fight after the first few minutes. Everybody ran out of breath almost immediately. On both sides, the muskets were useless after the first shot was fired—and even that rarely hit anything—so everybody fought with clubs and knives and axes. Two Suns enjoyed the noise and smoke made by the weapon, but like John Pennock, he used a blade when he really wanted to kill something.

The Abenakis were already attempting to find the captives they had selected or to locate valuable ones, like pretty girls or strong boys, that had been overlooked. Hair, his nose running blood, and Talks in His Dreams seized their milkmaids and were dragging them out of harm's way. The girls, misunderstanding, shrieked and struggled; English boys and men tried to save them and were tomahawked or knifed or speared.

Several houses were afire. Flames climbed up the steeple of the church while the bell rang inside it. Two Suns was still watching Pennock in deep admiration of his courage. Only a powerful man who had killed many enemies could be so angry while he died.

Clouds of swallows, driven out of the burning church, soared through the smoke. They were all scolding the Abenakis, and Two Suns was quite sure that one of the swallows was trying to tell him that Pennock was the natural father of Two Suns's lost daughter, the redheaded girl, Squirrel. That made him very glad.

His mood was broken by a piercing scream. A young woman was running toward him, shrieking in uncontrollable rage. Two Suns wanted to get out of her way because she was clearly mad, but then he saw that three huge dogs bounded beside her. Two Suns recognized them as the dogs the crow had warned him about. He hardly had time to think about that before he noticed that the woman was carrying a red-haired child in her arms.

That must be my daughter Squirrel, he thought happily. But then he saw that the child was a little boy. By now the dogs were on him. One of them knocked him down and bit him on the leg. Two others attempted to seize him by his shoulders and neck, but their teeth skidded on the heavy bear grease he had rubbed onto his skin. He hit the dog that was biting him on the head with his war club and it let go and gave him a look of befuddled surprise.

Two Suns jumped to his feet, snatched the child from the woman's arms, swung it by the legs, and smashed its head against a tree. Then he threw it high into the air and watched it fly end over end like a hatchet. Ordinarily Two Suns would not have done this. He had never liked to kill children, but in this case he reasoned that the dogs would run after the child with the idea of fetching it

back to its mother. He was right. The wolf dogs bounded along under the dead child until the moment it fell into the flames, and then stood with their heads at one side and their ears pricked, watching the little body cook. They did not make a sound. By now Two Suns was sure that these were not dogs, but ghosts.

At this moment, Hope Pennock, howling while strings of saliva flew from her mouth, knocked Two Suns to the ground and leaped onto his back. He thought that she might break his neck in the way Pennock had killed the other Abenaki. In fact, Hope nearly choked Two Suns to death before the bear grease saved him again and he managed to twist from her grasp and split her skull with his hatchet. She was the strongest woman the Abenakis had ever put into a story.

Squirrel was invisible to Two Suns until he had killed her mother, but the instant that happened, he saw the little red-haired girl standing calmly in the middle of the fight. Even though she was standing up with her eyes open, she seemed to be asleep. Two Suns picked her up, carrying her over his arm with her head in the crook of his elbow so that her little skull would come to no harm. He looked down into her face and asked if she wanted to wake up. Because she was asleep, she did not answer. "That's all right, daughter," Two Suns said. "Sleep. I'll make you a papoose frame as soon as we find some saplings and you can sleep while we run away."

After Two Suns killed Strong Woman and found Squirrel, the Abenakis decided that it was time to go, even though the old man, Flying Leg, had not stopped dancing in the fire. It would have been more polite to stay until he died, but the Indians thought that the English at Deerfield and Hatfield must by now have noticed the smoke from the burning town, so they tied the captured girls and the bigger children together with a rope looped around their waists and drove them up the hill.

They took the Jesuit's corpse and the bodies of the three slain Abenakis with them. Gustavus Hawkes, the oldest and strongest of the male captives, was detailed to carry the dead Jesuit. It took four warriors to hold Gustavus while Two Suns, who was the expert in these matters, tied the body to his back. The boy was terrified by the corpse, and Two Suns had to beat him to make him carry it. This was no easy matter, with the priest's legs wrapped around Gustavus' waist, the arms tied around his shoulders, and the bald head, eyes wide open, lolling on his shoulder. Three other big boys, brothers to Hepzibah Clum, carried the dead Abenakis.

The Indians expected to be pursued by a strong force of English. As soon as they were deep enough into the woods, they found a

stand of pines and hauled the bodies high into four separate trees.
Then they split up into three or four small groups, each Indian
keeping the captive he had claimed for himself; some had taken
more than one prisoner, reasoning that some were bound to die on
the journey.

There were five Indians and six captives in Two Suns's party.
Two Suns had claimed Thoughtful and a girl of thirteen as his
prizes; the other English were Gustavus Hawkes, who was still
trembling in disgust over the dead Jesuit, and the Clums. Two
Suns hit the boys on the fleshy parts of their bodies with his war
club a few times to frighten them and make them weaker. He
wasn't sure that he could win a fight with them, especially the big
one, because his wounds, especially the bite from the ghost dog,
were very painful.

Also, he did not want to die because he had finally found his
daughter and wanted Thin Ice to have the pleasure of seeing her.
Two Suns strapped Squirrel into a papoose frame made from a
green sapling and hung her on the older girl's back. So as to leave
no tracks or scent in case they were followed by dogs, the Abenakis
traveled in the brooks, splashing through the shallow water at a
dogtrot.

Birds spoke to Two Suns from the poplars and willows along the
bank. He asked them if they saw the ghost dogs coming. They
didn't answer, but then he heard a crow cawing about a mile away,
followed by the scolding of some blackbirds, and he led the party
into the woods to hide.

Before they could find a place to conceal themselves, however,
the wolf dogs attacked. In their absolute silence, they just materi-
alized in the middle of the Indians, knocking two men to the
ground.

Two Suns seized Thoughtful in her papoose board and climbed a
tree. Two other Abenakis did the same, tugging the Clum boys after
them by their ropes, but the dogs had the other two Abenakis
before they could move. The three dogs killed one Abenaki, and
by the time Two Suns stopped climbing and looked down into a
shower of blood, they were in the act of killing the other, a man
named Yellow Rain. One of the dogs held Yellow Rain's head
between his jaws like a ball.

Two Suns had never seen animals as strong and quick as these.
Of course he did not believe they were from this world, so he didn't
try to kill them with arrows. He began to sing his story, in case the
dogs killed him too. It would not have surprised him if they had
seized the tree he sat in in their jaws and uprooted it. But then
Two Suns saw that Gustavus Hawkes was running away through

the forest, calling to the dogs to follow him, and they bounded after him and disappeared.

The journey continued. The Abenakis and their captives dog-trotted, never stopping to rest, from morning to night. The smallest of the Clums fell in a brook and broke his ankle. The Abenakis killed him with a tomahawk because he would not be able to travel farther.

Squirrel was still asleep. At night, Two Suns gave her and the older girl and the surviving Clums a mouthful of nocake, a gob of bear grease on the end of his finger, and a long drink of water from whatever brook they were following. Then he hung Thoughtful up in her papoose board in a tree. The Clums were tied, lying down, to trees by their wrists and ankles. The girl slept with her hands tied in front of her, attached by a thong to Two Suns's left wrist. These details were an important part of the story because they told the listener that the Abenakis were observing the proper decorum in regard to captives.

Because Two Suns and the other Abenakis were very tired after the battle and two of them were slightly wounded, they slept very soundly at night. On the twelfth night, when the party was deep in a hemlock forest in the Green Mountains, the Clum brothers escaped. There was no time to stop, so the Abenakis made no attempt to find the boys, who were never seen again by anybody. The Abenakis and the two girls pressed on to the north, and after twenty-six days of hard travel, arrived in the village on the Saint Francis River.

Thin Ice loved her daughter Squirrel, especially when she saw that the ducks had been right about her red hair. This was something the Abenakis had never seen before. They realized after the first novelty of it that red hair was ugly. They had never seen freckles either, and tried to wash them off. Finally Thin Ice cut Squirrel's curly hair short on one side and long on the other in the Indian style, and that made her somewhat more beautiful.

Squirrel did not wake up until the snow was on the ground and the river froze. She ate in her sleep. Thin Ice and Two Suns and the whole family talked to her as if she were awake, telling her their stories and her story, which was naturally short as she was only three years old. When Squirrel did wake up, she spoke Abenaki in a deep voice, like Flying Leg, only softer. Nobody was surprised by this: what other language would she speak, how else would she sound?

Her skin was so pale that the Abenakis could see the light inside her, and that was the name, Light Inside, they gave her for the use

of her husband when she got one. All Abenakis had several names, some of which only the person himself knew.

Squirrel never grew more beautiful. Thin Ice did not think she would ever grow breasts, but outward beauty was not important in Squirrel; it was the light inside that made the Abenakis say that they would sooner part with their hearts than part with her.

Two Suns gave the girl who had carried his daughter to Canada on her back to the Ursuline nuns at Three Rivers. They were very glad to get her, and later on the mother superior asked if Squirrel could come to the convent in the winter to learn to read and write and speak French.

"We wonder," Two Suns said. "Squirrel was lost for many years, and we only found her two years ago, so we haven't remembered her entire story."

"She must learn the story of Our Father and the Savior and the Blessed Virgin," the superior said.

"We've already told her those stories in Abenaki. You don't have to talk to the Blessed Virgin in French."

"No. But it's the only way to talk to the French, and it would be a good thing to have a daughter who understands them perfectly."

Two Suns himself only understood one French word in every ten or twelve, and this had led to trouble; the French sometimes did stupid things, such as paddling into a rapids at night and drowning themselves, if they did not understand what you were saying to them.

"Very well," Two Suns said, "but if the English come to buy back their children, remember that this girl is not English. She is my daughter Squirrel, an Abenaki who got lost and was born from the wrong woman."

"We will be very careful with her, Two Suns," the nuns said. "We know your story."

"And when you came back to Alamoth with Hawkes," Fanny said, "did you recognize everything?"

"I remembered the things that were described in my story," Thoughtful replied. "The hanging rock where Two Suns ate the bear, the dead pine where the crow talked to him. But this is not my place."

"It would have been if the Indians hadn't carried you away. You do know that Alamoth and all the land around it belonged to your English father."

"Magpie told me that. But these people are very strange."

"Then why did you come back?"

Thoughtful looked at her in puzzlement. "Hawkes stole me. I

went for water with Thin Ice and the dogs killed her. Then he tied my hands and carried me here. I would not walk."

"The Abenakis didn't follow?"

"How could they? They don't know how to kill the dogs."

"Then you'll stay here forever."

Thoughtful stood up in her voluminous Puritan dress and looked to the north. She held a kitten against her cheek.

"Maybe not," she said.

# 17

Almost as soon as he laid eyes on Thoughtful Pennock, Oliver realized that her father's will had been a mistake. This strange girl who had the manners of an Indian and the voice of an old man was John Pennock's natural daughter, for whom he had searched the Indian villages until he died. Nobody, least of all Oliver, could possibly believe that the old soldier would have willed his possessions to a nephew by marriage if he had known that his own kidnapped child was alive.

Yet it seemed that Pennock may have known all about Thoughtful. She herself knew that Pennock had been looking for her. He had even come to Two Suns's village on the Saint Francis River, and she had seen him there.

"He came to the actual village where you were being held captive and did not find you?" Oliver said. "How can that be?"

Fanny translated. As was her way, Thoughtful answered what she regarded as a lie embedded in the question rather than the question itself.

"Captive?" Thoughtful said to Fanny. "Nobody ever wants to go back to the English, doesn't he know that?"

"No. That's not what he wants to know. How did it happen that your father didn't find you if he came to your village?"

"He did find me. But he did not see his daughter."

"How do you mean, Thoughtful?"

"He looked at me, standing as close to me as Oliver is now, but naturally he saw an Abenaki, not an English girl."

Oliver listened to Fanny's interpretation of these words. "Pennock

didn't notice an Indian with red hair and freckles?" he said. "Very mysterious."

"Not to Thoughtful's way of thinking," Fanny said.

"Magpie was there," Thoughtful said. "She saw me too."

Oliver waited a day or two before questioning Magpie about this episode. To divert any suspicion Rose may have had about his purposes—he had not told his wife that he was thinking about renouncing his inheritance—Oliver asked Magpie to guide him to the big firs that Captain John Pennock had mentioned in his will.

He and Magpie set off at dawn, walking up the river with Oliver's land, meadows and forest and mountains, lying all around them as far as the eye could see. It took the better part of the morning to arrive at the grove of firs. Not even the monumental oaks of the eastern forest had prepared Oliver for the reality of these trees, which were not European firs, as Pennock had thought, but North American white pines. None of the hundreds of pines was less than one hundred feet high. Some individuals, rising 250 feet into the sky, had trunks that six people holding hands could not have encircled.

After walking through the fragrant grove for half an hour or so, gazing upward at his magnificent, useless trees, Oliver sat down gratefully beneath one of them and pulled the corks out of the two-spouted pottery canteen filled with ale that he had brought along for his midday thirst. Magpie had brought a small chicken for his lunch. She tore it apart and fed it to him piece by piece. Oliver kept offering to share, but after he was finished, Magpie ate nocake instead, sitting in profile to him and gazing out over the valley at the blue hills beyond the river.

Magpie thought that Oliver would go to sleep when he finished, but instead, he took her hand and squeezed it. No Englishman had ever touched her before and she wondered, unlikely as it seemed, if he wanted to get on top of her before he took his nap. She knew that his wife did not lie with him, a circumstance that made Rose even more baffling, because all the other English people Magpie had ever known could think of nothing but copulation and drinking and talking.

But Oliver only wanted to ask questions. "Magpie," he said. "I want to talk to you about Captain Pennock and Thoughtful."

This came as no surprise. Thoughtful had told Magpie in signs what Oliver wanted to talk to her about. She was not eager to discuss these matters. Looking at his broad face, Magpie saw what a good-hearted man Oliver was. She gazed out over the valley in silence, wondering what to do. Oliver seemed to understand. He squeezed her hand again.

"Just tell me all about how you and the captain looked for Thoughtful all those years," he said. "We've got all day."

So Magpie told him, in her flat droning English, about every village she had visited with Pennock—Pocumtuck, Cowasuck, Penacook, and finally, when the war with the French was over for a little while, Abenaki and French. In Quebec, the governor himself had received Captain Pennock and had him to dinner, with Magpie sitting between him and the governor as the governor's wife smiled at her while listening to Pennock. The French kept lists of all the English captives, but there was no record of a three-year-old girl having been brought back from the raid on Alamoth.

"Of the twenty persons captured," said the governor, "fourteen died on the march and never reached Quebec. It was a very difficult campaign."

"It's terrible, the war," the governor's wife said. "My niece was captured by the Mohawks, ferocious savages sent against us by the English, and though she was an innocent girl, she was violated many times. God mercifully arranged that she should have no memory of these events."

"He is often merciful in such matters," Pennock said. "I should like to visit the Abenaki villages, if that is possible."

"It is possible, Captain, but on the basis of the facts, it will almost certainly prove to be futile."

"Nevertheless I must go. I have been searching for my daughter every since she was taken."

"Then naturally you must continue," said the governor. "Surprises are always possible. I will send an officer from my staff to assist you."

Pennock had already encountered surprises. He had brought a thousand pieces of eight with him with which to ransom the English captives from Alamoth. Of the six who had survived, five had refused to return to New England. The sixth was an Ursuline nun who was forbidden to talk to men and who was, in any case, too old to be Thoughtful.

All the captives had turned papist. Most had forgotten how to speak English; few remembered their own families, and none remembered Pennock when he appeared before them. They might all have suffered from some infectious disease that had destroyed their Englishness and left them with the illusion that they were Indians. More likely it was something other than a disease. There was Jesuit in every village, and Pennock naturally suspected that they had worked some sort of religious spell on the English children, having got them young. The youthful ensign from Saint-Malo who was escorting Pennock made a French joke of it, quoting an

English clergyman who had said, after his own children had re-
fused to return with him, that it would be easier to persuade
Frenchmen and Indians to go south with him than to redeem his
own people.

*"C'est fort aguichante, la joie des autres,"* he said—the joy of
others is mighty seductive.

In Two Suns's village, Pennock encountered the milkmaid,
Hepzibah Clum's older sister, who had been captured by Talks in
His Dreams. She was the only one who remembered who she had
been in her previous life.

When Pennock found her in Two Suns's village, she was grind-
ing corn on a stone with the children of Talks in His Dreams' other
wives all around her, and she looked to be seven or eight months
pregnant. She had come from a family in which all the girls were
pretty, and she had been the prettiest of all the Clum sisters. She
was still comely, but she was so much an Indian now, in dress and
manner and vacant mind, that you hardly noticed the color of her
hair and skin.

"Well, yes," she said in a resigned tone of voice when Pennock
asked her about religion. "I became a Catholic when I married.
The Abenakis believe in it, you see, and what would the children
have thought? 'They'll never obey a woman who's going to hell,'
Talks in His Dreams said, and I couldn't argue with that."

"What about their immortal souls?" Pennock asked. "What
about your own?"

"One doesn't hear quite so much about that here," the young
woman replied.

"You are content to live among these savages?"

The young woman dropped her eyes. "They have their own
ways," she said.

"But surely you must miss your own people?"

She looked up at him with a slow countrywoman's grin. "I do
wish they'd stolen my sister Hepzibah too," she said. "We always
had good times together."

Two Suns greeted Pennock outside his lodge and offered him
food. Pennock, who had visited dozens of Indian villages, knew
that he must eat when asked to do so, so he sank onto the ground
beside the old Indian with a groan. The women brought them corn
cakes and bits of meat. Like most Indian food, it tasted of singed
fur and was hard to chew.

After they had eaten, Two Suns lighted a long clay pipe, puffing
energetically until the burning tobacco glowed in the bowl, and
handed it to Pennock. The two old men finished the pipe, passing
it back and forth, before Two Suns spoke. He told quite a long

anecdote in Abenaki, pausing now and then when he came to one of the good parts to laugh in a sharp barking way.

The French ensign pursed his lips before interpreting.

"Two Suns says he remembers you very well and wonders if you remember him. To refresh your memory, he tells you that he is the man who tripped up your horse with his musket during the fight at Alamoth. It was he, also, who locked your neck in the pillory and burned you in the fire. He is delighted to see you. You are the bravest and the most famous enemy he has ever had. He also speaks well of your wife."

"I remember him," Pennock said. "Ask him if he knows anything about my daughter."

The Frenchman asked Two Suns this question. Two Suns replied at great length, but without the laughter. A row of women and girls stood behind Two Suns, listening intently to what he was saying. Occasionally they grunted in unison or uttered a peculiar high-pitched series of yips. There were ten or twelve of these females, all standing in full view of John Pennock. When Two Suns finished, the ensign turned back to Pennock.

"Two Suns says that the only girl of that age he knows about is his own daughter, who was lost among the English for a while but is now an Abenaki again. Her name is Squirrel. That is her, standing next to his wife, Thin Ice—the fat woman who fed you the porcupine meat."

Pennock, squinting, looked at the girl. Two Suns watched him, then asked a question.

The ensign translated. "He wants to know your daughter's name."

"Thoughtful," Pennock replied, looking at Two Suns again, but not at the girl. "Is his daughter a Catholic?"

"Oh, yes, like the others. He told me a lot about her. She was educated by the Ursulines."

"She's a nun?"

"No, she's too young. Besides, her mother needs her to help with the work."

"Is his daughter as happy as all the rest of the Abenakis?"

The Frenchman talked to Two Suns and interpreted his reply.

"Happier, he says, because she is with her real mother. He wants to know if the big dogs that killed Yellow Rain are still at Alamoth."

"Yes," Pennock replied. "It's the only place you will find them, besides Ireland."

In the pine grove, Magpie stopped talking.

"Magpie, this is very important," Oliver said. "Was Thoughtful there that day?"

"Captain Pennock did not see her."

"Did you see her?"

Magpie was silent for several moments. Oliver, who was not usually alert to the sounds of nature, heard the wind murmuring in the pines and the calls of the many kinds of birds that lived in the big trees.

"Captain Pennock always told me that he would give me Coffee if we found his daughter," Magpie said at last. "When he died, he gave me Coffee."

# 18

Magpie's account of John Pennock's visit to the Abenaki village did nothing to change Oliver's mind about Thoughtful's right to inherit her father's estate.

"The old man made a mistake," he told Rose. "Maybe it was a mistake of the heart, but it was a mistake."

His obstinacy was like a great weight lying on Rose's chest and pressing the air from her lungs.

"Mistake of the heart, mistake of the heart, that's all you know how to say," Rose said, barely able to breathe as she talked. "How do we even know she's who she says she is?"

"She's never said," Oliver replied. "We're the ones who say that she's Thoughtful Pennock, and we're right. Just look at that picture."

An oil portrait of eighteen-year-old John Pennock hung in the hall. Wearing a breastplate and a steel helmet called a lobster-tail burgonet, he looked straight at the painter, his wiry red hair escaping from the helmet to form a fringe around his face. Thoughtful looked like his female twin—the unruly curls, the candid eyes, the skeletal forehead and cheekbones, the captured light beneath the freckled skin.

"Suppose she *is* John Pennock's daughter," Rose said. "If so, he saw what she was in that Indian village."

"Oh? What was she?"

"A papist for one thing, a savage Indian for another. The two things Captain Pennock hated most in this world."

"But we do know that he found her."

"Then why didn't he bring her home, if he'd spent so much time looking for her? He didn't want what belonged to his family to fall into the hands of an idolatrous savage, that's why."

Oliver's face broke into a benign smile. "Then he did his daughter a very great wrong. I must write to Lebbaeus Williams and see what is to be done about it."

Rose could not believe her ears. "Write to Lebbaeus Williams?" she cried. "See what is to be done about it? Nothing is to be done! That girl has no right to anything under the law. Williams has already said so."

Rose gestured violently and her face flushed a deep red. Oliver had never seen her so alive. He gave her an easy smile and spoke to her in a tone of exaggerated reasonableness. "So he did. But that was before he was in full possession of the facts."

"Don't use that tone of voice," Rose said, "as though I'm the one who's mad. It's you that wants to give away ten thousand acres to a girl who can't speak a word of English, who says the rosary in front of everyone as if she couldn't be hanged for it, who doesn't even wear petticoats. Williams'll have you locked up for a lunatic."

"Better mad than greedy," Oliver said, calm as before. "After all, dear wife, we were all right before we had all this."

"All right?" Rose cried. "You think we were *all right?* Alfred Montagu almost pulled our house down around our ears and drove us out of England as paupers."

"Hardly paupers. We still have the *Pamela*—and the whole wide world."

"The whole wide world? The *Pamela?* We'll never see the *Pamela* again—your dago is gone forever and your ship and your lobsters are gone with him."

"Peters may be a dago, but he's honester than any Englishman I ever knew except Henry Harding. You're wrong about him, just as you are wrong about John Pennock's will."

Rose stared into his face but saw no glimmer of good sense.

"You can't be serious," she said at last. "You wouldn't give away everything, not the whole ten thousand acres, not the Manor, the fir trees. . . ."

"Of course I'm serious, dear wife," Oliver replied. "Never more so."

Oliver was happy. A burden had been lifted from him. He took off his wig and twirled it on his finger and gave Rose a broad slow wink. Then he went into the library and began to write his letter to Lebbaeus Williams. It was a long letter; Rose's bedchamber was directly above the library—they were the two biggest rooms in the

Manor—and she heard his quill scratching on the paper long after she went to bed.

Although she came from a well-known Buckinghamshire family, Rose had been poor nearly all her life. She remembered feasts and dolls from her very early childhood, but after that she had always been slightly hungry and slightly ashamed; her beauty made people look at her, and when they did, they saw how cheap and wrong her clothes were. At Lockwood Hall, Rose had lived on table scraps after Robert was killed; Sir Cecil had even denied her her own candle so that she had to find her way through the dark to a dreary room under the eaves that no member of the family had ever slept in before. When Sir Cecil had thrown her into marriage with Oliver, Rose had expected that her life would become even worse than it always had been, and when Montagu appeared, she knew that she had been right. Except for her victory in bed over Oliver, she had been powerless all her life.

Now, miraculously, Rose was mistress of the handsomest house in the Massachusetts Bay Colony. For the first time, she had something to lose, and the situation was absolutely clear: Thoughtful Pennock had the power to take it away from her.

The prospect was unbearable. Like an old penniless aunt who inherits the possessions of a family in which everyone else unexpectedly dies before her, Rose was passionately attached to every single item in the Manor—jewels, silver, pewter, porcelain, swords, armor, guns, the portraits of the bony Pennock ancestors, the English bedsteads, commodes, clothes presses, glass-front bookcases, chests, tables and chairs, musical instruments, all gleaming with varnish and wax.

Though it was built of wood and groaned when the wind blew, the Manor was the only house Rose had yet seen in America that could be called an English house; everyone else, no matter how rich, lived all tumbled together in a medieval lack of privacy, with nothing good to eat and nothing beautiful to look at.

"Is Rose Manor not beautiful?" she said to Ash.

"It is plain and simple like its builder," Ash replied.

In her heart, Rose knew that this was true by English standards. But there was no real Englishmen here in the wilderness to see the facts of the situation and make a point of them. As Rose understood from bitter experience, the whole idea of being on top in England was to have more of everything than your neighbors— land, money, influence, haughty children, glittering friends, servants, horses, works of art, beautiful women—so as to be able to

impress your inferiors by making a show of possessions that they could never hope to match.

Rose certainly owned more of everything than anyone else for hundreds of miles around, and in the time that she had been at Alamoth, her manner had changed so dramatically that she had undergone a physical transformation. Always before she had slumped a little in her discontent, but now she held herself gracefully erect. The sullen expression she had worn in Lockwood Hall, where she had been a ragged bride and then a widow living on charity, and in Catherine Street, where she had been an unwilling wife, was replaced by a look of perpetual amusement—not quite a smile, but an aristocratic twinkle of superiority, as if nothing could ruffle the happiness that was her natural right.

She applied the lessons in posture and deportment that had been drummed into her all her life: bend from the hips, not from the waist; stand with the back arched so as to lift the bosom and the buttocks; let the left arm hang loose and lift the right arm languidly always along its whole length; walk with the foot fully arched; open the eyes wide and part the mouth slightly a long moment before forming the first word of a reply. Rose spoke and moved more deliberately, especially when she went for her daily ride through the village. The velvets and silks that Oliver had bought her in the first days of their marriage were too rich to be made into dresses in a place where there was no society and no possibility of one, so she had them sewn into riding habits that would have been considered daring even in Versailles. Here they were so astonishing that the villagers looked up at the sky or down at the ground when Rose approached, not knowing whether they were permitted to gaze at such a display of uncovered neck and bosom.

On the other hand, everyone greeted Thoughtful like a princess returned from exile. The village girls took her by the hand and walked along beside her, older women gathered around her in groups of three or four to stare at her while they told each other stories about her when she was a baby. Old husbands brought her gifts of fruit in the evening when they came home from the orchards and told her what a great man her father had been. It was maddening. Thoughtful's birth had given her a power over these people; they did not care that she was ugly and ragged. She was the last of the Pennocks.

"You'd think she'd come back from the dead," Rose said in disgust.

"She has, as far as they're concerned," Oliver replied.

Rose spent a great deal of time alone, worrying about Thoughtful, in the big four-poster bed in the bedchamber where Captain

John Pennock had slept and died. Sometimes she would lie down in the afternoon and close the curtains. Then the bed was like a rich little room, with the cheveron dancetty and the winged griffin of the Pennock coat of arms carved into the headboard, and overhead—a peculiar scene to find in a Puritan's bed—a tapestry canopy depicting Paris in the act of judging three plump Flemish models who impersonated Hera, Athena, and Aphrodite. The look on Paris' face, wild and stupid, reminded her of the way both her husbands had looked when they saw her naked. There were two big mirrors in the room, and sometimes Rose stood between them when she was tired of thinking so as to look at herself, front and back at the same time.

Sometimes she could hear Oliver below her in the library, talking to Edward Ash about Thoughtful, or talking to Thoughtful while Fanny interpreted, or working on his letter to Lebbaeus Williams. Sound traveled upward in the wooden house, and of course Rose could hear every word that was said. Very little that she overheard was remarkable. Oliver and the others just kept going over the same ground: how Thoughtful had been captured, how she had lived, how she had been redeemed by Hawkes, what Thoughtful believed, what she deserved. The details of Thoughtful's life seemed to exercise some mysterious power over the imagination, especially Oliver's imagination. One afternoon Rose heard him talking quietly to Fanny—so quietly, in fact, that she had to get down on the floor and press her ear to the wood in order to make out the words.

"It's very odd, Fanny," Oliver was saying, "but I've come to love Thoughtful—love her as I love you, as a daughter."

"What's so odd about that?" Fanny asked. "She's a lovable girl."

"It's more than just that. She reminds me of Henry. I feel when I see her that Henry has come back."

"Do you really?"

"Yes, I do, Fanny. Look how everybody smiles at her. They can't help themselves, just as they couldn't help it with Henry. Don't you see it too? You must, to be such friends with her—the two of you are like sisters."

"Perhaps you're right."

Lying on the floor, listening to these words, Rose thought for a moment that she was truly lost. How could she combat the ghost of Oliver's only friend? She got back into the bed, drew the curtains, and lay for a long while with her eyes closed. When she opened them again, the first thing she saw was Paris and the three naked goddesses. Hardly knowing what she was doing—she certainly had

never done such a thing before—she stood up, took off her clothes, and looked at her nude body in the mirrors.

She smiled at her image because suddenly she knew what she must do. *She* had the power to make him forget about Thoughtful, even to forget about Henry Harding. She would have a child by Oliver. A child, a son, was what all men wanted. Rose did not understand this, but she knew that it was true. Her father had hated his daughters, but her mother had always said that he might have loved them if they had had a brother to tease them. Even Robert, who had seemed to have no heart at all, had talked about nothing but the sons Rose was going to give him, even before she was pregnant. After she was with child, Robert had listened at her stomach to hear the baby gurgling inside, and felt it kicking, and even talked to it, hallooing through her belly button.

She assumed that a boy would look like its father. She did not see how she could ever love a child that looked like Oliver. Perhaps it would not look like him. Perhaps it would look like Robert. He must have left something of himself behind as a result of all those penetrations.

Rose did not want to have what must happen, happen more than was necessary. She would let Oliver do as he wished once, then wait a month for a result, then give permission again if she was not yet pregnant.

Oliver had not touched her since the day Henry was killed. He had left her alone aboard the *Pamela*. Since coming to America they had slept in separate rooms. In fact, Rose did not know where exactly Oliver slept at night. When she went to bed, he was always still awake, drinking rum, or talking to Ash, or listening to Fanny play one of her instruments, or playing draughts with Hepzibah. At Rose's insistence—she said they needed twice as many servants as they had—Oliver had hired the Clum girl as a maidservant, giving her father ten acres of land and ten pounds, and paying Hepzibah herself six pounds a year, in return for a three-year indenture.

Rose always locked the door of her bedchamber, but Oliver had never tried to enter. It did not occur to Rose that this meant that his desire for her was any weaker than it had been in London. How could it be when it had never been satisfied?

Yet Oliver was suspicious when Rose suggested that they should sleep in the same bed.

"Sleep together?" he said. "What about the witches?"

They were alone in the hall. Oliver had drunk a good deal of rum, even for him, and his speech was slurred.

"The Gypsy told me not to worry about that," Rose said.

"The Gypsy? What Gypsy?"

"Henry's Gypsy—the one we went to see on the day he died. She said the witch would only come in the form of a bear, so there's nothing to worry about, really. I would have told you, but then the football game happened, and you . . . lost interest."

Rose looked modestly at the floor. Oliver uttered a gassy drunken laugh.

"Lost interest?" he said. "Is that what I did, Rose?"

What was wrong with him? Was he too drunk to realize what she was offering him?

Rose said, "I thought you might be pleased."

"Teased, you mean. No, thank you, my dear. I've had enough of fucking the air, thank you very much."

"I have no idea what you're talking about."

"Of course you don't."

Oliver's voice was hard. Rose tried to force tears from her eyes to soften his heart. None came. She thought about her years in Lockwood Hall—the cold, the nights the Lockwoods ate supper without telling her, the darkness, the look of contempt on the servants' faces because she was poor and because they all knew how Robert had used her. She began to sob.

"I never thought that you could be so cruel," she said to Oliver. "Not you."

Oliver was still grinning. "Come, Rose," he said. "We both know you don't want to be a wife to me. So what's all this about?"

Rose was sobbing uncontrollably now. Oliver shook his head violently to clear it of rum.

"By God, Rose, you really are something," he said. "You ruined me in London for no reason at all, and now you're going to spread your legs and jump onto it off the bedpost for appearance sake?"

Rose wiped her eyes. As soon as the tears were gone, all trace of distress vanished. She was as perfect as before.

"You were not *tender* in London," she said, pouting and looking sidelong. "The place was strange. I was frightened. You were so impetuous and so . . . masculine."

"Sorry about the tenderness," Oliver said. "There's not much I can do about the dimensions, lucky for you. You really mean this, do you?"

"Of course I mean it. We are husband and wife."

"Are we now? When do we start?"

Rose silently counted the days again. "Friday," she said. "But you must promise to be tender."

"Friday? It's Wednesday now. Why not a bit of tenderness today or Thursday?"

Rose looked modestly downward. She should feel the twinge by Thursday. "A woman knows the right moment," she said.

When the moment arrived, Oliver astonished her. Everything seemed to be as it had been before, but in fact it was all different.

The moon was full on Friday night, and the bedchamber was illuminated by moonlight when Oliver shook the door to see if it was locked and then entered. Rose stood looking out the window. she had combed out her hair so that it hung to her waist, sprinkled scent on her neck and bosom, and put on the same transparent gown that had so excited Oliver in London.

Rose identified Oliver's peculiar male odor and sweat and decay as soon as he entered the room, but to her relief, she smelled no spirits. Perhaps he would be less clumsy if he was not drunk, perhaps he'd be quicker; Robert always had been. Rose continued to look out the window. She could see Oliver's reflection in the wavy panes, remembering how she had kept him off in London by telling him that she couldn't see him in the looking glass.

Groaning like an old man as he bent over and straightened up again, Oliver undressed in his careless way, boots thumping to the floor, buckles and buttons rattling on the wooden floor as he threw down his waistcoat and breeches. The moon, hanging in a cloudless sky beyond the branches of the oaks, was as white as salt. Rose kept her eyes fixed upon it.

Just as before, she gagged on Oliver's tongue as he kissed her, then closed her eyes as he stripped off her clothes. He picked her up and dropped her on the bed. The frame groaned as he crawled in beside her. She kept her eyes closed, and began to think about riding in Buckinghamshire—that was what she had always thought about when Robert played the husband. She could see the horse, a tall chestnut with a white star, smell the leathers, visualize the cloudy sky making a quarter-turn around her as she pirouetted into the saddle . . .

Nothing happened. Rose opened her eyes. On the other side of the bed, Oliver lay on his back with his arms crossed on his chest, his big horny feet protruding over the footboard. He was not looking at Rose, but gazing upward at the tapestry canopy.

"Husband?" Rose said.

Oliver's eyes were open. He did not answer or change his position. Minutes passed.

"Husband?" Rose said. "Is something the matter?"

Still Oliver did not move. Really, what *was* the matter? Was he

asleep? Did he want her to make some gesture of apology for having denied him? She could not bring herself to kiss Oliver, but she did lift his hand and press the back of it against her cheek. The hand was limp, a strange condition in such a large object. When Rose let go, it fell back onto Oliver's chest with a thump.

Oliver's eyes were still open. He was breathing normally. But he seemed to be unaware of Rose.

Suddenly Oliver laughed explosively, a single derisive *Ha*! Then he rolled over onto an elbow and looked Rose's unclothed body up and down.

"Lovely," he said in a genial voice, as if remarking on a sunset.

Then, using a different tone, he began talking to someone else. "Just have a look at that, old boy, wake up and look, that's all I ask," he said. "You know you've never seen knockers like these on a mortal woman."

Oliver spoke with such gruff affection that Rose thought for a moment that he was having some sort of a vision, that he might have thought that Henry had come into the room with them. So strong was this feeling that she opened her eyes and looked around. They were alone.

Oliver lay beside her, up on his elbow with his grizzled head propped in one hand. He was looking at Rose's body, his face transformed by the look of wonder she remembered from their wedding night. With a shake of his head, he gave the flaxen hair between her legs a prolonged, painful tug. Rose sat up, gasping in surprise and pain. Oliver lifted her breasts one after the other, displaying them to the unseen presence he was talking to.

"Just feel that, old boy," he said. "Silk and honey."

Rose squirmed. Why wasn't it over with? Robert had carried butter in his pocket so as to be quick. "Hurry," she whispered.

Oliver seemed not to hear. He was still talking. "Nothing like it in this world, old boy," he said. "Only a fool would refuse it. You say you don't give a damn? Then you're the loser."

"What are you saying?" Rose said. "Whom are you talking to?"

"To my friend here."

Oliver lifted Rose's hand. She resisted, but he merely used a little more strength, guiding her fingers downward.

"Poor chap," Oliver said. "Lifeless and limp."

Rose snatched her hand away and leaped out of bed. "You bastard," she said. "How dare you?"

"Calling me names is no help. I'm as surprised as you. This is the first time he's ever refused to stand up for a lady."

"You foul bastard. You've had another woman tonight. I smell her on you."

"You smell another woman on me like you couldn't see me in the looking glass in Catherine Street because I was a witch," Oliver said. "I know you, Rose."

His tone of voice was mild. He wasn't even looking at Rose. Instead, he was looking beyond her, at something in the window.

"It's that skinny little bitch, isn't it?" Rose cried. "No wonder you want to give her the world. She's put a spell on you."

"Ah, it's witches again, is it?"

Oliver, smiling broadly, was still looking over her shoulder. "Look, Rose," he said, "in the tree outside the window."

Rose turned around. The oak was full of cats, eyes glittering like chips of moonlight.

# 19

Despite Rose's ban on cats, Thoughtful had kept one of the kittens she had saved from drowning. She took it everywhere with her, carrying it inside her dress for warmth. At supper on Saturday, the day after Oliver's visit to the bedchamber, the kitten crawled out of the neck of Thoughtful's dress, purring loudly. It was a pretty animal, black with a white face and white boots, and so young that its eyes were still blue. Thoughtful fed it drops of milk off her fingertips and talked to it in Abenaki.

"Fanny," she said, "please inform the Impostor that supper is at five, when Magpie rings the bell, and that she will not be given any food hereafter if she is late. And please ask the Impostor why she has no manners at all."

"Rose, be kind," Fanny said.

"I am *trying* to be kind. Tell her what I said."

"She understands."

"You mean the Impostor understands English?"

"She understands the look on your face. Some words are almost the same in English and French—including the name you call her by."

"Really? Teach me some more French words. How do you say 'ugly,' 'rude,' 'imbecile'?"

The kitten, purring ecstatically, clambered over the top of

Thoughtful's curly head and then down her shoulder before disappearing inside her dress again. Thoughtful peered down into her bodice and spoke gravely to the tiny animal again in Abenaki gutturals.

"Look, Mr. Ash," Rose said. "The Impostor has a kitten in her bosom."

Ash pretended not to hear. Yet Rose thought that Ash's eyes, set in his pallid face, were distinctly more melancholy than before. How difficult it must be for him to live in the same house, so near to her and yet so far! Certainly Ash, who did little except read books nowadays, had been unusually quiet since coming to America.

"Mr. Ash," Rose said. "*Are* there any witches in America?"

Ash sighed. "I have explained that point. They are everywhere because they are Satan's creatures and Satan is everywhere. Especially in America, if we are to believe Mr. Joseph Mede of Cambridge University. According to Mede, Satan transported the Indians to America long before the coming of Jesus Christ and made them his own chosen people."

"Satan's own chosen people? What for?"

"So as to put at least a part of mankind beyond the reach of salvation."

Ash recited the proofs of Mede's theory: the Babel of Indian languages, the tendency of the Indians to practice sorcery and black magic, the hellish torture and cruelty that Indians inflicted on Christians when they captured them, the great epidemic that God had sent to weaken the Indians just before the Pilgrims landed.

Listening to what Ash was telling her, and realizing what it meant, Rose felt her breath grow shorter.

"Then the Indians are all devils?" she said.

"Theoretically, yes. I can discover no scriptural support for Mede's idea, except by implication in the Apostle Paul's letter to the Ephesians in which he says that those who are without Christ are 'strangers from the Covenants of promise.' "

"How interesting," Rose said in her harshest voice. "The Impostor talks to the creature in Indian, the language of Satan, just as a witch will speak in tongues to a familiar spirit."

Fanny held up a hand in warning. "A familiar spirit?" she said. "What are you trying to do, Rose?"

Rose smiled at Ash, but would not meet Fanny's eyes. "I am trying to amuse you with this interesting theory about Satan and the Indians. What form can familiar spirits take, Mr. Ash?"

"In England, a rat, usually, sometimes a mouse or a toad," Ash

said. "But when Saul visited the woman of Endor, she raised up a familiar spirit that took the form of Samuel."

"And these familiars stay close to witches, and at night take their usual form, which is that of a devil, and play the husband to their witches?"

"That is the usual pattern. Witches, because they are female, are insatiable."

"But ugly. They have need of familiar spirits to satisfy their lust because men find them too ugly. Is that not so?"

Ash did not answer. He was astonished that Rose, who was so incurably stupid, had been able to remember so much of what he had told her in their many conversations on the subject of witchcraft, even if she remembered it faultily, and to make such a telling case as she was making.

"Could a witch make another woman, even a beautiful woman, appear ugly to her husband?" Rose asked.

"I know of no such case," Ash said, "but certainly it is possible."

"Rats, mice, toads—disgusting creatures," Rose said, her eyes fixed on the kitten, which was crawling out of Thoughtful's collar again. It looked around and suddenly meowed, one yowl after another, in a surprisingly loud voice. Hearing such a small creature make such a tremendous noise, everyone laughed but Rose.

She said, " A clever witch who knows Indian magic would have a pretty thing for a familiar spirit, I suppose—something that charms and amuses. A kitten, for example."

Fanny and Thoughtful slept in the same room at the opposite end of the Manor from Rose. As soon as Thoughtful was asleep, Fanny walked down the long central passageway and opened Rose's door.

Rose lay on the floor in her chemise, brushing her hair and listening at the cracks between the boards. She held a finger over her lips.

"Oliver and Mr. Ash are in the library," she whispered. "They are talking about the letter to Lebbaeus Williams."

Rose listened intently for several more minutes, then got to her feet. "They never say what's *in* it, only how to send it," she said, still whispering. "They are waiting for Hawkes to come back so that he can carry it to Boston." She handed Fanny the brush. "Brush my hair, Fanny. I can't reach—it's so long."

Rose sat down on a bench in front of a full-length mirror and crossed her legs. She was barefoot. While Fanny pulled the brush through her hair, she examined herself in the wavy glass. Even her

toes were shapely—each one mated perfectly to the one beside it, little pink toenails like mother-of-pearl.

Fanny stopped brushing and looked at Rose in the mirror. Rose held out her calf and examined its reflection.

"Don't stop, Fanny, please. I'll do yours. Then you can stay with me. I worry about you, sleeping with that Indian and her familiar."

Fanny tapped her on the crown with the back of the brush.

"Rose, you must stop this nonsense about witches and familiar spirits. You know perfectly well that there's nothing wrong with Thoughtful."

"Stop?" Rose looked away. "How can I stop? Awful things are happening in this house, Fanny. I can't tell an innocent girl like you how awful they really are. You wouldn't understand."

"Rose. . . ."

"Don't 'Rose' me. I know the signs. I've seen her walking backward and twining her fingers, and you all saw her with that disgusting thing she sleeps with, talking to it in Indian."

Fanny put down the brush and walked around to face Rose. She spun on her buttocks, turning her back to Fanny and the mirror, and began brushing her own hair. It crackled with static electricity in the cold room and stood out around her face.

Fanny tried to make Rose look at her, but instead she turned around again and looked knowingly at Fanny's reflection.

"She doesn't even have the voice of a girl," Rose said. "She sounds like something that lives under the earth. We *know* that she has a mark under her hair because Hawkes shaved her. Witches are always shaved so that the judges can see what's written on their scalps."

Rose brushed rhythmically as she spoke, one angry stroke for each word. Her eyes, like the eyes of a child who is just learning how to lie, were locked to Fanny's in the mirror.

"Rose," Fanny said, "you don't believe a word you're saying."

"No? You'll see. She's made you blind to what she is."

Fanny seized Rose's wrist; Rose struggled for a moment, then stopped brushing.

"Rose, listen to me," Fanny said. "It's one thing to have a joke about witches in London to get your own way with Oliver. It's another to call Thoughtful a witch because you're afraid that Oliver is going to give everything back to her."

Rose's expression changed. Watching her in the glass, Fanny recognized the look. It was the same panicky, helpless one she had worn on the day Montagu pulled down Henry's house in Catherine

Street and Fanny had had to yank her to safety by her hair. Tears wetted Rose's cheeks.

"You're against me too, Fanny," she said.

"I'm not against you. But you've got to stop. They hang witches in this country."

She began to cry again. "Oh, Fanny," she said. "You don't *know*! I've told no one what she's done."

Her eyes shone in the glass.

"Tell me," Fanny said.

Rose looked right and left, then beckoned Fanny close. She put her lips against her ear and whispered. Fanny could feel the moisture in her breath.

"It's a ligature," she hissed.

"A what?"

Fanny knew the word. But what did Rose mean by it? She drew away and looked at Rose, but she had covered her face with her hands.

"I don't understand," Fanny said.

Rose parted her fingers so that Fanny could see her eye. She was wearing her ruby ring.

"A ligature," she repeated. "Witches do it to men all the time. It takes away their manly powers, so they can't be husbands anymore. Oh, Fanny, what am I going to do?"

Rose let her hands fall limply onto her lap and watched herself weeping in the glass. She was as lovely as a picture. Fanny walked backward out of the room, leaving Rose alone, looking at herself.

# 20

As dawn broke the following morning, Fanny found Ash asleep on the floor of the library. It was a large square room, taking up the whole thirty-two-foot width of the house and containing one of the four big stone chimneys that anchored the Manor.

The light was still dim, and several minutes passed before Fanny located Ash, who lay on his stomach with his knees drawn up under him in a peculiar childish position. He now read himself to sleep at night instead of praying, and books were scattered around

him on the waxed floorboards. He mumbled in his sleep, trembling slightly from the cold. A west wind moaned down the chimney, and as the sun grew stronger, lacy patterns of frost appeared on the windowpanes and then evaporated.

Fanny sat down in a chair by the fireplace and waited for Ash to wake up. The windows, which faced the east, filled the pale glow of first light, then with pink, and then, as the sun rose above the ridgeline, admitted horizontal shafts of sunshine that illuminated the many portraits and paintings of dark northern landscapes which hung, frames touching, on the solid back wall. For many minutes, Fanny watched the light move from one Pennock face to another, disciplining herself to look only at the pictures that the sun touched. It was like watching the minute hand of a clock in order to see it move. She missed the ticking of clocks; there were none in the Manor. John Pennock had believed that the mechanical telling of time distracted the mind from God, who made the passing of the hours evident by the movement of the sun and moon, the gathering of shadows, and variations in temperature.

"Fanny," Ash said.

Fanny looked away from the paintings, parting her lips to say "good morning," but Ash was in the same contorted position, breathing like a person asleep. She realized that he was talking in his sleep. His voice was no less strong than when he was awake, but the words were unintelligible. Fanny tried to sort them out. At first she could make no sense of it, but then she realized Ash was speaking Latin and made out the words: *"Sciuris mortuus est . . . mortuus est . . ."*

Fanny giggled. What else but Latin would Ash speak in his sleep? He rolled his tongue in his dry mouth, coughed violently, and opened his eyes.

"What do you mean, the squirrel is dead?" Fanny asked.

Ash lay motionless, staring at Fanny, who was just being reached by the light. He had been dreaming his usual dream about her, but he realized after only an instant of doubt that the slight figure seated in the high-backed chair was not the inert nude in his dream but Fanny herself.

Waking from his dream, Ash was still in a state of desire. He sat up, hoping to conceal this from Fanny. He found it difficult to breathe. He had used his coat as a pillow and his face was marked by the buttons, two spots of dull red among the stubble on his whey-colored cheek.

"What?" he said. "What squirrel?"

"You were talking in your sleep. I thought you said *Sciuris mortuus est.*"

"Your Latin is better than my memory."

"You don't know what you meant?"

"I must have been dreaming."

"You do know what Thoughtful's Abenaki name is."

Why was she asking these obscure questions?

"Do I?" Ash said. "It's very early in the morning, Fanny."

He covered his mouth and coughed again, pressing a forearm into his bulging lap to suppress the sympathetic spasms that this created.

"Squirrel," Fanny said. "The Abenakis call her Squirrel. You were saying *Sciuris mortuus est* as you were waking up."

Ash nodded. "Perhaps I was. But my dream had nothing to do with Thoughtful Pennock, I assure you."

Ash's flesh would not subside. He could not move until it did. He searched the room for a means of diverting his mind. The sun flashed on a pair of crossed German rapiers mounted above the mantelpiece. These weapons were as plain as butcher knives—no elaborate basket to protect the hand, no engraving on the blade, just hilt and edge and point. They were nevertheless quite beautiful in a stern Lutheran way. Their purpose, the infliction of death, was much more unhypocritical than in English weapons. Ash concentrated on them, requiring himself to think of nothing but what his eyes beheld, an almost impossible task for him. Finally the rapiers became abstract objects, mere strips of shiny stuff that his conscious mind could not put a name to. His excitation passed. He stood up, ran his hands through his hair, and put on his coat. It was badly wrinkled.

Fanny watched him with curiosity, as she always watched men in their unguarded moments. Opening his surprised eyes and unfolding his limbs, Ash had seemed to be positively afraid of the morning. Gradually, however, he became himself again—the old Ash having taken shape out of the bewildered stranger she had watched regain consciousness. This composed, friendly Ash seemed to be waiting for her to say something to him.

"Isn't it cold," she asked, "sleeping on the floor without a cover?"

"Not cold enough. Why are you here, Fanny?"

"I want to talk to you." She spoke in a low, barely audible voice. "Let's walk outside."

"Why outside?"

Fanny pointed upward. Rose's bed stood almost directly above their heads. Ash nodded. He collected the books he had been reading, all of them Henry's, and put them back on the shelf.

Fanny went and stood at the door that led into the central passageway.

Ash shook his head, put a finger over his lips, and gestured her to come close. He spoke to her in Latin.

"There's another way," he said. "Do you know about Virgil? Second shelf, bound in blue leather, first three volumes on the left . . . so!"

He removed the books from the shelf, put them under his arm, took Fanny's wrist, and guided her hand into the empty space where the books had been. She felt a latch and lifted it. A section of the bookcase about three feet wide swung outward, revealing a narrow flight of stairs that led downward into darkness.

Ash lit the stub of a candle from the last coals in the fireplace and led the way into the passage, a narrow corridor passing between two stone walls. Fanny could stand up in it, but Ash had to stoop in order to pass beneath the ceiling, which was constructed of the large flat rocks that were common in this country. After a dozen steps, they came to a right-angle turn and then to another. Both were fitted with heavy frames and stout oak doors bound with riveted iron strips.

"Firebreak," Ash said, speaking English now. "If the Manor is set alight, you can close the doors, run to the end of the passageway, and survive the smoke and fire in this chamber."

They stood now in a square stone room furnished with a rough table and chairs and a row of bunks. Water, evidently piped in from a spring, ran through a stone basin in one corner, and out again through a drain. Everything was covered with glistening green mold. Kegs and crocks containing corn, potatoes, apples, salt beef, and salt pork stood along the walls. Two hams and a long rank of smoked salmon hung from hooks driven into the stone ceiling. There were two low, narrow alcoves like bread ovens with beds in them.

"John Pennock had this hiding room built after the attack by the Abenakis," Ash said. "The whole household could remain here for days, even in winter; as it lies below frost level, there is no danger of freezing even in the coldest winter. There are ducts for fresh air and an exit beyond the walls of the fort. Had this place existed when the Abenakis attacked, Thoughtful would have grown up in this house as a Protestant with a mother and brother instead of in Canada among savages."

"And we would be in England. How did you find out about it?"

"Its existence is a great secret, only revealed in a sealed codicil to Pennock's will. Only you and Oliver and I know about it."

Fanny looked around her, saying nothing. Ash had been sur-

prised, when she was his patient aboard the *Pamela*, by her habit of falling into a silence as soon as she understood what was said to her. She simply listened to the words, understood, and waited for the next subject to be introduced. That was what she was doing now. It was disconcerting to encounter a female who had so much intelligence. Because his head was bent beneath the low ceiling, Ash's face was quite close to Fanny's. It was chilly. His breath condensed in the air. Ash's face, usually so ghostly, was tinged with color.

He backed away and opened another low door. Fanny followed him through it. They emerged inside a thicket of raspberry bushes. There was no outer door, just a frame of stones that looked like the mouth of a shallow cave.

"It gives a very natural appearance," Ash said, unable to restrain himself from stating the obvious. "In winter, of course, it would be concealed by the snow."

Again Fanny was silent. It was difficult to walk out of the thicket, or into it, because of the thorns on the raspberry bushes. Ash led the way, holding back branches for Fanny. By the time they emerged, his hands were covered with bleeding scratches, They were standing a few hundred yards above the village. Woodsmoke rose from the dozens of chimneys, saturating the air with its acrid fumes. Even now, Fanny could not accustom herself to the constant sight and smell of smoke and the prodigal expenditure of fuel that it represented. Above them in the higher meadows sheltered from the sun, the dying grass was white with frost. Mist hung over the river. The long narrow fields along the river were turning many shades of yellow and brown.

"It must have looked very much like this on the day the Abenakis came," Ash said.

Abruptly he began to describe the battle in minute detail from Pennock's point of view, as if Fanny had never heard the story. "I have been reading Pennock's diaries," Ash said. "As he burned in the pillory that day he thought of God's words to Abraham as Stephen recounted them on the day of his persecution: 'Get thee out of thy country, and from thy kindred, and come into the land which I shall shew thee.' "

Though he hardly spoke, now, to anyone else, Ash could not keep quiet in Fanny's presence. She tried to catch his eye, to change the subject. He would not look at her, but examined the landscape as if he had never seen it before. Even when he was not talking to Fanny, he muttered to himself, a new mannerism. He repeated the Latin words he had spoken in his sleep. When he came back, he spoke them aloud.

"I can't remember the dream," Ash said, "or why I should have spoken the words *Sciuris mortuus est*. In Catullus' *Carmina* there is a similar line about a sparrow, '*Passer mortuus est meae puellae.*' My mistress's sparrow is dead, *et cetera*. Why should that line come to me in my sleep?"

Fanny lifted her palms to stop his chain of thought and speech. "Never mind," she said. "It's Thoughtful I want to talk to you about."

"In what connection?"

"In connection with Rose. What is a ligature?"

"The surgical term?"

"In terms of witchcraft."

"It deprives the male of his sexual powers, *impotentia ex maleficio*, usually by means of a potion. One seldom encounters it in England, but it is common in southern climates, where tempers are more amorous."

"Did you tell Rose about ligature as you told her about Satan and the Indians?"

"Perhaps. It's impossible to remember every question she asks."

"Rose believes that Oliver has one."

The corners of Ash's lips twitched. "Oliver? Who is the witch?"

"Thoughtful, of course. You heard Rose at supper last night. She doesn't understand what might happen if she goes on with this silly nonsense."

"You think the works of Satan are silly nonsense?"

"I think it's silly nonsense to say that a kitten is a devil in disguise and that Thoughtful is a witch who has it for a husband."

Fanny was speaking to Ash in a level tone of voice, with no sign of temper, but with such determination that she seemed to be rooted to the ground.

Ash said, "If Thoughtful is not a witch, then Rose can do her no harm by saying foolish things about her."

"No? How many witches have been killed in England?"

"No one knows. Perhaps thirty thousand, including Scotland. The Scots were very active witch-hunters but compared to the Continent the total was modest. In Saxony a single judge, Benedikt Carpzov, is said to have burnt twenty thousand witches."

"Rose must stop this nonsense," Fanny said. "She doesn't understand what can happen if she goes on."

"Doesn't understand? You think that?"

Ash looked down at Fanny, the straight white part in her glossy hair, her eyes shining with love for her friend, Thoughtful, and with ferocious disgust for Rose Barebones' accusations.

"If she does understand," Fanny said, "then it is worse yet. You can't want what will happen to happen."

"If Rose is misbehaving," Ash said, "then her husband should command her to stop. Speak to him."

"She won't listen to Oliver. It's you she listens to. If you tell her to stop, she will stop."

Fanny's expression changed. For once she looked young, uncertain, supplicating. What sign was she giving him? If he gave Fanny what she asked for, what would she give in return? Suppose that Betsy died in childbirth? Would Fanny be his new wife? Ash realized—this was an entirely new thought—that he wanted to have a child by Fanny.

This child was more vivid to him than the one Betsy was bearing him now, more real then his dead children, whose faces he could not really remember. He longed to see it, he imagined talking to it, smiling at it, teaching it Latin, looking on while Fanny taught it music. In his vision it had Fanny's face and his mind. No doubt God, when He endowed him with such powerful fleshly instincts, had wanted him to have children. That was mere instinct, this was revelation. . . . Stop! Think about something else. He held his hands before his face and stared at the tiny beads of blood oozing from the network of scratches left by the raspberry thorns.

Ash heard Fanny's voice speaking to him.

"Will you do it?" she asked. "Will you speak to Rose, tell her to stop?"

"God means Thoughtful no harm," Ash said. "Her present trouble is part of His great design, and He will deliver her from it. I am sure of it."

Fanny's heart sank. To a Christian like Ash, the gibbet was a glorious deliverance. Ash started to turn away, but Fanny would not let him go until he said more.

"No doubt God's eye is on my friend, as you say," she said. "But will you explain that to Rose?"

"I will speak to her. But it will do no good. She doesn't believe what she says, therefore she will go on saying it until she has what she wants. It is unimportant. Witches are merely a contrivance to her."

"Will you say *that*, if necessary?"

"If necessary."

"Then please be quick about it. There's danger here, Edward."

Edward? Until now Fanny had never called him by his Christian name. Why did she choose this moment to do so? Something was happening that he did not understand.

Ash had excluded the Scriptures from his thoughts for many

weeks, but now he began to consider God again, and to wonder about His design for his life. Surely everything that had happened to him meant something, if he could only see the purpose. Why had he been brought together in the wilderness with Fanny, with Rose, with Oliver, with Thoughtful who had been rescued so providentially? Why had he been taunted by the sailors, and why had such a little thing as that separated him from God? Why were the signs of Satan being made so plain in Rose's obsession with witchcraft?

Could it be that all this, and especially his passion for Fanny, was not a sign of his downfall, as he had feared, but a temptation sent to fortify him for some mysterious future that God had had in mind for him all along? Of course it was. Ash's faith, which had been driven out by lust, came back again. Lust had been a mere disguise! Fanny, whose beauty had made him blind to the intentions of the Lord, and now made it possible for him to see again. How symmetrical were the works of the Lord!

Ash's heart swelled with gratitude. All the prayers that he had not uttered in those long days and weeks swirled out of his soul and on to his tongue. He felt the pressure of all three hundreds of unspoken prayers as a dizzying physical force so strong that he lost his balance and staggered a few steps down the hillside.

Instinctively Fanny seized Ash by the arm and was pulled down the slope after him by his greater weight. When they came to a stop they had to hold on to each other for a moment to keep from falling.

Having been unconscious or under the influence of opium while Ash carried on his great struggle with his own flesh aboard the *Pamela*, Fanny had never before seen him in a religious state. The change was startling. A moment before, he had been quiet and morose. Now he was jubilant, charged with energy, his mouth open, his chest heaving, his eyes glowing, as if he were on the verge of babbling and dancing. He was shuddering with delight.

He looked into her face with an expression of such unguarded, exalted love that Fanny thought for a moment that he had lost his senses. She removed her hands from his forearms and stepped away.

Ash stumbled after her, reaching out his arms.

"There is something I must tell you," he said. "You need not answer, you need not even believe what I say."

Fanny said, "It would be better not to say it." But she knew that nothing would stop him.

"I love you," Ash said. "I have always loved you, from the first

day, with a love so strong that my soul and my body have hardly been able to bear it."

Ash's face glowed with happiness. Fanny knew that she must say something cruel, and say it quickly, or she would never escape from him.

"I am sorry to hear that," she said. "Because I don't love you and never could."

The words had no effect. Ash went on smiling. "Of course you would say that," he said. "I have a wife already. That is so. It is an impediment that no Christian could ignore, and I shall not ignore it. But one day I will be free. Something very powerful tells me so. And when I am, I will tell you everything that is in my heart, and you will know what love God can send into the lives of a man and a woman."

Ash squeezed Fanny's hand. His palm was damp but cold, an unsettling combination of sensations.

"I already know that," Fanny said.

"Then you have felt my love already!"

Fanny looked him in the eyes. He held her gaze.

"No. I have known about you for a long time and been sorry for you," she said. "But that's not what I mean. I love someone else. I could never love you, or anyone but him."

Ash staggered. He kept on looking into Fanny's eyes. He saw that she was not lying. Still, he could not believe her.

"Who?" he gasped.

"You don't know him."

"Because he doesn't exist! You are telling me this to drive me away."

"You know I wouldn't lie. He exists. He will come for me."

Fanny had no idea why she spoke these words. She had dreamt of Philippe often, always the drowning dream, but she had never spoken about him to anyone, or even imagined him in her conscious mind. But now she believed what she said. He had saved her life once; he would save it again.

"God!" Ash cried in his great voice.

Tears ran down over the scratches on his colorless cheeks. Then, without speaking again, he plunged back into the raspberry thicket. The barrier of thorns and springy canes held him back for a moment before he broke through and disappeared.

# 21

Fanny and Thoughtful spent as much time in the woods as possible, picking berries until the first frost and gathering beechnuts afterward. Thoughtful taught Fanny woodcraft—how to tell the hoofprint of a doe from that of a buck, how to recognize the scat of all the animals, how to tell where deer had been browsing by the ragged condition of the chewed leaves, as contrasted to the even edges left by nibbling rabbits, how to recognize the girdled pines left by bears who liked to eat the soft brown layer of stuff between the bark and the wood.

Because of her musical gift, Fanny excelled at recognizing and imitating the calls of birds and animals.

"You must never call out in your own voice in the woods," Thoughtful had explained. "The animals do not like it."

When Thoughtful spoke in the forest, she usually spoke in signs. This was a simple language, easily learned, and soon Fanny knew it well enough to follow Thoughtful's meaning and make the necessary replies.

Fanny also learned to use her eyes in a different way.

"Do not look at what you expect to see," Thoughtful told her. "Look at what is there." Gradually deer, rabbits, squirrels, partridges, snakes, and all sorts of other animals became visible to her in the dusty forest light. All around her, almost all the time, creatures stood frozen, in plain sight but invisible. The animals knew when their camouflage failed, and as soon as Fanny discovered them, they ran away. "It is because you sniff when you see them," Thoughtful said, imitating the sound Fanny made when she was surprised by the appearance of an animal. "Be quieter or you will never kill anything."

Above all, Thoughtful taught Fanny how to stay alive in the woods—how to move slowly, how to hide, what roots and plants to eat, how to kill porcupines and skin them. There were always porcupines about, and they died very easily—a blow on the nose with a stick would kill them. They were composed mostly of fat, and with their skin and quills removed, they looked like cats carved

from lard. Thoughtful roasted them over a little fire, caught the fat in a container made of birch bark, and poured the fat into the intestines of the animal. When it congealed, this sausage would be hung up in a tree as emergency rations.

"Why are you teaching me all these things?" Fanny asked.

"Because you don't know them already," Thoughtful said. "And because of Ash and Rose."

"What about them?"

"They are both crazy. Sooner or later you will have to leave this place."

"Where will I go?"

"Into the forest. You're in the wrong place. Nothing here is as it should be, so everything must change. I was born here by mistake, and now I have come back here by mistake. There must be a reason for all these mistakes, but I don't know what it is. Maybe Rose should have been born here instead of me."

"That is certainly true," Fanny said

Thoughtful's black-and-white kitten was big enough to walk now, and it had followed them to the forest. The girls were stretched out side by side on a springy carpet of pine needles. While she fed the kitten, pouring milk out of a crock the girls had brought along for their lunch, Thoughtful went on talking in her deep voice. Otherwise, the forest lay in a deep midday hush.

They had been picking blueberries. Thoughtful produced a small wooden bowl and a spoon from the pocket of her apron and mixed nocake, blueberries, and milk together. When the parched corn had absorbed the milk, creating a spongy porridge, the girls ate it, passing the spoon back and forth. Fanny stopped after the first few mouthfuls, but Thoughtful ate like an Indian, as much as she could hold, and then lay down on the pine needles.

"Before it snows," she said, "we must hide some nocake under the hanging rock."

"What for?" Fanny asked.

"In case everything changes."

As soon as she finished uttering these words, Thoughtful closed her eyes and fell asleep, as was her way. She lay on her back on the pine needles, a long narrow figure dressed in a gray linsey-woolsey dress with a prim white collar and Indian moccasins on her feet. Thoughtful's clothes fit her better now; Fanny, with help from Betsy Ash, had cut some of Hope's dresses down. Thoughtful still wore her beaded Abenaki headband.

Fanny took off her apron and rolled it up into a pillow. Falling asleep without delay was one Abenaki skill that she had been

unable to learn from Thoughtful. She lay for a long time with her eyes open, watching the clouds.

*In case everything changes.* She knew that Thoughtful believed that the Abenakis would come again and rescue her. She spoke about Two Suns and Hair and Talks in His Dreams all the time, describing them to Fanny and talking about the life she had led. It was impossible to have secrets from her because she observed every detail of everyone's behavior and knew, through some sense that only Abenakis seemed to have, exactly what was in everyone's mind.

"Ash is going crazy because he cannot have you," she had told Fanny. "Abenaki girls would not let this happen. If you did not want him you would tell your friends and they would all lie down with him, one after the other, until he forgot about you."

"How many girls?"

"As many as were your friends."

"But what if they didn't like the man themselves?"

"They would like him if he was Abenaki. Besides, the man would make love as though each girl was the one he couldn't have. It would be pleasurable."

"Would you do that?"

"Not here. But I was almost old enough to begin when the dogs killed Thin Ice and Hawkes carried me back to this place."

Smiling at her sleeping friend, Fanny herself fell asleep.

She was awakened by a warbling bird call. She had never heard this particular bird before. No two notes had the same pitch.

Thoughtful and the kitten were gone. There was nothing unusual about that; Thoughtful often vanished into the woods for hours at a time. The bird, which was quite nearby, called again and was answered by another warbler deeper in the woods. Fanny memorized the notes so that she could ask Thoughtful what it was.

Fanny looked at the angle of the light and realized that she had slept for two or three hours. Her mouth was dry. She got to her feet, shook the pine needles out of her skirt, and walked toward the spring. In the brown dirt beyond the pine needles she saw the nailed soles and sharp heels of her own small footprints, and a little farther on, the print of a cloven hoof with a drag mark behind it, the mark of a white-tailed buck deer. Thoughtful had left no tracks. This was unusual. Normally she left a plain trail so that Fanny could follow it and find her.

The strange bird was still calling. Fanny stopped for a moment and answered it. The call was difficult, but musically comical because it was so dissonant. The bird fell silent. Applying Thoughtful's teachings, Fanny quartered around the spring, and waited by

a tree to make certain that there were no bears around. They were very dangerous at this time of year, when they were likely to be drunk on fermented berries, and particularly dangerous to women at the time of the month when they smelled of blood.

Fanny and Thoughtful had never seen any bears among the blueberry bushes, but they saw droppings and fresh tracks nearly every day, and this was the spring in the little upland clearing where Two Suns and the other Abenakis had killed the drunken bear.

Fanny planted her hands in the damp soil beside the spring and lowered herself toward the water. She drank, then raised herself and gazed at her reflection in the surface of the water, dark hair and skin burned darker than usual by the sun. She saw nothing else. Her hands were splayed in the mud. The fingers were stained with blueberry juice. Because they had had so much exercise on musical instruments, her hands were blunt and strong and slightly larger than they should have been in proportion to the rest of her body.

The warbler woke up and called again, and was answered once more by its mate a few hundred yards away. Fanny, smiling, ran her fingers along an imaginary keyboard in the mud, turning the harsh treble call into a run on the spinet for the right hand.

The bird stopped singing. Fanny kneeled and looked at her handprints in the mud at the edge of the spring. She splashed water on them and they disappeared, roiling the water. From this angle she was able to see the other bank of the spring, as she had not been able to do when she was drinking. A moccasin print was stamped in the mud. It was a print left by a man, and it was filled with water; someone had tried to erase it, as Fanny had obliterated her handprints, by splashing water on it, but had not succeeded.

An Indian had been here today, while Fanny and Thoughtful were asleep only a few hundred feet away. Fanny stayed as she was, motionless, and searched the perimeter of the clearing. She saw nothing.

The warbler called again and was answered by the second warbler. They were close together now, somewhere near the hanging rock. Fanny decided to try to see these birds. As Thoughtful had taught her, she walked in the opposite direction from the rock, and then circled through the forest, gliding from tree to tree and keeping what little breeze there was in her face so that no animal could catch her scent as she approached. The birds were now answering each other more urgently, uttering five or six calls, then falling silent before calling again.

By now Fanny could see the hanging rock. She was approaching

from the rear, so the ledge seemed close to the ground. She felt, rather than saw or heard, that something large was nearby. Looking down, she saw the spattered droppings of a bear; the loose stool was yellower than any she had seen before, and blueberries had passed, whole and undigested, through the animal. At least he would not be drunk on berries that had not had time to ferment.

Fanny felt a loss of breath and realized that it was fear. Nevertheless, she wanted to see a bear, so she dropped to her hands and knees and crawled, slowly and carefully, toward the rock. She stopped every five or six feet to look all around her and listen. Finally she reached the hanging rock. The bird called again. She pursed her lips to answer, then decided to keep silent in case the bear could tell the difference between the real bird and a human imitator.

Crawling on her belly, Fanny moved along the back of the hanging rock until she came to the end. She pressed her cheek against its cool surface and moved her face, inch by inch, until she could see down into the clearing in front of the shelter beneath the rock. All the while, she kept on hearing the calling of the warbler, very close at hand, and the second bird answering as it moved away.

Moved *away*? There was something strange about that. Why would two birds of a feather call to each other, then separate?

Below the hanging rock, four men stood in the clearing—three Indians wearing feathers and paint, and a white man dressed in a blue coat and a tricornered hat with a red cockade.

One of the Indians, who had his back to Fanny, was imitating the bird and listening for the response. Each time his call was answered, he uttered a pleased chuckle and replied, and the other Indians poked him in the ribs, amused by the exchange of calls. They were smiling broadly under their paint, as if they were calling to another person of whom they were extremely fond.

These Indians—tall, muscular, and armed with knives and hatchets, bows and long-barreled muskets—were nothing like the Nipmucks. They were wild, as different from the Indians Fanny had seen so far as a stage is different from a horse.

One of the Indians, the one who was making the bird call, had only one ear. Fanny realized with a start that she knew who he was, who they all were. She recognized them from Thoughtful's stories. The man who was making the bird calls was Used to be Bear, the Abenaki who had had his ear sliced off in the fight with Captain John Pennock. The other two were Hair and Talks in His Dreams, the sons of Two Suns, Thoughtful's Abenaki brothers. Fanny realized that they must be calling to Thoughtful. But why

was she going away from them instead of joining them now that they had come for her?

As the Indians continued to imitate the bird call, then listen for the response, the white man turned on his face too. His eyes, his whole demeanor, was very alert. He was looking around, examining the perimeter of the clearing inch by inch.

"If an animal or an Indian is looking in your direction when you are trying to hide," Thoughtful had told Fanny, "close your eyes. If they are open, they will see the whites."

This white man obviously knew how to see like an Indian. Methodically his gaze moved along the rock, beginning at the end opposite to Fanny's position. As his head turned, his face became visible in the shadow of his hat brim. He had not shaved for many days.

Fanny recognized him. It was Philippe.

She looked him straight in the eyes. He returned her gaze, soberly, steadily, just as he had done in Honfleur, and then his eyes moved on.

Fanny backed away from the hanging rock, then ran through the forest, holding her skirts above her knees. Her petticoats flashed in the dusty light and it was this, she supposed later on, that had made it possible for Philippe to follow her so easily.

She had been running for only a moment when she saw him running easily through the trees on a course parallel to hers. She ran on for a few more steps, then stopped. He stopped too, and looked at her for a long time. He was alone. Fanny looked behind her and all around, but she saw no sign of the Abenakis. Nevertheless, they must be near. Her heart pounded. She felt like a wild animal.

When Fanny looked back at the place where Philippe had been, he had disappeared. Then she saw him walking toward her through the trees. He carried a peculiar short musket across his chest. His face was as grave as she remembered it. She stood where she was.

Philippe walked up to Fanny and took off his hat.

"I was sure it was you," he said, "but I couldn't believe my eyes. Why did you run away?"

"I don't know. I knew it was you."

"That frightened you?"

"No. But how could it be you?"

He looked exactly the same, except that his scar had faded.

"Your wound is better," Fanny said.

He looked puzzled, then touched the saber cut on his jaw.

"Yes."

They were standing in a grove of white birches, in a slightly

swampy place that seemed cooler than the surrounding forest. The light, falling through the pale birch leaves instead of dense pines, was brighter.

"Those Indians are Used to be Bear, Hair, and Talks in His Dreams?" Fanny said.

"Squirrel has told you her story," Philippe said.

"Yes, but she's called Thoughtful here. Have you come to take her back to Canada?"

"Not yet."

"That will be a disappointment to her. She's very unhappy here."

"She understands. Are you happy in this place?"

For some reason, Philippe smiled as he asked this question. He had not smiled when he came up to her, he had not smiled when she knew the names of the Abenakis.

"No," Fanny said, "I am not happy here. Thoughtful says it is the wrong place, that everybody is here by mistake. Why are you smiling?"

"Because I am glad to see you. Because now I know where you are."

Fanny lifted her hand, indicating the forest, the silence, the strangeness.

"You sound as though you intend to come back," she said.

Philippe did not reply. They had been holding each other's eyes all this time. It was Franny who looked away. She saw the Abenakis now. They had come out from behind the trees where they had been hiding and were watching Philippe and Fanny.

"What else would one do?"

With that, Philippe turned away and walked off among the chalky trunks of the birches. Used to be Bear, Hair, and Talks in His Dreams had already vanished, and in a moment Philippe was gone too.

Fanny walked back to the pine grove. Thoughtful was waiting for her, sitting cross-legged with the kitten playing on her lap. She was talking to the kitten in Abenaki and smiling. When she saw Fanny, she smiled again.

The two girls started down the hillside together. Behind them, the forest was perfectly silent again, but frogs were beginning to chirp beside the spring of the drunken bear.

"What was that bird that sang a little while ago?" Fanny asked.

"It has no name," Thoughtful said. "It's from the north. The Abenakis know it. I heard you call to it, but then it stopped singing because you sound so much like the bird itself that it didn't know what you were."

They walked on with their backs to the forest. In the nerves along her spine, Fanny felt Philippe's presence. Breathing deeply to keep herself from breathing too fast, she stopped and turned around. The edge of the woods, rank after rank of pine, was brightly lit by the rays of the afternoon sun.

"They're gone," Fanny said.

Thoughtful stroked her kitten.

"Maybe not," she replied.

# III

# THE RIVER

# 1

The great snow that covered Alamoth and all of New England that winter began to fall during the first week in November. Not even the Indians had seen so much snow so early in the season, but the storm came as no surprise to Thoughtful Pennock, who had been told what to expect by a wild gander. The month before, during the hunter's moon, she and Fanny, wrapped in the same blanket, had heard the Canada geese honking and bugling as they came down the river. Wings beating in a powerful slow rhythm, flying very low, the geese passed across the disk of the moon in a miles-long unbroken skein.

Thoughtful called to them. For a long time they did not respond. Then one gander, flying at the point of the wedge, broke formation and honked back to her. He told her, Thoughtful said afterward, that the sky was heavy with snow. The geese had never seen so much, and they saw it wherever they flew.

Ash, who had been studying the habits of migratory birds, told Fanny that the behavior of the gander could be explained by the fact that the leaders of any flock of birds often changed places while in flight, apparently because of fatigue. Fanny did not doubt that this was true, but by now she saw nothing odd in Thoughtful's conversations with wild animals. To her, communicating with a Canada goose was no stranger than talking to an Englishman, except that the goose was more likely to tell the truth. Gustavus Hawkes, returning from his long scout to the north, had heard the same forecast from the Indians he met along the way. The Pocumtuck, the Massachusett, the Penacook, the Cowass, the Sokoki had also heard the geese's warning. Up and down the Connecticut River, the tribes were getting ready for a hard winter, laying up corn and beans in underground barns and sending the women out to gather extra firewood.

Alamoth had had an excellent harvest. Like everything else there, it was organized along lines laid down by John Pennock. Each sex and age group was assigned specific tasks. Hay and clover, which grew on the high ground above the river, were mowed

259

in June and stacked in ricks that straggled along the slope like
another village of windowless houses. Millet, rye, barley, and
wheat were cut in turn by ranks of men with scythes, then tied in
sheaves by the women. Boys picked Indian corn and collected the
squashes and pumpkins that grew among the stalks.

Girls harvested and gathered potatoes and turnips after these
had been dug out of the ground by the men and boys. Few farmers
outside of Alamoth grew these little-known root vegetables. Pennock
had discovered the potato (*Solanum tuberosum*) in Burgundy,
whence it had come by the way of the Andes, Spain, and Italy.
The French, like Lebbaeus Williams, regarded it as an aphrodisiac;
Pennock, noting that it grew cheerfully in poor, stony soil, re-
garded it as ideal for the lands along the Scottish border, and for
the scrubbier fields of New England.

The Dutch had introduced turnips as cattle feed; these tainted
the milk, but increased yields. Pennock was an admirer of Dutch
husbandry, in which every inch of land was made to yield the
maximum in food, and all excess food was returned to the land in
the form of compost or excrement. No garbage littered the door-
yards of Alamoth; every house had a compost heap, and every
scrap of waste organic matter, along with the contents of chamber
pots, went into it. Red Devon cattle, merino sheep, and spotted
hogs, fatter than any others in New England, grazed on the second
crop of hay and were later let loose to forage among the stubble of
the grain fields.

The ricks of clover-hay meant that cattle could be fed through
the winter, and need not be slaughtered, salted, and pickled in the
fall merely to prevent their starving during the winter months, as
had been done in Europe since ancient times. Alamoth only slaugh-
tered as much meat as it needed for food. Clover formed the basis
of a nine-year cycle of crop rotation invented by the Dutch, and
was supported by the Dutch method of fertilization, using wood
ashes, sheep manure, and pigeon dung, as well as human excre-
ment and compost.

Once the sheaves of grain were dry, men skilled in the use of the
flail threshed the grain in a barn with two open ends, so constructed
that the wind funneled through it with great force. Afterward, the
grain was winnowed from the chaff by throwing it into the air with
wooden shovels. The wind carried the chaff away through the open
end of the barn, and a haze of dust hung over the village, softening
further the mellow light of the season. The grain was ground into
flour by Pennock's millwrights on millstones from Andernach on
the Rhine. Young people husked thousands of ears of Indian corn.

Girls and women soaked, pounded, and combed flax and later spun and wove it into linen.

This orderly division of labor and the strict rules of husbandry that Pennock laid down produced a deep contentment in his city in the wilderness, as he had foreseen. Everyone in Alamoth knew precisely where he belonged, exactly what was expected of him, exactly what his share of the village's wealth would be.

But no one knew when the Abenakis and the French might come again. Fall was the most dangerous time of the year, when there were crops to be reaped and no time to spare from work for military duties.

Fanny told Oliver what she had seen in the woods only a mile from Alamoth.

"What do you mean they were relations of Thoughtful's?" Oliver asked.

"Thoughtful tells stories about them."

"Did she see them too?"

"We weren't together. I didn't ask her."

"But did she?"

"Yes."

Oliver frowned, then suddenly beamed with pleasure. "She saw them, she talked to them, but she didn't go away with them. That means she's happy with us."

"Or that they're coming back for her," Fanny said.

Oliver did not hear what Fanny had said to him; his mind was elswhere. The idea of giving Thoughtful all his worldly goods had made Oliver love her. He wanted her to stay here and live to an old age with Pennock children around her. Any child she had would be a Barebones too—and if Thoughtful was John Pennock's only living child, she was also Oliver's flesh and blood.

"They *will* come back," Fanny said.

But Oliver turned his back and walked away.

Oliver posted boys on the parapets of the village and instructed them to watch the forest day and night for signs of Indian raiders. Hawkes and his dogs went north during the last quarter of the harvest moon, timing their departure so as to arrive along the Saint Francis River in late October, when the hunter's moon was full.

Just as the ducks arrived over Alamoth, Hawkes returned. He had a reassuring report to make. The Abenaki villages were quiet. Apart from the usual Jesuits, Hawkes had seen no Frenchmen among the Abenakis. The men were not painted. No more were missing than might be expected during the fall hunting season.

Hawkes had been spying on these villages for twelve years; he knew their populations, and could even recognize most individual Indians. He had watched Thoughtful for years before he kidnapped her. By the time he took her, he knew nearly everything about her life.

These were the good signs. There were other signs that might be less good. By a lake between the source of the Connecticut River and the Saint Francis River, he had stumbled onto a party of three Abenakis and a Frenchman. He recognized the Indians: Talks in His Dreams and Hair, who had made him carry the dead Jesuit, and Used to be Bear, the big ugly Indian who had had his ear sliced off by John Pennock. Hawkes did not know their Abenaki names—he had his own names for them—but he knew their faces.

The Indians had just killed a moose, but it was obvious they were not a hunting party. They wore paint, their clothes were torn, and there were raw places on their shoulders. That could only mean that they had been down the Connecticut, spying on the English settlements, and had worn the skin off their shoulders portaging their canoes across the miles of rough country between the two rivers.

The carcass of the moose lay half in the shallow water, half on shore, seeping blood. Minnows swarmed around the dead animal, thrashing in their frenzy to find something that was small enough to eat. The Abenakis sat in a circle with drawn knives, passing the raw liver of the moose from hand to hand. The liver was still quivering, like a small dog that had been skinned alive. They were very hungry; even the Frenchman gobbled the uncooked meat. That, too, was a sign that they had not stopped to hunt during a long journey. Two birchbark canoes were pulled up on the shore, suggesting that the Indians had seen the moose feeding in the water as they were padding by, and perhaps killed it while it swam.

Hawkes's dogs had not killed anything large for several days, and weak as their noses were, they were excited by the smell of blood. They lay down beside Hawkes on the pine-needle floor of the forest, but they were beginning to whimper and twitch and lick their jowls. They gave him imploring looks. Hawkes knew that he could not keep them quiet, so he let them go. He himself remained in hiding behind a ledge about fifty paces from the edge of the water. He did not know what to expect. He knew that Hair and Talks in His Dreams were sons of the woman the dogs had killed the year before. They would be terrified; it was possible that the dogs might kill one or more of them. It was also possible that the Frenchman, or even the Indians, might try to shoot the dogs.

Hawkes slid his musket forward and put the sight on the

Frenchman's heart. When the Abenakis saw the snarling wolf dogs burst out of the woods, they dropped the moose's liver and scrambled into the canoes, dragging the Frenchman with them. The dogs did not pursue. Instead they devoured the liver, tearing it apart like a woodchuck, then fell on the moose itself. They lay down in a row beside the ungainly carcass with its huge antlers, growling and yipping like sucking puppies as they worried the crimson meat.

The Abenakis paddled halfway across the lake, then stopped. Hawkes could hear the Frenchman's voice very clearly across the water. He was telling the Indians to return to shore. For a long time the canoes lay motionless in the water. At last they started back. As they paddled, the Abenakis tried to talk to the wolf dogs, barking and calling out greetings in Abenaki. The dogs pricked their ears and lifted their blood-smeared muzzles above the moose's rib cage, then went on feeding.

The Frenchman unslung his weapon, a musket with a very short barrel, and gave orders to the Abenakis to position the canoe so as to give him a clear shot at the dogs. This maneuver took some time because the dogs were shielded by the moose's carcass.

Hawkes was not worried; the canoe was sixty or seventy yards away from the dogs, and the Abenakis would come no closer. Few men could shoot accurately from that range even with a long-barreled musket. All the same, Hawkes called his dogs, imitating the rattle of the woodpecker. The dogs had been trained to respond instantaneously to this signal, and they twitched when they heard it. Hawkes called again. The Frenchman was getting ready to shoot; the stubby firearm was pressed to his shoulder and he was waiting for the canoe to stop rocking before he squeezed the trigger. At the third call, the dogs came slowly toward Hawkes, whimpering and looking back over their shoulders as they slunk across the pine needles.

The Frenchman fired just as they entered the woods, a shot of at least 150 paces. Hawkes expected the shot to go wild. The solid musket ball was seldom a perfect sphere, and as it flew out of the smooth barrel it had a tendency to curve in flight and strike ten or twenty feet to either side of the target or above or below it. A man of ordinary skill would seldom hit a stationary target at a range beyond thirty yards. Moving targets were usually struck by accident only, and the dogs were now moving very rapidly. To Hawkes's astonishment, the ball slammed through the trunk of a sapling, knocking a huge splinter off the back side and missing one of the dogs by no more than the breadth of a hand.

Who was this marksman? Hawkes peered at him. The Frenchman was enveloped in a puff of black powder smoke. The recoil of his

weapon had nearly overturned the canoe, which was rocking violently on the glossy surface of the lake. Was this luck? The Frenchman's musket was a curious weapon, at least a foot shorter than an ordinary French musket, and with a much smaller bore.

"It was a lucky shot," Hawkes told Oliver on his return. "No stubby little musket can come that close from more'n a hundred paces."

Hawkes said that he wanted to go back upriver to watch the trails from the north. The scouting party, its air of carrying important news, worried him.

But Oliver refused. "If they're coming, you won't be able to stop them," he said. "All we can do is get ready for them."

He handed Hawkes a letter. "Anyway, I want you to take this to Lebbaeus Williams," he said.

Hawkes looked at the red wax on the back of the letter. "Go to Boston?" he said. "I should be going north, not east."

"It's an important letter," Oliver said with his jovial grin. "Especially if the Indians kill me."

Hawkes left before the sun came up. At the top of the ridge, by the dead pine that Oliver had seen as a mast for a man-o'-war, he paused and looked down on the village. It was quiet, asleep, dreaming.

John Pennock began to make a new defensive plan for Alamoth even as he lay in the bloody brook after the Abenakis had departed. With houses and barns and the church burning all around him and strips of his blistered skin fluttering in the current of the brook, Pennock pondered the lessons he had learned that day. He realized that Gustavus Adolphus' tactics, which were designed to defeat a massed enemy army by attacking it in surprising ways at its weakest points, would not work in America. An attacking force of Indians could not be defeated in the open field like soldiers of the Holy Roman Emperor, but must be kept outside the walls of the town and slaughtered there. Pennock had the soul of a cavalryman, and the idea of hiding inside a fort violated every lesson he had learned in war. But he knew that defense was the key to Alamoth's survival.

Alamoth's stockade, made of thick maple posts set in the ground with the upper end sharpened to a point, had been roughly circular. After the battle, Pennock directed the villagers to build four V-shaped extensions pointing north, south, east, and west. This created a four-pointed star and eliminated the possibility of attackers creeping close to the walls, as Two Suns and Hair and Talks in His Dreams had done, without being discovered. Defenders, posted

along the rays of the stars, were able to see every foot of ground outside the palisade. They could fire down on the enemy from many different angles, setting up a crossfire in which no attacker could live.

Two underground tunnels were built, in addition to the secret tunnel leading out of the Manor, to provide the means for parties of defenders to sally forth and attack the Indians from the rear. Pennock's law for the defense of the village required every house to keep ten pounds of nocake, twenty pounds of dried beans, a sack of flour, sufficient fat and salt, and two dry cords of firewood (a cord being a stack eight feet by four by four) on hand at all times. Every house in the village was under orders to have at least one musket, fully loaded with buckshot and provided with fifty extra loads, within reach of the table at suppertime and within reach of the bed at night.

Pennock insisted on buckshot for a sound reason. Gustavus Adolphus' great invention, the infantry volley, was designed to compensate for the innaccuracy of solid musket shot by firing a great many balls all at once against a mass of disciplined soldiers. But, as Pennock had discovered, the volley would not work against a force of whirling savages; the balls simply passed between them. The old soldier realized that he needed to adapt the principle of the volley to new circumstances. He hit on the idea of using buckshot, many small bits of coarse lead sewn up in linen tubes for quick loading under battle conditions. As the tube burst under the force of the exploding powder, each musket fired a small volley of its own, scattering bits of shot over a radius of several feet with sufficient force to kill if a single pellet struck a vital organ. Even if it failed to kill, buckshot inflicted hideous wounds, being capable of peeling the skin off the muscles as neatly as a sharp knife could do, or blowing out the eyes, or severing an arm. The psychological effect of such wounds, even on savages, was not to be underestimated.

All these excellent military principles were written down in a large leatherbound book that was kept in a secret drawer of Pennock's big desk in the library. Ash, who had discovered it in its hiding place, read it aloud, a section at a time, to Oliver, who had inherited military command along with his lands.

"What does *he* know about being a soldier?" Rose asked.

"He need know nothing," Ash replied. "Pennock knew that his plans must be carried out after he died by men who had never been soldiers, and he wrote them down so that even a fool could understand."

"In that case we'll be safe," Rose said.

Oliver took to being military commander of Alamoth with en-

thusiasm. It was something like football—a lot of men all running in the same direction and shouting their lungs out. Oliver's size, his loud voice, and his jokey fearlessness would have made him a leader even if he had not been the richest man in the village. In his confidence and good humor, he reminded the villagers of John Pennock. He drilled the men and boys, posted sentries, sent out scouting parties, rehearsed attacks with the girls and boys playing the part of the Indians shrieking out of the orchards and the woods to carry out frontal attacks on the stockade. While the alert lasted, Oliver banned football. Like King Charles, he feared that broken shins and caved-in heads might deprive him of soldiers.

The snow fell before the river froze. This was the most significant fact about the weather, though nobody realized it at the time. The first storm came at twilight on a Sunday, blowing over the western mountains so unexpectedly that heaps of squash and pumpkins, and even a few shocks of wheat, were still lying in the fields. Oliver's drills had taken the men away from the fields before everything had been put under cover, and about an inch of snow had fallen by the time the villagers, indistinct figures inside the gauzy curtain formed by the big slow-falling flakes, went out at twilight to rescue the crops.

By morning the snow was knee-deep, and in the filtered light of the early sun, the blurry scene emitted a subdued glow, as if the snow had captured light on its way down from the sky and was now giving it back. It began to snow again at dusk, the same lazy descent of large flakes that stuck to everything. Clear, chilly weather followed for three days. Still the river did not freeze. Then a third, even heavier snowfall began. The paths of the village were like tunnels, higher than the eaves of the houses. Boys flung themselves off the stockade into the fluffy snow like penny-divers into the Thames.

"The danger is past," Ash said. "God has sent His snow to protect the English from the French and Indians. As in David's song of deliverance, 'the Lord had delivered him from the hand of all his enemies. . . . And he said, The Lord is my rock, and my fortress, and my deliverer.' "

It was also an article of military faith, laid down by John Pennock, that no body of men, not even the Abenakis, could march four hundred miles through deep snow, fight a battle, and then retreat another four hundred miles to their base. Everyone in Alamoth believed this.

The cycle of storms lasted exactly a week, from Sunday to

Sunday. Ash had constructed a device outside the library window to measure the snow.

"This is remarkable," he said to Fanny. "The amount of snow that has fallen in the three storms is precisely three cubits, a very clear indication of God's intentions."

Having decided that it would be impious to record its depth in any but biblical measure, Ash had redefined the cubit. The term, he explained, was derived from the Latin *cubitum*, meaning elbow.

"In Hebrew and Greek, the word means forearm," Ash said. "Why the Romans did not call it *bracchium*, I do not know. The cubit mentioned in Matthew and Luke is based on the length of the forearm from elbow to fingertips. The Roman cubit was just above seventeen inches, the Egyptian over twenty inches. I can't discover why they were different."

By measuring the forearms of everyone in the village and averaging their length, Ash had created an Alamoth cubit of exactly eighteen inches.

He and Fanny had been spending time together studying medical texts, because Oliver had assigned her to assist Ash in case of Indian attack. With Ash as her teacher, Fanny studied the techniques of amputation and probing for bullets, memorized the names and locations of all the arteries and veins and nerves, learned the purposes of the surgical instruments, practiced sewing up wounds on the shaved skin of a calf.

"You have the touch," said Ash, watching her. "You shall sew up all the wounds and hardly leave a scar."

As long as he and Fanny were concentrating their minds together, Ash seemed to forget his passion for her. In the pauses, he remembered what he felt and a look of deep melancholy came into his eyes. Knowing these signs, Fanny left Ash the moment their work together was finished.

With the help of Hepzibah Clum and two or three other women detailed as nurses, Fanny and Ash made arrangements to convert the church into a hospital. It was now stocked with bandages and lint and bedding and a table that could be used for operations.

Before the ground froze, Ash caused ten graves to be dug in the churchyard and covered up with boards. These were soon concealed by new snow. Ash showed Fanny one of the open graves, casting the boards aside in a flurry of snow.

"There may not be as many dead as we have provided for, but it is well to be prepared," Ash said. "Disease breeds in the dead."

On seeing the empty grave, dusted with bone-white snow, Fanny turned her head aside, reminded of Saint Andrew's churchyard.

"I'm very sorry if this worries you," Ash said. "But you must

know every preparation made and the reason for it. If I am killed or captured, you must carry on. There is no one else."

Suddenly he stopped talking and stared dumbly around him out of his red-rimmed eyes. In the pale light of the winter afternoon, he looked pinched and worn-out. He pointed to the snowdrifts that buried the village to the top of the palisade.

"Snowbound," he said. "We are imprisoned together—the one who loves and the one who will not permit herself to be loved."

The wind came up, driving the snow so that it stung the skin. Fanny turned her face away and wrapped her scarf around it.

Ash was trembling. "Who is the man you are waiting for?" he asked.

He was whispering. It was startling to hear him speak in such a tone of voice.

"Who?" Ash said. "Is he young? Rich? Poor? How do you know him?"

Another snow-filled gust struck them. Fanny turned her back against it. When she turned around again, Ash was running toward the Manor, stumbling and falling down in the knee-deep drifts.

The weather turned very cold. Thoughtful found snowshoes in a storage room at the Manor and taught Fanny how to walk on them. The woods were astonishing in winter, when it was much more difficult for the animals to hide. The surface of the snow was covered by the lacy pattern of tracks left by birds, squirrels, rabbits, and the predators. They heard a baby howling in a grove of trees and a moment later came on the torn remains of a rabbit and the tracks of a cougar.

Thoughtful led, moving silently over the top of the snow. They ran for half an hour, then walked for half an hour. The two girls, moving at a lope, skirts pulled up, stockings flashing, passed among the trees. Their bodies dripped sweat even on the coldest day. Finally Fanny was able to keep up this pace for hours at a time.

"Good," Thoughtful said. "You're beginning to be an Abenaki."

Thoughtful was eager to teach. She pointed out a feathery patch of snow, plunged her hands into it, and captured a grouse just as it exploded into flight. She rigged nooses in deadfalls and captured rabbits. She pointed out the ragged toothmarks of a deer on a stand of young willow and aspen. Thoughtful touched the torn browse, touched her top teeth, reminding Fanny that deer ripped their forage because they had no incisors on top, while rabbits nibbled it off evenly.

Then, very slowly, she moved into the thicket. There were no other sign—no tracks, no droppings, no indication that deer were

present. But in the center of the thicket a dozen deer were huddled together. Immobilized by the snow, they did not flee or even try to move. Every bit of bark had been stripped from the limbs of the saplings all around them so that only bright polished yellow wood showed. Thoughtful took the ear of a doe gently in her hand. The deer panicked, eyes rolling, spindly legs churning.

"We are not hungry today, sister," Thoughtful said to the doe. The animal tried to escape.

"She doesn't believe me," Thoughtful said.

Fanny and Thoughtful came to the edge of the woods. Oliver's great naval firs stood behind them, bent under tons of snow. They were standing on a bluff above the river.

It was frozen now, and people were skating on it. Fanny recognized Rose among the skaters. She wore her fur-lined cape, a very pretty garment for skating. It swung when she stroked, flared when she turned; she was the best and most graceful skater on the river.

A bonfire, burning on the ice, sent a plume of smoke into the cloudless sky. The frozen river, perfectly clear of snow, gave off a dull metallic glitter. The air smelled of ice.

Fanny, mildly hypnotized, washed her face in snow. Because the waters of the river were sealed beneath the ice, the silence was absolute. The skaters' voices drifted across the snowfield, amplified and undistorted like voices coming over the water.

All around, even and unmarked, lay the snow, like a vast prison of space.

"Snowbound," Fanny whispered to herself.

# 2

Oliver had noticed Hepzibah Clum on his first day in Alamoth. Her bouncing figure and her happy nature reminded him of the girls at the Widow's.

A week or two after she came to live in the Manor, he showed her the hiding room.

"In case the Indians attack I want you to come here and hide," he said. "Meantime, I want you to bring a bottle of rum and a pitcher of ale down here every night to keep the provisions up to

standard. Come late, after everybody's asleep, so nobody sees you. You *can* keep a secret, can't you?"

Hepzibah looked him in the eyes until they were both smiling, then nodded her head. After that, they met in the hiding room nearly every night when the house was asleep.

"How old are you?" Oliver said at the end of a week.

"Eighteen."

Hepzibah, wearing a shift, was straddling his lap as he sprawled on a chair. Oliver hefted her globular breasts.

"How long have you had these?"

"Since I was twelve."

"Then I wasted six years in London when I should have been in America."

"Nobody should be in America," Hepzibah said.

"Why not?"

She giggled. "Too little of this. Too many Indians."

Hepzibah was terrified of the Abenakis, but she understood Thoughtful. Hepzibah's own sister, the wife of Talks in His Dreams, looked on herself as a member of the tribe that had captured her. She had four children, all males, a fact that made Talks in His Dreams the envy of other men. Hepzibah knew these facts because Fanny had brought her news of her sister; she had long known that she was alive, and that she would not come back to Alamoth, as a result of the report John Pennock had brought back after his own journey to Canada.

"Does that trouble you," Oliver asked, "having little red nephews and a papist for a sister?"

"That's better than being lost and dead like my brothers," Hepzibah replied.

"Maybe Thoughtful will persuade this fellow she's married to to let your sister come for a visit."

"She wouldn't come—she told Captain Pennock so. She's afraid the English would keep her here. Nobody ever wants to come back to this life once they've been captured."

"Nobody? Why not?"

Hepzibah giggled. "You don't know? They say it's the Jesuits. But it's not—it's this." She moved her body up and down. "You can do as you like, with anyone you like. The Indians don't mind."

One night as they lay talking, Hepzibah amused Oliver with tales of the old religion.

"What's that?"

She tickled him. "You know—potions, spells, curses."

"You mean you're a witch."

"Not me. It's to keep the witches off."

As a child on Pennock's estate an old aunt had taken her with her onto the moors to collect frog spit and worts and simples and taught her how to mix them into potions.

Hearing this, Oliver sat up. "Is it, now? Would it work on Rose, do you think?"

Rose had been suffering from headaches. They began with a numbness in the lower lip and spread up through the face and into the skull, producing the sensation that two heavy spherical stones were lodged in the brain, one behind each eye. The stones rubbed together, producing an unbearable screeching noise.

Rose was sure that the headaches, like their cause, Oliver's ligature, were the result of witchcraft. After listening to her symptoms, Ash prescribed strong coffee and cold compresses to relieve the pain. He was fatigued by Rose's obsession with sorcery. As was his habit, Ash dispensed a scriptural prescription also. He was out of patience with Rose.

"Ponder Jesus' pain when the soldiers placed the crown of thorns on his head," Ash said, "and smote him on the head with the reed, and mocked him."

"What good will that do if I am under a witch's spell?" Rose asked.

"Picture the Cross and our Savior's poor body," Ash roared. "That will drive the demons out!"

Rose needed a nurse, and on Oliver's orders Hepzibah undertook her care. She brewed Rose's coffee and tended to the cold cloths. Rose hardly ever came out of her room now. Hepzibah remained with her, brushing her hair, helping her in games of dress-up, coaxing her to eat supper from a tray.

Rose had not ceased wanting a child to inherit the Manor and the rest of John Pennock's estate. She wandered the Manor at night, clutching a Bible for protection, hoping to surprise Oliver in sexual congress with a familiar.

"Do you think the creature comes to him in his sleep?" Rose asked Hepzibah.

"You shouldn't worry yourself, mum," Hepzibah replied.

When Rose's headaches were at their worst, she distinctly smelled the spermy odor of coitus, and it was then that she would dash into Oliver's bedchamber and strip the covers off him as he slept. Almost always she discovered him in a state of arousal.

However, as soon as he woke and saw Rose, even if she was naked and already in bed with him, the ligature would tighten and his male part would subside.

More often, Oliver wasn't even in his bed. When this happened,

Thoughtful's cat was invariably absent also. The cat, Rose believed, turned into a succubus and seduced Oliver in his sleep.

"I smell its stink on him," Rose said. "It smells just like a woman."

Hepzibah did not scoff. She listened sympathetically, clucking and making mewing sounds of agreement.

One day she said, "You can do something about witches if you will."

"Yes," Rose said. "Hang them, burn them. But nobody will do it."

"Let's start with the headache," Hepzibah said.

She told Rose what she knew about potions and spells.

"Do you know one for ligature?"

"I was too young. But I know the one for the evil eye, and maybe that's what gave you your headaches."

"It *is* evil eye," Rose said. "I've always known it. The Impostor stares at me just like a cat. She never blinks."

The next night, when the moon was up, Hepzibah brought everything necessary for a potion against evil eye—half a cup of mother's milk, borrowed from a cousin, and a cup of water from the river.

"The water has to come from a stream in which somebody has drowned," Hepzibah explained.

The gibbous moon, white as snow, shone through the stripped branches of the oak outside Rose's window. Hepzibah blew out the lamp, threw open the sash, and beckoned to Rose. She handed Rose the cup of milk and the cup of water.

"Now," Hepzibah said, "put three drops of mother's milk into the water by the light of the moon. Now look into the cup by the light of the moon. If the three drops of mother's milk remain separated, you haven't had the evil eye put on you. But if they run together on top of the water and make an eye, then you have."

Rose stared down into the cup.

"The drops came together," she said.

"Then it's the evil eye for certain. Now say, 'Get behind me, devil, get behind me, saint.' "

"Get behind me, devil, get behind me, saint," Rose repeated.

"Quick, look straight at the moon as if he's your lover, and drink half the cup—but only half."

Rose drank, shivering in the bitter draft that came through the open window. The mother's milk, oily and sweet, overwhelmed the taste of the cold water.

"Now," said Hepzibah, "you must pour what's left in the cup onto a living tree—the oak."

Rose flung the water out the window. It splashed on a limb that nearly touched the house. The cats used to sit on the limb, staring through the glass, before the snow and the cold drove them away. Remembering the cats, Rose shuddered and slammed the window shut. She wondered through her pain if Hepzibah knew a ritual that would drive the cats out of the oak once and for all.

Her headache seemed to be reduced to two small, ice-cold pellets. They ran out of her skull, down her throat, along her arm, into her hand, and out the finger on which she wore her ruby ring.

"It's gone!" she said, kissing Hepzibah.

"Do you think she's really cured?" Oliver asked.

"My old aunt swore by it," Hepzibah said.

"Then let's do more. What's good for the way she feels about cats?"

"The only cure for that," Hepzibah said, hanging over Oliver with her eyes squeezed shut, "is for the cat to turn into something nice."

But as the days passed and Rose still could not dissuade Oliver from giving everything to Thoughtful, the headaches came back, as bad as ever.

On the night that Hawkes departed for Boston with Oliver's letter to Lebbaeus Williams, the pain in Rose's head nearly drove her mad. The screech of the stones rubbing against each other was unbearable, and the odor of sex was so overpowering that Rose imagined that it was seeping into her pores, into the strands of her hair, so that she herself would smell of it for the rest of her life.

Rose whimpered from the pain as Hepzibah, who had made love to Oliver in the hiding room less than an hour before, applied cold cloths to her forehead.

"Shall we try the potion again?" Hepzibah asked. "I can fetch the milk from my cousin in no time, and water from the river."

"It won't work," Rose said. "The Impostor is too strong for us."

Rose reached out and touched Hepzibah. She had grown fond of her; it was such a relief to have someone about who believed what one said.

"It's not your fault," Rose said. "The spell would have worked with water from an English river. Nobody but Indians has ever drowned in the Connecticut—that's what's wrong with the potion, it doesn't have the right things in it."

She sat up. "Magpie," she said. "Magpie can go after Hawkes and stop him."

She ran down the passageway to Oliver's room. Oliver was

awake, sitting up in bed with a lighted lamp and a pitcher of ale beside him, a quill in his hand, and the many pages of a letter spread out on the coverlet.

"Hello, Rose," Oliver said. "Another headache?"

"Thanks to you. I'm sending Magpie after Hawkes to bring him back."

Oliver smiled at her.

"I thought you might," he said. "So I sent her with him for a visit to her people."

"Sent her with Hawkes?"

Oliver flinched, laughed, and reached under the covers. His big hand came out holding Thoughtful's cat. He rubbed the animal against his cheek, taunting Rose, and then let it hop down onto the coverlet.

A musket, loaded with buckshot according to Pennock's rule, stood against the wall. Rose snatched it up, pulled back the hammer with both hands, lifted the muzzle. As she carried out these actions one by one, she caught glimpses first of Oliver, whose face was lighting up with amusement as he watched her, then of the cat, which saw Rose and began to bristle.

Oliver's mouth opened to form a word. The cat put back its ears and gathered itself to leap, as if it were about to turn into something else. Oliver spoke Rose's name.

The musket went off with a thick gush of red flame and smoke, flying out of Rose's hands as it fired, obliterating the odor of lovemaking with the acrid stench of scorched powder. The bed, and Oliver lying on it, was enveloped in a cloud of gray-white smoke. To Rose, the report sounded as if the entire house had exploded. She fell to the floor, covering her ears.

Fanny and Thoughtful found her there when they came to the door. When she saw the girls she began to shriek, a high-pitched sound that went on and on. Inside the cloud of powder smoke, the cat was yowling. The smoke cleared a little. Oliver's face, stunned, and powder-burnt, appeared above the cloud. He was looking down at the bed.

"Jesus, Rose," he said, in the exact tone of voice he had used after she bit him on their wedding night.

The screaming cat, half the fur peeled from its body, was tumbling convulsively over the coverlet. Oliver reached for the animal and it fastened its teeth into the fleshy part of his thumb. He lifted his hand, gazing dumbly at the dying cat, and tried to shake it loose, but it would not unclench its needly teeth.

Fanny looked away. Her eyes fell on what she thought was a second dead cat. She wondered where it could have come from,

and then realized that she was looking at Oliver's left foot. The buckshot had nearly torn it off the ankle.

Oliver, struggling with the cat, shifted his weight. Blood spurted from a severed artery and splattered on the pages of Oliver's letter, which had been blown all over the bed by the muzzle blast of the musket. Oliver stared at the red stains, not yet realizing that they were blood. His eyes began to search for the source of the stains.

"Oliver, the cat," Fanny said in a distinct voice. "Look at the cat."

Oliver nodded obediently, grinned, weakly shook his hand with the cat dangling from it, and fainted.

"Squirrel, find Ash, quick," Fanny said in French.

Thoughtful ran out the door. Fanny grasped Oliver's foot, a mangled red nest of ripped flesh and shattered bone. She could not see the severed artery.

She said, "Rose, bring the light."

Rose was still shrieking. Fanny slapped her hard on the cheek, leaving a smear of blood from Oliver's wound on her skin, then handed her the light.

"Hold it close," Fanny said. "I must be able to see, Rose. Otherwise, you will have murdered him."

Rose, swaying and gagging, held the lamp. The spurting blood, sticky and warm, sprayed on Fanny's hair. She still could not see the artery. She seized Oliver's pitcher of ale and poured it all at once into what had been Oliver's huge hammer of a foot.

The blood washed away for an instant and she could see into the wound. She put her fingers into the chewed flesh, grasped the artery between the nails of her thumb and middle finger, and pinched it shut.

"The smell," Rose said, sobbing, "I can't bear it."

She staggered out of the room, holding the lamp high and vomiting.

"Rose, bring the lamp back!" Fanny shouted, but Rose was running down the passageway.

The cat meowed into the darkness, a series of long thin notes above the staff. Oliver lay perfectly still. After a moment, Fanny could hear him breathing.

# 3

Aboard the *Pamela*, after he had discovered that Fanny was intelligent, Ash had shown her a series of anatomical drawings by the Italian artist Berrettini, called Pietro da Cortona. He had peeled back the skin of a classical male figure and exposed the blood vessels and nerves, the tendons, the bones. The detail was exact, the draftsmanship exquisite.

As he prepared to amputate Oliver's foot, Ash spoke to Fanny about the differences between the drawings and the realities of the body.

"Paper and ink have many advantages over flesh and blood from the point of view of clarity and consistency," he said, touching Oliver's mangled foot with the point of a scalpel. "In the living body, nerves and veins are seldom where they should be. In the diseased or injured body, the form in which the surgeon invariably sees it, the artistry of God has been vandalized. Here the astragalus is destroyed, the metatarsus is shattered, the great phalange and two others are missing. No foot or ankle remains. Could Rose have imagined what complexity lay concealed beneath this skin? Proverbs: 'A foolish woman is clamorous: she is simple, and knoweth nothing.' "

Oliver's leg was propped up on two wooden blocks, the ruined foot dangling. Ash had every candle in the house brought into Oliver's bedroom and placed around the bed. Oliver's stripped body took on the waxy light of the candle flames. He had been slightly injured by the buckshot in many other places, and rills of blood from these untended wounds formed a scarlet network on his skin.

His hands and his undamaged ankle were tied to the bedposts. With a quill pen, the same one Oliver had been holding in his hand when Rose came into his bedchamber, Ash drew a line around Oliver's leg, just above the ankle.

There was no blood now. Fanny operated the tourniquet, a triangular device made of brass and leather and canvas straps that fitted around the leg. The tourniquet, operated by a screw,

compressed the tibial artery between the ankle and the knee. By adjusting the screw on Ash's command, she was able to regulate the flow of blood, leaving the flesh clear while the surgeon made his incisions, but permitting the blood to flow so as to cleanse the wound—Ash believed in the antiseptic properties of blood in combatting animacules—and to prevent the flesh from mortifying. Fanny was also charged with counting Oliver's pulse and respiration and reporting any fluctuation to Ash.

Ash picked up his knife again. "Tighten," he said.

Fanny rotated the screw on the tourniquet a half-turn. Ash made an incision completely around the leg along the inked line, cutting through the hairy skin and the fat beneath it down to the muscle at a single stroke.

He folded this flap of skin back into a cuff. He touched the rosy exposed muscles with the point of the knife: "*Tibalis anterior, peroneus longus, peroneus brevis, flexor digitorum longus.*"

He went on speaking in Latin: "See? The nerve is not where the Italian's pen said it would be. Flesh is not art. Loosen."

Fanny operated the tourniquet. Why was Ash speaking Latin? He had not done so for months. She had to concentrate in order to understand, and Oliver's life was at stake.

"Count his pulse," Ash said. "Tell me if there is any change."

Ash cut through the muscle in two swift motions, transferring the knife from his left hand to his right as he reached the halfway point of the circle. He picked up a saw.

"The blade is made of clock spring," he said in English, as there were no precise words for clock spring in Latin.

He went on in Latin as he sawed through the tibia and the fibula with assertive strokes: "The blade must be very strong and perfectly tempered. It was developed for use in cutting ivory, particularly ivory combs, where great precision is required. The teeth of the surgeon's saw are larger than those of the ivory saw so as not to become gummed with green bone, a most difficult substance to cut cleanly."

Oliver's leg was now severed. It fell onto the bed. Ash put down the saw. Working with amazing rapidity, he tied off the two tibial arteries and the other blood vessels one by one, naming them as he did so.

"Loosen."

Fanny turned the handle on the tourniquet.

"More. Open it completely."

Holding a lamp in front of a small mirror, Ash put his face close to the stump, searching for bleeding. There was none.

"Help me," he said. "Dip this lint in this bowl of oil, so much at a time, then hand it to me."

Fanny did as she was told. Ash packed the stump in lint, drew the flap of skin over the stump, sutured it with a large curved needle, and wrapped it in bandages. Oliver was still unconscious. Ash rolled back his eyelids, listened to his heart, counted his breathing, and wrote all this information down, sharpening the quill with his scalpel. The whole operation had taken no more than twenty minutes.

Oliver groaned and moved. His severed foot still lay on the bed. A wave of fear went through Fanny, the first emotion she had felt since the operation began. What if Oliver opened his eyes and saw the foot? Fanny picked it up, put it into a basin, and slid it under the bed.

Ash was already at work, probing for lead in Oliver's other wounds. As he extracted the pellets, he threw them into the floor. None had penetrated far. Fanny bandaged each wound with oil and lint while Ash probed the next. Oliver was now shuddering in his unconsciousness. They removed the wooden blocks, lowered his stump, and covered him with blankets.

Oliver shouted something—they could not understand what—and worked his tongue in his mouth. His eyes opened in a wild stare. Ash seized his lower lip between his thumb and forefinger, twisted, and squeezed. Oliver's eyes came into focus.

"Do you know where you are?" Ash thundered.

Oliver nodded.

"Who am I?"

"Ash."

"Who is this person?"

"Fanchon."

"No. Try again."

"Fanny. Give me a drink,"

The pitcher of ale had been refilled. Fanny poured some into a cup and held it to Oliver's lips. He choked, coughed, and when the spasm reached his stump, screamed in pain.

"*Jesus Christ!*" he cried.

Fanny put her arms around Oliver's neck and pressed her cheek against his stubbled face. He oozed clammy sweat and made noises low in his throat.

"Oh," he said, "oh, Fanny-my-love, what a fool, what a fool."

"Ssshhh," Fanny said. She knew he meant himself.

Ash mixed opium with honey. As soon as Oliver could unclench his teeth, Fanny put the medicine on his tongue with a spoon. It was a strong dose. In a matter of seconds, Oliver's eyes closed.

"Graves could never teach me Latin, such a fool," he said before he lost consciousness.

Ash untied Oliver's wrists and sat beside the bed, counting his pulse. Fanny picked up the basin containing Oliver's amputated foot and walked along the darkened passageway, holding her breath against the stench. Rose had been right about that. Why should human flesh smell so much worse than meat? No doubt Ash could explain.

On the landing of the stairs, a candle burned beneath a mirror in a golden frame. Fanny looked at herself in the glass. Her face was covered with dried blood; the bodice of her nightgown was caked with it.

Fanny's skin burned feverishly. She put the basin down and opened the window. Cold air gushed into the house; snow fell off the sill onto her bare feet. Her body stung from it. She washed her face in snow, handful after handful, and scrubbed the blood off her hands.

The window faced east. Venus, as white as the moon and as big, compared to the moon, as the stone to a peach, was just rising above the horizon.

Fanny remembered the ancients' name for it: Phosphorus, the morning star. When it appeared as the evening star, the Greeks had called it Hesperus. Henry had taught her these facts as a means of making Greek more interesting, holding her up to the window in Catherine Street and pointing out the yellow planet, no larger than a pea, that shone so weakly over London.

She stood by the open window, quaking in her blood-soaked nightgown. The wind had begun to blow, moaning down the chimneys and making the Manor creak like a ship, driving the snow before it and lifting it up in plumes and devils that raced across the open spaces.

# 4

The wind had been blowing for three days when Two Suns finally discovered the Abenaki name of Philippe de Saint-Christophe. Until then Philippe had had no name among the Abenakis, because they could not remember anything about him.

As always happened, his true name, Atelang, or Wind Hunter, came into being at the same time that his story began. At the time, the Abenakis and Philippe were walking down the Connecticut River, about two days' march from Alamoth.

It was midmorning. The ice under their feet was so clear that they could see the water running beneath it. Mountainous banks of snow shut the river off from the surrounding country, creating a little world of bluish ice and white snow with a strip of bleached sky above; they had not seen forest or animals, or even the tracks of animals, since the new moon. The moon was now just past the half.

It was very cold. The wind blew hard at their backs. The Abenakis could not run fast enough to keep warm because they were held back by the small sleds they were dragging behind them. This was very annoying. Without sleds, they would have been able to move much faster and work up a sweat. The sleds were Philippe's idea. They were loaded with rope, gunpowder, food, two small cannon, and many pairs of moccasins and snowshoes.

Because of the sleds, which kept on getting snared on the branches and rocks that were frozen into the ice, the Abenakis were always falling down. Hair, who was clumsy, had broken his nose the day before, and now he fell again. Something struck his testicles as he went down and he writhed on the ice. The other Abenakis stopped in their tracks and looked away from the injured man, as politeness required.

Hair, speaking to his injury, said: "This is very painful. Please stop. I think we should bury these sleds and go home and leave you here to hit some Cowasuck or Englishman in his balls when he digs them up."

Two Suns was the oldest man in the party, and the Abenakis had

learned that the French preferred to talk to old men, so he said to
Philippe: "Maybe my son Hair is right. We could bury the sleds
and try to find some deer that are stuck in the snow and kill them,
and then go home."

"*Jaghte oghte*," Philippe said. "Maybe not."

Just then a white-tailed buck plunged over the snowbank and
fell, head over heels, antlers rattling, onto the ice of the river. The
Abenakis, knowing that anything could happen in the world at any
time, were not startled by this event, but they were very interested
in it. How had the deer reached the river in such deep snow? What
could be chasing it?

Stunned by the fall, the buck lay where it was, oblivious of the
150 Abenakis in full war paint who were standing on the ice no
more than twenty paces away. It was not dead; its ribs heaved and
the Indians could see its breath condensing in the chilled air. The
deer lifted its head. As it regained consciousness, the wind howling
down the Connecticut dumped the scent of all 150 human beings
into its nostrils.

This overpowering whiff of mortal danger seemed to disconnect
the animal's spirit from its legs. The buck scrambled to its feet,
tried to run, fell, got up again, fell again, tried to run again, tried
to climb the vertical snowbank, and crashed onto the ice a second
time. The Abenakis saw that the deer had broken one of its
forelegs.

Finally the deer staggered to its feet. Legs splayed, it stood
broadside to the wind. The wind pushed the buck downstream. Its
hooves skidded over the ice, and after a moment in which the deer
slid faster and faster over the ice, it sat down on its white backside.

The Abenakis burst into laughter. The deer looked away, pre-
tending that he did not hear them. Used to be Bear got out his
bow and launched an arrow, but the wind took it away. Talks in
His Dreams tried too, with the same result. Soon the air was full of
arrows, but the wind, eddying in gusts of forty or fifty miles an
hour, blew them harmlessly away as if the deer were protected by
an enchantment. Dozens of arrows disappeared into the snowbanks
or clattered on the ice.

This was a very bad sign. "I think we had better go home," Hair
said again in a very loud voice. "This deer doesn't want us to go
any farther down the river."

Just then the buck seemed to come to an understanding of the
ice under its feet. It straightened its legs, lifted its head, and gave
Philippe, who was the human being closest to it, a long brotherly
gaze.

Then, as easily as if it were running over the springy floor of an evergreen forest on four good legs, it bounded down the river, stepped gracefully among the spent arrows.

*"Huh!"* the Abenakis said in unison. The deer heard them and bounded very high into the air.

Then the Abenakis saw that Philippe was chasing the buck. Knees pumping, greatcoat swirling, he sped down a long straight stretch of the river. The deer ran easily ahead of him, rack thrown back along its spine, white tail flagging. The Frenchman seemed to have no chance of catching up.

Philippe had insisted that every Abenaki bring a shield with him. For some reason he was now carrying the shield that belonged to Used to be Bear. The shield was strapped to his back. Because Used to be Bear was so huge, this was the biggest shield in the tribe. It was made of the doubled hide of an entire moose, and it was prettily decorated with the severed and tanned ears of the moose and of many other kinds of animals.

Philippe seemed to be gaining on the buck, which was still heading down the ice in a series of tremendous bounds. As he ran, Philippe fixed the bayonet on his short rifle.

He was moving at tremendous speed, faster than the injured deer could run. The Abenaki suddenly understood why. Used to be Bear's shield was acting like a sail; the wind was pushing Philippe along with it like a leaf.

The deer was tiring. It fell, rose to its feet, ran on, fell again. Philippe skidded past the prostrate buck and turned. He thrust the shield into the snow so that it wouldn't blow away and walked slowly back toward the deer. The animal, confronted by the man, and apprehending the overpowering scent of danger behind it, scrambled to its feet and tried to climb the snowbank. It fell, skidding down the ice with legs whirling.

Philippe, who was waiting for it, stabbed it through the heart with his bayonet. The buck reared onto its hind legs, heart pumping vermilion, and fell over backward.

Leaving his sled behind him, Two Suns jogged down the ice. Philippe was cleaning his bayonet in the snow. His chest was heaving after his long run after the deer.

Two Suns said, "That was interesting, Wind Hunter. You only had to stab the deer once to make it die."

Two Suns knelt down on the ice, cut open the buck, removed the liver, and handed it to Philippe.

"Wind Hunter!" he said, very low, so the owner of the name would not hear.

Philippe ate some liver and smiled at the old man. In his fur hat, with fresh meat on his breath, he looked like an Abenaki, fearless and big-nosed, except that he had blue eyes and wore no paint.

# 5

The wind died on the night of the November half-moon, a Sunday. By then the drifts, piled against the walls of Alamoth, were fifteen feet deep. Cold followed the wind, so that the snow squeaked under the snowshoes of the Abenakis as they approached the stockade. Because of the bitter weather, no guards were posted on the parapets. Even the dogs were inside.

Philippe and his Abenakis simply walked up the sloping drifts, stepped over the palisade as if it were a stile between two peaceful meadows, and fanned out into the village. The tunnellike paths, which resembled a network of trenches, concealed the Indians as they drifted through the town, taking up the posts Philippe had assigned to them.

Two Sun's objective was the Manor. At midnight, he stood on the crest of a snowdrift with Used to be Bear at his side, looking directly into Rose Barebones' window. Rose stood in front of a mirror in her shift, trying on a green velvet hat with a peacock feather pinned to the crown. She wore red stockings that were gartered at the knees. A dozen gowns—red, blue, green, white, yellow—were scattered over the floor.

The Manor was the only house in the village with the shutters down and light in the windows. Inside the next window, a big Englishman lay on a bed, sweating from a fever. A girl with a long black braid was bathing his naked torso, which was covered with small wounds. The Englishman's right hand was swollen to nearly twice the normal size. His left foot had been cut off; the stump was wrapped in bandages.

Two Suns recognized all these people from the stories Squirrel had told her brothers when they met her in the woods above Alamoth.

Down below, in the shadow of the house, Hair and Talks in His

Dreams were talking to Philippe in signs. A small cannon, mounted on a sled, lay at their feet. With great difficulty, because the runners of the sled kept sinking into the soft snow under the weight of the gun, they had pulled it up the path to the Manor.

Philippe, his bayoneted weapon slung across his back, carried a shielded lantern that cast a pattern of yellowish dots on the snow. He looked upward to Two Suns and Used to be Bear and signed that the attack was about to begin. They all dropped to one knee and their Jesuit, a tiny man with a big tonsured head called Father Nicolas Laux, blessed them, waving over their bowed heads the tall cross he had used as a walking staff on the long march.

"Remember your shields," Philippe said in signs as he rose to his feet. "When you see an Englishman with a musket, kneel behind your shield, let him shoot, then charge with the tomahawk."

He pointed the cannon at the front door of the Manor, swiveling the sled and kneeling to sight along the barrel, then opened the lantern and lit the match on its flame. Two Suns and Used to be Bear peered in the windows again, looking for Squirrel. The woman was standing by the mirror, wearing a different hat.

Philippe touched the match to the breech of the cannon. A tongue of red flame spurted from the muzzle as the charge went off with a loud bang. The recoil sent the sled hurtling backward over the snow. It disappeared into the darkness.

A small hole, burning at the edges, appeared in the heavy planking above the lock, but the door was otherwise undamaged. At the sound of the cannon shot, the village erupted in noise—the pop of muskets and pistols, the sound of battering rams pounding against doors and shutters, the peculiar scream of English women that had frightened the Abenakis the first time they heard it, and the shrill yammer of the Abenaki war cry.

Flames blossomed in the darkness—the wormy flicker of muzzle flashes, the inferno of barns filling up with red light and boiling white smoke as hay and straw were set alight, the weak flames of burning arrows stuck in wooden shingles.

Used to be Bear, holding his shield before him, launched himself through the air at the window of Rose's bedchamber. It was a double-size window, more than broad and tall enough to admit even a man of his size. The weight of his body knocked the entire sash out of the frame.

As Used to be Bear came through the shattered glass, Rose was in the act of removing a veiled hat that was a particular favorite of hers. Looking through the veil, everything appeared softer around the edges than it really was. But as soon as Rose saw Used to be Bear's demonic face, a blue mask with bars of yellow and red

drawn across the nose and white rings around the savage eyes, she knew that she was looking at a wild Indian, and at nothing else that had ever existed in the world.

Used to be Bear stamped his feet on the floor and uttered a war whoop. Rose covered her ears. Used to be Bear advanced on her, shouting even louder. He smelled like a dead animal. Rose's eyes widened, her nostrils dilated, her ears collected the tiniest sounds. All this happened against her will. Rose did not want to see, smell, or hear anything.

As Pennock's law required, a musket leaned against the wall beside Rose's bed. She ran to it and picked it up.

Wild-eyed, barely able to breathe, Rose struggled to draw back the hammer. Used to be Bear made no move to interfere with her. He stood where he was, watching her. He seemed to have no fear. Underneath his horrible paint the muscles of his face formed an expression of mockery. Finally Rose managed to cock the musket. She swung the muzzle upward, just as he had done in Oliver's room, and just as before, there was a tremendous bang and a cloud of smoke.

The full load of buckshot struck the doubled moose hide of Used to be Bear's shield, ripping off many of the tanned ears that decorated it, but doing no other damage. Used to be Bear, who had been kneeling behind the shield, stood up and shouted in glee. He was untouched.

"Squirrel, you were right," he shouted. "The English bullets are too weak to go through an Abenaki shield."

Used to be Bear came toward Rose, slamming his feet onto the floor one after the other in a parody of menace, like a boy playing bear.

She pressed her body against the wall. He rolled his eyes, bared his crooked yellow teeth, and shook his hatchet above his head. All the while he was crooning in a strange tremolo; Rose realized that he was singing. She darted one way, then another, trying to escape, but the Indian was always ahead of her.

He went on singing in his terrifying falsetto, repeating the same phrase over and over: *shonts-mwa shonts-mwa shonts-mwa.*

Suddenly, as Rose tried again to dart by him, Used to be Bear seized her by the arms and lifted her into the air. She struggled helplessly. This man was stronger, far stronger, than Oliver. He had a twisted waxy hole in the side of his head instead of an ear. He threw Rose onto the bed.

"Have pity," she cried. "Oh, have pity. Save me. Husband! Fanny!"

Used to be Bear rolled Rose over onto her stomach, yanked her

hands behind her and tied them together, then bound her ankles and pulled them up into the small of her back. He forced a green stick between her teeth and tied it tightly around the skull and under her chin with rawhide thongs.

Then he turned Rose over, rubbed paint off his own face with a forefinger, and smeared a bar of white and one of yellow across the bridge of her nose to mark her as his captive.

*"Shonts-mwa shonts-mwa shonts-mwa,"* he said.

Rose screamed, a strangled sound because of the stick between her teeth. Used to be Bear gave the rawhide thongs a sharp tug. The stick acted like a bit, tearing at her lips and tongue. While she was still gagging from the effects of being bridled, he slapped her hard on the bottom, knocking her breath out of her body. Rose subsided.

Used to be Bear put on Rose's green velvet hat, the one with the peacock feather, snatched a burning brand from the grate, and thudded out of the room, baying like a wolf.

Three more Indians, smaller than the first one and painted in a slightly different way, leaped into the room through the broken window. They paid no attention to Rose as they bounded across her bedchamber, baying too. She could hear them going through the house, shattering glass, overturning cupboards, smashing furniture.

Terrible cold came in waves through the window. Rose knew that she was freezing to death, she knew that the big Indian was going to come back for her before that happened, she knew that the worst was yet to come.

# 6

Two Suns knew that Squirrel had taught her friend Fanny to speak in signs and that she had told her his story. Therefore, when he went into Oliver's room, he made the sign for Two Suns, touching himself on the chest, so that she would not be fightened. He thought that this was necessary because his face was painted black, with gashes of yellow running down the cheekbones, and he

was wearing his wolfskin hat with all the teeth still in the wolf's mouth.

Fanny recognized him at once. His hair was gray under the wolf pelt and he was squat—much shorter than she had imagined him, hardly as tall as Fanny herself, but otherwise as Thoughtful had described him.

Fanny made the signs for *I know you.*

"My daughter Squirrel will be here soon," Two Suns said in signs. "My son Hair is looking for her. This is my other son, Talks in His Dreams."

Talks in His Dreams, a leathery middle-aged man who had painted his face red and his nose white, stood outside in the passage.

Inside the bedchamber, Oliver's musket still stood against the wall. Two Suns picked it up and cocked it. He tossed his shield to Talks in His Dreams, who crouched hastily behind it. Two Suns pointed the musket at the shield and pulled the trigger. The weapon, which had not been reloaded after Rose fired it, did not discharge.

Two Suns grunted and threw the musket out the door. Talks in His Dreams returned his father's shield, then vanished. Used to be Bear and Hair could be heard shouting and breaking things elsewhere in the Manor.

The noise did not interest Two Suns. He sank to the floor, crossing his legs as he went down, to wait for Thoughtful.

Oliver had slept through all this. He was awake only fitfully. Ash had prescribed large doses of opium to dull the pain of the amputation and to induce sleep. Now Oliver opened his eyes and saw Two Suns.

"Who the hell is that?" he asked.

Fanny did not answer. She hoped that Oliver would think that he was imagining Two Suns. He had been hallucinating for two days. He stared at Two Suns for a long moment, then lost interest and closed his eyes again.

Oliver's right hand, the one the cat had bitten in its death throes, had become infected. In the excitement of the amputation, nobody had told Ash about this wound, so he had not cleaned it when he tended to Oliver's other injuries.

Oliver woke again and looked out the window. It was filled with the red light of the burning town. Not more than half an hour had passed since the attack began, yet every structure in Alamoth except the Manor seemed to be in flames. Oliver heaved himself up on his elbows and gestured with his swollen hand.

"They've lit the fires along the Thames again, the bloody fools," he said. "Smoke doesn't bother the corpses or the rats. All the cats

are killed, the lord mayor paid out tuppence a cat, did you know that, Fanny-my-love?"

"Yes, Oliver."

He tried to get up and cried out in pain when the weight of his body came down on his stump. Fanny held a cup to his lips. The medicine, more opium, dribbled down his chin. Oliver tried to wipe it away and knocked the cup out of Fanny's hand.

Fanny covered him up. Oliver, sweating from the effects of opium and fever, threw off the blankets. He squeezed Fanny's hand and looked idly out the window. Screams floated up from the village, the figures of Indians flitted among the fires. One of Rose's hunters, an arrow stuck in its rump, bucked furiously up and down the steep path between the Manor and the town.

"Something should be done about the horse," Oliver said. He seemed to notice nothing else.

Two Suns lifted his blackened face, sniffing and listening. Thoughtful's deep voice, speaking Abenaki, came down the passageway. In a moment, Thoughtful herself came in, followed by Talks in His Dreams and two other Indians. One of them, who wore Rose's green velvet peacock-feather hat and was almost as large as Oliver, had no left ear. Fanny recognized him as Used to be Bear. Oliver lay on his back, asleep.

Two Suns took Thoughtful by the forearms for a moment, then ran his hands over her head, arms, torso, and legs, as if to make certain that all her bones were in place. With tears running down his painted cheeks, he delivered a long singsong speech. The other Abenakis grunted from time to time or sang little songs of their own.

Thoughtful turned to Fanny. "Two Suns thinks that we had better leave now, before the ghost dogs come back," she said.

"Thoughtful?" Oliver said.

Fanny drew Thoughtful away from the bed. "Just go," she said. "Don't say goodbye to Oliver."

"We are waiting for you," Thoughtful said. "The four of us can travel very fast."

"What four?"

"Two Suns, Hair, you, and I. But we must leave now, before the others."

"What others?"

Thoughtful gave her a puzzled look. "Women and children," she said. "The Abenakis will take the ones they want."

Two Suns was already tugging at Thoughtful's hand, pulling her out of the room. Talks in His Dreams took Fanny's hand. She

snatched her hand away. Oliver uttered a loud snore and woke himself up.

Fanny leaned over Oliver's bed. His face was running with sweat. She wiped it with a cloth.

"You know, Fanny," he said, "there's something wrong. I smell smoke and there are all these damned painted Indians around the bed."

"It's all right," Fanny said. "They're just friends of Thoughtful's."

"Jesus," Oliver said. "Is that Rose?"

Used to be Bear had brought Rose into the room. She was still trussed up, with the bit still in her mouth, dressed in her shift and red stockings, but now she wore her fur-lined cloak and unbuttoned boots.

Thoughtful put her arm around Fanny, the first time she had ever made such an English gesture, "Come," she said. "We must go now, Fanny."

"Go?" Fanny said. "How can I go? He'll die if he's left here."

Oliver said, "If you had looked like your father instead of your mother, Fanny, you and Thoughtful would look like sisters. God, but I miss Henry."

He smiled up at the two girls, wiping his eye with the back of his hand.

Thoughtful looked impassively out the window at the burning town. She was paying no attention to Rose.

"Two Suns says it is time to go," she repeated. "He's afraid of the ghost dogs."

Fanny gave her a long look. "Then why didn't you poison them?"

Thoughtful did not resent the question. "It will be better if the Abenakis kill them," she said. "Then they will be sure that they are dead."

Two Suns said something in Abenaki. Suddenly Talks in His Dreams put his arms around Fanny's waist from behind and lifted her off her feet. The force of the grip on Fanny's diaphragm expelled the air from her lungs and turned her face red.

Oliver lunged, seizing Fanny's wrist with his good hand. Talks in His Dreams set his feet and pulled, shouting. Oliver was a powerful man even now, but the force of the tug-of-war pulled him over onto his side, throwing weight onto his stump, and he screamed in agony.

"Oliver, let go," Fanny said. "It's all right."

She looked around frantically for Thoughtful, but she had disappeared. So had Two Suns and Hair and Rose and Used to be Bear. Talks in His Dreams grunted and tightened his grip around Fan-

ny's waist. Oliver, his face contorted with pain, held on to her wrist and tried to get a grip with his swollen hand on the bedpost, but the hand was useless. He shrieked as his raw stump was twisted under his own body, and concentrated every bit of his strength in the hand, huge and horny, that held Fanny's wrist.

Talks in His Dreams kept walking backward, planting his feet and throwing his weight and Fanny's weight against Oliver's grip.

Inch by inch, Oliver was being pulled off the bed. Fanny knew that he would bleed to death if he fell out of bed and his stump burst open.

"Oliver, let go," she said.

He bellowed in pain and anger. His locked hand quivered violently. Fanny closed her eyes, then twisted her wrist against Oliver's thumb, breaking his grip.

Talks in His Dreams fell over backward, arms still gripped around Fanny's waist. Oliver fell back on the bed, then pushed himself up again and reached out again for Fanny.

Talks in His Dreams ran out the door, carrying her like a sack, and plunged down the stairs and out into the snow.

# 7

"Your ordeal is over," said Father Nicolas Laux, the little Jesuit. "You're safe among those who love you now. Let us pray."

"A man is dying," Fanny said. "You must let me help him."

Father Nicolas made a gesture, dismissing her words.

"Many men are dying," he said.

Holding on to the staff of his long cross with both hands, he fell to his knees in the snow and then pulled Fanny down beside him.

He had a small man's voice, sibilant and uncertain. It could barely be heard above the noise made by the burning town. Fed by swirling drafts of chilly air, the fires made a throaty choirish sound.

Fanny did not listen to the Jesuit's prayer. Her eyes were fixed on the Manor. She expected it to burst into flames at any moment with Oliver inside it. The picture of this disaster formed in her mind: the paintings, the tapestries, the furniture, the harpsichord

and spinet, John Pennock's great bed, all afire, and finally, Oliver, drugged and crippled, trying to escape the flames.

"Father," she said, "I must go back."

Her hands hung inert in her lap. Father Nicolas clasped them together, lacing the fingers as if she were a very small child.

"Of course you must, God wants you to," he said, misunderstanding. "But there are many dangers ahead. When was your last confession?"

"More than a year ago. In England."

"Then this must be a general confession. Be brief but heartfelt."

He inclined his head, ready to listen.

Ten paces away, Abenaki warriors were painting the faces of half-naked women to mark them as their property. An adolescent boy, shrieking in fear and bleeding from many cuts, was running the gauntlet between two rows of Indians who were beating him with clubs and hatchets.

Fanny tried to get to her feet. The priest restrained her.

"What sins have you committed?"

Fanny answered him, knowing that he would not let her go until she did. "Unbelief. Despair. I have been angry at God."

"How many times?"

"Many times. Nearly all the time."

Father Nicolas gasped, as if he had never before encountered these transgressions, but his voice was mild: "These are serious faults, but you have been separated from the church and you are very young. For now, it is enough to be truly sorry."

Father Nicolas hurried on through the forms, muttering so rapidly and so softly in Latin that some of his words were lost altogether.

"Do not fear, my child," he said in French. "You will be in a state of grace during the dangers that lie before us."

He gave Fanny absolution, and to her amazement, prepared to offer her Holy Communion. She did not want the sacraments; she did not believe in their power.

All that was happening around her—the burning town, the massacre of innocents, the hate that would not die—proved the truth of everything her father had ever suggested to her about the true practices of the religious.

Fanny looked at the Manor where Oliver lay bleeding. Against the background of flames, Talks in His Dreams was jogging across the village green toward the big house, his silhouette wavering like a reflection in water. Fanny was certain that Talks in His Dreams intended to set the Manor on fire.

"That man," she said. "Stop him."

Father Nicolas followed her eyes and saw Talks in His Dreams disappearing into the smoke.

"He has his work," the priest said. "Trust in God."

Father Nicolas elevated the host, smiling beautifully. The pyx containing it was a powder horn slung over Laux's shoulder. The host itself was a morsel of barley bread. Laux sipped frozen wine out of the neck of a gourd.

According to the belief in which Fanny had been raised, these rude ingredients had now become, through consecration, the transubstantiated body and blood of Christ. She knelt in the snow and opened her mouth for the bread. It dissolved on her tongue, as tasteless as snow. Her eyes never left Talks in His Dreams; he was now so far away that he could only be seen when he passed in front of a burning house.

"What a brave girl you've been, praying in secret all these years, living among God's enemies," Father Nicolas said as he put away his Communion kit. "We know a great deal about your life. You must tell me about your confessor in England. What was his name? Possibly I knew him."

"Evans, Philip Evans," Fanny said.

"Ah, one of the English martyrs. He was hanged in Wales for saying Mass and hearing confessions. He is certainly among the blessed."

"Hanged?"

Until now Fanny had not known what had happened to Philip Evans. She asked Father Nicolas no questions. There was death all around her; she did not want to know more than she already knew.

Father Nicolas collected his things. "We march in an hour," he said, in his mild way. "Think about God and His blessed martyrs, not forgetting my martyred brother Evans, and the hardship will seem lighter. Every single one of us, French and Abenaki, has received the sacraments. The entire expedition is in a state of grace."

"Father, am I a prisoner?"

The Jesuit was startled. "No. You are a rescued Catholic."

"Then I will remain here."

"Remain? You cannot remain. These people have seen you receive Holy Communion from a Jesuit. They will execute you as a traitor."

He gestured to the herd of captives standing fifty paces away on the village green. Fanny looked at them. All but a few looked away, unwilling to meet her eyes.

"I cannot leave my godfather," Fanny said. "He will die if he's left alone."

Once again the priest appeared to be startled by Fanny's words; surprise seemed to be his chief mannerism. "This person is a Catholic?"

"No, but he was present at my baptism and he has always protected me and kept the secret of my faith."

"Then God will be merciful to him. Here are your clothes. Look, the Indian is coming back."

Talks in His Dreams appeared with an armful of things—Fanny's warmest cloak, woolen petticoats and woolen stockings, the little sack that Antoinette had sewn to be carried in the holy pocket in her petticoat. It contained Fanchon's crucifix, the fifty gold sovereigns Praise God had loaned her, miniature paintings of Fanchon and Henry Harding, and the ruby necklace that Oliver had given to Fanny aboard the *Pamela*.

Talks in His Dreams had also brought Fanny's snowshoes and three sacks of the nocake that Thoughtful had hidden in their bedroom.

No one but Thoughtful could have assembled these possessions or told Talks in His Dreams where to find them. Fanny asked in signs where she was. Talks in His Dreams made the sign for Two Suns and Hair, running, and north.

Father Nicolas had vanished. Fanny put on her coat and tied the other things into a bundle. Then she started up the path toward the Manor. Talks in His Dreams let her go halfway. Then he came up behind her, gripped her around the waist as he had done before, and, grunting with every step, carried her back between the high snowbanks to the village green. There he set her down and handed her one last gift from Thoughtful, a knife.

"Look," a voice said from the crowd of captives. "He's given her a knife. Papist whore."

Most of the captives still wore their nightclothes. Many were barefoot. The men were trussed up, hands and feet tied, bridled like Rose with sticks thrust into their mouths. From time to time one of them would fall down. When that happened, an Abenaki would strike the fallen captive on the soft parts of his body with a club until he struggled to his feet again.

One or two small children had already been brained for making noise. Mothers suckled their babies, and even some larger children, to keep them quiet. The Indians passed among the women and children, looking at teeth, feeling arms and legs and breasts. Twenty or thirty living men and boys hung in the trees along the green, suspended from ropes tied under their arms. A few had been kicking when Fanny first came down from the Manor, but all now hung limp and unresisting, turning slowly on the ropes.

The night grew steadily colder. The prisoners, even the men who were tied up, milled constantly, trying to prevent their feet from freezing. The captives stood at the edge of a pond of blood. The cattle of Alamoth, handsome quick-stepping red Devons with long spreading horns, had been driven onto the green. The Abenakis were slaughtering them one after the other by cutting their throats. The blood froze almost as soon as it was spilled, forming a brownish scrim on the snow. Captives, using axes, chopped the dead animals into chunks of meat, leaving the hide on according to the Indians' orders.

The captives were staring at Fanny and whispering. She knew very few of them. Betsy Ash was not there. Fanny searched the crowd, looking for Ash, thinking that she could send him to Oliver—surely the French would allow that. What would they want with Ash?

Then she saw Hepzibah Clum standing with her arm around her younger sister. Both had streaks of red and white paint on their round faces. They were barefoot; Hepzibah wore a nightdress with a shawl over her shoulders, while the younger girl was wrapped in a quilt.

Fanny went to them, Talks in His Dreams following close behind. The little girl, Totsie, buried her head in Hepzibah's bosom when she saw the painted Indian approaching. Talks in His Dreams took hold of the long auburn braid hanging down the child's back and pulled her face around so that Fanny could see it. He touched the paint on the girls' faces and the paint on his own to show that they belonged to him.

Gurgling the French words, Talks in His Dreams said, *"Elle sonts les soeurs de ma femme, quelle joie."*

To Hepzibah, Fanny said, "He says that he is your sister's husband."

Hepzibah hugged Totsie more tightly and gave Fanny a look filled with loathing. "You can talk Indian?" she asked.

"No. He's speaking French. Have you seen Ash?"

"What do you care?"

Hepzibah was running in place to keep her feet from freezing and slapping Totsie on the bottom to remind her to do the same. The snow under their feet had been churned into slush.

Fanny said, "The Indians have Rose, I don't know where. Oliver is up there. His stump is bleeding. I must find Ash."

Hepzibah, still running in place, began to sob. She looked up at the Manor. There was lamplight in its broken windows. The fires were dying out now, but the acrid smoke that still issued from the what was left of Alamoth was settling near to the ground.

Fanny handed Hepzibah the bundle of clothes that Thoughtful had assembled. Hepzibah, still sobbing, shook her head.

"Give them to your priest, he wears petticoats," she gasped.

The other captives, who had been listening, murmured. "Papist whore!" one said, setting off a string of insults.

Fanny looked at Hepzibah for a long moment, then turned away.

Used to be Bear appeared out of the darkness, moving at a trot with Rose's slender body draped over his shoulders. He set her on her feet beside Fanny. Rose was fully dressed now in a woolen dress and a fur bonnet and her fur-lined cape. Her face was painted blue, with dark lines underneath her lavender eyes and her lips painted white.

"It's all right," Rose said. "All he did was paint my face."

"Have you just come down from the Manor?" Fanny said. "What about Oliver?"

"I know nothing about him," Rose said, sniffling. "All this, everything, is Oliver's work. He wouldn't listen. That little bitch was a papist spy. You know that, Fanny; everyone knows it."

The whites of Rose's eyes, inside the painted blue mask, were red-rimmed from the smoke. Fanny realized that everyone else's eyes were red too, even the Abenakis', so that the whole company of people, victor and captives, looked as if they were weeping.

Used to be Bear stroked Rose's fur cloak, then reached underneath and squeezed parts of her body, grunting in satisfaction as he felt her arms, her buttocks, her stomach, and ran his hands down her legs.

Rose made no effort to resist; in fact, she appeared not to notice. She was serene, detached, aristocratic. She inspected the other captives. The sight of them, half-clothed, faces lifted up in pleading, seemed to disgust her. She turned away.

"*Shonts-mwa shonts-mwa shonts-mwa*," said Used to be Bear.

Rose looked at Fanny. "He keeps on saying that," she said in a clear drawing-room voice. "Whatever does it mean?"

"He's saying, '*J'ai de la chance, moi*,'" Fanny said. "It means 'Lucky me.'"

# 8

"Are you quite all right?" Philippe asked.

Fanny was not in the least surprised to see him. He wore a bearskin hat and carried his peculiar stubby musket slung across his back. He was taller than Fanny remembered.

"Are you in command here?" Fanny asked.

"I am the only French officer present."

"Good. Then you must tell Talks in His Dreams and the others to let me go up to the Manor. There is a wounded man inside."

"What wounded man?"

"My godfather."

"What wound?"

"His foot was blown off with a musket before you came. It was an accident."

Over Philippe's shoulder, Fanny saw the captives looking at the two of them with hatred on their faces. Philippe's own features, regular and handsome, were as deeply calm as before. The wailing children, the women shuddering barefoot in the snow, the burning town, seemed not to move him at all.

"You say this man is your godfather," he said.

Fanny did not repeat herself or plead. Their eyes were locked together again. Philippe nodded and took her arm.

"I will accompany you."

"Then hurry," Fanny said, and ran up the path toward the manor.

Rose and Talks in His Dreams had left a lamp burning inside the door. Fanny picked it up as they entered. Philippe had unslung his musket and now he held it across his chest. A long bayonet was attached to the muzzle. He went up the stairs first, probing the darkness with the blade.

Oliver lay on the floor of the passageway, unconscious. Evidently he had crawled after Fanny and fainted there. She kneeled beside him and felt the pulse in his neck as Ash had taught her. It was rapid and thready.

"Help me," Fanny said.

She and Philippe lifted Oliver onto the bed.

"The lamp," Fanny said.

Philippe held it closer. The bandages covering Oliver's stump were soaked in blood. Fanny unwrapped them. The whole flap of the wound had come undone from its sutures, spilling the bloody lint that packed the wound. Blood trickled steadily onto the bed from somewhere deep inside the wound. Fanny lifted the leg, directing Philippe to fold the bolster beneath it.

"I don't know what to do," Fanny said.

Philippe had been watching her in astonishment as she uncovered Oliver's wound.

"I think it may be too late," he said. "There is a great deal of blood."

"No," Fanny said. "Wait."

She ran out of the room, leaving the lamp behind. Halfway down the stairs she heard Philippe following.

"Stay with him," she said. "I'll be back in a moment."

In the library, working by the moonlight and firelight that filtered through the windows, Fanny pulled the books off the shelf and opened the masked door to the hiding room. At the bottom of the stairs she could already hear Ash's voice as he prayed inside the stone chamber.

Within, a candle burned. Ash lay on the floor, beating his fists on the stones as he prayed.

"Get up," Fanny said.

He lifted a face with wet tears.

"Fanny! Go! Don't come here!" he said.

His medicine box and surgical box stood on the table; he kept them by him at all times in case of Indian attack. Now the attack was over and he did not know that it had taken place. Fanny picked them up.

"It's Oliver," she said. "The wound is open."

Ash seized his boxes from Fanny and bounded up the stone stairs into the library.

"My God, the town!" he said when he saw the burning houses through the window.

"It's over now," Fanny said. "Come upstairs."

Ash seemed not to notice Philippe, who appeared to be standing guard in the bedchamber. He looked at Oliver's wound, listened to his heart, rolled back his eyelids.

"We must be quick," he said to Fanny. "The artery is leaking."

Working with his usual deftness, but keeping silent except to give curt orders to Fanny, he stopped the bleeding and repaired the wound. Fanny assisted him, dipping lint into oil as in the first operation to pack the stump. Ash sewed the flap of skin into place.

"Bandage it, using plenty of lint," Ash said to Fanny. "Cover him warmly."

Fanny wrapped up the stump, holding it in her lap as she sat on the bed. Oliver remained unconscious, pale-skinned. His breathing was shallow. Fanny knew that even Ash was not certain that he would live.

Ash sank to his knees and folded his hands to pray; the fingers were smeared with Oliver's blood. Lifting his eyes, he seemed to see Philippe for the first time.

"What are you, in that hat?" he said.

Philippe flinched a little in surprise; he had not heard Ash in full voice before. He ignored Ash, who now was staring at him in growing anger as he realized that he must be the enemy.

"Hurry," Philippe said to Fanny in French, using the familiar form.

"*Dépêches-toi?*" Ash said. "*Dépêches-toi?* What do you mean, *dépêches-toi?*"

"We are leaving," Philippe said.

"Leaving?" Ash roared. "Fanny! *Is this the man?*"

Oliver heard him even in his unconsciousness and cried out. Ash got to his feet, his face working. Philippe stood his ground with his arms folded, as calm as ever. He looked on Ash with curiosity, unsurprised that he spoke French, unsurprised by his anger. His musket stood against the wall behind him; he made no move toward it.

"Bastard!" Ash cried.

Fanny laid Oliver's stump gently down and started to slide off the bed. Before her feet reached the floor, Ash launched himself at Philippe, bony arms flailing. He made no sound at all as he attacked.

Philippe stepped aside, arms still folded. Ash crashed against the wall and fell to the floor, stunned. He saw Philippe's musket and seized it. Now Philippe moved, very quickly, and grasped the weapon too. The two men struggled for a moment, then Philippe twisted the weapon from Ash's hands and backed quickly away so as to have room to use the bayonet.

"No!" Fanny said.

Ash threw himself forward again. Philippe reversed his weapon and struck Ash over the heart with the butt. The blow paralyzed Ash but did not knock him unconscious.

Philippe handed his musket to Fanny and rolled Ash over onto his stomach. With a length of rawhide rope that he produced from inside his clothes he tied Ash's hands behind him and then trussed

up his legs, bending them at the knees and tying the ankles to the wrists.

His eyes still on Ash, Philippe held out his hand for the musket. Fanny gave it to him.

"Come," he said. "We can't stay any longer."

Ash was struggling now, rolling on the floor, but still he did not speak. The wind came through the broken window, blowing snow onto the floor. Philippe took Oliver's cloak off its peg and spread it over Ash, covering him up head and all.

He held out his hand. Fanny took it and he led her out of the house.

They had left the lamp behind. It burned in Oliver's window.

Inside the Manor, Ash was shouting. His voice was muffled by the cloak, but Fanny could make out what he was saying. He was calling her name, over and over again.

# 9

The dogs discovered the fire and woke Hawkes around midnight. They had all been sleeping together for warmth in a snow cave cut into a big drift about fifteen miles southeast of Alamoth. Although he was a light sleeper, Hawkes was so tired that he did not rouse immediately. He had been running on snowshoes for fourteen hours before he went to sleep. The morning before, moving west from Boston through the oak and chestnut forest, he had come upon a hunting party of Squakeag Indians. Game was scarce because of the snow, and they were a long way from their usual hunting grounds, which lay to the north of Alamoth on the Connecticut River.

After Hawkes gave them bacon, the Squakeags told him that they had been chasing a big buck across a field of snow three days before, wearing it down nicely because they were on showshoes and the deer was plunging through deep snow, when suddenly it leaped onto the frozen river. Though the Squakeags had no reason to suspect that they were not alone, they did not chase after it, but crawled to the edge of the high snowbank, covered their heads and faces with snow, and looked cautiously downward.

What they saw made their blood run cold: a war party of Abenakis, all wearing paint and shooting arrows at the buck. The wind made the arrows miss. A white man flew over the ice, running without moving his legs, and killed the deer with a long knife. After this the Squakeags traveled as far to the east as possible to get away from the Abenakis and to see if they could find another deer.

"Have you seen any deer?" they asked Hawkes.

"The dogs killed a doe yesterday," he said, giving them tobacco. "Follow their tracks."

Hawkes strapped on his snowshoes and started running westward. He counted a thousand paces, then walked a thousand paces, then ran another thousand. The open forest was ridged with big snowdrifts, some of them twenty feet high, so that crossing them on showshoes was like climbing and descending an endless field of sand dunes.

The dogs sank into the snow up to their bellies, floundering and whimpering. Hawkes had stopped to rest and eat nocake only once between dawn and moonrise. Even as he ran, sweating and holding his side, he did not think that he could reach Alamoth in time to warn the town about the approaching war party, but he believed that he might arrive in time to fight.

Finally Hawkes could go no farther without sleep. He dug the snow cave, flooring it with balsam boughs, and crawled inside with the dogs, closing the entrance behind him. His animals, three wolf dogs and two mongrels, were as exhausted as Hawkes was. It was the mongrels, not the weak-nosed wolf dogs, that smelled the smoke and heard the sounds of the massacre on the night wind and woke Hawkes. He watched the glow in the sky for a minute or two, then started a fire of his own and cooked what was left of his bacon. He wanted to have as much fat in him as possible, to give him endurance for what lay ahead.

Hawkes angled northwest on a course that would bring him to the river at the first big falls above Alamoth. He knew that the sentries at the English towns south of Alamoth would have seen the fire, and that a rescue column would begin marching north on the river as soon as it could be mustered. In his opinion this was a waste of time, and would probably be a waste of life—English farmers never had much luck battling Indians in open country.

The Abenakis would travel on the river for a while if it remained clear of snow. Then they would split up into small parties as they always did and scatter westward along the dozens of streams that led to Lake Champlain.

Hawkes's plan was to intercept the main body above the big falls

before it separated. After that, he would follow just one of the smaller parties—the one led by the Frenchman, because it would be entrusted with the most valuable captives: Rose, Fanny, Ash if they took men, and most of all, Thoughtful. Probably there would be five or six Indians in this detachment. Hawkes believed that he could kill the Abenakis one by one, using the dogs, then capture the Frenchman, rescue the captives, and return to what was left of Alamoth.

With luck he might capture the Jesuit too—there was always a Jesuit. The ransom for two French captives could amount to hundreds of pounds.

Dawn broke. Hawkes kept moving, using the column of smoke that hung over his left shoulder as a reference point. By sunrise he was traveling almost straight north along the back crest of the ridge that stood above the river. This was easier going than east-to-west travel had been because he was running in the direction of the snowdrifts instead of across them, and the dogs could run freely between the drifts.

The dogs were hunting hungrily, running down rabbits and tearing them to bits. Once, passing a deadfall, the mongrels smelled a hibernating bear and found the vent melted in the snow by the sleeping animal's breath. The wolf dogs had already begun digging, making the snow fly and woofing happily, when Hawkes came upon them. He called them off, kicking them with his snowshoes, in the nick of time. He felt sorry for the dogs—they loved a bear fight—but he could not afford to spare the time or have them injured now.

By noon Hawkes knew that he was opposite the falls and a little to the south of them, so he turned due west again until he came out on the ridge above the river. The forest was dense here, with big white pines buried to their lowest branches in drifted snow. Hawkes knew that the main party of Abenakis must still be several miles to the south, coming up the river, but it was possible that an advance party had reached the falls.

All Indians except the Mohawks, and especially the Abenakis, wandered off in all directions on their own. There was no such thing as a formation, a command, a common purpose. Every Abenaki did whatever came into his head whenever it happened to come into his head, and no other Abenaki would ever interfere with what he did. Hawkes had seen them sit down in the middle of a skirmish, or walk away into the trees singing with arrows flying everywhere. No one minded.

Until now, Hawkes had not bothered with stealth and woodcraft. He changed tactics. There was nothing Hawkes could do

about the tracks he and his dogs had left up to this point, but as they entered the grove of big pines, he took off his snowshoes and ordered the dogs to walk, all together in a pack, before him—or, rather, behind him, because he was walking backward, brushing away their tracks with a pine branch. Once inside the trees, Hawkes told the dogs to lie down and stay quiet. He dug another snow cave, hollowing it out with a snowshoe, and sent them inside.

Hawkes looked up at the tips of the pines, towering above him, and located the tallest tree. Strapping his musket across his back, he began to climb, slowly and carefully, so as not to shake the tree and cause snow to fall off its upper branches. Any such disturbance would be noticed by any Indian who happened to be within a mile of the tree.

The climbing brought a different set of muscles into play. Hawkes realized, for the first time in hours, how tired he really was. During the night he had developed an unusually severe stitch in his side. He had run through it, making his mind as blank as the snow, but it had taken hours, or what seemed to be hours. Now that he had stopped moving, the sweat on his body was turning clammy.

He shivered. His mouth was dry. He picked up a handful of snow from the tree and put it in his mouth. The snow had been lying on the pine needles for several days, and it was full of dirt and dead matter. His nose filled from inside his mouth with the odor of pitch. He spat out the dirty snow.

Hawkes continued to climb, very slowly. The trunk of the fir grew smaller, no bigger around now than Hawkes's stout body, and he could see the whippy tip of the tree twenty or thirty feet above his head. He paused and leaned back, looking upward for the best branch to stand on. He wanted to be high and have a clear view of the river and the valley below, but at the same time he wanted to be concealed.

The sun was strong now. It winked on something bright above Hawkes's head. He leaned back again, trying to see what it was. It might be ice, but how could there be ice in the top of a tree when there had been no thaw?

The object flashed in the sunlight again. Hawkes inched his way all the way around the trunk of the tree, looking upward, trying to make it out. He did not dismiss the possibility that an Abenaki was waiting for him at the top of the tree. It was unlikely—the mongrels would have smelled him—but it wasn't out of the question. An ambush in the top of a tree was just the sort of attack, combining a good joke with the ignominious death of an enemy, that the Abenakis loved.

Hawkes got out his hatchet and began to climb as fast as he

could without knocking snow off the tree. There was no point in concealment now if there was someone in the tree with him. He gritted his teeth, swinging his weight upward, and made a picture in his mind of an Abenaki warrior standing with his back against the trunk—the paint on his face, the hatchet in his hand. He had learned from the Indians that if you pictured what you were going to see, you were not so surprised when you saw it.

But in the end he was surprised at what he had discovered. A skeleton, the corpse of the drowned Frenchman, was bound to the trunk, still hanging where Two Suns had tied it. Every vertical bone was still bound firmly in place—even the skull, which was fastened to the tree by a thong passing through the eye sockets.

The glitter Hawkes had seen had been made by a silver crucifix, two inches wide, that swung from a chain on silver beads among the skeleton's ribs. Hawkes took the crucifix, lifting the skull off the neck bone in order to remove it, and put it into his pocket with Lebbaeus Williams' letter. Thoughtful might like it, not to wear but to look at, to remind her after she and Hawkes were married, of the days when she lived among the papists.

Hawkes climbed up a little higher in the tree and looked up and down the river. A mile or so to the south, the main party of the Abenakis was dogtrotting toward Hawkes in a long straggling file. Behind them, a smaller party halted on the ice, waiting for something.

Hawkes had time. The Indians would have to leave the river and climb through the snow to the top of the falls. They could not possibly do so before dark. He climbed down and crawled into the cave with the dogs. The air inside was as warm as skin. Hawkes ate some nocake and some snow from the ceiling and closed his eyes, making pictures in his mind of his pursuit of the Frenchman who had stolen Thoughtful.

# 10

The Abenakis took forty captives from Alamoth, eighteen young women, twelve children, and ten men to carry the meat from the slaughtered cattle. Five of the women were pregnant. The Indians wore snowshoes, but the captives had none, so they sank into the snow with each step. Those who carried extra weight, mothers with small children and people of both sexes who had slabs of raw meat on their backs, floundered and fell. The Abenakis beat them with clubs and kicked them, making them run.

At the river, the Abenakis unpacked their sleds and fed the captives nocake, placing a large pinch of the parched and mortared corn on each tongue. The male captives, using the bloody axes with which they had butchered the cattle, were directed to chop a hole in the ice for drinking water. Few of the English had ever drunk water by choice. Now, at the Indians' insistence, they swallowed far more than any of them had ever drank at one time before.

Each captive was then given a pair of dry moccasins to wear and a pair of snowshoes to carry. Finally, the Abenakis gave each of them a bit of beef tallow, still warm from the animal, and watched them chew and swallow it, clubbing those who hesitated.

By now it was three hours after midnight and the half-moon was well down in the west. Strangely, the women whose faces had been painted were more easily identifiable by moonlight than the others. Fanny recognized Betsy Ash, Hepzibah and Totsie, and a dozen other girls and women she knew. She went to Betsy.

"They didn't take Edward," Fanny said. "He's with Oliver in the Manor."

Betsy showed no interest in Fanny's words. Her face was painted yellow, with a bold stripe down the bridge of the nose. Now that she and her unborn child had been captured, she seemed calm, withdrawn. She wore nothing but a nightdress and petticoats. Fanny took off her cloak and draped it around the other woman's shoulders.

"Edward's alive?" Betsy said.

"Yes."

"Did he even know what had happened while he was praying?"

Fanny hesitated, then shook her head. "He couldn't know. He was in the hiding room."

Betsy shrugged her shoulders and Fanny's cloak fell into the snow. She was holding up her large belly in her two hands.

The column began to move up the river. Philippe formed it into three elements—a rear guard that sent scouts downriver to watch for any rescue column that might be in pursuit, an advance party that traveled fast upriver to make certain that the way ahead was safe, and the main body, consisting of about forty Indians and all the captives. The male prisoners pulled sleds loaded with beef, the two small cannon, and the powder and shot.

The women and children went with the Indians who owned them: Rose with Used to be Bear, Hepzibah and Totsie with Talks in His Dreams: blue paint with blue paint, red paint with red. Except for Rose, who was dressed for a stroll through St. James's Park, the women were as thinly clad now as when they were taken out of their beds, in voluminous woolen nightgowns with linsey-woolsey petticoats and pantaloons beneath.

The Abenakis started off at their usual dogtrot, gesturing to the women to move at the same pace. Some understood and tried to run. Most simply started walking with the ground-thumping, deliberate gait of countrywomen. The Indians signed for them to go faster. When the women did not obey, their captors pushed them forward, running along behind and switching them on the buttocks. But as soon as the switching ceased, the women stopped trotting.

The one exception was Rose. With her superb athletic gifts, and because she was in excellent physical condition as a result of spending four hours a day on horseback and several more skating on the oxbow, she kept up to Used to be Bear with ease.

Fanny, who knew from Thoughtful's stories what was required, also moved at the Abenaki pace. Because she had been almost the last to start, she found herself jogging through the entire stalled column. Women lay on the ice sobbing and gasping for breath or crouching in fear over their children. Each one, on seeing Fanny's unpainted face and her skirts and petticoats pulled up through her belt to her thighs, gave her a look of hatred.

She heard shrieks of pain and terror behind her and ran back downriver. At the very end of the column, Talks in His Dreams was driving Hepzibah Clum across the ice, beating her across the back with his unstrung bow. Trying to escape, Hepzibah plunged into a knot of Abenakis who were digging in the snowbank at the

edge of the river. Her big globular breasts leaped under her nightgown as she ran. Talks in His Dreams followed, flailing.

Fanny shouted at him in French and began to move toward him. Suddenly she felt herself seized by the arm and pulled off balance. She looked up to see who had grabbed her. It was Philippe, who had been standing among the Abenakis by the snowbank. The Indians had stopped what they were doing—they seemed to be digging a hollow in the snowbank—to watch the beating.

"Don't interfere," Philippe said. "He's doing her a kindness."

"He's killing her."

"No, he wants her to live; she has value to him. If she doesn't run, if they all don't run, they will die."

"Then why don't you tell them so in English?"

"Do you think they would believe me?"

Fanny realized that the Abenakis thought that the English were stupid: they did not even know that they would freeze to death in their thin clothes if they didn't run to keep their bodies warm.

Talks in His Dreams dragged Hepzibah back onto the ice. His hands was clapped over her mouth to stop her from howling. Her eyes, looking out of the red paint that covered her face from hairline to chin, were rolling in fright and pain.

"Perhaps *you* should explain it to them," Philippe said.

About a quarter of a mile ahead, Rose and Used to be Bear were dogtrotting steadily along, surrounded by Abenakis. Fanny was already warm. She took off her coat, rolled it up, and began to run after Rose. She caught up with her around a bend in the river and fell into step beside her.

"How long do they expect us to do this?" Rose said. She was still wearing her fur-lined cloak and did not seem to mind the warmth. "I'm getting a stitch in my side."

Fanny repeated what Philippe had told her. "The women don't understand, Rose. If they don't do what's wanted of them, the Indians will kill somebody."

"They've already killed half the town. Savages. Look at this one, he might as well have fur and teeth like a dog. How could this happen? Where were the men? Where are they now?"

"Rose, the women will listen to you. They admire you. You must tell them."

Rose did not respond. Dawn was breaking, and in its more intense light, Rose's blue face with its white lips was breathtakingly beautiful.

"I can't bear the stink," she said. "The fire, the dead meat, these savages, even you, Fanny—you're sweating like a butcher."

"Rose . . ."

Rose looked at Fanny, now that there was enough light to see her. "Why aren't you painted like everyone else?" she asked.

Behind them, far down the river, they heard a faint popping sound. It was not faint to Rose, of course.

"Thank God, muskets," she said. "We're rescued."

She turned around and started running in the other direction. Used to be Bear pursued her, caught up with her, thrust his arm beneath her crotch, and heaved her through the air. Rose, shrieking, landed on all fours and slid on the ice, tearing the knees out of her red stockings. Before she stopped sliding, Used to be Bear picked her up, lifted her skirt, and gave her a loud whack on the bottom.

Then he stepped back and grinned at her.

"Fanny!" Rose cried. "Tell him to stop!"

Fanny spoke to Used to be Bear in signs: "She was going back to tell the other women they must run like the Abenakis."

"I thought she was running away," he said. "It's hard, having a woman who can't talk. Will you teach her the signs?"

"Yes," Fanny said, "if you let her talk to the women."

Used to be Bear was listening to the gunfire. In the skimmed light of the dawn, Abenakis and the panting captives were running toward them, slipping and staggering on the ice.

A young woman carrying two small children in her arms fell down. The Indian at her side pulled her to her feet and pushed her forward. She fell again. He snatched the larger child, a boy of about two, out of her arms and flung him over the snowbank. The woman tried to climb the snowbank.

The Indian pulled her down and pushed her forward over the ice. She refused to move her feet and fell down again. He threw the other child over the bank. She crawled toward the snowbank, clawing at the ice. The Abenaki tried again to make her run, but she flung her body back against his strength, reaching for her children. He split her skull with his hatchet and left her where she fell, with blood gushing onto her bright yellow face.

Neither the woman nor the Abenaki had uttered a sound during their struggle, but one of the children could be heard crying convulsively, "ah-*lah* ah-*lah* ah-*lah*," as the rest of the captives and Indians ran upriver, everyone suddenly in step like soldiers marching in double time.

# 11

The Abenakis of the rear guard, scouting two or three miles downriver from the main party, encountered the English rescue column almost immediately. They let it go by, counting the smelly noisemaking militiamen as they lumbered upriver. Then they slipped past them and dashed across the snow to report to Philippe.

"Do they have scouts out ahead?" Philippe asked. "Do they have snowshoes?"

The Abenaki said no, the English were moving all together in a column of fours and had no snowshoes with them.

Philippe ordered two snow caves dug in opposite banks of the river. He hid six warriors with bows and arrows in each cave, concealed the entrances with snow, and fell back around the bend in the river with another twenty men.

The twenty lay down, head to foot, along the banks. The river made a sharp bend to the east here. With the rising sun behind them, shining into the eyes of the advancing English, they would be virtually invisible.

Although he did not intend to use them unless everything went wrong, Philippe loaded both small sled-mounted cannon with grape-shot and pointed them downriver. Then he unslung his musket and replaced the priming. One of the Abenakis hooted like an owl to let him know that he could hear the English coming. Philippe heard the enemy too, coughing and rattling and jingling like infantry anywhere.

Making no attempt to conceal himself, Philippe waited in the middle of the frozen river. The spot he chose for himself was somewhat more than two hundred paces, or four times the range of the most accurate musket, above the bend in the river.

The English came into view, powder horns jouncing, muskets at the slope, heads turning nervously in fear of ambush. Philippe recognized their leader by his full boots: clearly he was the local squire. He wore a sword belt diagonally across his chest with a big silver buckle just over the heart.

Philippe remained standing in plain sight until he was certain

that the oncoming English saw him. Then he dropped to one knee and cocked his weapon, placing the sight on a point just to the left of the English captain's silver buckle. He took a deep breath and squeezed the trigger while he let it out. The hammer fell on the flint, the priming ignited, and as Philippe slowly released the last of his breath through his nostrils, the weapon fired, making a flat report like the crack of a whip.

The bullet penetrated the chest of the booted Englishman an inch below the buckle, piercing the left atrium of his heart. It then passed through his ribs and the muscles of his back, tearing out a chunk of flesh the size of a kidney as it exited, and smashed into the abdomen of the man immediately behind him.

The next militiamen in the file stumbled over these two instantaneous corpses, causing the column to collapse on itself. At this point, the Abenakis who had been lying on their faces along the riverbanks leaped to their feet and charged, barking the Abenaki war cry. The English broke apart, firing a ragged volley at the Abenakis. The balls, flying in all directions from the smooth-bore muskets, fell dozens of paces short.

The enemy fell back with empty weapons. The Abenakis hidden in the snowbanks burst into view, launching arrows. The English formed into a protective scrum, with men on the outside bravely taking arrows in their bodies while their comrades reloaded their muskets, a process that involved pouring a measured amount of powder into the barrel, pushing a greased patch of cloth or leather and a lead bullet after it with a wooden ramrod, and finally filling the priming pan with powder. During the forty or fifty seconds that this sequence required, the Abenakis continued to launch arrows, causing many painful wounds but no deaths because the arrowheads were deflected by the heavy woolen clothing of the troops.

When the English began priming their muskets, the Abenakis broke contact, scrambled over the snowbanks, put on snowshoes, and set off across the fields on a straight line for the next bend in the river. A moment afterward, when the English looked up from loading their muskets, the river was empty of Indians, and fifteen of the fifty men in the column lay dead or wounded on the bloodstained ice.

Although the troops in the front ranks had clearly seen Philippe fire the shot that killed their leader, those who survived assumed that he had been shot at close range by an Abenaki who had buried himself in the snow. That was a more believable explanation of the event than that a man kneeling on the ice two hundred paces away had put a bullet through another man's heart.

Philippe's weapon, a .70-caliber jaeger rifle made specially for

him by the famous gunsmith Haaslak, was a revolutionary weapon, firing a precisely molded bullet with a precisely measured charge of black powder out of a rifled steel barrel that was only thirty-two inches long. Accurate at ranges that had not hitherto been imagined, the Haaslak jaeger was also a beautiful object, with an octagonal chased barrel and a carved walnut stock decorated with grapes, the noonday sun, heads of wheat, the Cross of Jesus, and other symbols of France, eldest daughter of the church. There was no other firearm like it in the New World.

# 12

Fanny could not take her eyes off the dead girl. Out of sight, the child that the Indian had flung over the riverbank was still crying. All around Indians were beating and kicking women, driving them upriver, away from the sound of the muskets. Used to be Bear, no longer interested in the noise of the battle, was making the sign for *run* over and over.

Betsy Ash, lumbering over the ice with her hands locked beneath her swollen, pendulous belly, had just fallen down. Fanny threw herself down beside her.

"Betsy," she said, "you must try to run. Rose and I will help you."

Fanny was not certain that Betsy could hear what was being said to her. Her eyes were unfocused; her chin quivered convulsively. An Indian whose paint matched Betsy's poked her, hard, between the shoulder blades with the handle of his tomahawk.

"Rose," Fanny said. "Help me."

Rose smiled. She behaved as though the Indian attack were some sort of fancy-dress ball at which she was wearing the cleverest costume. Fanny wondered if, at last, Rose had lost her mind altogether.

"Take her other arm," Fanny said.

Rose did so and the three women started dogtrotting, with Used to be Bear and Betsy's white-faced captor running backward in front of them, shouting for them to move faster. Soon they had settled into a steady rhythm.

Betsy moved her limbs automatically, obeying the pressure of Fanny's hand when it squeezed her arm to warn her of some object in her path, but responding to nothing else.

Late in the afternoon, just as they were passing the junction with the Pocumtuck River, a large stream that joined the Connecticut from the west, Betsy's waters broke. She gave a little cry and tried to stop running. Fanny looked around for Philippe, but he was far behind with the rear guard. Betsy stopped in her tracks. Fanny and Rose stopped along with her.

Franny crouched on the ice with her arms around Betsy.

"Don't tell them what's happening," Rose said. "They'll kill her."

Betsy's eyes had rolled back in her head.

"The women won't help," Rose said. "They say you'll give the child to the Jesuit and it's better off dead."

The Abenakis were standing over them now. Fanny didn't know the signs for this situation. She signed "baby coming, water running."

The two Indians covered their mouths with their hands, hissed in surprise, and stepped backward. Then, as the whole company came to a halt, they turned around and trotted into the woods, beckoning the women to follow.

Evergreen forest came down to the edge of the river here— balsam and hemlock along the banks and huge pines standing on the bluff to the east. Used to be Bear climbed a balsam tree and began chopping off branches. Betsy's owner cut down half a dozen willow saplings and constructed a frame, roofing it with balsam bows. He drove other boughs into the snow, while Used to be Bear crawled around inside, weaving a floor from the spring tips of the dark green boughs. When they were finished, they had constructed a lean-to, just large enough for two people. Its open end faced the woods. Used to be Bear and the other Indian went away to the far side of the river and sat down with their backs to the lean-to.

All progress had halted while these preparations were being made. Mothers nursed children. Women in their sweat-soaked nightclothes crossed their arms and gazed into the distance. One of the warriors made the bickering call of the blue jay and was answered by another jay downriver. A short while later Philippe came into view, his rifle cradled in his arms, the Abenakis of the rear guard jogging along behind him.

Rose had gone with Used to be Bear, leaving Fanny alone with Betsy. She had a clear view of the whole group of Indians and captives clustered together on the ice, and, beyond them, of a frozen waterfall. A tiny figure that might have been Father Nicolas

stood at the crest of the waterfall, signaling with the blade of a knife.

On the other side of the river, the Abenakis had built a big fire and thrown a chunk of beef into it. Fanny smelled the cooking flesh and watched Philippe as he walked from one group of women to the next.

Finally he crossed the ice and climbed the riverbank. Inside the lean-to, Betsy moaned. She lay on Fanny's cloak in the open air, outside the lean-to. She was already in hard labor, grinding her teeth and digging her fingers into the cloth.

"I have been asking the women, but they say there is no midwife among them," Philippe said. "Do you know enough to assist her?"

"No."

"Do you know anything at all?"

Fanny shrugged. "I've never done it. I've read medical books and Thoughtful told me how the Abenakis do it."

Philippe looked at her gravely.

"The others will not help," he said, "and I cannot help. The Abenakis are superstitious about men witnessing childbirth."

Fanny looked across the river. The women of Alamoth stood in a row, arms crossed, as they stared across the river at the lean-to.

"Can you help me get her inside?" she asked.

Philippe picked Betsy up and carried her to the mouth of the lean-to. Fanny followed with her cloak.

"It would be better to put the cloak on top," Philippe said. "The balsam is quite comfortable and fragrant, but you must walk on it on your knees, not your feet, or the twigs will break and poke into your back."

"Thank you," Fanny said.

"In any case, the Abenakis won't move until the baby is born," Philippe said.

He unslung his pack and unrolled his cloak, which had been tied up with thongs. He shook it out. Fanny watched, examining the garment closely. He saw what she was doing and smiled.

"It's the same one you borrowed the last time," he said. "Your man Pietro di Gesù returned it to me."

Fanny gasped. "You've seen the *Pamela*?"

Philippe nodded. "At Honfleur." Betsy began to sob. Fanny crawled into the lean-to and held her hands.

"Are the pains close together?" Fanny asked.

Betsy nodded. Then she looked upward into Fanny's face and said, "You must promise me there'll be no praying."

"All right."

When she looked outside, Philippe was gone.

The baby, a girl, was born at sunset. It was a violent labor. The books that Fanny had read had not prepared her for this experience. Thoughtful, who had described the Abenaki method, as she described everything else about the life of the tribe, had told her the story of the birth of Hair, who got his name by reaching between Thin Ice's thighs and tugging her long hanging braids as soon as he emerged from the birth canal. In the methodical Abenaki way, she had also described each stage of the birth. Fanny struggled to remember what she had heard.

Very little happened as it should. Fanny knelt between Betsy's upraised legs, holding her hands.

"It won't come," Betsy said at last. "Why would it want to come?"

"Of course it wants to come. I see its head, Betsy."

Betsy lay on her back, taking shallow breaths, with the crown of the child's head showing. Fanny stroked her face.

"Betsy, try something for me."

"I've no more strength."

"Please try, Betsy. Let me help you before the next pain comes."

Betsy was too weak to resist. Using every bit of her strength, Fanny helped her into a crouching position. Then, like Thin Ice in the story about Hair's birth, she crouched opposite her so that Betsy could lace her fingers together on the back of Fanny's neck.

The baby slid out, puckered and silvery and mysterious, with every part of it—fingers, toes, eyes, ears—already perfectly human.

Fanny tied the umbilical cord with a string from her bodice and cut it with the knife that Talks in His Dreams had given her. A moment later the baby cried. Betsy put it on her breast.

Fanny took away the balsam boughs that had been beneath Betsy and replaced them with dry ones. She knew that Thin Ice would have dug down through the snow and buried the umbilical cord in the earth, so that the child would never fly away from its own people.

Fanny turned her back and looked to the west. Beyond the forest, the sun was sending up shafts of light through a lowering sky. The evening star, a very small one like an English star—Mercury? Jupiter?—hung motionless while dark clouds swept by.

For no reason that she could understand, Fanny began to weep, covering her mouth so that Betsy would not hear her. When she was done, she turned around. Philippe was standing ten feet from her, still as a deer.

"I've brought you and the lady some food," he said, showing her a chunk of scorched beef impaled on a sharpened stick.

There was just enough light to see the tears drying on Fanny's cheeks. Her nose was bleeding slightly because Betsy in the last of her labor had smashed her skull against it. Fanny picked up a handful of snow and washed her face with it. She was wearing Philippe's cloak.

"Thank you," she said, smiling at him.

His eyes changed. "You've never smiled at me before," he said.

A few snowflakes were falling. They clung to Philippe's bearskin cap.

"Up to now there's been very little to smile about," Fanny said.

# 13

Betsy's daughter was crying. Dancing Beaver, their captor, heard her voice in his sleep.

A moment later he felt the teeth of a big animal sinking into his leg and then into his arm. A third reeking mouth closed over his face, crushing his cheekbones and blinding him. Because he lost his eyes before he could open them, he died without fear, believing that he was being killed by a three-headed animal the Abenakis had never heard about.

Philippe was half-awake, planning the next day's march, when he heard the mongrels barking among the lean-tos. He picked up his weapons and ran toward the noise. The wolf dogs had disjointed Dancing Otter's corpse and were tossing the severed parts playfully into the air.

Philippe realized at once that these were the same dogs that had driven him and his scouts off the moose by the lake. They were even more beautiful than he remembered—enormous, muscular, big-eyed, intelligent. But they were ill-kept. Their ribs showed under their skin and their coats were rough, as if they had just had an enormously long run after a stag. They would never tire. Nothing like them existed in France; he had not known that anything like them existed in the world.

The dogs saw Philippe almost as soon as he saw them. They stopped what they were doing and turned, standing all in a row.

He had his jaeger rifle, two Belgian pocket pistols, a bayonet, and a knife. The wolf dogs were about five paces away. He knew he could kill one of them with the rifle, but would not have time to use the other weapons.

To his surprise, the dogs did not attack. They gave a string of low sore-throated barks, opened their bloody jaws and panted, and gazed at him out of their liquid, inquisitive eyes. Philippe had the feeling that the dogs would come to him to be petted if he called. They were emaciated and it was clear that they had not eaten for a long time, but they did not offer to eat the dead Indians.

Abenakis were all around now, stringing bows and climbing trees. One man blundered into the small clearing where Philippe stood. The wolf dogs attacked him at once, splitting into two units as they swerved around Philippe as though he had no more meat on him than a tree. Philippe realized that the dogs were trained not to attack white people. He set off at a run for the river.

After they had eaten all the beef they wanted around the big fire, the Abenakis had hung the rest up in a big maple tree beside the river to keep it from being stolen by animals. The meat was half-frozen, but it was still raw meat. Philippe, slinging his rifle across his back, leaped into a tree, and climbing from one thick branch to another cut the rawhide from which the beef was suspended. Half a dozen slabs thudded onto the ice. A dozen more still swung from the branches of the maple.

Philippe could not see the wolf dogs. Indians and captives fled through the trees below. He whistled. The surviving mongrel dashed to the edge of the river, barking, head cocked. Philippe pulled his knife from its sheath, chopped off a chunk of beef, and threw it at the mongrel, who caught it in midair and bolted it down, then barked for more.

Philippe whistled again, louder. The wolf dogs appeared. He cut off more beef, throwing it to them and talking to them, drawing them nearer. All at once they spotted the big slabs of meat on the ice and fell on them, woofing happily as they had done when they leaped on the Abenakis' moose.

Philippe unslung his rifle and checked the priming. The dogs were beneath him, close to the trunk of the maple. He could not get one of them in his sights, so he ran farther out onto the thick limb. He stood up, bracing his back against a higher limb so that the recoil of the jaeger would not knock him out of the tree, and put the blade of the sight between the heaving shoulders of the middle dog.

He pulled back the hammer, inhaled, and began to squeeze the

trigger. The rattle of a woodpecker sounded in the darkness. The dogs lifted their heads. Philippe had heard this signal before, by the lake where the Abenakis had killed the mooose.

Out of the corner of his eye he saw the ragged red muzzle blast of a musket being fired. The hammer fell on the flint of Philippe's jaeger rifle and the priming began to burn. A shower of buckshot struck the branches of the maple. The dogs pushed themselves off the meat with their front legs and sped into the woods. An instant later, Philippe's bullet, perfectly aimed, slapped harmlessly into the beef where one of the wolf dogs had been feeding a moment before.

Talks in His Dreams, hidden in another tree, did not see Hawkes until his musket went off. Then, looking down, he saw the huge Englishman with his musket still to his shoulder. Talks in His Dreams launched an arrow. It struck Hawkes in the right shoulder, at the base of the neck. He staggered forward a step, reached back to feel the arrow sticking out of his flesh, and turned around.

His eyes searched the trees for the man who had shot him. Talks in His Dreams had already fitted another arrow to his bow. He launched it, striking Hawkes on the left side of his chest, just above the nipple.

Talks in His Dreams waited for the Englishman to fall dead in his tracks from this heart wound. But the man did not even stagger. With one arrow sticking out of his neck and another protruding from his chest, he began deliberately to reload his musket.

The ghost dogs came back almost in the same instant. They leaped on the big man and licked his face. He spoke to them and they followed him, frisking and whining, as he ran off through the trees with a long, powerful stride, with the two flint-headed arrows still buried in his body.

Talks in His Dreams, moving with great caution, followed the ghost tracks for a little while. They looked like ordinary dog tracks and snowshoe tracks, except that they were larger. There was no blood on the snow from the arrow wounds.

# 14

At first light, Father Nicolas came down from the waterfall to bury the dead, and then he went across the ice to baptize Betsy's child. Betsy refused the sacrament, shaking her head violently, and when the Jesuit fell to his knees and began to pray in Latin, she covered the baby's ears with her hands. Father Nicolas, thinking that she was suffering from an ignorant Protestant fear of the church's universal tongue, pulled her hands away and spoke to her in his foggily accented English.

"A little water, a little oil, a prayer, and your child's soul will be safe," he said. "If she dies she will not wander for all eternity in limbo, never knowing God. Don't you want your child to love Christ?"

"No," Betsy said.

Again Father Nicolas thought that she misunderstood his words or his intentions, or both. How, otherwise, could she make such an answer to such a question? "It is not a Catholic trick I'm playing," he said patiently. "Think of the child. There is very little time, and so much danger."

"No."

Betsy's impiety frightened him. Even as she denied Our Lord she was suckling her newborn daughter, tenderly touching the child's plump cheek with the tip of her finger. Giving birth had made her plain face beautiful. It shone with love for her baby.

Father Nicolas turned to Fanny. "There are great dangers ahead," he said. "Who will protect her now that Dancing Beaver has been killed? If the child dies unbaptized, it cannot know God."

"She understands," Fanny said.

"Does she? The others say that she's mad."

"Father, believe me, she's not mad."

While the Europeans talked, Used to be Bear had been sitting in the snow, removing the bark from a pile of willow switches. Now he bent the bright yellow wood into a papoose frame, trying it with rawhide thongs and attaching straps so that Betsy could carry it on her back.

When he was finished, he plucked the fur hat off Rose's head, ripped out the stitching, and tied it onto the frame as a coverlet. Rose gasped, feeling her hair with both hands for the missing hat while she watched with unbelieving eyes as the Indian reduced this fashionable object that she had loved so much to a rough pelt. Used to be Bear hung the finished papoose frame on the ridgepole of the lean-to, then crawled inside and gazed into the baby's face. When he came back outside, he spoke in Abenaki for several minutes.

"Used to be Bear has decided to be this child's father," Father Nicolas explained in French. "He doesn't know yet what her name is."

Betsy had long ago decided to name her daughter Solitude, and after the others went away she baptized her in snow, repeating the words connected to the ritual of the Church of England as best she remembered them and speaking the names of the baby's dead brothers and sisters—Enos, Seth, Adam, Raymond, Elizabeth, Martha—as the snow melted on Solitude's forehead.

The sun had only just risen. It burned weakly beyond the bowl of the clouds, giving little light. The morning had a cottony quality, soft and dim, and the air was heavy and much warmer than before. Philippe, who had been standing among the trees on the bank, moved; Fanny saw him for the first time. He dressed like an Indian, he was as still as an Indian.

"Mother and child are well?" he said.

"I am looking for some food for them," she said.

Philippe leaped down, kicking snow onto the ice, and handed Fanny his musket. It was heavier than she expected it to be.

"Rest the butt on the ice," Philippe said. Crouching, he probed the ashes with a bayonet. After a moment he stood up and offered Fanny a chunk of charred meat on the point of the blade.

There was humor in his face, interest in his eyes. He had a fresh wound on his face—a small reddened puncture on the left cheekbone with a black streak under the skin. Fanny had seen wounds like this one before.

"That's buckshot in your face," she said. "It should be removed. It's quite close to the eye."

"Is it?" Philippe said. "Then I am lucky to be able to see you. Here is your roast beef."

Fanny took the chunk of meat, which was warm to the touch and covered with ashes.

Two young Abenakis, scouts from the rear guard, came into

sight, running. They were dragging a third Indian behind them on a shield, leaving a broad smear of blood in the ice.

Philippe did not move—Abenakis were pouring out of the woods to meet the scouts—but waited, erect and expressionless once again, for them to come to him.

The scouts came straight to him and told him what had happened. They had been attacked during the night by an English column that marched onto the rear guard as they slept on the ice four or five miles downriver.

Half a dozen Abenakis had been beaten to death with musket butts or stomped to death by a mob of bellowing farmers. The rest had escaped by fleeing across the snow; these three were merely the first to arrive.

Philippe asked the same two questions as before: did the English have snowshoes? were they sending out scouts? The Abenakis replied that most of the enemy still had no snowshoes of their own, but they had the snowshoes of the dead Abenakis. But this new enemy force was much larger than the rescue column Philippe had ambushed the day before.

Reinforced with men from Alamoth and other settlements along the Connecticut, it numbered at least two hundred men. The English were less than an hour away, and they were singing as they advanced up the river, something the Abenakis had never known them to do before.

"Singing?" Philippe said. This information seemed to disturb him more than anything else he had heard.

The Abenakis left. He turned around. Fanny was standing behind him with the chunk of beef in her hands. He frowned and bit his lip.

"Can she walk?" he asked, lifting his chin to indicate Betsy's lean-to on the other bank of the river.

"She's very weak. Why not leave her, if the English are coming?"

"The Abenakis wouldn't permit that."

"But you can order it."

"No. She belongs to them."

"*Belongs* to them?"

Philippe did not argue. "Used to be Bear has decided to be the child's father," he said. "You had better do what you can to prepare your friend for her journey."

Abenakis were hurrying among the trees, dragging captives toward the ice and forming up into parties of half a dozen, usually with two Indians for every captive. The sleds, the beef, anything that could not be carried by a person running, were abandoned.

Philippe was upending the two small cannon into the hole in the

ice, leaping back after he let them go to avoid the splash. Indians streamed past him as he worked.

By sundown, unless the English were marching faster than the scouts thought, these scores of people would have disappeared into the wilderness, scattered among the dozens of small tributaries of the Connecticut and the Pocumtuck.

Rose came out of the woods with Used to be Bear. He had tied a cord around her waist and was pulling her along behind him as they came straight across the river toward the lean-to. Father Nicolas trotted along behind them, accompanied by Talks in His Dreams, two other Abenakis, the Clum girls, and another woman who carried a child in her arms.

The Jesuit led them to the lean-to. He fell to his knees at the entrance.

"I beg you to reconsider," he said to Betsy. "Many will leave their bones in this forest."

Betsy covered Solitude's head and shielded her from the priest with her body.

Father Nicolas rose to his feet and blessed Fanny.

"I will try to find you," he said, "but the forest is vast. If it seems that the worst is happening, you must baptize the child. Touch its head with water, make the sign of the cross, and say, 'I baptize thee in the name of the Father, the Son, and the Holy Ghost.' A soul is in your hands, my child."

Fanny said nothing. Talks in His Dreams was already dogtrotting toward the mouth of the Pocumtuck with his captives strung out before him. Father Nicolas ran after them.

Used to be Bear pulled the lean-to apart over Betsy's head. He made the sign for *run*. Fanny helped Betsy to her feet. She was warmly dressed now in the extra clothes Talks in His Dreams had brought to Fanny.

Solitude slept in her papoose frame. Fanny slung the frame onto her own back. Betsy uttered a cry and lunged for the child.

"It's all right," Fanny said. "I'll walk just ahead of you so you can see her."

Betsy nodded, her eyes fixed on Solitude. She seemed to be far more tired now than she had been earlier. Fanny gave her some of the charred beef, tearing off the dry stringy meat with her fingers and putting it into the other woman's mouth. Betsy was too exhausted even to chew.

"Betsy," Fanny said. "Try. It will give you strength."

Betsy looked at her dully. Fanny gave her water. It dribbled down her chin. Fanny took her face between her hands.

"Think of the child," she said.

There was no more expression in Betsy's eyes than before. Fanny picked up the half-chewed meat that Betsy had coughed onto the snow, and put it back into her mouth. Betsy chewed, gesturing to Fanny to turn around so that she could see the baby.

Betsy staggered forward a few steps, then lost her balance. Fanny caught her, nearly falling herself and shaking the baby in its frame. The child whimpered.

Philippe came across the ice, carrying his jaeger rifle and a sack filled with beef.

Fanny said, "Look. How can she travel?"

Philippe did not reply. Fanny turned to Used to be Bear and started to make signs.

"No, don't do that," Philippe said sharply.

Fanny stopped with her hands uplifted.

"If you tell him what you just told me, he'll kill her," Philippe said. "Also the child."

"You would do nothing to prevent that?"

"I'd have to kill him. He does not understand mercy."

Fanny took Betsy by the arm and tugged gently. Betsy took a step and fell. Fanny crouched, keeping her back straight so that the baby would not slip, and helped her up. She took two more steps and fell again.

Used to be Bear watched. Fanny tried to get Betsy up again, but she was a limp weight, too heavy to lift.

Used to be Bear strode over the snow—Fanny felt rather than saw him coming up behind her, a big body displacing snow and air and light. Putting all her strength into the effort, she got Betsy onto her hands and knees. Philippe seized her beneath the arms and set her on her feet.

Used to be Bear was holding the ridgepole of the lean-to in his hands. He gave one end to Fanny and the other end to Rose. Then he wrapped Betsy's fingers around the middle of the pole, made some signs, and walked away.

The woman followed. Betsy grew steadier with each step. When they entered the mouth of the Pocumtuck, threading their way among the rocks that rose above the ice, Used to be Bear broke into a dogtrot. Fanny, who held the leading end of the pole, began to run too. Rose picked up the pace, and soon Betsy was running, her shocked eyed fixed on Solitude's face as it bobbed along in front of her.

The Pocumtuck, a fast-running river that cuts through steep, heavily forested country, makes a deep loop to the south before it turns to the west and north again. After the first mile, Philippe caught up with Used to be Bear and talked to him. Used to be Bear

swerved into a small stream that joined the river from the north. Following the course of this brook involved a hard uphill run, and after another mile it ended in a spring.

Used to be Bear paused long enough to put on his snowshoes, then plunged into the woods. The women, with Philippe bringing up the rear in silence, followed along. It was far more difficult to move through the trees on snowshoes using the pole than to run on the open, smooth surface of the ice, and Betsy fell.

Philippe lifted her to her feet, then drew a map in the snow, showing the half-circle of the river and their route across the diameter.

"Much shorter," he said, whispering. "And there's a hill just here from which we can look back."

The silence was very deep. Fanny wondered how it was possible that there were two hundred English soldiers and nearly that many Indians and captives all around them in this soundless waste.

Rose said, "Ssshhh, I can hear them singing."

Nobody else could hear the music. But minutes later, when Betsy fell again and there was a quiet moment undisturbed by panting and the swish of the snowshoes, Fanny heard the English too, a bass chorus marching up the valley, and even recognized the tune, John Blow's "Arms, arms, arms," with its thudding succession of low E's.

But it was Rose whose ears and eyes and nose were made for the place in which she found herself. She saw, heard, and smelled things that no Indian could have detected. She pointed out an owl in a pine to Used to be Bear, and because this astonished him, showed him other things as well—a rabbit by a thicket, a gray lynx with brown spots on its back lying on the gray limb of a beech among dead brown leaves. He grunted each time.

Betsy moved forward like a sleepwalker, holding on to the pole. She nursed the baby twice and drank the water that Fanny gave her.

Near the end of the day, she took a bad fall, tumbling down the side of a steep ravine, and could not get up again. She was not injured, just exhausted. The baby began to cry. Used to be Bear plunged through the snow and lifted the baby out of its frame. With his hand clapped over Solitude's mouth, he scrambled down into the ravine and handed her to Betsy. She put the baby to her breast and fell asleep while it nursed.

The ravine, a long open place, was shielded to the north by a high ledge of gray rock that rose ten feet or so above the snow. A few snowflakes were beginning to fall, the same big flakes that had buried the whole countryside a few days before.

Fanny pointed at Betsy, asleep in the snow. "She can't go any further," she said.

Philippe got out his knife. "Then we must cut balsam boughs," he said.

While they worked, Used to be Bear dug out the snow along the ledge to create two shelters roofed with boughs. Fanny and Philippe, working together, lined the floors and walls with more balsam boughs.

Meanwhile, Rose wandered through the clearing, turning her head from side to side like a doe. Used to be Bear did not try to make her work, but from time to time he stopped what he was doing and watched her, as if she possessed some mysterious spirit that he was trying to understand.

By now Betsy and the baby were nearly buried in fresh snow. Fanny helped them into the shelter. After wiping away the snow, she looked for signs of hemorrhage in Betsy; there were none. Fanny offered Betsy some beef, but she did not have the strength to chew.

"All right," Fanny said.

She chewed up a mouthful of beef, spat it into her palm, and fed it to Betsy on her fingertip, just as Two Suns had given Squirrel her ration of grease.

It was warm in the shelter, dug deep in the hardened snow. Betsy and the baby fell asleep again.

# 15

Outside, it was snowing even harder than before. The balsam roof of the shelter was already covered and all but invisible. Neither of the men was anywhere in sight, but Fanny saw Rose standing a few paces away in the falling snow. She wore her fur-lined cloak with the hood pulled up over her head. She had scrubbed the paint off her skin. Her face glowed inside its frame of fur.

"Look," she said, pointing with her toe.

Fanny saw a round hole in the snow, about the size of a shilling. A jet of steam, faint in the warmish air, came out of it. The

rhythm was very slow—so slow that the vent would be covered by the falling snow, then melted by a fresh exhalation, then covered again.

"What do you suppose that is?" Rose asked.

She drew back her foot to kick the mound of snow. Suddenly she was lifted into the air. A big dirty hand, callused and hatched with scars, closed over her mouth. The thumb and forefinger pinched her nostrils shut.

Used to be Bear, covered with snow, had materialized out of the storm and seized her from behind. Rose, unable to breathe or speak, struggled for a moment, then subsided. Used to be Bear put her down, pushing her and Fanny away from the mound of snow with exaggerated caution. His face broke across in a yellow grin and he said something in rapid signs.

Fanny interpreted, whispering: "He says you mustn't wake up the bear."

They were standing in a grove of young birches. Used to be Bear selected two, growing some distance apart, and told Rose and Fanny to climb to the tops. The limber saplings bent under their weight, so that they were nearly horizontal as they clung to them. They had an excellent view of what followed.

Used to be Bear returned to the mound in the snow, approaching it inch by inch with such caution that he appeared not to be moving at all. On reaching the mound, Used to be Bear dug in the snow with equal care, removing one handful of snow, waiting, and removing another until the bear was uncovered. The animal was curled up in a ball. On a colder day it would certainly have awakened. As things were, the bear, protected by three inches of fur and four inches of fat beneath the fur, did not appear to notice any change in temperature. It twitched a little but slept on. Used to be Bear sat cross-legged in the snow and watched it intently for many minutes. The air was just cold enough to condense the bear's breath; it seemed to be breathing four or five times a minute. Without this sign, it would have been difficult to tell one end of the bear from the other.

Used to be Bear had no gun, no bow. He was armed, instead, with Philippe's bayonet. This was a long, narrow blade with a needle point. He held it in both hands. Used to be Bear was looking at the bear's head, which lay on its hip. First he saw the breath, then the black nose at the end of the whiskery muzzle, then the lip, then a brown tooth under the lip, then an ear, and finally the eye hidden in the fur.

Used to be Bear placed the point of the bayonet against the bear's eye. Through the steel, he felt the lid flutter just before he

threw his whole weight onto the blade, driving it through the eye socket into the bear's brain. Used to be Bear, following his own weight, somersaulted across the body of the bear. Rolling to his feet, he leaped into a birch sapling and scrambled to the top. Behind him, the dying bear undoubled convulsively and stood up on its hind legs, as if trying to escape from the blade that had passed completely through its brain and emerged from the back of its skull. Then it collapsed onto the snow and lay where it fell, inert.

Used to be Bear, after waiting in his tree for a long time to be sure that the bear was dead, skinned the animal, gutted it, and trotted off into the falling snow with a tangle of intestines in his arms.

Rose followed him—the ways of the Indians were beginning to interest her. Used to be Bear walked along the ravine, listening. Every few paces, he dropped to his knees and put his ear next to the snow. Rose understood, perhaps because she could already hear it gurgling beneath the snow, that he was listening for running water.

She showed him where it was. He dug through the snow, found the frozen brook buried beneath it, and chopped a hole in the ice. Then he washed out the bear's intestines, holding them under the icy water and letting the current run through. The elements seemed to have no more effect on him than they had had on the bear.

Back in the ravine, Used to be Bear, muttering a song under his breath as he worked, removed every bit of fat from the bear's carcass and packed it into the intestines, tying them off every six inches or so with a length of rawhide. When he had finished, he had a long string of capsules of bear fat. He cut two of these off and dropped them on the raw side of the hide, where the bear's liver already lay.

The rest of the carcass he hung in a tree. Then he rolled up the hide, made the sign for "come with me" to Rose, and dropped down into the shelter he had dug for the two of them.

This trench in the snow, roofed with balsam boughs like the other, was about three times the size of a grave, and like a grave it was deep enough to stand up in. It was very dark inside. Rose was glad of the balsam over her head and under her feet, because its fragrance intermingled with the stench of the fresh bearskin and the many smells emitted by Used to be Bear. After he spread the bearskin over the floor, he retreated to one end of the shelter.

Rose heard him breaking sticks in the darkness. Used to be Bear, singing a fire-starting song in a muffled voice, struck his flint and steel together. Sparks flew, illuminating his big sleeper's face,

which was something like Oliver's face except that it was the color of a saddle. The tinder caught. Used to be Bear blew on it gently, coaxing it into a flame. Then he placed it gently beneath the tipi of dead wood he had built on the rock shelf.

A moment later, he had a bright, nearly smokeless fire burning. It was a very small fire. Neither the smoke nor the flame could be seen, and it could not be smelled except by an Indian—or by Rose—as far away as the river. The English could not be as close as that.

Used to be Bear cooked bits of liver on the end of a stick and gobbled them. When he had had enough, he sat back and watched Rose cook and eat. The liver was very strong in taste and smell, but Rose ate as much as she could. Finally Used to be Bear growled at her and she stopped. Belching and smacking his lips and spitting out the inedible parts, he ate more liver, meanwhile toasting one of the bear-grease sausages over the coals of the fire.

When the sausage was hot, he untied the rawhide at one end and squeezed a blob of fat into his palm. He licked it up and grunted, then offered some to Rose. When she did not eat it at once, he gave her a hard dig in the ribs. She stuck her finger into the fat and licked it. The horrible taste of the stuff, like the secretions of uncooked meat that had lain in the sun for a long time, like cat, filled the entire cavity of her head. She gagged.

Used to be Bear was laughing. What was wrong? Rose had always been told, even by Magpie, that Indians never laughed. Used to be Bear was making signs. By now Rose could understand most of this simple language, so what Used to be Bear did next did not surprise her. He stood Rose on her feet and stripped her naked, tossing her fur cloak, her gown, her petticoats, her shift onto the balsam floor.

Then, grunting, he stepped back to look at her in the firelight. He seemed to be a little drunk. He gave himself another mouthful of bear grease in the same way that Robert or Oliver, in the same situation, might have taken another drink of brandy. Rose smoothed her hair, which had been mussed during the undressing. Used to be Bear rubbed bear greased into it, then turned her around so that she faced the fire.

He pulled her nearer to the flame and kneeled, absorbed. He had never before seen a woman with flaxen pubic hair; the other fair-haired Englishwomen he had captured, three of them in all, had had dark hair on their stomachs.

Rose began to make her plans to control Used to be Bear. She gave him a look filled with pain and wounded trust. He pushed downward on Rose's shoulders, telling her to lie down. She twisted

away and bent over, reaching for her fur cloak. Used to be Bear gave her a clout on the buttocks that knocked her into the wall of the trench and took away her breath and even her sight. She felt him pulling her onto the bearskin and pushing her over onto her back. When she opened her eyes, he was standing over her in the smoky light of the fire, removing his breechclout.

Used to be Bear, singing a song to summon a child that would look like the Abenakis but have this woman's eyes and ears and nose, ran his greased hand back and forth on his engorged member and threw himself on top of Rose.

Used to be Bear bellowed his song into her ear. Unbearable smells issued from his body, his great weight slammed against her pelvis, the wet bearskin scourged her back. After a very short time, Used to be Bear let out a roar and collapsed on top of her. He lay inert for a moment, snuffling, then recovered his size and started in again.

Rose tried to smell just the woodsmoke so that she would not have to smell the bearskin, the bear grease, the breath and the secretions of Used to be Bear. Woodsmoke reminded her of Norwood and the Gypsy camp; Rose had smelled so much woodsmoke since coming to America that she had forgotten what a rare aroma it was in England. That was the day the Gypsy crone had told her fortune . . . And then, as if the old woman were actually there in the pit in the snow with her, Rose heard her say, *"I see a bear. . . . You cannot hide from him. The bear will find you. You owe him this child from another life and he will make you give it to him."*

Rose *had* been cursed. Her fate, grunting and pushing, was entering her body like an incubus, just as she had known it would, but in a way she had never imagined. For the first time, she could feel the act as it occurred. Against her will, she became aware of everything that was happening to her. She could see in the dark, hear the brooks running under the ice and snow, distinguish every nauseating odor in the pit from every other odor. Her body moved against her will. Something grunted and screamed, using Rose's voice.

Used to be Bear fell asleep on top of her. Rose was herself again now. A plan formed in her mind. She let Used to be Bear lie as he was for a long time before she moved, so as not to wake him up. Finally she turned her leg, very cautiously. Used to be Bear woke up and began to sing.

# 16

Talks in His Dreams smelled the smoke of Used to be Bear's fire when he was still about half a mile away from it. He stopped where he was, in a grove of hemlocks, and waited for Father Nicolas and Sleeping Fox, a young man whose father, Yellow Rain, was the first Abenaki to be killed by the ghost dogs, to bring the women along the trail he had broken.

The going had been slow because one of the women had a child who was too small to walk in the snow and too heavy to be carried. Now that it was snowing, the child, a boy with watery English eyes, was more of a burden than ever; the women kept falling behind, each carrying him for a while, then handing him on to one of the others. He had a bad cough that made him whoop as he struggled to draw breath.

Earlier that day, while headed north and west along the Pocumtuck, they had come on the tracks of the fat English ghost and the ghost dogs. These tracks were several hours old, which meant that the ghosts had started up the river ahead of the Abenakis, and were waiting for them in the forest ahead. The ghosts were not traveling on the ice, but on a trail that followed the contours of the hills above the river.

Talks in His Dreams and Sleeping Fox had left the captives with Father Nicolas and tracked the ghosts for a mile or two. They were moving at a fast pace, which showed that the fat ghost was not troubled by the arrows that Talks in His Dreams had shot into his neck and chest. There was no blood on the trail and no sign that the fat ghost was dragging his snowshoes as a wounded man or an exhausted man will do; his prints, laid down by running feet, were clear and distinct mile after mile.

After observing all these signs, Talks in His Dreams and Sleeping Fox decided that it would be better to go home by another route. Therefore they reversed direction and headed due east toward a tributary of the Pocumtuck that ran north and south, parallel to the Connecticut. This was a much harder river to walk on because it was narrow and full of rocks, but it led to a point

only a few miles away from a bigger river that led to Lake Champlain.

Waiting among the hemlocks, Talks in His Dreams listened for the women. He heard them coming up the steep hill behind him, gasping and whimpering. The child was coughing again. Whoever had built the fire would hear this noise. A dog would be able to hear it over the distance of half a day's walking. Sleeping Fox was too far behind, watching for the ghosts, to do anything about it.

Talks in His Dreams stripped the child out of its mother's arms and looked around for a rock on which to smash its skull. Seeing none, he dropped the child on its face into the snow and pushed it under the surface with his snowshoe while he got out his toma-hawk. The mother threw herself to the ground, howling, and clawed at Talks in His Dreams's snowshoe. She would not let go even when he yanked on her hair and poked her hard with the handle of his tomahawk. Talks in His Dreams did not want to kill her; Sleeping Fox seemed to like her. But how could they travel through hostile country with a woman who made this much noise?

While Talks in His Dreams was thinking about this problem, an owl launched itself out of a tall maple tree, dropping steadily through the air like a stone with wings, and landed nearby in a hemlock. The owl had always been a friend to him; perhaps it wanted to tell him something.

The hemlock shook, snow falling off the laden branches, and Philippe jumped out of it.

"Hello, Wind Hunter," Talks in His Dreams said. "I thought you were an owl. Is that your fire I smell?"

"Not mine. Used to be Bear killed a bear."

"Then he's cooking the grease."

"He will be glad to see you. Why are you walking this way?"

"Because the ghosts are going the other way."

"Going the other way?"

"We saw their tracks on the trail above the Pocumtuck, near the place where Crow saw the snake."

Any Abenaki would have known what place Talks in His Dreams was talking about. Philippe did not know, but he did not question him further. The Indian's mind was on the bear grease; he sniffed the air, hoping to catch the scent of it.

The child coughed convulsively under the snowshoe, choking as it inhaled snow, and then fell silent. Its mother, still lying prostrate in her tattered nightgown, was trying to dig away the snow to give it air.

Philippe said, "I think you can take your foot off the child now. It has stopped making noise."

Talks in His Dreams lifted his foot. "I'm going to go see Used to be Bear now," he said.

Philippe dug the half-conscious child out of the snow. Its nose was bleeding, but it was otherwise unharmed. Father Nicolas listened to it cough and shook his shaved head.

"Whooping cough," he said.

Father Nicolas carried a small cooking pot with him. He built a fire in the pit where all the women were huddled together. Even Rose was there. Used to be Bear had sent her away when Talks in His Dreams and Sleeping Fox arrived, and the three Abenakis were now eating bear grease together and telling stories. The singsong sound of their voices drifted over the campground.

Fanny made broth in Father Nicolas' pot from a chunk of beef from Philippe's sack. The women sat in a circle, passing Father Nicolas' spoon from hand to hand. Fanny fed Betsy as well as herself.

Father Nicolas renewed his arguments for baptism.

"The child will die in the snow and the cold," Father Nicolas said, speaking English to Betsy. "Really, you must think about the soul of your daughter, madam."

"Have some of the meat," Fanny said to Betsy.

She tore it apart with her fingers and put it into Betsy's mouth. This time she chewed and swallowed without assistance. Solitude whimpered; Betsy gave her her breast.

"This woman does not seem to understand me when I speak to her in English," Father Nicolas said to Fanny. "I'll speak French and you can translate. Tell her that she is committing the sin of pride, and thereby placing the soul of her daughter in jeopardy. . . ."

Father Nicolas went on in his thin earnest voice. The convulsive coughing of the little boy who had whooping cough made it impossible to hear what he was saying.

"What is that man saying?" Rose said. "Why does he never stop talking?"

She was trying to dress herself in the dark, and the effort was exasperating her. Used to be Bear had put her out naked underneath her fur cloak.

"Papist poison, that's what he's talking," Hepzibah said. "He's trying to steal the babe's soul for the pope, and Fanny's helping him. That's why Betsy gets the broth, Betsy gets the kind words, Betsy gets to wear her cloak while the rest of us go hungry and half-naked. As soon as the papists get the baby, Betsy, you'll be as bad off as the rest of us."

"Be quiet," Rose said. "You don't know anything about anything."

"I know about her. I found her crucifix where she hid it in her room a long time ago."

"You think Fanny's a spy, do you?" Rose said, "Come here, Hepzibah, I can't see you."

Hepzibah crawled across her sister's body and kneeled in the dark in front of Rose.

"Is that you?" Rose said, feeling her face and hair.

"It's me, missis."

Without warning, Rose slapped Hepzibah hard on the ears. She howled in surprise and pain.

"I know who the spy was, and it wasn't Fanny Harding," Rose said. "Don't ever tell another lie about Fanny or you'll get worse than a box on the ears. Now, go lie down and keep your mouth shut until you're spoken to."

Father Nicolas had gone outside. They could hear his faint prayers and the Indians and Philippe speaking Abenaki in the next pit. It was impossible to know what time it was because the storm had blotted out the moon and the stars.

"Rose," Fanny said. "Come lie on the other side of Betsy, to keep her warm."

They arranged themselves on either side of Betsy, who was still singing under her breath. Solitude was asleep on her chest. Reaching across Betsy to find Fanny's face, Rose touched the baby by mistake. It was wrapped in fur.

"My beaver bonnet," she said. "It doesn't look much like a bonnet now. Oliver gave it to me, you know, when we were happy in London. It was lovely in London—always something new, jolly people all around, and you playing your musical instruments."

Fanny said nothing.

"Fanny," Rose said, "do you remember the day we went to see the Gypsies? . . . Fanny?"

"Yes, I remember."

"Do you remember what the old Gypsy woman told me when she read my hand? It's come true, Fanny. The bear has found me."

"What bear? You mean the one Used to be Bear killed? That was just a wild bear, Rose. They sleep like that in winter, they just lie down and let the snow cover them up."

"I don't mean that bear. I can't tell you everything, but it's horrible. You must help me, Fanny. What's happening is not what I thought would happen."

Solitude gave a weak little cry.

"Listen, the babe is hungry," Father Nicolas said, whispering through the balsam roof. "If the child is awake, the mother is awake. Speak to her, Fanny."

"No, Father, she's asleep."

"Wake her," Father Nicolas said in English. "This child's life is so new, so feeble, so threatened. It can end at any moment. If we let that happen without protecting its soul, how will God forgive us?"

Betsy stirred and spoke in a loud, distinct voice. "I can't bear it," she said.

Fanny laid a hand on her forehead. "Don't listen," she said. "Try to sleep."

Fanny climbed out of the pit and sat down on her snowshoes beside Father Nicolas. It had stopped snowing.

"Do you think it's possible, Father," Fanny asked, "to be alone in the world—utterly, completely alone?"

"But we are not alone," Father Nicolas said. "God goes with us."

"But suppose He doesn't."

"That is not something I would suppose, or anything you should suppose. Why do you ask such a question?"

Fanny wanted to say: Because I always believed that my mother died for me and now I have seen how women really die.

Instead she said, "Because I feel that I'm alone."

"That is because you have not had the consolation of your own faith. You have been living among God's enemies. But soon all will be well. You are so good, so pretty, so musical, you speak Latin and Greek. You will marry, have children, and at the end of your long life you will go to heaven."

"How do you know I am musical or about the Latin and Greek?"

"I know much more." Father Nicolas chuckled, as though he had been waiting for an opportunity to tell her what he knew about her. "I told you, you are not alone. Even in Quebec, so far from France, so far from everywhere, everything about you is known— your father, your mother, your ship. Everything."

"Everyone knows all that? How?"

"I did not say that everyone knows. I said that everything, or nearly everything, is known."

"But how? By whom?"

"Someone is interested in you and has collected the facts. So you see, God is never absent from anyone's life. He works in His own way to make certain that none of His children is ever alone. I assure you, my child, that God does not want you to be alone."

"So I have always been told. But who is this person who knows everything about me?"

"A spy," Father Nicolas said. "One of God's spies—they are everywhere. Now I am very tired."

He had made himself a bed of balsam boughs under the open sky. He lay down on it and went to sleep.

Fanny let herself back into the pit, where the little boy was still coughing and gasping for breath, and lay down beside Betsy. She and Solitude were asleep, breathing quietly.

During the night, cold and wind came in from the west. The morning sun was so brilliant, shining on the snow, that it was almost impossible to open one's eyes without being blinded. Betsy and Solitude had disappeared.

# 17

It was Father Nicolas who discovered Betsy's trail when he woke before dawn to pray and contemplate the mysteries of Christ's passion from the Last Supper to the Garden at Gethsemane. He had very little woodcraft, but even he could see that they were the tracks of a woman and that she was barefoot. It did not occur to him to follow her. He did not think that she would go far, and he knew that she was in no danger—no Abenaki would harm her, and if she stumbled onto her own people, an unlikely outcome, she would be safe with them too.

Accordingly, Father Nicolas commenced the contemplation specified by Saint Ignatius Loyola, the founder of the Society of Jesus, for the first day of the third week of the Spiritual Exercises. The sun had risen by the time he had said his preparatory prayer, formed a mental image of Jesus descending with his eleven disciples from Mount Sion, where the Last Supper was held, to the Valley of Josaphat, then leaving eight disciples in the valley and going with the remaining three to the Garden at Gethsemane, where he prayed three times to his Father, arousing his disciples three times from sleep, and his sweat became drops of blood, his enemies dropped to the ground at the sound of his voice, Judas gave him the kiss of peace, he restored the ear of Malchus which

Peter had cut off, he was seized like a malefactor and led through the valley and back up the slope to the house of Annas.

Having fully imagined these scenes, Father Nicolas visualized every detail of the road from Mount Sion and also the Garden—their width, length, and general appearance—and finally asked for himself that which he most desired: grief with Christ suffering, a broken heart with Christ heartbroken, tears, and deep suffering because of the great suffering that Christ had endured for him.

By that time Used to be Bear and Talks in His Dreams had seen Betsy's tracks and followed them out of the ravine and uphill through a grove of beeches into a thick hemlock forest where the trees grew so close together that she had crawled on her hands and knees and finally on her belly to get under the trees and through them.

There she had lain down in the snow with her baby in her arms and frozen to death.

Solitude seemed to be dead too, her small bloodless face pillowed on Betsy's breast, and the Abenakis were about to leave when the baby told Used to be Bear her name, Snow, and informed him that she was not dead.

She was so small and so cold that he nearly did not hear her, and when he picked her up and put her mouth against his missing ear, which was more sensitive than the good one, he realized that she was not breathing.

So he opened the baby's mouth with his forefinger and blew into it several times, saying, "Here is some breath for you, Snow."

Then he put her inside his shirt against his skin, which was smeared with bear grease, and ran back down to the ravine through the dazzling light.

Used to be Bear held Solitude's body against Rose's ear. She heard its heartbeat, but no breath. Used to be Bear, blowing into Solitude's mouth, seized the two fattest women, Hepzibah and the mother of the coughing boy, and told them in signs to put the baby between them, against their bare skin, and wrap their arms around each other, so that she would be warmed by their bodies.

"It's not breathing, the fool," Hepzibah said when Fanny interpreted.

"Do as you're told," Fanny said.

The other woman passed the naked child down though the neck of her gown, settled it between her breasts, and embraced Hepzibah. The two women looked into each other's faces in horror, feeling the rigid little body pressing into their own chilled flesh.

Every now and then Used to be Bear would call to the silent baby: "Are you alive yet, Snow?"

Finally Solitude cried. Used to be Bear applied a thick coat of bear grease to the child, wrapped it up in its fur again, and handed it back to the women, making the signs for suckling and watching the child drink as the mother of the coughing boy gave it her breast.

Father Nicolas, who had praying all the while and measuring the time by watching the movement of the shadow of the two women on the snow, said nothing about miracles, but his face was radiant. He baptized the revived infant without delay, giving her the names Solitude Neige Martha Genevieve Ignatius. The godparents were Used to be Bear, Philippe, and Fanny.

Watching Used to be Bear, who had painted black circles around his eyes, making the sign of the cross on his greased chest, Hepzibah shuddered.

"The babe would have been better off dead with its mother," she said.

There was no possibility of burying Betsy even if the Abenakis had been willing to touch the body of a mad suicide. With Philippe's help, Fanny dug a fresh trench in the snow at the base of a double beech tree, lined it with boughs, laid the body in it, and covered it up with boughs and snow.

Philippe removed his bearskin hat and bowed his head.

"No," Fanny said. "Don't pray."

Philippe opened his eyes. "But this is a dead person under the snow," he said.

"I know," Fanny said. "Leave her in peace."

# 18

Arctic cold moved across the forest on a fierce west wind that tore dead wood out of the trees and filled the air with a pall of blowing snow. Hawkes was not bothered by the cold. The two flint arrowheads embedded in the slab of hard fat beneath his skin did not trouble him greatly either. It was the layer of fat that protected him in both cases; as solid as lard to the touch, it insulated his body against the cold and made him very difficult to kill. He had been wounded by arrows before, and also by musket balls, knife

blades, and the teeth of animals. Nothing had ever penetrated so far into the fat as to damage muscle or bone.

Hawkes was not the first member of his family to be protected by this buckler of lard. On the morning of August 11, 1674, his father, John Pennock's faithful sergeant, was shot twice in the chest with wheel-lock pistols while strangling a French cannoneer during the Battle of Senef in the Netherlands. He fought on until both the Protestant and Catholic armies withdrew during the night. Pennock dug out the two .56-caliber lead balls with a penknife.

Because nerves were not usually involved, wounds in the lard caused little pain. If Hawkes moved his head too quickly, he felt the flint arrowhead buried in his shoulder, but this caused no inconvenience. The arrowhead in his chest was a different matter. Any pressure on it disturbed the anterior supraclavicular nerve, filling Hawkes's whole upper body with searing pain and depriving him momentarily of the power of movement.

Hawkes's mind was not occupied with these facts as he and his wolf dogs moved eastward on a contour north of the great bend in the Pocumtuck, looking for the Frenchmen and their captives. He knew that they had not gone west along the river, because he had inspected every party of Abenakis and captives that came that way before heading back. It was twilight. Hawkes, half-blinded by the blowing snow, was passing along the edge of a ravine when the surviving mongrel, who had been foraging through a stand of white birches in the bottom of the ravine, found the carcass of the bear that Used to be Bear had killed. It was spread-eagled in a tree, swinging in the wind. The wolf dogs, who had not eaten anything substantial in days, pulled it down and tore it apart. There was little left but the bones.

As soon as he descended into the ravine, Hawkes realized that Abenakis had camped here. The new snow and the wind had not obliterated footprints inside the sleeping pits. Hawkes examined these carefully, looking for some sign that Thoughtful had been here. Three sets of footprints toed inward, and the rest, including one set of male prints, toed outward: three Abenakis, one Frenchman, Six Englishwomen, probably a child or two—and one half-grown boy. It was possible that Thoughtful, who had large feet for a girl, had left one set of the Indian prints; it was difficult to be sure when she wasn't wearing her own moccasins.

While the dogs crushed the bear's bones, Hawkes ranged back and forth across the ravine in the failing light, looking for some sign that would tell him which direction the Frenchman had taken. The wind had erased most signs, but as last he found two sets of moccasin prints, those of the Frenchman and a small-footed En-

glish female, in the shelter of a huge double beech tree. There were only the four prints; all the rest had been blown away. Farther on, he found the place where the two had put on snow-shoes and struck out toward the north. Still farther away, near a deadfall that sheltered the trail from the wind, he found the tracks of the larger party, all heading northwest.

Hawkes was now satisfied that the Frenchman was heading for the Naquag. When he came to the headwaters, two days' march to the north for a party held back by women, he could run in three main directions—to Lake Champlain along the rivers, up the valley between the green mountains to Lake Memphremagog, or up the Connecticut. But for now, he could only go along the Naquag, moving slowly. Hawkes called the dogs into the sleeping pit the women had used and lay down on the balsam boughs. The wind howled through the trees, and as he fell asleep in a huddle of dogs, he heard wood splintering and branches falling all around him.

When the moon rose, bigger and brighter now as it fattened into its third quarter, Hawkes headed north, again following the trail along the contour just below the ridge of the little valley that the Naquag had carved in the schist and granite. It was a good trail, free of brush, tamped into the hillside by tens of thousands of years of use by hoofed animals. Just before dawn, in a tiny meadow along the Naquag, he found the Frenchman's camp. There was nothing to show that it was a camp—everyone was hidden in sleeping pits and the wind had blown away their footprints. The wind was blowing toward the camp, so the mongrel did not pick up the Indians' scent.

Hawkes might have missed it, but Father Nicolas was kneeling in the snow, contemplating the events of the passion from the house of Annas to the house of Caiaphas, where Peter denied Jesus twice, Jesus looked on Peter and wept bitterly, Jesus was left bound the entire night, and those who held him prisoner blindfolded him and struck and buffeted him and said to him, *Prophesy, who is it that struck thee?* Hawkes at once recognized Father Nicolas in his black robes as a Jesuit. Every now and then his small figure was obscured as the wind drove a cloud of snow across the campground.

Nobody except the priest seemed to be up. The Naquag ran nearly due north and south through the meadow, with steep hills on either side. Hawkes was sprawled on his stomach just below the opposite slope of the western ridge, about two hundred paces from the camp, with the dogs lying down around him. In the camp, an Abenaki rose up out of a sleeping pit, then another. One by one, the rest of the party got up. Hawkes recognized them all, even the

Abenakis—Talks in His Dreams and a younger man from the same village.

There were only four females—Fanny, the Clum girls, and a woman named Jean Judd who was nursing two babies. The Frenchman was missing. Where was the third Abenaki? Hawkes searched the camp and the woods around it, moving his eyes very slowly so as to cover one small patch of ground in every detail before moving to the next. He saw nothing except what might be a trail of filled-in tracks leading upstream along the course of the Naquag. Maybe the Frenchman and the third Abenaki had taken the most valuable captives, Thoughtful and Rose Barebones, and gone ahead by moonlight.

Off to the right, the bleached winter sun was beginning to rise. This was the moment to attack; he couldn't have these Abenakis and the Jesuit at his back while he pursued the Frenchman. He could leave the women here and collect them when he came back down the Naquag with Thoughtful and Rose Barebones. The Indians were not armed with muskets. They could not possibly get away from the wolf dogs.

Hawkes stood up on the skyline, a little stiffly because of the arrowhead in the back of his neck, and clucked to the dogs. The Abenakis saw their silhouettes and began to sing; Hawkes could hear nothing because the wind was so strong, but he knew that was what they were doing. Hawkes never looked forward to anything, but when this moment came in all its intense pleasure, he was always happy. He felt the dogs around him, whining and smiling and gathering their huge bodies for the attack.

Hawkes opened his mouth and called on the muscles of his throat and tongue to produce the call of a jay. As this sound formed, but before the dogs heard it, he saw a peculiar blossom of flame bursting from the snow on the opposite hillside.

With his eyes still fixed on the flame, which was turning into a cloud of powder smoke, Hawkes heard a hollow sound, like a palm slapping the ribs of an animal. The wolf dog nearest to him, the one that had torn off Dancing Beaver's head beside the Connecticut, rose onto it hind legs, waved its paws in the air, and fell over backward, with a gushing wound in the place where the hairless spot behind its near front leg had formerly been. The deafening crack of Philippe's jaeger rifle echoed from the hills.

The two remaining dogs, having heard Hawkes's imitation of the jay, attacked. The Abenakis below held their ground as the dogs came for them. Hawkes plunged down the slope after them, his eyes fixed on the point where the shot had come from. He could

see the Frenchman, who had risen up out of the snow under which he had concealed himself.

He was frantically reloading his weapon, pounding the bullet into the barrel with a steel ramrod that blinked in the sun. He was about two hundred paces away. Even on snowshoes this was a run of less than a minute. If he could get within twenty paces of the Frenchman before he reloaded, Hawkes could kill him with his musket. If he could lay hands on him he could break his neck. The two Indians on the other side of the river threw something at the dogs, then leaped into a sleeping pit and pulled the balsam roof over top of them. The confused dogs stopped, bolted several lumps of meat that the Indians had thrown to them, skidded to a stop, and attacked again.

Hawkes had covered half the distance to the rifle and was gathering himself to leap across the Naquag when Used to be Bear, dressed only in a breechclout, rose up out of a sleeping pit in the snow directly in front of Hawkes. He held a tomahawk in his left hand and a long glittering bayonet in his right. Hawkes, holding his musket aloft in both hands, had already left his feet to make his leap. Rose Barebones' perfect face looked at him out of the sleeping pit. He tried to turn his body in flight to avoid a collision, but it was too late.

He crashed into Used to be Bear, knocking him backward. The impact, which drove the flint arrowhead against the nerve in Hawkes's chest, made him scream in agony. He felt another fiery pain in his left arm, the wrong place. He heard another rifle shot. He and the Abenaki, who was the largest Indian Hawkes had ever encountered, came down in the snow. Blood spurted from the Indian's nose. He was snatching at Hawkes with his right hand and swinging a tomahawk with his left. Hawkes wrenched the Abenaki's hatchet from his hand and chopped blindly at him. A wolf dog appeared behind Used to be Bear and seized him by the arm, dragging him off Hawkes. He could not see the other dog.

The two Abenakis from the camp were running up the hill. Hawkes rolled over onto his buttocks and fired his musket, which was loaded with buckshot. Both Indians sat down abruptly in the snow. Waves of nausea rose out of Hawkes's stomach. He scrambled to his feet and began to run along the slope toward the woods. The wolf dog that had attacked Used to be Bear ran along ahead of him.

Inside the trees, the same mixture of birches and swamp maples through which he had traveled during most of the night, Hawkes paused to reload his musket, passing it from his right hand to his left, but his left hand failed to grip the musket and it fell to the

snow. Hawkes remembered the pain in his left arm, and remembering it, realized that he still felt it. Used to be Bear had driven the bayonet completely through his biceps. The wound did not seem to be bleeding much from either of its mouths. Hawkes, holding on to the slender trunk of a birch so that he would not fall down, vomited onto the snow.

Below, a wolf dog, shot through the skull, lay on its side in the snow-choked bed of the Naquag. The big naked Indian walked in circles in the blowing snow, holding on to his bitten arm. The other Abenakis gazed politely in another direction. Hawkes knew that they wouldn't follow him. The fight was over. They would want to look inside the wolf dogs and eat their livers, so as to mingle their enemies' strength with their own. Hawkes heard the sound of a pileated woodpecker and looked around, wondering if there were other Abenakis behind him. The last wolf dog licked his face, whimpering, and Hawkes realized that he himself was making the same sound.

Where was Thoughtful Pennock?

# 19

Philippe, his eyes fixed on the spot were Hawkes had disappeared into the woods, ran across the valley with his rifle in his hands. He had not been able to get off the third shot that he had intended for Hawkes. He plunged into the woods. There was blood on the snow and spilled gunpowder beside a yellow birch tree where Hawkes had reloaded his musket. Hawkes's tracks, intermixed with blood, went straight for the Naquag.

Philippe, running as hard as he could, ran away from the stream for a hundred paces or so, then parallel to it for a quarter of a mile, then back toward it. At the end of this half-circle he emerged onto a ridge above the stream.

Over the sound of his own hard breathing, he heard a series of loud grunts. Down below, Hawkes, with his wolf dog bounding alongside him, was running through the trees. He was grunting in pain with every step. Philippe put the sight of his jaeger on Hawkes's

back. He had been running too hard to hold the rifle steady, so he rested the barrel against the trunk of a tree.

Hawkes was passing through a grove of stark white birches about fifty paces away. He made a big target, but he was never in the open for more than an instant. No bullet could reach him before it hit a tree. Philippe lowered the hammer on his rifle and dropped its butt to the snow. He reached for his bayonet, thinking that he could outrun Hawkes and use the blade on him or the wolf dog after having used his bullet on one or the other, but the scabbard was empty. He remembered that he had loaned the blade to Used to be Bear. He was carrying two small smooth-bore pistols but he would not be able to draw them in time to shoot the dog if it attacked. Knowing that he could not kill both Hawkes and the dog with the equipment he had, and knowing that he must kill them both or die himself, Philippe did not pursue his fleeing enemy any farther.

"No hope, no hope!" Hepzibah Clum moaned, with tears running down her chapped face.

She and her sister and Jean Judd, who thought that Hawkes and his dogs had come to rescue them, threw their arms around one another and sank to their knees in the snow. They were bareheaded and unbraided, two windblown chestnut heads and Totsie's auburn one.

"Aren't they afraid Hawkes will come back?" Fanny asked Philippe.

The Abenakis, having used the women to gather wood, were building an enormous fire on their campground beside the Naquag. Talks in His Dreams had lighted it with a shot from one of Philippe's pistols. He reloaded the pistol while the flames began to catch.

"Is that his name?" Philippe said. "The Abenakis call him the fat ghost."

The wind whipped the fire, sending sheets of sparks dancing over the snow. The dead dogs roasted inside the flames like huge bubbling logs. Sleeping Fox had cut off the dogs' heads and propped them up on a pile of snow where he could peer into the eyes. He had been looking all his life for his father's head, which the wolf dogs had stolen, and he thought that he might be able to discover where they had hidden it.

There was a little blood on Sleeping Fox's chest where Hawkes had shot him, but he had not looked after these superficial wounds. Except for Used to be Bear's arm, which had sustained a compound fracture, the Abenakis' injuries were not serious. Talks in His Dreams was even less affected than Sleeping Fox; the shot had

barely pierced his skin after passing through the three or four layers of deerhide that he was wearing.

While waiting for the meat to cook, Talks in His Dreams had chopped a hole in the ice of the Naquag and spread Used to be Bear's bearskin beside it. Used to be Bear lay down on his face on the bearskin and plunged his broken arm into the freezing water. After a while he sat up and began to sing again. Talks in His Dreams sat down on the ice facing him, took hold of the other man's wrist, braced his moccasins against his chest, and set the fracture.

Fanny was quiet. Frowning slightly, she examined the buckshot lodged in Philippe's cheek. He had a black eye now and a swelling on the cheekbone. The discoloration improved his looks, she thought, by making his face less symmetrical, less grave, younger. Fanny touched the swelling with her fingertip and pressed. The wound oozed yellow matter.

"It's too late to probe for the lead now even if we had something to probe with," she said. "You should put hot saltwater packs on it, to draw out the pus."

They were standing between the steep banks of the Naquag, where there was some shelter from the wind.

Fanny touched his wound gently and said, "What is the sense of what you have done?"

Philippe did not pretend not to understand.

"Sense?" he said. "Shall we speak about the attack by the English and the Iroquois on La Chine in the summer of 1689? A hundred French dead during the attack, another hundred carried off and tortured to death afterward."

"I know it has all happened before, and what explanations have been made. Have you done it before—you, yourself?"

"No. I am just beginning."

Fanny's eyes did not waver. "It appears that you have a gift for your work," she said.

Philippe rose to his feet, cradling his jaeger in his arms, and studied the clouds as they scudded across the sky.

"We must move as soon as the Abenakis wake up," he said.

"Move? In the night?"

"The moon is very bright now. It was planned in this way. The march takes two weeks and a day or two, the retreat a little longer, so if you leave the Saint Francis with the full moon you return to its banks at the next full moon."

He began to walk away.

"Wait," Fanny said.

He turned around.

"Father Nicolas tells me that I am not a prisoner," she said. "Is that your opinion also?"

"Certainly. You are a rescued Catholic."

"Then I am free."

Philippe nodded.

"Good," Fanny said. "Then let me buy the others from the Abenakis and let us go."

"Buy them? With what?"

Fanny turned her back and lifted her skirt. When she turned around again she held Oliver's ruby necklace in her hand. Philippe looked at it without touching it. When he spoke there was a change in his voice.

"Put it on," he said.

Fanny unwound her scarf, opened her cloak, and clasped the necklace around her neck. She had never worn it before. The red stones and the gold in which they were set seemed to gather light from her skin.

"What you offer is far too valuable," Philippe said.

"I am willing to make the bargain."

"The Abenakis don't know about rubies," he said.

"Surely if the stones are so valuable, their value can be explained."

"No. How would you find your way back to Alamoth?"

"We would follow the rivers."

"The English would hang you."

"*Jaghte oghte*," Fanny said.

Hepzibah Clum was standing above her on the riverbank with Totsie beside her. Their lips and chins shone with grease. They stared at the ruby necklace.

"You whore of Babylon," Hepzibah said. "Poor Gus Hawkes, who only wanted to love his dogs."

Rose appeared and gave Hepzibah and her sister a shove, as if they were girls in the nursery. "You'd better eat, Fanny," she said.

Rose saw the necklace too. "What's that round your neck?" she said. "It matches my ring. It's beautiful, Fanny! Where did you *get* it?"

# 20

The wind captured Fanny like a net. To make herself smaller, she bent her body at the waist and gripped her knees. Snow whipped her face. The gale ripped a tree apart and blew through the forest with a volume that rose and fell, but in a low and somber pitch that never changed. Fanny, pausing chilled and exhausted in the whirling half-light of the riverbed, had the illusion that the wind was releasing bass notes that were too deep for her ear to apprehend. Probably Rose could hear these sounds. She was behind Fanny, walking in Used to be Bear's footsteps and using him for a windbreak.

The gust passed. Fanny completed the step she had earlier begun to take and reached over her shoulder and touched Solitude. Betsy's baby was asleep. In the pause in the wind she heard the Judd boy feebly whooping. The Abenakis paid no attention to him now. They appeared to believe that the death of the wolf dogs had put them beyond danger, and tonight they blundered across the country like a gang of farmers, making noise, lighting fires, ignoring sign.

Still, they moved forward under the waning moon as doggedly as ever, never stopping, never slowing down. They had been walking up the Naquag since early afternoon. It was now midnight, the hour of the first contemplation in the Spiritual Exercises.

Father Nicolas, trudging along ahead of Fanny, was engaged in imagining the words spoken by Pontius Pilate after he had examined Jesus. He spoke them aloud: " '*I find no crime deserving of death in him.*' " Father Nicolas' voice was carried back to Fanny on the wind. As he spoke each syllable, he drove his staff into the snow. "They all said, '*Let him be crucified!*' " Father Nicolas cried. "The procurator said to them, '*Why, what evil has he done?*' But they kept crying out the more, saying, '*Let him be crucified!*' "

Fanny slowed her footsteps and fell behind. Used to be Bear trudged along beside her. He had cut a slit for his head in the center of his bearskin and was now wearing his garment, fur side

inward, cinched at the waist with a length of rawhide. It was frozen stiff.

Rose fell into step with Fanny and gave her an ingratiating smile. Fanny supposed this meant that she was going to ask about the ruby necklace, but instead she pointed at the diminutive figure of Father Nicolas.

"What is the dwarf saying?" Rose asked.

Father Nicolas had been quoting in Latin from the Gospel According to Saint Mark. Fanny interpreted.

" 'I find no crime deserving of death'?" Rose said. "Is that what Pontius Pilate said?"

"Yes."

"He wouldn't say that about these papists or their savages, would he?"

Rose glared at Father Nicolas' hunched black-robed figure as it marched through dervishes of snow, shouting out Pilate's infamous claim to be innocent of Christ's blood. Rose was limping slightly.

"Your leg," Fanny said. "Is it all right?"

"It will be by and by," Rose said. "Tell me the secret of the necklace."

The Abenakis stopped at last just before moonset, an hour or two after they reached the source of the Naquag. They were in the mountains now. A dense evergreen forest lay all around, with smaller, greener trees than the ones in the valley. They seemed calmer in this dark woods than they had previously been. The wind hardly blew over the floor of the forest, and such noise as it made, whistling through the limber tips of the pines and spruces and hemlocks high above, seemed less wild than the demented gale they had been walking through.

The Indians built lean-tos, separating the party as they had been doing all along—women, including Fanny but not Rose, and the children in one lean-to, Talks in His Dreams and Sleeping Fox in an adjoining one, Philippe and Father Nicolas in a third, and Rose and Used to be Bear in the last one, some distance from the others.

Rose accepted these arrangements without complaint. The others had heard her cries coming out of the sleeping pit on the first night she had spent with Used to be Bear and knew what they meant.

They had all been raped too—the Clum girls one after the other by Talks in His Dreams, Jean by Sleeping Fox—but this had happened while they were still in the lean-tos along the Connecticut. The act had been perfunctory; the Indians seemed to be doing it not for pleasure but for the same reasons that they fed the

captives nocake or made them dogtrot or beat them when they urinated or defecated anywhere but in running water through a hole chopped in the ice—to establish the rules of the situation. The women had lain quietly while it happened, side by side, and said nothing about it to each other afterward.

Rose's outcry, the sound of blows, her undiminished haughtiness in the aftermath, all showed how different she was from ordinary women. Tonight Rose was in no danger. Used to be Bear had a fever. The dog had ripped the skin from his forearm and inflicted deep punctures in his muscles. The walls of these wounds had collapsed, providing ideal conditions for infection. Also, the pain was considerable. Used to be Bear's radius and ulna had not so much been broken as splintered by the pressure and rotation of the wolf dog's teeth and jaws.

As he inserted himself into the lean-to feet first, head just inside the open end, and laid himself down on his bearskin, he groaned in his discomfort and dug through the balsam-bough bed to scoop up handfuls of snow for his fever and his thirst. He paid no attention to Rose, who sat cross-legged on the snow near his head.

The moon was down. In the starlight that filtered through the roof of the lean-to, Rose could not, at first, make out Used to be Bear's features. Of course she knew where he was and what he was doing by smell and sound—the bear grease, the roast wolf dog he had been digesting since morning and which was now escaping from his body in the form of gases, the rasp of his fingernails on his scalp and stomach, the sharp squeak of breath when he moved his arm. Rose ignored sound and smell and concentrated on seeing. Gradually her extraordinary eyes adjusted to the dark.

For a while, Used to be Bear muttered to himself and scratched his skin aimlessly with his unwounded hand. Finally he fell asleep. Rose concentrated on his face—only the face, the lantern chin, the thin scarred mouth that let yellow teeth show through at the left corner, the flat planes of the cheeks, the smashed nose, the missing ear, the eyes. She was, of course, looking at him upside down. His face, dark skin surrounded by darkness, did not have the appearance of flesh and bone, but resembled a face seen in a mirror in an unlighted room.

Rose focused on his left eye, to the exclusion of every other feature. Used to be Bear, who was practically hairless, had no eyebrows and only the sparsest lashes. That morning, while Used to be Bear was walking around in circles holding on to his broken arm, Rose had picked up Philippe's bloody bayonet and concealed it in the skirt of her petticoat. It had bumped against her poor leg all day long.

Now she took it out, and holding it in both hands as she had learned from watching Used to be Bear, placed the point against his eyelid and drove the blade into his brain. Unlike the real bear, Used to be Bear died without moving or uttering a sound.

Rose retrieved the bayonet, crossed the campground to the lean-to where Talks in His Dreams, and Sleeping Fox were lying with their heads pointing outward, and sank quietly into the snow to study first one sleeping inverted face and then the other.

# 21

When Rose crawled into bed with Fanny, so stealthily that Fanny did not know that she was beside her until she heard what she was whispering into her ear, Fanny's heart froze.

"It's a very quiet death, Fanny, not like shooting or hanging," Rose said. "One must pinch them afterward to be sure it's really happened."

She reached up in the dark and pinched Fanny's lower lip to show her how—not nearly as hard, of course, as she had pinched the corpses'.

Fanny took several deep breath before she could whisper back.

"The Jesuit?" she said. "Philippe?"

"I haven't killed them yet. I don't know if I can. They're not Indians."

Fanny groped for Rose's hand. Rose squeezed her fingers; she really could see in the dark.

"Wait," Rose said. "What if they follow us?"

"They won't," Fanny said, squeezing hard. "We must get away. Now, as quick as we can, before the French wake up."

Two hours later, Rose and Fanny, running side by side between the high banks of the Naquag, were far ahead of the other women. With an unerring sense of direction, Rose had led them out of the forest, leaving the Frenchmen alive in their lean-to.

Rose slowed down and stopped in the middle of the frozen watercourse. The Clum girls and Jean Judd, stumbling through a whirlwind of snow, came into sight. They were more warmly

dressed now. Hepzibah wore Used to be Bear's bearskin like a jerkin. The other two women were wrapped in hides that Rose had stripped from the bodies of Talks in His Dreams and Sleeping Fox.

The Judd boy was still gasping for air. Solitude, strapped to Fanny's back as usual, was beginning to wake up and cry. Fanny jiggled her shoulders, rocking the papoose frame, and the child quietened.

"Let Hepzibah carry her," Rose said. She adjusted Solitude's swaddling, gently pinched her nose, and swung the papoose frame onto Hepzibah's broad back. Fanny had never before seen Rose touch a child.

After they had rested for a few minutes, Rose ordered the others to move on. They staggered forward, groaning, but they obeyed without complaint. If they had been Rose's servants before she killed the Abenakis, they were her slaves now. Only slaves or sleepwalkers would have consented to push on. Except for the two hours' sleep they had had before Rose woke them, the women had been walking or running for nearly sixteen hours.

While they were stumbling out of earshot, Rose held Fanny's hands. Her eyes were fixed on the papoose frame as it bobbed away into the darkness on Hepzibah's back. She uttered two or three long sighs.

"How mysterious God's ways can be," Rose said at last. She was speaking in the tone of voice used by Ash when he talked about God's will. "To think that Edward's child has been left in our care and Betsy is dead, and my poor husband is gone, and all impediments have been removed to what must be, and yet . . . It is cruel, Fanny, cruel."

A gust of wind jostled them. Rose lost her balance, took three of four quick sidewise steps, and then recovered herself. Fanny spoke to her as calmly as she could.

"What do you mean, Rose, your husband is gone, and all impediments have been removed to what must be? *What must be?*"

"Edward loves me," Rose said.

The words came out one at a time. Rose was gasping for breath. Even though they were no longer running, the mere act of breathing inside this maelstrom of snow was difficult.

Fanny's voice was unsteady. "Ash loves you?" she said.

The moon was behind Fanny, shining onto Rose's face.

"Oh, yes," Rose said. "He has loved me from the start—lucky for you, or you would have died on the ship. That's why he prays the way he does. I am the passion of his life. He's constantly asking God to be freed from it. He prayed for release on the ship, and all these months I have heard him through the floor of my

bedchamber when he prayed in the library at Rose Manor. His prayers were never answered."

Rose gave Fanny a look of intimacy, "Poor Betsy, poor Oliver. But they're gone. Edward's state was often . . . noticeable when we were in the same room together. On board ship it was embarrassing. Didn't you ever notice how he kept his eyes on you all the time when we were together? That was because he was fighting the temptation to look at me. I supposed he thought your innocence would purify his thoughts."

By now they had fallen many paces behind the others. It was nearly impossible to see or hear. Fanny placed her mouth close to Rose's ear.

"How do you know these things?" she asked.

"I know what I know," Rose replied.

She gave Fanny a brilliant smile and started off after the others with her easy, athletic stride. She looked back once and beckoned Fanny to follow. Fanny began to run in Rose's tracks. The course of the Naquag was very steep here and rocks lay beneath the snow. The others, trudging on, were nearly out of sight. Totsie tripped and sprawled on her face.

Rose's slim figure, the fur cape swirling around the hips, glided through the eddying snow. *What if they follow us*? Fanny slowed her pace to a walk. What if Philippe did follow? What would his fate be then—death in the mud, death by fire, death by examination for witchcraft, death because a Gypsy prophesied sexual union with a bear, death because Rose, instead of God, had heard someone's prayers?

Fanny stopped in her tracks. She could not go on; she could not go back. Rose had nearly caught up with the others. She ran through their struggling ranks and took the lead. As Fanny watched, standing quite still, their indistinct forms moved farther and farther away. A gust of wind filled the air with snow and Fanny lost sight of them. When the wind died, they had vanished into the storm—scrubbed out like chalk figures in a cartoon.

Fanny turned around and began to jog rhythmically in the other direction, toward Canada, straining her eyes to see the footprints she had made only minutes before, and which were now being obliterated by the wind.

# IV

# THE WILDERNESS

# 1

**P**hilippe's sister Marie-Dominique, Countess of Vallier, told fortunes with tarot cards. Seated at a marquetry writing table, called a bureau Mazarin, in the Hôtel de Vallier, her husband's house in Quebec, she shuffled the deck, turned up the Knight of Cups, the Star, and the Four of Wands, and said, "You will marry a brilliant man for love, but your love will be the great secret of your lives, so you will never suffer for it."

"Never suffer for love?" Fanny said.

"Hardly. The cards only say you will not suffer for *having* loved. As indicated by the Knight of Cups, the card of gentle spies, others won't make jokes about six months of love not being worth a lifetime of reproach, because you will be so clever that they will never suspect that you are madly in love with your own husband, and he with you. You and he will be very discreet, very correct when in the presence of others, hiding your passion, like lovers instead of spouses."

Marie-Dominique turned up another card, the Nine of Swords, which can mean doubt, desolation, or the death of a loved one.

"Never mind about that one," she said. "It's time to practice what we'll say tonight to dazzle the gentlemen. We'll tell them about the porcupines, I think."

On their march south to raid Alamoth, the Abenakis had killed dozens of porcupines and hung them in trees along the Connecticut as emergency rations for the retreat to Canada. Fanny, Philippe, and Father Nicolas had survived on these frozen porcupines during their long march back to Canada.

"The governor adores the story about the porcupines," Marie-Dominique said. "It's wonderful to watch him as he imagines you, the prettiest girl ever seen in New France, climbing the tree, skinning the horrible pricky little beast, roasting it over a fire, eating it so delicately with those little white teeth. One can see his appetites improving by the minute."

Marie-Dominique, indeed all the French, never stopped telling Fanny how pretty she was. As soon as she arrived, after sailing up

the broad unfrozen Saint Lawrence River aboard a patrol boat of the French Navy, Marie-Dominique has asked her if she had any money.

"Fifty English pounds," Fanny replied.

"Wonderful," said Marie-Dominique. "We'll give ten to the dressmaker."

Very soon afterward Fanny possessed morning dresses for walking and riding in carriages through the narrow streets of the steep little city, afternoon dresses for calling and receiving visitors, and evening gowns that exposed her shoulders and bosom.

"It's true," Marie-Dominique said, clasping the ruby necklace around Fanny's throat. "You *do* have the golden skin of Araby!"

Like her brother and Father Nicolas, and, it seemed, the entire city of Quebec, Marie-Dominique knew the basic facts of Fanny's life.

"How do you know these things?" Fanny asked.

"From the Spy," Marie-Dominique replied. "The Spy fell deeper and deeper in love with you as each secret of your life was revealed. You cannot imagine his joy as he learned that you are the granddaughter of Captain Harris, who fought against the English Protestants and married Liliane l'Ecossaise, that you are an orphan, Catholic, that you possess a beautiful singing voice and play both keyboard and strings, that you were secretly educated by a Jesuit and speak Latin and Greek, that your baptismal name is Genevieve, that the madman who tried to drown you in Honfleur also tore down your father's house with a span of oxen, that you own a ship. . . . The ship was the best part."

"But who is this spy?"

"Someone my husband commissioned to find out everything about you after he saw you on the quay in Honfleur. 'The miracle of the fishes,' Armand called it—this angel in mourning appearing out of the Channel mists with the morning catch, speaking French like a servant girl. Was this an English plot, was the angel an English spy?"

"What nonsense."

"So the Spy found out," Marie-Dominique said. "But one cannot be too careful about the English; even their virgins are treacherous, my husband says."

Marie-Dominique, who was only a year older than Fanny, was the second Saint-Christophe sister to have married Armand de Grestain, count of Vallier, captain-general of New France. He was twenty-five years older than she; after six months of marriage, she was in the sixth month of pregnancy.

Her sister, Edwige, the first countess, had been tortured to

death by the Iroquois at La Chine together with her two-year-old son. (Because the body of Grestain's heir was never found, a legend arose that a French nobleman was living, unsuspected and unsuspecting, among the Iroquois; Eleazer Williams, the redeemed English captive who later represented himself to the world as "the lost dauphin of France," may have based his imposture on this fable.)

"Armand *hates* the English," Marie-Dominique told Fanny.

"I thought every Frenchman did."

"They do. But what the English did to Edwige and her son made things worse for Armand. He was already enraged because nearly the entire male line of the Grestain family were slaughtered by lowborn English axmen at the Battle of Agincourt."

"But that happened nearly three hundred years ago."

"Nevertheless, Armand says it was a cowardly act. The Grestains were stuck in the mud in their suits of armor and were unable to defend themselves."

On Fanny's arrival in Quebec, after she had escaped from the English murderess and walked all night through a blizzard to find Philippe and then marched with him and Father Nicolas Laux across three hundred miles of wilderness, sleeping in the snow and subsisting on porcupines, Grestain had instructed everyone in his household and every officer on his staff to watch her with the greatest care, as she was probably an English spy.

"But we already know everything about her," Marie-Dominique said.

"One never knows everything about the English."

"My dear husband, she is a Catholic and part French."

"*Ainsi que Henri Cinq*," Grestain replied—just like Henry V of England, the victor of Agincourt.

Fanny lived with the Grestains in the drafty timber-and-stone Hôtel de Vallier on the heights above the Saint Lawrence. She paid for her food and lodging at the rate of a shilling a month. Normally Philippe also lived at the Hôtel de Vallier, but without charge because he was Marie-Dominique's brother and because he had no money beyond his army pay as an officer of artillery. Now he was absent, waiting for the last Abenaki to return to the village on the Saint Francis River before he came back to Quebec.

"He has a great sense of duty to the Indians," Marie-Dominique told Fanny. "He grew up among them."

"Grew up among them?"

"Yes, like an Indian boy, shooting arrows and living in the woods. Surely you noticed that he is just like an Abenaki when he is on a campaign against the English."

"I saw many similarities," Fanny said.

The Hôtel de Vallier, though it was by no means grand enough to be called an *hôtel* in Paris, was three times as large as an ordinary Quebecois house. It was old by North American standards, having been built half a century earlier. Because the Normans who settled Quebec did not at first understand the climate, it was built like a Norman house, according to the method called *colombage pierotte,* in which the walls were formed by filling wooden frames with loose stone cemented with lime mortar. It was soon discovered that lime mortar dissolved under the assault of Canadian rain, snow, and wind. To keep out the elements, later occupants sheathed such houses with lumber, covering even the chimneys with broad pine boards.

The expense of sheathing had been so great in the case of the Hôtel de Vallier that Grestain had declared that they could not entertain any person of less than noble rank, unless he was a member of the Sovereign Council of New France, for the remainder of their time in Canada. Being able to make this decision on economic grounds was a great comfort to Armand de Grestain: because Quebec was an outpost of empire, people who were eligible to dine with the Comte de Vallier here would have snatched off their hats in France as he passed by; Armand de Grestain never gave the impression that he had forgotten this fact. The governor and the intendant, as the treasurer of the colony was called, and the bishop came to dine once a month.

Otherwise, no stranger consumed food in the Hôtel de Vallier. Those who were not fed by the Grestains were known as *les soupirants,* the sighing ones.

When the servant passed among them at a soiree with tiny glasses and a decanter on a tray, he would ask, *"Desirez-vous une larme de vin?"*—will you have a tear of wine?

The *soupirants'* decanter contained a discreetly watered mixture of the leftover wines that had been decanted for the governor, the intendant, and the bishop.

Armand de Grestain believed that Fanny should marry a prominent man of the colony—though not, of course, a nobleman—as quickly as possible. Because he was clearly her protector, he reasoned that any dowry should come to him.

"I quite understand, of course, that you are, for the moment, without substantial funds," Grestain said to her, "although you seem to be able to wear charming gowns and a fortune in rubies around your neck. You will wish to write a letter to the man Pietro di Gesù, instructing him to call at Quebec in the *Pamela.* You will then be in a position to arrange a suitable marriage. Perhaps we

can arrange something between us as well—a cargo of furs, perhaps, in exchange for silk and scent and that excellent coffee. There is never enough silk or coffee in New France."

Fanny's accent, which had offended Grestain on the quay at Honfleur, was less noticeable, if no less grating, in Quebec. Champlain himself had sailed from Honfleur, and the province had largely been settled by Normans, most of whom sounded a great deal like Antoinette. That was exactly why Grestain thought that Fanny's speech was an impediment to a good marriage.

"But you must teach this girl to speak!" Armand said to Marie-Dominique.

"Nonsense, it's the best thing about her: that hair, that skin, that ravishing figure, those rubies, and then she speaks. If we were living at court, everyone would be trying to sound just like her."

Marie-Dominique was a tall, very thin young woman, almost skeletal, with long limbs and the greenish complexion and languid gestures of an anemic. She was as intelligent as her brother and resembled him physically: the Viking blood showed in her height, her eyes, her symmetrical face, her tawny hair. She was far more talkative than Philippe; Fanny required no spy to find out the details of Marie-Dominique's life or the history of her family. She was six months pregnant and ate horse liver and fried blood, which she detested, for breakfast to make blood for the fetus. She hoped for a boy, and then for another boy a year afterward; no girls. She wished to fulfill her obligation to perpetuate the male line of the Grestains as quickly as possible.

"Canada is a good place to have my babies, one cannot go out while it is happening no matter where one is, so one might as well be in the wilderness," she said. "Afterward, when Armand has defeated the English in America and made enough money to uphold his position, we will all go back to France while I am still young and live at court. Armand, of course, will be quite old by then."

"Leaving me in Quebec?"

"You must be wherever Philippe is. It's clear that you two love each other, and of course Armand is right about the desirability of finding you a husband. The sooner you're married, the sooner the two of you can become lovers."

"I thought your cards said that I was going to marry a brilliant man for love and live happily ever after."

"Yes, but there's no reason why you should not love two men at the same time—one brilliant, the other beautiful and brave as a lion."

"What will the two of them think of that arrangement?"

"What an idea! Men do not think as long as they get what they want," Marie-Dominique said. "One must be absolutely selfish, always doing the thing that makes one happiest, or else one will make everyone else very unhappy."

"If the object is to sleep with someone you love, then why not simply marry for love?" Fanny asked.

"Because then one would have had to sleep with the same man for the rest of one's life, and that would make the poor fellow very unhappy."

"Life was simpler before you read the cards."

"If you want life to be simple you should go back to the English."

Marie-Dominique had a perfectly composed French mind. In her view, the French had arranged their nation and their culture perfectly in order to let every person of suitable birth realize the possibilities of his or her life to the fullest. Her education, like that of most French people, was based on memorization, so that when she came to the end of her lessons at the age of sixteen she quite naturally believed that she knew everything. There was the church, unquestioned in its authority to teach and forgive; the king, unparalleled in his competence to punish and reward; the family, unquestioning in its loyalty to its members and more important by far than anything else; and the English, the Germans, the Dutch, the Spanish, and the other enemies of French, unspeakable in their un-Frenchness.

One did one's duty, which only occasionally required serious sacrifices, such as being hacked to death by the English, and was otherwise free to advance one's interests, acquire new privileges, get money, possess beautiful things, promote the marriages and careers of one's children, humble one's rivals, judge the worth of everything under the sun with absolute certainty, enjoy the company of one's friends, appease one's appetites, fall in love repeatedly. In a life properly lived, all these things occurred all the time, so that the mind was fully occupied in plotting to make them happen and the body was fulfilled as a result of their having happened.

"Above all, one must live for oneself," Marie-Dominique repeated over and over; this was her maxim. "Other's will not go to the trouble of looking after someone else's pleasure."

Marie-Dominique had been the youngest child in the large Saint-Christophe family, in which many children died. In the end only she and Edwige and Philippe remained alive. Marie-Dominique was five years younger than Philippe, who was himself five years younger than Edwige.

The two girls were greatly attached to Philippe. By way of their

mother they were distantly related to the Bourbons, and through their father to a hero of France who, though bleeding to death himself, stripped off his own armor and carried his wounded king, Philippe VI, across the River Maye after the French had lost the Battle of Crécy and some twenty thousand men-at-arms to English archers. The king made his rescuer a member of the nobility as Sieur de Saint-Christophe, an obscure but fertile estate at the edge of the Marais, the great swamp near the mouth of the Seine. The heir to this estate was always christened Philippe.

"The men of our family were probably larger in 1346, as the Viking blood was less mixed with the French," Marie-Dominique said, "but all the same, it's a wonder they didn't both drown. One can see our Philippe doing the same sort of thing, can't one?"

The family was not well-off. The conquest of Normandy by Henry V had deprived them of most of their lands, and ancestors who inherited the original Saint-Christophe's quality of blind loyalty had fought on the wrong side in most internal French wars. Somehow Louis XIV had heard about the heroism of the original Saint-Christophe at Crécy nearly 350 years before and appointed the present head of the family, Philippe's father, to a post in the army as a belated royal reminder to less audacious Frenchmen of how kings once were loved in France.

That action led to a meeting between the Sieur de Saint-Christophe and the Comte de Vallier and eventually to the successive marriages between him and the Saint-Christophe daughters. Because both families were members of the *noblesse d'epée,* the ancient branch of the French aristocracy that had won its titles through feats of arms, the match was suitable if not particularly advantageous to either.

In some generations, Marie-Dominique said, it was enough to hold one's own—except that the Saint-Christophes, in the same generation as herself and Edwige, had brought forth Philippe, the precise individual that thirty generations of breeding had been designed to produce.

Everyone in the family recognized Philippe's uniqueness. Almost from birth, he could do anything—ride, shoot, run, leap, make anyone fall in love with him. Yet he was quiet, modest, and loving, a mysterious mixture of soldierly and saintly qualities. When Edwige, at the age of seventeen, married Armand de Grestain and went with him to New France, she took Philippe along. Their father agreed with Grestain that it would be a good thing for the boy to live for a while in the wilderness, so that he would understand with his entrails as well as his mind and heart what wonders the French had wrought.

Philippe was twelve, already a cadet, and Grestain sent him to serve in the small garrison at Chambly on the Richelieu River. There he met Father Nicolas Laux, who acted as his tutor as well as his confessor. From boys in the Indian villages, including Used to be Bear, he learned woodcraft and the tongue-twisting, mind-bending dialect of Algonquian spoken by the Abenakis. He was already a first-class archer and a quick, aggressive wrestler. A *coureur des bois* who had killed seventeen Iroquois and possessed the wonderful name Aurélien Veron taught Philippe to shoot. He was too young to accompany the first expedition to Alamoth, but he had watched the captives come back and heard the Abenakis' stories about the raid.

Father Nicolas perfected his Latin by dictating accounts in that language of the atrocities committed by the Iroquois against the French. Father Nicolas himself had been hung by his feet from the beams of his church by Iroquois who then set the church on fire. One of the Indians, evidently a secret Christian, gave the little Jesuit a knife at the last minute and so he was able to escape and flee down the Saint Lawrence to Montreal.

When Edwige was raped and murdered by the Iroquois at La Chine, where she happened to be visiting a friend, and her baby was carried away, Philippe was allowed by his brother-in-law to join the party of soldiers and Abenakis who were sent in pursuit. At campsite after campsite they found the flayed corpses of French men, women, and children, more than a hundred in all, tied to stakes, pegged to the ground, flayed and hung from the trees like wild game. Any number of the slaughtered children might have been Philippe's small nephew; it was impossible to identify people of any age whose skin had been completely removed. It was August, and as the French proceeded through the forest, they came to know when they were approaching a place where the Iroquois had amused themselves by the loud buzzing of the flies.

"Philippe cannot bear the sound of flies buzzing to this day," Marie-Dominique told Fanny. "Of course he hates the English, too, who sent the Iroquois to attack La Chine, and that is why it was so disturbing to him, that day in Honfleur, to realize that the angel of the fishes might be an English girl. How could there be an English angel? Then, of course, we learned the truth through espionage."

Through espionage, the Grestains also knew about Fanny's musicality and took advantage of it. They possessed the usual keyboard instruments, and also a very fine violin signed inside the body by the same Italian, Nicolò Amati of Cremona, who had made Fanny's viola d'amore. When there was company in the

Hôtel de Vallier Fanny played and sang. The French loved Fanchon's old songs and even Armand sang along with Fanny, damp-eyed and homesick, on the tenderest lines, such as *Vivray-je toujours en soucy* and *Coulez dans une paix profonde, coulez moments delicieux.*

Even *soupirants* dressed well in Quebec, and after the drab butternut hues of Puritan Boston and Alamoth, the sight of iridescent silk gowns and swelling bosoms, with beauty spots pasted onto the swell, and powdered wigs in the reception rooms of the Hôtel de Vallier made Fanny remember the theater in Drury Lane. Owing to Grestain's meager hospitality, the French were never drunk, but they would have looked to Edward Ash as though they ought to be. Thanks to Marie-Dominique's seamstress, Fanny was dressed very much like the others, of course, except that no one had ever seen a necklace like hers.

The governor had an ear for Italian music and a knowledge of Italian musical instruments, and when he came to the Hôtel de Vallier he wanted to hear Corelli played on the Amati. Fanny played the violin parts of all the music she had memorized. Because Henry had ordered so much music from Italy, the governor, Philippe de Rigaud, Marquis de Vaudreuil, listened not only to Corelli but also to Vitali, Landi, Stradella, Cavalli, and others.

He wanted to hear more. Fanny's arms were tired and the tips of her fingers were swollen.

"I'm afraid I don't know any more, Excellency," she said.

"Tell his excellency about the porcupines, Fanny," said Marie-Dominique.

"I know all about the porcupines," the governor said. "Surely you have music written down on paper."

"Of course we do, my dear marquis," said Grestain, who was always eager to accommodate Rigaud because he was his superior in noble as well as administrative rank. "A whole drawerful of it. Give it to the young lady, madame, if you please."

Marie-Dominique called the servant, who brought a stack of music to Fanny on a silver tray. She took the piece from the top, a trio sonata in manuscript. She had never seen this music before, but reading as she played, she went through the 166 bars of two slow movements and two quick ones while Marie-Dominique turned the pages. It sounded vaguely like Corelli.

As soon as she was finished, Marie-Dominique whisked the pages away as if to protect her from requests for yet another encore. There was something written at the bottom of the last page, and as the manuscript was not signed and Fanny had never

before heard or seen the music, she took it back out of Marie-Dominique's hand. She had to tug to retrieve it.

"Marvelous," the governor was saying heartily. "What music is that?"

Fanny read the inscription. Written in English in a large youthful hand, it read: "To H. Harding, Gentleman, this poor composition, written by his generous commission in honor of his daughter's birthday, from his most grateful and admiring friend, Giovanni Ravenscroft."

"Marie-Dominique," Fanny said. "What is this?"

"Espionage," Marie-Dominique whispered, smiling brightly. She pulled the score gently from Fanny's hand and gave it to the governor.

"Here, Excellency," she said, "perhaps you'd like to run your eye over the score."

# 2

"Listen," Fanny said to Marie-Dominique on the morning after the musical soiree, "I want to know how you happen to possess a musical score that belonged to my father."

Marie-Dominique was still in bed with her hair inside her nightcap and the pages of the long letter she was writing to someone in France scattered on the coverlet.

"It's very important to write amusing things to people at court when you're out of sight in Canada," she said. "That way everyone laughs at your jokes, even when you're not at Versailles, and tells them to the king, and when you come back they think you're amusing no matter what you say. I'm just writing about your porcupines—it takes days to get it right."

Fanny was not distracted. "I want to know everything," she said.

"Everything?" Marie-Dominique said. "That's quite a lot. The violin belongs to you too."

"The violin? What else?"

"Philippe should tell you the rest. He's the one who took the game so seriously."

"The game? What game?"

"The family game," Marie-Dominique said. "It's called Spy. Philippe will kill me for telling you, but I owe something to my own sex, and you won't stand a chance against him when you're lovers unless you know how to play."

The wind shook the windows in Marie-Dominique's bedchamber. She opened the feather bed.

"Get in," she said. "You'll freeze if you stay out there."

At the time that Fanny went to Honfleur in search of the *Pamela* and Philippe saw her for the first time, Marie-Dominique was a bride of eighteen for whom time was passing very slowly.

"I became pregnant at once, on the first night—so much for Armand," she said to Fanny as they lay side by side under the feather bed. "There were only five people in all of Normandy with whom Armand would dine, and they all had very old wives who drove me mad with advice and tales of deformed babies and dead mothers. If Philippe hadn't been living with us as Armand's adjutant, I *would* have gone mad."

The Saint-Christophe children had always played games, with Edwige and Marie-Dominique seeing the chance for amusement and concocting the situations, and Philippe, with his charm and his physical prowess and his male freedom, acting them out.

"The best game was Spy," Marie-Dominique said. "We invented it when Armand came to inspect Edwige before he married her."

They did not like Grestain and told their parents so; their parents, called Sieur-et-Dame by their children, replied that they, the children, knew nothing about Grestain.

"Very well," said Edwige to her siblings, "we'll find out all about him; I doubt that Sieur-et-Dame know as much about this fellow as they should."

Spy was invented on the spot. To play it, one needed an Enemy of France, a Plot, and, of course, a Spy. Grestain became the first Enemy of France; the Plot was his suit for Edwige's hand. The Spy, always referred to in the singular in order to confuse the enemy, was in fact the three children, together with their network of agents and collaborators.

"You can't imagine the fun," Marie-Dominique said, "Secretly observing the Enemy of France, reading his mail, suborning his servants, questioning his friends, inquiring into his finances, and putting everything into a dossier from which his true intentions could be deduced at secret meetings."

From Grestain's manservant, who kept his master's accounts,

Philippe discovered that Edwige's suitor was a miser for the best of all possible reasons—he had no money. From his letters, stolen by Edwige's maid, they learned that he had an Italian mistress called Luisa d' Onofria, Marchesa di Mazzatenta, with whom he engaged in practices that involved the use of a velvet bastinado.

"It was I who found out that his hair was gray under his wig and that he had no back teeth on either side of his mouth," Marie-Dominique said.

"How?" asked Fanny.

"By sitting on his lap and wiggling."

"If he can't chew his meat, maybe he'll choke to death and leave you everything," Marie-Dominique said to Edwige; this was before they knew Grestain's exact financial position. The precise value of his estate and many other things came to light as the game was played out.

Once the skin of Grestain's haughty personage was pricked, it hemorrhaged secrets. They discovered that they could trade small secrets for large ones: telling a man something he did not know was a sure means of stimulating him to show you how much more he had to betray than you could ever hope to know. In the end, Edwige not only knew exactly what she was getting into by marrying her decrepit fiancé, but she possessed a great deal of useful information with which to astonish and confound her husband as the need arose in the future.

These same facts, refreshed by a new game, were equally useful to Marie-Dominique ten years afterward when she, in her turn, married Grestain. The motto of the game, also the password used by the spies and their most trusted confederates, was *Cogito, ergo sum*—"I think, therefore I am"—the famous statement of René Descartes.

When, after encountering Fanny on the quay at Honfleur, Armand de Grestain and Philippe came home to dinner, they could speak of nothing else: her simplicity, her lack of artifice, the light of intelligence and the shadow of melancholy in her eyes, the golden skin—especially the golden skin. It was evident that this astonishing creature was not in the least aware of her own beauty; perhaps the English, with their taste for pallor and yellow hair, did not realize how extraordinary she was.

"I suppose you scowled at her like a toad, Philippe—you always do when you see a pretty girl," Marie-Dominique said.

"Scowl? She's an angel."

"But she speaks French in a very common way, like a scullery maid," Grestain said. "It gives the whole thing away—don't you

agree, Philippe? She had an English father and she asked to be taken to an English ship. Why is she in Honfleur just as we are getting ready to sail for Canada? It's all very suspicious."

Marie-Dominique, who had quickly become bored by this rapturous discussion of a foreigner who was of no possible interest to anyone in France no matter how pretty she was, suddenly became animated.

"My dear husband," she said, "you don't think this angel of Philippe's is a spy, a beautiful English spy?"

"One never knows," Grestain said solemnly, as if he had had this thought about Fanny from the start.

"A spy?" Philippe said. "She can't be more than seventeen."

"That's exactly what the English would expect the stupid French to think if they sent a beautiful virgin to murder France," Grestain said. *"Jamais trop jeunes et jamais trop belles pour être perfides, ces anglaises"*—the English are never too young or too beautiful for perfidy.

Next morning, Philippe told them about Montagu's attempt to rape Fanny, and how she had thrown herself into the harbor rather than submit.

"And you saved the virgin's life?" Marie-Dominique asked.

"I helped her to swim back to the ship," Philippe said.

"Then she will always love you," Marie-Dominique said.

"Nonsense," said Grestain.

When the courier brought him the morning report from the Lieutenance, Grestain learned that the *Pamela* had sailed without clearance on the night tide. At breakfast, he ordered Philippe, as his adjutant, to find out everything possible about the English girl.

"Everything, Count?" Philippe addressed his brother-in-law by his title when they were discussing official matters.

"Everything; spare no effort. The master of that vessel knows my mind about our voyage to Canada. It would be very convenient for a British man-o'-war to hide among the icebergs and drown the captain-general of New France."

Grestain, agitated, gulped down an unchewed piece of bread and went into a paroxysm of coughing. A servant, stationed behind his chair in case this should happen, as it often did, brusquely stood Grestain on his feet and repeatedly bent him over at the waist like a jointed doll until he expelled the bread from his windpipe. Afterward Grestain sprawled in his chair with his head against the backrest, sipping watered wine from a cup held by the footman.

"The English would love to kill me," he gasped.

"*Cogito, ergo sum,*" Marie-Dominique said to Philippe, eyes shining with interest for the first time in months.

Marie-Dominique sent a servant into town at once to buy a quire of the best paper for the Dossier. She cut it into quarters herself, making one hundred normal pages out of twenty-five big ones.

"We know the Plot—to hide among the icebergs and sink the captain-general of New France to the bottom of the sea," Marie-Dominique said, folding and splitting the sheets with a paper knife. "We know the Enemy of France—the Angel of the Icebergs. What is the first question to be asked?"

"Is she acting alone or is she a cat's-paw?" said Philippe.

"Exactly."

From the captain and crew of the packet boat, the Spy learned that Fanny had traveled in the company of a Frenchwoman who had given everyone to understand that the girl's father had died in tragic circumstances. They all remembered that the woman had been happy and the girl had been sad. Some thought that the girl had taken a chill. No one had doubted that she was French. From the waterfront porters, who remembered Fanny as vividly as Philippe, and for the same reasons, it was learned that Fanny had come ashore with Antoinette, from whom she had parted after a tearful scene and the gift of a purse.

Philippe had one of his men pound on the door of Antoinette's family's house in the rue aux Chats with the butt of a rifle, crying, "Officer of the king! Officer of the king!"

After expelling Antoinette's relatives from the house, Philippe questioned her at the table while a clerk wrote down every word that was said on the crackling sheets of paper. The noise the expensive paper made when it was spread out on the table, its thickness and sheen, which made it fit for the king's own eyes, added to the impressiveness of the interrogation, just as Marie-Dominique had intended that it should.

"Family name, Christian names, parents' names, grandparents' names, place and date of birth, civil status?"

Philippe's uniform and boots, his scowl, his abrupt loud voice, caused the family to see Antoinette's adventures in London in a different light. By now her sisters and brothers-in-law, to say nothing of her nieces and nephews, were bored by her stories about London and the Hardings; they were tired, especially, of hearing about Fanny. Suddenly it all became fascinating: an agent of the king was interested.

Like an actress playing to the audience standing in the perpetual Norman rain outside the windows, Antoinette related every detail of Fanny's life that was known to her. She was sure that she knew

absolutely everything. After all, the girl had had no friends of her own age; every moment of her life, except when she was sleeping, had been spent in the company of herself, Antoinette, or Henry Harding, or the Jesuit who had baptized, confessed, and tutored her. Fanny might as well have been in a convent; certainly Antoinette had been as assiduous as any houseful of nuns could have been in protecting her from spiritual and corporal pollution, except, of course, that she had given the child a mother's love.

"Why then did she leave you so cruelly on the quay and sail away in an English ship?" Philippe asked.

"Cruelly, sir? There was no cruelty. Only sorrow. She paid me honorably."

"Nevertheless she sailed away in the night, a young girl alone, on an English ship. Where was she bound?"

"Who knows?" Antoinette sobbed quietly. "Who knows if she sailed of her own free will? Those were not honest Frenchmen on that ship. Of this you may be sure. Fanny is a daughter of France and a heroine of the true faith. There is no question of her English blood interfering with what she knows in her heart is right."

"A heroine!" Marie-Dominique said, on reading the transcript of this interview at the next secret meeting of the Spy. "What romance—no wonder she makes such an impression! We must know more. We must know everything!"

Others in Honfleur provided bits of the puzzle—ships' masters who were friends of Joshua Peters', old men who knew Fanny's grandfather and grandmother. The manuscript of the trio sonata written by Giovanni Ravenscroft, an Englishman who had gone to Italy to study composition, was discovered in a trunk that Peters left behind in his lodgings ashore, together with a dozen letters written to Peters by Fanny in excellent Latin. Evidently Peters was bringing the music back from Italy as a gift for Fanny's eighteenth birthday. Marie-Dominique studied Ravenscroft's score for any sign that the music was a code, but found nothing beyond the usual opening slow fugue, a fast and a slow movement, and a finale in 12/8 time. The trunk also contained a fine violin signed by Nicolò Amati which Marie-Dominique confiscated as evidence.

"If the Enemy of France turns out not to be an enemy of France," she said when Philippe protested this corrupt action, "the instrument will, of course, be returned to her."

From Jesuit gossip, Father Nicolas, who had come to France to report to his superior on the progress of his mission among the Abenakis, discovered Fanny's connection with the hanged Jesuit Philip Evans. Evans had kept a secret diary, smuggled out of England after his death and stored at the Jesuit college at La

Flèche, in which Fanny was clearly recognizable through the descriptions of her birth and the homely details of her religious life and education. Philippe, who, like Philip Evans and Descartes, had studied at La Flèche, consulted the diary in the college library. It contained prayers, observations on the will of God, and a long meditation on the possible meaning of Fanny having been born at London in the same hour (more or less) in which Charles II embraced the Catholic faith on his deathbed.

As he watched the child grow, Evans wondered about the significance of this coincidence—was it the source of Fanny's musical gift, the reason for her unchildlike calm? The diary contained many original songs, from childish tunes to complicated sinfonie, that Evans had written for Fanny, for whom he appeared to have had an uncle's warmhearted affection. The diary excited the Saint-Christophes. At their urging, Father Nicolas asked a member of his order who was on his way to England to make inquiries about the destination of the *Pamela* and the whereabouts of Fanny. The priest sent back a letter describing the *Pamela*'s voyage to Boston and her subsequent return laden with enormous live lobsters that created a sensation in The Rose Tavern, where they sold for a pound apiece. He added that Fanny had had pneumonia during the voyage and nearly died. She was now living in an English settlement called Alamoth, on the Connecticut River in the Massachusetts Bay Colony.

All this information, and more besides—the particulars of the *Pamela*'s construction and the probable value of her cargoes, the personal history of Henry Harding, including the incomprehensible fact that he appeared to have been an unbeliever who caused his daughter to be raised as a Catholic at the risk of both their lives—was broken down into categories and arranged in the Dossier, which Marie-Dominique bound in ribbons. Grestain was given a much more concise report. Even this digest of the facts fanned his suspicions. How could such an extraordinary person be anything but a spy? No girl of seventeen could have such adventures unless they were arranged by a hidden mastermind.

Philippe, playing Spy, never believed this. Poring over the Dossier, he tried to understand the mind, the emotions, the soul that dwelled within this lovely Enemy of France.

("You see?" Marie-Dominique said to Fanny. "He was already in love with you. In his eyes you are completely virtuous, you are a mystery to him.")

The game had uncovered no reliable clue as to her invisible nature. She wrote to the old sea captain about the weather, about her father, whom she appeared to love very deeply, about music.

Why did she write in Latin? Her style was clear and logical and so dry that her letters might have been written by a man of her father's age.

In Antoinette's stories Philippe encountered Fanny riding through the London in the beautiful frocks and fashionable hats of her childhood, at prayer with her hair combed down the back of her nightgown, doing her lessons without being wheedled.

"Not once," said Antoinette proudly, "did she ever ask me a silly question; she would look, listen, and know."

On the theory that a father's bombast always has an effect, good or bad, on his child, Philippe had compiled Henry Harding's favorite sayings. These seemed to be divided equally between compliments to his daughter's beauty ("You have the golden skin of Araby") and warnings about the excesses of religion and the probable nonexistence of a Supreme Being.

Philip Evans' diary was little more than a priest's inventory of reasons to praise God, but because Evans had been an amateur of drawing as well as a musician, there were sketches of Fanny as a little girl—her small face scowling prettily while she learned music and Latin, her hands on the keyboard of the spinet and the harpsichord, her eyes looking inward as she played the viola, her smiling mouth singing old French songs and new English ones.

These images and accounts of Fanny's life had one thing in common: in them, Fanny herself never spoke. She was always silent, always alone, a child among adults, a beauty among ordinary faces. Philippe conceived the idea that for all her beauty, knowledge, and goodness, Fanny was somehow not fully . . . What? Awake, aware, alive? She was a sleepwalker, watching others live while she waited for her own life to begin.

("Philippe wanted to wake you with a kiss, of course," Marie-Dominique told Fanny. "He was helpless. After he saved you from drowning, his fate was sealed. You should have seen his eyes. I thought you *had* drowned, he was so devastated. The thought of your dying was almost as bad as the reality.")

When he returned from Honfleur to Boston, Pietro Di Gesù, as Marie-Dominique called Joshua Peters, told Philippe exactly where Fanny had gone.

As soon after his arrival in Canada as possible, Philippe proposed a scouting mission down the Connecticut River.

Grestain readily agreed. The New World was a natural theater for the new war between England and France—the War of the Spanish Succession, in which the Bourbon Louis XIV was claiming the vacant Spanish throne for his second grandson, Philip of Anjou, while Leopold I, the Hapsburg emperor of Austria, claimed it for

his second son, the Archduke Charles. Philippe had already distinguished himself in this war by leading a scaling party over the walls of a fortress in the Spanish Netherlands and overcoming the garrison with no loss of French lives. Who knew what this daring young man might accomplish with a few Indians in Massachusetts in a cause that was of intimate dynastic and paternal concern to the king of France?

In the week that he spent in hiding in the woods above Alamoth, studying the fortifications of the town and the habits of its people, Philippe saw any number of ways to convert the village and the idyllic countryside around it into a battleground in a religio-dynastic war that was taking place three thousand miles away.

The military possibilities were obvious, and when Thoughtful provided him with the book containing John Pennock's secret plan for the defense of Alamoth, he realized that he only had to devise the simplest countermeasures in order to conquer the town.

Talks in His Dreams and Hair, along with Used to be Bear, had accompanied Philippe down the Connecticut in the hope of finding their sister, Squirrel, who had been stolen a few months before by the Englishman they called the fat ghost.

They encountered her and Fanny on the very first morning. The two girls were picking blueberries. The Abenakis called to Thoughtful, using the difficult false warbler song that Philippe had learned from Talks in His Dreams himself when he was a child. When she answered, Fanny turned around and smiled, as beautiful as Philippe remembered.

That night, Thoughtful rendezvoused with the scouting party. Philippe, who knew Thoughtful's English identity and how much importance that gave her in Alamoth, explained to the Abenakis that she could not be rescued. To do so would betray the existence of the scouting mission to the English and eliminate the possibility of surprise in the attack to come later. Although she had hoped for immediate rescue, Thoughtful understood.

After the other Abenakis had greeted her, rubbing faces and offering food and telling stories, Philippe asked her about Fanny.

Her description of Ash, bathing Fanny's unconscious body aboard the *Pamela* and then being possessed by lecherous memories, drove Philippe into a jealous panic.

("That was why he attacked in winter," Marie-Dominique told Fanny. "He told Armand it was to surprise the English, but it was really because he could not bear the thought of another man wanting you in that way. You are his bride, Fanny; no one else must even think about you.")

During the next days, when he wasn't watching the town, Philippe

stalked Fanny. Thoughtful brought her to the woods every day so that Philippe could look at her. He watched her as she picked berries, as she drank from the spring, as she lay on her back and dreamed, as she passed silently through the woods with her skirts pulled up to her thighs. Philippe was an Abenaki when in the forest, but Thoughtful had taught Fanny a great deal about woodcraft, and several times she nearly saw him. On the last day he deliberately left a footprint by the spring, and then called to her. To his astonishment, she faultlessly reproduced the warbler's call, as if she were reading notes off a staff. He called again, leading her through the woods as he ran toward the hanging rock so that she could see him. Would she know who he was?

Fanny looked across the pillows at Marie-Dominique.

"I knew," she said.

"Of course you did," Marie-Dominique said. "It's all in the cards: a dark woman, a fair soldier, danger, love."

# 3

In the village on the Saint Francis River, Philippe went to the village church to pray for the souls of the departed Abenakis. He was deeply religious in a tender hearted soldierly way, and he loved the rude beauty of Saint-François-de-Sales, which smelled of pitch and sap and was filled, day and night, with a peculiar smoky light. Long and narrow and somewhat taller than the eye expected it to be, the cruciform structure was made of whipsawed spruce lumber laid over maple beams and joists that were mortised and tenoned and joined by wooden pegs. It was sheathed with gummy hand-split spruce shingles and leaked only when the three or four feet of ice on the roof melted in the spring. When the bell, cast from the bronze of Spanish demiculverin cannon captured at the Battle of Rocroi, rang in the steeple, the timbers of the church quivered sympathetically, setting up a softer counterpoint to the humming of the vibrating bronze.

Stained-glass windows, one at either end of the transept and one in the vault of the apse, depicted Christ's miracles, the healed lepers and blind men and cripples being portrayed as Algonquian

Indians in buckskin and feathers. Along the curving wall of the apse stood figures of the saints,carved in wood and brightly painted, that looked like the fathersand mothers of some of the Abenakis present, in the way thatstatuary in a provincial cathedral in France will sometimes resemble the long-dead notables of the town.

Because they seldom had money, the Abenakis were in the habit of leaving furs or freshly killed game beside the poor box. Talks in His Dreams had once deposited an entire female moose, the meat butchered and bundled up in the hide, on the floor of the narthex. Philippe had accompanied him on the hunt, in which Talks in His Dreams, famous for this archery, killed seven moose, shooting them through the heart one by one with flint arrows while the others grazed on dreamily like bison, never suspecting that death was lying concealed in the grass a few feet away.

The Abenakis had given Philippe the name Otter because he had dived into the river one day and risen to the surface with a huge spawning salmon in his hand. He had lived among these people for four years, wrestling with Bear, who was the strongest boy of his age, and racing against Sleeping Fox, who was the fastest afoot, and learning, in addition to their language and the use of their arms, three great lessons from the Abenakis: how to listen, how to wait, and always to point with the chin instead of the finger so as not to puncture the spirit of another person.

Because of the power of these lessons, Philippe made no effort to discover why the Abenakis did not remember him or his boy-hood name when he returned to the village five years after leaving it for France. Father Nicolas thought that they had not actually forgotten him, but simply did not believe their eyes when he reappeared as a man after having gone away as a boy, because they had never known any living person to come back from France; the Jesuit was not certain that this was the case because he did not ask the Abenakis questions, either.

Philippe's prayers for the dead—he realized that he had been murmuring their stories as a way of commending their souls to God—were interrupted by a hubbub in the village. Members of the force that raided Alamoth, having followed so many different routes, had been straggling into the village for several days.

Philippe now heard a party coming in. Because what would happen next was no concern of his, he climbed into the belfry to watch. The Indians and their captives were still some distance away, jogging up the Saint Francis River, but the entire population of the village had gone outside to greet them. Ululating calls of welcome and triumph, tuneless and bloodthirsty to the European

ear, melodious and jubilant to the Abenaki, filled the winter air. A nimbus of chilled breath lingered over the crowd. Wisps of smoke rose from the wigwams. The many new birchbark canoes built by the women while the men were at war lay upside down on a long rack made of saplings.

The Abenakis led the captives, half a dozen women and their children and two or three men, out onto the ice of the Saint Francis River and painted their faces vermilion. Meanwhile the Indians on the riverbank, still screeching and beating on drums, formed two parallel lines that defined a pathway between the riverbank and the wigwams. The captives recognized the gauntlet.

Resisting, weeping, trying to shield the children, the English were led one by one by the hand into the gauntlet by the Abenakis who had captured them. The purpose of this gauntlet, as soon became obvious, was not to beat the captives but to permit every Abenaki to touch them; as they passed between the two lines of Indians, each English person was lightly tapped on the shoulder by each Abenaki. Then the Indians formed a circle around the captives, teaching them the words of the song they had been singing by shouting out the words slowly and distinctly:

The men fought like men
   the women will be wives to the Abenakis
sisters to the Abenakis, aunts to the Abenakis
   the boys will hunt with the Abenakis, ho-ho

The Abenakis then drew the captives into the circle with them, and danced, singing this song over and over again, *ho-ho ho-ho ho-ho,* for some hours. Two Suns then made a long speech in which he told the story of the Abenakis and how the fish, first the shad and then the salmon, swam up the rivers in the spring, filling the water with their silver bodies from bank to bank. He then gave each captive some wampum. Then they dispersed, being guided by their owners to their respective wigwams. Before they went to sleep, they would be told by their new families that they had been adopted into the tribe and they would be taught the Abenaki words for brother and sister, the form of address the Abenakis used with each other, because it was impolite to speak another person's name in his presence.

Philippe, watching from the belfry, remembered what Bear had said to him when they were fourteen: "If you see a girl that you like and she doesn't ask *you,* then you must go into her house at night, being sure that nobody sees or hears you, and lie on top of her. If she opens her eyes, that means go ahead. Sometimes they

wait a long time, but in the end they always open their eyes. Women are very curious: they want to know who it is that's lying on top of them."

Tonight this would happen in every house in the village.

Philippe, whispering through the grate, confessed to Father Nicolas. "Father," he said, "I tell you that I made this girl the reason for everything. If I had not known that she was in Alamoth I would not have urged my brother-in-law to let me attack the village. No one would have died. The truth is, I thought a winter attack was impossible. All I wanted was to rescue her."

"But it was not after all impossible," Father Nicolas said. "The ways of God are deep and mysterious."

'What will I do?"

"Already you are beginning to purify your heart. Keep on with that."

Philippe said, "I cannot stop thinking about her."

"Why should you stop if you think the thoughts of a virtuous man? When we all slept together on the march out of enemy country, night after night, pressed together for warmth in the snow, did you feel lust?"

"No," Philippe said. "But that is changing."

"Do you with to marry this girl?"

"Everything separates us," Philippe replied. "She is not really French, she is not really Catholic, she has no family."

"Then what?"

"I am ravished by her beauty."

"Your soul is in great danger, my son," Father Nicolas said. "You covet this chaste and innocent girl."

"But that's not all that I feel; it is far from being all."

Father Nicolas' weak voice was even more difficult to hear when he was closed up in the confessional box. Philippe concentrated hard in order to understand what he was saying.

"Think back to the wilderness," the Jesuit said. "If you felt no lust when you slept with your arms around this virgin, Who do you think was protecting her, and why? Remember her actions—the birth of the child, her love for the child, the way in which she preserved us from the madwoman, the journey through the blizzard. What will happen to your soul if you ravish such a girl, even in your thoughts?"

Suddenly Philippe remembered what Thoughtful had told him about Ash. Jealousy and hot anger rushed through his body. What right did this madman have to possess Fanny in his thoughts?

*But in what way am I less mad than he except that I am young?*
Philippe asked himself.

And with that question in mind he performed the mild penance
that Father Nicolas had prescribed for his sins.

# 4

On Quasimodo, the first Sunday after Easter, a ship arrived
from France bearing a letter in which the king commended his
cousin, Philippe de Saint-Christophe, on his singular victory at
Alamoth.

" 'Cousin,' yes, 'cousin,' his majesty used the word 'cousin,' "
said Armand de Grestain three days afterward as the family dined
alone in the Hôtel de Vallier. "And then he speaks of a 'singular
victory.' These are very good omens."

Easter fell on March 28 that year, but it was still winter in
Quebec, with bone-numbing cold and winds that drove snow into
the face like darts.

The Saint Lawrence River, broad and tidal, never froze between
Quebec and the sea. Armand de Grestain saw no reason, there-
fore, why the *Pamela* should not cross the North Atlantic in
March, sail up the river to Quebec, and relieve him of his worry
about the expense of keeping Fanny all winter as a houseguest in
the Hôtel de Vallier.

Every day at dinner he raised the subject. When would the
*Pamela* arrive? What cargo would she carry? The *Pamela*'s exotic
cargoes and their probable value were subjects to great interest to
Grestain.

Reopening this subject after a respite during which he had
talked of little but the king's letter, Grestain revealed what he
knew about the cargo of lobsters, and Fanny learned for the first
time that the *Pamela* had reached England after sailing from Boston.

"But how many lobsters did the *Pamela* carry?" Grestain asked,
drinking soup between questions and letting it cool in his open
mouth betweentimes. "Five hundred, a thousand, more? How
were they kept alive during such a long voyage? Was there an
apparatus of some sort?"

Marie-Dominique looked fixedly at her husband. "Perhaps the captain tied up the ship and the sailors took the lobsters for walks on icebergs to let them graze and relieve themselves," she said.

"Not possible, my dear," Grestain replied, swallowing his soup. "Suppose there were a thousand lobsters. If the tavernkeeper's profit was half the asking price, that is still five hundred pounds, less expenses, for the shipowners. No doubt there were many more than a thousand. Truly, Philippe, this young lady is an heiress."

He winked; Fanny's fortune, which he imagined to be very large notwithstanding the Spy's report on her finances, often made him flirtatious on behalf of whoever was going to become her husband. The closing and reopening of Grestain's eye was barely detectable. Although it was only three in the afternoon, the early northern twilight had already fallen.

Except for Grestain's military orderly, who stood in readiness behind his chair, the family was alone. The servants, working in the dusk, were preparing the house for a reception in honor of Philippe. The governor would read the king's letter aloud. Grestain had frequently mentioned that it was within the governor's power as the king's lieutenant to make Philippe a suitable gift of money or land, or even give him a title.

"I hope it's money," Marie-Dominique said. "Maybe Philippe will buy some lamp oil or a few candles."

No lamps or candles burned in the Hôtel de Vallier; Fanny and others ate by the light of the log fire. It was not necessary to see the food. The menu was the same every day: soup from the big iron pot to which all cooking water and leftover solids were added, heavy bread with a thick crust, like the parings from a horse's hoof, salt cod boiled in milk, stewed apples, wine diluted by half with water.

Today was one of Marie-Dominique's days to eat liver. Twisting her lips in distaste, she ate the last morsel of a cod's liver and placed her hand on her belly. Her baby, soon to be born, moved about vigorously in the womb, but was always quiet for several hours after its mother consumed liver or fried blood.

"It's asleep," she said. "I wonder if we will have to give it blood after it's born to keep it quiet."

"Enough," said Grestain in a loud voice.

Marie-Dominique meekly bowed her head and looked down at her plate. Jokes about the unborn child were forbidden. It seemed to him, Grestain said, addressing himself to Philippe as though Marie-Dominique were unable to understand French, that his wife, the mother of this child on whom the whole future history of the family depended, was laughing at the dead Edwige, laughing at her

dead nephew (now also her dead stepson), laughing at him and all the Grestains and the house of Vallier.

"Yes, laughing at everything," Grestain said.

"I hardly think so, Armand," Philippe replied. "Marie-Dominique is frightened, you know. And so she makes jokes. She doesn't want to die like Edwige."

"There's no possibility of that as long as she remains in Quebec. The city is invulnerable to the Iroquois, even to the English fleet. I've seen to that."

"I meant, die in childbirth."

"Why should she die in childbirth? It didn't happen to Edwige. The cod's liver and the fried blood have a very good effect, you know. Edwige took it too. My mother took it. It's very dear, but the blood quickens the child and strengthens the woman."

Grestain finished the last morsel on his plate and snapped his fingers for his cloak and hat.

"You must be home at eight for the soiree," Marie-Dominique said.

"No *soupirants,* I hope," Grestain said.

"The entire city will be here. The governor will be reading the king's letter about Philippe."

"All the more reason not to clutter up the place with lawyers and people who sell us fish."

"The governor was very kind to let us have the reception here. It's a royal occasion, after all."

"Maybe we can lead the governor into the library, away from the *soupirants,* and plan your next campaign," Grestain said to Philippe, leaning across the littered table to grip his forearm.

Grestain wanted to give the king another victory in America as soon as possible. He and his staff were already choosing objectives, weighing tactics; Philippe would almost certainly lead any new force that might be sent against the English colonies.

*"On dit que les généreaux sont toujours en retard de la guerre,"* said Marie-Dominique—they say that the generals are always preparing for the last war.

Grestain lifted his eyes and drew in his breath through his nose.

"Marie-Dominique," Philippe said in a tone of warning.

"The saying does not refer to my husband, of course," she said, smiling brilliantly in the half-darkness. "It is well-known that the count is an excellent general. Everybody says so. Sieur explained to me that Armand never attacks until he understands the plan of battle perfectly, and by that time every private in the army has known it by heart for a year, so there are never any mistakes."

After a long pause, Grestain chose to speak to Fanny instead of

Marie-Dominique. Because he never called either woman by name, and because it took him some time to come to the point, it was difficult in the dim light to know which one of them he was addressing.

"Perhaps you should write another letter to the man di Gesù or even to your manager in London," he said. "When did you send the first letter?"

Fanny had answered this question many times. "On the Friday after Advent Sunday," she said again.

"Exactly. And Easter has come and gone. The letter about Philippe's victory over the English went out on the same ship, and the palace has already replied. When a Genoese seaman is slower to answer than the king of France, something is wrong."

He rose from the table. "Write to this fellow again. I will leave Philippe to wait for the letter. A ship sails for France tomorrow and your letter can go with the dispatches; I'll add a laissez-passer so that your man can have no doubts about his safety. There are excellent fat lobsters up and down the coast of Canada; mention that."

"Eight o'clock, no later," Marie-Dominique said. "The governor doesn't like it when he's not the last to arrive. Fanny is going to play."

"Charming," said Grestain. "Make sure the servants know who gets which wine."

His orderly helped him into his cloak, fitted his cockaded hat square on his head, and handed him his sword. These accoutrements transformed Grestain from an aging man cooling soup in a toothless mouth into a stern soldier. He waved away the servant who had brought Philippe's less magnificent cloak, hat, and sword.

"Wait for the letter," he said. "Then bring it to me directly, Philippe."

"At your orders, Count."

"My, how the lobsters have excited him," Marie-Dominique said. "Maybe the Spy shouldn't have told him about them."

"Maybe not," said Philippe. "But the damage is done."

Fanny had already left them and was sitting in the library writing a letter to Joshua Peters. So as not to waste candle wax, Marie-Dominique sat down on the opposite side of the writing desk and laid out the cards. She sat on her favorite chair, a *voyeuse* upholstered in yellow silk; this chair, designed for card-playing, had a padded rail built into the top of the backrest. Philippe leaned on the rail and watched Fanny as she filled a page with her rapid clear hand.

Marie-Dominique turned up the Two of Pentacles (gaiety), the

Hermit (silence, prudence, secret advice), and the Three of Swords (tears, a lovers' quarrel).

"The cards are cold," she said, wrapping up the deck in a silk cloth and tucking this parcel into her bodice to warm it up.

She looked over her shoulder at Philippe. "What gives you the idea that I'm afraid to die in childbirth?" she asked. She never forgot an accusation.

Philippe said, "Of course you're afraid; it's your first child. Anyone would be."

"Anyone? Certainly not. I shouldn't be afraid if I were Fanny. I'd go into the forest, build a lean-to, and come out a bit later with the last of the Grestains in my arms."

Fanny wrote on: "The captain-general of New France, the Count of Vallier, is especially interested in shipping lobsters in the *Pamela*, as he has heard from a spy that you sold the last lot in London for the astonishing price of one pound apiece."

Marie Dominique read Fanny's letter upside down. " 'From a spy'?" she said. "Oh, dear; I don't think that will amuse my husband."

"He won't read it."

"I shouldn't count on that," Marie-Dominique said.

Fanny blotted the ink with sand, poured the sand back into its box, and handed the letter, unfolded and unsealed, to Philippe.

"To make matters easier," she said.

Philippe averted his eyes. "Do you think the *Pamela* will come?" he asked.

"No doubt the Spy will know more about that than I do," Fanny said.

"That's three times she has denounced the Spy," Marie-Dominique said. "How unlike Fanny."

Fanny's own eyes were averted, her face flushed.

Philippe said, "You aren't obliged to write a letter just because Armand wants you to do so, you know."

"The alternative is to be asked again tomorrow, or even tonight, if the Spy has fresh news for your brother-in-law. It's easier to appease stupidity than to cure it."

"What an epigram," Marie-Dominique said. "How can she be only half French?"

Fanny went to the narrow Norman window with its tiny glass panes and looked down over the steep jumbled town at the boats lying at anchor along the waterfront. Their stern lanterns were the only lights showing in Quebec. She saw the wavering images of Marie-Dominique and Philippe in the windowpanes and turned around. Her eyes shone with tears.

"Fanny," Philippe said, reaching out the hand that held the letter.

He took a step in her direction, but she turned her back again. This time she looked at her own face in the dimpled glass, something she hardly ever did. She was hardly visible in the feeble light: dark hair, dark eyes, skin pigment. She had been eighteen years old for fifty days. She saw a tear squeezing out of the corner of her eye, caught it on her fingertip, and smeared it on the windowpane. It congealed immediately on the cold surface.

Marie-Dominique, studying her brother as he watched this tiny action, said, "Perhaps it's time to hang the Spy."

# 5

At a quarter after eight the governor arrived at the Hôtel de Vallier with an escort of a dozen infantrymen and a pair of drummers. Fanny stood by herself at the window of the grand salon. Over the chatter of the guests, she heard the drums a long way off, then heard marching feet crunching on the snow and an officer shouting commands. Outside the door the soldiers formed two facing ranks and presented arms.

Philippe, escorted by the governor, passed between them, saluting, and entered the house, where they were saluted by Grestain and his staff. The soliders tramped inside, still responding to the shouts of their officer, and took up positions along the walls of the big reception room, crashing the butts of their muskets onto the parquet floor.

"Don't let these fellows trample on your violin, my dear," the governor said as he passed by, taking Fanny's hand briefly in both of his and touching the callused tips of the fingers on her left hand.

He wore a wig and his full-dress uniform with sword and ribbons and orders. So did Grestain and the other senior officers. Owing to his low military rank, Philippe was less splendidly dressed, but he, too was wigged—the first time Fanny had seen him in one.

The whole company, civilian as well as military, had turned out in their best clothes and jewels, and the grand salon, which was really a gallery that ran along the whole length of the south wall of

the house with tall windows on one side and mirrors alternating with tapestry panels on the other, was brilliantly lighted by dozens of candles in chandeliers, torchères, and candelabra. Usually this room was unfurnished, without even a chair to sit on. Tonight all the best furniture in the Hôtel de Vallier had been brought in. A row of gilded chairs and stools upholstered in pink silk damask stood along the interior wall, interspersed with carved and gilded side tables and console tables, slightly chipped, that must have been brought from storage; Fanny had never seen them before.

The bureau Mazarin from the library, the ebony veneer commode from the hall, the ormolu clock from the petit salon, and statuary from all over the house had been placed between the windows. Even though she had examined them all one by one, Fanny had had no idea that the house contained so many beautiful things. These splendid objects had a good effect on the guests, who could see themselves in the mirrors as they bowed and curtsied to the governor.

The governor took up a position in front of a tall mirror and waited for a hush to fall. As soon as the silence was complete, the drums rolled, a startling sound in a room that was designed to amplify music.

"We know with what ferocity the English hate France," the governor said in a loud voice, "and what a danger to France are their perfidious schemes to draw other nations into the web of their plots against us French and our great and noble king, his majesty King Louis. But France will prevail. French civilization, French arms, will prevail. God must surely wish to destroy a nation that turned against His Son's true church merely because Henry VIII lusted after a woman whom he could not marry acording to holy law. Our brave friend Saint-Christophe has lately given us new proof of the truth of these thoughts."

The company murmured its approval.

"The deeds of brave Frenchmen reassure us that there is nothing to fear," the governor said. "We are protected by God, by the destiny of France, and by the wisdom of a monarch chosen by God to re-create the army of France into the greatest army ever known, led by sons of France such as Philippe de Saint-Christophe, may his name be remembered for his splendid victory on the Connecticut."

The governor read the king's letter about Philippe and promoted him to the rank of captain. The drums rolled again, the troops presented arms with another crash, the company cheered. Toasts were drunk.

"No money, no land, no Sieur de Quelquechose, nothing but

kind words and a new badge for Philippe; poor Armand," murmured Marie-Dominique.

She sat down in the *voyeuse* chair that Fanny had been saving for her and lifted a glass of wine off a servant's tray.

"Philippe doesn't care," Marie-Dominique said. "He has what he wants."

"Does he?" Fanny said.

For the first time since the massacre, she permitted herself while waking to remember the scene at Alamoth and the events of the march up the Connecticut.

"Of course he has what he wants," Marie-Dominique said. "Glory. Love. Philippe is a Viking."

Philippe was surrounded by men who embraced him or pumped his hand, and by women who smiled at him in a particularly feminine way, as if to say: Alas, what happiness the two of us could have known if only we had met in time. The governor himself stood beside Philippe with his hand resting on his shoulder, grinning like a father.

Philippe's eyes never left Fanny's. She looked back at him steadily, as always. Was this really why he had done what he had done? Fanny shifted her gaze and looked from face to face in the pack of males around Philippe. All wore the same half-dreamy, half-bloodthirsty expression. Every one of them knew the story of his bravery. They murmured, they waited, they stood at a respectful distance, sipping their wine, heads at one side, smiling confidentially, waiting for Philippe to say something that only he and they, who could be as brave as he if given the chance, could understand.

Philippe himself was still looking at Fanny. He smiled, a sudden joyful grin that involved his whole face. He freed himself of the crowd, smiling, answering questions, letting his hand be pressed as he moved toward Fanny.

He arrived at her side still smiling. The room, crowded with more than two hundred people, had grown very warm. Sweat trickled down the faces of the soldiers in their thick woolen greatcoats and bearskin hats, and nearly everyone else was beginning to display streaks of dampness down the spine and wet black semicircles under the arms. Nobody minded the odor, salty and onionlike; there was nothing unusual about it.

A new crowd, both men and women, gathered around them. Philippe looked at the circle of rapt faces.

"Forgive us," Fanny said, "but we must greet some friends."

Philippe followed her out of the grand salon and into the entrance hall.

"Cloaks," Fanny said to the servant at the door.

Outside, Fanny walked quickly, the heels of her slippers sinking into the compacted surface of the snow. The sky was filled with stars—the Little Dipper, the Bear, the Crab, the Giraffe, the Dragon, the Twins, and Cassiopeia, which could not be made to resemble any creature on Earth. The constellations looked more familiar here than in Massachusetts. They looked like the stars over France.

Wherever they went, Fanny thought, the French took France with them, building French houses, eating French food, wearing French clothes, thinking French thoughts, taking deep satisfaction in French prejudices, regarding the natives as Frenchmen in the rough. They did not think in terms of what already existed in a new world but concentrated instead on transforming it into something that was French and therefore ideal. The English in America, on the other hand, seemed to want to escape from their Englishness. In two or three generations they had changed over to different houses, different clothes, different food, different ideas, even different speech.

She stopped and faced Philippe.

"Antoinette—you know her, she was one of your best informants at Honfleur—told me that I am not French and can never be French," Fanny said. "She was right. All I could think about while the governor read the letter from the king was Betsy."

"Betsy?"

He did not remember the name. It was difficult to see the expression on Philippe's face in the starlight.

"The mother of the child Used to be Bear saved."

"Ah. The woman in the snow."

"You actually remember."

Philippe took her by the shoulders. He had not put his hands on her since he saved her from drowning. He was as strong now as he had been then. He looked years younger, even, than he was, with the white hair of his wig framing his smooth face with its two neat scars.

"Oh, yes," Philippe said. "I remember. The fields of glory. Does this mean that you are English at heart and hate me?"

"No. I am nothing at heart—not even a rescued Catholic."

"Quite suddenly you're telling me a great deal."

"It's a swap. Did you want to do the things you did in Alamoth?"

Philippe did not hesitate. "Yes. Certainly. Soldiering is what I do."

"It's what you love."

"Yes, but not the only thing. What do you love?"

"I don't know yet."

Fanny moved. Philippe did not try to hold on to her. She turned and walked off again. Philippe kept pace, taking one long stride in his boots for every three or four that Fanny took in her slippers. His sword, the same one he had worn in France, clanked in its scabbard and shone dully in the starlight.

They arrived at the waterfront. It was easier to see here. The black river, still as ice, was dappled with amber light from the stern lanterns of the boats tied up along the wharf. Philippe's peruke had the effect of isolating his face from the rest of his body, so that the expressions seemed stark and slightly false, like an actor's caricature of feelings.

Fanny's own face was hidden inside the hood of her cloak. Her feet in their thin evening slippers were freezing. The chilled gold chain of the ruby necklace formed a cold ring around her neck. Philippe's body emitted a little heat. Fanny had noticed this phenomenon during the long run north from Alamoth. At the end of the day, when they slowed down and searched the trees for frozen porcupines, they would sometimes be quite close together, unaware of each other, walking under the trees, staring upward into the branches with all their concentration. Then, sometimes, Fanny felt the warmth of his body as it seeped through his clothes, not enough really to warm the skin, but enough to deceive the nerves momentarily. She felt it now.

At night on the trail, sleeping between Philippe and Father Nicolas, she had known the difference between them, one male and the other something else, even in her sleep; when the Jesuit rose before dawn to pray, she would sometimes turn over to warm the other side of herself against Philippe. She had not had a single dream in this whole time; only afterward. She would wake up, still feeling what she had felt in the dream, and wonder: How do I know about that?

The wharf curved with the river, hiding the upstream bank. As Fanny and Philippe walked along it, a glow appeared in the sky, and then they saw a big campfire billowing sparks into the darkness about a mile upriver.

"The Abenakis," Philippe said. "Listen."

"Why are they here?" Fanny asked.

"The king sent them gifts. They received them from the governor this afternoon and now they're singing about the victory. At dawn they'll go back to the village."

The singsong Abenaki chorus came clearly over the water, changing keys and time and pitch in every bar. Automatically Fanny tried to imagine the music—the actual notes on the staff—that the Indians were singing. Of course there were no bars. This was music

that had been stored in the brains of the Abenakis, whoever they were, for most of their history, whatever that was. Fanny realized that she could not understand it as musical notes. It did not matter what the words meant.

"Do you think it's possible to understand anything?" she asked Philippe.

"Oh, yes. Even Alamoth."

Philippe had taken off his wig.

"You should know at least one secret about me," he said. "I did not come down the Connecticut with these Abenakis for the sake of a French victory. I came for you."

They stood five or six paces apart, the light of the Abenaki bonfire behind Philippe, the bulk of the city behind Fanny, the singing growing louder. A big birchbark canoe was coming over the water surrounded by little bursts of phosphorescence where the paddles bit into the water.

Fanny said, "You came for me?"

"Yes," Philippe said, "because I wanted to know everything."

The canoe was quite close now. The paddlers were resting on the thwarts, letting the current carry the boat along. Fanny recognized Two Suns and Thoughtful among them.

The canoe, the largest one Fanny had ever seen, touched the wharf. Thoughtful and the Abenakis kneeled in the hull, waiting.

"May I come with you?" Fanny asked.

Thoughtful pointed to the place where she should sit. Fanny picked up her skirts and stepped down into the canoe. The Abenakis showed no surprise; Philippe made no attempt to stop her.

"You are leaving Quebec?" he said.

"Forever," Fanny replied.

She settled herself, kneeling in the bow. Philippe put his wig back on his head, fitting it to his crown with the fingertips of both hands. Finally he bowed to her.

"*Je te rattraperai*," he said—I'll catch up to you.

"Will you? Why?"

"Because I don't know everything even now. And I don't like all this disappearing. First a ship, then a blizzard, now a canoe. What next?"

The canoe, airy and swift, drifted away from the dock and pivoted, then moved away slowly against the current.

Two Suns, grunting as he paddled, said something in Abenaki. Thoughtful interpreted.

"My father says that something is going to happen between you and Philippe," she said.

"Does he know how long it will take?" Fanny asked.

# 6

Someone—Ash never knew who—untied him before the night was out. He seized John Pennock's rapier off its peg by Oliver's bed and dashed out into the smoldering town. Dozens of people were coughing from the smoke, bodies hung from the trees on the green, corpses and dead animals lay helter-skelter on the snow.

Ash seized an old man. "Where did they go?"

"Up the river," the old man said. "Over the ice."

Ash ran down the path to the river. The ice was rough underfoot and the leather soles of his boots slithered with every step, throwing him off balance, but he kept on running north, the rapier in his hand.

After a while—he had no idea how long he had been running—he saw a flash of reddish light above the riverbank and then the sound of a musket discharging. Immediately there was more shooting and the sound of Indians shrieking and Englishmen cursing. Ash ran faster, coming around a bend in the river, and found himself in the midst of the battle between the miltiamen and the Abenakis.

He saw Philippe ahead, standing on the ice away from the others. He knew him at once. With a wordless roar, he pointed the sword at Philippe's heart and ran straight at him. He had taken only a dozen strides when an Abenaki slipped out of the darkness and struck him on the head with a club.

When he regained consciousness, he found himself back in Alamoth, lying on a pallet in the church with wounded men all around him. He seized a passing woman by the skirt.

"Where am I wounded?"

"The head."

Ash unwound the crude bandage around his skull.

"Examine the wound," he said, asking questions and directing the woman as she worked.

"Help me up," he said when she was through and he had diagnosed himself as having a possible fractured skull. "Now, remain with me. If I faint, place my head low and my legs high and wait by me till I wake, then help me up again."

For the next ten hours he set bones, sutured hatchet wounds, amputated mutilated arms and legs, put frostbitten feet to soak in pans of warm water, examined horrifying burns that he had no means of treating.

One of the women who was assisting him brought in an unconscious castrated boy of sixteen, already half-dead from loss of blood and exposure.

Ash said, "Are you his mother? Take him out and lay him down again in the snow; it is the best thing for this wound."

The dead militia captain in his full boots was already laid out in the snow beside the church, next to the man who had been wounded by the same round from Philippe's jaeger rifle. After perforating his bowels, the bullet had touched the second man's spine, paralyzing him; he screamed until dark, then died. It was the burned and the tortured who were the worst.

Most of the other wounded soldiers were only superficially wounded. Covered with blood to the elbows and spattered with it from head to waist, Ash shouted at them in his terrible voice: "On your feet! You, you, and you—find tools! Cover the windows in the Manor! You—salvage whatever meat you can from those slaughtered cattle outside, then clear away the rest! You—find whatever food is left and take it to the Manor. We must all live there until we can build up the town again."

Ash had no clear idea of what had happened during the attack. The men were silent. The women, whispering, told him that not a single Abenaki had died, that every house in Alamoth had been set on fire while they slept, that the muskets loaded with buckshot had been useless.

"We were betrayed," they said. "Fanny was a spy—the papist whore. She was a Catholic all the time, sir. We saw her confessing to the Jesuit and eating Communion bread while the boys of Alamoth were hanging in the trees and we were all standing barefoot and naked in the snow and the savages were murdering the cattle.'

"You must be mistaken," Ash said.

"There's no mistake. The French knew just who she was. And they stole poor Thoughtful Pennock again."

Hawkes returned. Ash removed the flint arrowheads from his chest and neck and cleaned and dressed the bayonet wound in his arm.

Ash had never observed a phenomenon like Hawkes's layer of lard; once freed by the scalpel and subjected to the pressure of a thumb on either side of the wound, the arrowheads popped out of the yellowish subcutaneous fat, leaving a practically bloodless cav-

ity that soon closed itself. Even during surgery Hawkes did not complain about pain.

"You saw the captives?"

"Not close. It was dark.

"Did you recognize anyone at all?"

"The Abenakis built a lean-to for your wife. I heard the baby crying."

Ash stopped what he was doing and gripped the ledge of the operating table. His head swam.

"Will they let them live?"

Hawkes did not answer at once. Ash opened his eyes.

"She'll live if she can keep up. I saw Fanny carrying the child on her back and helping her."

In the late afternoon of the fifth day after the massacre, Ash was examining a boy whose leg had been amputated. The light was uncertain; Ash could not see the patient's features very clearly. He felt his forehead. The skin was feverish, a normal symptom. But Ash felt something else on the skin. He rotated his palm gently on the forehead, then felt the cheeks. The boy's face was covered with small hard pimples that felt like shot. Ash fetched a candle, shooing away a woman who wanted to hold it. Then he stripped the boy. There were no pimples on the chest, none in the armpits, none in the groin. The face, the forearms, the feet were covered with them.

To the boy he said, "Have you any pain apart from the stump? "

"My back aches," the boy said.

"It will soon be better," Ash said, holding a cup containing a strong dose of opium to his lips.

The symptoms were unmistakable. The boy had smallpox.

Ash washed his hands with soap a second time before touching another patient. He examined them all very thoroughly. Of the fifteen wounded in the church, none but the boy with the amputated leg displayed the symptoms of smallpox. As soon as it was dark, Ash loaded the boy onto a sled and hauled him to the Manor. Then, laying his unconscious body on a rug, he tugged him over the wooden floors to the library and down the steps of the hidden passageway to the hiding room.

Smallpox had always interested Ash. He believed that it was transmitted by animacules that lived in the pus discharged from the unbilicated vesicles, the pustules, which developed out of the original pimples. The fact that the complete isolation of this patient appeared to have prevented the spread of the disease tended to confirm the theory. Taking great care to avoid contact with his

own skin, and washing himself afterward with soap, Ash took scrapings of pus from the boy and studied them under his microscope. Animacules were clearly visible.

Although he had found nobody except Thomas Sydenham who was willing to listen to him, Ash believed that inoculation, which had been practiced for a long time by the Turks and other peoples in the Orient, could reduce the high rate of mortality and disfigurement associated with smallpox.

The theory of inoculation held that by deliberately infecting a patient with smallpox, one could induce a milder case than was likely to occur through natural infection. The Chinese had accomplished this by smearing pus from an active case into the nasal membranes of an uninfected person. The Turks had developed a method of scratching the skin and applying crusts scraped from smallpox pustules to the scratches. In both cases, the hoped-for result was a spreading of the disease from the point of inoculation to other parts of the body.

Usually, though by no means always, the result was a superficial case of smallpox which neither killed nor unduly disfigured the person, and rendered him immune from reinfection for the rest of his life. Sometimes, of course, the case was severe and the patient died just as he would have done if he had contracted the disease in the normal way.

It was best to collect crusts for inoculation from the running pustules of a victim who had a mild case of smallpox. The boy's case was not mild, but as it had not killed him, it was clearly not the most severe variety. Ash therefore decided to inoculate himself and observe the result.

The objection that had in the past prevented him from doing so—that if he died, God might reasonably condemn him to hell on the grounds that he had committed suicide while blasphemously eating from the tree of knowledge—no longer seemed to apply. Ash wanted to die; he was even willing to believe that a self-induced death might be the act toward which his passion had been driving him.

"If I do not die," he cried in his last prayer before inoculating himself, "then I will know that Your purpose is yet to be revealed to me. But oh! reveal it soon!"

Working while the patient slept, Ash scratched an X on his left biceps, collected three samples of crust from three separate pustules, and rubbed them into the wound.

Hour by hour in the days that followed he watched and recorded the progress of his symptoms—the reddened skin on the inoculated arm, the hardened swelling, the growing lassitude—with an excite-

ment that was heightened by the inevitable appearance of a high fever. Finally the pimples appeared—a dozen on the face, a few on the extremities. Four days later, the eighth day after inoculation, these erupted into pustules.

The sores were especially noticeable on Ash's colorless skin, but no one said anything about them until Rose Barebones came through the gates of the town. Her eyes shone brightly and her exquisite face was slightly flushed as she stood on the snow-covered green with Ash's daughter in her arms and the Clum girls and Jean Judd slumped in the snow at her feet.

"Your wife is dead, but I have brought you your daughter, Edward," Rose said, proffering the sleeping infant in its papoose frame.

Then, seeing the pustules, Rose pulled the bundle back. "What's that on your face?" she asked.

"A slight rash," Ash replied, very surprised when his words were followed by a loud sob, and then by another.

He stared at his child.

"A slight rash," Ash repeated, sobbing hysterically and groping for his daughter Solitude as Rose walked backward to avoid his touch.

# 7

Philippe waited outside Two Suns's wigwam in the early morning, sitting cross-legged on the beaten dirt like an Abenaki until Fanny appeared. She was not surprised to see him.

"Are you still yourself," Philippe asked, "or have you been adopted by Two Suns?"

She wore Indian dress: moccasins that laced to the knees, a short skirt, a red blouse cinched at the waist with the belt of wampum that Two Suns had given her as a gift of welcome. Her hair hung down her back in a thick plait.

"I am still myself," she said.

"Then we can talk. You asked me about the forest. When I was a boy, Bear and I went down Lake Champlain, where our canoe was capsized by the wind, and across the edge of the Mohawk

country, where we found a deer strangled in a Mohawk snare, and then through blue mountains covered with hemlock forest. Just as the moon was turning full, we came to a big grove of beech trees, where we saw a lot of black bears, a whole herd of them, it seemed, eating the beechnuts. They are tiny things, the nuts, but there are heaps of them on the ground in the fall. There was a small river, full of trout, at the edge of the grove, running very fast through a narrow slot between high cliffs. There is no French word for a place like this."

"A gorge," Fanny said in English.

"Yes, a gorge. I think this is the place that you wanted to go to."

Fanny looked at Philippe very carefully. He was dressed for the forest, his jaeger rifle slung over his back, knife and hatchet stuck into his belt, his belongings lashed onto a willow pack frame.

Philippe was smiling at her with compressed lips. She smiled the same smile back.

"What is this place called?" she asked.

"From today it is called the Gorge," he replied in English, then returned to French. "Formerly it had no name. As you are a canoeist, we will go part of the way by water. And as we will not be accompanied by a priest this time, I think we had better be married before we leave."

"Very well," Fanny said.

"Wait," Philippe said. "Before you consent, let me tell you about my fortune and my prospects. What I own is what you see, except for a sword and some uniforms, which you have also seen— and my wig, of course. I am the only son of the Sieur de Saint-Christophe, who is penniless, and if I live longer than my father I will inherit his small cold house in Normandy and five hundred *arpents* of boggy land."

Fanny had not heard Philippe speak at such length before. Perhaps he had thought out his speeches beforehand. She asked, "Have you discussed these plans, this marriage, with your family? I am not, as you know, French."

"My family is preoccupied with other matters," Philippe said. "Marie-Dominique gave birth to a healthy son who has been named Philippe Jean Armand Louis Marie Edwige Dominique de Grestain. My sister advises you to accept my offer of marriage. She says that the cards are emphatic about this, but to remember the importance of secrecy. I don't know what she means by that. But I assure you that the Spy has been hanged."

"And your brother-in-law?"

"Armand is waiting for your ship to come in. I didn't receive his blessing."

Suddenly Fanny said, "Tell me about the forest. How far into it have you gone?"

"To the Great Lakes to the west, to the sea to the east and south to Alamoth. I don't want to talk about the forest. There is something I must tell you about Alamoth."

"I have decided that I don't need to know that particular secret," Fanny said. "Have you ever found a place where there are no people and never have been any people?"

Philippe was interested now. "There are some mountains about halfway between the Hudson and the Connecticut where nobody lives," he said. "I went there with Bear when we were boys. The Mohawks go over to hunt moose in the winter, and they've driven some other Indians called Mahicans into the southern valleys. But in the north it's empty."

"Empty? What is it like?"

"Forest, rivers, rocks, mountains, wild animals."

"That's where I want to go."

"Go there? How? Why?"

"With you, since you know the way," Fanny said, "to live in silence, to be something that is not French or English or anything else."

"Silence I can promise," Philippe said.

Father Nicolas married them the next morning in Saint-François-de-Sales as soon as the light was strong enough to illuminate the stained-glass windows.

Philippe insisted on waiting for that moment because one of the disciples, Timothy, closely resembled Used to be Bear. Speaking her vows, Fanny spoke Philippe's Christian name for the first time; he called her by her given name, Genevieve, but whispered "Fanny" into her ear when he kissed her by the altar.

Afterward Thoughtful gave Fanny a gift of seed corn and bean and pumpkin seeds.

"Plant them in the sun," she said. "Water them every day. The beans will climb the corn."

Two Suns gave Philippe a bow and quiver. "Don't make your wife run too much before you get her with child," he said. "Seed doesn't catch in a woman who runs. The year my daughter Squirrel was born in the wrong place was the year Thin Ice was running away from the Iroquois."

Paddling down the Richelieu, and then along the eastern shore of Lake Champlain, Philippe sang in Abenaki, smiling at

Fanny when she turned around in her place at the bow to join him.

At its southern end, Lake Champlain narrowed into a long strip of water that was hardly wider than a small river. The western bank lay in Mohawk country. Long before they reached this point, Philippe stopped singing and forbade noise of any kind. They paddled at night, never speaking, stopping often to look and listen.

Philippe fell into a hypnosis of woodcraft and caution. If Fanny rattled her paddle against the gunwale, Philippe would poke her hard on the back with the dripping blade of his own paddle. If she coughed he would cover her mouth with his hand, half-smothering her. They lit no fires and made no camps, but carried the canoe ashore before dawn and hid it, and then slept a long way off from it.

They slept in turns, never at the same time, so that one of them was always on watch, and ate in turns too, so that one was always listening while the other went about the ear-plugging business of chewing up nocake. They urinated and defecated in running water, one squatting while the other watched the surrounding scrub.

Philippe checked the priming pan of his jaeger ten times a day. Before setting out he had taught Fanny how to load and shoot the jaeger, and also his Belgian pocket pistols. He gave her one of the pistols to carry in a pouch slung across her chest. She also carried a knife.

"If you see a Mohawk, make yourself small," Philippe whispered. "Say nothing, do not move. If he sees you, cock the pistol. Do not let him see it until you shoot. Hold it in both hands. Fire when he is three steps away, aiming for the heart. Then run."

"And if I miss?"

"Then use the knife, quickly."

He meant use it on herself, because he, himself, would already be dead.

After a week they were far enough away from the Mohawks that they could risk a fire. Philippe kneeled by a stream, building a little tipi of sticks with which to light a fire. He had just caught two large trout and they flopped on the moss beside his knee. Fanny had snapped a handful of dead stubs off a hemlock. He added these to the tipi. Then he lifted Fanny's hands one at a time and kissed the palms.

"Your skin smells like honey."

"It smells like pine pitch."

"Then it's a trick—I'm smelling its color. Listen!"

Fanny did so, making herself motionless and small at the same time, thinking that he had heard something moving. She could

hear only the wind in the canopy of the forest and the twitter of birds—unmistakably birds and not a Mohawk imitating a bird because so many of them were calling all at the same time.

"I don't hear anything," Fanny said.

"That's because there is nothing to hear, just as you wanted. There are no people here—no Christians, no Turks, no Indians, no English or French, only you and me."

By the time they reached the Gorge, the moon was full, which meant according to Fanny's calculations that they had been married for three weeks. They had not yet become lovers.

At night they slept in each other's arms, fully clothed in their deerskins, and often she would be awakened by Philippe's kisses. She kissed him back, able to see his face and the desire in it as the moon grew larger and brighter night after night, and feeling the change in her own breathing, a lightness in her body, a change in her racing mind so that at last she thought of nothing but making him her lover.

Philippe would hold her body cradled against his own, breathing deeply like a sleeper, but not asleep. They went no further than that. When they walked through the forest they walked in single file, with Philippe always in the lead, many paces ahead. Often he would stop on the trail and watch her as she approached. When she reached him they would kiss again, sometimes for a long time.

Fanny did not know why they were behaving in this way instead of doing what they both longed to do, or how much longer it would last. The kisses, the smiling glances, produced a constant state of desire, strong enough to give off a ferny scent, new to Fanny, that lingered on them both.

After lying for a long time in Philippe's arms with her eyes closed, apprehending him with senses that had nothing to do with sight, she would wonder who he was when she looked at him again. She never doubted that he had some reason for conducting the courtship in this way. Philippe was subject to ideas, to plans; Fanny had learned that much about him even before she knew that she loved him. He formed an intention about nearly everything and then carried it out. He had formed an intention about Fanny, about Alamoth, about the angle of the sun at the precise moment that they spoke their marriage vows in Saint-François-de-Sales.

Now, evidently, he had formed an intention as to the circumstances in which they would consummate their true marriage. He called it that, afterward: *le vrai mariage*.

When Fanny saw the grove of beeches and the Gorge itself, she understood why they had waited.

Of all the American trees, the virgin beech was in every way the

most beautiful and the most haunting. Fanny loved its pallor, its
serenity. The smooth bark was gray, of a shade somewhat whiter
than wood ashes, and when struck by the sun or even by the moon,
it absorbed light in a way that made it seem translucent. The trunk
could be huge, sometimes fifteen feet in circumference, rising
straight, clean, and symmetrical to the first branches twenty or
thirty feet above. The delicate leaves, pale green on one surface
and silvery on the other, turned in the slightest breeze, creating
ripples of changing color and the sound of whispering. The wood,
when cut, was pallid too, and beaded with fragrant sap. Dozens of
fearless red squirrels scampered through the foliage, scolding and
hurling down twigs on the intruders.

Philippe and Fanny walked hand in hand among the beeches,
toward the sound of the water. There was water in the air—not
spray or dampness, but the smell and coolness of water. Fanny was
overwhelmed by the belief that she had been in this place before.
The colors, the patterns of light and shadow, the hue of the sky
which was darkened by the elusive tints of gray and green inter-
posed between it and the eye, the roar of the water growing louder
with each step—it was all as familiar to her as her own body.

How could that be?

The edge of the Gorge was quite close now. The noise of the
water was far louder. Spray rose above the lip of the cliff, wetting
the rocks. Fanny started to go closer, but Philippe pulled her back
and led her toward a high ledge. Pointing out the steps and
handholds as he went, he climbed to the top.

Fanny followed. They were standing on a huge sheet of gray
rock. Beyond it lay the mouth of a cave. Philippe signed to her to
wait and not move; he went inside, returning after several minutes
with the brittle skull of a bear. He poked his finger through a hole
in the cranium and mouthed the Abenaki name for Bear.

They went into the cave. It was divided into one large room at
the front and two or three smaller ones farther in. The floor was
littered with rocks, large and small, that had evidently dislodged
from the ceiling over a period of thousands of years. Philippe
rolled aside a boulder, revealing a small low chamber leading off
the main room. He put his pack and rifle inside, and then Fanny's
pack and weapons, and rolled the boulder back into place. Al-
though the rush of the water was still audible, it was far quieter in
the cave than it had been outside. Philippe, silent and serious,
looked down on Fanny.

She smiled with her lips, thinking that he was going to kiss her.
Instead he turned her around so that he was standing behind her
and began to undress her, blouse, skirt, leggings. He fumbled and

she tried to help. He removed her hand gently and went on. He kneeled and unlaced her moccasins, lifting first one foot and then the other and stripping them off. When she was naked he unbraided her hair and shook it out so that it hung like a shawl down her back, touching her buttocks.

"Wait," he said.

From the sound of his movements, Fanny knew that he was undressing too. She was facing the mouth of the cave. On the other side of the Gorge, a hundred yards away, she saw different trees—birches, maples, oaks. Birds wheeled in the afternoon sky, silenced by the roar of the water. The sun was well down below the tops of the trees. The mist was more visible in this horizontal light, and larger drops of water leaped into the sunshine too.

"Come," Philippe said, taking her hand.

At first Fanny did not look at his body. She did not think that he was looking at hers either. When they walked outside, the watery breeze from the Gorge played over her skin, touching every inch of it in the same instant. Her hair moved around her, her nipples hardened, she felt the whetted surfaces of the rock beneath the soles of her feet.

Philippe led her to the edge of the Gorge. The river, after passing over a series of waterfalls, a very high narrow one and then three lower ones, boiled through a narrow gash in the rock. Spewing out of this stone nozzle, it crashed against a series of huge ledges, sending spume twenty feet into the air. Then, after flowing over a long bed of boulders, it spread out into a wider place and became calmer.

Fanny had never seen anything so wonderful; her heart pounded. Philippe stood behind her again and put his arms around her. No naked body had ever been pressed against hers before; Philippe's body, muscular and slightly scratchy except for the smooth, very warm part pressed along her lower spine, felt much as she had expected. He was trembling slightly.

"Look toward the sun," Philippe said.

Fanny turned her head and saw a rainbow in the spray. Philippe cupped her breasts in his hands. He moved his right hand and laid the palm flat on her stomach. She touched the backs of both his hands. He turned her around and looked into her face. He wore the same mesmerized expression as when they were passing among the Mohawks.

She still could not see his body; he was too close. But now she saw that he had more scars—a long white saber slash on his chest, the puckered pink eye of a healed bullet wound on his shoulder. Her own body did not have a single mark on it; except for the

THE BRIDE OF THE WILDERNESS

wine-dark areolas of her breasts, her golden skin was the same glowing color everywhere.

They stood at the very edge of the cliff. At the bottom, twenty feet below, the water had collected into a calm pool between the bank and a huge dark rock.

"Do you love me?" Philippe asked.

Fanny nodded.

"Say it."

"I love you."

She could see his entire figure now with the mist behind it. She had not dreamed that the male body was so beautiful, so perfectly made for its purposes, so much fleeter and stronger than her own.

Philippe took her hand, looked into her eyes, smiled, flexed his knees. He went through the sequence a second time, teaching her something. The third time, Fanny flexed her knees too and sprang outward with him off the edge of the cliff.

Instinctively she pressed her feet together and held her arms stiff against her sides. Like two knives, Fanny thought, their naked bodies fell side by side down the gray face of the cliff. Fanny's hair, falling more slowly, streamed above her. The descent took place in less than a second, but Fanny nevertheless saw Philippe smiling beside her, saw the high waterfall, saw the birds wheeling above the birches and recognized them as swallows, felt the spray on her skin.

She struck the water feet-first, having glimpsed Philippe as he cleaved the surface an instant before her, and then plunged into the bone-chilling water, sinking to the bottom. There she met Philippe, who looked at her solemnly through the greenish water and took her hand again. Her hair floated all around her. They pushed against the bottom and shot to the surface.

It was only two or three strokes to the black rock. The granite was bathed in sunlight, and the smooth heated surface seemed warmer than it really was against Fanny's skin. They began kissing while they were still wet, but soon they were dry.

A moment later Fanny gave one little sharp gasp of surprise. Philippe paused. She opened her eyes and lifted herself toward him, hearing the roar of the water, smelling the oil in his skin coming back to the surface, touching his hair and his scars, seeing his face change, then become itself again, then change back.

He throbbed within her like a heart. Fanny changed too.

# 8

Because the muscles of her abdomen were so strong, Rose's pregnancy did not begin to show until the sixth month. Even then, the presence of Used to be Bear's child in her womb could only be detected when she was undressed. Rose was not surprised by this; during her two pregnancies by Robert her belly had been so flat that her husband had only believed that she was pregnant when he felt the fetus moving.

This new child, on whom Rose's whole future depended, was late to quicken, but kicked more lustily than either of her stillborn girls had ever done.

"I'm quite sure it is a boy," Rose told Oliver when she informed him of her condition. "It is very lusty."

She had come into Oliver's bedchamber in her nightclothes. Standing beside his bed, she opened her robe, lifted his hand, and placed it firmly on her bare stomach. The baby's foot thumped against his palm. Rose put Oliver's unresponsive hand back on his chest where she had found it and gave him a tender look. This was the first time they had touched each other since the accident with the musket, and only the third or fourth time they had spoken since Rose returned from captivity. Rose was unchanged by her adventures and her pregnancy except that her complexion appeared to be somewhat more luminous.

"Virgin birth agrees with you," Oliver said.

"We're so fortunate that it happened before your injury," Rose said. "I know that we'll never be husband and wife, in the old way again after what has happened. You're right to blame me; I should never have been so upset about a cat, but you know I hate all cats. At least you'll have a son to carry on in Alamoth."

By now, six months after the burning of Alamoth, Oliver's stump was nearly healed. He swung his legs over the side of the bed. One of them ended in a big bunioned foot, the other halfway up the shin in a withered purply stub. Rose turned her face away.

"Are you saying," Oliver said, pointing to the small mound

beneath the silk dressing gown, "that whatever it is you're carrying around in there belongs to me? Look at me, Rose."

"Please cover yourself before I do," Rose said, tugging at his coverlet. "The child will be marked."

"How in God's name did you manage it?" Oliver asked.

Rose opened her eyes. Oliver was counting on his fingers. A look of comprehension came into his face. He began to guffaw.

"The Indians!" he cried. "Which one was it? Or was it all of them?"

Rose's eyes glistened. "How could you?" she asked, biting her fist. "How could you?"

Oliver's own eyes were merry. "Ten little Indians," he said. "By God, Rose, it must have been something to see. Pinned at last."

"Oh, how can you be so cruel?" Rose said. "How can you laugh? If what you're saying was true, instead of a filthy lie, it would be even crueler to say it. You've spewed all over me often enough, horrible sticky stuff."

"Not on this side of the ocean," Oliver said. "You'll have to scrub the paint off it before you have it baptized."

Oliver shouted for Hawkes, who slept in the passageway with half a dozen other refugees from the burned town. Six months after the disaster, the Manor was still packed with homeless men, women, and children. They spent their nights on the floor, all mixed in together, so that even during the day, when they were working in the fields, the house smelled of sweat and dung and the pungent fluids of copulation.

By the time Hawkes appeared, Oliver was standing on one leg beside his bed. "I'm giving you this room, Gus," he said. "Guard Missis Barebones well; she's had a terrible ordeal. With your help, I'm moving with all my worldly goods to a safer place. First me, then the worldly goods."

Oliver threw his arm around Hawkes's shoulder and hopped past Rose's immoble figure and down the stairs.

"I want all the rum brought to the hiding room," Oliver said. "Then send me my nurse."

Supplied by Hawkes with plenty of rum and food, quills and ink and paper, and the companionship of Hepzibah, Oliver remained below ground. He wrote to Fanny nearly every day, although he had no means of sending the letters and nobody was sure that she was alive.

As his physician, Ash disapproved of this arrangement. It was damp and dark in the stone chamber, and as Ash knew better than anyone, night and day were the same to the person inside.

While Ash examined Oliver's stump, Oliver sipped rum from the

bottle. He drank a quart of the stuff every day, a sip at a time, so that he was never insensible, but always just one dram short of falling down unconscious.

"If you go on drinking rum in this way you will die," Ash said, rolling the healed but still-tender stump between his palms.

Ash had done a splendid job; the stump was curing perfectly. There would be no need to operate again or scrape dead tissue from the bones, as often happened in cases of this kind.

Oliver was not bothered by Ash's warning. He held Hepzibah on his lap and a bottle of rum in his hand.

"Die of drink, will I?" he said. "That must be the Almighty's design. He sent His Indians to burn and smash everything in Alamoth except the kegs of rum."

He pulled the bodice of Hepzibah's dress outward and peeked down it to observe the quivering flesh beneath.

"It's been days since you've seen sunlight," Ash said. "It's nearly Midsummer. The farmers are haying, the carpenters are building. It would put heart into them to have you outside watching and encouraging."

"Yes, they'd all say, 'There's the toadstool come up through the ground.' I'd rather come up down here where it's nice and dark."

Hepzibah flushed and giggled. Guffawing, Oliver lifted her large left breast, closing one eye in concentration as if guessing its weight.

"Does he eat?" Ash asked Hepzibah.

Hepzibah shook her head. A bowl of food stood on the table, untouched. Ash wrapped up Oliver's stump and laid it back down on the stool. Oliver grinned at him.

"Will the foot grow back by next Shrove Tuesday?" he asked.

"No," Ash said. "Not as soon as that."

"Fanny told me you'd buried my foot so I'd have it in the next world. Is that so?"

Ash did not reply. It was the first time Fanny's name had been mentioned to him in weeks, and he was overcome by strong feeling. Oliver did not notice; he was frowning and shaking his head in bafflement as he tried to overcome the effects of the rum and remember exactly what he had intended to say. At last it came back to him.

"Something about Fanny," he said. "Wait, I have this letter from Joshua. He's bringing the *Pamela* to Boston to see if I want to go to Canada to fetch Fanny home."

"For certain she'll be very welcome," Hepzibah said.

Ash gave Hepzibah a stern look. She gazed saucily back at him. Oliver pushed her off his lap.

"Get out," he said. "Bloody lies. I saw the savages steal her—
*saw* them. She was screaming. Get out!"

Hepzibah left. Slanderous talk about Fanny infuriated Oliver.
Her supposed treachery was still the talk of the village: the papist
whore, the spy, the secret Catholic, the child-thief.

"I can't go to sea on one foot," Oliver said. "It will have to be
you. Ransom, that's what the Frogs want."

Oliver swayed on his stool. Ash tried to take the rum bottle out
of his hand, but Oliver closed his fingers tightly around it and
swung it out of reach.

"About Fanny," Oliver said. "I've sent Hawkes to Boston for
another paper from the lawyer. I'll sign it and then you can sail to
Canada and give it to her."

"What paper?" Ash asked.

"The deed to the ship. I'm giving Fanny my share in the *Pa-
mela*," he said. "Then she can do as she likes, marry or not, go or
stay, be mistress to the Prince of Wales or take holy orders. She
must go back to England. These Christian bastards in Alamoth
want to kill her."

"What about yourself? Your wife is with child. What will they
do if you give everything away?"

"That's nothing to do with me."

Oliver's face, shiny from drink, was a mask of indifference.

"Wait until you see the child before you burn every bridge,"
Ash said. "It's only two more months."

"Wait? What for?"

"You may love it more than you think possible," Ash said.

# 9

Philippe sensed that the buck was coming, and so he looked
for the last time at the place where he knew the deer was going to
be and drew the bowstring back to his right ear. Then he closed his
eyes. Now he was absolutely motionless. Fanny lay beside him on
the powdery floor of the forest and fixed her eyes on a patch of
sunlight a few paces farther down the hillside. Earlier, a doe had
passed through it. Off to their left, Philippe had explained in signs,

a buck was circling, following the sexual musk secreted by the glands located in the split between the female's hooves.

The buck came into sight. It was still some distance from the patch of light. The animal froze, one forefoot raised high, and smelled the air. The wind was blowing across its nostrils from left to right; Philippe and Fanny were on its right, so it did not detect them. Its long ears twitched and swiveled. In another place it might have heard the hunters breathing, but the roar of the river muffled sound.

The buck was a fairly big animal, well-fleshed and young, with a wide rack of antlers. The horns were just out of velvet; in recent days Philippe and Fanny had been hearing the rattle of antlers as rutting bucks fought over does. As the buck moved along the contour of the hillside, walking a few steps, then stopping, it vanished and reappeared repeatedly as its coat and antlers blended with the foliage. A fallen tree blocked the trail. The deer collapsed its splindly legs, laid its antlers back along its spine, and slipped beneath the trunk like a dog wiggling under a fence. On the other side of the barrier the buck paused, stepped, sniffed the trail, froze again, and walked into the patch of sunlight.

Philippe released the arrow. Then he opened his eyes. The deer saw the two minute flecks of white that were the balls of Philippe's eyes, saw the vibration of the straightening bow, and heard the twang of the bowstring because the arrow that severed a carotid artery in his withers did not kill it instantaneously.

With the arrow still in its flesh, it leaped straight up into the air to the height of its own head, came down, looked around alertly as if it expected to go on living. It bounded along the hillside in five or six prodigious jumps that resembled an attempt to fly, and fell down dead.

Philippe was already running after the animal with another arrow fitted to the bowstring, but by the time he reached it, nearly all the blood had run out of it. He pricked the buck's moist eye with the arrow to make sure it was dead, then rolled the warm carcass over onto its back and began to skin it.

Fanny crouched down to watch; she did not yet know how to do this. Philippe went slowly, demonstrating. Working with his left hand because his right was trembling violently from the strain of holding the bow, he cut around the anus, slicing off the scrotum, turning the knife edge upward and slitting open the belly from vent to breastbone. As he made this cut, his whole hand disappeared inside the deer to protect the viscera from the knife point. He pulled out the guts, wrapping the liver and the heart in ferns.

Then he drew his bloody forefingers along the lines of his cheeks

and across the bridge of his nose and did the same to Fanny. The fresh blood, which was slightly warmer than her skin, itched a little and smelled of salt.

"You shot before you opened your eyes," Fanny said.

"Did I?" Philippe said. "Be careful not to let the hair of the deer touch the meat. It spoils it."

Philippe sliced off a strip of liver and ate it raw. Fanny shook her head no when he offered some to her. She had not smelled blood since Rose showed her Used to be Bear's corpse. Philippe grunted like an Abenaki as he chewed up the last of the liver.

"Tell me about shooting arrows with your eyes closed." Fanny said.

"The deer can see your eyes if they're open, so you must close them when you hunt."

"Then how do you see the deer?"

"With your eyes closed."

Philippe kissed her. He tasted of the deer he had killed. He lay back, carrying her with him in his arms, looking into her eyes with great seriousness as if her existence had made it possible to invent the act of love. He was always like that. He held her face between his hands and kissed her lips, delicately tracing their outline with his own lips, then tasting her tongue.

"It's a useful trick," Philippe said, "seeing things with your eyes closed."

Fanny tasted nothing now but the familiar flavor of her husband's mouth. They were lying on a bed of moss. Philippe stood up and got undressed. So did Fanny. Sunset bathed the tops of the beeches, tinting the small fluttering leaves with salmon and violet lights. Lying on their clothes, which Fanny had spread over the moss (after a summer together they could wait the extra moments), the tastes and odors of their bodies altered.

Philippe lifted Fanny up and fitted her onto himself. She crossed her ankles behind him, and as she was drawn toward the center of their marriage she smelled on his skin the earlier sleep-blurred scent of their morning lovemaking, in which, feeling Fanny's lips, Philippe woke to find his wife's head in his hands and then drew her into his arms, tasting salt on her tongue and then tasting the tongue beneath the salt and feeling her skin and the grip of her body as she had been the night before and all the times before that.

*Ah*, Fanny whispered as she always did as it began again, body joining to body, thinking, *How can this be true, how did I always know these mysteries that we have taught each other, how can I ever live for a day without this, what if he dies like all the others?*

Reading her mind, Philippe told her silently, *Stop thinking*. He closed his eyes. What did he see?

Fanny listened to the river in the Gorge and thought about the deer, slowly, from the beginning, watching it approach the pool of sunlight, watching Philippe with the bow drawn and the gray mottled feathers of the Abenaki fletching against his tanned skin, the thumb and forefinger pinching the arrow and holding back the whole force of the bow, the tendons taut on the back of the hand, the raised muscles in the forearm, the buck with his hoof drawn up ready to spear the earth, the pool of sunlight waiting, the buck and the sunlight in Philippe's mind, the animal sensing the man, knowing the danger but knowing it too late, and then with its wonderful eyes seeing the arrow in flight, seeing the eyes of the hunter as they opened just as the arrow struck.

Fanny shuddered and cried out, the deer flew upward in her memory and dissolved. Philippe opened his eyes. He looked down into Fanny's face with such sympathy that Fanny thought, when she opened her own eyes again, that perhaps he did not love her after all, that she was like the deer, something he had imagined in its innocence and beauty and then made real by killing it.

He touched her cheek and put his finger to her lips. She kissed it, tasted salt, and realized that her face was wet with tears, as it always was when she thought that she would die of love.

Now that the beechnuts were beginning to fall, Philippe carried the jaeger rifle again. He was on the watch for bears, but never again observed them in a flock as he and Used to be Bear had done when they were boys. All the same, the grove of beeches was a paradise for bears, and Philippe warned Fanny to be careful; she already was.

In strawberry time she had seen individual bears grazing in the meadows along the bluff, and later, while raspberrying, she heard one gobbling fruit and snorting on the other side of the bush. She backed away slowly, and after taking four or five steps she was able to see the bear. It was standing on its hind legs, salivating; the white patch on its chest was stained pink by berry juice. One of its ears had been chewed off.

The bear lifted its hoglike snout and swung it from side to side. Fanny was menstruating. The bear smelled the blood and gave her a slow puzzled look with its weak eyes. Fanny kept on walking backward, slowly and steadily. The thorny branches of the raspberry bush were tangled in the animal's fur. The bear attempted to crash forward through the bush, but the springy branches held it

back. It rose to its hind legs once more, gave Fanny another look of deep puzzlement, and decided to ignore her.

Once she was out of the bear's sight, Fanny broke into a run, arriving at the cave sweaty and out of breath. Philippe listened to her story. He did not know why the bear had not attacked. Possibly the bear had never smelled a human being before, he said, or perhaps it had never smelled the combination of blood and human scent.

"This bear has only one ear," Fanny said.

"Then maybe Used to be Bear has gone back to being a bear. But you shouldn't go berrying when you're unwell."

"I know; I thought that it might not happen this month."

"Also," Philippe said with his lips against her cheek, "stop all this running. It's not good for you."

The next month Fanny's menses did not occur. She decided to wait another month before telling Philippe, but he remembered.

"We must name this child Henry," said Philippe, who knew Fanny's father well from the game of Spy and now from Fanny's stories. "That will please Armand de Grestain because it will remind him of the victor of Agincourt."

Although they spent nearly all their time together, Fanny and Philippe only spoke to each other when they were in the cave or near it. Like the Abenakis, Philippe had a superstitious reluctance to speak in any language except signs or the calls of birds and animals when he was in the woods.

Fanny's imitations of the crow, the jay, the red squirrel, the distress call of the rabbit, the bawl of the doe in heat, were the truest Philippe had ever heard. One day when she had half the birds in the forest calling back to her, he broke his own rule and gave her an Abenaki name, Speaks to the Birds.

Sometimes in the evening Fanny sang Fanchon's songs for Philippe, who had, of course, known them all his life. They made jokes. Otherwise, they lived, as Fanny had hoped, in silence.

On the day after they arrived, Philippe had woven a long conical fish trap out of willow branches and set it at the mouth of the Gorge. The thundering water filled the trap with fish every day. The first time Philippe dragged the trap ashore and dumped out the dozens of flopping speckled trout, Fanny picked out a large one for Philippe and a smaller one for herself and then began to return the rest to the river.

"No," Philippe said, taking a foot-long fish out of her hands and killing it by thrusting his thumb into its mouth and bending its head back against its spine. "The trap won't always be full."

He had brought salt in his pack, so they salted some of the

bigger trout. The rest they butterflied and dried in the air or smoked over the coals of a beechwood fire in a pit. By August, when the trout grew scarce, one room of the cave was nearly filled with preserved fish laid out on racks made from beech saplings.

Fanny had planted the seeds she had received as wedding gifts in a sunny meadow between the cave and the Gorge, fertilizing them with dead trout and training the beans to climb on the cornstalks in the Indian way. She hoed the ground with a stick and strung strips of birchbark on a length of rawhide to keep the birds off. Late in the summer this garden began to yield. They dried the vegetables and dug an Indian barn, a square hole in the ground lined with stones, in which to store them.

As the trout ran out, Philippe began to hunt for game. In beech-nut season this could have been a simple matter. On any morning, a dozen deer and scores of rabbits fed among the beeches; the branches teemed with squirrels and raccoons; grouse nested among the cavernous root systems of the older trees. An Indian, like Talks in His Dreams slaughtering the herd of moose, would have bagged as many of these animals as possible before they disappeared. Philippe killed sparingly, preferring to stalk deer in the woods and take small animals in traps. He set snares to catch rabbits and spread a rawhide net to entrap grouse.

"Henry must have red meat," he said.

"Very well," Fanny replied, "but no liver."

There were other hunters in the grove besides Philippe. One morning, coming home with a string of grouse from the net, they heard the buzzing of flies. Following the sound, they found the half-eaten remains of a deer hidden beneath a deadfall. From a safe distance away, Philippe examined the tracks and other sign and showed them to Fanny. There was a strong odor of cat urine.

"We must come back," Philippe said.

That night they climbed high into a huge beech and waited. Philippe had brought the jaeger. Several hours after the moon rose they heard the sound of a baby crying, and then saw the cougar that had made this eerie sound. Soon the big cat itself appeared before their eyes, a skulking dun creature with a round intelligent face. It dragged the deer's carcass into the open and fed on it in a leisurely way until it was satisfied. Then it hid its kill again, scratched a pile of leaves and dirt together, and urinated on it. After that, it lay down in the forest much like a house cat and washed its paws and face, which were marked in white. After its bath the cat stood up, twitched its long tail, took a single step, and dematerialized.

"Is it so stealthy because it's afraid?" Fanny asked.

"No, because everything else is afraid of it," Philippe said. "Like the Mohawks."

He hardly ever spoke of the Mohawks, but Fanny knew that they might appear at any time. Like all Indians, they traveled along riverbanks, and this river, called the Woronoco by the Mahicans, formed a natural east-west highway between the frontier of Mohawk country and the Connecticut River.

Week by week, as Fanny's pregnancy progressed, Philippe began to worry about the dangers of the forest. Her condition did not seem to affect her in any way except that she required more sleep. Nevertheless, Philippe warned her frequently to be careful.

Adders and blacksnakes, and also a few rattlesnakes, lived in the rocks around the cave; they came out in the morning to warm their blood in the sun, then disappeared to hunt for field mice, chipmunks, and squirrels. Philippe, who in the early days had killed two or three rattlers with his tomahawk but otherwise ignored the reptiles, now warned Fanny every time she walked over the rocks to watch for poisonous snakes.

He was afraid, too, that she might fall.

"Have you ever seen me fall?"

"Only off a ship," Philippe replied. "But be careful, especially at night when you go out alone—it's a long way down to the bottom of the Gorge."

The leaves began to turn—first the vermilion swamp maples, then the amber birches. The river was now too cold for swimming, but late as it was, Philippe had seen several big trout pointed into the current just below the big falls, and had set up his trap in an attempt to catch them for Fanny.

One afternoon, when Fanny slept longer than he did after love-making, Philippe left her in the cave and went down into the Gorge to check the trap.

Leaping from stone to stone across the river, he felt the intrusion even before he saw the signs of it. The air, the ground, the stones rising out of the water were not the same. He looked downstream and saw birds rising straight up into the sky.

Someone had come and gone. Philippe drew himself back into the trees on the far bank of the river and made a half-circle, looking for tracks or other sign. He didn't see any. Making another half-circle, he reached a point, under the cover of the trees, from where he could see the fish trap. He searched the rocks and trees, saw nothing, then watched the trap for a long time. It had been moved—not by much. The water could have nudged it out of position. But it had been moved.

When he examined the trap, he saw that a human being was responsible. Several trout had been removed—only very small ones remained—and carried away wrapped in skunk-cabbage leaves that had been torn from the plants growing beside the river. Signs in the gravel told him that several more fish had been consumed on the spot, but not by the man.

Philippe plunged into the forest and ran through the trees to the next bend in the river. In the mud he found the heel mark of a moccasin and other sign. These were fairly fresh; they had not yet filled with water. Philippe ran on, pounding through the woods without caution, to the next big loop in the river. This time he found an intact human footprint, but again he was too late to catch a glimpse of the man who had made it.

There was no point in running farther; the man was traveling fast, the river turned every few yards so there was no possibility of getting in a shot at long range. Philippe knew that he could not make an accurate snap shot with the jaeger after such a hard run.

Philippe knew, also, whose tracks he had found; he had seen them, and the tracks that always went with them, before. To make certain that he was not deceiving himself about the identity of the man he was following, Philippe followed the tracks another mile or so, and found sign—a skunk-cabbage leaf floating in an eddy, the paw prints of a leaping excited animal—which told him that Hawkes had fed his wolf dog the rest of the trout on this spot, and then continued to travel west. What was this man doing here? Why was he traveling in the direction in which he was traveling? Why had he not searched for the owner of the fish trap? Why was he in such a hurry?

Philippe said nothing to Fanny about what he had found. The moon was in its third quarter. He started to watch the approaches to the Gorge, always keeping Fanny close to him, and one morning just before the full moon they heard the deer whistling in fright in the beech grove and the squirrels scolding.

Philippe knew that no enemy would approach so carelessly, so he stood out in the open where the Abenakis could see him.

Soon Two Suns and his surviving son, Hair, appeared among the birches. They wore paint and carried new French muskets.

Philippe read the letter they had brought to him from Grestain, then squatted with them as they told him from beginning to end how Hawkes and his one remaining wolf dog had killed five people from the Abenaki village on the Saint Francis River. All the victims had been decapitated and the heads had never been found.

Meanwhile, an Englishman with a loud voice had sailed down

the Saint Lawrence in a ship and was trying to buy Squirrel from the governor of New France.

"I think he wants to buy you too," Two Suns said to Fanny. "He wants to buy Hair's wife, and the widow of Talks in His Dreams. He thinks they can remember when they were English."

They started for Canada the next morning, going downriver, then striking north along the Connecticut. Two Suns did not want to travel by this route until Philippe told him why it was safe.

"Why is the fat ghost going west toward the Mohawks?" Two Suns wondered.

Philippe had never before heard an Abenaki ask a question.

# 10

Hawkes had arranged to meet the Mohawks about twenty miles west of the Gorge, at a waterfall near the source of the Woronoco. He arrived just before moonrise, lighted a fire, and cooked the last of the trout that he had stolen from Philippe's trap.

He was eating this fish off the cooking stick when the Mohawks arrived. The wolf dog, the only one Philippe had left alive, snarled when he saw the Mohawks and the coarse fur bristled on its ruff. The Mohawks, who were seeing this animal for the first time, stared at it without fear. There were twenty of them and they knew that they could kill anything they wanted to kill.

The Mohawks were darker and leaner than the Abenakis, and appeared to be taller because of their hairstyle, which consisted of a stiff roach growing from forehead to nape down the center of shaved scalps. Most of the warriors in this party were bare-chested despite the deep autumn chill that had settled on the country; heat still rose from the river in the form of mist as the water cooled after a day of strong sunlight.

The Mohawks, smallest but most famous of the five nations of the League of the Iroquois, were the most warlike and ferocious people the English had so far encountered on the American continent. Until recently the Mohawks had regularly raided New England from their fortified villages west of the Hudson, killing, torturing,

and capturing slaves. The English paid the Mohawks a fee for destroying the enemies of England.

Scalps were the reason why Hawkes was meeting the Mohawks. After the attack on Alamoth, the General Court in Boston had offered a bounty of forty pounds for each Abenaki scalp. He knew that he would never be able to marry Thoughtful and live in peace with her on the lands that Oliver Barebones had given back to her as long as the Abenakis believed that she was an Abenaki and Thoughtful agreed with them. As Hawkes saw it, the only way to overcome this difficulty was to lure the Abenakis from Thoughtful's village into battle and kill them all. He could not do this single-handed, and the half-trained, half-hearted English troops had shown on many occasions that they could not do it either.

Only the Mohawks could do it.

Hawkes looked around the circle of painted faces. War had made these Mohawks prosperous; each carried a good musket in addition to a bow. Some had pistols; all were equipped with excellent knives and hatchets. One or two had arrows fitted to bowstrings and Hawkes saw that the arrows had iron points; a metal-tipped Mohawk arrow was capable of passing completely through the body of a deer or the torso of a human enemy. These men were better-nourished and better-clothed than any other Indians Hawkes knew about.

The friendship of the Iroquois for the English, and earlier for the Dutch, had been based on the relationship between trade and warfare. With firearms obtained from the Dutch in the middle of the seventeenth century, the Iroquois subjugated the Huron, the Tinontati, the Erie, the Illinois, and other Iroquoian tribes to the west and north of their base in central New York, driving these powerful peoples out of their palisaded villages, their lands, and eventually, out of history. At different times they terrorized all of what later became Virginia and parts of North Carolina, transplanting an entire Iroquoian tribe, the Tuscarora, from Carolina to New York State. Meanwhile they carried out their incessant raids against the French and the Algonquian allies of the French in Canada.

Hawkes began to talk in signs; the Mohawks' language bore no relationship to the Algonquian tongues spoken by the Abenakis and many other tribes, including the Blackfeet, the Cheyennes, the Arapahos, and other plains tribes still unknown to white men. The Iroquois were different from the Abenakis in many other ways. Husbands left their own villages when they married, to live in the villages of their wives' clans; the Iroquois traced their descent through the female line rather than the male, they were hardly

Christianized, they were successful farmers, and they were highly organized politically, with chiefs and councils and laws and a rudimentary religion that encouraged military virtue and otherwise served the political purposes of the united tribes. Hiawatha, one of the two founders of the League of the Iroquois, was a Mohawk. (The other was Dekanawida, who may have been born a Huron; like other American peoples, the Iroquois, whose population was repeatedly decimated by European diseases such as smallpox, sometimes adopted slaves into the tribe.)

The Mohawks watched impassively as Hawkes made the sign for his own name, for Abenaki, for war, for the Connecticut River, for French Officer, for scalps, for forty pounds sterling, and for hunter's moon, which was the next moon after the present full moon.

A long silence ensued. Then one of the Mohawks said, in English: "Why will the Abenakis come down the Connecticut as you say they will?"

"Because I killed five of them and cut off their heads to make them angry and two weeks ago I followed two Abenakis who were carrying a message to the Frenchman who has been living near the other waterfall with his woman. His name is Christopher and he's the one who led the Abenakis against Alamoth."

Christopher was the name the English had given to Philippe Saint-Christophe after the massacre at Alamoth. By now even the Mohawks had heard of him.

The Mohawks remained silent; nothing in their code of manners made it necessary for them to give any sign that they understood the words being spoken to them by a non-Mohawk. At this point in the conversation an Abenaki might have suggested killing Philippe, who was only a five-hour run away, stealing his woman, and then ambushing Two Suns and his son.

The Mohawks were a more advanced people who knew that the future existed; they understood strategy. Every warrior present realized that the possibility of killing a lot of Abenakis, and taking their scalps at forty pounds each, depended on letting this smaller party escape. Without Philippe to lead them, the Abenakis would not come south in profitable numbers to a place where Hawkes and the Mohawks could attack them.

"What will we be given?" the English-speaking Mohawk asked.

"You already know that. Forty pounds for every scalp."

"How many scalps?"

"I can't say. When they attacked Alamoth there were about a hundred and fifty in the war party."

The Mohawk interpreted this to the man who appeared to be in

command of the war party. He responded in two loud bursts of Iroquoian.

"What else will we be given?" the English-speaker asked.

"Three hundred pounds," Hawkes said, naming the total he had earned by rescuing Thoughtful and scalping the five severed Abenaki heads. "Half now, half after we kill the Abenakis."

"That's only fifteen pounds each."

"It's all I have."

The interpreter spoke to the leader, a leathery bowlegged man whose eyes popped slightly when he talked. He had the loudest voice—almost as loud as Ash's but much higher in timbre—that Hawkes had ever encountered in an Indian.

"Where are the other two dogs?" the English-speaker asked.

Hawkes was not surprised that the Mohawks knew about the wolf dogs; probably they also knew that the dogs were dead and how they had died. Indians generally knew such things. They also knew that white men lied, and Hawkes realized they were testing his honesty.

"Christopher shot them," Hawkes said. "He has a musket that is accurate from a long way off."

"How far?"

Hawkes looked around, trying to find a landmark two hundred paces away. He settled on a dead tree on the bluff beside the waterfall; its jagged form was silhouetted against the moon.

"As far as the dead maple, maybe farther," Hawkes said.

The English-speaker interpreted that. The chief barked again.

"We don't believe you," the English-speaker said, "but we want the whole three hundred pounds now in case you're killed by the Abenakis or they capture you."

"All right," Hawkes said, "but I get Christopher's gun."

"Done," the English-speaker said.

The Mohawks spread a blanket over a flat rock and Hawkes poured out the coins. The English-speaker, who seemed to be the clerk of the expedition, sat down opposite the leader and counted the money, stacking it into twenty-one precarious piles of fourteen coins each. The English-speaker poured the six extra coins into Hawkes's hand without explanation. Evidently this was some sort of gesture of honorable partnership.

The Mohawk dangled the silver rosary that Hawkes had taken off the skeleton of the first Jesuit in the big pine tree above the falls of the Connecticut. It had been in the wallet with the coins.

"Are you giving us this also?" he asked.

"No," Hawkes said, taking it back. "It's a present for my future wife."

# 11

There were no canoes on the bank when Fanny and Philippe arrived at the Abenaki village on the Saint Francis River, and only Thoughtful met them at the landing.

"Everyone has gone to the forest," she said. "There's a sick white person here."

The Abenakis, like the Mohawks and many other woodland Indians, had seen whole villages die of measles and smallpox. They were terrified of any sickness carried by whites.

"Sick with what?" Philippe said.

Thoughtful directed her answer to Fanny. "A fever. It's Ash's child, the one you birthed. Ash came on the *Pamela* to ransom the people from Alamoth."

"And brought the child with him?"

"They say he loves it too much to be separated from it. He carries it around with him on his back like a woman, singing to it."

Two Suns and Hair were already paddling upriver, away from the pestilence. Philippe watched them for a moment, then got back into the canoe he and Fanny had arrived in and paddled after them.

Ash and Solitude were staying in Father Nicolas' wigwam. When Fanny arrived, the Jesuit was seated outside his wigwam, listening to a voice that came from inside. It was lower than Fanny remembered, as if the speaker was exhausted, but it was unmistakable.

Father Nicolas hurried down the path, gesturing.

"He is in great distress," he said. "He seems unable to think or act. Or pray. He speaks about you."

Fanny drew in her breath.

"What sickness is it?"

"A fever. It's not clear. But the Abenakis are afraid and the nurse is frightened to let the child suckle."

"What nurse?"

"The Englishwoman we knew on the trail, the one whose little boy had whooping cough. The madwoman hung him up in a tree and left him while they were running away in the blizzard, she says."

"Ask Mr. Ash to come outside," Fanny said.

Father Nicolas called to Ash through the wall of the wigwam. After a moment he came out, the same gaunt gray man, but with deep smallpox scars in his gray skin. It was noon. Ash squinted into the light as he came out of the dim interior of the wigwam. He did not recognize Fanny. She was burned darker by the sun and dressed in skins with her hair in a braid, and she had changed in other ways. He looked at her without curiosity for an instant. Then she moved and he saw who she was. He took a step backward, as if he had been pushed.

"Is it safe for me to come inside?" Fanny asked.

"Safe?"

"I'm pregnant."

Ash blinked. "There is always a risk, but you can wash. I have soap."

Solitude started to cry, a shrill high-pitched wail that was full of pain and fear. Ash lifted the flap on the door of the wigwam. The baby's cries grew frantic as light poured inside. Doubling his long body, Ash stooped and entered, carefully closing the flap behind him.

Father Nicolas gave Fanny a look filled with sympathy.

"You realize what child this is?" he said.

"Yes. Have you seen her? Is there any rash, any pimpling?"

"No. She's a pale thing like her father. The skin is clear."

Fanny went inside. Ash knelt by a cot, gazing down at Solitude, whose shrieks once again grew louder as the flap was lifted and a bar of light flashed into the wigwam. Ash crooned and covered the child's eyes with his hands.

"She cannot look at the light," he said.

Jean Judd, the nurse, cowered at the other side of the lodge. Like Ash, she looked incuriously at Fanny without seeming to know her.

Fanny kneeled opposite Ash and spoke his name. The wigwam was crowded with Father Nicolas' religious objects: a painting of Christ, a half-finished log sculpture of a long-faced saint that Fanny supposed was Saint Francis of Sales, painted saints carved out of pine, rude crucifixes. Father Nicolas was the artist; the painted windows in the church, showing Agbenaki warriors as the Apostles, were his work. Ash seemed to be oblivious of the popish articles all around him.

"What is wrong with the child?" Fanny asked.

"I can't make sense of the symptoms," Ash said.

"Is there any rash, any token?"

"Only fever," Ash said listlessly, "and the fear of light."

Fanny feared for her baby, but it was clear that Ash was not himself. He took no interest in the clinical aspects of his child's case. He seemed merely to be waiting for Solitude to die.

"Let me see," Fanny said. "Guide me."

She opened the child's blankets. She looked at once at the groin for the nutmeg tokens of plague. They were not there. The fever was not severe. The lymph nodes were enlarged. The pupils were contracted. The child had retracted its neck into its shoulders. Every muscle was tense, the trunk was slightly bowed already. The sensitivity to light was a symptom of many illnesses.

"Say something," Fanny said to Ash. "Anything." She spoke in French.

"She is very sick," he whispered.

"Speak as loudly as you can."

The command was so strange that Ash obeyed it without thought. "*Pourquoi?*"

Solitude screamed in agony at the sound of his voice.

"She also fears noise," Fanny said. "Had you noted that?"

Ash shook his head. Fanny waited until Solitude grew quieter, then bent the child's knees back against her chest. Solitude shrieked again.

"The hamstrings are painful," Ash said, showing interest for the first time. "What do we see?"

Fanny listed the symptoms. Ash nodded after every observation that she made; he himself had already observed each of them, but he had not been able to admit their meaning.

"You've seen this in children before," Fanny said.

"Have I? What is it, then?"

"According to what you taught me, meningitis."

Ash looked at her with disbelieving eyes. "No. It cannot be."

"Anything can be," Fanny said.

Ash's expression grew wild. Tears streamed from his eyes. He fell back on his haunches and began to sob quietly.

"Come, Jean," Fanny said in English. "This child must have a warm bath now, and another every day at this time. Keep her wrapped as you bathe her, washing only one part at a time so as not to chill her. When she cries, put a cold cloth on her head; she has a headache. Don't let the light in, don't make any noise. Both are very bad for her."

"And who are you, Indian, to know so much?" Jean asked.

"Do as she says," Ash said.

"Has she made water?" Fanny asked.

"No, she's dry all day."

"She must."

Fanny searched among the bottles in Father Nicolas' paintbox until she found turpentine. She held the bottle under the screaming child's nose and let it inhale the fumes. A few moments later, Solitude urinated.

Ash watched these procedures helplessly, as though he had never before observed a medical treatment.

Ash had loved his daughter with an overwhelming love from the instant that Rose placed her in his arms on the day of her return from the wilderness. All the tenderness he had never felt before, all the earthly happiness that he had believed to be an illusion, welled up in his heart at the sight of her. He did not connect this phenomenon to Betsy, whose death among the Indians had meant nothing to him compared to the capture of Fanny; yet when holding Solitude in his arms, he felt himself in the presence of the young, merry Betsy, and even of the infant's dead brothers and sisters. This love had grown stronger as the child grew older. Solitude was nine months old; she knew her father; she turned toward his voice when he spoke her name; she spoke words.

"He spent every minute with her in Alamoth," Jean Judd told Fanny, "rocking her, carrying her on his back all through the town, singing her to sleep. People laughed to see a man so moon-struck over a babe."

He slept in the same room with Solitude, and when she woke, he carried her to Jean, picking his way through the dark Manor among the sleeping figures, and then listening to the sound of suckling.

Finally he had brought her to Canada with him aboard the *Pamela* when Oliver sent him off with a box full of gold to ransom the Alamoth captives. He had brought Jean along to feed the child.

Fanny remained with Solitude during the day, bathing her to reduce the fever and keep her clean. At night, while Ash and Jean looked after the child, she returned to Two Suns's wigwam.

Philippe had not returned.

"He is waiting for Two Suns to say it is all right to go fight the English." Thoughtful said. "If Snow doesn't die I think they'll go." She called the child by the Abenaki name that Used to be Bear had given her.

Solitude was now at her worst—convulsive, violent, delirious if a child of her age could be said to be delirious. Ash sat dumbly by her side, awaiting the end.

"Will she live?" Father Nicolas asked.

"I don't know."

"Will Ash accept help?"

"You mean your prayers? I don't think so. He's a very strong Protestant."

"I mean more than prayers. This child has already died once. Surely God does not mean to take her after what happened in the snow."

Father Nicolas opened the vault in the altar and took out the relic of Saint Francis of Sales that was the church's greatest possession. He brought it into the wigwam in its locked case.

Ash picked up the relic from its velvet bed and turned it between his fingertips.

"It is the second phalange of the left index finger," he said. "A knuckle bone."

"It is more than that, my friend. Permit me."

Father Nicolas touched the child's forehead with the relic, making the sign of the cross. Ash watched but did not interfere.

"We shall see what God decides," Father Nicolas said. "Do you know of the miracle of the snow, when your daughter was dead and woke up again?"

"Miracle?" Ash said. "Temperature of the body, circulation of the blood."

But in the morning, Solitude was better. A day later she began to suckle again.

Ash brought her out into the sunlight. She did not cry. He sang to her, softly at first, and finally in his full voice, which brought the Abenakis out of their houses to see what was happening. The noise did not trouble Solitude.

"Was she cured by a piece of bone and the sign of the cross?" Ash asked Fanny.

"Father Nicolas will say so."

"And what do you say?" Ash was looking at Fanny with his old intensity now.

Fanny looked at the child in Ash's arms. "There are no miracles," she said.

"Perhaps not," Ash said. "I came here with money to ransom everyone—English pounds, gold louis, pieces of eight. But no one will come home. They are happy here. Thoughtful wouldn't sign the paper giving her back her inheritance."

Ash told her what had happened to Oliver and Rose.

"The child's name is Olivia," he said. "She is quite dark, darker than you."

"She would be," Fanny said. "Will you go back to Alamoth?"

Ash was looking beyond her. Fanny turned around and saw that Philippe had come back. Behind him a mob of painted warriors

were coming ashore in canoes. He was walking toward them across the village, dressed for the forest. He carried his jaeger rifle.

"I wish to say this to you before I go," Ash said. "I cared nothing about the others who were captured, not even my wife. You were all I thought about."

He was speaking to Fanny's back, and at first he was not sure that she had heard him. Then she turned around so that he could see her face.

"For the rest of your life you must think about something else, Edward," she said.

Ash smiled. "That is what I have always striven for. Here, hold Solitude for a moment."

Philippe was advancing across the beaten floor of the village. Fanny took the baby into her arms. It looked up at her with Betsy's eyes, calm and mild.

"War," Ash said, gazing at Philippe. "It is a very odd world that God has made. Here comes your husband, a man who burned an English town and stole its people and inflicted unspeakable suffering on them, and they speak of him half a year afterward as if he were a god. They can't pronounce his name, of course, so they have their own name for him. 'Will Christopher come again?' they asked. 'Be good or Christopher will come,' they tell the children. He made them love him for his cruelty. What do you call him?"

"Philippe."

"And do you love him for the same reasons as the others?"

Instead of answering—she did not want to talk about love with Ash, or about Philippe—Fanny made as if to give Solitude back to him.

"No," Ash said. "Hold her a moment longer. You are the only woman I ever wanted to bear my child, I dreamed of it, and— how odd—you've given me this child's life twice."

Philippe arrived beside them. Ash took his daughter out of Fanny's arms.

"I was just thanking your wife for all that she has done to save me from a loss I could not have borne," Ash said in his flawless French. "I thank you, too, sir."

Philippe bowed.

Without looking at Fanny again, Ash walked away through the village.

"Come," Philippe said. "We have a little while before I go."

# 12

The *Pamela*, so long awaited, had sailed down the Saint Lawrence in ballast, her hold filled with rocks from Massachusetts. Joshua Peters explained that he had discharged his cargo in Boston and had been unable to find another one in that city. In the hold were a few sacks of corn, a few kegs of rum and Canary wine, a dozen bolts of common cloth, and some wool blankets suitable for trade with the Indians.

"These are gifts for natives, not a serious cargo," Grestain said when he came aboard to inspect the hold.

"I didn't come to Canada to trade, but to bring Mr. Ash to see the governor about ransoming English captives and to consult with my owner."

"What about the famous lobsters?" Grestain asked.

"The lobsters were a great deal of trouble," Joshua replied.

"But profitable."

"Not so very."

"What can that Genoese of yours be thinking of?" Grestain asked Fanny. "Who ever heard of sailing hundreds of miles in a ship filled with rocks? Does he think he can get something for nothing in Quebec—furs, no doubt—and sail away never to come back? When I told him that this was a typical bit of Genoese trickery, do you know that he said? He said, 'I remind you, Count, that it was the Genoese crossbowmen who took the first storm of arrows from the English longbows at Crécy *while the French knights in their tin suits crouched behind us!*' Crouched behind them! *Crouched!*"

Grestain choked on his watered wine. The servant pounded on his back while the Indians watched impassively.

"Fanny will go down to the ship and speak to the master tomorrow, Count," Marie-Dominique said. "But as you can see, she has had a difficult journey and must rest."

Later, while Fanny lay soaking in the big tin tub that the servants brought into her room, Marie-Dominique came in to read

her fortune. She looked down at Fanny's body with the bold appreciation of a man.

"Lucky Philippe," she said. "When is your child due?"

"In March."

Marie-Dominique smiled, having won the point. "I'll show you mine after your bath. He isn't bad for a Grestain, in fact he's quite sturdy, like Sieur. I've given him up to a wet nurse so that I can conceive again as quickly as possible, though I must say it's taking a long while this time. The next one I'll nurse until he's five."

Marie-Dominique laid out the tarot cards, still chattering.

"Remember what the cards told you—the only way to keep love secret is to pretend that it's the farthest thing from your mind," she said. "My husband thinks that Philippe married you for your ship. If he finds out that there is love between you he'll try to take advantage of the fact. He'll keep on sending Philippe off to kill Englishmen until you bribe him by giving him the ship."

Marie-Dominique tapped the table with the edge of the tarot deck. "Even the cards say so," she said. "Look: the Emperor reversed, then the Tower, then the Fool coming up one after the other. What can it mean?"

The cards meant injury in battle and the loss of inheritance; catastrophe and bankruptcy; ruin caused by the folly of another. Marie-Dominique did not explain all that.

"Be careful of money, be careful of fools," she told Fanny. "Keep love a secret."

When Fanny went down to the wharf the following morning, still dressed in her Indian clothes, she found Joshua waiting for her on the deck of the *Pamela*. He led Fanny over the deck toward his cabin.

"No, not there," she said. "I'd like to see the hold with all those famous rocks in it."

At the bottom of the ladder, the smell of coffee was a little fainter than Fanny remembered (the *Pamela* herself seemed to be somewhat smaller after only a year), but the open space between the ribs of the ship with its kegs and crates and coils of rope, and the splinters of dust-filled light standing still while the hull rocked in the tide, were just the same.

"Before anything," Joshua said, "we must go over the accounts."

Joshua gave her a leather bag containing six hundred pounds, her share of the vessel's profits over the past year. They had had good luck with a cargo of Madeira wine and with another of Venetian glass. Nine hundred lobsters survived the ocean voyage; Praise God Adkins had sold them all to the Rose Tavern for nine

shillings each. After expenses the profit had been less than two hundred pounds, and every man in the crew had had his fingers pinched by live lobsters while removing the dead ones from the vats. The smell had been awful.

"The crew will desert if we try lobsters again," Joshua said. "They became sailors so that they wouldn't have to be fishermen."

"That will be a tremendous disappointment to my husband's brother-in-law," Fanny said.

"If I were you, Fanny, I'd keep my profits out of sight."

This was the second time in twelve hours that Fanny had been given this advice. She felt the weight of the six hundred pounds in the palm of her hand. She had never thought of money as having value, but now, she thought, with this sum Philippe and I can have a house in which to be alone.

"I've brought you a lot of letters from Oliver," Joshua said.

He handed them over, a thick packet wrapped in oilskin and a second, much thinner bundle.

"Oliver wants you to read the small one first," he said.

"Then you've seen him."

Joshua shook his head. "Ash brought the papers to Boston."

Fanny sat down on a box and read the deed transferring Oliver's share of the ship to her.

"Why?" she said, after reading it.

"Perhaps he tells you why in the letter."

Fanny broke the wax, which was sealed with Oliver's old signet ring, a B made of bones, that Henry had given him, and not with the Pennock seal that Oliver had used after he came to Alamoth.

When Fanny saw the formless handwriting wandering over the page, she knew that Oliver had written the letter while drunk. "I don't want Rose to have any claim on the *Pamela*," he wrote, "but if her child is needy at some future time, and you know of this and are satisfied that the girl is not a monster like her mother, then help her. Meanwhile take the money and the ship and return to England. Peters and Adkins will help you. Do not come here under any circumstances or the fools will hang you as a spy. You can be happy in England; Henry was and so was I."

He signed himself "O. Barebones, Gentleman."

Fanny lifted her eyes from the page. "What does this mean?" she asked.

"According to Ash, Oliver has decided to die."

"Decided to die? How? There's nothing the matter with him."

"There doesn't have to be. People do it all the time. I've heard of savages just lying down and dying on a whim, but never an Englishman."

He left Fanny alone while she read the rest of the letters. It was one long letter, really, a confession filling dozens of pages that described Oliver's great error in falling in love with Rose and marrying her.

"The joke is on Rose," Oliver wrote, "because Hawkes has now murdered a few Indians to provoke the French into sending out this Christopher at the head of an Indian war party against him. Then he'll kill them all with the help of the Mohawks, who are happy to work for scalp money—kidnap Thoughtful, and make her his wife."

Fanny ran up the ladder to the deck. Joshua was at the rail. She opened her mouth to speak, but she was not sure what sort of noise she might make if she tried to form words.

# 13

Beavers had dammed the little stream that the Abenaki war party had been following, creating a shallow pond that flooded many acres of forest. When he and his men came to the edge of this sheet of water, Philippe sent three scouts ahead. They waded thigh-deep among beaver lodges and the limber trunks of birches. It was a windless day. The passage of the scouts created ripples on the calm surface of the slew, breaking up clear mirror images of white trunks and golden foliage. Many trees had been girdled by the beavers and were dying; the rest would perish more slowly by drowning. An unusual number of beaver lodges rose up out of the water—low tangled half-submerged structures made by the animals out of mud and brush—and Philippe could see that the scouts were counting the pelts as they waded by.

The scouts disappeared into the woods on the other side of the lake. Philippe waited until the water was absolutely calm again, with the paper birches etched on the gunmetal surface, before he ordered the rest of the men forward. While watching their scouts advance, they had virtually disappeared among the trees and grasses, so that when Philippe gave the signal and the Indians all moved at once, the whole aspect of the forest altered. One moment there was nothing to be seen but trees and water and the vaporous

autumn sunlight, and in the next, an Abenaki was standing beside nearly every tree. Philippe had watched this occur many times, and it always seemed to him when it did that a very old secret was being revealed to him. He watched the Abenakis fan out into the pond, seventy-five men walking through three feet of water without making a sound.

The silence was so unspoiled that Philippe could hear the brook spilling through the dam fifty paces away. Even the birds were still. But why should they be, with so many human beings underneath them? Philippe looked at the sky to see if any flew overhead.

A man named Smoke, who had been almost the last Abenaki to enter the water, had also noticed the silence. He, too, looked upward for birds. When his head tilted back, Philippe saw the streak of vermilion paint in the part in his braided hair.

Smoke uttered a sudden loud grunt, which was followed by a burst of rapid grunts from other Indians in every part of the pond: "*Uh . . . uh . . . uh . . . uh. . . .*"

Smoke sank to his knees, then fell forward into the water with a splash. All around him, other Abenakis were falling down too, clutching at the iron-tipped Mohawk arrows that had thudded into their bodies.

The unwounded Abenakis were frozen in place. They did not even look around for the source of the arrows because there was no place they could have come from.

Philippe, shouting the Abenaki war cry, threw the jaeger to his shoulder and sighted on the beaver lodge closest to the place where Smoke now floated on his face with a sluggish fountain of blood pumping out of his back.

The lodge rose out of the water with a violent motion, sailed through the air, and splashed back into the pond. The Mohawk warrior who had hidden himself inside it now stood in the open, drawing his bowstring back to his ear.

Philippe placed the front sight of his rifle on the bridge of the Mohawk's nose and squeezed the trigger. The Mohawk was thrown backward by the impact of the bullet and landed spread-eagled on the surface of the water among earlier splashes created by chunks of bone that the bullet had blown out of the back of his shaven skull.

There were six Mohawks in the center of the lake, naked wet shrieking men with stripes of vermilion and white under their hate-filled eyes and bristling roaches of varnished hair rising up from their scalps. They stood in a loose circle, facing outward, methodically launching arrows from six-foot bows at the silent, unmoving Abenakis.

Philippe saw an arrow enter the stomach of a very young Abenaki named Gull, pass completely through his entrails, and emerge from his back, encased in a twisting sheath of blood. The bloody arrow wriggled like a snake into the water. While he watched, Philippe reloaded his rifle. He knew that he could accomplish this in less than a minute. By the time he was ready to shoot again, twenty dead or dying Abenakis were floating in the water. The rest appeared to be too stunned to defend themselves.

Philippe saw a flash of movement on the other side of the lake. Two of the three Abenaki scouts were running at top speed toward the fight. Half a dozen Mohawks burst out of the screen of trees behind them and killed them with hatchet blows.

The Abenakis in the water started to run back the way they had come. The Mohawks let them go. As they approached the dam, it erupted in flame and smoke as the remaining Mohawks, who had crawled up the streambed after the Abenakis and concealed themselves behind the tangle of brush and fallen trees, fired a musket volley. Half a dozen more Abenakis were felled. The Mohawks did not reload, but clambered over the dam with bows in their hands.

A flight of iron-tipped arrows from the dam killed five or six Abenaki archers. The Mohawks in the water launched another flight and more Abenakis fell. Philippe realized that he had been hearing the same soft grunts all during the fight that Smoke and the others had uttered when the first Mohawk arrows, driven by a bow that developed a hundred pounds of force, thudded into his liver. The surviving Abenakis, perhaps thirty in number, began to sing.

The only dead Mohawk was the one Philippe had killed with the jaeger. The smoke from this shot was still drifting over the pond in the form of a puffy blue-white cloud. On the other side of the lake, the Mohawks were scalping the men they had hatcheted to death.

In the trees behind them, Philippe saw the broad figure of Hawkes in his Puritan hat with his wolf dog panting beside him. Philippe lifted his rifle and sighted on Hawkes's heart, and as he did, saw a Mohawk running straight for him through a gurge of water, and shot him dead to save his own life. Then he turned and ran into the forest, fixing the long bayonet on his jaeger as he pounded through the drifts of rustling autumn leaves that lay among the maples and birches and stunted upland oaks.

Nobody seemed to be pursuing Philippe, but probably that only meant that the Mohawks were circling to intercept him. He stopped to reload his rifle and listened hard. Behind him, the Abenakis

ceased singing all at the same time and after a few minutes one or two of them began to scream.

In the ambush at the beaver pond, the Mohawks took fifty-one Abenaki scalps, many of those from men who had not yet died, and twenty-four prisoners. The monetary value of this victory, counting the prisoners, who would be scalped after being tortured, was three thousand pounds. Only two Mohawks had been lost, the ones that Philippe shot.

The Mohawks knew that Philippe, who could be ransomed back to the French, was worth more than all the Abenaki scalps together. Even while he was running through the trees, they began to discuss ways to capture him alive.

"You don't need to chase him," Hawkes said. "He'll chase you."

In the pond at his back, the other Mohawks were inspecting the floating corpses to make certain that they had scalped them all. On the opposite bank, one of the dozen Abenakis who had been stripped and hung upside down from the trees was being flayed alive. He thought that he was singing his story, but the sounds that he made were much louder than that.

"Christopher can hear what's going on," Hawkes said. "He ain't going to leave his men. He thinks it's his fault all these Abenakis are dead or being skinned alive."

The English-speaking Mohawk asked a question.

"His fault? Why?"

"Well, he's a white man. So he reckons he should have been smarter than you. And besides that, he's ashamed. He ran away from a fight."

The English-speaker translated this to the Mohawk leader, who thought it over for a while and then began to guffaw.

The Mohawks struck south for a few miles, then turned west on a warpath through the mountains that they had been using for generations. Because they had no interest in keeping Abenakis alive as slaves or breeding stock, the Mohawks tortured one prisoner every night. The Mohawks were learned anatomists, and these flayed, blinded, and otherwise mutilated Abenakis nearly always lived for many hours. The steep terrain, with only a thin membrane of dirt and moss stretched over monoliths of ancient rock, captured and amplified the sounds of this sport.

Philippe, listening, was never more than a mile away in the darkness, and next morning he would find the victim's raw carcass hanging by its ankles in the grove where the Mohawks had camped.

Philippe looked very closely at the flayed Abenakis, remaining with them until he knew who they were and remembered their stories. He was a professional soldier, and identifying the dead was a duty to him. He would sit down on the ground near the corpse and stare at it as it twisted on its rawhide bonds, the ruined face appearing and then disappearing as the body turned. What made recognition difficult, he realized, was not that the nose and ears and privy parts of the dead had been sliced off, but that they had no eyes. Philippe would imagine one set of Abenaki eyes after another in the sockets of the red skull until, at last, he visualized the right pair, and then the whole face would take its original shape in his memory. After that happened, Philippe would sing the dead Abenaki's story, pray for the repose of his soul in French, and apologize for having led him into defeat and death. Then he would haul the body up into the tree in which it had died and tie it to the trunk with rawhide thongs.

On the fifth morning, Philippe came into a campground by a deep brook. The Mohawks had killed a deer the day before and what was left of its carcass—the head, with its frightened yellow eyes, and the hide—was hung by the antlers next to the flayed Abenaki on the low limb of a maple tree. The Abenaki's red marbled body was covered with blue jays.

"Go!" Philippe said in French.

The birds rose up, beating their wings with a fluttering sound, then flew into the tree. As Philippe examined the Abenaki, putting eyes into the skull, the jays scolded him from the upper branches of the maple. This dead Abenaki looked slightly different from all the others, and after a moment Philippe realized why: for some reason the Mohawks had not cut out the tongue. The tip of it, pink and moist, was gripped between the teeth inside the lipless mouth. One by one, the jays began to come back, clinging to the Abenaki's body with wings still moving and bold eyes watching Philippe, then flying away with morsels of flesh in their beaks.

"I am sorry that you are dead," Philippe whispered to the corpse.

The corpse's tongue flickered in its mouth and it said, "Is that you, Wind Hunter?"

By now a dozen big blue birds clung to the corpse. Philippe leaped to his feet and chased them away. Then he opened his mouth to speak, but no words came out. He cut down the Abenaki, whom he recognized by his voice to be a young man of seventeen or eighteen called Sings in the Snow. Philippe meant to lay him on the ground, but then he realized that this would cause terrible pain, so he held him in his arms instead. Close up, Sings in the

Snow smelled clean and slightly salty, like the meat of a freshly killed deer, and he was very light in Philippe's arms.

He turned his eyeless face toward Philippe. "Please kill me," he said. "Use the bayonet as you did with the big buck that jumped onto the ice."

Sings in the Snow did not whisper; his voice did not tremble. He spoke in the ordinary tones of one Abenaki speaking to another.

Philippe tried to reply, but no words would come. His throat closed, his tongue and lips would not move; he had forgotten how to speak and he closed his eyes and struggled to remember, as one will try to recall a name that has escaped the memory. But words would not come.

The dying Abenaki seemed to understand what had happened. Was he so close to death that he already had the wisdom of the dead?

"If you can't talk to me, it's all right," Sings in the Snow said politely. "But kill me. The Mohawks left me my tongue, so I have told my story. Also, I am sorry for all my sins and ask our Lord Jesus Christ and His merciful Father to forgive me."

Suddenly Sings in the Snow twitched violently in Philippe's arms and uttered a loud sob. Philippe had never before heard an Abenaki make this sound. Philippe put Sings in the Snow down on the rocky ground as gently as he could, but when he felt the coarse grass, the pebbles, the dirt, the dead twigs against his exposed nerves, he screamed in a voice that sent the blue jays up into the air.

Philippe picked up the jaeger, fixed the bayonet (Sings in the Snow screaming all the while), and drove the blade through the other man's heart. Sings in the Snow sighed when he felt the steel.

Philippe fell to his knees beside the body and tried to say a prayer for the dead, but no words came. Later, after he had tied Sings in the Snow to the trunk of a hemlock, he tried to speak again, but even in the privacy of the tall evergreen his tongue refused to obey his brain.

Finally Philippe started westward again along the trail left by the Mohawks. There was no reason to speak now, so he did not try to form words. But he knew that he had lost the power of speech. It did not matter to him that this was so because he expected to be dead very soon. He followed their tracks day after day, and from hiding places higher up on the mountainside than the pretty glens in which the Mohawks always seemed to camp, watched the festive glow of their big fires on the leafy ceiling of the forest. The Mohawks made no attempt whatever to conceal themselves; on the seventh day, coming close to their line of march, Philippe heard

one of them conversing easily with Hawkes in English, as if the two had fallen into step while strolling through a public park.

"Where'd you learn to talk such good English?" Hawkes asked.

"At Harvard College," the Mohawk replied. "There were a fair number of us there in the Indian college, studying for the ministry."

"You're a minister?"

"No, I didn't finish. Only one Indian ever did. I think he was a Mohegan. His Christian name was Caleb."

"Did they teach you Latin and Greek?"

"Scriptures and good manners, mostly," the Mohawk replied.

This matter-of-fact conversation penetrated Philippe's shocked mind. Hearing human voices speaking a civilized language, he began to think rationally again. The truth about the massacre became evident to him: Hawkes had laid a trap and Philippe had walked into it and lost nearly every man of fighting age in Two Suns's village. Why? Was Hawkes revenging his dogs? Did he have some other equally mad reason for this slaughter?

Philippe told himself to stop asking questions that were designed to absolve him, Philippe, from blame for this military disaster. It did not matter what Hawkes's reasons had been: he had achieved a brilliant victory, an English victory over the French. Nothing could be more sane than that. He was clearly the most dangerous enemy of France now at large in this part of America. The shame of defeat, the horror of his men dying without a fight or being tortured to death with a ferocity that could only mean that the Mohawks considered them to be cowards, had clouded Philippe's mind. Now, thinking clearly again, he formed an intention.

That night he slipped past the Mohawks, and when he was well clear of them, ran west along the warpath until daylight. After sleeping for an hour he ran on, arriving at dusk at the summit of a mountain from which there was a view in all directions of somewhat lower hills. The sugar maples that grew down the mountainsides and the valleys in their tens of thousands were now in full autumn colors along with all the other brilliant trees.

The warpath, describing a series of hairpin turns as it followed the contours of the mountains, wound through this vivid panorama. Philippe found a big gnarled maple that commanded a view of the path to the west, then located another tree, three hundred paces beyond the first one, that provided an equally unobstructed view in the same direction. He was now about twenty miles ahead of the Mohawk war party. If they camped where he believed they would camp, in a glade where a spring gushed out of a rock about three miles away, he would be able to hear them in the night. Then, quite early in the morning, he would see them. He climbed the

first tree, stretched out in the fork of a huge leafy limb, and went to sleep.

When he woke, the morning sun was behind him. Below him, the Mohawks walked along the trail with the glare of it in their eyes. The captives stumbled along behind, yoked together by saplings lashed with rawhide on either side of their necks; the Mohawks made no effort to guard them. How could they run? Where would they run to?

Hawkes in his high-crowned ecclesiastical hat trudged along in the center of the file like a moose among deer. His wolf dog was nowhere to be seen, but that did not surprise Philippe; he knew that the dog hunted constantly.

Philippe had picked out a big quartz outcropping beside the trail as his aiming point. The sun glittered on the chips of mica embedded in the white stone. Lying on his stomach on the forked branch of the maple, Philippe moved the muzzle of the jaeger rifle, to which the bayonet was fixed, inch by inch to the left of the rock until the sight was fixed on the imaginary heart that was his target.

Eleven Mohawk warriors walked through the sights before Hawkes filled the space that Philippe had reserved for him in his plan. Philippe found himself looking directly into Hawkes's eyes. Hawkes did not see him. Philippe moved the muzzle of the jaeger downward a bit, let out his breath in two even streams through his nostrils, and squeezed the trigger.

Hawkes dodged sideways, then was thrown backward. The Mohawks started running up the path. Philippe, still enveloped in the smoke from his weapon, stood up on the springy branch of the maple and looked downward. The wolf dog stood on the ground ten feet beneath him, barking in its weak phlegmy voice.

Philippe leaped straight downward. His weight, multiplied by the speed of his fall, drove the needle-pointed three-foot-long blade completely through the animal's body and into the ground beyond. It did not kill it outright. Philippe tugged at the carved stock of the jaeger, trying to withdraw the bayonet, but the enormous dog, bred for courage and stamina, was driving itself onto the blade as it tried to attack him even as it died, and he could not back away fast enough to free the bayonet from its lunging body.

By now the Mohawks were very close. Philippe let go of the jaeger and began to run.

The Mohawks ran him down about two miles farther on, having worn him out by sprinting behind him at top speed one by one while the others conserved their strength by lagging behind at a dogtrot. When he turned at last, he killed one of them with a pistol, firing into the heart, as he had instructed Fanny, when the

Mohawk was only three feet away, but before he could draw his knife the others had shot arrows into his thighs, so that he was paralyzed by pain.

The Mohawks recovered their arrows by pushing them out the other side of his body, afterward wiping the blood off the fletching on his shirt. They did not humiliate him further, but packed his wounds with leaves and moss and then sat down on the roots of trees and waited for the rest of the party to come up.

Philippe drifted in and out of consciousness many times during the hour or so that this required, seeing Fanny with her eyes closed one moment and the staring face of a Mohawk the next, hearing the Woronoco pounding through the Gorge and then hearing his own heart, tasting Fanny's golden skin and then tasting the blood in his mouth.

He heard English being spoken and opened his eyes to see Hawkes, pasty-faced and unsteady, standing over him. There was a big bloodstain on the front of Hawkes's shirt and he was holding the jaeger in his hands.

He said, "What the hell kind of a gun is this?"

Philippe attempted to reply. He could see that Hawkes's whole mind was concentrated on his answer.

But the words would not come; like a stammerer, Philippe was able to visualize the objects he wished to name, but he hadn't the strength to force the words that described them out of his brain, where they seemed to be imprisoned, and onto his tongue and lips.

Hawkes held out his hand, as though Philippe's answer was something that had long been owed to him. Blood ran down his right sleeve and dribbled from the tips of his fingers. He swayed, nearly losing his balance. His eyes were clouded and his breath wheezed in his lungs like an exhausted runner's. His Roundhead hat was missing and his thick hair was matted on his skull

He looked down at the blood in his hand, noticing it for the first time. Philippe was still struggling to speak. Hawkes gave him a reproachful look.

"To hell with you, then," Hawkes said.

His eyes stopped seeing, and still holding the bayoneted rifle across his chest, he fell forward with a crash.

# 14

Because Philippe did not recover the power of speech for a long time, the details of the massacre at the beaver pond were not immediately known to the French or to Fanny. She knew only what the Abenakis had learned by reading the sign a week after the fight was over. Two Suns and Hair, having run all the way from the Saint Francis River, found the scalped bodies of the men they had come to warn floating peacefully among the dead golden leaves that now covered the surface of the pond.

They followed the tracks of the Mohawks and their prisoners westward over the war trail as far as the Taconic Mountains, identifying the Abenaki captives by their moccasin prints and reconstructing Philippe's actions by the signs he had left.

They found the bayoneted wolf dog half-eaten by birds and small animals, but Hawkes was untouched. His thick body, naked to the waist, sat upright under the ancient maple where he had fallen at Philippe's feet. His Puritan hat was square on his head and his eyes were open, so that he looked like a Calvinist patriarch waiting for someone of his own religion to come along so that he could accuse his murderer. His face was pallid and angry. His arms were folded across his chest, and the silver crucifix he had taken off the drowned Frenchman's skeleton dangled from the fingers of his right hand.

Two Suns and Hair watched Hawkes for a long time from hiding. When they were sure that he was dead, they came out in the open and approached him. The dead-white skin of his torso, which was as hairless as an Indian's, bore many puckered scars of old wounds. His chest and belly were caked with dried blood. An open bullet wound about a hand's breadth to the right of the sternum had been stuffed with moss and leaves. A huge bruise had formed around this wound that Two Suns knew could only have been inflicted by Philippe's jaeger rifle.

Hawkes said. "You're the one that keeps on stealing Thoughtful Pennock. Why?"

Hawkes spoke in a harsh whisper, as if the words were coming

out of his wound instead of his mouth. Even though he was sure
that Hawkes was dead, Two Suns was not surprised to hear him
speak: Hawkes was a ghost; he had always been dead. Two Suns
did not recognize Thoughtful's English name, but he knew that
Hawkes must be talking about Squirrel.

"She is my daughter," Two Suns said.

Hawkes sat as he was, every muscle frozen.

"Give her this," Hawkes said.

Still Hawkes did not move, but Two Suns realized that he meant
the silver crucifix. The beads were wound around Hawkes's blunt
fingers and it took several minutes to untangle them. Two Suns
never forgot any object once he had seen it, and he recognized the
crucifix at once. He supposed that Hawkes had met the drowned
Frenchman in the next world and stolen the silver cross from him,
or traded for it.

"She's my wife," Hawkes said.

This time he spoke in English and Two Suns did not understand
his words. Two Suns hung the crucifix around his neck and left.
Because the trail ran uphill for a long distance, he and Hair were
able to see Hawkes sitting under his tree as they went away. His
massive figure grew smaller and smaller, but it did not move.

When news of the disaster that had overtaken Philippe's expedi-
tion reached Quebec, Armand de Grestain took it as a personal
affront. Why should he be put into the position of sending news of
this kind to the king?

"Every man dead, himself captured, and nothing to show for it,"
Grestain said to Fanny. "Your husband has ruined the family,
madame."

"Then he is free of it," Fanny said.

"Oh, he'll be ransomed in two years' time. By then it will be
safe. The palace will have forgotten him."

"Sooner than two years," Fanny said.

Grestain raised a forefinger. "I forbid you to spend money
belonging to the family on this matter," he said. "Ransom is the
responsibility of the intendant."

The *Pamela* was still in her berth below the city. Fanny sailed in
her on the next tide.

# 15

Because it was impossible to penetrate Iroquois country from French territory and live, Fanny sailed in the *Pamela* to New York, then traveled up the Hudson to Albany in a riverboat. It was late November by the time she arrived. With the help of the English authorities, who seemed to have a regular postal service between Albany and the Mohawk villages, she sent word that she was prepared to ransom her husband. Hawkes's Mohawks came to Albany to negotiate: the war-party leader (who carried Philippe's jaeger), the English-speaker, and two gaunt women covered with ornaments.

Philippe, his arms bound with braided rawhide rope to a stick thrust between his elbows and his back, looked like what he was, a prisoner. He was bearded and ragged and he limped very badly, pausing at every step to concentrate on his balance as he swung one leg forward, then painfully lifted the other.

"Cut his bonds," Fanny said.

Evidently Philippe belonged to the women, because the English-speaker looked to them for permission before he did as Fanny demanded. Fanny took Philippe by the arm and helped him to a chair. He was still very weak from his wounds, and there was a look in his eyes, as if he were trying to hide the light of his intelligence, that Fanny had never seen there before.

"He has not been mistreated," the English-speaker said, vouching for the goods. "But his wounds are not yet healed."

Fanny ignored the man. Speaking French, Fanny told Philippe how much ransom she had been advised by the English to pay, and what plans she had made for them after he was released. Philippe listened to what she said but did not reply.

"Does all that suit you?" Fanny asked.

Still Philippe did not reply. He closed his eyes, concentrating, then opened them. His head twitched like a mute's. He bit his lip. Fanny was afraid that she understood what was happening, but to be sure, she spoke to him in Latin.

"If you are trying to tell me not to speak before these people, close your eyes," she said.

Philippe stared at her, unblinking.

"Are you telling me that you cannot speak?" she asked, again in Latin.

Philippe blinked. Fanny doubled her fists tightly and drew as much breath into her body as it would hold. Behind her, the English-speaker was saying something.

"He does not talk," he said. "We don't know why."

The negotiations were very brief. The ransom was one thousand pounds. Fanny handed them a letter of appraisal from a Dutch jewel merchant in Manhattan, and then showed them the ruby necklace. The Mohawks understood its value. One of the women spoke in Mohawk.

"My sister wants to see the necklace around your neck," the English-speaker said.

Fanny tried it on. The woman came close, looking for a long time at the necklace and then at Fanny's face. She unhooked the necklace, examined every stone, then held it against Fanny's cheek. She turned her head and spoke again; all the Mohawks laughed.

"She says we captured the wrong spouse," the English-speaker said.

The woman put the necklace around her own neck.

"Done," said the English-speaker.

"There are conditions," Fanny said. "My husband and I and our child must be able to live in peace from now on near the Gorge on the Woronoco and travel there from here without being molested."

"It's a poor place to go in the winter."

"Nevertheless, we wish to go there. And you must give back the jaeger rifle."

"What else will we be given for these things?"

"Only the necklace. It is worth more than you asked, and my husband is not the same as before."

The leader of the war party laid the jaeger on the table along with its bayonet and Philippe's bullet pouch and powder horn. The Mohawks, standing in a row, stared at Fanny for a long moment, as if memorizing her features. Then they left. Fanny put her hand on the stock of the jaeger. The carved grapes and other ornamentation, once so familiar to her, seemed strange to her eye and touch, as though she had recovered a duplicate instead of the original object. The baby moved, drawing a line with its hand or foot along the interior of its mother's body. Fanny followed this movement with her own hand.

She turned around. Philippe, seated on a low stool, looked up at her with eyes that she still did not quite know. She took his face in her hands and turned it to one side, placing his ear against her belly, and while he listened with his eyes closed, began to weep.

# 16

Living beside the Gorge, Philippe gradually became himself again, except that he did not speak and could not run. After the first few days, he stopped struggling to form words. He would not even speak in signs. Fanny had to guess at his intentions. She talked to him in French as she had always done, and sometimes, at night, sang French songs that made him smile.

Fanny had seen the muscles, nerves, and blood vessels of the human leg laid open by a scalpel, and she knew that Philippe was lucky even to be walking. He still limped severely, but this was no handicap to him in stalking game. He never used the bow now, but hunted with the jaeger, despite the noise that it made. The Mohawks had made their bargain; there was no need to fear discovery.

Just as the February thaw was beginning, Philippe saw the tracks of a moose leading into the trees, and then glimpsed the animal itself walking through the beech grove. He and Fanny followed, thinking that they could kill it close to home and carry the meat to the cave at their leisure, but the moose stayed ahead of them hour after hour, turning away from them as they circled around to intercept it.

Finally the moose stopped walking. Swinging its clumsy head as it sniffed the air, it stood within a hundred feet of them and regarded them with an unwinking stare, as if seeing his pursuers for the first time. The air had become progressively warmer during the long stalk, and now a glimmering rain was falling. The moose's antlers glistened.

Philippe started to lift the jaeger. Fanny placed a hand on his arm. The moose gazed mildly at them as it waited patiently for the bullet. Philippe lowered the rifle. The moose watched, still interested and unafraid, as Philippe and Fanny walked away among the

beeches over a crust on the snow that buckled like leather beneath their moccasins.

Rain was falling more heavily as the light failed. By the time they reached the cave, which was only a couple of miles away, the rocks were coated with ice. When they took off their coats they saw that these, too, were frozen stiff.

About midnight Fanny felt a mild sensation in the muscles of her abdomen. It was more noticeable than the movements of the baby, but not quite a pain. She lay quietly, with Philippe sleeping beside her, and listened to the rain pattering on the rocks outside the mouth of the cave. Philippe murmured in his sleep as he often did. Evidently the power of speech came back to him when he dreamt.

The sensation now involved Fanny's back as well as her abdomen and was stronger. The waters broke, the contractions became stronger. Soon they were hard enough to prevent her from using her mind while they were going on, but between the pains she followed the instructions that were given to Abenaki girls and began singing the story of her child's ancestors, her great-grandfather the Christian soldier whom she had never known, and the Hardings and Fanchon, whom she had only known through her father's story. So as not to disturb Philippe, and because she wanted to be alone with her baby for a few minutes longer, she whispered, telling the child Henry Harding's story and her own story and as much of Philippe's as she knew.

Now the pains were very powerful. She got to her knees, then crouched. The movement woke Philippe. Knowing at once what was happening, he kneeled, facing her as they had done when rehearsing this moment, and she locked her hands behind his neck.

He was smiling at her, so she supposed that she must be smiling at him too. She tried to continue with the story but instead let out a cry that filled up the stone cavern, and then many more, one after the other so that she mistook them for echoes. She could not stop the noise she was making or anything else that was happening to her.

Fanny's body and the strong body of her child carried her away into some place, strange yet well-known to her, where her mother had been before her, and as her son left her body, so did her grief for Fanchon. She was sure that her mother's breath, after its long years of captivity in Fanny's heart, was passing into the breast of the newborn child.

Fanny came back. She watched Philippe tie and cut the umbilical cord. Smiling radiantly, he made the sign for *son* with glistening hands, then mutely held up the baby. The child was dark, like Fanny.

Fanny reached for him. At that moment, without warning, the birth pains began again. She shouted in surprise and seized Phillipe instead, pulling herself into the crouching position. Philippe's face was very close—the deep blue eyes, the white sword cut on the left cheek, the blue buckshot wound on the other.

"Fanny!" he cried. "Fanny!"

In her helplessness, Fanny thought that she was imagining the sound of his voice. She knew that he could not possibly be speaking to her.

"Fanny!" Philippe said again, as if pronouncing her name in his old precise voice was the most unsurprising thing in the world. "Do you know what's happening?"

Shouting wordlessly, unable to stop herself, Fanny crushed her face against Philippe's. Each time she screamed, he answered with her name. At last the second of her twins swam into its father's hands. Philippe held it aloft, the bulging cord still attached. It was a girl.

Philippe wrapped the babies in wool and gave them to Fanny. They nursed dreamily; the boy was warmer to the touch and a stronger feeder than the girl. Fanny went to sleep while they were still drinking. The faint sweetish odor of milk rose from their quiet forms. All around them in the forest, trees splintered and fell under the weight of the rain that had frozen on their branches.

In the morning, which was lit by a brilliant white sun, Fanny and Philippe took the babies outdoors. The ice storm had transmuted the forest from wood to crystal. Every twig and branch, every rock, the earth itself, were coated with ice and filled up with dazzling light. There were no shadows, only reflections.

Philippe melted ice in his hand and dripped it onto the twins' foreheads. Each uttered a sharp cry of surprise. A black bear, awakened from its hibernation by the thaw and attracted by the scents of birth, bounded out of the grove of beeches and skidded to a stop on the icy ledge at the rim of the Gorge. There it rose on its hind legs, putting its head to one side and dreamily regarding the little group of human beings at the mouth of the cave. Fanny recognized the bear: it was the same one-eared animal she had encounted the summer before.

The bear coughed hoarsely and chattered its teeth, then staggered clownishly in its dark coat along the edge of the cliff as it lost its footing on the ice. The sun was directly behind the bear, so that the bent light, shining through the prism of the ice, flashed red and blue and yellow all around its whirling figure.

"Say good morning to Bear," Philippe said to his children.

Without fear or surprise, Henry Philippe Oliver de Saint-Christophe and his twin sister Lily Genevieve Edwige, the first Christophers born in the New World, opened their eyes and gazed at the bear, which seemed to be dancing for them in a forest of jewels.